Heirs of the Blade

Adrian Tchaikovsky was born in Woodhall Spa, Lincolnshire, before heading off to Reading to study psychology and zoology. For reasons unclear even to himself he subsequently ended up in law and has worked as a legal executive in both Reading and Leeds, where he now lives. Married, he is a keen live role-player and occasional amateur actor, has trained in stage-fighting, and keeps no exotic or dangerous pets of any kind, possibly excepting his son.

Catch up with Adrian at www.shadowsoftheapt.com for further information about both himself and the insect-kinden, together with bonus material including short stories and artwork.

Heirs of the Blade is the seventh novel in the Shadows of the Apt series. Have you read *Empire in Black and Gold*, *Dragonfly Falling*, *Blood of the Mantis*, *Salute the Dark*, *The Scarab Path* and *The Sea Watch*?

BY ADRIAN TCHAIKOVSKY

Shadows of the Apt

Empire in Black and Gold
Dragonfly Falling
Blood of the Mantis
Salute the Dark
The Scarab Path
The Sea Watch
Heirs of the Blade

SHADOWS OF THE APT

BOOK SEVEN

Heirs of the Blade

ADRIAN
TCHAIKOVSKY

TOR

First published 2011 by Tor

This edition published 2012 by Tor
an imprint of Pan Macmillan, a division of Macmillan Publishers Limited
Pan Macmillan, 20 New Wharf Road, London N1 9RR
Basingstoke and Oxford
Associated companies throughout the world
www.panmacmillan.com

ISBN 978-0-330-54129-9

1 3 5 7 9 8 6 4 2

A CIP catalogue record for this book is available from
the British Library.

Map artwork pp.x-xiv and illustration on p.v by Hemesh Alles

Typeset by CPI Typesetting
Printed and bound by CPI Group (UK) Ltd, Croydon CR0 4YY

For Doctor John Vandenbrooks,
Arizona State University

Acknowledgements

Firstly, an enormous thank you to my wife, Annie, not just for all the usual, but for her invaluable assistance in reading through and commenting on the manuscript during the editing process, when I was greatly in need of another point of view.

Secondly, the usual round of people, 'Without Whom': Simon Kavanagh, Peter Lavery and Julie Crisp, Chloe Healy and everyone else at Tor; Pete Bayly and the regulars at Oxford and Reading. In particular thanks to Helen Walter for being my consultant armourer.

Finally, for diverse secret reasons, a special thanks to Lasse Skjalm, Johnny Burlin and Anders Åström.

A glossary of characters and places can be found at the end of the book.

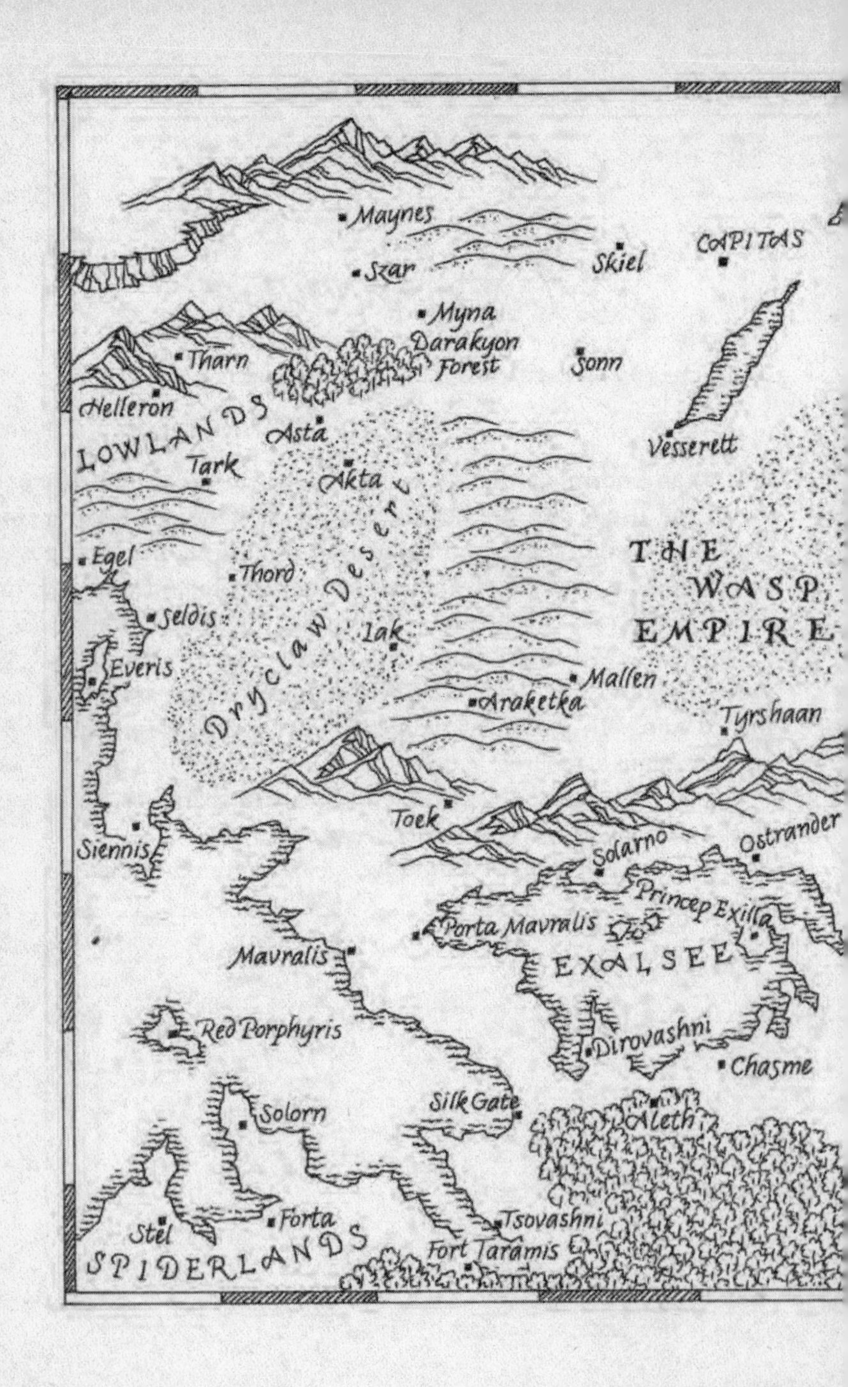

Maynes
Szar
Skiel
CAPITAS
Myna
Darakyon Forest
Sonn
Tharn
Helleron
LOWLANDS
Asta
Vesserett
Tark
Akta
Egel
Thord
Dryclaw Desert
THE WASP EMPIRE
Seldis
Everis
Iak
Mallen
Araketka
Tyrshaan
Toek
Siennis
Solarno
Ostrander
Princep Exilla
Porta Mavralis
Mavralis
EXALSEE
Red Porphyris
Dirovashni
Chasme
Solorn
Silk Gate
Aleth
Stel
Forta
Tsovashni
Fort Taramis
SPIDERLANDS

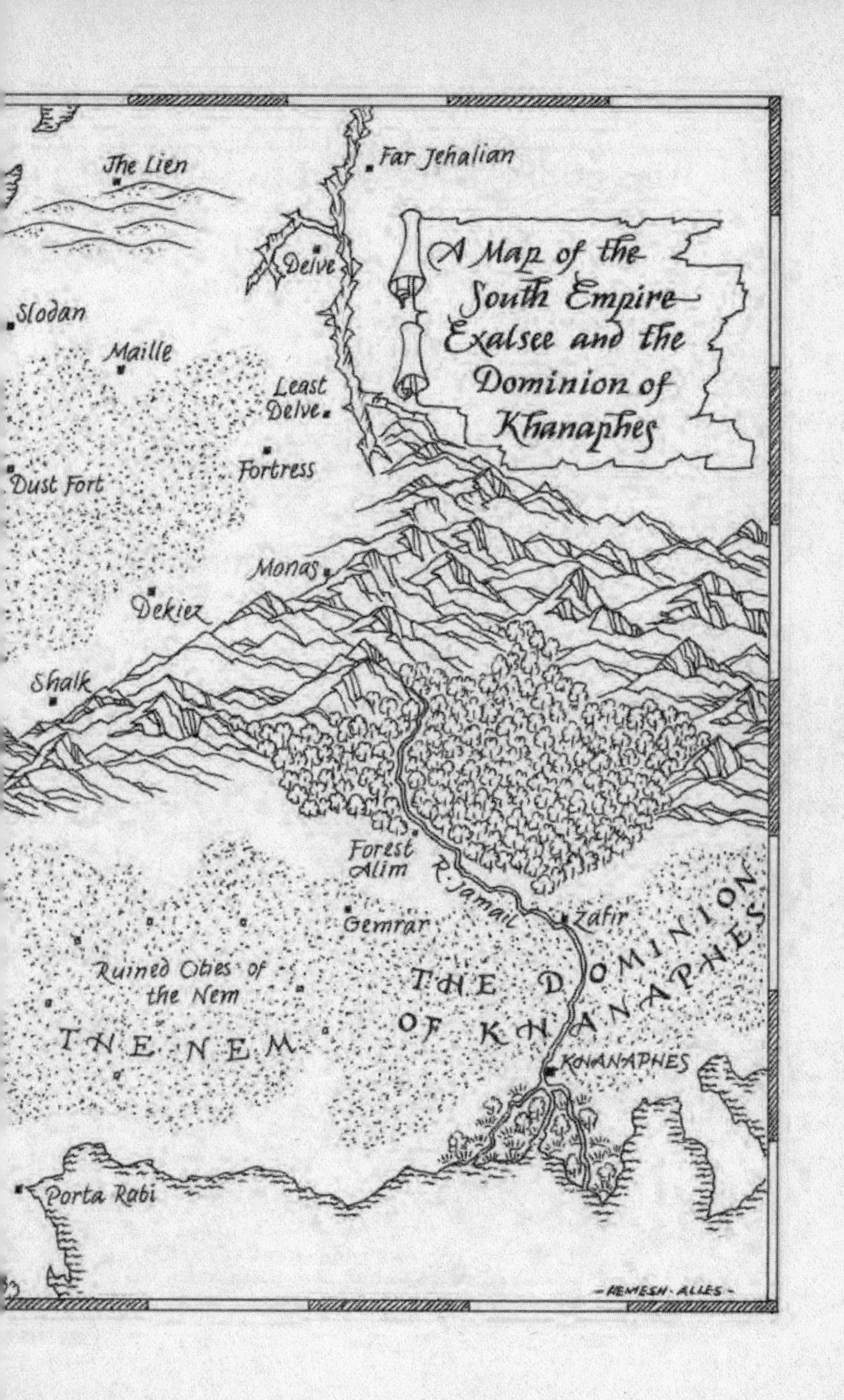
The Lien
Far Jehalian
Delve
A Map of the South Empire Exalsee and the Dominion of Khanaphes
Slodan
Maille
Least Delve
Fortress
Dust Fort
Monas
Dekiez
Shalk
Forest Alim
R. Jamail
Gemrar
Zafir
Ruined Cities of the Nem
THE DOMINION OF KHANAPHES
THE NEM
KHANAPHES
Porta Rabi
HEMESH ALLES

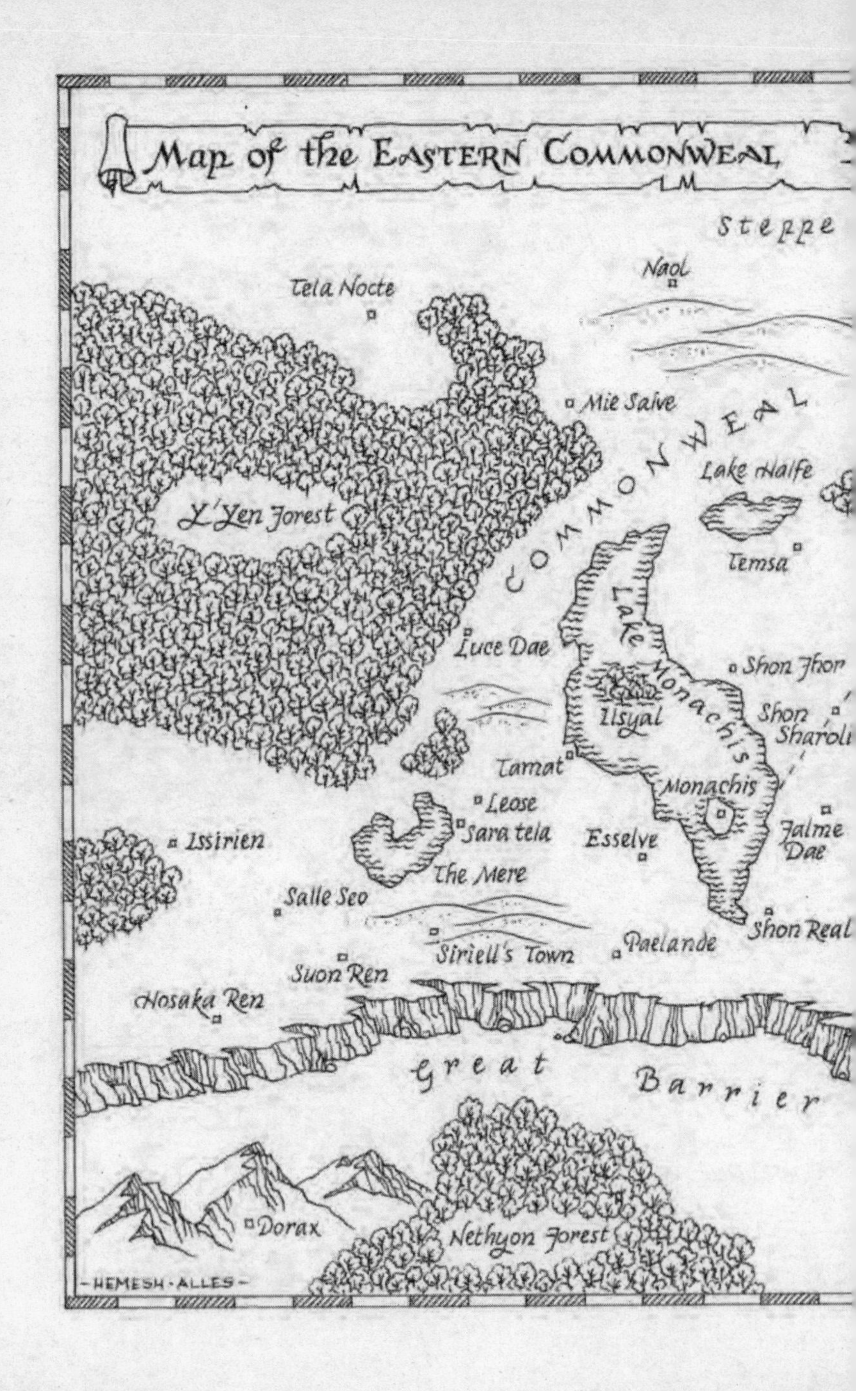
Map of the Eastern Commonweal
Steppe
Naol
Tela Nocte
Mie Salve
COMMONWEAL
Lake Halfe
L'Yen Forest
Temsa
Lake Monachis
Luce Dae
Shon Jhor
Ilsyal
Shon
Sharoli
Tamat
Monachis
Lease
Sara tela
Issirien
Esselve
Jalme Dae
The Mere
Salle Seo
Shon Real
Siriell's Town
Paelande
Suon Ren
Hosaka Ren
Great Barrier
Dorax
Nethyon Forest
-HEMESH-ALLES-

Braem
Fiol
T'soka Forest
Arche
Line of Pearl
Del Halle
PRINCIPALITIES
Povre
Mallie
Lake
Limnia
Ualla Rae
Te Sora
JEREZ EMPIRE
Luscoa
Lose
Derosaka
Masaka
Mian Lae
Sa
Shon Aeres
Solamen
Maynes
Landstower
Nalfes
THREE CITY ALLIANCE
Ridge
Szar
Myna
Darakyon Forest

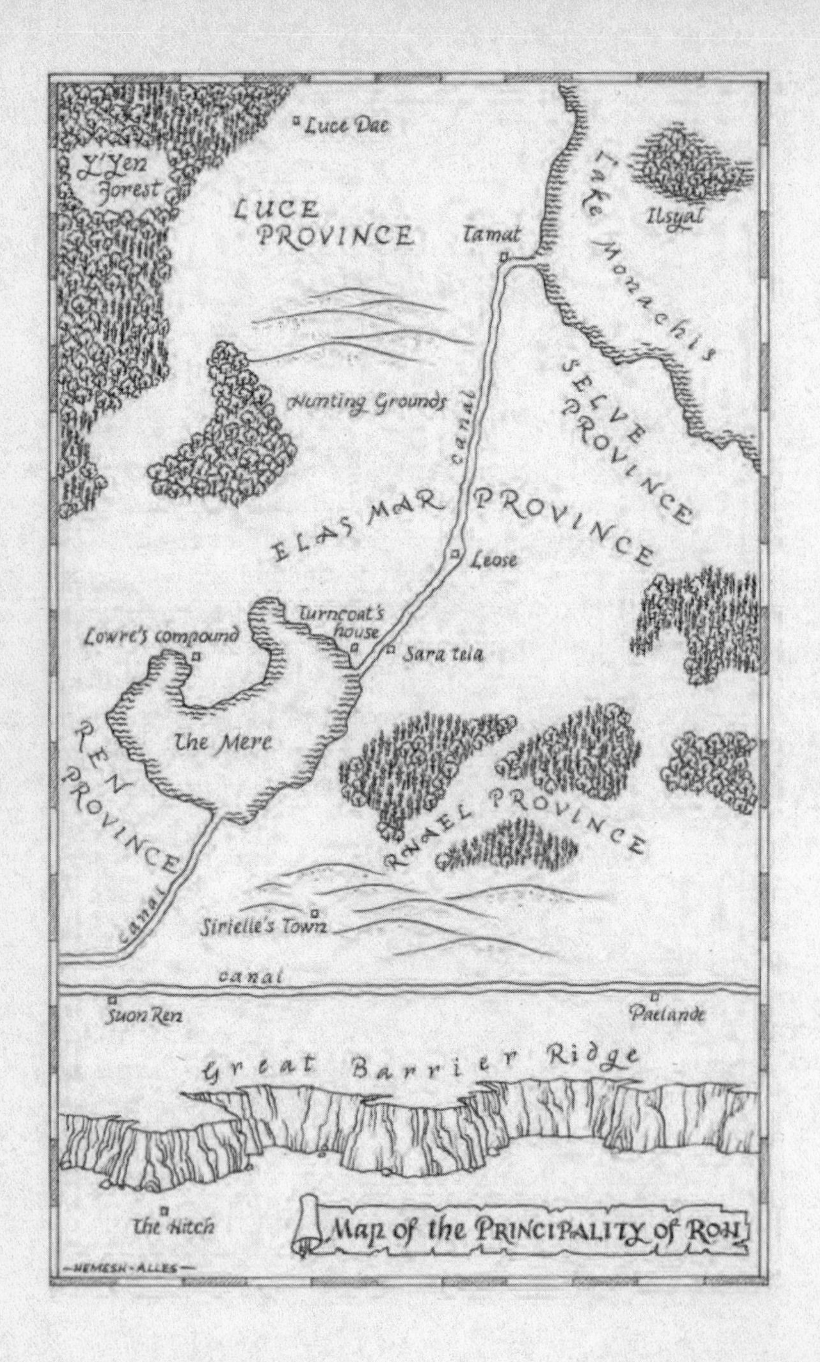
Luce Dae
L'Yen Forest
LUCE PROVINCE
Tamat
Lake Monachis
Ilsyal
SELVE PROVINCE
Hunting Grounds
canal
ELASMAR PROVINCE
Leose
Turncoat's house
Lowre's compound
Sara tela
The Mere
REN PROVINCE
RNAEL PROVINCE
canal
Sirielle's Town
canal
Suon Ren
Paelande
Great Barrier Ridge
The Hitch
Map of the PRINCIPALITY of ROH
NEMESH-ALLES

Summary

The war against the Empire concluded in a troubled stalemate with the newly crowned Empress Seda dealing with those rebel governors who refused to accept her claim to the throne. Now the Empire has quelled its internal dissent and is rebuilding its power. Unknown to most, Seda herself has lost her Aptitude and fallen victim to bloody and unnatural appetites.

In an attempt to come to terms with her own newly Inapt nature, Cheerwell Maker has travelled to the ancient city of Khanaphes and met with the immortal, subterranean Masters, who claim to be the first lords of mankind and the first great magicians. Having spurred them to defend the city above from the hordes of the Many of Nem (attacking with Imperial support), Che is now heading north with Thalric, intending to stand between her fugitive foster-sister Tynisa and the vengeful ghost of her father, the Mantis Weaponsmaster Tisamon.

The former First Soldier of Khanaphes, Amnon, has travelled to Collegium with his lover Praeda Rakespear, a Master of the College, but news of an open Imperial invasion of the old city have sent them both hurrying back to help Amnon's people.

Tynisa herself has been missing for some time, having fled Collegium shortly after the end of the war which claimed both her father, her close friend Salme Dien, and Cheerwell's lover Achaeos, the latter of whom died from a wound that Tynisa inflicted.

Part One

The Recluse

One

She remembered how it felt to lose Salma, first to the wiles of the Butterfly-kinden girl, and then to hear the news of his death, abandoned and alone in the midst of the enemy.

She remembered seeing her father hacked to death before her eyes.

But of her murder of Achaeos, of the bite of her blade into his unsuspecting flesh, the wound that had sapped him and ruined him until he died, she remembered nothing, she felt nothing. In such a vacuum, how could she possibly atone?

The world was a wall.

The Barrier Ridge was what they called it. In Tynisa's College lectures she had seen it marked on maps as delineating the northernmost edge of the comfortable, known territories referred to as the Lowlands. Those maps, set down by Apt cartographers, had been hard for her to follow, and the concept of the Ridge harder still. How could there be a cliff so great as the teachers claimed, and no sea? How was it that the Lowlands just stopped, and everything north from there was . . . elsewhere? The Highlands, by logical comparison: the mysterious Commonweal which had, for a fistful of centuries, rebuffed every attempt by the Lowlanders to make contact diplomatic, academic or mercantile. *Everyone* knew that, just as everyone knew so many things which, when looked at closely enough, were never entirely true.

On those maps, the Ridge had been a pair of long shallow curves with regimented lines drawn between them, like a stylized mouth with straight and even teeth. The imagination had been given nothing otherwise to go on, and year after year of students had left the College with the inbuilt idea that the world, or such of it as was worth learning about, somehow came to its northern limit by way of a cartographer's convention. Now she looked up and up, seeing the heavens cut in two. To the south was a sky swirling with grey cloud. To the north, ridged and corrugated, rose a great, rough rock face that had weathered the spite of a thousand years and then a thousand more, that had cracked and split and had sloughed off whole fortress-weights of its substance in places, but which remained the barrier keeping the Lowlands and the Commonweal apart. Only the greatest of climbers could have attempted scaling it. Only a strong and confident flier would trust his Art to take him over it, penetrating the foul weather that traditionally boiled and clawed over the land's division.

To her back lay the northernmost extent of a tangled forest that housed two Mantis holds – and too many secrets. The airship that had brought her this far had sailed high to cross it, far higher than weather or hostile natives might otherwise account for. Its pilot, Jons Allanbridge, had simply shrugged when queried.

'I don't like the place,' was all he would say on the subject, while beneath them the dark sea of trees remained almost lost in mist and distance. 'Now Sarn's behind us, I'll not make landfall before the Hitch.' Seeing her expression, he had scowled. 'Who owes who for this, girl? You're in no position to ask any cursed more of me. Got that?'

Which was true enough, Tynisa had to concede. The knotted, clenched feeling inside her had twitched at being balked in such a way, but she held on to it, fought it down. Her hand stayed clear of her sword hilt, and it, in turn, stayed clear of her hand, in a tenuous pact of mutual non-aggression.

It had been cold in the upper reaches of the air, but she had planned ahead for that, remembering their journey together to Tharn. She had packed cloaks and woollens, and still she shivered, crouching close to the airship's burner, while Allanbridge bustled about her. That voyage to Tharn had been in his old ship, the *Buoyant Maiden,* and Allanbridge's status as a war veteran had proved currency enough to finance his trading the *Maiden* for this much grander vessel. She had the impression that he was finding the craft difficult to run single-handed; not that she would have been able to help him even had he asked.

He called this new vessel the *Windlass*, which Tynisa thought reflected a lack of imagination on his part, but then he was her benefactor, and she the one who had so unfairly imposed herself on his conscience, and so she had said nothing.

They had been aloft many days now, with Allanbridge stoically rewinding the *Windlass*'s clockwork engine each day. He cooked their meagre meals and did incomprehensible things to the airship's mechanisms in response to changes in the *Windlass*'s handling which Tynisa was unable to perceive. He was not one for conversation so their days together passed in silence. She slept in the hold, while he had the single cramped cabin that was the benefit of having acquired a larger airship than the little *Maiden.* This lack of talk, of any meaningful human contact, suited her very well.

Sometimes she had company other than Allanbridge, or at least her eyes twisted the world to make it seem that way. From the corner of her eye she would see a slender, grey-robed figure hunched at the rail, his posture twisted as if racked by illness, and she would think, *He always did hate travel by airship*, then close her eyes hard, before opening them to see the rail untenanted again. *I killed you,* she reflected, and she could not deny his ghost its place in her mind.

Or she would come up from below decks to see a familiar golden-skinned face, that damnable smile that twisted in her heart, but he faded, he faded, so much less real than Achaeos's image had been. *Salma*, she cried silently, and she would have held on to him if she could. Where the murdered Moth put the knife in her with his presence, Salma rammed it home with his departure.

Then, again, sometimes it was Tisamon – who she had actually seen die. When the vibrations of the airship denied her rest, when the other two hallucinations had been stabbing at her conscience, as she looked over the *Windlass*'s rail and could find no reason not to simply vault it and find briefly another kind of flight, then she would look along the length of the airship's decks and see her father, exactly as she had seen him last.

The sight calmed her. She knew he was not there, that her mind was breaking up and these images were leaking out, but he calmed her nonetheless. She knew that, if she looked at him directly, he would be gone, and so she would stalk him, sidle up on him, creep closer until she could sense him at her elbow: Tisamon the Mantis-kinden, Tisamon the Weaponsmaster, just as he had left the world: a tall figure dressed in blood, hacked and red from a dozen wounds, half flayed, swords and broken spears rammed into him where the Wasp soldiers had desperately tried to keep him away from their Emperor.

And she would stand there companionably beside him, leaning on the rail or holding firmly to a stay, and feel comforted by the riven and ruined corpse her mind had conjured up here beside her. It was almost all she had left of her father.

She was not sure what she intended once Allanbridge at last got her to her destination. The inner wounds that surrounded her motives were too painful to bear scrutiny. The one vague feeling that she huddled close to, as vital as the airship's burner in keeping her warm and alive, was that she should say sorry, somehow, to someone. Possibly thereafter she should accomplish her own death, and she had reason to believe that, for the people she intended losing herself amongst, this was a practice that they respected, and therefore would not interfere with. Her own people were not so understanding.

My own people! she had reminded herself dismissively, when that thought occurred to her. *And which people are they? I have no people.*

And now Allanbridge had set down at this place with half a sky, which was indicated as 'The Hitch' on his maps, and that in his own practical Beetle-kinden script. People actually lived here, where there was only half a sky.

Tomorrow, Allanbridge's airship would make that journey up, and although he anticipated a jolting passage, its physical dangers did not concern him. After all, he had made the same trip on four occasions before now.

'Why stop here?' she had asked him, as he began to lower the *Windlass* earthwards, in the face of that appalling wall of stone.

'Morning crossing's easier,' he explained. 'There're tides in the air, girl. Just after dawn and they'll be with us, draw us up nice and soft, without breaking us on the Ridge or chucking us ten miles in any direction you please.' When her enquiring expression had remained unsatisfied, he added, 'Also news is to be had here, and I want you to think about whether you really want to do this, 'cos I reckon you think it's all light and flowers up that way but, let me tell you, it's no easy place to make a living if you're not born to it.'

Making a living's the last thing on my mind, she had considered, but for his benefit she had shrugged. 'The Hitch it is,' she had replied.

Now the *Windlass* was anchored, and resting its keel lightly on the ground, the airbag half-deflated to make it less of a toy for the wind. She and Allanbridge had descended to find the local people clinging to the Barrier Ridge like lichen. Viewed from the forest's edge, the Hitch would barely have been visible. The collection of huts – little assemblages of flimsy wood that looked toylike in their simplicity – lay in the shadow of the cliffs. And behind them, what seemed like deeper shadow became a regular arch cut into the rock itself. Glancing upward Tynisa saw a few holes higher up, too: entrances and exits for winged kinden perhaps, scouts' seats or murder holes. She looked away hurriedly once her gaze strayed too high, though. Mere human perspective could not live with that vast expanse of vertical stone, and it seemed to her that any moment it must tumble forward, obliterating the Hitch and the *Windlass* and all of them.

Allanbridge had been checking the airship's mooring, and now he returned to her side. His expression was challenging; he knew enough, had been through enough with her, that he could guess at part of her mind. He did not approve, and did not believe that her resolve would last, and yet he understood. He had brought her this far, after all.

If he will not take me over the Ridge, she determined, *I shall trust to my Art to make the climb.*

'Who lives here?' she asked him.

'Fugitives, refugees,' he grunted, stomping off towards the shabby little strew of buildings, and making her hurry to keep up with him.

'But it's not the Imperial Commonweal above here, is it?'

The look he sent her was almost amused. 'More things in life to run away from than the Black and Gold, girl.'

She thought about that, seeing the ragged folk of the Hitch creep out to stare at her and Allanbridge, at the sagging balloon of the *Windlass*. Her first thought was: *Criminals, then?* She had mixed with criminals before – thieves, smugglers, black marketeers. A crooked trading post here between Lowlands and Commonweal, unannounced and half hidden, made a certain sort of sense. *Wouldn't it look grander, though, if there was money to be made here?* she considered, but then Jerez had been a mudhole too, for all the double-dealing and the villainy . . .

But enough of Jerez. She was not yet ready to think of Jerez.

. . . imagining her hand on the sword's hilt, surely she had felt the indescribable satisfaction of driving it in? She had never liked the man, never . . .

She stopped, fists clenched, looking down until she was master of her expression again, forcing that image from her mind, driving it back into the darkness it had arisen from. Was that a flutter of grey cloth at the edge of her vision, the hem of a Moth-kinden robe?

Allanbridge glanced back for her, but she was already catching up.

And there are other reasons to flee the Commonweal, she told herself, desperate to move her imagination on. *Their sense of duty, their responsibilities, that drive them to such madness, some surely must fail and seek to escape from the demands of their fellows.*

She stopped walking then, ending up a step behind Allanbridge and to his left, as though she were his bodyguard or a foreman's clerk.

The people of the Hitch that had assembled to receive them numbered perhaps a score. At least half were Grasshopper-kinden, tall and lean and sallow, with hollow cheeks and high foreheads and bare feet. There were a half-dozen Dragonflies as well, looking just as impoverished. They were as golden-skinned and slender as Salma had been, but if these were fallen nobility, they had fallen very far indeed. There was a Roach-kinden couple, white-haired and stooped, and looming over them all was a single gigantic Mole Cricket woman.

Tynisa had encountered a couple of that giant kinden since the war, both of them Imperial deserters and both of them male. They had been half again as tall as a tall man, enormously broad at the shoulder, massive of arm, with skin like obsidian, and in manner quiet and wary, although that might simply have been the escaped slave in them. This apparition before her was something again. The woman stood surely a foot taller than those two men she remembered, and her body fell in enormous curves – of shoulders, breasts, belly and thighs – so that beneath her brown woollen robe she looked like a melting idol shaped from mud. She had a riotous flow of silver hair and her face, many-chinned and broad, was beaming at Allanbridge with rapacious cheer.

'Why, it's my favourite Lowlander!' she boomed, loud enough that Tynisa feared for the solidity of the cliffs above them.

'Ma Leyd,' Allanbridge named her, making a brief bow. 'Always a pleasure.'

'This man's a friend,' Ma Leyd assured her followers, who were clustered about her colossal waist like children.

'He's the one with the trade boat?' one of the Grasshoppers piped up.

'You see it there,' Ma Leyd replied cheerily, pointing out the *Windlass* with a finger not much smaller than Tynisa's wrist. 'You're on your way up to Siriell's Town, Master Allanbridge?'

'If so advised,' the Beetle confirmed.

'Then I'll have some freight for you on your return,' she promised him. 'For now, come inside. Come talk, come drink.' The Mole Cricket's eyes flicked towards Tynisa. 'Got yourself a wife there, Jons?'

'Not likely,' Allanbridge assured her. 'Just . . .' He looked at Tynisa as though suddenly unsure about her. 'Just an old friend who needs help.'

Ma Leyd lived in the cave at the back of the Hitch. Indeed, Tynisa guessed the big woman's hands had shaped it from the rock of the Barrier Ridge, using Mole Cricket Art to mould and carve the solid stone as she saw fit. Inside were high, groined ceilings, and oil lamps hanging from sculpted hands that reached out from the walls. The whole could have been one of the Great College's grander cellars, an impression reinforced by a small stack of casks at the back.

The lanterns had been dark, but Ma Leyd lit them with a steel lighter without even having to stretch, for all that they were well above Tynisa's head. The enormous woman then settled ponderously on to a threadbare cushion, and one of the Grasshopper-kinden locals hopped in a moment later with a steaming pot, before ladling some of the contents into three bowls.

'Fortified tea,' Allanbridge identified the liquid. 'Not real Commonweal kadith, mind, because frankly that's something of an acquired taste – the taste in question being gnat's piss. This stuff is better.'

Tynisa sipped it, and used all her willpower to keep a polite expression. The fortification involved was plainly some type of harsh grain spirit, whose aftertaste destroyed any virtue in whatever it was fortifying, like a boisterous army sent to defend a small village.

'Now, tell me how things stand, up top,' Allanbridge prompted.

Ma Leyd stretched monstrously. 'Well, dear heart, I hear the Prince-Major has yet to make any serious decrees likely to cause you problems, although his lackeys are all demanding justice from him regarding these terrible bandits and criminals that they see lurking in every shadow. Not just the Town in Rhael, either, but I hear half of Salle Sao's gone rogue as well. All the princes-minor want action, but your man in charge there, he must want it to be someone else's problem. After all, raising levies was what caused half the problems last time.'

Allanbridge nodded, although Tynisa could make little sense of it. 'I might have some more additions to your menagerie then, Ma,' he considered. 'Depends how bad it's got. Tell me about the Town.'

'Still there, such as it is. A year ago and I'd have a whole new list of names for who you should deal with, and those you should avoid, but it looks like Siriell has it straightened out now. The same faces as you met last time are all mostly still in place and not knifing each other. 'Cept for Hadshe, who's dead, and Voren who left. Looks like the current order at Siriell's Town is there to stay.'

Tynisa glanced between Allanbridge and the massive

woman, because whatever dealings were being spoken of were not what she had expected. *I should have known better*. Before the war, Allanbridge had been a smuggler, and it looked as though he had decided to take up his old ways on his visits to the Commonweal.

'Now everyone says the Monarch won't stand for it,' Ma Leyd went on. 'They say that Felipe Shah and his neighbours will get a rap on the knuckles, and a million Mercers will set the land to rights: peace and plenty, love and wonder, all that nonsense. *But* they were saying that almost a year ago and the Monarch does nothing, and frankly it seems even Shah isn't exactly bailing his fealtor princes out like you'd expect. Mind you, that's the Commonweal princes all over: dance and paint and hunt and write poetry and whatever the pits you like, except for actually *doing* something.' Her leer dismissed all the lands extending above them with utter derision.

'And what would you know about it?' Tynisa snapped, the words bursting from her against her will. She knew about the Commonweal, for all that she'd never been there. She knew because the moral standards of the Commonweal – those strict, self-punishing demands that it made of its people – had driven to his death someone that she had loved dearly. He had been too honourable, and the world had not been able to live with him. So he had died. She found that to hear this bloated woman carp on about the shortcomings of the Dragonfly-kinden was more than she could bear. In her heart the poison was stirring restlessly.

Ma Leyd's expression became as stony as her home. 'I saw all too much of the Commonweal, dear, when I travelled across it to find where the Empire had left my husband's corpse.'

'So you've seen the occupied principalities. That's not the *real* Commonweal at all,' Tynisa shot back, quite happy to take this woman on in whatever field of combat she preferred. She discovered that she was standing, though she had no memory of rising to her feet. Even so, she was forced to look up in order to lock eyes with the sitting Mole Cricket. Her hand itched.

In measured stages, the enormous woman also stood. 'You'd best not tell me what I know, dear.' She was surely strong enough to tear Tynisa limb from limb, but the rapier's whisper told her that speed would defeat strength always, so she tensed . . .

'Enough!' Allanbridge burst out, leaping to his feet as well. 'You,' he said, jabbing a finger at Tynisa, 'you want to be on my ship tomorrow, you go outside and cursed well keep your mouth to yourself.'

Tynisa stared mutinously at him, grappling with the frustrated anger within her, but already she was regretting her outburst. Her temper seemed to be a thing apart these days, something she had less and less control of. Her hand twitched again, belated and unbidden, near her rapier hilt.

'I'm sorry,' she forced out, and left Ma Leyd's cave hurriedly, to find that a misting of rain was feathering down outside. It fitted her mood.

Months ago the plan had been made, back in a city that had been home to her for so long. Now Collegium had changed, and she had changed. She was marked with blood, every bit as much as the Mosquito-kinden magician who had enslaved her in Capitas.

She had been shipped back home like a slave, a calculated peace offering made by a Wasp named Thalric, who had been spymaster and turncoat in his time, and was now luxuriating in the title of Regent Consort, or some such – or so Tynisa was given to understand. Of all of them in that war, he had slipped through almost unscathed, to claim power and glory at the end of it. She loathed him, and perhaps she loathed him still more for thinking to bring her back. She had departed the Empire with only some slave's shabby clothes and a pair of matching gold brooches, one hers, the other her dead father's. Not even with the rapier: she had lost that when the Mosquito caught her. Its return would come later, inexplicable as dreams.

Stenwold, who had raised her as his own daughter, had been waiting for her when she alighted from Thalric's flying machine. His face had been all relief at seeing her alive, but deep in his eyes she had seen a condemnation of her failure. She had not done enough. She had gone to rescue a man, and brought back only an eyewitness account of his bloody end.

Tisamon.

And then the news had kept coming: the fallen leaves of war; the blood on her own hands become indelible. Each day some new word had come to trouble her, peeling away what little armour she had retained against the privations of the world, until she could not stay in Collegium longer, nor could she remain amongst those that she had failed, for all they told her it did not matter. She could not stay, yet she had nowhere to go.

There had been one night when she had awakened, screaming, from her dreams . . . *arm red with blood to the elbow – his blade running with it, the Wasp soldiers stabbing and hacking as though what they struck was a piece of butchered meat and not a man . . . his smile, always his smile, the last to fade* . . . She had awoken from that dream and known that she had reached the end of her time in Collegium. Either she must flee or she must bring matters to a close. In the darkness of midnight, her hand had reached out, unbidden, to close about the hilt of her rapier.

How had it come to be there, when it had last been consigned to adorn some Imperial collector's wall or treasure vault? Had some agent provocateur read her mind, and placed it ready for her?

She had never believed in the magic that her mother and father had sworn by, but at that same midnight, suddenly and inexplicably provided with the means to end herself, she wondered if this was not the voice of the universe telling her that it had no further place for her.

With that thought, something of her old fire rekindled, and

she took the blade in her hands, feeling blindly its old familiar weight and grace. Her father had won this blade to give to her mother, and then he himself had kept it for so many years, until their daughter was grown and had proved her skill against him. She chose to believe that he had sent it to her, from beyond the veil of death – from where Mantids went, when their time came.

She had looked up and seen him for an instant, for the first time: the ravaged hulk of her father standing at the window, and then he was gone. A trick of her mind, a holdover of the dream, but she had understood the warning.

I am losing my grip on the world, she realized. *I have killed a friend once and I will kill again unless I do something to stop myself.* The rapier, the agent of that murder, hung there in her hand, sleek and balanced. *There must be work left to do that I can devote myself to, because, if I have nothing left to distract me, I shall go the last few steps and be mad indeed.*

It only remained for her to invent what work that might be. By dawn she had decided the goal, but had no means to accomplish it. How could she get herself to the notoriously isolated Commonweal?

Jons Allanbridge had visited there, she knew. He had shipped Stenwold over there during the war, in a failed attempt to enlist Dragonfly aid against the Empire. Amongst all the bad news, word had come to Tynisa that Allanbridge had since made a return visit or two, joining the many merchants who had tried to strike up a trade with that sprawling nation's insular inhabitants. Still, Allanbridge was more persistent than most and, anyway, the Commonweal was not what it had once been.

She had tracked the man down when he next arrived in Collegium. Now she had a goal, she could hold out in the face of her guilt and the accusing stares of others. She had sat down with Allanbridge over a jug of wine, and told him she wanted to go to the Commonweal.

'I know that Spider-kinden live there,' she had pointed out, for one of Stenwold's companions, on his abortive mission there, had been such a man.

Allanbridge had shrugged. 'Maybe,' he said carelessly, as though her entire future did not depend on his answer. 'What does old Sten Maker say?'

'He doesn't know. He must never know. I don't want him coming after me.' Her confession had come rushing out in a jumble of words.

She had known that he must surely refuse her. She had fumbled away her one best chance of accomplishing the end that she had set herself. Allanbridge was an old acquaintance of her foster-father's, so he would hardly agree to such deception.

But Allanbridge had taken a long, deep breath, staring at her. 'I hear your old man killed the Emperor, and paid for it,' he had murmured at last. The truth was not entirely thus, but it was the story everyone was telling – even the Wasps themselves, it seemed – and Tynisa saw no reason to correct the historians. She had simply nodded, silently waiting out the long pauses the Beetle aviator had now fallen back on.

'A shame,' the man had grunted, ' only Mantis I ever got on with. But this is more than just him, right?'

Another small nod from her.

'I remember Jerez,' Allanbridge had said, unwillingly. 'A lot of bad business there – lots of stuff I don't even *want* to understand. But I hear the news, since. I know what's happened to . . . to the Moth. So maybe I see level with you.'

She remembered that she had been holding her breath at this point.

'Spit and sails, I don't like dodging Sten Maker, but he wasn't there,' Allanbridge had continued sadly, a man finding an unwelcome duty at his door that he could not avoid. 'I *was* there, though, so I can take you to the Commonweal and keep it quiet. That kind of shipping's been my business for twenty years, after all. What you do to make ends meet after that is your own affair.'

Now she sheltered in the *Windlass* until Allanbridge sought her out again. In the hold he sat down with a sigh, frowning at her.

'I'm sorry,' she said, and sorry she was, not for the words spoken but because she had jeopardized her tenuous hold on his good will.

'Commonweal hasn't been open to men like me since forever,' he pointed out gruffly, 'so don't you judge. Just so happens there're people there who'll trade with the likes of me now, only all right, it's not the princes. There are no official channels open to a Lowlander, see? And it's not as simple as you think. Ma Leyd keeps me informed. I need her.'

Tynisa nodded. 'And what does she ask in return?'

'Those from the Hitch that want it, I carry free, when I head back south. Princep Salma's an attractive second chance to some. Plus there's some trade I do for Ma, but that's the main thing. For years there's only been pissant places like this for those that want out of the Commonweal but don't know where else to go. Princep's a little slice of the north in the middle of the Lowlands, and word of it's spread.'

She must have looked doubting, because he shook his head, standing up to go back above. 'Tomorrow morning I'll put you down close enough to Suon Ren for a brisk walk to get you there, and then you go off and . . . well, from there you're on your own. I've a feeling that you won't find the Dragonflies quite what you're expecting, girl, but that's none of my business, and the best of luck to you.'

Two

Salma, Prince-Minor Salme Dien: the only Commonwealer student to attend at Collegium in living memory. He had been sent there because the Commonweal had lost its war with the Wasp-kinden, and Prince-Major Felipe Shah had foreseen that the Lowlanders might become allies against a common enemy. The boy had come to Collegium in his grand finery, with his exotic manners and his golden skin and his inimitably mocking smile.

That year at the College, he and Tynisa had danced around each other like two moths circling the same lantern, closer and closer and yet . . . always when she felt she could reach out and find his hand extended back towards her, he was away again. She wove her webs but never caught him. Always his dance took him away from her, until it was she who followed him, trying to match his steps.

But she would have had him eventually, she knew. Given time, shielded from distraction, he would have been hers. This was an article of faith with her.

But Salma had been distracted along the way by a Butterfly-kinden dancing girl who seemed to change her name every other day, but these days just called herself Grief, as though she had some kind of monopoly on that emotion. Tynisa had never believed in magic, but she found that she could readily concede that Salma had been enchanted by the glow-skinned Butterfly witch.

Even then, she had known in her deepest heart that it would not last. Salma was a fighter, a flier, a man who lived his life without chains. He would need more in the end. He would come back to Tynisa, who alone could match him in all things.

The Empire had not given him the chance, though. Salma, because of who he was and the society that had given birth to him, had become a rallying point for the dispossessed and the refugees. He had led his makeshift army against the Imperial advance, and there, crossing blades with a Wasp general, he had died. And thus the adamantine cord of their joint destiny, which she was sure had been on the very cusp of drawing them close again, had been parted for ever.

She awoke with a start, baffled by the curving contours of the room about her, by the turbulent swaying of her surroundings. Most of all she awoke into the evaporating sense of Salma. Sometimes she dreamt of him rather than of the others, and those dreams were warm and bright. Waking from them cut as deep as any number of nightmares.

He was there as she woke. She did not see him, but his presence was unmistakable, sitting on the edge of her bed and watching her sleep. She even reached a hand out and, in the uncertainty of waking, fully believed that she would touch his golden skin.

The weakness came upon her which had oppressed her since everything had gone so fatally wrong. For a moment she could not move, could not stand, could not even bear to think. Some part of her tried its very hardest *not to be*.

But the world would not oblige, and she understood that she was still aboard the *Windlass*, of course, and it was aloft. Catching her balance against the constant shifting motion, she went aloft to find Allanbridge at the wheel. Normally she would have been woken by the *Windlass*'s oil-drinking engine, but today the airship was moving under clockwork power alone, and using as little of that as Allanbridge needed to keep the craft steady. Instead, most of the work was being done by the burner hoisted up beneath the balloon. The aviator had tried to explain how it all worked, how there was some special gas in the canopy that pulled *up*, and how it pulled up more when it was heated, but none of it had made a great deal of sense to Tynisa.

Now, though, whatever the gas was, it was pulling like a team of draught beetles, and the *Windlass* was ascending with all the ponderous grace of a Collegium matron taking to the air. The cracked and riven wall of the Ridge coursed past them to port, and it seemed that at any moment the airship would be dashed against it, its balloon ruptured and hull smashed to splinters, but Allanbridge knew his trade, and so the *Windlass* maintained her steady climb.

'Suon Ren's just over the edge?' Tynisa asked him.

'A little further than that, but close enough,' he agreed. 'I'll put you down in sight of it.'

Tynisa glanced up at the looming curve of the balloon above. 'I thought you weren't welcome there. If you're in sight of the city, then they'll be able to see *that*,' pointing at the great swell of inflated silk above them.

Allanbridge shrugged, his expression closed. 'Your man there, Felipe Shah, he's progressive, so if he looks out of the window and sees an airship, he won't think the sky's falling on his head – not unless it's black and yellow, anyway. As for the rest of them, you'd be surprised what they can make themselves not see.'

They cleared the crest of the Ridge shortly after, and suddenly the sky was whole again, the late autumn sun crisp and clear over them. Allanbridge made adjustments that sent the *Windlass* scudding over a rugged landscape of abrupt hills and heavy jutting outcrops of stone. It looked to Tynisa almost as if some great cresting wave of rock had been rolling forward with the intention of burying the Lowlands for ever, but here it had frozen in a rubble of stony foam.

She watched shadows duck and bob as a trio of bees, bigger than she was, bumbled over the rough ground. 'Where are the people?' she asked. The land was green enough, but wild and devoid of human life.

'Commonweal's a big place, girl,' Allanbridge told her. 'Galltree told me that the locals reckon it drives you mad to live too close to the edge. Given most of 'em can fly, seems strange to me. Maybe the lords and princes and what have you spread that word, to stop people getting ideas about heading off elsewhere, eh?'

Soon after, the *Windlass* was making her leisurely way over irregular fields ribbed by the plough. Some were deformed by the contours of the land, but a little further on the land had been cut to fit them, each hill stepped and tiered so that, from their lofty perspective, the land appeared as a series of concentric rings.

'There,' Allanbridge prompted. 'See there?'

'What's that?' She spotted a little arrangement of buildings ahead, though still nothing much that she would call civilization.

'It's Suon Ren, girl.'

'That's a village.'

'It's Suon Ren,' Allanbridge repeated. 'Round these parts, that kind of place qualifies as a centre of trade and culture.'

At this distance it was hard to tell, but there were just three stone-built structures that looked like civilization to her. Beyond that, there stood some absolute fantasy of a building on a hill overlooking the rest, four floors high, but most of it either wooden-walled or with no walls at all, and crowned with an overflowing roof garden that cascaded trailing vines and creepers halfway to the ground. All the rest of the place was a loose-knit circle of small dwellings around a central space, nothing but little slant-roofed wooden buildings, and each far enough from its neighbours that the community seemed a collection of hermits. North of it all, the sun caught two silver lines that must be rivers, save that they were too straight to be natural. On one, a long boat of some kind was making a slow, sail-less progress.

Allanbridge was now guiding the *Windlass* down by some

complex artifice, cutting even the clockwork and letting the vast bulk of the airshop ghost silently along, its keel almost brushing the flattened peaks of hills. At the last, he did something that caused a rattling within the ship's bowels, and shortly after that they had dragged to a stop.

For a moment the Beetle aviator stared at her, his face fought over by expressions of sympathy and dislike. At last he sighed, plainly about to make some gesture he fully expected to regret. 'I'm heading north, you hear me? Siriell's Town, it's called. No place that Felipe Shah and his like would be seen dead in, either. North of here the land runs lawless – or else the only law is Siriell's, and she's no noblewoman nor princess.'

Tynisa was not even trying to keep the look of disdain from her face. *Those were the same people that Salma's family must have fought against, the enemy of the Commonweal before the Empire came. But Master Allanbridge needs his profits, is that it?*

'Look . . .' Allanbridge got out a scroll and a reservoir pen and began sketching, quick, rough outlines. 'Here's us, Suon Ren there . . . canals, you see them north of us . . . hills . . . woods, just the basics, the lie of the land. There's no road, but if you keep to this course' – a dotted line on the map – 'you'll see Siriell's Town soon enough. Can't miss the place.' He thrust the makeshift map at her as though it was a weapon, making some part of her instinctively twitch for her sword. 'Going to be doing business there, and then a round of some other contacts in the vicinity, and then back there to pick up what goods I've asked after. Then I'm gone, set for Collegium, and won't be in these parts for half a year at least.' When she still seemed not to understand him he sighed mightily and went on. 'You'll want back. This Commonweal is a madhouse. You come find me at Siriell's Town, I'll take you back home, and maybe neither of us need to mention this entire journey.'

'I won't be going back,' she told him firmly.

'I'm just saying.' When at last she took the map from him, Allanbridge stepped back, plainly indicating that his work was done.

Minutes later she was standing on the earth of the Commonweal, and the *Windlass* was receding like a dream.

She set a good pace for Suon Ren, keeping her eye on the three stone-built structures that clustered together as though ready for an attack by the savages. As she grew nearer, the closing of distance mended some of her initial impression. The Commonweal houses were delicate, looking as though a strong wind would blow them away, but equally it was plain that they had been where they were for a long time. One moment she was the surrogate child of Beetles, born to stone and brick and tile, amid the foundries and the factories and the bustle of industry. Then some inner voice in her called out to awaken her vision, and she saw Suon Ren as its makers had intended.

The graceful dwellings of the Commonwealers were built from wood, true, but also from artistry and exacting skill. Each was like a puzzle-box, its walls composed of sliding panels so that this building was open down half one side, the next one open from halfway up to its roof, the very boundaries mobile and changeable. The roofs were each a single slope, and all sloping in the same direction, as though the entire town was a field of flowers angled at the sun.

She saw it then, although she could never have put it into words. She saw the world from which Salma had sprung.

The largest of the three stone-built structures would be the Lowlander embassy, self-proclaimed, and that was where she went first, waiting at every moment to be challenged by the locals. She knew that the Commonweal enforced its own isolation. She knew that theirs was not a society devoid of martial prowess. Any moment, she expected winged challengers to drop from the skies to arrest her.

Instead, she walked through the scattered buildings of Suon Ren as though in a dream, and nobody so much as looked at her – rather, they ignored her pointedly. She was not part of their world. The Dragonfly-kinden peasants toiling in the fields, the lookouts atop tall platforms, the citizens of Suon Ren as they strolled between its buildings, or spoke together in low voices, they none of them admitted to her existence.

She found the Collegiate ambassador outside the embassy. Stenwold had mentioned this man, one Gramo Galltree, an academic long forgotten in his home city and now on a one-man diplomatic mission. He was an old Beetle-kinden, his hair white and wispy, his dark face creased by time and the sun. He could have been any elderly merchant or College lecturer, save that he stood with the ease of a younger man, and he wore a yellow knee-length tunic with a dark green sleeveless robe over it, clothes in the Dragonfly style. After she had stood, for some minutes, watching him tend a little vegetable garden, he looked up and bobbed his head at her, seeming unsurprised to find her there.

'Master Galltree?' she asked, and saw him instantly revise his opinion as he heard her accent.

'Ah, official business, then?' He carefully leant his rake against the embassy wall. 'I apologize. There are a few communes of Spider-kinden here in the Commonweal, so I'd thought you were local. Please, please, I'm a terrible host. Won't you come in? You have letters for me perhaps?'

Before she could stem the flow of his words, he was bustling inside, forcing her to either follow him or abandon him.

'So, what matters has the Assembly sent you to me about?' His voice drifted from some other room as she entered. The interior of the embassy had once been dominated by a few items of Collegiate furniture, making her wonder just how grand Galltree's enterprise had originally been, when he arrived here decades before. Everything had now been shoved back against the wall, though, and mostly shunted together into one corner, so as to leave as much open space as possible. The windows were thrown open to try and counterbalance the heaviness of the stone walls, and those walls were hidden behind light hangings in tans and faded reds. The overall impression was that Galltree seldom thought much about his original home.

He bustled back in, even then, carefully holding a steaming pot and a little tripod, and set them up in the centre of the floor, as though he was going camping. He sat down, with remarkable ease for a man of his years, and gestured for her to join him. Everything about him, and about her surroundings, was subtly off, with nothing working as she expected, and she felt obscurely threatened, keeping a hand on her rapier hilt for comfort. In the corner of her eye was the suggestion of spectres waiting for their moment: her doubts and fears in a grey robe, with a blank-eyed, accusing face.

'My name is Tynisa Maker,' she told him. 'I'm Stenwold's ward.'

He nodded amiably, as if he had expected no less. 'I knew that Master Maker would not forget Collegium's most far-flung outpost. He sends word?'

Galltree's expression was painfully earnest, and Tynisa took a moment to reorder her words. She was no emissary, yet surely she would secure an audience more swiftly if everyone assumed she was. She would never have to claim it as a fact, when Galltree already seemed to have made the assumption. 'I wish an audience with Prince Shah,' she told him.

He looked a little disappointed that he was not being let in on her supposed official business, but he nodded amiably enough, filling a couple of shallow cups from the pot, and then let a little wrapped package steep in each of them. 'I cannot say whether Prince *Felipe* is in residence at the moment. He has been in and out, as we say, in the last month or so, visiting his fealtors to the west mostly. However, let us sup, and then we can present ourselves – and at least let the castle staff know that a dignitary from Collegium is here.'

The drink tasted mostly like some sort of soup, surprisingly rich and savoury. 'Kadith,' Galltree explained. 'Very popular with the nobility. Each breeds his own, you see, with different herbs and grasses. It's quite a commodity for barter between provinces.' Seeing her frown he hooked out his little bundle. 'The larvae build their little homes from what plants are given them, you see, so the flavour varies from pond to pond.'

'Oh, *caddis*,' she declared, as sudden understanding came to her. The strangeness of it was lost in the fact that the drink was so good. She had the errant thought, *We should import this to Collegium*, before she reminded herself that she was not going back there.

They passed amongst the dispersed buildings of Suon Ren, the locals breezing past, but ignoring her, and barely acknowledging Galltree himself. Tynisa had a sense of their contentment, everything around them part of a grand and changeless pattern that had endured for centuries – a pattern she had yet to earn a place in. An echo of Salma glittered and danced amongst them, teasing her memory for once without drawing blood. The Commonwealers walked, meditated or wrote, practised their archery or took off into the sky on shimmering wings. There was precious little talk at all between them, as though everything worth saying had already been thoroughly discussed by their grandparents' parents. Aside from a single man hammering away at a forge on the edge of town, the loudest thing in Suon Ren was the younger children, who chased about between the buildings in some game that involved tagging one another and then running away. Tynisa smiled to watch them, until she heard one child cry out, while tagging another, 'You're the Wasp! You're the Wasp!'

'The war never came this far, did it?' she asked Galltree, realizing, as she did, that her knowledge of Commonweal geography was almost entirely lacking.

'No indeed,' he replied, 'but many of Prince Felipe's people travelled to meet it.'

Then they were ascending the rise that led to the castle, and Tynisa began to appreciate what a bizarre folly the place truly was. The structure seemed to make do with half the walls of any other building – not that whole sides of it were open but, instead, great sections of its exterior, at various heights, had simply been omitted, allowing both sight and access into the building's interior. Much that was there was strewn with green, a profusion of vines tumbling in a verdant mane from some manner of roof garden, and other gardens within, also, to merge seamlessly with the outside. There were inner walls, too, but they were no more complete than the outer, so that, looking into the heart of the castle, Tynisa experienced a feeling not unlike vertigo – finding her Lowlander sense of boundaries and borders constantly violated.

Gramo stopped abruptly, and for a moment she could not work out why. Only after a moment's reflection did she guess that a few more steps would actually have brought them notionally *within*, a separate space whose limits were entirely invisible to her.

'Do we . . . Is there a bell we ring?' she asked.

'We wait,' Gramo advised. 'You must realize, the Commonwealers do not have that sense of urgency you may recall from Collegium.'

She could see people further within, who she guessed were servants busy about the tasks of maintaining the place, but none of them seemed to see her. The unseen walls of this place evidently blocked her from their notice.

With a little creaking of joints, Gramo seated himself. 'Ah, but there is no such thing as idle time in the Commonweal. This is a time to reflect and to meditate upon one's life.'

The idea brought a sour taste to Tynisa's mouth. *I have no more need of that kind of introspection. Anything but.* 'I can't see how this sort of building can have stood them much stead during the war,' she remarked, to burn away the silence.

'Oh, this is no castle, in that sense,' Gramo admitted. 'This is Prince Felipe's new home, built after the loss of his family's original seat of power. There is little enough change in the Commonweal, but this is a new . . . interpretation, shall I say, of their architecture. Mind you, I'm afraid their stone castles hardly fared better than this one would. Perhaps that's the point.'

There was a flurry of wings and a Dragonfly landed a few yards away, a lean man with high cheekbones and hollow cheeks, his hair a steely grey. As he approached them, he moved like a man in his prime, and nothing in his manner or stance suggested age. His clothing was in green and blue, a robe and under-robe as Gramo wore, but of far finer quality, being silk embroidered with gold. For a moment, Tynisa thought that this must, in fact, be the prince unexpectedly answering his own door.

'Seneschal Lioste,' Gramo named him. 'You do me much honour with your presence.'

'Ambassador,' the seneschal replied, neither warmly nor coldly, but a simple statement of fact. His eyes flicked to Tynisa questioningly.

'Ah, well.' Gramo gestured vaguely in her direction, 'we have a visitor from the Lowlands, as you may guess. She is sent by Master Stenwold Maker, who visited with the prince so recently.' The full year that had passed did not make a dent in that 'recent', Tynisa guessed. 'Tynisa Maker is here to pay her formal respects to the prince, or to his retinue during his absence.'

Seneschal Lioste stared at her and said nothing.

'Your prince, of course, welcomed Master Maker on his visit, as did the Monarch, since when your prince has taken a refreshingly open stance, of course, towards my homeland,' Gramo went on, hands worrying at the cloth of his robe. The Dragonfly glanced at him, face carefully blank, and then his eyes returned to Tynisa.

'Mistress Maker is here at his behest – Master Maker's, that is – formal greetings from the Lowlands . . . in this new, this day and age . . .' Gramo faltered to a stop.

'Prince Felipe has yet to return,' the seneschal said, and

Tynisa decoded his expression at last. Here was a man faced with something that he had no idea what to do with.

'Mistress Maker was hoping to be admitted to the castle,' Gramo tried gamely. 'Master Maker, when he was here, was summoned, of course . . .'

'Master Maker had brought home one of the Monarch's subjects,' the Seneschal reminded him, apparently seizing on something that he at last understood. It was plain that, however progressive the prince himself might be, in his absence his staff fell back on what they knew. 'My prince shall return to Suon Ren shortly. Perhaps the Spider-kinden shall be sent for in due course.' He was meticulously polite in words, manner and expression, but Tynisa could almost see the panic leaking out at the edges. The idea of allowing a stranger, a foreigner, into Felipe's home behind his master's back was obviously more than the seneschal could countenance.

Descending back towards the embassy, Gramo was full of apologies, defending the natural reticence of the Dragonflies, assuring her that the prince himself would send for her eventually. 'You must get used to the slower pace, is all it is,' he explained. 'One does not rush, here.'

Gramo prepared her a room at the embassy, which mostly involved hooking up a hammock-like affair for her to sleep in. Her new chamber was dominated by a solid Collegium desk, the sort that a well-to-do academic would write his memoirs on. She was willing to bet it had seen no use in ten years, and there was no chair.

They ate later, still no word having come from the castle. Gramo prepared a meal of beans and roots and other vegetables, his choice of spices too subtle for her palate, the flavours seeming bland or else more bitter than she was used to, the variety broad, the quantities mean. Everything came from his own garden behind the embassy. He appeared to be entirely self-sufficient.

'What about the people of Suon Ren?' Tynisa pressed him. 'Surely they don't just ignore you?'

'Oh, they're very good,' he protested. 'The prince invites me to his castle sometimes. There are recitals, music, theatricals . . . Hunts and dances also, although I am somewhat unsuited to such diversions. It's just,' the old Beetle smiled wistfully, 'I can never *be* one of them. It is not that they keep me out . . . only, I cannot fly with them, cannot think with them. I have become as much a Commonwealer as any son of Collegium, but it is not enough sometimes. And then there are their beliefs . . . Of all things, it saddens me most that, being Apt, I cannot understand them.'

His words baffled Tynisa. 'Surely you don't believe in ghosts and magic,' she stated. Inwardly, something twisted awkwardly at the thought. Tisamon, her father, had believed in such things, and in his company she had occasionally witnessed too much: sights that still hung on her mind the next morning, ones that sunlight could not dispel. She had been brought up and tutored by the practical people of Collegium, though, who believed in nothing that artifice and philosophy could not confirm with experimental proof. She had learned every year in College that there was no such thing as magic, for all that the old Inapt kinden might claim otherwise. Magic was a crutch, a convenient excuse to cover all manner of crimes: *A magician made me do it.*

Gramo gave her a weak smile. 'Of course, of course, and yet . . . I see the Dragonfly-kinden live every day of their lives as though magic was a real force, as potent and wild as the weather. I have come to terms with it. I do not pretend to understand it, but at the same time I will not mock them for it. And I have found that I cannot explain the way . . . everything works here, the chances and the odd coincidences, that they call fate and predestination. It seems to serve them well enough.'

Or it did until the Wasp armies reached them, was Tynisa's thought, but she left it unspoken.

'Who can say what may be true, so far away from Collegium's white walls?' the old Beetle murmured softly, and in his voice there was a young man's longing, for far vistas and lost secrets, and for the world to be something grander than it was.

At the evening's end, when Gramo had tidied away the supper bowls, he stopped her just as she was retiring to bed.

'You're not here on official business, are you?' he said sadly.

She shook her head. 'I mean neither you nor any other here any harm, I swear, but I do need to speak to the prince.' *Because I have burned all my other bridges, and this tenuous link with Salma is the only thing I have left.*

'May I ask what has brought you here, perhaps?'

She was at first not going to answer, but the shadows seemed to be building in the room around him as the fire guttered, and there were silhouettes there, clawing their way out of the grave of her mind. 'Three dead men,' she told Galltree shortly, then retreated to her hammock.

Three

By objective standards, her father Tisamon had failed at almost everything in his life.

He had failed as a Mantis, giving his heart to one of the Spider-kinden they so despised. Later, he had failed his second lover, the Dragonfly Felise Mienn, by abandoning her. He had failed his oldest friend Stenwold Maker by leaving his side in his hour of greatest need.

At the last, brought to bay in the Imperial arena, he had failed to kill the Wasp Emperor. It was his greatest deed, already immortalized in song and celebrated on stage: the Mantis that brought down an empire. Except that the Empire was already doing a good job of climbing right back up. Except that the Emperor had been dead even as Tisamon was at the centre of a knot of furious Wasp soldiers, shedding blood and being hacked at like an animal. The Emperor had been a victim of a Mosquito-kinden who had caught Tynisa, and had brought her to the arena so she could watch her father die.

She remembered, though. The blow he had struck, as he had fought his bloody, tattered way clear of the Wasp throng, was not against the Empire's overlord, but to slay the Mosquito-kinden who was tormenting her. She had come all that way to save her father but, instead, at the end he had done what remained in his power to rescue her.

And he had died. The Emperor's guard had made sure of that, cutting and slicing at the corpse long after life had made its exit. She had witnessed that, and felt her gorge rise, felt the horror and despair . . . but then all those feelings had burned away, for a moment. Her Mantis blood had risen within her, the half-heritage that Tisamon had bequeathed her. She had seen their butchery as the tribute it was, for he had shaken them so deeply, pride of the Empire as they were, that they could not risk even the slightest chance that he might yet live.

In one part of his life only could dead Tisamon claim success. He had been a killer, a relentless, poised and deadly killer, bearing as his credentials the sword and circle badge of the Weaponsmasters. To his daughter, he had given the only gift he had, by passing to her all he knew of the ancient art of separating lives and bodies.

She clung to it now. Here, alone and far from home, crippled by lost friends and by her own victims, she needed his guidance and his strength. All she had of him, though, was what she carried within her.

So it was that Tynisa found herself abandoned in Suon Ren.

That word would have been considered unkind by Gramo Galltree, who was doing everything in his power to make her stay a comfortable one: cooking and cleaning and making polite conversation about the weather, or trying to get her to talk about Collegium, his long-lost home. As a day passed, though, and then another, Tynisa became increasingly aware that Gramo's power here was minuscule: he just did not *matter* to the locals, and neither did she. She could walk every one of the broad, almost unformed streets of the town, and it was as though she was invisible to all but the children, and even they kept clear of her – parental warnings no doubt ringing in their ears.

Sometimes the castle seneschal, or some other functionary, would come to the embassy for a few brief words with Galltree, and each time it was plain that the question was the same: *Is she still here?* Sometimes they came to stare at her, as though she was some grotesque piece of artwork, but they would not answer her questions, or even recognize that she was capable of speech.

With so little outside stimulus, she sank deeper into herself. Her days were spent hunting between the Commonwealer buildings, looking for she knew not what, but sensing others moving on parallel paths, always just out of sight, but constantly in her mind. When darkness fell they closed in, so that she would sit in her little room at the embassy and listen to the ghosts have their way with the place, moving just out of sight, the whisper of a robe's hem, the harsh scrape of Tisamon's boots. Sometimes she heard the distant echo of Salma, laughing gently at some remark made by who-knew-which shade, and she would hunch tight in her hammock, turning her back to the world and trying to blot it all out.

After two days, she took to her practising again, because that was the only part of the woman she had been that she cared to revive, and because it was a gift from her father. While Gramo pottered about in his garden, she used his large room as her Prowess Forum, rapier tasting the air, darting and stepping through all the intricate passes and guards of the Mantis styles, each coming unbidden and unrusted to her mind, a smooth-running sequence of steel. For two hours she strung her body through them all, and back again, fighting imaginary duels in her mind: against one, against many, against overwhelming odds; rehearsing that final dance that all Mantis warriors hoped for.

She completed her pass, blade glittering in the air, and found the rapier's point falling into line with the chest of a Dragonfly man now standing in the doorway. He looked to be another of the seneschal's stamp, wearing clothes of the same green, gold and blue colours, but more practically made and harder-wearing. His hair was a little longer than the fashion in Suon Ren, and bound back, and she guessed he was older than the seneschal as well.

'I hope I do not interrupt,' he said mildly. 'I am sent from the castle.'

The surprise of actually being spoken to dried her throat,

and it was a moment before she could speak. 'The ambassador is not here . . .' Abruptly a thought came to her, a certainty: 'The prince is returned.'

'As you say,' the Dragonfly confirmed. 'Seneschal Coren has reported a petition that disturbs him, a Lowlander demanding an audience.'

'You are sent for me?'

'I am sent here to find out what it is you want with the prince,' he corrected her. There was a straightness in his bearing that was almost reminiscent of Tisamon, a pride rooted in ancient places. She wondered if the man was a Dragonfly Weaponsmaster come to kill her, if her answers did not suit.

Her rapier found its home in her scabbard, and she let out a long breath. 'What do you want me to say?' she asked him, finding the locals' elaborate politeness too standoffish.

'When Stenwold Maker came here, he spoke of war. Are you sent on the same mission?'

She sensed that this was the question that could see her turned away, although she could not quite grasp the significance the man was putting into his words. 'I have come to talk to the prince about Salma – about Prince Salme Dien.' She stumbled over the formal Commonweal name, because he had always just been 'Salma' to her. 'Did you know him? The prince became his guardian after Salma's father died.' Uncertainty was evident in her voice, and the Dragonfly shook his head slightly.

'He was kin-obligate to the prince.' It was another polite correction. The Commonweal tradition that saw children find surrogate homes with those of other castes and trades was something alien to the Lowlands. 'It is true that Prince-Minor Salme Dien had the honour of being chosen by Prince Felipe as such. It is a rare thing indeed for a prince to so bless the children of another noble family. We all remember him fondly. To my prince, he was as a son.' Something was softening in the man, his cold manner melting away, and she felt a connection with him, tenuous but present – the first time she had found any echo of humanity in this reserved people since Salma had died.

Tynisa realized how she was clenching her fists, nails digging painfully into her palms, as if in readiness for her next words. 'You know that he is dead?'

There was no surprise. 'Your Master Stenwold Maker brought a letter from Salme Dien: a farewell to the prince. Clearly Dien knew that he would die, or guessed at it. You were his friend, I see. His death has marked you.'

More than his friend, Tynisa thought, but she just nodded. Somewhere in Gramo's house that irresistible smile of his winked and wounded, the echo of the man she had known and loved. 'I just thought . . . he did so much for the Lowlands. Perhaps in the end nobody did more to stop the Wasps. I just thought that someone should come and speak of him to Prince Felipe, and about what he did. I don't know . . .' Her voice began to crack and she scowled, reaching for her Weaponsmaster's core of self-control, and finding it slippery in her hands. 'I don't know if there has been a messenger, or if Stenwold sent a letter, or . . .' She finished lamely. 'And that's why I've come.' Laid out like that, it seemed a pitiful excuse for such a journey.

The Dragonfly was staring at her so intensely that she thought she must have delivered a mortal insult somehow. His casual manner had evaporated entirely. 'No one has come,' he said softly. 'The prince has waited, but no word has arrived from your Lowlands, for this duty of duties. No doubt your great men of the Lowlands have much to occupy them.' He took a deep breath. 'Tell me of him.'

'Will your prince not hear me?' she asked, frustrated all of a sudden. She imagined briefly an infinite sequence of servants, each one demanding every detail of her tale before passing her into the hands of the next one, until her words grew stale and hard as month-old bread. The next words escaped before she could stop them: 'Please, I've come so far . . .'

He sighed. 'Forgive our poor hospitality. When our seneschal brought word of your arrival, perhaps it was natural to assume that Stenwold Maker was attempting to further his campaign against the Empire by some other means. We have not treated you as befits a guest, and certainly not as befits one on such a gracious and solemn errand. Please, tell me of Salme Dien.'

She stared at him, trying to recast him as something other than simply a Dragonfly man, not young and yet ageless, wearing clothes that were surely less fine than Lioste's had been, but then, of course, he had been *travelling*, and these were clothes meant for the road.

'Master – my lord – Your Majesty,' she stammered, making him a College magnate and a Spider Aristos and finally an emperor.

'Prince Felipe,' he said quietly, 'or "My Prince", if you were a retainer. Or Shah, if you prefer. But please' – and his voice shook just a little despite his iron control of it – 'tell me of my kin, of my boy. Tell me of Salme Dien.'

And so she did. As he sat on the floor like a child, she told him how Salma had formed his own army, his own nomadic principality of the lost and the fugitive. She spoke of how the errant prince had won the respect of the Sarnesh Ants, and how he had led the assault on the Imperial Seventh Army, breaking their lines and destroying their siege engines, so that the Ant-kinden could make their assault.

She told him how Salma had died in that battle, but sensed that those were not the details he wished to hear. Instead she passed on to the city that Salma's followers were building west of Sarn, to which they had given the name Princep Salma in his memory.

Of the Butterfly-kinden woman who had been Salma's lover, she said nothing.

Felipe Shah listened in silence to every word, nothing of his thoughts showing in his expression, and his gaze remained clear when she had finished. 'He met his destiny well. Would that we were all so lucky. My Salme Dien became a true prince of the Commonweal before he died, and that is something that many of us who bear the empty title never achieve. What would you have of me, Tynisa?'

The question caught her unprepared. 'I'm not here to ask for anything.'

'Nonetheless, I am in your debt. If you will not barter for my favour now, then return to seek it, or send word. You have done me a courtesy fit for princes, one that I would not have expected to come from the Lowlands, where such things are not understood. You have brought Salme Dien back to me.'

She felt embarrassed at the praise, not knowing what to do with it.

'Prince Felipe, I seek nothing . . .' *I have nothing.* She now realized that she had come to the end of her road. *And what now? Walk on to Capitas and attack the Empress? Is all my life shrunk to this moment?* She thought of asking to stay in Suon Ren, but the idea of living as a recluse in the midst of all of these elegant, alien people, with nobody but Gramo and perhaps the prince to talk to . . . She would become a shadow, a nothing, waning and dwindling in the vacuum of their turned backs. 'I . . .' she began, but there were no more words.

'I am a prince-major of the Commonweal, whose only master is the Monarch,' Felipe Shah told her. 'And I am in your debt, so you have but to ask.' He stood up to go, and she tried to speak, tried to beg him for . . . but there was nothing, a void where the future had been.

He bowed, and took his leave.

That same evening found the seneschal, Lioste Coren, back at the embassy door, brushing aside Gramo Galltree and seeking out Tynisa.

'The prince has spoken,' he declared. 'He advises you to leave.'

Tynisa stared at him open-mouthed, even though she herself

had decided she could not stay. 'He said he owed a debt . . . He wants me to go?'

A battle fought its way briefly across Lioste's face. 'Do not . . .' he started, and then his dislike of her finally gave way before his duty to defend his prince. 'He does not banish you. He does not cast you off. My prince has some small talent with the future, however. He sees only grief for you here. We are well aware that the Lowlander merchant is at Siriell's Town. My prince advises you to leave his domain – to leave the Commonweal, to return home. He says you will be happier there. It is because he owes you a debt that he gives you this advice.' The effort of being civil to her was plainly stretching him. '*Please.*'

'What shall you do?' Galltree asked her later, after she had listlessly picked at the late supper he had prepared.

'Would you let me stay here even if the prince wanted me gone?'

Galltree twisted the silk of his robe wretchedly, and she held a hand up to forestall his crisis of conscience. 'It doesn't matter.' She took a deep breath. 'This Siriell's Town, it's a rough place?'

'Lawless.' Galltree nodded emphatically. 'Rhael Province – the family that ruled there under Felipe's, they're all gone, long gone, I think. In such places, others creep in, fugitives from the order of the Commonweal. These days, there are many such provinces, especially since the war.'

Her hand was on her sword hilt again, and she could sense the ghosts gathering close, waiting to hear her decision. 'I'll go,' she said. *Home or die, and how convenient that both are to be found in the same direction. I don't even have to choose right now.* She found that she had no intention of rejoining Allanbridge, if indeed he was not already on his way back to Collegium. Home held nothing but sharp edges for her now. She could not look Stenwold or Che in the face without seeing dead Achaeos reflected in their eyes – and how she felt him close and gloating with that admission – and she was being forced out of Suon Ren so very politely. How good of the world to provide a sink like Siriell's Town to drown herself in.

She took out Allanbridge's rough map, and looked Galltree straight in the eye. 'Anything to add to this?' she asked.

The road to Siriell's Town was a matter of heading north-east as best she could: bridging the canals, and then heading over increasingly hilly country until she had made the subtle transition from land that still knew the hoe today all the way down through a gradient of neglect, to land that had not been sowed in a decade or more. She saw a few villages on the way, and avoided them by choice. There were no other travellers, no merchants or messengers, no flying machines overhead. The sense of the land was one of quiet desolation. She knew she would feel different if the Commonweal had accepted her in any way, but aside from Felipe Shah's brief moment of openness, she felt more a stranger here than she had done when she arrived – and even the prince thought it would be best if she left.

Each morning, and sporadically throughout the day, she checked her bearings as best she could by Allanbridge's landmarks, thinking, *So I can't miss the place can I, Jons? As if I believe that.*

But when she came within sight of Siriell's Town – having veered west some distance from her intended course – she found that Allanbridge had been telling nothing but the truth. It was indeed a town, or something resembling one, but at its heart was a castle upon a hill, and Tynisa saw instantly that it looked something like the exemplar of Felipe's own. Complete, it had constituted a six- or seven-floored hexagonal tower, narrowing towards a point at the top. The walls were lanced with arrowslit windows, so that no attacker on the ground or in the air would have been safe from the defenders' missiles. Tynisa, having observed the sturdy walls of Collegium and the Sarnesh fortifications, could see only absences here: nowhere to place artillery, not that the Dragonfly-kinden would know what to do with it; no reinforcing of the walls, so that catapult or leadshotter assault would hammer them down all the sooner. This was a castle that had been designed to hold off men from another age.

It would not even serve for that purpose, any more. One whole side of it had sloughed off and tumbled down the hill years before, leaving a teetering rotten tooth of a place latticed with the shorn-off stubs of internal walls. The hollow shell of the interior had been colonized haphazardly by its new masters, for there were tents and shacks and wood-frame structures not only about the walls and within the castle's hollow footprint, but straggling up the walls themselves, as though growing there like mushrooms. A further shambles of makeshift dwellings had spread out from the castle's collapsed side in a jumble of huts packed far closer than the homes at Suon Ren. The entire place looked foul and squalid to Tynisa.

There was a clear effort to try and farm some of the land around Siriell's Town, with a hundred little plots scratched into the soil. Several of these had adults or children standing guard over them, as though protecting seams of precious metal. They stared at her suspiciously, as she passed between them on her way to the town proper. Drawing closer, she saw that the narrow streets radiating out from the broken face of the castle were cluttered with people, many of whom seemed to be drunk or unconscious, and a couple of whom were clearly dead. The air washing over Tynisa reeked of sweat and refuse, and resonated with arguments and shouting, the clatter of pots, singing, the odd scream and the roaring declamations of some kind of street entertainer.

Most of the resident scum were Dragonfly-kinden, she noticed, and it was plain that noble paragons such as Salma or Felipe Shah were only setting an example that many of their fellows failed to match. Most of the other outlaws were tall, lean Grasshopper-kinden, but there was a fair quota of halfbreeds and other kinden, including some Mantids and even a few Wasps.

A middle-aged Dragonfly in a ragged robe reached out to tug at her sleeve. 'How much?' he slurred. 'How much for it?'

She slapped his hand away, and in that moment her rapier was a comforting presence, resting against the man's neck. He seemed too drunk to quite understand, so she kicked him in the parts for good measure, rousing a murmur of appreciation, or sympathy, from some of the degenerates nearby.

She had not thought to find Wasps in the Commonweal, but their pale faces kept leaping out at her as she passed through this filthy town, and she could see that they were prospering here too. There were only a handful, but people got out of their way, and wherever they sat, each held court with a gang of local ruffians at his beck and call. Watching a few of them, and the craven way in which most of the locals bowed and scraped, she soon made the connection. The Empire had dealt the Commonweal the most savage beating in that nation's history.

At the end of the Twelve-year War three whole principalities – perhaps a third of the Monarch's domain – were under the black and gold flag, and the Imperial forces had only halted their advance because of an uprising in one of their subject cities back along the supply chain. Even though a treaty had been signed, pledging future peace, and even though the three captured principalities were now nominally free, following reversals suffered in the Empire's war with the Lowlands, everyone knew that the armies of black and gold could return at any time. Their repeated defeats had wormed their way into the consciousness of the Commonweal, and even people who had not taken up arms knew that the Wasp-kinden were to be feared.

After that, she was looking out for each renegade Imperial, her fingers constantly hovering near her sword hilt, some part of her mind plotting her own glorious fall. To rid the Commonweal of Wasps? To rid Felipe Shah's principality of the vermin of Siriell's Town? What might she not set her blade to? To die in the pursuit of some grand and bloody ideal, was that not the Mantis way? There was no past she wished to face, no future she could conceive, but Siriell's Town offered her an eternal bloody present: fighting as Tisamon had fought, and losing herself here just as he had sought oblivion in Helleron after her mother had died.

For surely the world has no better use for me, she thought and, even as she did, her eyes lit on a face she recognized – bold as the sun, a man she had never wanted to see again.

She had been fleeing Jerez, as much as Collegium, when she came to the Commonweal, but here was Jerez mocking her on the streets of Siriell's Town.

Jerez had been the idea of doomed Achaeos. There was some box, he said, just a little thing that a man could grip in one hand, but the Moth insisted it was of vital importance. Somehow, in the middle of a war, Achaeos had talked Stenwold into backing an expedition to retrieve it, and Tynisa had gone with him, to nobody's gain.

Tisamon had been with her, watching her back as she watched his; and Jons Allanbridge of course, to get them there. Then there had been the two Wasps. One, the arch-traitor Thalric, had subsequently escaped to become a big man away in the Empire – yet another sack of blood she had never quite managed to cut open, for all he deserved it. And then there had been Gaved, who claimed to be independent of the dictates of the Empire. Tynisa had long decided that if he was genuinely something other than a servant of the Emperor, then he was something even worse: a freebooter, a mercenary, a thief and a kidnapper. Like Thalric, though, and unlike Achaeos, he had come out of the business untouched, and had been the only one to make any kind of profit from the whole wretched expedition.

While others had bled and died, Gaved had left Jerez with a Spider-kinden girl on his arm, and an eyewitness familiarity with Tynisa's own crimes.

And here, on the stinking streets of Siriell's Town, was Gaved himself, with his intolerable burden of knowledge practically shrieking out to her. She watched as he spoke to some halfbreed who seemed to be a taverner, passing over several trinkets in return for some information or other – then the Wasp was off down the street with that light and easy step only truly owned by the utterly guilty.

And the irresistible thought came to Tynisa: *I can kill him. I can start by ridding the world of Gaved, right here, right now.* Because, although killing Gaved would be a pitiful gift to the world, at least it would give the drift of her life some meaning before the end.

Four

She had never been in Siriell's Town before, but instinct had taken over and she skulked along in Gaved's wake, without any suggestion that he was aware of her. He seemed a busy man, too, with plenty of people to talk to: darting from hovel to shack, exchanging words, paying his way with what looked like some little cut stones. Sometimes she caught him looking over his shoulder, and she guessed she was not the only person here who wished him ill, something that seemed entirely understandable to her.

Twice she thought he was going to get into a fight. The first time, he was accosted by another Wasp and she heard angry words exchanged, the man accusing Gaved of some disloyalty – perhaps to the Empire that both had patently abandoned – but Gaved smoothed matters over with some joke, fending off the man's anger. The aggressor looked more than a little drunk and Gaved was able to evade him quickly.

The second time a half-dozen or so Grasshoppers tried to accost him, and although his hands threatened them with Wasp Art they only kept their distance but did not disperse. They were armed with spears and staves and knives, and they clearly wanted Gaved to go along with them to some local tyrant or other. Tynisa watched, interested to see if she would have to save the man's life in order to have the pleasure of killing him herself.

One of the Grasshoppers became too bold, reaching for the Wasp's sleeve, even though his fellows were still holding back. A bitter expression crossed Gaved's face briefly and Tynisa saw his hand flash fire, knocking the grasping man off his feet, still alive but with one leg scorched. In the next instant the Wasp had taken to the sky, his wings lifting him back over the adjoining buildings. The Grasshoppers cursed and gave chase, as their own Art sent them leaping and bounding along at rooftop level, determined not to let Gaved get away. The wounded man yelled after them, demanding aid that was not offered, and then he began to crawl away, weeping with pain.

Tynisa loped into action. She did not possess the Art to follow either the Grasshoppers or their prey, but she could see the net of his pursuers as it spread. Hurriedly, she climbed up to the creaking roof of the largest shack, spying them out, seeing who gave up soonest, who continued following a trail. She took only moments to make her guess, and then she dropped back down to street level and went hunting.

It felt good – and so little had felt good recently – to be moving swiftly and silently through the shabby streets, rapier swaying at her side like a faithful companion beast. This was more a taste of life than the world had afforded her in a long time now, since the war.

Sometimes people got in her way, but they got right back out of it once they noticed her expression, Wasps as well as locals, for she was not someone to stop, just then.

She slowed as she neared the wretched district her instincts had led her towards, and began to quarter it more subtly, street by street, her eyes not actively searching so much as taking it all in – letting the filthy sights and sounds wash over her while sifting them for familiarity. She encountered a few of the Grasshoppers, angry and frustrated at their failed search, turning back now to make their excuses to whoever had hired them. She paid them no mind.

As she shifted sidelong into the shadows beneath a shed's

sagging eaves she found a core of stillness, a Mantis's watchful invisibility before the strike, as though the shade of Tisamon stood beside her, hand on her shoulder, lending her his kinden's Art. The other ghosts had been left far behind.

There. She had him. The cloaked figure walking almost – not quite – like a Dragonfly, but a little too burly despite his best efforts. She watched as he slipped out from between two buildings, a little astray from where she had predicted, but close enough. There was a brief pale flash of Wasp skin as he glanced about, and then Gaved hurried off, not at the idle saunter of before, but like a man in a hurry to get somewhere.

She flowed after him, like a ghost herself, keeping up with him at a distance, street for street. When she saw he was heading out of Siriell's Town her satisfaction only increased. She would be able to kill him cleanly and without interruption, before returning to this festering pit to begin earning her atonement in blood.

He made good time after that, but always on the ground, not wanting to take wing and be too visible. Shortly, he was at the outskirts, where Siriell's Town petered out into the most wretched of slums, amid the utter squalor of those too weak to fight for something better. Shacks and hovels had become just makeshift tents, cloaks propped up on sticks. The stink was vile, with flies rising in whirling clouds from makeshift latrines, and from bodies.

Gaved did not stop for any of this, and nor did Tynisa, although her stalking had become more careful as her cover diminished. She fell further back, changing her tactics from crowds and walls to using the curve and lurch of the land against him: creeping low, meandering left and right as the contours took her, but always managing to keep him in sight. His track took him through barren farmland in which some of the locals were trying to scratch a living, and she followed him field by field, crossing their boundaries, slinking along irrigation ditches and taking the occasional stand of stunted trees as a gift.

Dusk was on its way now, a bloated moon having already hauled itself clear of the horizon. Gaved had passed the last patch of farmland, too stony now for anything but a handful of scrawny sheep watched over by a Grasshopper youth, and his red and black beetle that circled the animals constantly in a vigilant trundle. One hill beyond, Gaved turned down into a sheltered defile, and there made camp.

Watching his quick, professional movements as he set a little fire beneath the overhang and hung a tiny pot over it, she almost forgot why she had followed him. Thinking himself alone out here, he had become an honest man, quietly competent and well able to brave the wilderness, seemingly more at home than he had been on the streets of Siriell's Town. She watched for longer than she intended, out in the cold and the dark, as he cooked up something almost scentless to eat, over a fire that gave no smoke.

At the last, and shivering slightly from the chill, she drew her rapier in one smooth, silent motion. His wings and sting would give him all the advantages when at range, yet she could not bear to simply kill him from behind. This was not squeamishness: she wanted him to know the agent of justice before he died.

Even as she took her first step towards him, his voice called out, 'About time. Now come out where I can see you.' He was standing up, one hand out with palm open, but not quite looking at her – knowing that he was observed but unable to make her out in the darkness beyond his fire. She edged closer, in inches and steps, and he cast about, frowning and tense, but unwilling to flee from mere shadows. In her slow progress there was a fierce battle being fought, his eyes and the moon against her stealth, until she was almost within rapier's reach. Then the firelight caught her, and he saw at last who she was.

His expression was almost all she could have wanted: utter shock at first, but swiftly replaced by an intense loathing that mirrored her own thoughts exactly. She had to kill him, because he was a reminder of all the things she was trying to forget. He, in that instant of recognition, had made a similar resolution – and quite possibly for similar reasons.

'What are you doing here?' he demanded. 'You've got the whole of the cursed Lowlands! Why can't you keep there?' The immediate hostility was gratifying: no wheedling, no excuses, no feigned friendships, nothing to tempt any uncertainty; just a man who very plainly did not want to see her.

'Perhaps I'm the new Collegiate ambassador,' she said. 'Why are you fouling the Commonweal, Wasp?' And it was a release to be able to speak so frankly – and viciously – to someone, for a change. She was already calculating angles, distances. If he took wing, there would be a moment sufficient for her to rush forward and impale him. If he lashed out at her with his sting she would trust to her reflexes to read the motion, to be casting herself aside and in again even as he formed his intention to shoot. Poised on a knife-edge of reflex, his death within her gift, she could afford to talk, to make him understand, relishing his hatred and casting it right back at him.

'No fool would make you ambassador,' he told her. 'Wait – this is where the airship visits. Did Maker send you here?'

When she neither confirmed nor denied it, he bared his teeth. 'Just do what you came for and go back to the Lowlands,' he told her. 'I don't want trouble. Just go.'

That was too much for her. 'And how do you imagine I can just go *back* after what happened?' she hissed, bunching herself to spring. His hand was slightly lower now, the talk taking him off his guard. In a moment, she would have him.

'Oh,' he said, almost to himself, 'the Moth boy died, then.'

It froze her even as she was about lunge for him. *The Moth boy died, then.* For, of course he had. Not when she herself had run him through; nor even later in the Collegium infirmary. While Tynisa had been off chasing her father, *the Moth* had levered himself up from his sickbed to try and save his own people from the Empire and there, in the remote mountain fastnesses of Tharn, he had died. The delay had been just enough, after her terrible deed, to fool Tynisa into believing that she might not, after all, be the woman who had killed her half-sister's lover.

'Is that what this is about?' Gaved asked Tynisa, seeing the struggle inside her. 'You're running away?'

Every instinct howled for him then, but her own guilt was like a grey anchor that held her back, so that she twitched for action but did not lunge, sending him two steps back with his palm directed squarely towards her forehead. She wanted so very badly to kill him, but something within her continued withering and shrinking away from her own thoughts.

'Look,' the Wasp was saying, 'I'm doing all right here. I'm clear of the black and gold for the first time in my life. We've settled down. They don't . . . know how it was, with me.'

His own past was surely sufficiently larded with bloody-handed deeds that the Commonwealers would want to be rid of him, if they knew. Probably he had turned his hunting talents upon them during the Empire's war, and even Siriell's renegades were unlikely to forgive that. Just as his reaction to her had mirrored hers to him, so might he have kindred reasons for seeking her silence.

Besides, he had said 'We', and that meant he was still with the strange Spider girl, Sef, he had taken from Jerez, and surely Tynisa bore that wretched woman no ill will.

I should have just killed him.

Suddenly there were repercussions and uncertainties, no matter how honest he was being with her, and an uncomfortable part of herself said that was because life was never as simple as she was trying to paint it.

But she had come this far, and she knew that, after killing him, she would be able to paint again, to interpret the result however she wished. What other witnesses were there to gainsay her? She realized that she was on the brink of a precipice within her mind, and to go one step further would be to lose some fraying but fundamental connection with the world.

She felt her body flow into line, taking up her fighting stance within herself, even though nothing showed outwardly, so that, when the attack came, she would be sublimely ready for it.

Gaved must have sensed something, too, for he exploded into motion that was a counterbalance for her poised stillness. His wings took him back, ten feet away from the fire, his hands outstretched, one before him, the other pointing upwards.

Already the Dragonfly-kinden were dropping down towards them. A half-dozen came sleeting down around the fire like random arrows, while Tynisa could hear at least a dozen more approaching from all round. In their bickering, she and Gaved had let them get perilously close.

That they were Siriell's Town natives was clear enough: there was nothing of Prince Felipe's court about them. All wore a mismatch of armour, from leather and chitin to fragments of glittering noble plate and discarded Imperial war leavings. Several carried bows but, as their grounded infantry approached cautiously, she saw the bulk of them had spears, along with the occasional long-hafted sword. Some were lean and lanky Grasshoppers, but the bulk were Dragonflies, and she looked in their faces, feeling such a sense of *waste*. They were poised and elegant, but where they should have been beautiful, their harsh lives and harsher deeds had marked them with scars and filth and ugly expressions.

'Now then,' Gaved said quietly. He had his hands each directed at one of the archers, and in return most of the arrows were angled his way. Tynisa had attracted her share of the spears, but they were misreading her calm quiet and seeing her as the lesser threat.

'You've got an invitation, Gaved,' said one of the few swordsmen, thus helpfully identifying himself to Tynisa as the leader of this little rabble. 'Siriell has a few more questions for you, about just what your business here is.'

'Not a problem,' the Wasp replied, his easy tone belied by his stance. 'I'll drop in on her when I'm next passing through. I always have time for Siriell.'

'Now, Gaved,' the leader demanded. 'Tonight.'

Their numbers should have been overwhelming, of course, but they hung back. *They don't want to hurt him? Want to keep him alive for Siriell?* Tynisa wondered, but she noticed how they swayed back a little, whenever Gaved moved. *It's because he's a Wasp,* she realized. *These cowards think he's got the Light Airborne hidden in his pocket or something.*

'Take him,' the leader snapped, with the confidence of a man who isn't the one having to do so. Two spearmen stepped forward unhappily, weapons held aside as they reached as hesitantly for the Wasp as for a nettle. They stepped into the aim of the archers as they did so.

'Enough of this,' Tynisa decided, and let fly all the pent-up anger and frustration she had been nursing since before she ever reached Siriell's Town.

She ignored the leader, in that first moment, hoping he would prove a challenge later. There were two archers within reach and she impaled one through the eye – after slashing the throat of a Grasshopper spear-carrier to get there – and whipped her blade back to sever the other's taut bowstring. Her momentum carried her past the archer even as the cut string lashed the woman's face – then she was standing between two spearmen who desperately tried to drag their weapons towards her, but too cumbersome and too close. She let the razor-sharp edge of her blade open one up, feeling her steel keen through layered leather as though it was not there – a move that served to draw back her arm so that she could ram the point into the other spearman's chest. She watched her blade hardly bend as it punched through chitin plate and then between ribs, before sliding out again like water.

She heard Gaved's stings crack and sizzle and knew, without looking, that his targets would be the other archers, the greatest threats towards him, who would now be turning to look for Tynisa in the spot where she had been standing just a moment before.

Then she had spears all about her, their wielders fighting to keep distance, the long, narrow points trying to fence her in, so that for a few tense moments she almost lost the rhythm, batting them aside with blade and offhand, vaulting and stepping aside to keep out of their lancing approaches. She kept lunging at every gap, making individual brigands draw back, but without breaking the cage that enclosed her. Then an arrow flowered in the shoulder of one, providing the key that unlocked it all, and she was out from their midst – two Grasshoppers spinning bloodily away, to mark her exit.

She felt it was time to engage the leader, who had been backing away since things had gone so very badly wrong. That she would be confronting four or five of his followers at the same time was just grist to her mill. Gaved's sting spat again, and she caught its flash in the corner of her eye. Another arrow picked off the last archer, striking him low in the gut and doubling the wretch over.

The spearheads flurried for her like fish, but she turned sideways to them, her sword point-down as she advanced, parting their little hedge of spines until she was right amongst them. Even then, they nearly had her, moving faster as individuals and more cohesive as a group than she'd expected. Two closed with her, their spear-shafts walling her in, whilst another two stepped back to gain distance. She felt one spear point graze past her cheek and another cut her biceps as she twisted away, putting a knee to someone's groin to her left, and her sword's jagged guard into a face over to her right. The trap opened up again, and she cleared the air about her with her sword, forcing them to retreat or fall.

Close, too close. But wasn't this just the sort of death that she was looking for, after all?

For a bitter moment she thought their leader was going to fly off, but then he screamed in her face and went for her, bringing his long sword down in a vicious strike that would have cut her in two had it only landed. He was fast, though, wielding the sword two-handed with a nimbleness she had not expected, turning each attack into the next without overextending, so that he drove her before him in a mad blaze of steel.

She watched, and learned his patterns and his limitations, and understood that what she saw was all there was: speed and fury but no precision, no flexibility. When she moved with his strike, letting the sword chop to her left as she moved right, so that he was past her before he realized, he could not recover in time. She almost held off, in the fond hope he might have something more, but the rapier itself had decided to end it, and she pierced him under the armpit, where his armour left off, and dropped him in mid-yell.

That was enough for the survivors, who went flying, running and leaping away into the night, leaving a litter of bodies behind them. At least one more dropped, with an arrow in his back.

So whose arrows are those then?

Even as she thought it, the archer was approaching, stepping into the firelight while Gaved was brushing down his cloak and looking about him at the bodies. Tynisa turned to the newcomer – and her world stopped dead.

Her hallucinations had always been corner-of-the-eye things, melting before her direct stare as if unable to bear the weight of her attention. But here he was in plain view, the bow in his hand, as though he had never been killed by the Wasps after all. As though it had simply been some raconteur's exaggeration to say that Salme Dien was dead.

She couldn't breathe. She felt that her heart had ceased to beat. Her fingers twitched nervelessly, though her sword still clung within her grip.

'Salma?' she managed.

And the man before her, the Dragonfly-kinden with that oh-so-familiar, cocky smile, said, 'Yes?'

Five

Heedless of her expression Salma walked over to the dead men and studied them. 'So, this is what lurks in Siriell's Town,' he remarked. 'Ugly characters, certainly.' He glanced up suddenly. 'Turncoat?'

Tynisa jumped at the word, but it was Gaved who stepped forward.

'My Prince?' The Wasp was now studiously ignoring her.

'Losing your touch with the vermin?' Salma eyed him. 'You're lucky I was coming to meet you.'

Gaved's face remained studiously neutral. 'You're here alone, my Prince?'

'A little reconnoitring for Mother,' Salma said, self-mocking, and still everything about him was maddeningly as she remembered it: his expression, his tone. When he flashed a smile her way, she felt her heart would break. She was not sure, standing there in the moonlight, whether she had simply gone mad behind her own back, her mind snapped and flying free. The impossible situation refused to resolve itself. *Salma*? It was Salma.

The Dragonfly prince had taken hold of an arrow, setting one foot on a corpse's head to yank at it, but the shaft remained securely embedded. 'I'm too skilled a shot for my own good, it seems,' he murmured philosophically.

'Salma . . .' Tynisa said involuntarily.

The Dragonfly glanced up, and his smile was painful. 'Another one of yours, Turncoat? You're collecting Spider-kinden?' He was grinning through it, though, and sketched her an elegant bow with much flourishing of hands. She had seen him do just the same once, at the College, to impress a magnate's daughter.

'Don't you . . .?' *Don't you know me?* was the plaintive cry within her, but of course he could not know her. He was Salma: he was Salma to the very last detail as she had known him at College, three years ago. But this was a man who had never come south to learn the ways of the Lowlanders, never signed on with Stenwold Maker, never come too close to death while fighting the Wasps at Tark. This was a man who had never been enchanted and seduced by a stray Butterfly-kinden, or given his life in a desperate, heroic bid to defeat the Empire.

'She's none of mine,' said Gaved forcefully.

'Too clean by far to be Siriell's get,' Salma finished for him. 'And she fights. You've hired yourself a bodyguard, Turncoat?'

'An old acquaintance,' the Wasp got out between gritted teeth, and sudden panic overtook Tynisa, the forgotten weight of Gaved's knowledge slumping back on her like a landslide. One word now from Gaved and this miraculous dream would shatter. *She's a murderer,* was all the Wasp needed to say.

But she caught Gaved's eye, and saw her own thoughts reflected in his face: a tightly contained panic that at any moment she might give him away. He was a rogue and a thief, she knew, but what lies had he told to find himself a place here in the Commonweal? *One word from me . . .*

In that moment, within their conjoined silence, a guilty pact was made between them. Omission for omission, they would cover for one another and bury their pasts.

'Tynisa Maker of Collegium,' said Gaved wearily, 'I present Prince-Minor Salme Alain of Elas Mar Province.'

Tynisa stared, caught off guard, because somehow she had never even considered the idea that Salma would have had *family* here beyond his mentor Felipe Shah. And she had already thought that the Salma that this Alain resembled so much was more that youth who had first come to Collegium, not the later man she had last seen planning battles against the Empire. A younger brother, but such a likeness nonetheless.

'Why, then, what chance has brought you to grace our lands, Tynise?' The flowery words were all mischief, but then *he* had always been like that.

There was a void in her heart where the answer to that question should have been and, as she opened her mouth to answer, she knew that she had no words. She had come here to the Commonweal because being anywhere else had become intolerable. She had come to Siriell's Town because she wanted to find a Mantis death, and no amount of equivocation would hide that, now that she looked on her motives again. Looking into his face, though, and reaching for a response, the void was abruptly filled with one word: *You*. Salma had brought her here – and here he was, both in image and in manner. She felt the world was yawning open beneath her, the brink of a chasm at her very feet.

'I . . . am travelling to your family,' she finally got out, the words stopping and starting, and utterly beyond her ability to predict. 'Salma . . . my Prince, I knew your brother. He was my friend. I bring word . . .' She could say no more, but Salma was already looking towards Gaved.

'Seems Dien made quite an impression,' the Dragonfly said philosophically, but then the warmth of his smile was focused back on her, and she met his gaze boldly. 'Well, such things have been known, and you make a better messenger than a turncoat Wasp. Will you come to Leose, then?'

She had no idea what Leose was, but she nodded nonetheless. *Let me go with you,* she thought. She was terrified that, if he left her sight for an instant, she might lose him for ever.

But already he was waving a hand at Gaved. 'Bring her with you, Turncoat. I must report to Mother, of course, but no doubt we'll meet at the castle.'

She wanted to ask why they could not all travel together, but

Alain put his fingers to his mouth and whistled piercingly. A moment later she heard a low drone that quickly built up into a buzzing roar of wings, as something descended on them from the skies above. The downdraught of its wings battered her, and Gaved's little fire leapt and danced madly to the point of extinction. The dragonfly glittered like silver in the light, surely twenty feet from its stubby antennae to tapering tail. It hovered for a moment and then found a perch on one side of the defile, claws digging deep for purchase.

Seeing her expression, Alain was all smiles. 'Lycene,' he named the animal. 'Only the Salmae breed dragonflies that can fly so well at night. You have your report, Turncoat?'

With a start, Gaved dug in his tunic to produce a messy fistful of paper. 'There's more. I've learned today—'

Alain waved it off. 'Then it can wait until you get to Leose. You have a horse nearby?'

The Wasp nodded glumly.

'Good, make best speed, and bring our new guest with you.' Again the flash of teeth. 'I will look for you in more civilized surroundings,' he told Tynisa, 'and I'd wish duty didn't lay its hand on me so hard, but I must go.'

She tried to say something but her throat had dried up, and a single flick of his wings lifted him into Lycene's saddle, where he holstered his bow. Then the insect was aloft again, its wings thrashing up a gale, and seconds later he was gone, swept across the vault of the sky far enough that even her eyes could no longer pick him out, as the sound of Lycene's wings became a diminishing hum.

Horseback riding was not something Tynisa had been called upon much to do, and she would have found it uncomfortable and awkward even if not sharing a horse with a Wasp-kinden. After the fight, Gaved had broken camp and relocated to another sheltered place, but neither of them had slept much, constantly jabbed awake by mutual suspicion.

Before dawn he had tracked down his errant mount and they had begun their journey in silence. The land around them was inhabited once, for they passed a patch of lumpy, mounded earth and rotting sticks that had clearly been a village. The rolling countryside had been cut into tiers for agriculture in the past, but many years of neglect were softening the contours. Grass, nettles and thistles grew tall, even at the approach of winter, and the land was broken up by knots of densely growing trees.

'Did the war do this?' she asked, the first words uttered for more than two hours. Even as she asked, she was thinking that the abandonment looked far older. 'Was there a plague here or something?'

'More than a generation ago, the family of little princelings who ruled this province ran out of heirs, I think,' was Gaved's response. 'And by the time some other petty nobles came round to claim the place, after decades of duelling genealogies, the locals weren't exactly ready for someone lording it over them.' He did not sound particularly disapproving, but then that prospect was probably inviting to him. 'All over the Commonweal, there are whole provinces gone fallow. More so since the war, obviously, but it's been going on for ever, from what I can make out. Place is falling apart. If it's not bandits setting themselves up as princes, it's princes going bad and turning bandit. Raids across principality borders, villages burned, or village headmen declaring independence, thieves on the roads and in the forests, peasants deciding they'd rather be free, or lords taxing the shirts off their backs. The Monarch's a long way away, and the Mercers do what they can – the proper ones and the provincial sort like we've got – but how many Mercers can there be?'

'And yet you're working for Salma's family. I'd have thought you'd be on the other side,' she said darkly.

'Me? I'm making a living,' Gaved declared, glancing back at her briefly. That she could stick a knife in his back at any moment was something he was apparently managing to deal with phlegmatically. 'When I left Jerez and headed west, I only had one name to conjure with, and that was your friend's.'

'Salma? You got here through trading on his name?' she demanded.

'Once I heard his family mentioned, I made my way over and talked myself into a job. Maybe tomorrow Sef and I'll move on, turn brigand even, but for today I'm on the side of the Monarch. It's that kind of world. I keep my options open. Or I try to. There was no need for that bloodshed, last night.' His voice was careful and measured, and he must have felt the flash of anger going through her.

'They were going to kill you.'

'I could have talked my way out of it, with them, or with Siriell if need be. It's part of what I do. She was probably only going to make me an offer.'

'Oh, and that would suit you well, wouldn't it?' she accused him. 'Just waiting for the chance to jump flags to join the outlaws, after Salma's people took you in.'

'I like to keep my options open,' Gaved repeated. 'But killing people closes doors. Who knows when I might need to go back there, on whoever's business? Now I don't know if I can.'

'I'm not going to be anyone's prisoner,' Tynisa hissed through gritted teeth. She was starting to see flickers at the edge of her vision, one or other of her imaginary companions keeping pace with her. Achaeos, was it? Had he come to reproach her now for the blood she had spilled?

'It's not so simple—' Gaved began, but she hissed at him so fiercely that he stopped.

'I have been a prisoner once,' she snapped. 'You have *no idea* what that cost me and what parts of me I left behind, when I got out.'

The Wasp scowled at her over his shoulder. 'Well, it's done,' was all he could manage. 'But they'll have people in the air, searching for us. Nobody kills that many of Siriell's people without being hunted.'

'So we'll fight them again.'

'No, we'll lose them,' Gaved decided. 'We'll keep riding as fast as the land permits and as long as the horse can keep the pace. We'll head uphill, too. I know a good road for us to throw them off.'

'There's a forest?' Tynisa asked, because tree cover was always the best way to hide from airborne spies.

'Of sorts,' Gaved confirmed, 'but I doubt it's what you're expecting.'

They settled into a steady pace, with the Wasp refusing to be drawn on where he was guiding them. The land about them was already looking more promising, their trail winding between stands of gnarled trees which grew only denser ahead of them.

They kept up a pressing pace for hours, with Tynisa spotting the occasional dark shape high above that might have been a man or a hunting insect. Gaved was now angling them along the broad flank of a hill that was creased into a series of slopes and valleys still heavily hung with morning mist. The scrubby trees had given way now, left behind on the hill's southern skirts. Here, down in the valleys, was a dense forest of another kind altogether. The mist contained a maze of tall, leafy canes, some as slender as a finger, some as thick as Tynisa's thigh, as though a regiment of giant archers had loosed a thousand shafts at the hillside itself. This bristling cane forest seemed to preserve the mist even past midday, so that their progress deteriorated into a groping through a constantly shifting landscape of vertical shadows. Gaved led with apparent confidence, but Tynisa spotted him consulting a little aviator's compass more than once. She was glad of that since, between the mist and the sameness of the landscape, she felt she would become lost almost instantly.

Some time later, Gaved let their weary mount plod to a halt, swinging from the saddle to feed and water it.

'Won't they catch us?' Tynisa asked him, her eyes seeking

their airborne pursuers. The mist about them was so heavy that even the sun was just a brighter smear.

'They won't come here,' Gaved said. 'We've lost them.'

'Then what's wrong?' she pressed, because it was obvious that something was amiss.

'Just imagine,' Gaved said, 'that you're in the house of someone very polite, but very dangerous. Behave as a good guest and we'll be fine.'

Tynisa glanced about, seeing only cane-striped mist. 'What lives here?'

'Oh, some fair-sized mantids, some spiders, centipedes,' Gaved replied casually, 'but people too, of a sort. I've come through here twice before, under similar circumstances, and I can't say I've definitely seen any of them, but I'm told they're here, and I believe it. The brigands don't come raiding here and the nobles don't hunt. This place is supposed to be Stick-kinden land.'

'There are Stick-kinden?' Tynisa demanded incredulously.

Gaved held up a hand to indicate that she should keep her voice down. 'I don't know. I've never seen one. But you don't, apparently. I heard that a travelling noble decided to pass through here with his retainers, and killed the animals and had his people burn the cane back. He got a five-foot arrow in his chest, while he was taking his supper, and nobody ever saw the archer. I heard that one of Siriell's predecessors tried to use this place for launching raids from, and he and those few that got out of here talked like the forest itself had come to kill them. So we won't draw any weapons, and we won't make too much noise, because they prefer the silence. And when we're done camping I'm going to leave a few thank-yous about the place, just in case.'

He was as good as his word, though Tynisa never found out exactly what was in the pouch he left beside the ashes of their campfire. The rising sun made inroads into the mist, but never quite dispelled it, and it was easy to see the tall, thin shadows looming on every side as something more sinister. *And probably there are no Stick-kinden,* Tynisa told herself, *for whoever heard of stick insects having a kinden?* But she was far from home now, and many unthinkable things might turn out to be true.

Towards evening when they were, according to Gaved, nearing the cane forest's edge, she thought she saw one of the shadows shift and fall back between its brethren, giving her a momentary impression of a fantastically tall and attenuated figure carrying a staff that might have been a bow, and trailing a grey cobweb cloak off into the mist. Later she was sure that she had imagined this, as she imagined so much else, but by then they were clear of the cane and crossing the border into the next province.

Leose was the princely seat of the Salmae, Gaved explained. Unlike Felipe's family, they had not lost their stronghold to the Empire. The war had come close, chewing at the edge of Felipe's great domain and gnawing away odd provinces, but in the end the Treaty of Pearl had put the Wasp-kinden territorial ambitions on hold.

The Wasp spoke of his own people with a studied detachment, neither condoning nor apologizing for them. He was working hard at being someone in no position to have an opinion on Imperial affairs.

They had now passed a number of smallholdings, isolated stretches of farmland where the hillsides had been amenable to step agriculture, with clusters of low buildings with sloping roofs on the hilltop above. The land here was both more rugged and more heavily forested than Prince Felipe's southern holdings, and Gaved's chosen path meandered wherever the clearest land went, avoiding the deep woodland. Those trees extended easily over the border of Leose province, he explained, and then into the lawless lands to the south which they had just escaped from. Those thick woods were known as 'bandits' roads' by the local peasants. Sometimes, when the brigands were bold, they played deadly hide-and-seek games between the trees with the Salmae's Mercers. At other times the woods were left for the peasants to herd their aphids through, or for the hunting excursions of nobles.

They were obviously nearing the province's heart, but they had seen few others travelling, and none following the same route as they did. There was none of the traffic Tynisa would expect, when approaching a town. 'So how far to this Leose?' she pressed.

'Depends what you mean by Leose,' Gaved replied. 'Every part of Elas Mar within a few miles of the castle is Leose. There's no town as such, just villages dotted about the place. Remember, Suon Ren's almost the closest to a proper city the Commonweal has – after the capital. Most of the Commonwealers live spread out like this, making the best use of the land. What you're looking for is Leose *castle*, and we'll see that by tomorrow. That's where the Salmae live, but their people are spread all over.'

The castle, when they had sight of it, did not disappoint. They had been following the course of a canal for some hours before the edifice came into view, and Tynisa saw that it had been placed to command the watercourse where it had cut a deep valley between two hills. It was a broad, squat mass of stone surmounted by tapering battlements, held in place against the land by a half-dozen spidery buttresses, seeming as though it might at any moment pick itself up and walk away. Two of the arching buttresses spanned the river itself, forming narrow bridges leading from the far side to the castle's very door.

'So that's where you live, is it? Very grand,' Tynisa remarked.

'Me?' Gaved shook his head. 'They wouldn't let me past the door, believe me, but I'm useful enough that they found Sef and me a little abandoned place not too far away, and we do all right there. There's a little lake you can see from the door. That's important . . .' He made an awkward face.

'So what now . . .?'

'Now I report to my betters,' Gaved explained. 'I'll tell them how Siriell's in a restless mood, anyway. Then perhaps some peace and quiet over winter? That would be nice.'

The castle seemed to grow and grow as they approached, so that what had seemed a mere fort, at a distance, became a great architectural sprawl. Even the slender buttresses were revealed as a marvel, suspended impossibly against the universal pull of the ground. This arching stonework seemed to spring from utterly different hands to the light wooden walls of Suon Ren.

The great double doors were barred, and apparently unguarded, but there must have been watchers above, for Tynisa had a glimpse of flurried movement within, at a higher storey. Then again there was nothing, and little enough sign that the place was occupied at all.

'So who lives here?' she asked.

'The Salmae and their retainers and, yes, they rattle about in there like dried peas when some other noble hasn't come to guest with them. These castles, all of them, they're built like they're for people nine feet tall with a thousand servants each. Very few of them are even half used: the same way as half the land in the Commonweal seems like it's given over to outlaws or beasts because there aren't enough law-abiding folk to till the soil. Place isn't what it was.'

The doors opened then, before Gaved could expand on his theory. A pair of Dragonfly-kinden warriors, in full scintillating armour, scrutinized them uncharitably, before a slender, grey-clad Grasshopper woman hurried out to greet the newcomers. Behind her, Tynisa could see a courtyard of some kind, that was crossed by strange shadows.

'Ah, Turncoat,' she observed, 'you come with news?' At his nod, the Grasshopper inclined her narrow head. She was tall and sallow, like most of her kin, and her long hair was pulled back into a tail. Tynisa guessed that she was on the far side of middle age, but she had a straightness of bearing and lightness of step that belied it.

'You'd better come in then, you and your . . . woman,' the woman suggested frostily.

The iron gaze of the guards still did not trust these arrivals in the least.

Behind the gates, Tynisa saw that the courtyard had a roof of sorts, but one that was no more than a lattice of sturdy timbers that would keep out neither enemy nor weather. She presumed that some manner of covers or hatches could be put in place if there was ever an assault on Castle Leose, or perhaps the courtyard was intended to be abandoned to the foe, who could then be penned in and shot at from the castle proper. In the end she was forced to admit that her grasp of siege warfare was lacking, and that whoever had gifted the Commonwealers with these edifices had been of a strange turn of mind.

There were servants, though: Dragonflies and Grasshoppers who led their badly used horse off for feeding and grooming in stalls that were set into the castle walls to the left and right. Before them was another grand portal, this one inlaid with symmetrical patterns of brass, or perhaps gold. A smaller portal was set into a corner of one of the grand doors, and the grey-robed woman now sent a youth of her own kinden hurrying through it.

'The princess has been sent for,' she explained. 'She will come in her own time, as I'm sure you know, Turncoat.'

Gaved nodded. 'We can wait.'

A jug of good honeydew was brought to them by another servant, whereupon Gaved simply seated himself on the ground in the middle of the courtyard, on a blanket he had already scavenged from his saddle.

'You know her, I take it,' Tynisa noted, nodding towards the Grasshopper woman, who was currently chastising one of the grooms over some point of detail. 'She seems a barrel of laughs.'

'She's not so bad,' Gaved said mildly. 'Her name's Lisan

Dea, and she's been seneschal to the Salmae since before the old man died.'

Tynisa realized, with a vertiginous lurch, that 'the old man' meant Salma's father, of course. Feeling suddenly off balance, abruptly too close, too soon, to the heart of things, she changed the topic with, 'I'd get tired being called "Turncoat" all the time.'

Gaved gave her a glance without expression. 'I reckon they might have chosen something worse, so I'll settle for it.' A moment later he was scrabbling to his feet, as both of the grand and gold-chased doors swung open.

A woman stormed through them, outpacing her retinue of attendants. She was tall, for a Dragonfly, and more imperious than a regiment of Wasp-kinden. Her heart-shaped face was perfect and, although she was clearly a peer of Felipe Shah, her cold beauty admitted nothing of her age. She wore high-shouldered formal robes in red and pale blue and spotless white, starched and edged with gold plates, and Tynisa caught her breath, because she had seen Salme Dien wearing just such a garment in Collegium.

'Turncoat!' the woman snapped. 'Where is my son?'

Gaved was down on one knee, but Tynisa hesitated for a moment, pride battling with propriety, before grudgingly doing the same.

'He had set out on his Lycene for Leose before me,' Gaved reported, staring down.

'Feckless boy,' the woman exclaimed, obviously not caring who heard her. 'Probably having the run of every bandit camp and village from here to Tela Nocte. Idiot child.'

Tynisa stole a glance at her, seeing her regarding Gaved with distaste. By now her retinue had caught up with her, somewhat raggedly. There were a dozen or so finely dressed Dragonflies, either privileged servants or attendant lords, but Tynisa's eye was drawn away from them towards one particular figure. For a moment, as his presence impinged upon her, Tynisa took him for yet another hallucination, mimicking her father's intensely focused poise at the noblewoman's shoulder. Then Tynisa's gaze lifted further, and she realized that this was a different man, a living man. *It is getting hard to tell,* she recognized unhappily. First Salme Alain and now this newcomer. There would come a time when she would no longer be able to trust her eyes, and then where would she be?

The man was dressed in an arming jacket and breeches of pale grey leather, obviously far from new, and his boots were of a similar vintage, well crafted and just as well worn. Looking up furtively from her low vantage point, what caught her attention first was his utter stillness, for she had seen that particular brand of motionless calm before and she felt that this man was like a bow drawn back and ready to strike at any moment. She had known him for Mantis-kinden from the first glance. He was paler than the Dragonflies, and older than Tisamon had been when he died. This Mantis had hair gone completely white, and a hook-nosed face creased with lines of bitter experience. For all his years, Tynisa shivered when she saw him. A moment later her eyes picked out the brooch over his breast. The style of it was different, but she recognized the sword and the circle and knew him for one of the same order that she herself had been initiated into, and that Tisamon had been a master of.

'My Princess, I have important news of the bandit communities to the south,' Gaved added hopefully.

The woman, Salma's mother, dismissed that comment with a wave of her hand. 'Tell it to my seneschal and my champion,' she told him. 'If you've no more news of my son, I am done with you.'

'Alas, no, Princess,' Gaved replied, but the woman had already turned and was about to walk away.

Tynisa found herself on her feet so abruptly that the Mantis took a step in, to put himself between her and the princess.

'My lady. Princess.'

The Dragonfly woman turned and regarding Tynisa blankly. 'What is this?'

Gaved grimaced, and took a moment too long in deciding how to answer, and Tynisa declared. 'My lady, I am come from the Lowlands.'

From the Dragonfly's expression, she might never have heard of such a place. 'On what business?'

'I was a friend of Prince Salme Dien,' Tynisa declared, pronouncing his full name carefully.

Salma's mother stared at her for a long moment. 'You are seeking employment – like this one?' She threw Gaved the smallest nod imaginable.

'No, my lady, I only wished . . .' For some reason, though her mission to Felipe Shah had seemed utterly natural, before the cold gaze of this woman she faltered. 'I aided your son Salme Alain at Siriell's Town, and had hoped to meet him here. And I would speak with you of your elder son, if I could.'

The princess's expression, already cold, froze entirely. 'As you have heard, Prince Alain is not here. As for Dien, no doubt there were many Lowlanders he was . . . *familiar* with.' Then she had turned and, with her robe flowing behind her, was gliding back through the gold-chased doors, her retinue following her hastily. Tynisa had her mouth open, wanting to call the woman back, but was suddenly aware of the line of etiquette that would transgress. The Grasshopper seneschal's stern frown did not encourage her to push her luck.

Then the doors were closing again, and only Lisan Dea and the Mantis-kinden remained with them.

'We passed through what they're calling Siriell's Town . . .' Gaved started, but the Mantis was paying him no attention.

Tynisa took a step back, to allow herself fighting room. Since she first saw the man she had been waiting for this. Mantis-kinden and Spiders did not get on, and it would make matters considerably worse if he found out she was not a pure-blood Spider at all. His face did not betray the kind of fierce loathing she had encountered in the Felyal Mantis-kinden, when she had travelled there with Tisamon, but nonetheless he regarded her sternly, and his eyes were like steel.

'Show me your blade,' he instructed her, and it was as though Gaved and the Grasshopper were simply not there.

At first she misunderstood, taking the weapon half from its sheath, wondering whether this was some trick to disarm her, or whether he was a smith or a collector – or whether he just wished to satisfy himself that here was a Spider bearing a Mantis-crafted rapier, before he attempted to kill her. But something in his stance belatedly communicated itself to her, and she realized that his words were a ritual challenge.

She dropped back into a defensive stance, blade out and levelled at his heart, along the straight reach of her arm, weight poised on the back foot. He had a leather and steel gauntlet on his left hand, she noticed, with a short, slightly curved blade jutting from between his fingers, but folded back along his arm for now. That was a weapon she knew well. She waited for him to take up his own stance, the last formality before the inevitable duel, but instead he just regarded her.

'Good,' he said, at last, with a nod of approval reminding her of nothing so much as her old sword-master, Kymon of Kes, dead these several years past. 'I see the Lowlands contains some virtue in it yet.'

She blinked, surprised enough to straighten up from her guard. If he had struck at her then, she might not have been fast enough to parry him.

Without warning she was abruptly conscious of her own badge. For all that it was hidden out of sight, the Mantis had marked it in some way. Weaponsmasters acknowledged their own, she now discovered, and she would have spoken further with him then, save that he had already turned to Gaved.

'Report,' the Mantis ordered, and Gaved gave a concise account of Siriell's Town and its circumstances, numbers, factions, in a dizzying blur of information; names such as Pirett,

Seodan, Ang We, Dal Arche; rivalries and alliances, and little of it meaning anything to Tynisa.

'Nothing may come of it,' the Wasp finished up. 'Siriell wouldn't manage to mobilize one in three of the fighting population there, and there will be a dozen contenders ready to take what she has away from her. If we were to strike there, it might cut off the centipede's claws – or it might just stir them all up.'

Lisan Dea nodded, looking thoughtful. 'It will be the princess's decision, of course,' she said, but unhappily.

'She will listen to her advisers, I am sure,' Gaved remarked.

It was clear that the Grasshopper was far less certain of that, but the Mantis nodded briskly.

'No doubt we shall call on you again, Wasp-kinden.' He said the words without much relish, but to Tynisa's ear *Wasp-kinden* sounded a great deal better than *Turncoat*.

Then, just as Lisan and the Mantis were turning for the gates, Tynisa spoke up: 'What about me?'

'You say you are an acquaintance of our young prince?' the Grasshopper enquired.

'I am, yes,' Tynisa replied with some force, perhaps more to convince herself than the other woman.

'When he returns, he may send for you,' Lisan Dea suggested simply.

'Can I not . . . wait for him here?' Tynisa asked, aware that she was breaking delicate rules of conduct that stretched like a web all about her.

There might even have been some sympathy in the Grasshopper's expression. 'Without the invitation of my lady, you may not enter.'

After the two of them had gone, Tynisa felt as though some part of her had been ripped out. The princess had not wished to hear of Salma. Tynisa had been turned away at the Salmae's very gate. Alain was not here, her purpose was evaporating, and she had nowhere to go.

'That was . . .' Gaved said awkwardly, and Tynisa rounded

on him, expecting him to mock her. Instead he was shaking his head. 'What was that between you and Whitehand, anyway? I thought you were about to fight each other.' At her questioning look, he elaborated, 'Isendter, the Salmae's champion – Whitehand, as they call him.'

'I thought he would call me out because of my kinden,' Tynisa said numbly.

Gaved was shaking his head again. 'That's a Lowlander thing. Mantids here don't care. None of them ever had any issues with Sef. They just keep to themselves mostly, or serve the nobles.' He was already turning his back on Leose, heading for the stables to saddle up a new mount. When he came out, leading the beast by the reins, she was still standing there before the closed gate, and he stopped to stare at her.

When she rounded on him, expecting a smug look, a snide remark, his face remained carefully closed.

'You're going to wait until the boy comes back?' he asked her. At her nod, he went on, 'Could be tendays. You know winter's almost on us, right?'

'So?'

'So this is the Commonweal. Winter kills here, if you're not ready for it. A lot of my kinden found that out during the war. You can't just camp outside the castle gates until he gets back.'

Of course. Because that would be too simple. The thought came to her of heading south to Siriell's Town, finding some place there amidst the scum and the outlaws. Killing and killing until they . . . But her own internal reaction surprised her: *I don't want to die. I have something to live for now.* The iron drive towards self-destruction that had goaded her this far had rusted as soon as she had set eyes on Alain. 'I'll manage,' was all she replied.

Gaved stared at her thoughtfully. 'You were going to kill me, before. I could see it in you.' It was not even an accusation, more an observation. She could only shrug at the comment, so that he continued, 'I don't see it now. Do I get to sleep in peace? Or am I living in fear?'

At that, she really did try to summon up some ire, and to remember what it had felt like when she had stalked him from Siriell's Town, when ridding the world of him had seemed such a self-evidently noble aim. That state of mind had deserted her utterly, leaving nothing but doubt in place of those certainties.

Gaved studied her for a long time. 'Sef and I live a few days from here, on the lakeshore,' he told her, at last. 'We can find room for one more.'

'Why . . .?' Tynisa breathed. She felt as if she was engaged in some kind of duel, the rules of which she did not grasp. Gaved was plainly unhappy with the offer, even as he made it, but something had driven him to it.

'Not for me, but Sef . . . speaks of you, sometimes. And of the Mantis, Tisamon. You rescued her from her masters, back in Jerez – and I *know* what happened there after, but I've left my past behind, for now, so let's leave yours there too. I know full well how you wanted to put a sword in me back at Siriell's Town. To tell the truth, if I could have gotten rid of you without consequence, I'd have done the same. But now we're both here on the Salmae's graces, so killing each other isn't an option.'

'Why?' she asked again, still infinitely suspicious, but something within her was breaking before this unexpected mercy.

He shrugged. 'Because Sef owes you – and because of the things we both saw in that place. The same thing that we'd kill each other for, when you think about it.'

Six

In Suon Ren, Tynisa had noted that Commonwealer houses comprised a strange double structure, with their central rooms surrounded by an encircling space shaped like a squared ring. She had noticed how the external walls to this outer chamber could be slid aside, or even removed, turning it into a sort of all-encompassing veranda. For the life of her, she had no idea what the point of this all was, but she learned a few days after coming to Gaved's home.

The Salmae had ceded to their Wasp servant an isolated site beside a broad lake that Sef called the Mere. The inner house had three small rooms joined by a fireplace – no more than a single hollowed stone without a chimney. Tynisa felt the smoke should have filled the place in moments, but the angled slope of the roof gathered it up against the higher end in a roiling fug that eventually seeped out from under the eaves of the lower, yet losing no heat and almost impossible to see from outside. The weather had grown chill on their journey from Castle Leose, and as soon as they arrived Gaved took an hour making sure that the outer walls were securely in place, and sealing the gaps between them with some kind of grease.

Tynisa watched all this in bafflement, since in Collegium winters were barely worthy of the name.

The welcome she received was awkward. Sef, the Spider girl, was an escaped slave, and her habits had been honed by fear and subjugation. Since Jerez, she had grown bolder, Tynisa noted. Living with Gaved obviously suited her: she had not simply exchanged one master for another. Still, Sef remained shy and kept her distance, all the more so considering the tension that continued to twang between her and Gaved. For the first day, Tynisa could not understand why the Wasp had taken her in, rather than abandoning her at the gates of Leose.

Then, that evening, while Gaved was off scrounging for wood, the girl approached her, eyes downcast. 'I did not think I would see you again,' she whispered. Tynisa, who had thought of Sef not at all since parting, just shrugged.

'I have carried a debt ever since. So few ever show my people any kindness in the place I once lived, so we hold our debts to our hearts. I had not ever thought that I could tell you how much it meant to be away from the masters, and to be free.'

'You've spoken of this to Gaved, haven't you,' Tynisa guessed.

'He knows how I feel.' For a moment, the woman met her gaze, in a flash of personality that she would not have dared back in Jerez. 'I know he does not like you, nor you him, but he knows that to show you thanks and to repay my debt in some small way will make me happy. He is a good man.'

Tynisa tried to equate 'good man' with a renegade Wasp-kinden, and failed, but she said nothing, just nodded.

During the following days Gaved went fishing, and Sef swam in the lake despite the cold. Tynisa's hosts were wary of her, and inside the house's small space they managed to leave her to herself a surprising amount of the time. In turn, she did not know what to do with the hospitality they tentatively extended, but then she did not know what to do with herself either. She slept under their roof and she shared their food, which was cooked for them by a Grasshopper girl from some nearby peasant family. Gaved was embarrassed about it, or pretended to be, but he told her that the Salmae would not hear of one of their retainers shifting for himself, not even the least-regarded one. Tynisa was not sure whether to believe this or not.

Then the cold came, dispelling Tynisa's former assumption that it was already upon them. One evening she was in the outer room, practising her footwork as Tisamon had shown her. While she moved, she barely noticed the change, but as soon as she stopped, she saw that her breath was pluming pale in the suddenly chilling air. Outside, the darkening sky was crystal-clear, the stars like pinheads set in velvet. She was shivering even as she backed away from the small window, and a moment later Gaved slipped past her to fasten a shutter over it.

They retreated to the inner rooms and the hearth, closing themselves off from the surrounding space, letting the cold prowl between the walls until it succumbed to the slow advance of the fire's heat. Even so, Tynisa slept in her hammock bundled up in two cloaks and a horse blanket, and still sensed the biting frost as though it was an enemy stalking outside the walls of the house, rattling the shutters and hunting for a way in.

It was hard for her to live thus in that double-walled house. Lying in the inner compartment at night, the outer house was busy with the sound of creaking wood and the battering of the wind. As the nights grew even colder, her mind grew tired of simply presenting her with shadow puppets of the dead, and diversified instead into footsteps – so that she could lie there awake, with Gaved and Sef and their servant all asleep, and listen to Achaeos's shuffling tread, his nails scraping on the wall as though his figment was searching for a way in, out of the cold. *But he has already gone to that final cold – and, if he found his way in, he would bring it with him.*

And she knew he was not with her, but was dead by her hand, and that she was slowly losing her mind over it, but she felt fear stealing up on her even so.

One morning she awoke and knew that something must be wrong. There was a peculiarity to the light that pried through the edges of the house. She slipped from her hammock, a motion she was now practised enough to be confident with, and ventured into the outer section of the house, wrapped in a blanket.

There was a strange pale glare showing at the edge of the shutters, and limning each panel of the walls, as though the light of the sun had swooped very close to the world, but without bringing any of its heat. Bewildered, Tynisa wrestled with one of the wall-panels, until she could move it aside.

She stared, caught utterly unawares by the sight. The world outside had died, and some vast hand had draped it in a shroud. Everywhere the contours of the land had been smoothed by a universal covering of white, flurrying whenever the wind picked up. The lake had shrunk: clear water still lapped at its centre, but a shelf of solid ice had reached out from the shore as far as Tynisa could make out. She stared at it all, awestruck in a way that she had not been since her childhood.

She realized that she was shivering, and withdrew into the house, where she found the servant eating some oatmeal for breakfast.

'Is that *snow*?' she demanded.

The girl looked at her as if she was mad.

'You've never seen snow before?' Gaved stepped out, pulling on a tunic as he did so. 'This won't last. Two, three days and it will melt, is my guess. Still, when winter really gets into its stride there'll be more.'

'Oh.' She found the prospect disappointing. The sight outside had seemed so utterly unprecedented to her that she had needed it to be universally significant, as though it was a sign of the end of the world. The blanched landscape had seemed to speak to her: *I am changed, so shall you be. Something different is about to find you. Your life will not be the same.* That was a message that she had badly needed to hear.

Sef came out too, then, wrapping a thick robe about herself, and Tynisa realized sourly that she and the Wasp had been busy in her absence. It was a bitter thought that the happiness of others should have become as hard to bear as freezing. Living with two people who were apparently content with one another was becoming untenable: they were forcing her either to feel her own solitude too greatly, or to find some excuse to look down on them for their lack of ambition and dearth of spirit.

A change did come, though, as if some part of her had turned magician and foreseen it. Past noon, with no sign of a thaw, and Sef spotted a rider approaching, around the rim of the lake.

The three of them gathered to watch as that single dark shape against an argent field resolved itself into a Dragonfly youth swathed in a russet cloak. There was a shortbow and quiver at his saddle, and the line of his cape was wrinkled by a short sword at his belt, but he approached them openly, his horse high-stepping in the snow, and when he drew nearer they saw that there was no bulge of armour beneath his cloak.

Tynisa's rapier was in her hand, quivering in readiness, but the rider barely glanced at it, which seemed the clearest indication that he was no enemy. Instead, when he had reached what he clearly felt was the boundary of Gaved's little fiefdom, he slung himself easily off the saddle, with just a flicker of wings, and waited there.

'Come closer,' Gaved called out to him. 'All friends here.'

The visitor bowed elaborately, his hands moving in arabesques that Tynisa associated more with stage-conjurors than courtiers, but then both Salme Dien and Salme Alain had favoured the same kind of extravagance.

'I seek Maker T'neese.' Leaving his horse untethered and on trust, he stepped over towards them. He was very young, some years Tynisa's junior.

It took her a moment to disentangle what he had done with her name. 'That would be me,' she said.

The youth smiled brightly. 'My master has no wish to impugn the hospitality that you receive here, and places no obligation upon you, but if it be your pleasure, Lady Maker, you are invited to be the guest of Lowre Cean for whatsoever span of this winter you wish.'

The name meant nothing to Tynisa, but she saw its impact on her companions, and therefore concluded that this Lowre Cean was obviously important in some way.

'May I confer with my host?' she asked cautiously.

'As much conference as you should wish,' he allowed, 'though I'd ask for some feed and water for my mount, if I may?' This last, with raised eyebrows, was directed at Gaved and Sef. The Wasp turned back to the house, on the point of hailing their servant girl, but then some ghost of his old freelancer's pride overtook him and he set to the task himself, leaving Tynisa to trail after him.

'You're honoured,' Gaved told her, as he broke the ice on their water trough.

'Why's that? What's this about?'

'As to what it's about, no idea. The man's got a big old estate within Salmae lands, though, few days to the west of here. Couple of farming villages and his own compound, servants, soldiers, scholars, that sort of thing.'

'He's, what, a local chieftain? A bandit prince made good? What?'

Gaved uttered a strange sound. 'Don't – seriously don't – ever say that to anyone around here. *Prince-Major* Lowre Cean is probably the greatest war hero the Commonweal has. He was just about their only general who had any luck against the Empire, and he's also one of the Commonweal's greater nobles, on a par with your friend Prince Felipe. So, no, he's not a bandit prince made good, or if he is, the making good happened a few thousand years ago, when the Commonweal was putting itself together.'

'Then what's he doing living inside the Salmae borders?' Tynisa asked him, somewhat put out at his obvious amusement. 'How can he be all that important? Why's he not even on his own lands?'

Gaved gave her a look, and she understood, feeling abruptly chagrined.

'Right,' he confirmed. 'The war. All gone. At least Felipe survived with the majority of his principality intact. Cean lost his lands, all his people, children, grandchildren, everything. Now he's basically living on the charity of Prince Felipe and Princess Salme, and pretty much waiting to die.' His gaze appraised her. 'But for some reason he's taken an interest in you.'

'You think I should go?'

'I'd go myself, if he asked for me, only I imagine he's seen enough Wasp-kinden to last him for the rest of his life. I don't imagine he wants to murder you or force you into marriage, if that's what you're worried about.'

'I don't know what I'm worried about,' she told him, but at the same time something had stirred inside her. She realized she agreed with Gaved, that this did not look like trouble, and she realized also that danger was what she would have preferred. Even this, though, would be something. She had a new purpose, a new direction. It might keep her going for only a tenday, perhaps, but it was better than nothing.

The road to Lowre's home, his *manse* as the messenger described it, was longer than Gaved had told her to expect, although that was probably due to the encumbrance of the snow. Caught frozen in white, the Commonweal seemed like a dream place, or some make-believe land that some scholar might write a fanciful book about, a land unfinished, half shapeless and awaiting detail from some great moulding hand. They encountered precisely one other human being, a herdsman's daughter trudging through the snow as she followed the tracks of an errant aphid that had somehow escaped its pen and blundered off into the cold.

The world was white as a fresh page, Tynisa thought, and each living thing left a scrawl of writing that told all who cared precisely what manner of creature had passed, and where it had gone. She herself had left a similar travelogue that stretched all the way back to Gaved's door, and would do so until it snowed again, or a thaw came.

At last, after several nights so cold that she and the messenger practically slept on top of each other inside his small tent, necessity easily overcoming propriety, the home of Lowre Cean presented itself. That day the sky was clear, and the snow around them starting to dissolve back into the earth, or so it seemed to Tynisa. The ground, which had been hard, now became muddy with it, and they had to pick their way carefully down towards the little walled village which Tynisa understood to be the exiled prince's home.

The scene within the walls was reminiscent of the aftermath of a siege. In the centre of the compound, a band of ferocious-looking warriors had built up a grand fire and were now singing raucously and handing round a skin of some potent liquor. They were long-haired and bearded, and wore furs and brightly dyed homespun, and Tynisa had no idea what kinden they might be, save a very noisy one indeed. Around them, a fair number of Dragonfly peasants hurried about, carrying bundles and buckets, lifting, cleaning, clearing and obviously doing their best to ignore their barbarous guests.

There were a dozen buildings within Lowre's little domain, and Tynisa was surprised to see that many of them were of stone, and not the ancient stone of the Commonwealer castles, but something more like the civilized architecture she was used to. One such was plainly a forge, from the ring of hammers issuing from it, but there were a couple of larger buildings of unclear purpose, although back home she would have labelled one as a workshop.

The prince's own home must be the largest structure there, its lower storey stone-built and the upper two constructed sturdily of wood. The general shape was borrowed from the local castles – as Felipe's had been – but unlike that fragile construction, Lowre had obviously retired here to somewhere that could be defended. Tynisa read in this that he was, in some way, still fighting the war.

The messenger, who had never volunteered his name, had a boy come and lead her horse away, then informed her that he would go find his master and announce her arrival. He left Tynisa standing somewhat bemusedly in the centre of the compound, with all the business of a noble's estate bustling away on all sides. One of the uncouth-looking warriors called out some unintelligible suggestion to her, and she glared at the lot of them, to their great amusement. Then there came a Roach-kinden man leading a string of horses, whom she was forced to stand aside for, which in turn put her in the path of a peasant woman, two buckets yoked over her shoulders, on her way to fill the water-troughs. One of the savages had meanwhile started up some ferocious howling noise which she realized belatedly was intended as a song, and from the far side of the buildings she heard a fierce chirring, as a pack of house crickets began stridulating in protest.

And then the messenger appeared at her elbow once again. 'My master will see you now.'

Lowre Cean was neither enthroned like a prince nor practising at arms like a warrior noble. Instead she found him in a strange room lined with little wooden hutches, each fronted with latticed wire, so that she assumed this man kept crickets or jewel beetles, both of them common pets back home. He was a tall old figure, his hair white and thinning, and his long face was creased by the echoes of a hundred strong emotions. He wore a long grey smock, looking nothing like a prince or a war hero. There was a sharp, sour smell about the whole room that was utterly unfamiliar.

'Maker Tynise, my Prince,' the messenger announced, then stepped back and away to leave the two of them alone.

Tynisa could only wonder at the way these Commonwealers seemed to have no fear of strangers bearing ill intent. Were there no assassins in Dragonfly-kinden history?

She was indeed no threat, or so she hoped. That cold rage had not touched her again since Siriell's Town. Perhaps this equally cold winter had put it to sleep.

'My lord.' She tried something like their type of formal bowing, got it wrong, but Lowre Cean was not watching. Instead, he was cupping something in his hands with infinite concentration. She took a step forward to get a look at the things in the cages, and recoiled back to the doorway with a yelp. She had never seen anything like them.

They were tiny enough to fit into the palm of his hand, and they were manic, leaping and darting inside their little boxes as though furious at their captivity. They had two stick-thin legs ending in little clawed hands, and ragged paddles for arms – no, for wings, she realized, although they hardly seemed the right shape for taking to the air. Their little round heads had madly staring little round eyes and a beak like a tiny blunt dagger-blade, and their skin was furred with something a little like the scales of a moth's wing. They had been quiet, but her approach had set them off into a twittering, piercing cacophony of sound, a random and tuneless assault on the ear.

The lean old Dragonfly in their midst turned and gave her a wry smile. He was actually holding one of the vile creatures in his hands, a thought that made Tynisa's skin crawl. 'Forgive me,' she heard him say, over the racket. 'I had forgotten how my little pets are an acquired taste. My family has always bred these little singers, and since the war I have begun to devote more of my time to our old fancy here.' With infinite care he replaced his charge in one of the boxes and closed the grill, whereupon the little creature began yammering and twitching like all the others.

'You are Prince-Major Lowre Cean?' Tynisa began uncertainly. She had seen Felipe Shah eventually behaving like a prince, and Salma's mother most certainly like a particularly arch princess. This man was not conforming to her expectations.

'That is the curse I bear,' he confirmed, washing his hands before removing his smock. Beneath it he wore a plain, pale robe, something even a servant would look drab in. 'And you are the Lowlander? Fascinating.'

'Please, master, why did you send for me?' she asked. 'How did you even know about me?'

'Why magic, of course. Your coming was foretold centuries ago.'

She goggled at him in astonishment, and it was only after he had stepped out of the menagerie that she saw how a mischievous twinkle had entered his tired eyes.

'Or perhaps it was a Fly-kinden messenger from Suon Ren bearing word from my old friend Felipe Shah,' he added. 'Shah believed that you might find yourself a little stranded here in Leose, so asked that I extend to you all hospitality due to an honoured ambassador from the Lowlands.' For a man of his age he stood very straight, and despite his dress and circumstances she had a brief glimpse of the man he had been during the war. 'If you wish it, that is.'

Tynisa thought again of Salme Alain, who would no doubt return home sooner or later. She thought of Gaved and Sef, whose resources were meagre and who would doubtless prefer to retain their privacy over the winter.

More than that, though, she thought of Felipe Shah, and of this old man now before her, two Dragonfly nobles whose war-wounds were borne on the inside, but who could still find charity for a stray Lowlander out of nowhere, penetrating all her angst and guilt and fretting about her purpose, she felt a moment's sunlight touch her.

'I wish it,' she told Cean with profound gratitude.

Part Two

The Widow

Seven

The Empire had no great tradition of receiving ambassadors, yet these were not the first who had stood before Seda. They were the strangest, and most of her court did not know what to make of them. The great and good of the Wasp-kinden could not decide whether this was some kind of joke, or a calculated insult from an unknown power, on seeing these three cadaverous creatures standing before the throne.

The small proportion of her court who *did* understand what these visitors were, and what that signified, had gone quite still – like a cricket that spots the twitch of a mantis amongst the leaves. Those were themselves newcomers, a strange detritus of the Inapt that Seda had been quietly cultivating since she had secured her throne against the other would-be emperors who had begun carving off pieces of her rightful domain after her brother's death. These other ambassadors – the Moth-kinden, the Grasshoppers, scholars and mystics and magi – stared at the three dark-robed creatures as though they were a nightmare come to life.

It was not just what they represented, that sparked such horror. Nor was it because these things were standing in the Empress's court in broad daylight, whose true place was in the furthest, darkest holes away from the wrath of civilized peoples. It was a fear that these creatures might have a proposal for Seda: a promise of power that would be both greater and darker than those scraps of support that the Moth-kinden had been trying to get the Empress to accept. The price that would be exacted, in return for their gift of tainted power, threatened to undo centuries of bitter history.

The Mosquito-kinden had come to Capitas.

Seda watched them curiously. She had known only one of their kind before, although that one still cast a long shadow even after his death.

They had come to her in her dreams, these three. She was not sure whether they were scapegoat delegates forced by their fellows to undertake this task, or perhaps the boldest and most ambitious of a people sly and retiring by nature; or whether they were renegades cut off from their own kin and seizing on her unique position for a chance of reprieve. It was in dreams, however, that they had made themselves known, whispering promises of power, of understanding, even a twisted kind of comfort, extending a helping hand to draw her from the sea of blood that they knew she must be drowning in.

In her dreams they had been huge and cloaked in the night sky, their gaunt faces commanding. She had felt tiny before them.

Before her now, they were shorn of such grandeur: three haggard, pallid things, wrinkled and sexless. If it were not for those eyes, they would have seemed just some pack of ancient, mongrel beggars, not even worthy of the Slave Corps' time. But their protuberant and glistening red eyes dominated their every expression with a naked, hungry gleam. One of them, too, had a patch of red across his brow, like a birthmark save that it seemed to shift fluidly as he glanced about the room in jerky motions.

There had been a war, she knew, for her adviser, Gjegevey, had told her that much. In some forgotten corner of the lost centuries, before her race had come into its own, the Moth-kinden, in their strength and wisdom, had broken the power of the Mosquitos, cast them down and saved the world from their thirst for blood and for dominion. Of course, as all the records were kept in their clever, grey-skinned hands, Seda had only their word for the rights and wrongs of it. As the Moths themselves were long since banished to a few mountain fastnesses by their own triumphant slaves, one might think the issue moot. Official Imperial history certainly did: the squabbles of the Inapt kinden in bygone days were not taught in Wasp schools.

She had surprised them, in the end, for as they had pillaged her dreams, whispering and promising, she had shown them only need and weakness, enticing them to creep from their haunts and converge on Capitas. *Come to us*, their voices had rustled in her mind. *Be ours, sworn and sealed. How else will you ever control your new heritage?*

When they were close enough to her walls, she had sent soldiers out for them with a polite but forceful invitation to the Imperial court. Here they were: three scraps of old night caught now in the daylight that her artificers funnelled into her throne room, through shafts and high-set windows. Had they come after dusk as they planned, they would have found no less of a glare from the gas lamps. She could see them flinching from it, all the progress and the newness, trying to steady themselves against the moving tide of history.

But she owed their kinden something, and that had earned them a public audience. Also, it did no harm to remind the Moths and the others that she was no creature's toy, not theirs, nor the Mosquitos'.

'You have travelled so very long to present yourselves to me,' she said now, looking down on them from her central seat. On each side of her throne were three lesser seats where her brother had seated his advisers, but these days she seldom shared her glory with anyone. Had her regent been here, then perhaps she would have permitted him a place beside her, but they told her he was dead in some far-off city. Oh, the lies they thought she swallowed, when she could see through them all.

The three Mosquito-kinden had no doubt pictured this meeting differently: they as the masters, and she the meek supplicant. Their obvious discomfort amused her. 'Speak,' she encouraged them. 'Surely such a great journey is of some great import. Have you a boon you wish to ask of me?'

Because they did not know precisely the corner they were backed into, or perhaps because they did, they found their courage from somewhere. One, the oldest and most haggard of the lot, stepped forward.

'Empress,' he began, his voice quiet yet carrying, which was an old trick of the Inapt. 'Your most royal Majesty, you know who we are. The name of the Mosquito-kinden is not foreign to you.'

Seda heard the murmur echo about her court, among the Apt segments of it anyway. There were many there who still clung to the idea that the Mosquitos were nothing but a myth to frighten children with, either lost to time or merely a fiction from the start. There were enough, though, who remembered the Emperor Alvdan's favourite slave, red-eyed and hungry-faced, a creature akin to these. Uctebri the Sarcad, he had called himself, and few recalled him fondly. Perhaps a few there even knew something of Uctebri's appetites, of the servants and slaves he left pallid and shaking, and sometimes dead and withered, in his wake. In this new age of a young empress, perhaps it was time for the people of the Empire to reconsider their beliefs, Seda thought.

She had essayed a cautious nod, and the Mosquito-kinden spokesman took this as encouragement. 'We bring you gifts,' he claimed. 'Gifts not of simple treasures, for who could match the treasury of an empire, but gifts of understanding. We see the old faces here at your court, of those who have persecuted and oppressed us throughout the ages. No doubt they claim that they will give you wisdom. We know all too well their narrow-minded creed, Majesty. They will piece out knowledge to you with a parsimonious hand, and pass you only those scraps from their table that they think you fit for. They would presume to judge an empress, believing that their own power is anything but a shadow in these days.' The visible reaction of those he railed against emboldened him further. 'Majesty, we are a people in hiding, for they would slay us even now, if they could. Let us serve you, let us teach you our lore, let us be your mentors in all the old ways. You shall find us more open-handed by far than these.'

He waited, but she let herself seem thoroughly absorbed by his words, perhaps a little cowed by them. He shuffled closer, until her guards tensed, and she lifted a hand to hold them back. She let the gaunt, robed figure approach until its hushed next words would be lost to most of her court, intended only for herself.

'Majesty, we *know* what has happened to you, and what inheritance has come to rest within you. The Moths may claim it, but you must know they lie. Perhaps there are some dregs of their power in you, but Uctebri was your master, before now, and it is his tradition that has claimed you – *our* tradition. Who else can teach you of it, save us? And what will become of you, if you do not learn our ways?' His lips quirked into a smile, showing the translucent needles of his teeth. 'Or do you think the might of an empire is sufficient to master what lies within you?'

She stood up abruptly, and her court fell silent even as she did.

'You are in error,' she said, letting the soldiers and magnates of her court try to piece together precisely what words she was replying to. 'You recall to us our brother's slave, whom you claim as kin. You think to presume upon our favour through his name? I will not deny I knew him, and a cunning trickster he was, whom my brother found an endless fascination. Until he died, creature – until my dear, beloved brother was murdered.'

She sensed the tension all around her now, for this had been a topic brought out frequently in recent months. 'Though a fighting slave held the blade, no single man could suffice to make an end to my brother,' she said, and she had practised the emotions so well that nobody could have guessed how much she had laughed, the first time she mouthed those words. 'We are even now uncovering the depths of the conspiracy that contrived his death.' It was remarkable, how far that conspiracy had spread, starting from a Rekef general and a Mantis-kinden pit slave and then working outwards, like a plague caught by those who had incurred the Empress's displeasure, that was uniformly fatal. 'We know, though, for our Rekef has confirmed it, that at the heart of the knot was none other than my brother's slave, so trusted and so well placed to betray the throne. You come here thus on a traitor's business.'

Even as she finished speaking, the guards were moving in, but she was more interested in the peculiar sea-change affecting her courtiers. They were not themselves under the lens – none of them would be hauled off to the fighting pits or the crossed pikes today – and so abruptly they started putting on expressions of vengeful outrage, and looking forward to some entertainment.

'We shall see them meet a fitting end, for the blood their kind has shed,' she declared. 'Have them hung by their heels, then have them bled by the wrists until not one drop remains within them.' And she did not now say, *and have that blood brought to me*, but there were those of her staff who knew the drill, and went about her business with fat purses and lips sealed, lest they, too, encounter the same fate. The Mosquitos understood, though, for she saw it in their red eyes. 'Do not assume,' she told them, 'that I am not fully educated as to your *traditions*.' Though her court would not understand, it was worth it for their expressions, before they were hauled away.

Invisible to her, there were some hundreds of people making ready within the palace and all across the city. Quartermasters, officers, engineers, chandlers, scouts, cartographers, diplomats, merchants and an army of slaves were smoothing her way so that the Empress's path should be effortless, greased as it was with the sweat of all their brows.

Her brother Alvdan had never set foot outside the capital. If he had been able to avoid it, he had never left the *palace,* the scene of his one mean triumph where he had ordered the murder of his siblings at the hands of General Maxin. That the late and unlamented Maxin was now a keystone in the grand and convenient 'conspiracy' that Seda had woven around her brother's death was a source of constant entertainment to her.

The Empire was changing, she knew. Its recent history, even its defeats, had strengthened it and broadened it, and she was not content to sit at home and merely try to fill her father's shoes, the ones that her brother had tried on for size so many times and found too large for him.

My grandfather Alvric unified the tribes and defeated our nearest neighbours, and he was great in one way. My father Alvdan the First built an empire, and was great in another. My poor brother's failing was in never finding his own path to greatness, but living off the table scraps of our family history. I have my own road now. And she did, and her forebears would never have guessed at it.

From the shade of her rooms she stepped out on to a balcony, into the bright sunlight, looking down the tiered flanks of the palace, over Capitas the golden city. The sky above it teeming with Wasps and Flies engaged on her errands, the streets coursing with her subjects, warehouses crammed with her treasures, barracks thronging with her armies. Above and to either side of her balcony, several of those soldiers tensed as soon as she showed herself, instantly casting their gaze skywards, in case any of her loyal subjects should harbour conspiratorial designs. Wasp Art furnished its devotees with wings and hands that were deadly at a distance, and for the Empress to stand thus in the open would be a gift to any assassin, which perhaps explained the late Emperor's reclusive habits.

But I know more than you ever did, Seda reflected, because castigating her dead brother was another source of amusement to her. She was slowly mastering her newfound skills, but the ability to read others and to know of danger, and to turn minds, all these were increasingly within her grasp. Last year an assassin had broken into her very bedchamber. She had talked to him all through the night, and when the guards eventually found him, he was ready to swear undying allegiance to the throne.

She had ordered the intruder skinned alive.

Her shadows moved with her, her constant guards. They were gifts from the Moth-kinden of Tharn, and she knew that her regular soldiers worried about exactly where their loyalties lay. Only Seda could see their hearts, however, and she had twisted them, and twisted them again, by gifts and words, promises and understandings, until the half-dozen Mantis-kinden killers were hers through and through, pledged inviolably to her by their ancient knots of honour. They carried bows and the short-bladed clawed glove that only the Mantids cared for, and any assassins that wished to try their luck would find the Empress's bodyguards waiting.

She heard the shuffle of feet behind her, and sensed her Mantis-kinden escort tense for a moment. There were few allowed in her chambers unbidden, though, and once they recognized the Woodlouse-kinden, Gjegevey, they relaxed again. The old slave was her favourite adviser, and a supporter of hers since before the Emperor's death; and if she had learned one lesson from her brother's failures it was to reward loyal service. More than that, though, Gjegevey understood what she was, what she had become, and what she wanted.

'I, ahm, understand all is in readiness.' To the Wasps he was a bizarre spectacle, outlandishly tall and thin, yet so crook-backed that it seemed that he was meant to be taller still. His skin was a pallid greyish-white, with darker bands starting at his forehead and patterning the top of his bald head before disappearing down beneath his robes behind. He claimed to be older than the Empire itself, but his eyes were sharp in their nest of wrinkles. His people dwelt north and east of Wasp lands, she understood, in some steaming swamp-forest of eternally rotting trees, and his kinden were seldom seen. Once, he had been an agent for whatever nebulous leadership existed amongst his scholarly and retiring fellows, but time had eroded the particulars of his original briefing, so now he was hers entirely.

'Khanaphes,' she pronounced it carefully, 'is known to your people, I am sure, in far greater detail than you have described it.'

'Memory fails me . . .' he said vaguely. 'But perhaps the sight of it will stir some, ah, recollection in me. Without much, hmn, hope, it behoves me to sound my old note of caution once again, Majesty. There are other ways.'

'We will exhaust them all in time, but why cast away this opportunity? The Empire has come to Khanaphes,' she told him. 'My artificers and officers tell me of diverse reasons why we must make the city ours. My soldiers walk its streets even now. You know what I must have, Gjegevey.'

He nodded unhappily, but she knew he would come with her and aid her, if only to retain some hope of influencing the future, of affecting what she might become.

'Gjegevey, you shepherded me into this world, as much as ever Uctebri did. You opened my eyes to the old magics. You prepared the way that made me this . . . *thing*.' She saw the pain in his eyes, saw him about to remonstrate with her, but she pressed on. 'What am I, slave? The ritual that killed my brother stripped me of my birthright, and gave me only rags to hide myself with. Am I to be content in that? The Mosquitos spoke truth in one thing: at the moment I am a beggar at the Moths' table for what little they deign to share. I have been reborn into a new world, an ancient and terrible world. I therefore see all the things my people are blind to. Am I to be a slave in this new world and only play the empress, as Uctebri designed? Or am I to seize that world with both hands and sting it into submission? You know this, old slave.'

'But Khanaphes . . .' he whispered. 'They are, hmm, ancient there, or were . . . perhaps the power is fled from that place, or perhaps . . . perhaps it remains too strong even now . . .'

'You can't have it both ways,' she told him drily. 'If they are strong, then I shall be bold and conquer their strength. If they are dead, I will turn over their tombs for what fragments they have left.' Her face hardened. 'But I know they are not dead.'

That was news to the old man. 'Majesty . . .'

'I dream, Gjegevey, I dream of lightless halls, of statues that wake and walk. Each night another page to the story. My dreams whisper the name "Khanaphes" to me, over and over. I am called there, as power calls to power. They made themselves the heart of the world in an age lost to my people, an age dim even to the Moths.' She smiled. 'And to your own folk, and their rotting libraries?'

'We . . . remember,' he said softly. 'There was once a time when Moths and Spiders called us brothers, mm? But never did the Masters of Khanaphes. My folk turned away from the world long before the, ah, Moths lost their domain to their slaves, and yet even at our greatest height, so the influence of, hmn, Khanaphes was already in decline. Its greatest golden days were behind it, even then. *Old*, Your Majesty. Old so that you, or even I, can barely, ah, comprehend. All that is left is the worn stub of what once was.'

'I will be Empress,' she told him flatly. 'Empress of both worlds. The one I shall move with armies and machines, the other . . .' She turned from the balcony at last, stepping back into shadow. 'Do you not wish to walk the secret halls of Khanaphes, Gjegevey?'

His long face always provided a burlesque of melancholy, like a fantastical actor's mask. 'I fear I do not, hm, Majesty. But if you walk them, I shall be there beside you.'

Eight

The Wasp-kinden were a young race, but they had developed their own art forms nonetheless. Spider-kinden merchants making the long trek to Capitas were favourably impressed by the degree to which they had advanced the art of the pit-fight. Scorpion chieftains arriving with their strings of human goods admired the Wasps' ability to control and manage so many slaves. Many foreigners of all kinden were struck by the delicacy and care with which the Wasps ordered and categorized their prisoners, although their unfavourable critiques were usually coloured by their own position on the wrong side of the bars.

There were professionals, former Consortium clerks or retired Slave-Corps officers, whose sole business was to find prisoners a fitting place of durance – either until their eventual fate was decided or enacted, or because that imprisonment represented that fate. Cells, mines, shackles, the quick mercy of the blood-fights – or as one of a small but mysterious number who were sent to the palace and simply . . . disappeared.

Many prisoners laboured, too. Often this was not even as a result of a sentence, just a good use of resources that would otherwise be sitting idle while being fed for free. There were the parched-dry quarries of Shalk, the winding mines of the Delves, logging camps, fields, masons' yards, each penitent fitted to his interim fate with a master's expertise as delicate as that of a matchmaker.

Then there were the factories, which were always hungry but seldom fed with the bodies of prisoners. Most of the workers were slaves or citizens, and all of them were not just Apt, but artificers of some mean grade or other. The vast machine-noisy halls were operated day and night, and if it was possible they were run even while errant machines were being fixed. Fingers and toes were a cheap currency in those chattering, clattering rooms, but it was better work than the mines, less dangerous than the army. The free workers there held themselves to be a curious aristocracy, standing together against the bureaucrats, the taskmasters, and the grafters of the Empire. They might only be churning out standard-issue breeches by the hundred, but where, as they pointed out, would an army be without its trousers?

Sometimes an artificer fell from grace, and then the factories were always waiting. Even murderers, even traitors, if they had a spark of mechanical skill, would be chained to the machines and put to work while waiting for sentence. A little knowledge was too precious to waste.

Angved hated it. It was fair to say that he was being unreasonable, given all the other ways a prisoner could be spending his time, but even so . . . He had been a lieutenant in the Engineering Corps – an officer! – and now a burly slaver came each morning to chain him up in front of all these others, as even the slaves were not chained, and he worked at the most menial, repetitive tasks, and risked his hide between the teeth of the looms if they jammed, and he had to bear the mockery of the rest of the workforce, because he had been better than them, and had failed.

He had never been a high-flier. Past forty now, his hair greying, and when he was young he had thought he would be a major by this age, perhaps with some comfortable teaching post. Then there had been a string of poor decisions, the wrong horses backed, unavoidable failures that had drawn the ire of his superiors. He had never made captain, whilst the declining quality of his assignments had eventually ensured that he never would. Then had come the bastard Rekef with their make-or-break plan for Khanaphes, and he had seen it as a desperate chance to regain his place on the ladder, for all that it would probably have ended with a knife in his back had all gone according to plan.

All had most definitely not gone according to plan.

With the exception of two old women who ran the kitchen, the other factory hands were not Wasps. They had a curious two-tier organization, two separate tribes side by side yet passing through one another as though existing in fractionally shifted worlds. The Beetle-kinden, and the bulk of the slaves – Ants, Bees, even some halfbreeds who were inexplicably *not* despised by their comrades as Angved would have anticipated – worked at one level of detail, whilst a host of Fly-kinden men and women were busy in amongst them, passing under and over and sometimes even through the machines, trusting to their small size, delicate fingers and quick reflexes to preserve them from injury. The only fifth wheel in the factory was Angved himself, the size of a normal kinden – by his standards – and yet put to the most menial jobs during both shifts, by specific decree.

For a man formerly of the Engineers, it was pure gall, insulting, demoralizing, as good as receiving a beating any day. It showed that the clerks who had assigned him here knew their business.

He had made his pleas. He had shown them his findings. Still, they had been dead set on his excruciation and then a public execution, on general principle. Then it had all been dropped. There had been one night when he was dragged before a triumvirate of hooded men – Rekef for sure – and they talked amongst themselves about him, and he understood that the Khanaphes expedition was now an embarrassment best removed from history entirely, and him along with it.

But he had lived on for another night, in fear, and then

another, and then a quiet, lean man had come and explained to him how he had best forget the name of that desert city, unless someone should mention it to him first.

A tenday later, and the factory had got him. Since then he had been here, the butt of every joke, hearing the snickering of slaves, the laughter of *women* – Fly-kinden women no less – wasting his training in the manufacturing of the banal and the commonplace. Only one thought kept him sane, for, while he would not converse with his fellows there, he overheard their copious gossip. As he eked his days out amongst the menials of the machine world, one fact went round and round in his head.

They've gone to Khanaphes.

The Empire had taken Khanaphes as easily as he had known it must, having seen the city's primitive defences first hand. But why would the Empress stretch her reach so far, and for so little gain, unless . . .

After he had returned from there, he had cast his die. He had given his report, his numbers, the results of his tests. He had supposed them since burned, lost, misfiled, sitting in an unread stack of trivia on some uneducated Rekef thug's desk. But what if an artificer had got hold of them, after all? What if something Angved had said had penetrated as far as the Engineering Corps?

They've gone to Khanaphes.

Of all the world, he had no wish to return to that cursed city, but nowhere else would rescue him from this humiliating penance, and he still had enough frustrated ambition to overcome his fears and his memories.

They've gone to Khanaphes.

It became his mantra, his hope. And one day, after tendays and tendays of wretched picking at the factory machines, they came for him as well.

They came halfway through the working day: serious, solid men in uniform, who muscled into the factory without a word and struck his chains off in a manner that made it clear that being shackled to an automated loom would be luxury compared to where he was going next. The rest of the workforce had gone quiet and diligent immediately, their chatter and gossip killed in an instant.

When they hauled him out of that place, he had assumed it would be to the interrogation table for sure, since their grim manner suggested nothing else. They always claimed that doctors and artificers broke first, for every junior machine-hand ended up running the tables for the Rekef questioners once or twice, and, after that, little imagination was needed to proceed through all the ways a body could be broken beyond any engineer's repair.

They hustled him across the city until he recognized the district. It was a home away from home for him, the workshops and familiar halls of the Engineering Corps in the little quarter of the city they had made their own. It did not look so welcoming now, for nobody met his eyes. Nobody would admit to knowing this old washed-out former lieutenant who had somehow managed to bring so much wrath down upon his own shoulders.

A moment later and he was inside the Severn Hill, a squat ziggurat named after the Corps' first colonel. Rather than the well-lit debating rooms and the grand hall, however, he was hauled downstairs, away from the sun, into the tunnels beneath.

A tribunal, he realized. He was not sure, just then, if he might not have preferred the Rekef and its interrogation tables. Every engineer knew of the tribunals, although nobody ever formally spread the information. They were not admitted to by the Corps, internally or externally, but apprentice artificers whispered the rumours one to another. They were the Corps' own internal disciplinaries, for engineers who had betrayed the Corps to some other branch of the services. All nonsense, of course, for any such rivalry between the different wings of the army's support corps would be damaging to the Empire, and thus never tolerated. And yet it was true, and it happened, and the Engineers looked after their own no less than did the Rekef or the Slave Corps or the Consortium. They were a young elite, the artificers of the Empire, and ruthless in keeping their secrets.

He found himself, at last, in an eight-sided chamber that he guessed must lie beneath the very centre of Severn Hill. The ceiling was a casual marvel, a piece of mechanical elegance that he realized must only ever be seen by the condemned and their judges. From a mosaic setting of geometric patterns set out in thumbnail-sized blue and green tiles depended a veritable orrery of lamps, circling one another in complex, perfect patterns to the gentle ticking of its clockwork. From a professional point of view it was admirable, but it peopled the scene below it with disturbing, circling shadows, and the blue-green of the ceiling reflected a gloomy, undersea radiance on to everything there.

There was a high dais to one side of the room, a long table set out upon it which was scattered with scrolls and papers, and at least one map that looked – from the brief glimpse Angved caught of it – to be a chart of the Lowlands. Angved himself was not destined for that table, of course. There were three rows of benches on the far side of the room, and they dumped him on one without a word and left him there, abruptly forgotten and abandoned.

Surreptitiously, he peered at the high table, trying to work out what was going on. There were a half-dozen men there, conferring in hushed voices but with a fair amount of animation, showing that, whatever was at stake, they had a great deal invested in it. Another man sat back, listening but not contributing, and displaying an indefinable air of wrongness. *Not one of us*, Angved realized, although he was not sure if he himself still counted as one of the Corps. The seated man was Rekef, though: he'd bet his life on it. An observer from the secret service – Outlander probably – brought to the secret heart of the Engineers' little dominion. *What is going on here?*

The arguing men were four Wasps and two Beetles. After his eyes had adapted to the light, Angved could place at least half of them, and from that he guessed they must all be very senior engineers indeed. In the centre of the knot was Colonel Lien, his gaunt face looking as bitter as ever with the knowledge that his inferior rank was all the authority the Engineering Corps could muster. They had never been granted a generalship, and the others would all be mere majors.

Abruptly there was movement from behind Angved, with more hard and unsympathetic-looking guards arriving, and for a moment the engineer thought that he would just be hauled away again, his brief glimpse of this place just a mistake, punctuation on his road to some worse fate. The newcomers were delivering, however, rather than picking up, and someone slumped on to the bench next to Angved with a clink of chains.

This newcomer had not been employed on factory duty. Angved would find out later that this was the difference between being blamed for the demise of a halfway secret and deniable desert skirmish and being blamed for the failure of a major invasion. He was thin enough to look starved, with a wild growth of beard and his hair matted and tangled. Between that and the dirt, it was hard to see much in his face save the creases and lines. Grime and harsh treatment went a fair way to bridging what was in reality a fifteen-year gap in their ages, and perhaps it was this that broke through Angved's shell of self-absorption. For the first time since the Khanaphes business had gone sour, he found himself looking on someone else as a human being, a kindred spirit.

The guards had stepped back to the door, and up at the high table the senior engineers were arguing again. A slim book was being passed back and forth, almost torn in half as they fought to point out various pages in it.

Angved saw the newcomer looking at him, the eyes lurking in that overgrown face surprisingly sharp.

'Varsec,' the man told him, keeping his voice low enough not to drift over to the guards, 'former captain.'

'Angved, former lieutenant.' It was a curious brotherhood, and if the other man had once held a higher rank, still he had fallen further.

'Engineers?' the other man pressed.

Angved nodded. 'You're not?'

Thin shoulders shrugged. 'Have they worked out where the Aviation Corps fits yet?' he asked wryly, to Angved's surprise. The aviators were virtually independent of their parent artificers, a young, arrogant and elitist band. This man did not seem to fit the mould, but then a few beatings and a turn on the rack would take the shine off anyone's pride.

'And you're here for . . .?' Varsec wondered.

'Khanaphes,' Angved found himself answering without hesitation.

'Ah, I didn't hear much of that. Still, I've not been best placed to get the news recently.'

'You?'

'Solarno.'

Angved blinked. That *was* a matter of public record, even if the doomed Khanaphir expedition was not. The Empire had taken Solarno as part of a daring experiment, an invasion planned and spearheaded by the Aviation Corps. They had lost the city at around the same time that the big war had turned, when suddenly there were too many battles to fight, and too few armies, and when the Lowlands had pulled together and everything else fell apart. He understood then that Varsec must be the ranking survivor of the Solarnese force, just as he himself was the scapegoat for Khanaphes.

He was about to pass a comment, his intended words surprising him by being solicitous rather than scathing, when something in Varsec's pose alerted him. The men at the high table, those important engineering magnates, even the seated Rekef intruder, were looking back across the room. Their eyes fell on Varsec, and then on Angved, passing back and forth, finding each as unpalatable as the other, and yet they kept looking, snapping and growling at one another even as they did. The level of tension in the room, the bowstring-taut nerves of all those powerful men, was almost enough to taste. Words drifted across the room, odd snippets of hissed and urgent demands. 'Are you sure . . .?', '. . . the tests showed . . .', '. . . would never let us do it . . .', '. . . the Empress . . .'

Angved swallowed, but one fragment of their conversation had lodged in his mind. *The tests,* they had said. *My tests? Have they read my report?* And the only conclusion he could come to: *There is nothing else in the world that could have landed me in this room, save the results I handed in – the tests I conducted in the Nem desert.* A little piece of side-business undertaken while the Rekef team and their Scorpion-kinden tools had been cracking open Khanaphes; a little experimentation with some of the local resources that had borne an unexpected yield. He had thought it might provide a useful nest egg to retire on, but now it might be the only thing that could save his life and career.

He glanced at Varsec. The man wore an almost defiant expression as he looked at his superior officers, and Angved felt a leap of confidence in just seeing him. *He is like me and, just like me, he's found something that they need.*

Then the talking was done. In the end it was Colonel Lien who finished it. Lean and stone-bald, and yet barely Angved's senior for all that, he spoke quietly and with purpose, and all the others listened. He even cut the Rekef man off with a sharp gesture when an interruption was threatened. *We are decided*, Lien's stance said, and nobody challenged him on it.

He was the first to leave, stepping down from the dais and striding towards the door. He slowed, though, as he neared the two prisoners: grey-haired Angved and the raggedly hirsute Varsec. His calculating eyes flicked between them, and on his face the distaste could not quite edge out something more thoughtful. On a younger, less cynical man it might have been hope.

After that, the guards dragged Angved out, but not back to the factory. He learned soon enough that the Engineers had their own cells beneath Severn Hill, windowless and comfortless save for a pallet bed and the constant glare of gaslight. Angved had reckoned that he'd had enough of the sun out in the desert, but spending a day sealed underground did away with any such illusion.

When he awoke, stiff and aching from the hard bed, he found his jailers had already been and gone. They had left him some water, a jug of weak beer, and some stew that had at least seen some meat around the time it was cooked. Luxury it was not, but nor was it food to waste on anyone facing a death sentence. More important than that, though, they had left him a book. It was slim, densely typeset and printed in the manner of all Engineering Corps texts, but certainly nothing on the standard syllabus. It was something *new*.

He looked at the title page, holding it up to the hissing lamp.

Towards an Efficient Mechanized Air Force, its Design and Deployment. Beneath that was stamped the name and rank of the author: *Varsec, Captain, Southern Expeditionary Aviation Corps*.

For a moment Angved was quite blank as to why he might have been passed this document, but some helpful clerk had already thought of that, and a stub of black tape marked out a particular page towards the end of the book. The section there dealt with key problems that the author, Varsec, had not been able to solve. Angved had to read it three times before the pieces clicked into exquisite place in his mind, and it was all he could do to stop himself whooping in the narrow confines of his cell.

He read, from start to finish despite the poor light, devouring Varsec's words voraciously, poring over the diagrams, the carefully printed sketches and schematics depicting wings, streamlined bodies, joints and couplings. He skipped only those sections that dealt with Varsec's mooted reorganization of the Aviation Corps, for that interested him not in the slightest. He had eyes only for the technical specifications.

At the end of it, he put the book down and just stared at the wall, his mind's eye painting it with all the wonderful colours of the future.

Stab me, he thought, *but we'll take down every last living one of them. The Lowlands won't know what's hit it.*

Nine

Khanaphes, city of a hundred thousand years – or, at least, old enough that calendars failed to have any relevance. Even the ancient, opaque system of the Moth-kinden, with its animal years marching in erratic and seemingly random procession, was nevertheless younger than this ancient city. The Collegiate dating system, so popular now, had yet to reach the year 550. Perhaps Khanaphes possessed its own calendar, but if so it was locked in the ubiquitous, impenetrable carvings that were incised on every wall and every stone surface. The locals themselves did not count the years. Time for them was the year's cycle: the flooding and the growing and the harvest, year without end, lives lived in annual segments that followed precisely the footprints that parents and grandparents and more distant ancestors had trodden. The Khanaphir had no use for time's progressive arrow.

But that had changed.

The Khanaphir themselves, those solid, shaven-headed Beetle-kinden, were doing their best to pretend that they still possessed that unbroken line back into the deepest past. All of them, farmers, traders, clerks, soldiers and artisans, they were desperately mumming the lives that they remembered from only a year or so before, casting themselves in the grand mystery play of eternal Khanaphes. It was a lie, though, for change had come to Khanaphes with two swift dagger strikes: the first to wound and the second even now poised above them, ready to kill.

The Many of Nem, the wild Scorpion-kinden, had always been their enemies, and the Khanaphir had fought them since time out of mind, as part of their eternal rote. When they had come last, though, the Scorpions had brought new weapons, allegedly gifted to them by the Wasp Empire, and with these they had knocked holes in Khanaphes's walls and rampaged through half the city. That they had been driven away at last did not go far towards disguising the damage they had done or the appalling number of the city's people they had slain.

Still, had the city been left to its own devices, the old timeless cloak might have fallen across it once more. History is insistent, though, and now it had its hooks into Khanaphes. It was not long after the attack of the Many that the Empire had arrived.

Word had come to Collegium swiftly, following on the heels of the scholarly visitors who had become caught up in the fighting with the Nem. Scarcely had they returned home than some of them were embarking again, finding the first airship back east, bound for Solarno and the Exalsee and, from there, to Khanaphes.

Or not quite Khanaphes. Word had come that the Imperial hold on the city was tight, as always the case with a new addition to the Empire. The harbour was crawling with black and gold, and any ships that docked were subjected to a rigorous search. Still, there were plenty of convenient places to hide on a merchantman, and Praeda and Amnon might have risked it had they managed to find a ship's captain willing to chance his cargo being confiscated by the Wasps' Consortium.

Praeda Rakespear was a College scholar, an artificer and architect, young and keen-minded and mostly fed up with Collegium's hidebound attitudes these days, whether it was towards foreign policy or the advancement of female academics. Back in Collegium, she had cultivated a reputation as possessing armour that was proof against any man's advances. The presence of Amnon at her side was testimony to the only time that armour had been breached.

Amnon was Khanaphir, although he was now wearing Lowlander clothes. He was huge, massive-shouldered, tall and broad, and yet swift and precise with it, a true warrior's warrior. In Khanaphes he had been their First Soldier, who led their armies and organized the city's military forces. He had been exiled, too, which was just one of the topics that he and Praeda had not got around to discussing.

Their transport was a Solarnese ship, low and single-masted, that crept up the coast of the Sunroad sea until the desert had given way to the marshy delta of the Jamail. The vessel's master, a lean woman, with grey hair shading to white and her sand-coloured face sun-weathered, had her two-man crew set a fire on an islet there, settling down to wait for the unnamed parties she was to meet. Praeda and Amnon knew little of her business, save that the protocols she was following had been put in place in case business went bad – and Imperial invasions certainly counted as that.

'You did something like this when the Scorpions attacked?' Praeda dared to ask.

The master nodded briefly. 'He showed up then, sure enough, with bags all packed,' was all she would say.

'This friend of yours, he can help us into the city?' Praeda pressed.

'If he's going back there.' The ship's master shrugged. 'If he thinks it's worth the candle.'

They waited a day before the marsh people came to investigate the fires, unconcerned by the crossbows the three mariners lifted against them. They were slight Mantis-kinden with grey-green skins, silent and staring, but the master offered them some token that looked just like a red stone to Praeda. They accepted it from her, in the manner of a contract concluded, and vanished into the thronging green again.

'Now we're running out of time,' the master had declared.

'Half a day more and we'll have to catch the tide, so come along with us, or stay on your own.'

'And your friend?' Praeda asked her, but the woman shook her head, lips pressed together.

The friend never showed, and the master abandoned her hopes brusquely, as though it was nothing of any particular import. Nobody mentioned the Empire, even though it was the prime culprit in the man's absence. Only as the little ship cast off, turning back for Porta Rabi, did Praeda see the Solarnese woman's shoulders slump and her ramrod posture collapse. Their last view of the woman, as her vessel tacked swiftly away, might have been of her weeping.

'Well,' Praeda said soberly. 'We're on your ground, so what now?'

Amnon considered slowly. 'We cannot travel the marshes, not so far from the city. The shipmaster's token will be no good to us now. We must reach the desert and then take the long road to the Jamail.'

'But surely the marsh-kinden will know you – you were First Soldier. They're hardly going to sell you to the Ministers or the Empire, are they? Can't they help us?'

His smile was fond. 'Your people have such a belief that other kinden are just like you beneath the surface. Your logic is like bad wine, Praeda: it does not travel. You know a little of our histories?'

'I know what you tell yourselves about your histories, but I don't accept it as the truth. History never is,' she replied defensively.

'Then just this: the marsh people are pacted to us – rather, to Khanaphes.' That self-correction was hasty and awkward. 'Sworn to send their people to serve us, but in return we leave them their ancient ways. Stray from the river, stray into the delta, and you enter their domain and they will hunt you. They are very skilled in the hunt.'

They followed the borderlands of the marsh, where the

ground was still damp but firm enough to walk on, where the riot of ferns and cycads and arthrophytes gave way to long, lush grass and thornbushes. A day and a half of muggy heat it took them, resting up beneath what shelter they could find during the hottest hours, pressing on after dark to make up the time. They encountered the marsh-kinden just once, when they had camped past midnight in a stand of cypress trees. The Mantis-kinden came padding up, five of them, to investigate Amnon's fire, but they seemed to recognize that they were beyond their boundaries. Instead, they regarded the travellers solemnly, until Amnon offered them some of the fish he was cooking. Hesitantly they came forward, three women and two men, slight enough almost to be children. Those of their kin that Praeda had seen in Khanaphes went about as shaven-headed as the locals, but these had white hair, worn long and braided back, then twined and knotted in intricate patterns.

One of them reached out to touch Amnon's stubbled scalp. The rest kept stealing glances at Praeda's own head of long, dark hair. *Such a small thing, but so important here.* Shaving the head signified submission to the will of the mythical Masters of Khanaphes, the invisible lords of the city in whose ghostly name the Ministers governed. Praeda's professional academic opinion was that they were long extinct, merely a convenient rod with which to keep the people of the city in line.

Amnon spoke with the marsh-kinden, trying to coax some news from them, but they would admit to no knowledge of recent developments within the city itself. If the pickings of their hunts had been richer, with refugees fleeing from the Empire's advance falling into their hands, they made no mention of it.

How did the fight go? Praeda wondered. The magnificent army of the Khanaphir had been devastated by a Scorpion-kinden host armed only with obsolete Imperial cast-offs. How would they have coped when the Empire itself stood before their gates, rather than merely by proxy?

Towards the end of the next day the two of them had put the huge swathe of the delta behind them, and could now see the farmland lining the Jamail extending northwards along the river's course. Khanaphes itself appeared brilliant in the sunlight, its stones fairly glowing. Praeda could make out those walls that had served it so poorly in the fighting, and beyond them the greater edifices of the city government. Nothing seemed to be on fire or even smouldering.

'They'll have guards on the gates,' she said, recalling all she knew of the Empire. 'They'll be searching all the people coming in and going out. Anyone slightly suspicious will get thrown behind bars, interrogated, fined, made to disappear. In fact, a fair few people who aren't suspicious, too, just to spread fear. Fear keeps people in line, especially the fear of arbitrary punishment. Nobody wants to be noticed, when that kind of regime's in place. Nobody causes trouble when they don't know for sure where the lines are drawn. So no doubt there's some secret back way into the city, that only the First Soldiers know about?'

Amnon regarded her quizzically. 'Why would anyone devise such a thing?'

'But you have a plan,' Praeda insisted. 'If we just walk in, well . . .' She swallowed, tilted her chin up. 'I'll shave my head. Then we'll be locals. Will that be enough?'

'Perhaps. As you say, I have a plan.'

Before dusk they had trekked through a mile of farmland, tracing an erratic path of roads and irrigation dykes to reach one specific farmhouse out of dozens. There were a few Khanaphir about, who watched them arrive, more of caution in their eyes than curiosity. At the door, a broad-shouldered old man met them, nodding at Amnon as though he was a tax collector.

'I'd expected it,' was all he said, and he plainly recognized the former First Soldier. 'Inside, then, you might as well. Food?'

'If you have spare,' Amnon said with careful deference. He had to stoop some way to get under the lintel, Praeda trailing after him.

Most of the house consisted of a single room, where a long table had already been set. A woman of the old man's years was bustling about it now, rearranging the places to find space for two more. She glanced from Amnon to Praeda, her dark eyes unreadable. Praeda realized that she herself had never seen a peasant home belonging to the Khanaphir, what with living out of an embassy and being the honoured guest of the Ministers. She had assumed that the foundation on which Khanaphir rested must be crushed down by its weight, impoverished and sullen – deprived as they were of anything like Collegium's enlightenment and standard of living. Instead, the inside of the farmhouse was surprisingly well furnished, chairs and table all finely carved and clearly ancient, and the walls liberally adorned with those baffling carvings. Even these Khanaphir peasants lived neck-deep in history, she saw, and they bore their servitude with stubborn pride.

The Beetle-kinden they had seen outside now trooped in to take their places, and Praeda found that she and Amnon were directed towards the table's head, sitting at the right hand of the old man. She guessed that it was the senior pair that owned and ran the farm, and the rest were hirelings and farmhands. The fare itself consisted of some kind of thick soup, flat bread, and some fish that had been pickled to within an inch of its life at some point in its distant past.

There was little conversation around the table, and even Amnon said nothing, just ate dutifully as though he was only a labourer himself. Nobody commented that an ex-First Soldier had just turned up out of nowhere, with a foreign woman. Praeda suspected that they were all buzzing with questions, but that it was not in their nature to ask them, and the presence of strangers had killed off any other kind of talk.

At last, as the meal was drawing to a close, Amnon grunted, 'Need to get into the city. Going that way?'

'What sort of question is that?' The old man's expression was openly disparaging. 'Market, you well know. What of it?'

'Room on the cart for two more?' Amnon said, not even looking at the farmer.

This was greeted by an exasperated sigh. 'Then you'll work, load and unload, for I need all the hands I have, and you'll leave two men sitting idle here, if you have your way.' Both his tone and expression stated, clear as day, that Amnon had been personally sent by the Masters to inconvenience him.

Instead of rallying at this, Amnon's head sank even lower and he shrugged, not in any way the man that Praeda knew. She looked about the table, but nobody met her eyes.

'Excuse me,' she said at last, almost relishing the shocked silence that greeted her words, 'but you do know this is the First Soldier? That he saved Khanaphes from the Many of Nem?'

For a long while she thought that nobody would respond, that she had killed off all chance of anyone in this house ever saying anything again, but then the old man snorted with derision.

'*Was* First Soldier. And who ever heard of such a thing as a man who *was* First Soldier, hm? And not such a great one even when he was. Now Thamat, before him, *he* was a great First Soldier. He'd never have let the Many get close to the walls.' He shook his head, lamenting the youth of today, as any elderly College Master might – or any old man anywhere.

The next morning the old man had some of his fieldhands load up a wagon and hitch it to a tired-looking draught beetle, all without Amnon actually making any further request that Praeda could see, or anybody suggesting a plan. On to the bed of the sturdy wagon went sacks of flour – that Praeda guessed must be hand milled – and some dried fruit, and a surprising number of jars of some kind of liquor.

By that time the old woman had plucked up the courage to approach Praeda, though still saying nothing, but offering her the curved copper strip of a razor.

For a moment she closed her eyes against the thought,

reluctant because her long hair was such a part of the way she imagined herself, but reluctant even beyond that, for some obscure reason she could not name. If she was to creep into occupied Khanaphes, however, she would have to pass as a local, and if the Wasps looked closely then a mere headscarf would not serve.

'Will *you* do it?' she asked. The woman nodded, and in her eyes was a fair measure of sympathy – and perhaps a little awe at ever seeing an adult Beetle-kinden with a full head of hair.

Most of an hour later, and it was done. Amnon's reaction was the worst, trying to adjust to her transition from the exotic to the familiar. *I am still the same woman*, she told herself, but she did not feel like it with her bare head cold and itching.

Then they were on the wagon, and the old man flicked at the beetle with his crop until it began its weary plodding towards the city.

There were indeed Wasp soldiers stationed at the gate, but Khanaphes was large, and not even occupation by a hostile military could keep its doors closed, not if the occupiers themselves wanted to eat. There was a steady stream of locals going in and out, the oil on the wheels of commerce. When their wagon reached the gates, there was a cursory search, the confiscation of a few jars of homebrew, a narrow-eyed squint at each of the passengers, especially the large figure of Amnon, but they were all Beetles in a city and a nation of Beetles, so the Wasps waved their wagon on without hindrance. That one of the sacks also contained all of Praeda and Amnon's possessions, the Wasps never knew.

Those few foreigners trying to enter or leave, they saw stopped and searched far more diligently, and most of them were turned back, either trapped inside or kept out.

After that, they were within the walls. The old man just nodded once at Amnon, again with no need for a word between them, then the big man slipped off the wagon, pulling Praeda with him.

'Where now?' she whispered, resisting her hand's natural inclination to drift up to her scalp.

'I know places,' he murmured. 'Near the docks first, maybe. We'll see how the Wasps are dealing with the river trade.' He cast a single glance back at the old man and the wagon, before heading off.

It was only three streets later that Praeda enquired, 'Amnon, have I just met your parents?' The thought had been absurdly slow in coming, and even then she was not at all sure until she saw his face. 'Did you . . . did you not think to introduce me?'

'I did. After you slept,' he mumbled, looking awkward for a moment. 'They liked you, I think.'

'What . . . did you tell them?' she demanded, but just then he pretended to spot a Wasp patrol and picked up the pace, leaving her glaring at his broad back.

Then the city had encompassed them, and she was abruptly wrestling with memories of how she had seen the place last, before her return to Collegium. The western half had been occupied by the Scorpion-kinden then, as the Many of Nem ravaged the farmland up and down the riverbank seeking for a way across, while she and Amnon and the mercenary artificer Totho fortified the bridge against them. Beyond that, she remembered the still dignity enveloping the city before the Scorpions came: the austere calm of its ministers, the solid and elegant lines of its architecture, the noiseless bustle of its shaven-headed citizens.

She remembered her colleagues who had died when the Wasps, and their Scorpion tools, had made their move. Seeing the black and gold now at every street corner made her clench her fists, wanting to lash out at them with all her tiny might. She remembered waiting after the battle, to learn if Amnon had lived or died.

It was strange that she remembered Che most of all, for there was no reason that Stenwold Maker's niece should serve as a linchpin in her memories of this city. The girl had been a dismal failure as an ambassador, going missing half the time and seeming almost deranged, fixated on strange parts of the city's history even when the walls themselves were tumbling. She had even been absent during the fighting, had not contributed to it at all, instead had gone off with the Imperial ambassador, who seemed to have gone rogue in the interim. Oh, Praeda had quite liked Che as a person but, still, the woman had hardly been an influential figure in the disaster that had been Praeda's original visit to Khanaphes.

And yet somehow she had been. Praeda could not account for it, or explain her feelings on the matter, but Cheerwell Maker had been the hub of the wheel, standing at the heart of all things. This fact was inexplicable and yet undeniable.

Praeda suddenly stopped dead, so that Amnon went on another five yards before sensing her absence, and turning with a quizzical look. Praeda met his eyes but was not equal to the task of explaining, hiding her sudden shock by rushing to catch up with him.

I did not just see Cheerwell Maker, she reproached herself. *That face in the crowd, it could have been anyone's.* Except no Khanaphir woman had hair like that. *I did not just see the crowd part, and Cheerwell Maker, in that inexplicably open space, staring at me and then gone the next instant. It's the heat. It's the stress. My mind plays tricks.*

They were almost at the docks by the time Praeda's heart had stopped hammering.

Ten

She awoke to darkness and a moment's utter panic because the man who had awoken her, by slipping out of the bed and pacing across the room, was not Achaeos.

Cheerwell Maker's mind remained blank. Her dream, something wild and horrible, was now gone from her head, and nothing came to replace it – just the sound of someone, some unfamiliar body, confined within the same four walls.

The thought returning to her first was that darkness was optional, given the Art that she had been blessed with, and so she banished it. The Mynan boarding-house room came into sharp relief, picked out in a whole other spectrum of greys, and with it came a fuller recollection of where she was and why.

Over by the window, Thalric was peering out through the shutters, wearing only his breeches. She stared at his broad back, picking out each scar in turn to read his history there, whose gaps she filled in as he turned back to her.

'You're awake,' he observed. 'Your breathing changes when you're awake.'

She made a noncommittal noise. *Here* was the vertical line that Tynisa had drawn down his abdomen, that Che knew continued even to his thigh. *There* was one of the narrow jabs he had received from a former governor of Myna, in a fight he had told her about when they returned to this city and he got maudlin drunk on the memory, a curious lapse for Thalric.

That, of course, was the near-fatal wound another Rekef man had dealt him, after the Empire had decided he was expendable, and close by it was the curious, puckered mark where a snapbow bolt had penetrated, after chewing its way through layers of metal and silk.

Whatever else he had been, and all the different colours he had worn, Thalric was undoubtedly a survivor.

'Can't sleep?' she asked him. 'Conscience troubling you?'

He smiled a little sourly. 'It's nearly dawn.'

That surprised her, but she would have realized it herself after allowing her eyes to adjust. Her Art-sight, which cut through the dark, robbed her of the visual cues she had grown up with. 'Today's when Hokiak said to come back to him,' she recalled. 'I don't imagine the old man gets up this early, though.'

Thalric shrugged. 'I get twitchy in this place. Too many bad memories. I keep thinking that one of the locals is going to creep in here and cut my throat.'

Che and Thalric both had a curious relationship with the city-state of Myna. She had first come here as his prisoner, and while her uncle had been orchestrating her rescue, Thalric had been killing the aforementioned governor on Rekef orders. Later still, they had come back here together to try and foment revolution, and she had narrowly avoided being executed by the very resistance fighters who had helped rescue her in the first place; whilst Thalric had ended up as a prisoner of the new governor. Whom, she could hardly forget, he had *also* killed – an act that lit the flames of rebellion in the city, as a result of which Myna was currently free of Imperial rule.

They had been in the city now for two hard days and the first half-day had been spent in separate cells.

I had not considered we were fugitives, after all. Oh, being on the run from the Empire had become almost standard practice, and there had been no whiff of the black and gold here, but they should have entered Myna like war heroes. Instead they had been arrested: he for being a Wasp, she for being with him.

Che had told them a name, over and over: 'Kymene', and after the first hour or so she had begun to wonder whether there had not been some disastrous shift in Mynan politics, and that the woman who had led the city's liberation had somehow been displaced, even executed. After about six hours, in which various blue-grey-skinned Mynans had asked her unsympathetic, suspicious and occasionally meaningless questions, she had started to think she might have simply dreamt the woman.

Then had come Kymene, looking anything but pleased to see Che.

'So you're back.' They had been standing in that stone-walled, windowless cell lit by erratic gaslight, whose sporadic death and rebirth was more to do with the ongoing rebuilding effort than any attempt to disconcert the prisoner.

Kymene had looked older, and Che had wondered how much of the city's current governance fell directly on her shoulders, how much of her strength she expended in fighting other factions. Myna had been united by Imperial occupation for all of Che's life, and most of Kymene's. Freedom demanded difficult adjustments that were slow in coming. The city had been at war, on each street, in each citizen's heart, for too long.

'We're just passing through,' Che had said urgently.

'You and your Wasp.'

'Thalric, Kymene,' Che had told her, searching the woman's hard face for any clues to his fate. For a moment there was nothing, and Che was abruptly sure that they had killed him. For that sliver of a second, the pain had been shocking, utterly unexpected.

'I recognized him,' Kymene had admitted reluctantly, and even that had provided no reassurance. How it must grieve her, to be beholden to a Wasp-kinden. 'I've signed the orders to release both of you.' The words were virtually spat out. 'Cheerwell Maker, what do you want?'

There must have been some hurt and betrayal in Che's face that got past Kymene's armour, however, for the woman's expression had shifted, a little ashamed perhaps, and a little defensive. 'Maker, I've been all morning trying to keep this city together, to balance the warmongers and the cowards in the Consensus – if our government deserves to call itself that! – and then your name falls into my lap, you and your cursed Wasp both, and what am I to make of it? The last two times that man came here, he brought down the government. Is he going to make it a third?'

Che had almost laughed at that, save that Kymene was being so deadly serious. 'We're heading west.' She was conscious of the Mynan woman burning to be elsewhere, *anywhere* else perhaps. 'Heading into the Commonweal. I was hoping for your help in crossing the border.'

New suspicion had then clouded Kymene's face instantly, but it had drained away to leave an expression that Che had become tiresomely familiar with: someone's contempt at her naivety. 'The Commonweal? You're going west out of the Alliance?'

That name was new enough to feature only on the most recent maps. Three former slave-cities, Myna, Szar and Maynes, had broken together away from the Empire after two decades of subjugation, and were fighting to hold on to their independence even as the Empire regained its old strength and ambitions. Che had assumed the Mynans must have plenty in common with the Commonwealers, whose conquered principalities must also have rid themselves of Imperial rule: the Alliance's combined uprising had cut them off from direct contact with the Empire. Nothing in Kymene's face had suggested that was the case.

Do they fear that the Dragonfly-kinden will invade them, now? Do they trust nobody?

'The border?' she had repeated hesitantly.

'There's little can be done about that,' the Mynan woman had told her. 'Alliance relations with them are . . . strained. The border is patrolled on both sides, travellers are not being let through. If you wish to risk the crossing, I can give you papers to get past our troops, but as for the Principalities . . . I will not be able to assist you.' For a moment her face had remained nothing but stern: the Maid of Myna, the woman who had unified the resistance and freed her city. Then came the tiniest twitch, an acknowledgement of old times. 'But if you're asking about crossing borders with goods or people, you know where to ask as well as I do.'

Freed from the cells, their first look at the streets of free Myna had not been inspiring. Life under the Imperial boot had taught harsh lessons to the Mynan people, which would not soon be unlearned. There were plenty of weapons on display, and soldiers drilling with sword and crossbow, and even a few of the new snapbows that had made such an impact during the war. The red and black flag of Myna was displayed everywhere, as though people were afraid it might be taken away from them again. Non-Mynans were regarded on a sliding scale of suspicion. The Ant-kinden of Maynes and the Bees of Szar were tolerated, as they represented Myna's neighbours in its Three-State Alliance. Others, like Che, were treated coldly, as though every one of them was suspected of being a Rekef infiltrator. Thalric had resorted to a hooded cloak, but was still stopped several times by guards, to be searched, questioned and insulted. The papers Kymene had provided were pored over, creased, frowned at. The Mynans would take a long time to grow easy with their new freedom, and Che only hoped that such time would be granted to them.

Since their release they had found their own lodgings in the city. Thalric's gold had sufficed to get them a room, but it was a dwindling resource that they needed to save for other tasks, and so this single chamber, this one bed, was all they felt able to afford.

Sleeping beside Thalric was a strange experience. Achaeos had slept quiet and still, breathing so softly she could hardly tell he was there. Thalric seemed to take up all available space, and in the darkest pit of the night he would twitch and start, pursued by all the bad dreams that his varied career had gifted him with.

Sleeping beside him was all that had happened, so far. Twice now they had come close to something else but, like a ship's master suddenly seeing hidden rocks, she had steered away from it. She was a little scared of him, and feared what his effect on her would be. And then there was Achaeos, poor dead Achaeos, whose ghost she had been trying to exorcise ever since his death during the war. The revelation that the spectre that had formerly tormented her had not been his at all had not driven away that host of memories. The greater part of her felt that she was teetering over of an abyss of guilt, and that to give in to Thalric's wishes would be to fall.

And the rest of her, a minority vote, wanted to jump just so she could be rid of this burden of propriety that was tying her in knots. *Would Achaeos truly have wanted me to be chained to his corpse for ever?*

The obvious riposte to that was: *Achaeos would not under any circumstances have ever wanted to see me with Thalric.*

They hit the streets early, leaning into those ubiquitous hostile stares as though into inclement weather. They managed to get a street away from the boarding house before the first guard stopped them for their papers. Looking into the man's face, Che had a sudden revelation: *not hatred, not loathing, not a lust for vengeance, but fear.* The man now staring at Kymene's signature was of Che's own age. He had never known his city be free, until the uprising a few years back. It must seem that the least breath of air could snatch it away from him.

The guard had turned away, his initial interest subsiding into mere dislike, and in that instant Che had stumbled, leaning for support against Thalric, conscious of a ripple passing through the people around her, as they shrank away from her as though she had the plague.

'Che, what . . .?' Thalric had been asking, but she had only stared: bright sunlight, not Myna's overcast skies; a beating heat she recognized. And the stone walls inscribed with legion upon legion of tiny carvings, spilling a thousand years of history across every surface . . .

Khanaphes.

And for a moment there had been a Beetle woman staring at her from amid the Mynan crowd, clad in Khanaphir peasant dress but with a Collegiate face. *Praeda . . .?*

And Thalric was virtually shaking her, as the crowd ebbed back from them, and there were guards approaching, so they would be arrested again, or worse, if she did not . . .

'I'm fine.' She felt anything but fine, though. Each night she woke to find shards of her dreams scattered about her like broken glass. Ever since Khanaphes, where she had been changed. Ever since awaking into the presence of the Masters. She had gone to that city because the war – and Achaeos's death – had robbed her of her Aptitude, stripped from her the mechanical inheritance of her people, and thrown her into a world of magic she had never entirely believed in. In Khanaphes she had begun to understand, however, and the ancient, callous Masters had taught her more. But more doors had been opened than she knew how to close: her mind was leaking visions every night, fleeting and unremembered, just bright but receding shards inside her mind as she awoke. But this . . . never before in daylight, not like this.

She never remembered those dreams, save for one thing: they were dreams of Khanaphes.

'Let's move,' she said shakily, wanting to lose herself in a crowd that would only reject her.

With the Mynan authorities unwilling or unable to help them further, she and Thalric had fallen back on an old acquaintance. Hokiak's Exchange had not been changed much by the city's liberation. It still possessed the same shabby emporium at the front, a drinking den at the back, and no doubt the same constant flow of smugglers, criminals and fugitives looking to use the old man's services. Che was vaguely surprised that the new, iron-handed Mynan leadership had not decided to curb their old semi-ally's practices, but then, no doubt, the ancient Scorpion-kinden had gathered a lot of incriminating information over the years which would be awkward if made public. Whatever the reason, he was apparently still operating as freely as during the Imperial occupation.

The man himself had barely changed, either. Che and Thalric had both encountered a great deal of the Scorpion-kinden in the recent past, in all their hulking and brutal glory. Hokiak was what happened when that glory burned out and withered away. He was a hollow-chested, paunchy, stick-limbed old creature, his white skin wrinkled and baggy, with one thumb claw become nothing but a broken stump. He walked with the aid of a stick, had developed a rasping cough, yet still exercised a remarkable amount of underhand influence over a great many people.

That he remembered Che and Thalric was clear. He did not welcome them effusively, not quite, and indeed the circumstances of their last meeting had been ambivalent to say the least, but something lit up in his yellow eyes when they found their way into his back room after so long.

Perhaps things are quieter here, with the Wasps gone, Che wondered. *Perhaps the old man's getting bored.*

'Well now, who's this, eh? Maker's girl, and the Wasp assassin.' He leered at them through the stumps of his fangs. 'Trouble coming, is there? For certain there is.' He used his stick like a lever, prying his laborious way across the room before dropping down into a creaking chair. 'Come join me,' he invited. 'Tell me what trouble you've brought us.'

'No trouble, I hope,' Che replied, and Hokiak chuckled.

'They hanged two Beetle-kinden yesterday,' he remarked, without further explanation.

Che and Thalric exchanged glances. 'Who did?' she prompted.

'The militia. Said they were Rekef. For once I believe it. They were asking questions before they were caught, these two stretch-necked fellows. There's a certain stink off them, more even than normal Rekef, and that stink goes all the way to Capitas.'

'What questions?' Thalric asked.

Hokiak's rotting smile was hideous. 'You don't need to ask it, assassin.'

'I'm no assassin,' the Wasp said irritably.

'I know two governors of Myna who'd call you a liar,' the Scorpion pointed out. 'No wonder the Consensus is twitchy, if you're back in town.'

'What have you guessed?' Che asked, annoyed at all this obfuscation.

'Rekef from Capitas will be here looking for me – or they soon might be,' Thalric explained. 'General Brugan might not have given up. Which makes our business with you that much more urgent, Hokiak.' He fixed the old man with a stern look. 'Unless you've decided I'm merely a commodity again.'

Hokiak scowled, less the villainous broker and more – or so it seemed to Che – the put-upon merchant. 'You flatter me, assassin. Those were the days, eh? Sell the resistance and the Empire to each other, and have both of them paying you for the privilege. Good times, good times. The current lot lost their sense of humour when they took over, I'll tell you that straight. Her up top, Kymene, who I personally kept out of Wasp hands, she came down here after they chose her to run the Consensus. No more deals with the Wasps, she told me. No deals with the Empire. Keep your smuggling, your racketeering, your private work – but the moment anyone looking like a Wasp agent heaves into view, it's pass them over to her, and I can whistle for a profit.' The old man shook his head disgustedly. 'So, tempted as I am, I wouldn't be selling you to the Rekef, Master Assassin, even if I could find one with his neck kept short.' The ruined smile returned. 'Though I thank you for giving an old man credit.' He looked from Che to Thalric, and back. 'A man could wonder, it's true, how come the two of you are still on the same road as each other, so long after, and whether there wasn't something in all those suspicions we all had about the pair of you last time. But me? I stay out of politics these days. Consensus wants to interfere with my business, then I'm damned if I'll go an inch out of my way for them.'

Che shivered, only now appreciating that narrow escape, for of course the Mynans had thought she and Thalric were Imperial agents last time, and Che herself had narrowly avoided being tortured or killed for it. And yet here the two of them were, together again, and it was bound to make Hokiak wonder.

'We need a guide westwards,' Thalric announced. 'You must know someone. We have a little wherewithal.'

'West?' Hokiak grimaced. 'West ain't so easy these days, with troops on both sides of the border.' Seeing their downcast expressions, he held up one hand. 'But, yes, I do business with types whose work takes them that way. Easy enough to find one who's willing to take a couple of friends over. There are a few kicking their heels in the city even now, waiting for a commission to take them back across the border. I'll send word out, and you can just wait here. That's it then, is it?'

'Nothing more troublesome than that,' Thalric started, but Che took a deep breath and added, 'One more thing.'

Thalric plainly had not expected this from the look he gave her, but she pressed on valiantly. 'I would like to speak to a . . .' She could not form the word *magician* before the old Scorpion's pragmatic stare. Thalric might just understand, after all they had been through together in Khanaphes, but Hokiak? 'Somewhere in Myna there must be someone . . . a fortune teller, or a mystic, perhaps . . .'

But Hokiak's expression was not encouraging. 'Plenty of those where you're headed, maybe, but in *Myna?*'

'Do you have anyone Inapt working for you?' Che pressed, ignoring Thalric's doubting expression.

Hokiak made an exasperated face, a feat in itself. He had one of his people run off, to return a moment later with a cadaverous old Spider-kinden in tow. Che recognized the man as Hokiak's business partner.

'Gryllis,' the Scorpion said, sounding embarrassed to even be asking this, 'you know any fortune tellers or quacksalvers or anything like that in this city?' A thought obviously struck him. 'Wasn't there that deserter . . . what was her name, Wheezer?'

'Uie Se,' Gryllis pronounced it carefully, and Che reflected that there would be plenty more names like that to be found in the Commonweal. 'She's clinging on.'

Hokiak gave him a sidelong look. 'You don't ever go have your fortune told, do you?'

'Old Claw, when you get to our age, money spent on a seer would be money wasted,' Gryllis replied drily. 'Who wants to know about Uie Se, then?'

'*I* do.' Che interrupted. 'Thalric, can you wait here for the guide? I won't be long.'

'So long as you know what you're doing,' Thalric cautioned her. 'And so long as this guide of yours,' he added to Hokiak, 'won't run a mile if they see a Wasp.'

'Oh, I don't reckon there's a chance of that,' the Scorpion replied, obviously finding the idea amusing.

Hokiak's opinion of seers and magicians was sufficiently low that even he threw in this Mynan fortune teller's whereabouts for free. Che learned also that the mystic had been one of the Auxillian troops the Empire had used to keep the peace in Myna during the occupation, that the woman had aided the resistance and then deserted once the Wasps were driven out.

It was an indictment of the current Mynan paranoia that all the risks Uie Se had taken on behalf of the locals had resulted in bare tolerance of her presence, rather than any true acceptance. She lived in a single room, in a house that had plainly belonged to a well-off family some time before the occupation, but was now falling to pieces a day at a time. The room itself was grimy, and the partitioning of the house's interior had left the seer with a bare sliver of window, so that inside it was so dark that only by Art or magic could one see anything at all.

Che, whose understanding of magic was in its infancy, fell back on her Art, exchanging the darkness for a palette of greys. Uie Se, she saw, was a tall, lean and angular woman, a Grasshopper-kinden as all the other Mynan Auxillians had been. Her hair was kept long and tied back, and she wore a simple and much-darned smock reaching down to her bony knees.

The seer was staring at her bleakly. 'You've come to the wrong room, Beetle,' she said, her voice dry and hollow, and tried to close the door again. 'Don't bother me.'

'Wait,' Che said hurriedly. 'I need your help.'

'There's nothing I can do for such as you.' Abandoning her attempt to close the door, Uie Se turned and shambled back to sit down on a filthy straw mattress.

'I have money.' Meaning yet more of Thalric's, and she suspected he would not approve, but her need was great.

'Oh, then come in,' said the Grasshopper, with a loose-jointed gesture, and Che realized that the woman was drunk. 'Buy me a chair, so you can sit on it. What do you want, Beetle? Are you a scholar come to record stories of a vanished age? I will talk. I will talk all you want.'

Maybe this was a waste of time. 'I want to talk about dreams.'

Uie Se was abruptly more still. 'You have aspirations for the future, rich lady?'

'No, dreams. I am having *dreams* that I know are important, but they never stay with me. I know how important dreams are to seers and magicians, so there must be some techniques to help me recall them.'

The Grasshopper eyed her edgily. 'You have money?'

'Some.'

'You are . . .' The woman could not bring herself say it, but her fascination was that of someone observing some bizarre freak of nature.

'Inapt, yes.' Che could say the word with equanimity now. The admission no longer hurt as it once had. Spending time away from the eminently Apt city of Collegium had helped. No doubt Uie Se assumed she had been born different, a throw-back amongst her own people, but of course most of Che's life had been spent amongst the technical elite, trained in mechanics and artifice and dismissing all those old stories of magic as deluded Moth-kinden propaganda. Then Achaeos had entered her life and touched her with his very real magic, coming to find her when she was captured by her enemies, and then taking her to that ghastly, haunted Darakyon and forcing her to witness its hideous ghosts.

And when he had needed her, when his people had been trying to raise their ancient magic against the Wasps who had occupied their home, he had begged her for her strength, and she had somehow found the capacity within herself to give it. Their minds had touched, and she had funnelled her stoic Beetle endurance towards him, given him the extra reach so that he could cast his net further.

And his call had rung out from the mountain top above Tharn, where the ritual was being enacted, and the things of the Darakyon had heard and answered.

If some magician had offered Che the chance to forget the feel of those cold, ancient, twisted things inside her head, but taken as his price all her memories of Achaeos, she would have thought a long time about the proposal.

But the things had come when Achaeos called, charged him with strength, set the Moth-kinden ritual ablaze, terrorized the Wasps out of Tharn, driven them mad and set them against one another. And Achaeos, already badly wounded, dragged from his sickbed to join the Moth-kinden's dark venture . . . Achaeos . . .

She had felt his life wink out amidst the cackling and rustling of the Darakyon things. She had felt him leave her.

'Dreams,' she repeated to the Grasshopper seer, and there was a tone to her voice, dead and angry at the same time, that made the woman shrink back.

'Yes, yes.' Uie Se scuttled into the further shadows of her room. 'There are herbs. I have some. You shall know them by their smell. They have been used for ever as a net for dreams. There are talismans, and I shall ready one for you now, soon, soon, now. Only a moment, great lady. They shall be a spider's web, yes, to catch your dreams, so that you may feast on them when you wake. You shall have your dreams.'

'How much?'

'No money, none,' the wretched creature told her instantly. 'No, no, no.'

'How much?' Che repeated. 'Look, I will pay for your services. This is just . . . business.' Something about her had so clearly rattled the Grasshopper, and she wondered if the rush of memories that had briefly overwhelmed her had bled out of her and into this woman's head. From somewhere the words came: 'I absolve and forgive, and will leave nothing behind me but footsteps.'

The seer paused, staring back over her shoulder, her hands stilled for a moment where they had been sifting through pots and jars by touch. 'Thank you, great lady, thank you.' The tension was abruptly gone from her.

What have I said, and why did it matter? Belatedly Che recalled from where she had pirated the words – a play, of all things: a Collegium play set back in the time before the revolution. Supposedly it had been adapted from an older Moth-kinden work, but updated for a modern audience.

But they must have kept some of the original, nonetheless. She would have to be careful with that kind of trick. She had the unwelcome feeling that certain words and phrases uttered by her, that would have been just wind before her change, carried a mystical weight now, whether she knew their import or not.

Uie Se had gathered together her herbs, and handed Che a pouch full of them. 'You should steep them in water, let the water boil as you sleep. Do you keep to any of the Apt?' she asked and, at Che's nod, made a sour face. 'They will complain, so ignore them. As for this,' she held up a ring of twisted copper wire, 'hang it near your bed – anywhere there are spiders smaller than your fingernail. Let one spin its web within it, and your dreams shall not escape.'

When Che returned to Hokiak's Exchange, the guide had arrived and, to Che's surprise, turned out to be another Wasp-kinden. He was a big, broad-shouldered specimen, decidedly bulkier than Thalric, with a heavy jaw and hair trimmed close to his skull, looking every bit the thug. Thalric and he had been sharing a jug of wine, though and, given Thalric's history among his own kind, were clearly getting on remarkably well.

'Cheerwell,' he greeted her. 'This is – Varmen. He'll be guiding us over the border.' A moment's pause before the name told her that he had been about to assign this man a military rank, before checking himself.

Deserter, then, she guessed, *rather than a lifelong mercenary*. 'You're a smuggler, Master Varmen?' she asked doubtfully.

The big Wasp shook his head. 'Been back and forth a few times, riding escort mostly. Still, I know the best places.'

'I'd have thought getting into the Commonweal was hard enough with one Wasp, let alone two,' Che commented, sitting down and reaching for a wine-bowl.

Varmen grinned. 'Not so hard, at that, but we're talking about Principalities, anyway. Commonweal laws don't hold there, you'll see.'

Eleven

The ring of twisted copper wire dangled above her, suspended from a thornbush branch. The walls of Myna were behind them now, and they had made good time heading north-west before nightfall had caught them. They rode, which Che found easier than she had expected – easier even than the two Wasps seemed to, who had at least a little more experience than she did.

They had found a suitable hollow and had tethered their mounts, with Varmen using his sting to start a campfire, after a few explosive false starts. The man's pack-beetle had its leash still tied to the pommel of his horse's saddle, presumably so that they could get moving that much faster if need be. It was a ridiculously small creature, around the size of a Fly-kinden, and almost obscured under the heavy load of luggage that Varmen apparently felt compelled to travel with.

Varmen was not overly talkative, nor aloof either, for he responded readily when questioned. He and Thalric exchanged anecdotes intermittently, a well-travelled round of Imperial localities, favourite drinking dens, family names and public figures. Che hovered at the edges of their laconic conversations, feeling excluded by their shared race and past. Even she, though, could detect the huge gaps in their exchanges, the vast areas of personal history unvisited. Neither of them was keen to pin down any specifics of the respective military careers that each had abandoned.

The road that he was now guiding them along had provided the Empire's invasion route, all those years ago.

Now that they were camped, Thalric was taking first watch, while Che had taken to her bedroll and let sleep overcome her. She had left her herbs simmering over the fire as instructed, although the two Wasps wrinkled their noses at the smell of them.

Above her head, a small spider had already begun to build its trap within the ring of twisted wire.

Just the other side of sleep, the fierce sun of Khanaphes blazed down, fragments of day and night, times past and present, faces she had known. Her newfound heritage was clawing at her, seizing control of her head and forcing her eyes open to see . . .

The sun over Khanaphes was a bronze nail-head driven into a cloudless sky.

Ethmet, the First Minister, stood on the steps of the Scriptora and watched his world teetering on the brink of destruction. It was an unexpectedly peaceful sight, for the second sun above him was descending with gentle grace: a black and gold orb blazing back the light of the true sun, suspended impossibly over his city like nothing he had ever witnessed. He could hear a faint insect-like drone, but he could not tell whether it came from this floating giant or from the dozen smaller machines that buzzed in wide circles, keeping a vigilant perimeter.

The city of Khanaphes, which had stood changeless for countless centuries, was now becoming unrecognizable to the old Beetle-kinden minister. It seemed that he had been serving the unseen, unheard Masters for ever, just one link in the chain of First Ministers stretching back into the golden dawn of time. He had thought, in time, to pass on the mantle of responsibility to one of his like-minded colleagues, had thought to become another name carved on the lists adorning one wall of the Scriptora's hall of records. A legacy of honour, surely, but also a curiously anonymous one, in no way marked out from his predecessors or his successors. But that was not to be, for history had chosen him to be significant after all, and the thought made him weak.

Khanaphes could have recovered from last year's unpleasantness, he knew. For the Scorpions to come from the deep desert and conquer half the city, aided by agents of the Wasp Empire, that was a terrible thing. The Scorpions had gone, though – the power of the Masters had put the rabble back in their place, the river Jamail overflowing its banks to wash Khanaphes clean of them. Ethmet should have rejoiced at this clear sign of favour, unprecedented in a thousand years, but even then he had fretted. He did not want to carry the burden of importance. *Let me pass on and be gone, and let my name survive only in stone.*

But then the Wasp-kinden had come, in force. They had come with ambassadors who had explained to him that it was rogue elements fleeing the justice of their Empress who had been behind the Scorpion attack. Ethmet had recognized the lie, though even the men they had sent to him believed their words to be true. Nonetheless he thanked them on behalf of the city, and had assured them that the Dominion of Khanaphes bore them no ill-will.

It was not quite as easy as that, they then explained. The Wasp Empire felt dishonoured by the incident, cut to the bone by shame and guilt at the way its renegades had injured a neighbouring power. They had come to put matters right, to ensure that Khanaphes was properly defended whilst rebuilding its strength.

Ethmet had assured them that the Khanaphir trusted to the Masters, and therefore such kindness really was not necessary. By that time, messengers from upriver had been flocking to the city with further news.

You should not put yourself to any trouble, he had assured the Wasps, and they had told him that there would be no further trouble, and that was what the soldiers were here for – the soldiers who had been marching south from the Imperial border, come to defend Khanaphes from . . . From just about everything, it seemed, including any aberrant belief amongst the city's leaders that it might not require defending.

So far there had been little trouble: Ethmet had ordered it so. The Khanaphir guardsmen and militia had stood by as the Empire entered their city, not raising sword or spear against the intruders. For tendays now there had been Wasp soldiers on every street, in every marketplace, on the city walls, watching the rebuilding. Ethmet had wrestled with his conscience, for there had once been a rod of iron to his spine, which countenanced no deviation from The Way Things Were Done – as set down a millennium ago by the Masters themselves. Surely, having witnessed what must have represented the Masters' intervention on behalf of their favoured city, that rod should be even more inflexible now? Surely he should be exhorting his people to rise up and slay the Wasps, to defy their new-minted Empire?

And yet, when he reached out for that rod of iron, he found that it had rusted through. Something within his proud heart had shattered quietly when the Scorpion-kinden had sundered the walls of his city, and captured every street and building as far as to the western bank of the river. Now his former strength of purpose was gone, and he hid a terrible fear inside him: that if the Khanaphir fought against this new invader, *the Masters might do nothing to save them.* Ethmet did not think on the flood that had driven away the Scorpions, but only upon all those losses they had suffered before the flood had come. *What more might be lost? Would the hand of the Masters serve only to sweep the Wasps from a barren ruin?* It was blasphemous, such thinking, yet he could not rid himself of it. He could not give the order to go to war.

He had meanwhile called on the Masters, night after night, praying for guidance. *There are foreigners profaning your city, great ones,* he had told them. *Shall we do nothing?*

And an echo had come back, *Nothing, only nothing* – so that he could not know if he had been answered or not. He had eaten the drug called Fir to open his mind to them, and reached for their guidance, but still that empty *Nothing* had returned to him. He felt as though the Masters themselves were waiting, and likewise holding their breath.

And worming in his gut was the knowledge that it had not been his prayers that had inspired the Masters to drive away the Scorpion-kinden of the Many of Nem. For all that he had entreated them, as their pre-eminent servant, they might as well have been no more than the statues they had left behind.

As yet the hand of these new conquerors had been felt only lightly. Some foreigners within the city had been exiled, others arrested and taken away. Traffic in and out now had to pass Wasp checkpoints. Ships were searched at the docks. There was a curfew, though enforced erratically. A few deaths, a few more beatings: the Wasp soldiers were being kept in check. A few who had killed or raped in a manner that, by some invisible yardstick, was unacceptable had been executed publicly on crossed spears thrust up through their living bodies. So far, the Wasps were being very considerate conquerors, but Ethmet had an unpleasant feeling that this must surely change.

And then, only this morning, the Imperial colonel serving as chief ambassador had come to him with news which was plainly scarcely less new to the colonel himself.

The Empress is coming to Khanaphes.

In fact, the Empress had been on her way for several days, but the news had been carried only a half-day ahead of her, in case some enemy of the Empire might choose to take it as a challenge. The news the colonel had brought him was that the Empress would be arriving in Khanaphes by *noon.*

And now Ethmet looked up at this descending airship – the world of the *now* descending to destroy thousands of years of carefully husbanded history – and he felt like weeping.

There had been a Rekef mission to Khanaphes which had gone painfully awry, that much Seda knew. The few survivors who made it back to the Empire had not been Rekef people but Engineers, and so, instead of the secret service keeping its errors secret, matters became widely known in a variety of circles.

Seda knew that nobody had expected her to take much interest in this business. It had been meat and drink for General Brugan's enemies, ammunition for their broadsides at him, when her advisers met. She was their grand figurehead, the beautiful, whimsical Empress, and they knew she left the minutiae of government to them. She made a great show of acceding to their requests, validating their decisions, making herself the unchanged catalyst by which every other thing happened, but she left them to get on with their areas of expertise, which they appreciated.

But when Khanaphes had been mentioned, as a ranging shot aimed at General Brugan's high standing in her eyes, she had announced, 'We will go there.'

There had been silence amongst her advisers then, and they glanced at each other uncertainly. Her brother, the late Emperor, had kept to their ridiculous tribal custom of leader and advisers all sitting in a line, not facing one another. That did not suit her, though, so she had changed it effortlessly, without anyone being able to muster an argument against her decision. Now the Empress would meet with her advisers outside on a sun-warmed balcony, sitting or even reclining on comfortable couches in the Spider style, while plied with food and drink by the palace servants.

'There is nothing there,' had ventured Colonel Thanred, an old soldier who was the nominal governor of Capitas. 'Just a backward Beetle city full of simpletons.'

'The Rekef clearly believed there was something there worth seeing,' a Consortium magnate had suggested snidely.

'Lowlander agents were present in the city, so it was our duty to ensure they did not secure a base from which to strike at us.' General Brugan had retained his composure magnificently, for which Seda indulged him with a small smile of approval that did not go unnoticed by his peers. *He lies so well*, she had thought, almost proudly.

'We have quelled the rebel governors and generals, have we not?' she had asked them, affecting a slightly bemused smile. 'Our Empire is whole once more, thanks to your efforts. Our wounds are healed.' She included them all in the smile, even those who had patently done nothing but stand on the sidelines and wait to see how matters would turn out. She had then locked eyes with the old Woodlouse-kinden, Gjegevey, adviser to her brother and their father before him, a man whose counsel was more valuable to her than any dozen Wasp-kinden dignitaries.

'You word it perfectly, of course,' a second Consortium man had observed, fat, old and ugly, but a man endowed with a rare sense of art and poetry. While her duller brother had demanded blood-fights in the arena, this man had been quick to arrange more refined entertainment for her, and thus won himself a place amongst her favourites – for now. 'Empress, you should know that some of the Consortium have been considering a move eastwards. There are cities across the Jahalian Rift that our factors claim show great promise . . .'

'But if we do head east, who would know of it?' she had asked him pleasantly, and he was shrewd enough to remain silent and wait for her to elaborate. She was positively beaming now, letting them bask in her radiant expression. 'We must not forget that we are no longer a solitary power surrounded by small cities who barely feel our approach before we snap them up. We now stand amongst those who think themselves our equals; even if we still stand head and shoulders above them, we must not forget that we are *watched*. We must remind them what it means to be an Empire.'

She had gauged their expressions in turn, reading worry, anticipation, a certain dormant bloodlust coming to the fore again.

'We shall break no treaties,' she had declared, 'and so the

Lowlander city-states will merely fret and protest. Yet we can extend our protective hand to a neighbour in need, a neighbour who is just within their sight. A city of Beetles, sorely oppressed by Scorpion barbarians, shall come to see the wisdom of sheltering beneath the black and gold flag. And their kin in Collegium will wring their hands and tell each other how terrible it is. And do nothing.' Her smile, as it toured the balcony, had been sharp as a razor. 'Or not, perhaps. Maybe it is just a fancy of mine, this thought of Khanaphes. What think you, my advisers?'

She had them immediately, of course. It was a perfect plan, bold and cautious in equal measures. It would remind the world of the Empire's power but, more than that, it would remind the Empire's own soldiers and citizens.

Two days later saw completion of the debriefing of those Engineers who had survived the Rekef fiasco. It had been assumed that they would be punished for their failures, but something very strange had happened during their interrogation, for their leader had produced a remarkable report. Suddenly a colonel in the Engineering Corps, the highest-ranking Imperial artificer there was, was *also* trying to promote the possibility of an Imperial expedition to Khanaphes, not realizing that his Empress had already pre-empted him. The idea had gathered momentum fast, until . . .

Until here I am, Seda thought. The army had gone in first, of course, and her airship had departed Capitas only after the expedition leaders had confirmed their control of the city. Such control had come about swiftly, for there had been no resistance from the Khanaphir, and she had her own good reasons to be glad about that.

Her reasons presented to her advisers for this expedition had been lies – just as much lies as Brugan's dissembling about why he had sent men here originally. The Engineers' quest here was a useful sideline, one that she did not understand but was prepared to indulge.

She had come to Khanaphes for her own private reasons. She had come here seeking *power*.

'It's a woman!'

For a moment Praeda held the telescope steady, expecting the honour guard and dignitary that had disembarked from the airship to be merely some vanguard for an even greater potentate, but it was plain that this slight-framed girl who had stepped down the ramp from the gondola was the whole and purpose of what was going on. She seemed a mere slip of a Wasp-kinden female, for all that she was dressed with an elegance any Spider might envy. She was clearly precious to the Empire, though, for as well as a dozen Sentinels in the heaviest armour, and a further dozen of the Imperial Light Airborne, Praeda's glass identified the four warriors closest to the woman as Mantis-kinden, decked out in black and gold as though they had surrendered a thousand years of heritage in exchange for Empire coin.

'What is so remarkable about that?' rumbled her companion.

Praeda Rakespear gave him a quizzical look, but then nodded. 'I suppose you've no reason to know of the shameful way in which the Empire treats its womenfolk.'

'She must be the Empress,' Amnon declared. He was squinting at the far spectacle from the rooftop they had commandeered, hidden in the shadow of a row of statuary.

Praeda laughed harshly. 'Oh, of course,' she said sarcastically. 'First place she'd stop, here, on her journey to the moon.'

'Why not? The Dominion of Khanaphes has influence yet,' Amnon said, obviously chastened but being stubborn. In his mind, no doubt, his home city *did* still have some shred of the power that it once had wielded, a thousand years ago and more.

From force of long habit, Praeda opened her mouth to make some scathing comment, and stopped herself when she remembered that Amnon sometimes took her vitriol to heart. Her glass was still trained on the mysterious Wasp woman, waiting for some clue as to her identity. The old First Minister was bowing to her, but then the Khanaphir bowed a great deal, even their leaders.

The Wasp woman reached out and laid a hand on the First Minister's forehead, and Praeda's reaction was, *She's going to kill him!* because she knew that female Wasps could also use that stinging Art of theirs. The gesture was not a physical attack, but it seemed an attack nonetheless. Praeda watched the old Beetle man drop to his knees, swiftly enough for her to fear that he might not easily get up again. After a moment of uncertainty, the other Ministers present began following suit. The woman watched them with a proud air.

A *proprietorial* air.

'Fire and forge,' Praeda murmured, finding her view through the telescope suddenly quivering. 'Amnon, I'm a fool, and I should listen to you, because you see things more clearly than I sometimes. I think you're right. I think it's her.'

Amnon grunted, happy at the validation, and reached for the glass. He took it clumsily, but soon had it to his eye, twisting its sections to bring the view into focus. He would never make an artificer, but he had taken surprisingly swiftly to many of Collegium's innovations. His reverence towards the Masters of Khanaphes, pounded into him as a child, had been extended into a kindred awe of machines which Praeda, an artificer herself, found endearing and not a little gratifying.

'If only I had a snapbow,' Praeda breathed.

'I had not thought you had such unfond memories of my home that you would wish to complete its ruin,' Amnon stated mildly.

'Well, of course not,' she admitted. 'Still, she is very bold to expose herself to any public-spirited assassin who might come along. But you're right. I am no killer and your people would suffer.'

'I am glad you see matters so, for I have brought just such a thing with us,' Amnon continued, unperturbed.

‘A *snapbow?*’ she demanded.

‘I thought it might be useful.’

‘Maybe it will be, at that,’ she allowed, retrieving the glass from him. ‘So, what’s the woman doing now . . .?’

Seda stood perfectly still, watching a score or so of old men and women, the pick of the Ministers of Khanaphes, bow their heads to her.

Of course, my brother never set foot out of Capitas, she reflected. *Where our father and grandfather flew with the armies, he buried himself in the Imperial palace for fear of encountering the hatred of his subjects. How different a man might he have been, had he been welcomed like this in Szar or Myna or Vesserett.* And was that so unlikely? If any city wished to avoid the Imperial scourge, how better to do so than with such a complete display of supplication as this? The Khanaphir government’s public obeisance to her was a gesture to melt the heart of the harshest tyrant, and surely she was not the fear-ridden monster her brother had been.

Surely, surely? She knew what they said about her: her servants, her advisers, her generals. Those near to her had heard the rumours by now, for all that she had done her best to keep the knowledge contained: *the Empress has strange tastes.* Missing slaves caused no great comment, but there would inevitably be some palace steward who had done the relevant arithmetic to work out just how many were vanishing, and other servants of her private chambers who had to deal with the detritus . . .

But that is for a reason, she assured herself. *It is not like my brother’s pointless cruelties. I need . . .* And she did need, and she could feel that need within her even now, which would have to be slaked sooner rather than later.

Behind her, Gjegevey the Woodlouse was picking his way down the airship ramp, leaning heavily on his staff. He paused to see the Ministers in such submission.

‘Ah, remarkable,’ he murmured, and she knew from the faint

unsteadiness in his voice that he, too, suspected it was more than diplomacy that had brought them to their knees.

'Rise,' Seda commanded. 'The Empire thanks you for your reception, and it knows that you will have prepared suitable chambers for us.'

There were Khanaphir servants scurrying away even as she spoke, and she had no doubt that the city's bounty would be laid bare for her by the time she reached the Imperial embassy, or wherever it was they chose to receive her. She tried to focus on the political and material matters in hand, while keeping at the back of her mind her very personal reasons for demanding to come here.

Still, some instinct she could not name had prompted her to touch the First Minister's brow like that, and she would swear that, as she did so, she had heard a distant voice echo from out of the very earth itself, and it said: *Kneel.*

Kneel.

And Che awoke to see the first pale skies of dawn, her heart hammering in her chest as though she had been running, clutching at the very ground itself to remind herself of where she was.

Twelve

They stopped briefly in Szar, just a night's rest, while Varmen spoke to some Way Brothers about the road ahead. Che had not been happy about their guide going off on his own. It seemed easily possible to her that he could be going to meet with brigands, to arrange an ambush. She expected Thalric to dismiss this idea, given how well he and the other Wasp seemed to be getting along together. Even before she mentioned her fears, though, she found Thalric already setting out to keep an eye on the man.

'And I thought you liked him,' she accused him.

Thalric laughed bleakly. 'Let's just say I've lost faith in my ability to judge my own kinden.'

The Wayhouse had been vacant for several years during the tail end of the Imperial occupation, and inviting the Brothers back had been one of the first moves of the Szaren Bee-kinden. The Brothers themselves were all Lowlander Beetles, for the sect had originated in Collegium as a charitable organization providing board and lodging for poor travellers.

Small wonder the Empire didn't approve of it, Che reflected. Sitting downstairs in the Wayhouse's common room, she watched the Brothers curiously. It was not unknown for men and women with dubious pasts to seek the absolution of anonymity wearing the plain brown robes of a Way Brother – the title was used by both genders within the order. Certainly, several of the Brothers she could see looked as though they would know what to do in a fight, for all that their order was ostentatiously pacifist. She wondered about the nature of the individuals Varmen was meeting with upstairs, and hoped that Thalric would find a good vantage point from which to spy on them.

Szar itself had surprised her. She had already heard a certain amount about the place: ground under the Imperial boot for a decade and a half after the Empire had taken the Szaren queen into custody. She had heard a great deal more about the circumstances of the city's liberation – a Wasp secret weapon had been triggered within the governor's palace, wiping out thousands of soldiers, servants and slaves at a stroke, in an action now notorious wherever Szar was spoken of. She had expected to find the city wounded, half broken, grim and drab and as bitter as Myna. Instead the native Bee-kinden had since been working hard to reverse all those years of Imperial domination. Szar was becoming green. The local buildings were all low, little hexagonal cells, with far more investment in cellars than rooms above ground. Under the Wasp rule that was all there had been, but now they were planting again, and each little dwelling had its garden border, each roof its bright bursts of transplanted foliage. This greenery made the whole city seem lighter and more spacious, and Che knew that the place's true glory would reveal itself only with the spring.

Thalric returned shortly, with time only for a nod of reassurance before Varmen himself rejoined them.

'We'll be heading south of Maynes,' their guide explained. 'The Ant-kinden are worse than the Mynans – barely any time for their own allies, let alone strangers. Let alone Wasps, 'specially.'

Che nodded. 'And yet here you are posing as our guide, Varmen.'

He gave her a big, uncomplicated grin. 'Trust me, you'll be glad of my services.'

Heading west, they merged with a respectable number of travellers going between Szar and its Ant-kinden allies in Maynes, despite Varmen's words. As soon as they turned off the Maynes road they were nearly alone, however, and making their own way across an unforgiving country, too uneven for agriculture and with patches of close-packed pine forest sending them miles out of their way. Once or twice, when stopping to camp, they saw the lights of other fires, but Varmen's advice was to avoid them. Travellers heading west from the Three-city Alliance seldom welcomed company.

Each night, Che hung up her little ring of copper, but her dreams were intermittent. Often there was no spider, and finding one and trying to coax it into place yielded no results. When she did recall her dreams, though, they were always of Khanaphes: not the place of her memories, however, but a city that time and the Empire had caught up with.

She had wanted to broach the subject of her dreams with Thalric, but she was not sure how much he would understand. He had seen plenty of the old magic of Khanaphes during the time the two of them had spent among the tombs beneath the city, but what would he admit to now, months after? Aptitude divided them.

But tonight he turned to her even as she was stringing up the dream-catcher, and said, 'What is it?'

She tried to look baffled, but the look he gave her in response was just exasperation. 'Che, for a tenyear I ran agents for a living. You were twitchy when we were in Khanaphes, and you've been twitchy ever since, but since we left Myna something's changed.'

Varmen cocked an uninterested eyebrow in their direction, then burrowed into his bedroll and turned over. He had already demonstrated a soldier's ability to find sleep at a moment's notice.

Che opened her mouth, but suddenly found the words hard to come by. *Dreams? Thalric will care nothing for dreams.* That was not what stopped her being candid with him, though. Some deeper prohibition was at work, one that she could not entirely identify. 'I was thinking about the Empress,' she said, hoping this half-truth would be enough for him.

Thalric's face darkened, as well it might. Of course, he had been Imperial Regent for a brief space of time, an acceptable male face that Empress Seda had stood behind while she consolidated her power: someone to appease the traditionalists amongst her subjects who recoiled from the idea of being led by a woman. By the time Thalric had jumped ship yet again, however, the Empress Seda was firmly ensconced, combining charisma, ability and the support of the Rekef in an unshakeable combination.

On the back of that history, Thalric's reluctant, 'Why?' was hardly surprising.

'Because we are alike, she and I,' Che reminded him.

'You are *not* alike.'

'You know what I mean,' she pressed.

He glanced at Varmen, who appeared dead to the world, and then leant close to her, keeping his voice low. 'So you have lost your Aptitude,' he told her, as though she might any day now rediscover it on the road. 'So the Empress has the same . . . condition. Believe me, you are not alike in any other way.' He did not voice his reasons, because she already knew them, but perhaps also because to give voice to them would be to somehow invite Seda's attention – for all that Thalric was Apt and did not believe in such things.

Because of the blood, Che thought. He had told her, when they had been trapped in the tombs: how the Empress lived off the blood of others, mostly slaves. It was as if she had become, in her own body, a personification of the Empire's own creed of rapacious conquest. By Thalric's account, the Empress Seda drank and bathed in the spilt lives of others.

And draws power from them, came the thought to Che then. It seemed perfectly obvious to her that it was so, that such behaviour was not simply the excess of an absolute ruler whose Empire overflowed with expendable human property. When Che tried to examine her certainty regarding this, she could find no train of logic in it, and yet she knew it to be true. *The blood itself is power. It is an old and evil magic.*

'The old fortress at Solamen, or whatever the 'Wealers used to call it,' Thalric enquired, 'is that back in use now?'

'Surely,' Varmen replied. 'Crammed full of Principality troops, more of 'em every month, seems like. Now, you said you had pass papers for the Three-city soldiers, that right?'

'Signed by the head of the Consensus, no less,' Che agreed.

'Makes it easier not to have to dodge them,' their guide allowed. 'In that case, if you're happy they're good, let's call in with the locals.'

An hour after that and they were being escorted through an armed camp amid Mynan soldiers in their black and red armour, and a small detachment of Szaren Bees who seemed to be engineers. Che caught the outlines of some manner of siege artillery but, in her present state of Inaptitude, she was unable to identify what kind.

'They seem to be a little anxious about something,' she remarked to her companions.

'Oh, you'll see the reason soon enough,' Varmen assured her. 'I reckon they've got cause. Don't blame 'em at all, me.'

The Mynan in charge of the camp studied their papers lengthily enough for Che to begin wondering if Kymene had not betrayed them by some hidden message. Eventually the man reluctantly agreed that they could pass through, although he was clearly suspicious of anyone who might want to. He herded them out of his camp immediately afterwards, as if worried that they would be stealing secrets or counting the number of his soldiers.

'Friendly folk around these parts,' was all Varmen would say about that.

Solamen, which had been called Shol Amen before the war, held the only pass between the Barrier Ridge and this side of the mountains. For centuries it had marked the easternmost point of the Commonweal, denying the barbarous tribesmen the road to the wealthy and civilized lands beyond. Then, a few generations back, those same tribesmen had been united by a man who became their first Emperor, and proceeded to conquer a great many of their neighbours, absorb a great deal of artifice and military theory, and decide that the lands of the Dragonflies were ripe for conquest.

'It was the Sixth that captured this place, wasn't it?' Thalric asked, as they gazed up at it.

'None other,' Varmen replied, with such fierce and automatic pride that Che knew he must have been present when it happened.

Solamen had then comprised a grand castle built high up the mountainside, with a good view of the road. Che could imagine defending troops sallying forth , in the air and on horseback, to chase down any strangers trying to breach the Commonweal's veil of isolation.

Perhaps half of the original structure still stood, pocked by cracks and craters from the assault of the engines. Commonwealer architecture had never been intended to stand up against heavy siege, and such engines had not even existed when places such as Solamen were built, nor foreseen by even the greatest of sages.

There had been some new construction, to balance the damage: a stone-walled compound at the castle's base, within which less magnificent but more durable buildings had been installed. The Empire had used the place as a way station for its troops, but it had not been considered a fortress by the Wasps. The initial Imperial advance of the Twelve-year War had taken the battle far enough west for Solamen to have served no useful defensive function.

Since the Empire's hand had been lifted from these lands,

however, it was clear that the old fortress had returned to its original purpose. Most particularly there were now dots circling the sky above, and as the three travellers drew near it was clear that Solamen's current masters had sent out a welcome for them.

Thalric watched the soldiers get closer, wishing he had invested in a telescope. Varmen had already halted the horses and climbed down, instructing his employers to let him do the talking.

'Is that . . .?' Che was squinting up. 'Do I see Imperial colours?' Her Art let her see in utter darkness, as Thalric had cause to know, but he was aware that her eyes were less acute than his own in daylight. All the same, he realized that she was right. There was definitely a touch of the black and gold to their welcomers.

But that's not right, he thought, still trying to discern the details. *They're Dragonflies – they must be. No Wasp flies like that.*

There were half a dozen of them landing in a loose arc across their path, and Varmen need not have worried about his companions. Thalric and Che were too busy staring to have anything to say.

They were Dragonflies indeed, the same slender, golden-skinned breed that Thalric remembered well from the Twelve-year War, and that for Che presumably recalled her dead friend, the Commonwealer prince. Four men and two women, they held their bows at the ready, arrows nocked but not drawn back. All had armour of chitin and leather, except for one man who wore most of a full suit of proper Commonweal noble's mail: iridescent plates of insect shell over fine chain.

Each of them was decked out in black and yellow, but instead of the Empire's uniform stripes, the patterns varied wildly. Only the colouring was the same, dyed or painted on. Even the fletchings of their arrows followed the theme, and the man in fancy armour had half his face tattooed black.

As the Dragonflies inspected the three travellers, their look was not wholly that of suspicious border guards. There was a wariness there that Thalric could not immediately place.

'Why do you seek to enter the Principalities?' demanded their leader, he of the painted face.

'Me?' Varmen responded casually. 'Just a guide, me. Don't want any problems. Just paid to show these two the best roads.'

'And what's their business?' the Dragonfly countered, pointing at Thalric with one end of his bow.

'Oh, traders,' was Varmen's explanation. 'Merchants, you know.'

Thalric winced, because traders would be travelling with a great deal more baggage than Varmen's little pack-beetle could accommodate. The Dragonflies seemed to be of the same mind, for they closed in a little, and the arrowheads were wavering upwards along with the level of their suspicions.

'Traders?' their leader spat disbelievingly.

'You know, fresh out of Capitas,' Varmen continued, for all that Thalric was on the point of telling him to shut up. 'Long way, you know, from Capitas, but they're very keen to, you know, *trade*.'

It was as if there was some mindlink between Varmen and the people out of Solamen, because one by one they clearly leapt to some conclusion that his words alone could not account for. There was a nervous shuffling amongst them.

Fear? Thalric wondered, but there was more than simple fear there.

'Capitas, is it?' the leader asked cautiously.

'Oh, there are plenty of traders out of Capitas who want to know this part of the world better. News of your princes has reached them there, and they see a lot of, you know, *profit* in making deals over here, if you see what I mean.'

The Dragonflies apparently did see what he meant, for all that Thalric did not.

'We should . . .' one of them began, as their leader actually looked plaintively at Varmen for guidance.

'Best not to trouble your chief. It's all a little quiet, you know – trading *on the sly*, if you see?' Varmen was studying his dirty fingernails with exaggerated unconcern.

'I see,' the Dragonfly chief confirmed. 'You should pass through swiftly. I'm sure the Colonel would agree.'

At the mention of that Imperial title, Thalric almost choked, but he held it in and kept it there whilst the Dragonflies rose aloft and flew back towards Solamen.

'Glad you're with me now?' Varmen asked them, grinning broadly.

'What was that?' Thalric demanded. 'For that matter, why in the pits were they dressed like that? And a *colonel?* Has Solamen been taken over by madmen?'

'Not just Solamen, the whole of the Principalities – all the land the Empire bit out of the Commonweal during the war,' Varmen explained. 'You've got to think – this was all Imperial until the Alliance cities kicked us out, and the Commonweal never actually took them back.'

'But why?' Che demanded. 'Surely they're free now?'

'Oh, *free*,' replied Varmen dismissively. 'Free for what? Free to wait until the Empire comes back? Look, most of the noble families that were lording it over places like this got wiped out, right? Down to the last little snapper among them, is what I heard.'

Thalric nodded, lips pressed together, but Varmen failed to notice his reaction.

'So who takes over? Some peasant farmer? Who else knows how to run things, 'cept us?'

'And so they let us through because we were Wasps?' Thalric demanded. 'What was all that about merchants?'

'Well, you know . . . *merchants*,' Varmen echoed, with a peculiar emphasis.

'Explain,' Thalric insisted, but at his side Che was laughing. She was doing her best to contain it, but it was leaking out all over: her shoulders shaking, muffled snorting noises from behind her hand.

'Well, come on,' Varmen said, 'what would you think: two people who really, honestly aren't merchants come in, and they'd come from the capital, and they had, you know, secret business to attend to, all hush-hush, you know?'

'Oh, you bastard, they thought we were Rekef,' said Thalric, finding himself momentarily unable to know how he should feel about that.

Varmen shrugged. 'They know about the Rekef here. They know how the Rekef killed off all their old nobles, and they know they don't exactly want a new crop coming in from the Commonweal just yet, given how badly the old lot did. So, yeah, Rekef. Why not?'

Thalric gave in, and a moment later, catching Che's eyes, he gave out a bleak laugh at the absurdity of the situation.

'All right, all right,' Varmen said, slightly put off now. 'It's not *that* funny.'

'Oh, it is,' Thalric told him. 'Believe me, it is.'

That night, when they were well past Solamen and after Che had gone to sleep, Varmen said, 'I've got to ask. You and her, what's going on?'

Thalric stared at him coldly. 'None of your business, *Sergeant*.' He had guessed the man's rank within minutes of meeting with him in Myna.

Varmen held his closed hands up before him, a gesture of appeasement. 'It's just that, I reckoned you were in charge, and she was your woman, you know – or your slave, or maybe a scribe or something. But this is her journey, isn't it? And you're tagging along.'

'Like I said, it's not your business to worry about. Just get us to the Commonweal.' Thalric was annoyed at how transparent the situation had become. *Perhaps I should put a hand on the rudder of this little trip?* As a Wasp-kinden man, he felt that he should be offended that a woman of a lesser kinden was expecting him to trail after her. If he worked at it, he could get up quite a head of self-righteousness, but he did have to work at it. To his surprise, he found that, left to his own devices, he wouldn't care much.

Of course, I have no idea precisely where *we're going, or why, so a fine fool I'd look by demanding to take the lead and then having to ask the way.* Che had decided that she had to save her foster-sister, Tynisa. Save her from what? Thalric had no fond memories of the half-Spider girl who had tried to kill him on two separate occasions. In his opinion, it was not saving that she needed, so much as putting out of her misery like a mad animal. *She stabbed Achaeos, after all. Why doesn't Che want her dead, after that?*

Unless the girl's playing her cards close, and that is *what she does want after all . . .*

His memories of that brief sequence of incomprehensible events was far clearer than he was comfortable with. They had all been in Jerez, and had just recovered that wretched piece of tat that Achaeos the Moth had called the 'Shadow Box'. Why the nasty little relic was so important, the Moth-kinden was never able to explain to Thalric's satisfaction, but then Thalric was in no position to make demands, being there on sufferance, nominally as their prisoner and still recovering from his wounds.

Anyway, they had got hold of the thing, and Achaeos had been fingering it avariciously and then, without warning, he and Tynisa – and even Tynisa's murderous father Tisamon – had just dropped as though simultaneously struck on the head.

I should have taken the opportunity to kill the lot of them and take the box myself, Thalric thought, but it was almost by rote, old motivations grown stale since he had abandoned his role as a Rekef officer. What had actually happened was that he and Gaved, the other Wasp present, had just goggled at one another uselessly, tried and failed to rouse the sleepers, and then Tynisa had jumped up and put her rapier into Achaeos – very nearly a fatal wound there and then.

Thalric and Gaved had done their best to subdue her, but

in the end only the intervention of one of Gaved's local cronies had managed that. *It was a wonder she didn't kill the lot of us*, Thalric admitted in the privacy of his own mind, where he could afford to be honest with himself.

And yet Che seems to want no kind of revenge, but instead seeks to save the bloody-handed halfbreed woman from some indistinct threat. Unwelcome memories stirred inside Thalric, and he fought them down. *I have no idea what that threat is,* he insisted to himself. He was not ready to face such thoughts, and he might never be.

He was, however, aware that Che did not seek revenge, because Che was not Wasp-kinden, or Mantis-kinden, or even Spider-kinden. Her people did not place such a premium on personal honour. Moreover, Che saw the world very differently even from the bulk of her own people, for she suffered under a peculiar curse that had fallen upon her at the end of the war.

When Achaeos died, Thalric reflected uncomfortably, trying to dismiss any possible connection between the two. Still, the thoughts hounded him: *When Achaeos died, when Tisamon died . . . why do I believe there is a link?*

Che had then lost her Aptitude. She had lost that world of reason and mechanics and light that was her birthright, and instead she was groping through a new world of charlatanry and ignorance, living off scraps of esoteric knowledge left over from the Days of Lore. That Che's new viewpoint had saved both her and Thalric more than once was something he was unhappy to consider, but that he could not avoid acknowledging. This thought was a grain of sand in his mind that no amount of explanation could turn into a pearl.

There was only one other person that Thalric could name who had suffered the same reversal, and the fact that she had done so was a closely guarded secret. Seda, Empress of the Wasps, was likewise become Inapt, and on nights like these, when sleep kept its distance from him, he was forced to confront that curious web of interdependence: Che and the dead man Achaeos, Seda and the dead man Tisamon. *Why do I feel they are linked? Why?* There could be no connection, and yet some part of him remained sure of it, beyond any rational argument.

And now Che is asking me questions about the Empress? Thalric sat before their guttering fire, Che sleeping beside him, Varmen snoring gently on the far side of it. He felt as though the night was full of huge, monolithic *things* moving silently but massively, coming together to built some terrible edifice that he would be afraid to look upon.

I should leave, he told himself, not for the first time. *Che is not in her right mind. This entire business is madness.*

But he made no move to go, just looked down at her face in the firelight. *We have travelled a long road together, since my men caught you in Helleron*, he considered. *We shall walk a few miles more in each other's company. Why not?*

She shifted and twitched in her slumber, and he felt an unplaceable sense of danger.

Be careful what you dream of, Che.

Thirteen

Gathering information in Khanaphes was like reaching into briars, a delicate and unrewarding business. Amnon himself could have gone and spoken to a hundred people who would remember him as First Soldier, as saviour of their city, but each one of them was still tied by invisible, unbreakable strings of responsibility and duty that led all the way to the Ministers. That the Empress had been welcomed, and more than welcomed, suggested that a former First Soldier asking awkward questions might become an inconvenience. Without knowing precisely what game Ethmet and the others were playing, Amnon was loath to announce his presence in the city. It was not fear of the Wasps, Praeda knew, but fear of having to go up against his own people, those loyal servants of the city whom he had formerly led into battle.

Besides, the general feel about the city's populace was one of bafflement. Khanaphes' dealings with outsiders had not changed in centuries. Even the disastrous assault recently by the Scorpion-kinden had fitted a particular pattern: the Many of Nem had always been the city's enemies, after all, and it was only a matter of degree. The sudden imposition of an Imperial garrison on the city, the obeisance of the Ministers, the utter lack of reaction or statement from the Khanaphir administration, had left the people at large unsure of precisely what was happening. Patterns had been broken, but in a way that demanded no immediate reaction from them. Instead they were very pointedly going about their business as if nothing had happened, paying the Imperial troops as little notice as possible, and yet cooperating with them abjectly whenever they were forced to acknowledge the invaders' presence. Amnon and Praeda witnessed several examples of the Wasps taking their customary liberties with a subject population: goods taken from merchants, insults and beatings inflicted on locals who got in the way or looked at the soldiers too boldly, spontaneous and seemingly random arrests. Throughout it all, the Khanaphir simply bowed their heads, following the example of their Ministers and presenting their backs for the lash, as docile as broken slaves. This sheer calm acceptance of it all was plainly thwarting the Wasps' natural instincts. They had come here ready for a fight, assuming that the Khanaphir would resist, however primitive their methods. Instead the city had fallen into their hands pre-subjugated. They did not know what to do, and their expressions, as they castigated some cringing, wretched porter or servant, were almost embarrassed – apologetic for the duties forced on them by Imperial policy.

If not from the Khanaphir themselves, Amnon and Praeda still needed some source of intelligence, and there remained a body of people in the city who were very keenly interested in what the Empire might be planning. In the inns and open houses by the Estuarine Gate, they found the foreigners: sailors, merchants, adventurers and mercenaries who had not been thrown out by the Wasps, yet, nor crept or bribed their way out of the city. They were waiting to see what happened, tied to the place either by their investments, their optimism or their curiosity. Praeda and Amnon's appearance in their midst raised no questions, and it was plain that, while asking questions about the Wasps was an accepted custom, asking questions about the questioners was not.

After trying a few places, with Praeda doing most of the talking, they fell in with the right kind of company, meaning people that no self-respecting scholar of the College would have had anything to do with back home. As evening fell, they found themselves sharing a table with a trio of reprobates all evaluating their current fortunes, namely the merits and drawbacks of being stuck in occupied Khanaphes. There was a battered and ill-used-looking Fly-kinden man, sun-beaten and balding, who never quite admitted that he made a living by robbing the ruins of the Nem, but Amnon plainly knew the type, and would have disapproved furiously had he been in any position of authority any more. A Spider-kinden woman was also some manner of adventuress, not young and yet somehow ageless, the worn hilt of the rapier at her hip testifying to her chosen method of resolving disputes. The third was a Solarnese man, a publicly declared trader in gems and jewellery, or a smuggler when read between the lines. The three of them were plainly well matched, with enough petty villainy between them to give any number of Wasp-kinden pause for thought. Worse, they were waiting for a fourth who must surely be even more of a rogue than themselves, but they were not averse to Praeda and Amnon's company while they passed the time and drank and talked politics.

'It's the same every time,' the Solarnese merchant was holding forth. 'Must be standard practice for the Jaspers. As soon as they've seized a place they go into a frenzy of imposing laws, curfews, taxes, all that, but never reliably. Sometimes you can get away with murder; other times they'll throw you in a cell for sneezing. When Solarno fell, it was an absolute lottery: some real crooks were let in to moor at the high-end piers – without bribes, too – while respectable Spider-kinden traders got turned away as though they were plague ships.'

'Keeps people off balance,' the Spider considered. 'Makes them fear. Still, you can only do that for so long. At the start, if people are getting arrested for the slightest reason, or no reason, they'll toe the line. After a month, they'll just think they have nothing to lose.'

‘Oh it calms down,’ the Solarnese agreed. He was a pleasant, prosperous-looking man whom Praeda wouldn’t have trusted an inch. ‘Even Wasp-kinden can’t maintain that level of arbitrary hostility for long. They’ll get a basic administration in place, a governor and the like set above the Ministers here, and then things will find their own rut and stay there.’

The Fly spat. ‘The Empire, stay here? What in the pits for?’

‘Don’t worry, little man. They won’t cut into your sort of trade,’ the Spider jibed.

‘That’s what you think.’ The Fly bared yellow teeth. ‘Scouts are already heading off into the desert, have been almost since the first soldiers arrived. What are they after, eh? Or is it to invite the Scorpions back?’

‘That wasn’t the Empire, they say,’ the Solarnese opined, but rather uncertainly.

‘It *was* the Empire,’ Amnon declared. They glanced at him thoughtfully, and read a great deal of certainty on his face.

‘You’re local. You fought them?’ the Spider asked. ‘On the bridge, was it?’

‘On the bridge,’ Amnon agreed heavily, and the weight of memories bled into his words, lending them conviction that could not be denied.

‘I was there too,’ Praeda put in. ‘There were Wasp-kinden directing the artillery, flying in with grenades. In the city, too – Rekef, they said.’ She did not mean to, but she gave that word a hushed and fearful emphasis. From the reactions of the others it was entirely appropriate.

‘They’re after Solarno, for sure,’ said the smuggler-merchant savagely. ‘Flanking us, that’s what they’re doing.’

‘There’s the whole of the Nem between Khanaphes and the Exalsee,’ said the Spider woman dismissively. ‘What sort of flanking manoeuvre sees half your army dead of thirst before it arrives? The Spiderlands is next on their menu, you take my word. They know that, if they want to push their ambitions anywhere south of Toek, they’ll have to make a sustained assault on the Houses, and they're looking for a way in. Probably air armada over the Forest Aleth.'

The Fly-kinden shook his head. 'You're not listening. First thing when they got here, they're looking west. Not Solarno but the *desert.* They've had surveyors and artificers and wildsmen out there for days now. This isn't just a staging post. Solarno and the Nem are *it.*' The others stared at him, and he glowered right back.

'You think they're going to rob your tombs before you can get to them?' the Spider said somewhat disdainfully.

'Know what?' The Fly snorted. 'I don't know what in Waste's name they're after, but they're after it with all their bastard hearts. And while it won't be *my* business they're muscling in on, they won't want someone like me anywhere close by, I can tell you. Maybe it's time I went and followed up some leads down Tsovashni way.'

'And at last!' The Spider woman stood up, as their missing fourth had finally arrived. 'Someone who can give us the real story. Grab a chair, Emon.'

Praeda looked over, seeing a short, dark man, his greying hair cut almost to the skull: a Bee-kinden with an artificer's toolstrip slung over a dark tabarded breastplate. Only when she saw the symbol on his chest did she start. A grey gauntlet embroidered on grey cloth, yet some trick of the weave made it catch the light differently, making it clear and distinct and ominous.

'Iron Glove?' she exclaimed. 'I'd have thought you'd want to be well away from the city. Surely the Empire are shooting you people on sight.'

'And hello to you too.' The Bee, Emon, sat down and snagged a mostly empty jar of wine, draining the dregs of it. 'Who are these?'

'Travellers who want us to think they're locals. Or the other way round,' the Spider woman said wryly. 'Does it matter?'

'Perhaps not.' The Bee then squinted and appeared to change his mind. 'Or perhaps, yes. You're . . .' his eyes widened, staring at Amnon, and there was a tense moment in which revelations and violence hovered very close together. 'Never mind,' the Bee concluded. 'None of my business.'

'They fought on the bridge, they reckon,' the Fly explained, watching the Iron Glove man carefully.

'Oh, to be sure. I, on the other hand, fought on the river.'

'The *Fourth Iteration?*' Praeda pressed, for it was the name the Glove had given to their ingenious ship that had taken such a toll of the attacking Scorpions, until the Imperial artillery had finally silenced it.

Emon nodded. 'A lovely craft it was, too, but in the end it was swim or fly, when sailing couldn't keep us afloat any more. Not that many of us made it to shore.'

The Solarnese merchant had called for more wine, and the Bee accepted a jug gratefully. 'So I can see why you'd think I was tempting fate by sitting here, but it's not so. We're just arrived, and here because we're invited.'

That brought all the others leaning closer, waiting for the catch. *A trap?* was the plain thought on their faces, as if the Empress herself would go to such lengths to punish a cartel of weapons traders.

'Himself's shadow is here,' Emon murmured darkly. 'He's not exactly talked it over with the crew, but word is that the Glove is about to shake hands with the Empire, after all this time. Over in Chasme, we've made some remarkable advances, they tell me,' meaning the squatting little artificer town on the Exalsee that the Glove virtually owned these days. 'A poor sailor-engineer like myself wouldn't know where to start second-guessing Himself and his adopted son, but the Empire's the biggest market in the world. Makes sense that we'd want to set things straight and makes sense that the Wasps would want to let us. Nothing but the best for the army, after all, and we surely do make the best.'

Himself's shadow? Praeda wondered. 'But what if the Empire won't talk . . .?'

'It's like I said,' Emon explained, 'the Empire asked first. I reckon we probably sent them a catalogue, like merchants do sometimes, when they have special goods for sale. I reckon the Imperial artificers just about must have had a fit when they saw what we've cooked up.' He gave a crooked smile. 'I reckon the world's about to change in all manner of directions, I do.'

To Angved's surprise, Varsec had proved surprisingly good company. The Engineer was used to always having to compete with other officers, and all too used to failing at it, too. He and the aviator were still prisoners, and yet still being treated in a curiously tentative manner by their captors, who were all from the Engineering Corps themselves. Angved had meanwhile got a look at the machinery that had travelled the dusty road south to Khanaphes ahead of them, and he now felt cause to be hopeful.

Of course, they might have decided they don't need me to make it work, but why bring me along at all, in that case? And if they needed Angved, having decided to roll the dice and gamble on his discovery, then the same seemed to be true of Varsec, who was housed in the same cell and given the same uncertain treatment.

Of course the Khanaphir expedition didn't have a direct bearing on Varsec's particular work, but he and Angved had already got past their initial caginess regarding their plans, and it was clear to both that the one could help the other. Aboard the airship – the *Empress's* own airship! – they had taken every piece of paper they had been given and begun scrawling schematics and plans, diagrams of force and tension . . .

There had come a moment, far into the morning hours of a night that had slipped past almost unnoticed, when the two men had suddenly stared at one another, the plans spread out between them. Their shared gaze had spoken eloquently of a small part of the world changed for ever, the toothed wheels of progress moving on a notch.

They had called for the guard and demanded access to a messenger. The Fly-kinden who arrived was on the Empress's own staff, as he informed them in extreme annoyance at having been woken at the whims of prisoners. He then refused to take their messages until Colonel Lien had been summoned and shown the schematics.

The Fly was on his way north almost immediately after that, dropping from the airship and speeding for the factories of Sonn, where some of Varsec's initial ideas were already being worked into reality. *It must change. It must all change. It will be better.*

Now the two of them had been transferred to a room inside one of the embassies, still not considered quite as dignitaries but not quite as prisoners either, without rank and yet treated with cautious deference. Varsec was sketching again, drawing wing joints in delicate detail. He had kept the beard, trimmed down neatly now that they had given him a razor, but still a departure from the Imperial norm, and if his clothes were the simple tunic and sandals of a slave, at least they were clean and intact. He seemed at peace with it, too, their curious half-life. Angved himself still felt the pinch of ambition, of his additional years and his lack of success. *I must be close, though, now.* Close to an end or a new beginning, anyway. *Khanaphes again, and I didn't even need a leadshotter to get within the walls.*

He had been ready for some time, when the message finally came. For the last few hours both he and Varsec had sensed the approach of it. Whatever they were here for, death or glory, it was coming.

Dusk had come and gone, as the messenger arrived, and Angved caught himself wondering what precisely they were being called to that had to be done under cover of darkness. The bland-faced, efficient Wasp-kinden come to fetch them had brought uniforms with him: tunics in the black and gold. 'We need to make a good show,' he explained, and neither of the prisoners asked for whom.

They were taken to a vast mass of stone shot through with small windows, encrusted with glyphs and friezes, fronted by vast colonnades. 'The Scriptora,' Angved guessed aloud, obscurely proud of having amassed some little local knowledge, even if it had only been for the purposes of knowing which parts of the city to knock down. From this gigantic mausoleum of an edifice, the Ministers governed their backward city. There were no Khanaphir in sight, though, only some Wasps guarding the entrance. The city's leaders and their staff had been given the night off, it seemed.

As he was about to enter, Angved glanced back. In the centre of the square fronting the Scriptora was a truncated pyramid topped with an uneven ring of statues that resembled no Khanaphir he had ever seen. In the torchlight, their white stone took on a ruddy glow, and they seemed to dance a little, and even watch him, the flickering flames lending life to both limbs and eyes. Angved shuddered, obscurely unsettled, and hurried inside.

Bald, stern Colonel Lien was waiting for them, staring at the pair as though they were some faulty mechanism that might or might not be worth the fixing.

'Stay behind me,' he instructed. 'Watch and learn.'

Angved was already watching. There were a half-dozen soldiers inside the Scriptora's grand hall, but it was plain to his eyes that they were not simply the Light Airborne that their armour denoted. The way they stood, the nuances of their physiques, their ages: these were Engineers, and most likely men who had outranked Angved even when he had still been a lieutenant. *Whatever's here, it's not to be known outside the Corps*, he thought, and in that he was at once quite correct, and quite wrong.

There was the scrape of armour, and a handful of newcomers came striding into the Scriptora as though they owned it. Not the Khanaphir Ministers, though, but four men and a woman wearing a badge that made Angved twitch. The last time he had seen that open gauntlet, grey on grey, these people had been his enemies.

Lien must have expected some reaction from him, because he cast a warning glance over his shoulder. Angved was calm, though. Artificers were a practical, pragmatic breed, and he had not been deaf to the Corps rumour mill, even after being stripped of his rank. A look from Varsec suggested that Angved's fellow prisoner was thinking just the same thing. The Iron Glove cartel had been working some remarkable miracles of artifice down on the Exalsee's southern shores. Who they were, who led them, was a matter of some debate and of considerably more lurid speculation, but their credentials as artificers could not be denied, for all the Corps might wish otherwise. The Empire had never been shy of borrowing the inventions of other states and kinden for its artificers and, whilst this process usually resulted from armed conquest, trade was also an option wherever force would not yield results.

Still, what was this? The Glove and the Empire had been doing tentative business for a while now, but this piece of cloak-and-dagger promised rather more.

Four of the Iron Glove wore dark leathers, with blackened breastplates showing under their tabards, more like mercenaries than merchants. The woman and two of the men were Solarnese, the last man a thuggish-looking Bee-kinden. They were plainly no more than an honour guard, however, for the man in their midst was armoured head to foot in elegant, fluted plates – a perfectly machined carapace that looked as though it could withstand anything up to and including artillery. Angved held himself perfectly still, for he had witnessed just such armour in use, through a telescope, while he had watched the fighting on the bridge last time. It had been worn by the handful who had turned back the ambitions of the Many of Nem.

The armoured man took off his helm, and an uneasy ripple passed through the Wasp-kinden, for here was an insult, a slap in the face to Imperial doctrine – the Glove were being led by a halfbreed, a close-faced man who looked to be some mongrel of Ant and Beetle stock.

'Colonel Lien, I take it?' the halfbreed nodded to the lean, bald Wasp. 'Here we are, as ordered.'

The chief of the Engineering Corps visibly steeled himself, before stepping forward to face the Iron Glove's spokesman. 'You have authority to negotiate for your cartel's leader?'

'You have the same for the Empire?' the halfbreed shot back.

'Believe me, what's said here will bind the Empire. Of that you can be sure,' replied Lien, with a heavy emphasis that caught both Angved and the Iron Glove man off guard.

What don't I know? Angved asked himself and then, quickly after that, *Who else is with us?*

The halfbreed glanced about the hall, the same thoughts clearly on his mind, but then shrugged his armoured shoulders. 'Then let's get to it. Let us be blunt. We have what you want. We had a delegation from your Consortium guesting with us last month, and they made plenty of notes on what they saw. The Empire has completed its reunification, and you're casting your eyes towards your neighbours again.' He held up a hand even as Colonel Lien opened his mouth. 'I'll say no more. Feel free to pretend that I mean you're concerned about *their* territorial ambitions. Maybe Myna's going to make a strike for Capitas? Who knows? However, the sort of thing that your buyers want isn't our normal stock in trade. We save that for *special* customers – so special, in fact, that we've yet to sell them to anyone. And then the Empire pays us a visit.'

'And you start thinking of a price,' Lien interrupted. 'And you agree to meet us here, not quite Empire yet, and therefore safer for you, because you mistrust us. So tell me your price.' The current of dislike in his voice could not be hidden, but both he and the halfbreed plainly understood that personal feelings – or even the prejudices of whole kinden – could not be allowed to get in the way of business.

'Oh, money – lots of money,' the halfbreed agreed. 'You've

seen the greatshotters in action, and your Consortium men took away with them the cost of those per unit. More, the artificers in that delegation were asking a lot of questions about improved war automotives and, after we're friends again I've some plans to show you that will have you sending to the treasury all over again. But we have a few additional concerns – and that part about being friends again is one of them.'

'You're merchants,' said Lien carefully, 'isn't that so?'

'We're being honest with each other. We're artificers, we deal with realities. Let's leave the pretences and the lies to the Inapt, Colonel.'

For a moment it seemed that Lien was going to press on with his prepared position, but then his narrow shoulders rose and fell. 'Well, then . . . is it true?' In that last word there was almost a note of pleading, although it was not clear whether he was seeking the halfbreed's confirmation or denial.

'Our first condition is a pardon,' the halfbreed announced, 'for the Colonel-Auxillian.'

Angved choked, loud enough to draw all eyes towards him. *But he's dead!* he wanted to shout. The Colonel-Auxillian was the only man to bear a rank that they had invented specifically for him, for he was the genius halfbreed who had captured cities for the Empire in a dozen ingenious ways before falling victim to his own devices at Szar. The master artificer, Colonel-Auxillian Dariandrephos, was most certainly dead – except that his name was revived by Engineering Corps rumour-mongers almost every tenday, and recently more and more of those murmurings had also mentioned the Iron Glove. Angved would rather that creature was dead, but he sensed relief in the way that Lien stood.

So the genius outweighs the man's tainted blood, the arrogance, the apparent desertion and betrayal? Angved considered. Those Consortium artificers guesting with the Glove must have been extremely impressed.

Colonel Lien glanced aside, seeking guidance from the shadows. 'Dariandrephos wishes to return to the Empire?'

'He wants the air cleared, no more than that. We're happy there in our workshops in Chasme, thank you,' the halfbreed stated flatly. 'A public pardon, retirement with honours, and no reason for any Rekef man or ambitious Slave Corps officer to get ideas about him. Unambiguous and exact, just as we artificers like it.'

'It may not be out of the question,' Lien hedged, before another voice took the initiative.

'Of course, a pardon. The Empire can hardly reach agreements with those still considered deserters and criminals, after all.' The new voice was a woman's, and it echoed with peculiar impact between the carved walls of the Scriptora. There was the softest shuffle of footsteps and the speaker stepped into view, although later Angved was never sure quite where she had emerged from. The same went for her escort, a pair of armoured Mantis-kinden with the steel claws of their killing gauntlets very much in evidence. Everyone went absolutely still and silent, as she stepped into their midst – even Lien, who had plainly known she was watching.

It's her! Angved had never seen the Empress before, yet he had no doubt whatsoever that this was really the mistress of the Wasp-kinden, the last scion of her Imperial bloodline. Where her youth and beauty had once made her seem vulnerable, she seemed to be gathering some invisible strength from the stone walls and endless hieroglyphs, growing in stature without ever growing taller, each footfall resounding with a thunder just outside hearing. Here, in this ancient, torchlit hall, even the shadows seemed to throng at her beck and call, and Angved felt her physical presence almost like a blow. In that moment he would have done anything for her, obey any command, fall on a blade for love of her. The next morning, such memories of this meeting would horrify and shame him, and all the more so because the chains forged this night would bind him also in sunlight. The thought of turning against this woman would be like a knife point pricking at his eye, making him wince away at the very notion.

For now, though, her attention was focused on the halfbreed, who swallowed convulsively, staring back. She gave a small, cruel smile as she advanced toward him.

'Yes, a pardon for the Colonel-Auxillian, but more than that surely? What about a pardon for those of his followers who went with him into exile? Surely you are not throwing yourself on my mercy, Sergeant-Auxillian Totho?'

The halfbreed jerked as she spoke his name, and then she was abruptly very close to him, taking his chin in one hand before he could pull away, and studying his face. The Iron Glove people remained tense, confused, and her Mantis bodyguards were plainly ready for any kind of casual violence at any moment – but then Mantis-kinden were always like that. The situation was suddenly unreadable.

'I am told by my artificers that the Iron Glove has great plans for machines and devices that they lust after,' the Empress declared. For a moment she studied Totho's expression, and he kept as still as if she had a sword to his throat, but then she let him go. 'I am told that my own inventors would match them, in time, but history is pressing on us. The Empire has a destiny, and we cannot wait. I am no artificer, but I know sincerity when I hear it. So we are here. You shall have your pardon, and so shall your master and such other deserters as walk in his shadow. Any other Imperial subjects that might find their way to you subsequently are to be returned, however, or purchased for full value. Remember that you are merchants, and not some band of idealists like the Broken Sword.' She had looked away, her keen gaze sweeping across Lien, Angved, Varsec, all the other artificers dressed as soldiers.

Now her eyes pinioned Totho again. 'You shall have your money, but I leave the tawdry details to the Consortium. We shall have your machines, and moreover, we shall even let your master come and see them put to use.' She grinned at Totho's start of surprise, for a brief moment seeming her true age. 'But that was your request to make, was it not, and I have answered it too early.' And the steel was back in her gaze. 'Tell your master that we understand him, even if we do not understand his machines. People are transparent to us, and he is no exception. He needs us more than we need him, because what point is there to his machines if they are never used, and who would ever use them properly if not the Empire? So when the armies march again, you shall march with us, not sporting your old ranks and titles, but doing the Empire's work nonetheless. That was all your master sent you to ask for, was it not?'

Totho stammered, then nodded, words failing him, but she had not finished yet, had not dismissed him.

'It is not all,' the Empress continued. 'There is one thing we will have of you. Khanaphir and the Nem belongs to the Empire now, whatever face we put on that fact for the rest of the world. From dusk tomorrow, the Glove is forbidden – and any other foreign influence will disappear into the sands, never to be heard from again. You shall remove your people from these walls. You shall retrieve all your expeditions and agents from the Nem, all those diggers and robbers that you think we do not know of. This is non-negotiable, and no pardon shall save any of you from retribution if you disobey. We shall wipe the whole of your Chasme off the map if we must, and you know how the rest of the Exalsee shall cheer us on. Do you understand?'

Totho was silent for several foot-dragging seconds, no doubt weighing the odds in his mind: what could be gained where, and what were the percentages in trying to play both ends. The eyes of the Empress brooked no equivocation, however, fixing him like a specimen skewered on a pin until he finally nodded.

'Of course,' he got out. 'It shall be as you say.'

'It always is,' she said sweetly. 'And now I shall not keep you further. I will let my artificers and Consortium factors manage the details, but you may tell your master he shall have the pardons signed by my own hand. He cannot ask for any greater surety than that.'

*

After the Iron Glove people had departed, the Empress turned to Lien.

'They will be gone by dusk tomorrow. The day after, you shall commence your work.'

'If they keep their word, Majesty,' Lien muttered darkly.

'Do you doubt me, Colonel?' The words were said quite pleasantly, but a deadly silence descended instantly upon the Scriptora's echoing hall.

Lien shook his head convulsively. 'Majesty, of course not.'

She nodded, easily satisfied, it seemed. 'These are the men you spoke of?' And to Angved's alarm she was looking in his direction. He missed Lien's confirmation, his heart hammering, as she stared at him. He found himself terrified, out of all proportion even to the temporal power she wielded, and yet at the same time a shock of attraction surged through him as their eyes met, a physical desire such as he had not felt in a decade.

'This man is Varsec, from the Solarnese expedition,' Lien explained distantly. 'While in prison pending trial, he wrote the book you saw, about a new model air force, and how it might be accomplished, the adjustments, the Art . . .'

The Empress waved a hand. 'The technical details I leave to you, Colonel. It is enough that you have confidence in it. That is, after all, your role. I understand that this Varsec's proposals are drastic, and I approve the measures required. The Empire must move forward. We cannot cling to the past.'

'And this is Angved, of the . . .' Lien paused awkwardly, because of course the Empress had publicly denied any responsibility for the mission that had sent Angved to Khanaphes the last time. 'Who was in the Nem recently,' the colonel finished lamely. 'You recall his reports on the Nemean rock oil and its properties.'

She nodded, it being clearly another matter she was happy to rely on her artificers for. 'Proceed in all things as you have described to me,' the Empress instructed. 'The work in the desert and the adjustments back home. The Empire will make use of every tool to hand, whether it be the discoveries of these men or the inventions of the Iron Glove. We will be strong and we will break down the walls my brother balked at. We have a future to claim, Major Angved, Major Varsec.'

There was a moment of silence before the two men realized what she had just said, and after that Angved could have wept: not a prisoner now, not even an over-age lieutenant. *I've done it. I'm made.* He saluted, catching sight of Varsec copying the gesture from the corner of his eye.

'There will be an expedition heading into the Nem. You have seen the machinery we have brought here. You know the operation you must begin. Before you return from the desert, matters must be well in hand,' Colonel Lien reminded him. 'You have seen the trust the Empress has personally placed in you and you can imagine your fate if you get this wrong, Angved.' It was plain that Lien would rather see him rot than profit like this, but the man was an artificer, as pragmatic as that trade demanded. He would use what tools he had. 'Varsec, you'll accompany him while measures are put into place back home – factories converted, the recruiting sergeants briefed. You'll be sent for when they're ready for you. Expect to see Capitas in two months, at the latest, but until then I'll leave you with Angved. You've witnessed, how his oil will solve some of your problems.'

Varsec nodded thoughtfully. 'I have that, Colonel. I've a new sheaf of notes to send on to Capitas already, for the attention of the factory foremen.'

Lien turned away from them and saluted the Empress. 'Your Majesty, you have shown a faith in the Engineering Corps that your brother, whose loss we mourn, did not. With your support, we shall build for you the future that you have envisaged. I am only glad that you understand our craft so well.'

In response to that, something about the Empress's face struck a momentary wrong note, revealing some bitterness that Angved could not account for, but then she was smiling again.

'I shall hold you to your promises,' she told Lien. 'The dreams of my grandfather and my father and my brother are relying on you, *General* Lien. It is time that the Engineers took their proper place within our Empire.'

Fourteen

As the weather grew colder and the snow began to flurry, Varmen earned his keep, guiding them safely to empty little crofter's huts or searching out tiny hamlets, no more than three or four shabby hovels occupied by the most dismal-looking peasants Che had ever seen. These people were terrified enough at the sight of Wasps to abandon entire dwellings to give them shelter, and Che would never know if that was because of the past war or the current regime.

When there was no village or hut available, Thalric and Varmen showed her an old soldier's trick by heading for the nearest copse of trees. There would almost always be a hollow somewhere amongst the roots, which they would curtain off with a cloak to create a little pocket of body-heat against the cold outside. Che was uncomfortably aware that she was surviving through the skills of the Imperial army, learned through bitter trial and error during the first few winters of the Twelve-year War.

Some time later, they had stopped in a town that Thalric remembered: it had been marked as Lans Stowe on the Imperial maps during the war. He had not seen its capture personally, for there had been a great deal of ground to cover for an agent of the Rekef Outlander. The defenders here had held off the Empire for a long time – long after the land on all sides had fallen under the black and gold flag. The town was large, and built into the steepest side of a high hill, topped by one of the Commonweal's most defensible castles. It had been a low, solidly built, crown-like affair and, uniquely, the castle walls themselves had extended to encircle the entire town, sloping inwards to a height of twenty-five feet, then shelving outwards, at a sharp angle, to support roofed walkways, nests of arrowslits and a barrier of wooden spikes. Many of the buildings in the town had been similarly fortified, and Lans Stowe had boasted a great many archers and arrows. Had the place been more tactically essential at the time, it would have fallen far sooner, but a combination of its strength, the defenders' prudence in laying down supplies, and a lack of any pressing need to do anything about it had left Lans Stowe standing, besieged and surrounded, to within two years of the war's end.

They had brought in the artificers, Thalric recalled, and used this place as an experiment in new artillery, for the maverick halfbreed Dariandrephos had then been forging his reputation. Imperial soldiers had never needed to charge the strong walls of Lans Stowe. The Light Airborne had never risked themselves against the wings or arrows of its defenders. Instead, the artillery, far out of bowshot from the walls, had begun levelling the place systematically. The ingenious architecture, which had held off the Empire's desultory efforts for years, was as ancient as any other stonework in the Commonweal, the product of long-dead masons who had seemingly not passed their skills on to any worthwhile apprentice.

After a tenday of ruinous bombardment that had given Drephos the opportunity to experiment with various solid, explosive and incendiary missiles, the surviving defenders had sallied forth: all the glorious chivalry of the old Dragonfly-kinden with their glittering nobility and massed spear-levy. The Wasps had been ready for that, indeed it would be safe to say that the besieging forces had been ready for several years. By all accounts there were few survivors, the Wasps working out their long-harboured frustration on the city to such a degree that the Slave Corps raised an official complaint at the meagre pickings.

And here the three of them were at Lans Stowe, where Thalric had expected anything but this. A Commonweal shanty town of their little stick buildings, perhaps. A deserted ruin, certainly. But this . . .

In the centre of the town there rose a ziggurat in the Wasp-kinden fashion. It was, in its own way, a triumph of design. The lower two tiers were formed from blocks of broken stone mashed together, caged in wire and wood and then mortared in place. Had the upper reaches been of the same construction, then the whole edifice would have crumbled under its own weight, but they had presumably run out of suitable stone around that point, so had continued their work in cane and wood, the Commonweal's traditional building materials. The shape, however, was wholly Imperial.

Of the rest of the town, perhaps half the buildings followed the local pattern: the slanting roofs and, presumably, twin-walled interior. The rest of it, which Thalric guessed was put up to replace structures Drephos had beaten down, was devised to the Imperial pattern: solid, low buildings, often with a second floor smaller than the first; flat roofs and little walled compounds. A surprising amount was constructed of the same salvaged stone, the rest of wood.

There were plenty of soldiers out on the streets, and Thalric felt instinctively at home. It had the feeling of any occupied town in the Empire, with a good garrison on hand in case of trouble. The soldiers wore black and gold, in varying degrees, through most of them were Dragonfly-kinden. Perhaps one in five was a Wasp, with a scattering of other Imperials, mostly Beetle-kinden and Flies.

There was clearly a stratification at work here amongst the townsfolk, and again one that was innately familiar to Thalric. There was a definite ruling class composed of Dragonflies and Wasps, well dressed and armed, often with retinues of followers.

Then there were the Grasshopper-kinden making up the majority of the town's populace who, by contrast, were poorly clad, and they worked. Some were chained.

Their masters, especially the Dragonflies, made a point of naming their home Landstower, as the occupying Imperial forces had done before the Empire's borders had retreated so violently – after the death of the Emperor and the liberation of the Alliance cities. Thalric and Varmen were nodded to on the street, as though they had become people of consequence here purely because of their kinden.

'This is insane,' murmured Che. 'It's like they're putting on a play, or we're in . . . some kind of hallucination. A warped reflection.'

'What are we doing here, Varmen?' Thalric asked of their guide.

'Taking another sounding,' the big Wasp explained. 'Believe it or not, the Principalities aren't exactly the most stable of places. If there's fighting westwards of here, I want to know about it. Also, we need supplies, and personally I could use a proper bed for just one night.'

Che caught Thalric's gaze and her expression said clearly, *I don't want to stay here*, but she voiced no actual objection.

'So there's an inn?'

'Wayhouse,' Varmen explained. 'I like Wayhouses. Best thing the Lowlands ever exported.'

'What on earth are the Way Brothers doing out *here*?' demanded Che, still staring about them at this Empire in miniature.

'Keeping a Wayhouse,' Varmen replied, and then grinned at her exasperated expression. 'I'm not saying the Empire was ever full of the little fellows, but they were always there. Beetles mostly, but a few of them were offshoots of decent family, enough clout to stop the places getting burned down. And the soldiers liked them 'cos, when you got to stop at a Wayhouse, you knew they wouldn't rob you blind. 'Course, some of them got burned, all the same. You know how the army always is with cults and the like.'

Thalric nodded, remembering.

'But they were like the Daughters – you know, those healer bints that always went trailing the pike. The men liked them and so the high-ups tended not to notice them so much, you see?'

The Wayhouse itself was one of the flimsy-looking Commonweal structures, to their surprise, and quite a sprawling one, clearly having been extended recently. The four Beetle-kinden men running the place wore the comfortingly familiar brown habits of the Way Brothers. That they had a staff of a dozen slaves was jarring to Che, but she decided, unhappily, that being a slave to the Way Brothers was probably doing relatively well, as a slave's lot went.

The common room was already busy with travellers, and all of them sitting on the floor or on cushions – none of the tables and chairs that a Lowlander or a Wasp would have set out. Aside from a family of white-haired Roach-kinden bundled close together in one corner, the rest all seemed relatively well-to-do. There were several merchants – a Beetle, a Wasp and three Dragonfly-kinden – and one striking Dragonfly woman with a guard of four Mantis warriors. Then there were two important-looking Wasp-kinden with an entourage of a dozen men apiece, taking opposite ends of the room and pointedly keeping a no-man's-land of strangers between their respective followers. In the Lowlands a Wayhouse catered to all travellers, down to the very poorest, but Che guessed that the truly poor in these parts did not get to travel very often.

'Let me go and ask some questions,' Varmen suggested. 'Someone's bound to have come from the west.' He paused, considering. 'Or else, you know, if nobody has, then we can probably guess it won't be an easy road.'

Left to their own devices, Thalric and Che studied the varied throng.

'We should do a little information-gathering of our own

while we're here,' the former Rekef man decided. 'No real news of this place was reaching Capitas when I was still there. The Principalities must be changing every day, and I want to know how this place has turned out like it has.' Che could only nod.

He glanced from one to the other of the two influential-looking Wasps. The younger man looked like a merchant factor or quartermaster, the kind of Consortium type that Thalric had never much either liked or trusted. The older one still wore his Slave Corps tabard over his finery, as the badge of the Empire, no matter how debased, seemed to be a harder currency here than within the Wasps' own lands.

In the end he chose the merchant, as the lesser of two evils. The thin-faced man looked to be about thirty, with a great deal of locally crafted gold about him. His retinue included a few Wasp guards, but they were outnumbered by the Commonwealer servants or slaves attending on him, including a pair of well-favoured Dragonfly women taking turns at feeding him sweetmeats.

'May we join you, sir?' Thalric asked. As he had guessed, the Imperial term of respect carried disproportionate weight here. The merchant, who would have been far from a 'sir' to Thalric back in the Empire, smiled as broadly as his narrow face would permit.

'Well met, travellers on the road,' he announced, indicating that Thalric should find a space of floor close by. 'We have business together?'

'We might, sir.' Thalric was already fleshing out the details of his lie even as he spoke. 'I'm but recently arrived here from Capitas, scouting for markets.'

The merchant raised his eyebrows. 'A factor, then? Who for?'

'Consortium,' Thalric confirmed, but allowed the man's sly smile to prompt an addition, 'Horatio Malvern.' The Malverns were well known as a powerful family in the Consortium, and Horatio as one of their aspiring sons. Thalric's grasp of the intricate politics of the Imperial merchant clans did not run deep, but it was broad enough to fake a first meeting like this.

The Wasp merchant's smile in response was knowing, and told Thalric a lot. 'Well, the Malverns must know that we have all marked out our territories already, those of us Left Behind.' He put a formal stress on the words. 'If the Consortium wishes to run things here, then we may have difficulties . . .'

'On the other hand, if my masters were simply looking for someone to deal with, for Commonweal goods . . .' Thalric ventured. He was aware of Che, at his elbow, watching him with mixed amusement and fascination.

'Then we will no doubt get on extraordinarily well,' the merchant announced. 'I am Merchant-Colonel Aarth, and we are clearly well met.'

Thalric was at pains to nod solemnly at the absurd rank. Clearly those 'Left Behind' by the Empire's formal withdrawal from the Principalities had wasted no time in handing out the promotions. He guessed that, when the world around here had still been sane, Aarth had been no more than Thalric was currently pretending to be: a merchant family's roaming factor, lacking in either power or respect.

'Aulric, Consortium sergeant,' Thalric replied humbly. For impromptu identities, best practice recommended a name close enough to the truth for him to respond to it without hesitation. 'Tell me, Colonel . . . My masters told me that there were Wasps still in the conquered principalities, but I had expected to find . . .'

'War?' Aarth completed for him. 'All of us holed up in castles and forts, surrounded by a besieging horde? Not at all. Oh, there were some that were worried. The top people, the magnates and generals and governors, they all got out as soon as the news came and left us to our fate. They'd been keeping well apart from the locals, see? They were expecting this to become another Myna.' He smiled, not without a touch of self-mockery that made Thalric like him more. 'I won't deny that we were worried, but then we realized we weren't the only ones. Everyone left alive here was looking at each other and seeing that the nobles are dead, the generals are gone . . . You might not credit it, but a lot of locals here were just as concerned about the Commonweal coming back and lumbering them with another pack of princes.' A broad grin, from a man who plainly thought he had made the right choice back then. 'So most of the enterprising Dragonfly-kinden, those who had been something better than dirt farmers, started to look for someone to lead them. Sometimes they chose locals, more often they picked us. We were used to leading them, see? The main thing they remember about us is that we *won*, that we're stronger than they are. We'd won the battles and we still held most of the castles and defensible positions, even if we were short on men.'

For a moment he paused, as if to savour his petty victories. 'Pretty soon everyone was taking on any locals who wanted in just to protect us from all the others. Then we started talking to each other – sorted out a new hierarchy based on how many swords, how much land, all the basics. Those Dragonflies willing to deal with us, we accepted them as our near-equals, gave them ranks like proper civilized people. The others got to go to the bottom of the pile and, with our new allies, we had strength enough to keep 'em there. For about half a year it was . . . well, you know the North-Empire at all? The hill tribes? It was like that, every village and town for itself. But you know how *we* are, Aulric: we're better than that. We sorted it out. And those locals we've taken in and taught, they're proving good students. One of the governor-generals is a reformed brigand chief of theirs. I've met him – he's mad for all things Imperial, splendid fellow.' A shadow crossed the merchant's expression. 'Of course we hear things have calmed down back home, with herself in charge at last.'

Thalric made a quick judgement. 'I've seen no sign of armies pointed your way, Colonel. The Alliance cities are a problem, but . . .' He glanced briefly at Che. 'Seems to me the Lowlands are likely to be foremost in people's minds.'

'That's fine, because we'd value good *relations* with the Empire,' Aarth explained carefully, and Thalric understood him perfectly well. They wanted trade and the chance to visit home, but not to return to the bosom of the Empress. They were on to a good thing here, as lords of their own little backwoods empire.

After that, he and Aarth discussed matters mercantile, Thalric improvising well enough to keep the man happy. Shortly thereafter, Varmen was back with them.

'It's not what I'd call safe, west of here,' their guide explained, after Thalric had bid Aarth farewell. 'Still a few places holding out against the governor-general, which is what the local crook calls himself. We'll have to go carefully, and be ready for a fight.'

When they left Lans Stowe, or Landstower, Varmen's little pack-beetle had taken on a more sprightly gait entirely, and Varmen had transformed himself. He wore head-to-toe chainmail, from the coif framing his face like a hood, to the long hauberk falling most of the way to his knees, to . . .

'I've never seen mail trousers before,' Che declared, staring. 'I think that's more armour than I've ever seen anyone wear ever, Varmen.' She had kept her distance from him so far, but the sight of the man so heavily protected evidently struck her as almost comical.

'This?' Varmen just grinned. 'This isn't *armour*, mistress. This is just clothes you need to keep the rust off.'

As soon as they were beyond the farmland attached to Landstower, they travelled away from the roads, at Varmen's suggestion. The terrain was surprisingly hilly, with irregular patches of dense forest, but there were plenty of goat tracks, and Varmen explained to them that the roads themselves dated only back to the occupation, and were little better, just hard-packed earth. 'You see, the locals never did travel much,' he explained.

Oh, I know, Thalric recalled. All these lands were places where he had fought, undertaken Rekef missions and cut throats. Imperial policy had been strict concerning the longevity of noble families in all areas under conquest.

Also at Varmen's suggestion, they travelled on after dusk each day despite the intermittent snow, making several hours' careful progress along the animal tracks before camping for the night, so as to make better time despite the short winter days, and to make life more difficult for anyone hoping to catch them unawares.

That was why their enemies, instead of ambushing them at their camp, were eventually forced to descend on them raggedly as they progressed.

The three of them had been moving along a lightly wooded track between two hills, when Che called out the warning, her own eyes better in the dark than either of the Wasps'. A moment later, there were forms gliding down around them, half a dozen, and then more. Thalric had his sword out, his off-hand extended to sting, and Che had a hand to the hilt of her own blade.

'All right, what's this?' Varmen demanded, with weapon already to hand: a sword longer and heavier than army-issue standard.

'Give me a lantern!' someone snarled, and one of the figures produced a rush-light from beneath a cover, lending a faint illumination to their surroundings. The newcomers were mostly Dragonflies, partly armoured in their borrowed black and gold. Standing between, and a little behind two of them, was the speaker: a Wasp-kinden, not Aarth but the slaver at the Wayhouse.

Thalric made a quick count and found eight Commonwealers gathered in a loose half circle around them. Most of them carried spears, but a couple had bows with arrows to the string.

'Your name's Varmen, no?' the slaver asked.

'I owe you money?' the big Wasp asked. 'I don't know your face.'

'No need to worry yourself. I don't want you. You can just take off,' the slaver told him.

'Is that so?' Varmen said, looking round at all the Dragonfly-kinden. 'Kind of you.'

Thalric was not sure what he had expected from Varmen, but when the big man grabbed his beetle's halter and just backed off into the trees he found he was not overly disappointed. Che obviously had possessed more faith in their guide, for she shouted after him vainly, even as a curtain of driving snow took him from view, and then rounded furiously on the slaver.

'What do you want with us?' she demanded. Her own sword was out now, a short Collegium piece.

'With you, nothing. Go follow your man there, if you wish,' the slaver replied.

'I don't wish.' She stood closer to Thalric, despite the odds. Just then, he could have wished for her to take the man's offer, because he was faster than she was, both on the ground and in the air, and protecting her would get him killed all the sooner. Still, the odds were hardly favourable even without her.

'What's this?' he asked them. 'Who are you?'

'Captain Halter, at your service.'

There was an awkward pause, because clearly the man expected his name to mean something, but Thalric could not place it.

'I don't know you . . .'

'No?' Halter's face betrayed a twitch of annoyance. 'But I recall you, Major, or your description at least.'

This use of Thalric's old rank sent a dangerous jolt through him. *This may suddenly become worse than I thought.*

'I wasn't always the man of means you see before you,' Halter continued, clearly delighting in having a captive audience. 'I used to be a very lowly man indeed. But not entirely abandoned: I still got the lists.'

Thalric stared at him. 'You're not serious.'

'I used to spend a lot of time memorizing those lists,' Halter explained, positively beaming over his own cleverness. 'We got plenty of fugitives coming through the Principalities. It was one of the few ways I could really attract my superiors' notice, by turning in a few decent traitors. Names and descriptions, I memorized every one. Used to recite them to myself before I slept, most nights.'

'I don't know who you think I am,' Thalric started. 'My name's—'

'Aulric, you told the merchant,' Halter finished for him. 'So he told me, but I remember a man who matches your description nicely – a man who was right near the top of those lists, not so long ago.'

'Listen, I'm not—'

'Then you won't mind stripping off and letting me and my lads look at your scars,' Halter proposed, leering. 'You see, Sergeant Aulric, this *Thalric* I remember had picked up a big old scar running from his navel to just about his knee. The description was very specific.'

'Those lists . . . they must be years old, though.'

'Oh, but once you're on a list, there's only one way off, as everyone knows. Imagine the reward I'd get for turning in such an inveterate traitor.'

But I'm not a traitor: I was the Regent . . . And of course such a revelation would make matters a great deal worse. Thalric steeled himself, reasoning that this slaver would want him alive. Once again, he wished Che had fled, but to order her away now would surely give Halter the idea of using the woman as a hostage. Right now, the man probably thought Che was a servant or slave or something.

'So, you're going to strip, or shall we just fly you off to the Empire and see if they want you?' Halter demanded.

Thalric was formulating a line concerning the wrath of his notional Consortium masters, when a voice shouted out from behind Halter.

'Right now, you sneaky bastards! Face a real man!'

Halter whirled around, and half his men with him, to see an apparition come striding into the lamplight, out of the drifting snow, approaching almost within spear-reach before they could react.

The newcomer appeared colossal, but that was mostly the armour. A full-face helm exposed nothing of him save a narrow eyeslit, whilst segmented pauldrons encased his shoulders, and his torso was locked into a massive breastplate and backplate, from which hung curved tassets that descended clattering to mid-thigh. Brutal-looking gauntlets encased his hands. All of this was worn over the full layer of mail that Thalric had last seen the same man wearing, for that voice, despite its hollow echo, was Varmen's. He had his heavy-bladed sword in one hand, and a broad heater shield strapped to his other arm. The man had transformed himself into a ghost of the Imperial past: here was the heavy armour of the Sentinels, who until not so long ago had been the Empire's pride and joy and the unyielding fist of its line battles.

The only flaw in all this barrier of solid steel was a small, jagged hole in the breastplate, low-down to the left and barely noticeable.

'Oh, piss-damn,' Halter swore, shaken, and Thalric let fly a sting-bolt that killed one of the archers, whilst lunging at the other in a flurry of wings. The bowman twitched backwards, out of reach, but Thalric's backhand swing smashed his bow before he could bring it to bear. Then Varmen was charging down on Halter, an unthinkable weight of both metal and man in smooth, furious motion. The slaver rapidly let fly with his sting three times, twice caught on the shield and once searing harmlessly off the breastplate. One of the Dragonfly spearmen, undergoing a surfeit of loyalty, tried to get in the way, but Varmen did not even give him the courtesy of a sword stroke, barging him aside as though the man was irrelevant, bellowing 'Pride of the Sixth!'

At last, Halter tried to fly, wings suddenly sparking from his back. He had left it too late, though, and Varmen's blade chopped down to catch him neatly between neck and shoulder and slam him to the ground.

The Dragonflies had joined in the fighting, and Thalric had been hard pressed to keep the spearmen at bay in those first few seconds, until Che had lanced one through the ribs. Once Halter was down, however, they scattered instantly into the night. Had there been a free archer left amongst them, Thalric would have expected some long-range reprisal. As it was, he reckoned he and Che were probably safe from at least that particular pack of villains for the rest of the night.

He turned his gaze to the armoured behemoth that Varmen had become, and saw that the man had not yet sheathed his sword, but instead was now staring at him through that dark eyeslit.

'The lists,' came the man's voice, hollow from within the helm.

'What?' Thalric asked, with a sinking sensation in his stomach.

'He said your name was on the lists,' the other Wasp stated flatly.

Thalric felt himself tense, so as to be ready if the man came for him. Halter's sting had barely marked that solid armour, but Thalric's Art was considerably stronger than most, and he would aim for the lighter mail over Varmen's throat.

'What's going on?' Che wanted to know.

'Lots of people were on the lists,' Thalric said defensively, enlightening her not at all.

'Oh, I remember the cursed *lists*, and all the names on them were Rekef,' Varmen spat. 'It's true, isn't it? You watched me doing all that mumming for the Dragonflies, all those hints about how you were a sneak, and all the time you were laughing at me 'cos it was true all along.' His voice had turned raw and angry.

'Varmen, listen,' Che said hurriedly. 'It's not what you think—'

'I remember your *lists*,' Varmen snapped. 'When we were waiting to march on Sarn with the Seventh, two or three times some pack of Rekef executioners would come from down the rail line, with their cursed lists. They'd haul someone out from inspection, hustle them off, and then it was an unmarked grave and no questions asked. Because they were on the *lists*. And, you know what, I don't care. Let Rekef kill Rekef, I'm not going to piss any blood for that – but those poor bastards they hauled out, we knew them. We'd known 'em for years, you know? Ate with them, diced with them, trusted them to watch our backs – and they'd been Rekef all along, spying on us, writing down every last thing anyone said that sounded like it might be treason.'

'So what are you going to do about it?' Thalric demanded of him.

The faceless helm shifted left and right, seeming something less than human, a mute animal in pain. 'If I'd known . . . I'd never have agreed to guide you, if I'd known.'

'Listen,' Che told him, 'I'm not Rekef, right? I'm a Lowlander from Collegium. You're . . .' She remembered his cry: *Pride of the Sixth*. 'Sixth Army? You were at . . .' She got her recent history straight and blinked. 'Malkan's Folly, that must mean.'

'Malkan's *Stand*,' Varmen corrected, giving the Wasp-kinden name for the battlefield on which Imperial ambitions towards the Sarnesh Ants had been smashed . . . and where the Empire's heaviest line infantry had met the new dawn of the snapbow. Her eyes were drawn to that single flaw in the man's mail, a finger-sized hole punched effortlessly through that thick armour plate.

'I'm no Rekef, and Thalric hasn't been one for years. That's probably why he was on this list to begin with.'

Varmen's carapaced shoulders slumped. 'I'd never have said

yes,' he muttered, but he sheathed his sword in a single motion, through long habit able to find the scabbard's mouth without searching, and then he was fumbling at the buckle to his helm, dragging the weighty thing off and then drawing back his coif, showing a tousled, unhappy man underneath.

'We're glad you came back, even so,' Che told him. 'And that you could get all your armour on so fast.'

'All?' he said, with a faint smile. 'Woman, this isn't *all*. This is just what I could, you know, throw on in a hurry. Most of it's still on the beetle.' His eyes found Thalric's and the smile faded.

'What can I say?' Thalric shrugged. 'So I was Rekef. As she says, not for a long time – and the Empire has gone to some lengths to get rid of me since. Putting my name on the lists is the least of it.'

Seeing Varmen's grim expression linger, Che pressed on. 'I promise you. Nothing about this journey relates to the Rekef, or even to the Empire.' She essayed a smile. 'Let me tell you about my sister.'

Fifteen

A crowd had gathered in one of Khanaphes's great plazas. Merchants and artisans and farmers clumped together, looking up at the balcony from which, traditionally, the city's leaders had formerly made pronouncements, passing on the words of the unseen Masters.

Now the balcony bore a less familiar burden, as a handful of Beetle-kinden Ministers was overshadowed by the presence of the Empire. However, the most imposing presence belonged not to the Wasp-kinden officers, nor the Mantis bodyguards, but to the Empress Seda herself. For all that she was such a slight and unassuming figure, something about her instantly drew the eye and held it. No Spider Arista possessed such raw presence as she did, looking out over the anxiously milling people of Khanaphes.

Across the street, from the window of a merchant factora, Praeda and Amnon watched as one of the Ministers stood forth to address the populace.

'That's not Ethmet,' the big man murmured. 'Why isn't the First Minister there?'

Praeda shrugged. 'You tell me,' she replied, resting a hand on his arm. 'These are your people. When I was here last I'd have said that very little the Ministers did made many kinds of sense.'

The foremost Minister standing on the balcony – at this

distance just an anonymous old man – held out his hands, and the citizens below quietened swiftly. 'People of Khanaphes, rejoice!' he declared, with all apparent sincerity. 'Rejoice for the friendship of a new Empire!'

The people below did not seem minded to spring into instant celebration, but merely stared upwards cautiously. Praeda guessed many of them would have heard how this selfsame Empire had been behind the ruinous Scorpion attack of the previous year, from which the city was so plainly still recovering. To have such a large Imperial force insert itself effortlessly within their walls caused them understandable concern.

'The Honoured Foreigners of the Wasp Empire have heard of our troubles,' the Minister pressed on stoically. 'They are deeply grieved that renegades from within their own borders may have incited the Scorpions of the Nem to attack our walls.' Nothing in the Minister's assured delivery acknowledged just how swiftly those walls had been brought down, or the terrible cost of that assault. Khanaphes, city of ten thousand years, did not like to dwell on its own defeats.

Praeda shifted at the window, wishing she could get her telescope out, but knowing that, at this angle, sunlight might flash from the lens and draw Imperial attention. Amnon had talked his way into this place, the merchant that owned it was surely somewhere in the crowd outside, and she was still worried that word might already have reached the government that their errant son, their former First Soldier, had returned.

'So it is,' the Minister was saying, 'that the Honoured Foreigners wish to make amends. Even today they will be taking their soldiers off into the Nem, with all their fearful artifice, there to confront and slay as many of the despoiling Scorpions as they can find. These foreigners, our friends, shall thus take the blood of the Many in recompense for the harm their rebellious subjects have done here. They tell us that, after they are done, we need not fear the return of the Scorpions for five hundred years!'

For a moment there was silence, as the listeners digested this statement. Then a few scattered cries of approbation heralded the floodgates opening, and a moment later, everyone was cheering – cheering the black and gold. Praeda wondered whether any of it was spontaneous, or whether the Ministers had orchestrated every last echo.

'This is how they hope to keep the Wasps off their backs, is it?' she mused aloud.

Amnon hissed, 'Praeda,' in warning tones, and a moment later she heard the sound of sandals scuffing on stone steps as several people ascended the stairs from the factora's ground floor. She turned to see that Amnon had already drawn his sword: a well-crafted Helleron piece, and not the leaf-bladed weapon he had taken away on his departure from this city. She had a similar short blade herself strapped to the inside of the pack lying at her feet, and now she rested a hand on the hilt, waiting.

She had certainly not expected to see Ethmet, but the leading pair of feet to arrive belonged to none other than Khanaphes's First Minister. The man and woman following him were outfitted in the gorgeous gold-edged scale mail of the Royal Guard, but they themselves looked young and green: surely replacements brought in after the Scorpions had been defeated. Though not amongst those commanded by Amnon during the city's defence, they still eyed the big man with awe and reverence. Exiled though he was, his name still resonated within the city's walls.

There was an awkward silence between them that the sound of the crowd outside could not break into. Then Ethmet spoke: 'They told me you had returned.'

Amnon still held his sword to hand. 'If you believe that I have come begging for pardon, you are mistaken,' he stated. 'If you intend threatening me with the law of Khanaphes for defying my banishment, then you have forgotten who I am. These children will not suffice.' He looked directly into the faces of Ethmet's guards. 'They will not even stand against me.'

'No, no.' Ethmet's voice, that had quieted angry crowds in its time, emerged weak enough that Praeda had to lean closer to hear it. 'I just came to . . . to see you. An old friend . . .'

Amnon frowned suspiciously. 'You seem to like your new friends well enough to have no need of old ones. We saw you bow the knee.'

'Amnon, you do not *understand*.' The old man's voice cracked on the last word and, suddenly shaking, his legs gave way. One of his men lunged forward to catch him, and guide him over to a stone bench. To her embarrassment, Praeda saw tears on Ethmet's withered cheeks.

'The Masters,' he got out. 'The Masters . . .'

'There are no Masters,' Amnon said firmly. He put a lot of conviction into those words, and indeed Praeda had talked with him repeatedly about the archaic beliefs of the Khanaphir. Most of the time, Amnon came across as quite the rationalist Beetle-kinden, interested in machinery and progress and better ways of doing things. She knew him well, though, and there were times when his mind still played host to the superstitions of his upbringing.

'You are wrong!' Ethmet hissed. 'You saw them sweep the Scorpions from the city, at the last.'

'At the *last*?' Amnon demanded hotly. 'Old man, you had better hope that there *are* no Masters, for if there are, what manner of creature are they to let their servants suffer so, to see so many of their people die, to see their own army defeated, if all along they possessed such power?'

Amnon obviously expected Ethmet to rally at this, to curse him for his blasphemy, but the old man's shoulders kept shaking, and his words were momentarily lost as he fought to control himself.

'I believe in the Masters,' Ethmet forced out at last, 'and I believe I have always done their will as best I could. But it is for me as a man hearing the echo of a voice from distant rooms, so perhaps I have not always understood. Perhaps, sometimes, I thought I heard them when they were silent, or they spoke and I did not listen. But . . . I believe in the Masters now. They are awake. They speak, and if I myself can hear only the faintest whisper of their words, *she* hears them clear, whether she knows it or not. Oh, I knelt, Amnon. I knelt because the Masters told us to, all of us. It was only the echo of an echo, but I have never heard them clearer. I could not have kept a straight leg if I had wished to. *She* is here because of the Masters, Amnon. She means more to the Masters than do I and all my ancestors together for five hundred years.'

'I don't understand,' Amnon admitted. He glanced at Praeda, who put a hand on his arm, trying to comfort him.

Ethmet was crying quietly again. 'We have served them all this time. We have done what we thought the Masters . . . the Masters . . . what they wanted. We have failed them. We have grown away from them, from generation to generation. We are not fit tools for them, and so they reach out to others: first that Collegium girl, and now the Empress of all the Wasps. Even these foreigners are more beloved of the Masters than we are.'

Amnon and Praeda exchanged uncomfortable looks, on seeing the First Minister of the Khanaphir so comprehensively undone. In Praeda's mind, though, a phrase resurfaced. 'That Collegium girl' . . . *Che?*

That morning, in her mirror, she had seemed to see another face. She was Seda the First, Empress of the Wasps, a countenance revered and reproduced across the Empire, and yet, for a moment, her pale, fine features had been overlaid by those of a Beetle woman, of all things: a serious-looking girl of close to her own age. Seda had locked eyes with that phantom until it had faded.

It was not the first time, either. She knew the same face from fragmentary dreams, briefly glimpsed in standing water or reflected in glass. Most of the time the face itself went unseen, though, for her own mind's eye sat behind it and stared out . . .

Seda had stood on the city's western walls, those parts that had not been tested by the Imperial ordnance brought against them by the Many of Nem, and watched the Empire's punitive force set off. It was expected of her, for all that she understood very little of it. It reminded her of that strange little meeting in the Scriptora: the colonel of Engineers, the two disgraced artificers and the Iron Glove's halfbreed, all talking so knowledgeably about things that she could not understand. Not one of them had guessed at her ignorance or, if they had, they had assumed it was the simple lack of knowledge fitting for someone Apt but untrained. In reality they might as well have been making animal noises when they spoke of their craft, but she had been well briefed. She did not need to know how their machines worked. She only needed to know the *result*. They might claim to have an engine that would tear down a wall, but all that mattered to her was that the wall fell. She relied on people such as Gjegevey to brief her.

She knew, for example, that an observer from a more mechanically minded city than Khanaphes might wonder about the large quantity of machinery that this punitive force was taking into the desert with it: machinery that would seem to serve little martial purpose. However, once away from the city walls, any such observer would be advised to keep his or her distance.

And it was not all lies, either. Certainly the Scorpion-kinden were in for a rude awakening in the near future, for any tribe of the Many of Nem luckless enough to get within sight of this expedition would be wiped out. There would be Scorpion heads aplenty to satisfy the Khanaphir. *After all, we are here as friends, and the enemy of my friend is my enemy.*

So now Majors Angved and Varsec had departed, off to undertake their incomprehensible task in the desert: their peculiar mechanical mining for this mineral oil that the artificers had been so impressed with. So much for the Empire's formal purpose in coming to this place.

She was left here as an honoured guest in the city, with enough well-trained soldiers to ensure that she could make the place an Imperial protectorate at any moment she chose. No doubt her people expected that, once having shown her face here, she would be back inside the airship and heading to the capital soon enough.

But she had another purpose, too. Gjegevey's stories of the city had whetted it, but she had forged the idea for herself beforehand.

My dreams, she reflected, but that was not quite accurate. Better to say '*the* dreams', because, for all that she had woken from them, they came from another's mind entirely: the stone halls, the statues, the carvings, the darkness, the colossal tombs that were not tombs at all . . .

And the power, that naked, palpable power, it had called out to her across all the miles, until she had woken three nights running with the name 'Khanaphes' on her lips. And now she was here, and this mundane city was hers, but beneath her was a power unmastered and ancient.

Waiting . . .

Nights in Khanaphes were cool but not cold. The stone of the city seemed to have some secret treaty with the sun, holding back just sufficient of its daytime heat to stave off the dark's chill. Outside the Imperial embassy, the vast star-pocked sky seemed to suck all warmth and light towards itself, untrammelled by cloud, the constellations seeming to loom impossibly close.

Seda stood in the Place of Foreigners, the ornamental square at the heart of the various embassies that the Khanaphir had put up for their foreign guests, a thousand years before, when their city had still been clinging to the skirts of greatness. The statues of the great powers of yesteryear regarded her and judged her impartially: Spider, Mantis, Moth, Woodlouse, and of them all perhaps only the Spider-kinden remained a power in this world. Her own people were not represented: when these stone faces were chiselled out with such exacting skill, the Wasp-kinden had been no more than savages. Even in her grandfather's day they had been so. That they were now the greatest nation the world had ever seen made her proud of her people, of her bloodline. *We were not born emperors and conquerors. We have earned the right to own the world. But my people know only half of the world, can see and touch only a part of the whole. How lucky for them, then, that I am here to provide a bridge to those invisible powers that they cannot guess at.*

Overhead, the constellations drew pictures in the sky for her, patterns that the Moth-kinden had names for back when the Wasps had barely grasped the skill of metalwork, and perhaps those names had been coined here, originally, from the wisdom of the Masters of Khanaphes.

Before she had changed, before Uctebri's rituals and her brother's death, she had seen only points of light up there. Now she saw great forms striding across the sky, and she knew that the same forms had been known to the Inapt peoples of the world since the start of time.

Her guards had not seen her come out to stand here, and her staff believed her asleep in her chamber. It was a simple piece of misdirection to have them look elsewhere as she passed. In all the embassy, only one knew that she had departed it, and he had followed, his footsteps dragging softly on the stone flags. That *he* had stepped outside would not be remarked on. He was an old slave, for all his prestigious influence, and few cared where old slaves chose to walk, so long as they were present to fulfil their duties later.

'Gjegevey,' she said.

'Your, mmm, Imperial Majesty,' came his quiet voice. She sensed the presence of the tall, hunchbacked Woodlouse-kinden at her shoulder.

'It must be tonight,' she said. 'The call is too strong, and I feel that if I let another dawn pass me by, then I will fail in some test. Or they will think me afraid. I am not afraid, Gjegevey.'

'I am sure you are not, although were I, hmm, in your position, I would fear for my very being,' he said diplomatically.

She turned then and took his hand, feeling it lean and angular with bone, his skin dry and smooth, his Art making it feel harder than skin should. He had gone still, knowing that Empresses did not touch slaves, or at least not slaves who wished to live.

'Do not fear me, Gjegevey.'

He said nothing, but when she looked across to the archway leading from the Place of Foreigners to the square before the Scriptora, his eyes followed hers.

'This is not wise,' he whispered.

'I came here for no other reason. The old powers of this place must respect me, must *recognize* me, and they shall never do that if I slink away like a whipped slave. I will go to them tonight. I cannot take my guards or my servants, my spymasters or my artificers. None of these can understand, and likely they would die. There is only one of my retinue who might be of use to me in penetrating those dark tombs.'

He met her gaze, but only for a moment before he lowered his eyes. 'Surely your, ahm, Mantis-kinden . . .'

'Not there, Gjegevey. Not in that place. Faced with what we shall find there, I do not know if my bodyguards would remain true to me. Only you shall accompany me.'

'You ask a great deal of your slave, ah, Majesty.' For a moment his withered face was screwed up, lines upon lines, but then he mastered himself. 'Well, it has been many centuries since one of my kind went to visit the Masters of Khanaphes, even assuming the old stories are true. I shall be your guardsman and your servant and your, mm, intelligencer on this journey, Majesty, and should we ever see the sky again I shall be thankful.'

'Then follow me,' she said imperiously, and strode off towards the arch that linked the Place of Foreigners with the government of Khanaphes. The night, as well as her own skills, would prevent any Apt eyes from seeing her. Her soldiers kept a close lookout, but of all things, they did not expect to see their Empress walking past in a white gown, all alone save for her aged Woodlouse adviser.

The Scriptora was dark save for one window picked out by the dim glow of a rush-light, some diligent clerk labouring into the night. Even should he look up from his calligraphy, she trusted in her skills to cloud his eyes. These Khanaphir were but Beetle-kinden, chained by their Aptitude, and yet without any of the material advantages their cousins elsewhere enjoyed.

That is because the Masters do not desire them to change, the thought came to her, and she knew it to be true. *The lurking power that dwells beneath this city has influence yet.*

At the centre of the square fronting the Scriptora stood that squat, stepped pyramid with its flat top, about which stood an irregular placement of statues in white stone. They were not Beetle-kinden, nor Wasp nor any other race that Seda had known, and they were carved to be twice the height of normal men and women, giants looking over the city with a proprietorial eye.

And there they are. They were but stone, but Seda felt an echo there in their cold, disdainful likenesses, their distant beauty. *They are the Masters, whom I must now seek out.* Her dreams recurred to her: the darkness below, the pale forms striding through it. It was as though she had made this journey before. Even as she ascended the pyramid's steps, she knew that there would be a shaft at its apex, ringed and guarded by those statues. That was the path. It was the only path.

She took the steps carefully, wondering partway whether the city had been this silent for long or whether, as her imagination fancied, she had stilled all other sound by her ascent. Some part of her felt that, on reaching the top, she should somehow become of equal stature with the great stone forms, and ready to take her place amongst them, but instead they dwarfed her, which made her feel angry.

Gjegevey took longer to join her, struggling over each step. At the last he stopped and doubled over, and she let him catch his breath while she stared up at the stars.

'The most ancient tales of my, ah, people,' the Woodlouse slave got out, 'said that we were taught our earliest crafts by this vanished kinden, that our letters, our philosophy, all have their seed in the learning brought to us in the elder times by those who had been Masters here, and left Khanaphes to travel and teach the savage lesser kinden elsewhere.' He smiled sardonically. 'Of course, I am reminded of the, hmm, Spider-kinden, who will have you believe that without them the sun would fall from the sky – and they'll convince you of it, too, if you let them. There is no story ever told that can be separated from the interests of the teller.'

'You urge caution, then?' Seda asked him.

'My Empress, if to urge caution would help, then we would not be here. But . . . if they should stand before you in the majesty and grandeur of ten thousand years, do not forget, mn, all *you* are, and all *you* have achieved. There are many kinds of greatness in the world.'

For a long time she regarded him with a solemn scrutiny that would have made any other subject tremble and sweat, but he knew that a smile would appear eventually.

'I shall not forget,' she promised. 'Now, we shall descend and then, if I have a destiny, I shall find it here in that darkness, or not at all.'

Che awoke, staring upwards into pitch darkness, her Art nevertheless picking out the spider in its circular web.

What was the ruler of the Wasp-kinden doing in that ancient city? And why did Che's mind send her there every night that her dreams were lucid enough to remember?

And when I was there myself, walking beneath Khanaphes and seeing what I saw, was the Empress seeing me the same way as I see her now?

She had no control over this strange link with the Wasp Empress. It was part of the great magical world that she had been thrust into, vast and trackless and hostile, and yet it had become her new home.

The thought came to her, not for the first time, that there were magicians aplenty in the Commonweal. If anyone could help her understand this new life, then surely some Dragonfly mystic would spare her the time. Surely that was the reason for this lunatic journey in the first place?

No. I am here for Tynisa, to save her . . . Each day Che had to remind herself of that, at least once. Her concern for her foster-sister was steadily being eclipsed by her dreams, and by something else, too: this new world she was a native of concealed a wellspring of power, a power able to change the world in ways that the Apt could never conceive. If she learned just a little more, surely she could reach out and take a little of that power for herself? And then what might she not do? Even if it had fallen into decay, surely magic could still accomplish *anything*.

Tynisa, she reminded herself. *Just think of Tynisa.*

But her dreams were all of the Empress and her kindred quest to understand the ancient powers. However far Che travelled, Tynisa seemed ever more distant.

Sixteen

Praeda awoke because of someone shaking her. For the briefest of moments she was unsure where she was, but the very air said *Khanaphes* even before her eyes had opened to the ancient city's distinctive architecture.

Or to see Amnon, already clad in his battered, piecemeal armour of dark, fluted metal, with a snapbow over his shoulder and his sword ready at his belt.

'What's happening?' she demanded.

'Trouble,' he told her. 'We have to move.'

'Trouble?'

'The Wasps have gone mad,' he said shortly, thrusting the snapbow at her and slinging a pack about his shoulders.

She dressed hurriedly. The snapbow felt strange in her grip, like handling a dangerous animal. Of course she knew the principles of its air battery – could have given a lecture and drawn diagrams if needed – but she had never used one before.

Amnon had reverted to his roots, though: he was always best with a sword. It therefore seemed that she would have to uphold the honour of the Apt, in whatever engagement he had now dragged them into.

'Amnon, what have you done?'

'I? Nothing. There are Wasp soldiers out on the streets. They say the Ministers are arrested. They say all foreigners are being arrested, too. The Marsh Alcaia is being raided and the ships in dock searched.'

'Searched for what?' Praeda demanded, dressed and ready in less time than she would ever have thought possible.

'They say the Empress is missing,' he spat.

The Empress? 'Amnon, you didn't . . .?'

'No, I did not,' he said, frowning. 'But they will arrest us, if they catch us. Then they will discover you are a Lowlander, and they will kill you. We must leave.'

'How do you know all of this?'

'One of the Royal Guard remembered me fondly enough to bring me the news,' he explained, and then the two of them were out of the room and down the stairs.

Two dead Wasps lay at the foot of the steps. One of them had been struck so hard in the chest that the plates of his armour were split apart.

'You said you'd done *nothing*,' Praeda snapped.

'Nothing much,' Amnon replied, slightly shamefacedly. 'I did not think it was the time for details. Nor is this.'

Well, he's right there. 'Where are we supposed to go? You have a plan?'

'Out of the city,' he told her. 'If the Marsh Alcaia is already taken then I know of no place to hide for certain. But in the marshes themselves the Wasps shall not find us.'

'And your marsh-people, the Mantis-kinden?'

'I do not know.' He grimaced. 'I do not see any other choice than to risk the desert itself, and their winged soldiers would see us far easier on the sands than in the marsh.'

She shrugged, arranging her cloak so that the snapbow was well hidden beneath it. 'I can't fault your logic. Let's go.'

Had Amnon not known the streets of his own city so well, they might have fallen foul of the Wasp-kinden much sooner. His role as First Soldier had been more than a purely military one, however, and he had often gone out into Khanaphes to enforce the city's laws against those who would disregard them.

He had, he claimed, brought light into the shadows, which meant that he knew the shadows better than any.

The Imperial soldiers were out in force. Small groups of them hurried through the streets or coasted overhead. Any they found on the streets were stopped and questioned. Praeda saw doors kicked in, and soldiers flurrying into an upper storey through an open window. *What can they hope to achieve?* But it seemed they had lost their Empress somehow, and they were going mad trying to find her.

From elsewhere in the city could be seen the red glow of fire. She heard screams and cries in the night, from adults and children both. The two of them progressed through the city in fits and starts, hiding under awnings or in doorways, crouching on steps leading down to cellars hugging the walls at all times, because the skies were busy with the Light Airborne buzzing back and forth in search of . . . who knew what?

Abruptly Amnon hauled her around a corner of a building, holding his sword low, ready to ram it up into an enemy the moment a target presented himself. A moment later, a mob of Khanaphir stumbled past – men and women, old and young, dressed and half-dressed – with Wasp-kinden herding them, shoving and pushing and jabbing them at sword point. There was no hint of where they were heading, or for what purpose, or even suggestion that the Wasps themselves knew. Praeda had a horrible feeling that these soldiers were just doing *something* so that they could later say to their superiors that they had not stood idle in the Empress's sudden absence. And if that *something* should include slaughtering the Khanaphir, then no moral qualms would outweigh their fear of the Wasp chain of command.

She half expected Amnon to move, because these were his people and she knew his fierce sense of duty, but he remained still, terribly still, holding his own feelings down. It was then she realized just how strongly he felt about her, because her safety was now the sole reason he was restraining himself.

Oh, curse the lot of them. With that, she brought the snapbow up, sighting her target in the moonlight – a Wasp standing furthest away from the group – and pressed the trigger. The sound of it, that infamous 'snap', seemed laughable, the jolt of the weapon in her arms hardly worth mentioning. The Wasp dropped with a brief bark of surprise, not even pain, but she realized that she had killed him.

It was a drastic way to grant him permission, but Amnon took her gesture for what it was and he was already rushing the remaining quartet of Wasps, swift and remarkably quiet, his mail just a susurration of metal.

They did not see quite what he was at first, as their stings flared off the planes of his armour. Then he was right amongst them, his sword making swift, ugly work of the nearest two, even as they tried to put their own blades in the way. Of the remaining two, one hopped into the air with a brief flash of wings, intending to drop on him, and the other fled.

Praeda had reloaded the snapbow, and the escaping man's fast, erratic flight gave her one shot at him before he was lost over the rooftops. She missed, but in that time Amnon had dealt with the remaining Wasp, slamming him to the ground and lashing his sword's edge across the man's throat. He turned to the former prisoners, most of whom would surely recognize him.

'Go. Run. Hide,' he instructed them. Then Praeda was at his side and they were running themselves.

Trying to leave the city by any of the regular gates would be to chance Imperial checkpoints, and tonight it was plain that no amount of bribery or subterfuge would get them past the sentries. Quite possibly, anyone trying to leave at all would be shot on sight. Amnon continued moving through Khanaphes with a purpose, however, and Praeda could only trust his judgement. She realized that they were heading for the Estuarine Gate as its colossal pillars loomed close enough to blot out slices of sky and blot out the moon.

'Can you climb?' he murmured suddenly, and she stared at him in puzzlement before understanding that he meant using her Art. It was not exactly a dignified occupation for a College scholar, but her active adolescence had endowed her with a few advantages.

'I need to know if the gate is up,' he explained. 'If so, we've come a long way for nothing.'

She nodded, glancing around to try to assemble a plan of the nearby buildings in her head: which of them was high enough, and which offered a useful vantage point. Then she had chosen her best prospect, and put her hands against the stone, feeling the contours of close-packed carvings underneath her palms. She kicked off her sandals, for the Art gripped just that little bit better with bare feet. Out of practice, for a moment she was just scrabbling at the wall, but then the familiar pull of the Art returned to her, and her hands and feet clung wherever she wanted, released when she bade them, allowing her to creep up the side of the building in a slow, deliberate crawl, keeping three points of contact with the stone at all times.

It was hard work, draining in a way more than merely physical, and in the end the only thing that got her to the top was the thought that she would be letting Amnon down if she gave up. At last she reached a window recess that was high enough for her purposes and hauled herself, gasping, onto the sill. There was a swift whicker of wings at that moment, and she froze as an unseen flier passed by, doubtless a Wasp on some scouting errand. A moment later she turned her eyes towards the river and the gate. It was a grand piece of machinery, as she already had cause to know, and absurdly old by all accounts. The Khanaphir had a vast, metal-shot gate buried in the river bed, that chains and drop-weights could haul up in order to block any attempt to leave the city by water. Perhaps the Empire did not know about it, or had not yet found the mechanism, because the gate was still sunk beneath the surface. One road at least was left for those wanting to leave Khanaphes.

She saw movement by the pillars, and beyond the gate something was on fire. Parts of the covered market known as the Marsh Alcaia had already been put to the torch, the city's criminal element displaced by a more disciplined band of thugs entirely. There would be soldiers watching the river, too, and surely every boat at the nearby docks would have been seized or even sunk.

I hope you know what you're doing, Amnon.

The fires burning at the Marsh Alcaia cast a leaping and unreliable light over the Estuarine Gate, but they also inevitably drew the eye. Somewhere in that warren of stalls and tents there was fighting going on. Although Praeda could make out a fair few Wasps, they were all looking away from her, waiting for the denizens of the Khanaphir underworld to counterattack. Here, at least, they had found a substitute enemy to take out their anger on, in the absence of the Empress's presumed kidnappers.

And what can have happened? That the Empress would come here at all was frankly absurd, but for the most powerful woman in the northern world to have somehow vanished beggared belief. And yet the proof was all around them in the punishment the Wasps were now inflicting on Khanaphes.

Praeda dropped down and let him know what she had seen concisely, and Amnon squared his shoulders, plainly readying himself for some plan of action, more than likely a rash one.

'Amnon,' she murmured warningly, because the Wasps ahead of them were not so distracted that the two of them could just walk past. He was scanning the quays, though, and the various docked vessels. One ship was actually on fire, but the Wasps had evidently suffered a change of heart, maybe realizing that their vandalism could get swiftly out of hand. Even as she watched, the blazing two-masted Spider-kinden trader was cut loose from the docks, and airborne Wasps armed with long spears began trying to herd it further out into the river, where the current would take it swiftly away from the city.

'We must act quickly,' Amnon declared, and for a moment she thought he was proposing they get aboard the burning ship. With the city being stung so savagely all around them, the suggestion did not sound all that outrageous. Then Amnon had crept to the waterside, and was hanging his head over the edge of the docks, apparently inspecting the underside of the nearest quays.

'Amnon, what—?' she started, but then he grunted in satisfaction. 'Can you swim at all?'

Childhood summers spent swimming in Lade Sideriti surfaced briefly in her mind. 'Probably. I certainly used to be able to.'

'That will make this easier. I cannot. See there?'

She followed his pointing finger, but it was a long while before she spotted them: a few small boats moored right underneath the arches supporting the jetties themselves. From her last visit here, she was familiar with their construction: narrow craft of wooden planks held together only with taut ropes, gathered at bow and stern into a raised carving that mimicked bundled reeds. Amnon was already creeping along the waterfront to try and snag one. It seemed that the Wasps must spot him at any moment.

With a curse she kicked off her sandals, hesitating a moment on the brink before letting herself down into the water. She had expected cold, but the sluggish river retained the day's heat, and the flow was not so strong that she could not brace herself against the quay before kicking her way towards the nearest boat. It almost tipped over as she wriggled into it, scrabbling about inside it for an oar. In the end she gave up on actually paddling, but by pushing against the stonework she levered the craft to beneath where Amnon was waiting, and held it steady while he clambered down.

There followed the slowest and most agonizing minutes of her life, as Amnon took the slender boat out on to the river, just catching the swell created as the burning Spiderlands trader lurched past. There were Wasps darting overhead almost constantly, and if just one of them looked down, or if the eyes of their fellows on the shore had strayed from the blaze, then Praeda and Amnon would have been dead in short order. A ship on fire provided sufficient distraction, though, and Amnon was able to bring their tiny vessel into the hulk's shadow, paddling until their two hulls scraped, and letting the river's current then draw them sluggishly out past the Estuarine Gate, even as embers started drifting down about them.

That should have been the end of their difficulties, and Praeda never did understand why the Wasps had patrols flying out over the marshland, save perhaps that they were expecting some attack from the natives there. In any event, they were not quite out of sight of the city walls when the cry went up above them, and a moment later a sting sizzled into the water in a flash of gold.

Amnon was instantly paddling for the shore – on the water they offered too much of a target. Praeda scanned the skies but, with only a sliver of moon, she could not work out how the Wasps, as night-blind as she was, had ever spotted them. Stingshots came lancing down erratically, still off the mark but getting closer, and she could hear one high voice shouting instructions to the shooters, correcting their aim.

Abruptly their boat was grating on mud, and Amnon leapt out, pulling her with him. They had beached on a mudbank with only a few gangly, spider-rooted trees for cover, and he was leading her towards deep marsh, into a twisted maze of ferns, horsetails and gullies that could swallow an army.

Two more blazing shots pursued them, still nowhere near, then a sharp *snap* that whipped the water almost at Praeda's heels. She recognized that distinctive sound instantly, and whoever wielded the snapbow clearly had a much better idea of where they were.

They splashed on through clear, shallow water for a moment, then there was plantlife all around, more mud underfoot, and a fog of gnats that seemed almost solid. Amnon began slowing down, and Praeda only hoped that he had some destination in mind, rather than just charging blindly into this maze of mud and vegetation. She could hear the enemy voice shouting directions again, and sensed the Wasps coursing overhead, still searching.

There was no real silence in the swamp, for the stridulations of hundreds of nocturnal denizens kept up a constant racket, but still she felt that the enemy had lost their trail, their wings lending them too much speed and sending them ahead of their quarry.

'Where now?' she hissed.

'Come dawn, we shall work our way back to the river,' he told her. 'If we see a ship, we shall warn them of the Wasps, and with luck they shall carry us to the stone town.'

'To Porta Rabi, yes,' she agreed. 'And what about until dawn?'

She did not find out what his reply might have been, because that same voice above suddenly cried out, 'I see them! Get the lamp on them!'

The swamp was abruptly on fire, or that was how it felt. A white light sheared over everything and, had Praeda been looking in that direction, it would have blinded her. The source was a mirrored lantern mounted on the shoulder of one of the Wasp fliers, the sort of device used by explorers heading underground. Its bearer hung well back, but the blazing light made stark silhouettes of his two companions, who were even now advancing. Praeda understood immediately how they had managed to follow a trail at night, for one of them was a Fly cradling a cut-down snapbow.

Amnon rushed at them with a bellow, drawing their attention. Praeda saw the Wasp's sting flash off his breastplate, but then the snapbow spoke again, and punched Amnon off his feet. She shouted incoherently, lifting her weapon and pressing the trigger without even considering whether she had remembered to reload it. Plainly her hands had attended to that task without her recalling, for her shot slapped the closer Wasp off his feet, without a cry, and then she and the Fly were both busy trying to reload ahead of the other, while the lamp-man came rushing in clumsily under the offset weight of the lantern.

And then the light went out, as Praeda heard the glass break. Absolute darkness descended, but her hands kept following the motions: slotting a new bolt into place and winding up the pressure in the battery.

She wanted to call out to Amnon, but that would give the Fly something to aim at. She strained her ears above the monotonous sounds of the swamp, willing her eyes to reaccustom themselves to the night, take advantage of that sliver of moon.

She could make out a little more now, the faint glimmer of water against the deeper darkness of the plants, but of course the Fly's eyes would be so much *better* than hers.

She heard his quiet sound of satisfaction at reacquiring her position, and she loosed in that direction at once, feeling certain that she had missed and that she might as well have shot blind.

There came a grunt not quite from the direction she had aimed her bolt towards, and she stared wide-eyed, trying to make sense of the shadow play before her with the unreliable assistance of the moon. At last it came to her that the shape over *there* must be the Fly, and the straight shaft protruding from it was therefore . . . an arrow.

'Be very still,' Amnon's voice reached her, sounding pained. 'They are all around us.'

Despite the grim news her heart leapt to hear him. 'You were shot,' she reproached him.

'When the Iron Glove make armour, they make it well. The bolt pierced enough to draw blood, but the metal slowed it down,' he murmured back. 'Now be quiet and let me speak to them.'

She had absolutely no sense of there being marsh-kinden around them, those slender Mantis-kinden that called the Jamail delta their home. There could be ten or a thousand of them, silent and invisible, and she would never know for sure.

'You know me,' she heard Amnon announce. 'You are bound by the old covenants. Let us pass.'

Praeda strained her eyes, trying to make out the swift, small forms of the Mantis-kinden. It was all too easy to imagine their flint-tipped spears, their arrowheads of poisoned bone.

'We know you,' came a woman's voice. 'You are Amnon, who was First Soldier, but you are exiled.'

Praeda had known Amnon long enough, now, to sense his stance even in the faint moonlight. He had been ready to prove himself to these people in some savage trial, or to bluff his way back into their good graces, or to threaten the wrath of the Masters of Khanaphes. What he plainly had not expected was that they should be so well informed of his current status, and therefore his lack of the Masters' protection. For the first time in many years Amnon was without a plan.

She raised the snapbow again, realizing as she did so that she had not reloaded it since their skirmish with the Wasps. All around them she heard a faint creaking as a dozen of the Mantids' savage little compound bows were drawn back.

'The Loquae will be pleased with us,' their leader remarked with satisfaction.

What happened next was something that Praeda would never remember clearly.

There was a gasp from the Mantis-kinden, one arrow leaping from its bow to skim directly between Amnon and herself. The Mantids already were backing away, all stealth forgotten, their circle widening and widening, and for no apparent reason, save that . . .

Praeda would later decide that the night's exertions had begun to tell on her by then. She was hot and tired, and possibly poisoned by insect bites or marsh water. It would be easy, in such circumstances, to imagine things.

But she knew with an absolute certainty that there were

three of them. She and Amnon were now standing a little further apart, because someone invisible was standing between them. No – not invisible, because the *Mantis-kinden* had already spotted whoever this third traveller was. They had seen it, and they recognized something in it that overawed and terrified them.

'We will,' the Mantis leader was promising. 'We will lead them to the sea, we swear. We did not know . . . We could not have known . . .'

'What is this? You recognize your oath to Khanaphes, after all?' Amnon demanded.

'There are other oaths,' the Mantis replied, her voice trembling. 'There are other loyalties. We did not know what you brought with you.'

Praeda was feeling light-headed by that point, for while she stared straight ahead at the shadowy Mantis-kinden, she could also glimpse a third figure out of the corner of her eye. It was someone she knew, someone who could not possibly be with them.

'*Che?*' she whispered.

Seventeen

When Varmen had pulled ahead, Thalric found a moment to murmur to Che, 'You look terrible. What's wrong? You're ill?'

'Not ill,' Che assured him. Her dream last night had stayed with her this morning with unwelcome clarity. When she had embarked on this business of pretending to be some kind of magician, she had perhaps anticipated some manner of prophecy, portentous images that she might decode after much thought, and no doubt riddle out too late to be of any use. Achaeos had always spoken of dreams thus, but then he had ranked low by the standards of Moth magicians. Only the fact that he had somehow attracted the notice of the spirits of the Darakyon had marked him out in any way. The ancient Mantis-kinden dead of that abandoned forest had used him as a tool, in their quest to recover the Shadow Box that had held their collective heart, and when he called, they had come.

Che retained the memory with perfect and unwanted clarity: Achaeos touching her mind whilst she fought in Myna and he undertook a ritual in Tharn. Achaeos borrowing strength from her, even as his own failed, and using that same strength to call out to the Darakyon.

And the Darakyon had invaded both their minds, cold and hideous and thorned, and Achaeos, still weak from half-healed wounds, had died.

She had felt every moment of his passing through the bond that had connected them.

She was beginning to wonder if the world of magic would do for her as well. She would have liked to convince herself that it was merely her own imagining that had put her back in Khanaphes, but she found she could not stretch credulity so far.

I cannot be seeing these events as they occur, she complained to herself. *Sometimes it is day in Khanaphes, whilst I sleep here. But last night . . .*

She had never intruded into the dream before, never been anything other than a bodiless observer, watching the Empress and Praeda and the others, and coasting on their thoughts, seeing pictures in their minds, dreams within dreams. But the Mantis-kinden had seen her, as though she had physically been standing between Amnon and Praeda. And then, just for a moment, Praeda had seen her too.

Che had woken up with a start then, and not dared go back to sleep.

I really need to talk to someone knowledgeable about this. But she had already made cautious enquiries of Varmen. Hunting magicians was an old practice here in the Principalities, though the game had grown scarce indeed. During the occupation, the Wasps had singled out any who had claimed such powers, not because they believed the claims, but because supposed seers and mystics were often a focus of rebellion amongst Commonweal loyalists. Since the Empire itself had receded, the new lords of the Principalities had apparently kept up the practice with gusto, and if there were any magicians left, they were certainly not announcing it to the world.

But we near the Commonweal proper, assuming Varmen can get us across the border. I will find all the magicians I want amongst the Dragonfly-kinden.

'What's your plan for getting over the Commonweal border, then?' she asked Varmen.

'We need to hop a barge soon,' he said. 'Easiest way, always.'

When Che looked puzzled he explained, 'They have these canals all over. A couple cross right between the Principalities and the Commonweal proper, see?'

Thalric was frowning. 'Why not just cross by land. Surely that's easier?'

'Oh, you'd think so.' Varmen gave a grin, then repressed it. Since his discovery of Thalric's former role in the Empire, his manner had become odd: now friendly, now standoffish, as though he had to keep reminding himself that he didn't like Thalric any more. Che found his attitude almost endearing. Clearly he was not a man who held grudges well.

And a Wasp, too, like Thalric – and who knows how many other Wasps there are, that I would like if I ever got to know them? She felt a stab of anger at the Empire, and at the Empress who was invading her dreams piecemeal. *These people could be so much more, if they were only allowed, but their kin and their rulers sharpen them into weapons, over and over.*

'What?' said Varmen suspiciously, and she realized that she had been staring at him.

'Nothing,' she told him. 'You were saying about a barge?'

Two days later found them camping beside a slipway, on the banks of a canal that looked as though it had been old when Collegium was built. The great grey stones of its walls had crumbled and fallen away in places, and the water was green and ribboned with weed, dancing with the golden flecks of insects.

'You see, there's a whole load of raiding that goes on across the border, heading both ways,' Varmen was explaining. 'This side, the local captains and what-have-you are all men who have just a little slice of things, pushed to the edge of power, and so they're basically bandits in all but name, stealing from their neighbours 'cos they want something to bargain with, with their betters, right? Only, on the other side there's not much better. No princes or nobles, much, because this is where the army stopped, and the nobles who used to hold all these lands are dead or driven off. So the Commonwealers raid right back, fighting all over the place. Couldn't tell you where the actual border was, it moves about so much.' He pointed along the straight line of the canal, where it was cut into the hillside, a water-road running east–west as far as the horizon. 'There's trade, though, and 'cos the trade comes from the big noises in the Principalities, and goes to the bigger brigands and the dodgier princes on the other side of the border, it's not a good idea for your little fellows around here to get in its way. Nobody wants a hundred soldiers turning up and asking awkward questions, right? So the way things work is that only the big boys use the canals – and anyone on land is fair game.'

'That sounds utterly unworkable,' Che told him. 'How could they be sure nobody would try and rob them?'

'Well, they have guards and the like, and I reckon some of them do get hit, but it must work out all right, most of the time, or they'd not still be doing it.' He shrugged. 'Anyway, the next boat comes past, we'll hop a ride, offer our swords, tell them the . . . you know, the Rekef story or whatever feels right. Then we're over the border, and I'll find me someone wanting an escort back.'

After a day and a night's tense wait, a barge came as promised. Its master was a surprise, neither local nor Wasp but a spindly Skater-kinden, hunched up in a Commonweal-styled robe that failed to hide his fantastically long limbs. He had a face that was all sharp angles, down to the forked beard he affected. Varmen clearly recognized him, and seemed moderately glad to see him, naming him 'Skelling'.

Skelling needed suspiciously little cajoling to take them on as additional guards, though he had half a dozen armed Dragonfly-kinden already on board. While they waited for the barge, Che had spotted two roving parties of what she took for bandits, so she had the impression that the border troubles Varmen had mentioned were now going through an active phase.

The barge itself was a long, graceless thing built of heavy timbers, its hold stuffed with all manner of crates and sacks that Skelling expressly forbade them to meddle with. The vessel moved ponderously, and at first mysteriously. There was a sail but it seemed ludicrously small to shift such a weighty craft, nor did the crew seem to be doing anything to contribute to its motion. The vessel was double-ended, too, and it was clear that, had Skelling wished, they could simply have headed back the way they had come, as the canal had very little current to it.

However, as they moored up after their first day's travel, Che noticed a great disturbance at the vessel's fore, as something broke the surface there. She caught only a glimpse, but divined that it must be some manner of insect nymph trained to the task of hauling. One of the Dragonflies appeared to be the creature's handler, for he had spent the day's journey at the bow, and he now threw chunks of something into the water where the beast had last surfaced. She wondered whether the man possessed that elusive Art that allowed him to speak to the creature.

'Skelling reckons we'll get within the general region of the border tomorrow,' Varmen explained. 'Exactly where the border runs is a matter for debate, as they say, but by dusk we'll be inside the Commonweal proper. Assuming nothing bad happens.'

Che merely nodded, She was holding her dream-catcher in one hand, uncertain what to do with it. Last night she had left the thing inside her pack and, as a result, whatever dreams had come to her had failed to remain in her waking mind. Instead she had suffered all morning with a terrible feeling that *something* was going wrong: that some threat was approaching that she had thus blinded herself to.

But the dream of Praeda and Amnon had frightened her. They had been in great danger, in that dream, and she had been moved to step in. *Or it was just a dream, and none of it happened.* She could not believe that, even for a moment. She had already crossed some line, in coming to their aid, and she knew, beyond understanding why, that she had somehow opened herself up now, made herself somehow both vulnerable and powerful.

Achaeos never spoke of influencing the world thus, through a dream. Nor had any of the old tomes she had read in Collegium mentioned such a thing. *What is going on? Even if I am a magician now, I must be the most wretched and powerless of them all. What is happening to me?*

She put the dream-catcher down, knowing that whatever she did now, it would be the wrong choice.

The next day, Skelling set off before dawn, and everyone knew, without being told, that there would be trouble. The Dragonfly crewmen all had their bows ready strung, with spare quivers of arrows hooked on to the side rail, within easy reach. They also erected boards on either side of the barge, big solid pavises that would give them some protection from inbound arrows. Che had wondered if Varmen would take out his suit of mail, but in the end he obviously decided against it. He would vanish forever into the murky water should he go over the side in so much steel.

Sunrise showed them sparsely wooded canal banks providing ideal ambush territory, and the local brigands were predictable enough to take advantage of it. The first arrow whipping from between the trees actually fell short, a remarkably poor shot for a Commonwealer, but soon there were plenty of other shafts in the air. Skelling's crew and passengers crouched behind the pavises, waiting for a more personal introduction to their assailants. Che had the impression that these wooden shields were Skelling's own innovation, rather than standard fittings aboard Commonweal barges.

– dark stone halls, and only a guttering lamp to guide her –

Che blinked and shook her head uncertainly. The sun was bright in the east behind them, and the sporadic thud-thud-thud of arrows into wood had slowed as their assailants evidently realized they were simply wasting ammunition. Everyone around her was now drawing weapons: the Wasps with their cross-hilted shortswords and the Dragonflies with their punch-swords, whose blades jutted straight out from the knuckle-guard. She hesitantly laid a hand on her own weapon's hilt.

'Che?' she heard Thalric address her, obviously noticing something in her face that worried him.

'I'm . . .' she began, but lacked the words to say just what she was. 'I'm fine,' she said, which turned out to be a gross exaggeration because—

– the slave Gjegevey leading the way, his own eyes proof against the darkness, and how she envied that now. In her dreams, these tombs had been visible by a curious grey half-light, devoid of colours, and she had wondered if that was how the Moth-kinden saw through their blank white eyes –

There was combat all around her. She heard a clatter of steel on steel, and the brief crack and sizzle of Wasp stingshot, the very sound of it striking fear into her stomach, but its wielder was standing right over her, defending her prone form.

'Thalric?' she called out.

'Che, get up!' he shouted down at her, as his hand spoke golden fire again. She heard a man scream, and a dying Dragonfly-kinden dropped to the deck before her eyes, a hole charred into his leather cuirass.

I'm with Wasps, fighting Dragonflies. The thought rattled through her mind. *I was in Khanaphes . . .*

No! I wasn't in Khanaphes. That was the dream, but last night I didn't catch any dreams. I let them go.

Thalric was crouching beside her, in a moment of stillness while the barge's crew and Varmen continued fighting on every side.

'Che, what's wrong?' the Wasp demanded.

'Thalric . . . I don't know. Help me.'

His face said eloquently that he had no possible way to do so.

'The Empress . . .' she started. And then—

*

The walls and floor of this place were slimy, so that each foot set down skidded slightly, then came up trailing threads of ooze. The lamp that Gjegevey had started for her set every surface glistening unhealthily.

They had been underground for long enough that Seda knew it would be dawn already above, but down here was a labyrinth of vast halls, lined with statues, every wall inscribed with the ancient glyphs of the Khanaphir. For hours they had walked, at first with the old Woodlouse choosing their path, and later with Seda herself taking the lead. By then she realized why they were finding nothing but empty chambers: the power here had been turning them aside.

'Stop,' she ordered the old Woodlouse.

'We have been travelling for some, mm, considerable time,' he admitted. 'One might almost think that we were, ah, going round in circles.'

'It is a test,' she decided. 'One I do not appreciate, but I shall pass it nonetheless.'

'There is, hm, a great deal of, ah, latent power here,' Gjegevey conjectured cautiously. 'I would hesitate to . . .'

'Yes, you would – and you would be wise to. I am of a different order, however. I am the Empress of the Wasps.'

'I am not sure such titles will, ahm, mean a great deal to our hosts.' The Woodlouse-kinden's hollow eyes glittered in the lamplight.

'Then I shall enlighten them,' she replied pleasantly, and thrust a hand in the air as though grasping for something invisible.

The power awoke in her, digging its roots into the stonework of this place, then feeding, cannibalistic, on the ages of magic laid down here when the world was younger. She felt her blood stir and sing with all the borrowed life and youth she had taken into herself. In my dream she *gained an audience with the lords of this place, and so shall I.*

For a moment the monolithic grip of the place seemed immovable, and she was worried that she might not have enough reserves of strength within herself, for then her only option would be to seek the blood of another. And to lose Gjegevey would be a true tragedy, for he had been one of her very first supporters – since before she had even come to her throne.

But then she had hold of it and she twisted, with little finesse, but drawing upon that strength that she had been given, to make up for all that she had lost.

She felt the Masters of Khanaphes, sensed their slow minds come to a decision, and then they struck—

Che opened her eyes, expecting to find the fight still ongoing, but there was no sound of it. She was not even on the barge.

'Ah . . .' She hurt, but it was all inside. She bore no wounds.

At her faint sound, Thalric was kneeling again beside her. 'Che!'

'What's happening?'

'You tell me! You were . . . it was as though you were sleeping, but I couldn't wake you.'

She sat up painfully, seeing that they were camped beside the canal: Thalric, Varmen, Skelling and his crew. The crew was two men short, she noticed. 'We're . . .'

'Right up near the border, in so far as there's a definite "border" at all,' Thalric confirmed. 'Che, what in the wastes happened to you?'

'Thalric, she's there.'

He opened his mouth to question her, but the pieces fell into place before he had to.

'She's seeking the Masters,' Che told him urgently, as though there was something he could do about it. The world around her now seemed different, but then she realized that it was her senses that had changed. She had become charged with magic, connected to the world's weave like a spider at the heart of its web, feeling the strands tug and twitch. Not only was she still aware of Seda as a dull and distant ache in her mind, but she felt that, if she could turn her mind *just so*, then she would be able to sense each and every magician, each ancient site of power across the hills of the Commonweal and beyond, even to the furthest horizon. Her mind remained locked inside her skull, but only just.

'Thalric, I can . . .'

But an old, familiar taint had just touched the edge of her consciousness, snapping her back to the business at hand.

Is it . . .. is it him . . .?

Pressing on Thalric's shoulder for purchase, she stood up abruptly, staring wildly about. For a moment there she thought she had caught a glimpse of . . .

Tisamon . . .

Why is it so hard for me to remember what I came here for? Her quest to control her dreams, to know more about the magic that seemed to be engulfing her, that was secondary. She had come to save Tynisa from the spectre of her father. Only now did her roving mind fix on that task again – and only because she sensed the Mantis-kinden's ghost ahead of them, for the very first time since inside the tombs of Khanaphes.

There was no mistaking the touch. She had carried that twisted presence in her mind for a long time, believing it to be the bitter shade of her lover, Achaeos. Only through the power of the Masters of Khanaphes had the truth come out – and by that time the creature was freed from her. Immediately, Tisamon had set off to find his daughter. In life he had been an intimidating man, a fierce killer whose life was hedged about by an untenably harsh code of conduct that had, in the end, left him no other goal but to seek his own death. Oh, he had been an honourable man, and loyal to a fault, but the spectre that Che had faced seemed to have been pared down, cut away until only that self-destructive slayer remained.

Che reached out, trying to ascertain how far ahead the spectre was, though in truth she was unsure whether such a concept had any real meaning for what Tisamon now was. Again, as she touched him, there was a feeling of bitterness and ashes, but this time she heard his voice inside her head.

What will you do, Beetle child?

I will stop you, she told him flatly. *Tynisa does not deserve this.*

She is mine. *What can you do to stop me?*

From nowhere, or perhaps from some forgotten conversation with Achaeos, the word surfaced. *I shall bind you in a tree perhaps. I shall lock you away.*

I shall kill you before you have the chance, came his cold reply.

Will you so? She had thought long and hard on how she might compel this creature, on the journey from Khanaphes. *Would you kill Stenwold's kin?*

The silence that followed told her that she was right; that some vestige of the man he had once been still remained within Tisamon.

She gathered her strength then, while he seemed uncertain, for she was not sure herself how long such a leash would hold him. She tried to reach out again. *Almost, almost there, and then at least Tynisa can find her own way . . .*

—she was hiding under her bed, because she knew the bad man was coming, the man that had called her father 'friend' and never meant it—

'No!' cried Che, feeling the shade of Tisamon slip away from her. 'Thalric!'

'I'm right here,' the Wasp snapped in frustration. 'Che, what is happening to you?'

—steps echoed outside the children's bedchamber, and the door pushed open—

The world was sliding away from her, or she was falling aside from it, as though some giant hand had tilted it upon its side. She clutched impotently at Thalric, trying to stay with him. 'Hold me! Don't let me go, please!'

His arms were about her, but she could feel his bafflement in every movement. 'Che, I'm right here . . .'

'I'm losing you . . .' she got out.

And then she was gone.

Eighteen

Airborne war has been conducted for too long by airship. The fates of our Starnest *and the Collegiate* Triumph *show how foolish that is. The age of the war-dirigible is past. Orthopters and fixed wings will rule the skies . . .*

Varsec's treatise, *Towards an Efficient Mechanized Air Force*, was a light enough burden in Angved's hands, but he found that if he read it for too long, his fingers began to tremble ever so slightly. Between the cheaply printed words, History was waiting. Angved wondered how much he would be able to sell this crude copy for, by the time he finally retired. The book itself would be required reading for the Engineering Corps, but a discerning collector would no doubt advance a considerable sum for one of its very few first editions. He turned the page, needing no lamp: the thick material of his tent still admitted enough light in the mid-afternoon to read by.

He could not imagine the promises and bribes or the favours Varsec must have called in to get this work printed in even so coarse a form. Yet the man had known what he had been about, for both his future and the Empire's were set out in that book. The words had secured the former, and would now go about building the latter.

Approximately half the Solarnese air fleet was composed of orthopters, compared to perhaps eight out of ten among the

Imperial flying machines. At the end of the battle, according to my personal observations, perhaps two fixed-wing fliers remained operational – with the entire balance of the surviving machines on both sides being orthopters. It is my experience and that of every fellow aviator I have spoken with, and the inescapable conclusion from examining the reports of other conflicts where flying machines have confronted one another, that mobile-winged aeromotive craft have a substantial superiority in manoeuvrability that will, all things being equal, give them command of the air.

Angved was no aviator, but then Varsec had not been writing for his fellow pilots. He had been writing instead for the technically educated body of the Engineers as a whole, those men like Colonel Lien that he would have to convince. Still, his cool language somehow managed to convey the strength of his belief in the future. Angved looked down over the man's figures, anecdotes, facts and comparisons: airships could carry greater loads but were too vulnerable to aerial attack; the heliopters that the Imperial army had relied on from the first could achieve a delicacy of positioning in the air but were slow and cumbersome compared with other fliers, unable to escape or give chase and incapable of engaging in the aerial duelling that Varsec was a personal exponent of.

Angved flicked on towards the book's heart, those key paragraphs that had set his own heart racing.

And yet the demands of a future aerial war are more than simply about which flying machine will outperform its rivals in an airborne fight. There is a world of potential in air war that remains untapped, because the mechanical capabilities of the machines that we rely on, even our most sophisticated designs such as the Spearflight orthopters that were used at Solarno, are too limited. While they are so greatly limited in range, orthopters will only ever hold a supporting role. The fuel demands of mobile-winged flight are great, resulting in an air force tied closely to a ground base of operations: a flying force with clipped wings, therefore. Conversely, it has been repeatedly demonstrated that fixed-wing engines are capable of a far greater fuel efficiency, and therefore a greater striking range from their base, had they only the ability to survive against enemy air resistance once they arrived . . .

After that, the book descended into theory and dream: Varsec's hypotheses, his 'if only' thoughts, his tentative sketches of joints and mechanisms, his list of requisite developments that would make his future come to pass.

If I had not come along, with what I know, he would be in a prison cell still, or dead. He had spoken with Varsec on that very subject, and they both knew it, just as the reverse was surely true. Their projects were mutually reinforcing innovations, and they had fallen into the hands of ambitious Colonel Lien, who was aware that the Engineers *should* have been taking a greater place on the Imperial stage, but had previously been at a loss as to how to further his cause. The resurrection of Drephos, not dead but only defected, could have been the death knell for the Engineers' rise, with the Empire coming to lean more and more on outside inventions and becoming dependent on creatures like the loathed halfbreed. Even though Drephos seemed to have won the argument as far as ground-based machines went, however, Varsec and Angved had given Lien just enough ammunition to paint the skies of the future in pure black and gold.

A soldier tugged the tent flap open a little, but without looking inside. 'Sir, the enemy's moving. You said you wanted to see.'

'I did, thank you, Lieutenant.' Angved closed the book and stuffed it back into one of his belt pouches. A true artificer could never have too many pouches.

He let his wings carry him to the wooden parapet so that he could get a commanding look at the surrounding terrain. There he discovered the book's author sitting in a folding chair, one hand holding a little board with a sheet of paper tacked on to it, the other wielding a pencil. When not revolutionizing the world of mechanical flight, Varsec fancied himself as a landscape artist.

The landscape here was not what Angved considered inspirational, however. They had made considerable progress towards the heart of the Nem, the desert lying between Khanaphes and the cities of the Exalsee. Angved knew it well, for he had lived out here for tendays as a guest of the violent and unruly Many of Nem, the local Scorpion-kinden, while his then commander had armed them and pointed them towards Khanaphes. The Imperial force was now in what was referred to as the mid-Nem, which the Scorpions claimed as their own territory. The fringe of the desert remained a constant skirmishing zone between the Many and their neighbours, whereas the desert's heart . . .

Well, perhaps we'll see. They had made remarkable progress inwards, and the first drilling site they had chosen was nudging the inner edge of the mid-desert, closing on the central reaches. The Scorpions would not go there, so the ruined cities remained free of their scavenging, and Angved only knew that they feared it. *Well, we shall see just how much they fear it, then.*

Setting up their machinery where they had could not but be viewed as provocation by the Many, and Angved was surprised only that it had taken the locals three clear days to put a force together. *Of course, the Many aren't that 'many' any more, not after the Khanaphes debacle.* Not only had the Scorpions failed to take the city, despite the Empire handing them every advantage, but they had ended up getting a few thousand of their warriors killed, which was a serious blow to their overall population. *And in the end that's worked out nicely.*

Extending his glass, he put his eye to it and let his gaze rake the sandscape, watching the host of Scorpion-kinden advance determinedly, with stragglers still coming out of the dunes to catch up with them. Angved reckoned that there might be perhaps six hundred, a sizeable force indeed, almost three times that of the Wasp Light Airborne currently ranged against them. The Nemean tactics were plain: they were fanning out in a loose crescent already, obviously intending to sweep away anything that stood in their path before pillaging the camp, destroying, killing and stealing whatever presented itself.

The camp itself was not overly ready to oblige them. The Wasps had assembled a travelling fort, the sort of ready-made fortifications that had served the Second Army so well on its march to Collegium during the war. The walls that the soldiers had fitted together were angled, barbed with stakes, defendable by a fraction of the soldiers available, and easily large enough to encompass the drilling and pumping engines. Angved had discussed the best means of defence with the captain in charge of the Airborne, however, and it had been agreed that cringing behind walls was not the Imperial way.

Two-thirds of their Airborne were now standing in loose ranks between the camp and the Scorpions, and Angved knew that they would look like a pitiful force to the eyes of the locals, even those who had fought alongside Wasps at Khanaphes. The Scorpion force was already breaking up into individual war bands, he noticed, the main thrust gaining speed as it rushed for the camp's defenders, but substantial numbers breaking off left and right, looking to encircle their enemy and fall on them from all sides. Angved noted a remarkable amount of cavalry there – or rather insectry, as the proper term went, for horses were unknown in the Nem. Given his choice of animals, a scorpion would never have been his chosen mount – or any beast that might impale the back of his head if he had to rein it in suddenly. However, the Many of Nem had long ago designed a sort of offset saddle to put them out of harm's way, and now a full score of these creatures were scuttling along on either flank, not much faster than a running man, but considerably more dangerous.

'They make quite a show, don't they,' Varsec remarked mildly. Angved glanced down to see that he had sketched a bristling dark stain across the desertscape that he had already pencilled out: no details but just a riot of aggressive motion worked into the simple lines of the drawing.

'A show is all they'll make,' Angved declared.

'I see more than a few crossbows.'

The engineer shrugged. 'They have no idea, none at all.'

Abruptly, in almost perfect unison, the Wasp soldiers out beyond the walls were airborne. No doubt a few crossbow quarrels were even now winging their way, but the Scorpion-kinden had no experience of hitting targets in the air, and it was unlikely that any of them would be learning any useful lessons here for the future. The Imperial force split off into four groups, as the drill required. Two detachments flew left and right, in order to threaten the Scorpions' own flank, and the balance ended up in two clusters *behind* the charging mass of the Many. A good two-thirds of the Scorpions ignored them and continued on towards the walls, while the balance turned to face their relocated enemy.

'I notice you haven't sketched *that*.' Angved pointed out the single most dramatic feature of their surroundings. To the west stood a great ruin, half sand-swallowed, its maze of walls and the shells of its buildings worn down by the wind, buried in some places and stark like unearthed bones in others, the whole giving the impression of a nest of broken skulls. It meant they had come close enough to the desert's heart to see one of the cities of the Inner Nem.

'It's worth a picture all its own.' Varsec put down his drawing board with care and took up a snapbow. All around them, those of the Airborne left in the compound were already sighting. Angved himself, as commanding officer, had decided it was beneath his dignity to actually do any of the killing today. And besides, he was not much of a shot.

Not that long ago the Empire had introduced the Scorpions to their future, gifting them with leadshotters and crossbows and rousing them against their ancient enemies, the Khanaphir. The joke was that the future the Scorpions had then reached out for was already in the Wasps' past. There was not an Imperial soldier on the field or behind the walls who had not been training for the best part of a year with a snapbow, and most of them had been given plenty of chance to practise during the Empress's campaigns against the various pretender governors.

Angved had no love for the Scorpions – in fact he had a considerable amount of dislike for them – but even he flinched a little when the first volley of snapbow shot struck home and slapped the Scorpion charge to a standstill by killing them three-deep all the way across their front line. At the same time, the other detachments also began loosing their weapons, sergeants shouting out the orders so that their weapons discharged all at once, not as individual pinpricks but a collective hammerblow.

'At will,' bawled the lieutenant commanding the defence, and the Wasp snapbowmen picked their targets, even as the mass of Scorpions seethed and milled. Varsec raised his own weapon, aiming along the length of the barrel with an artificer's exacting care before loosing a shot, then calmly reloading and recharging.

Out beyond the wall, the Scorpion flanks had caved in, leaving a scatter of dead men and animals. Angved read the patterns in the corpses as though he was a seer, noting where the insectry had tried to charge the newly landed Wasps, only to have their targets simply take to the air again, shooting all the while. The two detachments at the rear had been exacting a similar toll, preventing the Many from retreating to regroup. *In all honesty we could wipe them out to a man, right now, and I'm being too clever by half,* he told himself, but the plan was laid, and he was going to have his curiosity assuaged whether he liked it or not.

One of the Wasp detachments waited until the Scorpions pulled together some semblance of unity, and then they broke away, taking wing and making a wide circle until they had landed within the walls of the encampment. Abruptly the deadly box had been compromised. The Scorpions now had somewhere to go, away from the lethal needles of the snapbow darts.

They were reluctant to take it, though, and Angved was not surprised. Once they were on the move the survivors of the Many repeatedly tried to break north and south, but the Wasps moved faster, always setting down in front of them and killing a few more – herding the Scorpions ever west.

To the west lay ruin, the half-hidden carcass of a dead city, and Angved wanted to see what would happen when the savages were finally forced to confront their fears.

He had to wait for the captain's report, for the ruins were some distance away, and by then there was so much dust raised that his glass could not penetrate it. Still, it was not quite dusk when the officer finally presented himself, saluting smartly, as though Angved had not been working as a menial in a factory only tendays before, when Varsec was a prisoner in a cell.

They received the report on the wall, looking out at the ruins that were now slowly sinking into twilight as though the desert itself was swallowing them up.

'What happened when the Scorpions reached there?' Angved asked.

'Not that many of them did, sir. A surprising amount tried to turn and fight, again and again. They were desperate to avoid being driven there. I'd estimate no more than forty or fifty of them reached the first stones.'

'And then?'

The captain's expression was that of a man without much imagination being faced with something that troubled him nonetheless. 'Screaming, sir.'

Angved frowned, and Varsec murmured, 'Does that pass for a report in the army, these days?'

'I apologize, sir. It was difficult to make out what happened, and those of my men I've questioned tell contradictory stories.

The Scorpions scattered amongst the buildings, losing all cohesion, as if each was looking for a different place to hide. Then we heard them start screaming, just some of them, then others. None of them for very long. I did my best to keep some in sight, but amongst the ruins it was difficult. Many of the structures there seem relatively intact, some almost completely so, and I thought I saw . . .' There was a pause, signifying a soldier trying to couch his experience in permitted language. 'Movement, sir. Terribly swift movement between buildings. Something large and fast. Others have reported the same . . .' His tone indicated that there was more, but that it would require prompting.

'Speak, Captain,' Angved duly ordered.

'One squad hasn't returned, sir. Sergeant Stasric and his people didn't come back with us.'

'You passed on my orders for nobody to enter the ruins?' Angved asked sternly.

'I did, sir, word for word.'

'What's this Stasric like, would you say?'

A diplomatic pause. 'He is a man who seizes opportunities as they come, sir. He has been reprimanded in the past.'

Angved and Varsec exchanged glances. 'Any other casualties, Captain?' the aviator asked.

'Eleven men lost, sir, all to enemy crossbows,' the captain confirmed. 'Twenty-one in total, including Stasric's men.'

Twenty-one dead to six hundred of theirs, Angved considered. A mere skirmish, but the numbers would look good when sent home. 'Have your men stay ready, since we can expect further attacks by the Many. They're a stupid, brutal people.'

Midnight was approaching when the watch lieutenant awoke Angved, sounding panicked. 'Something's outside the wall, sir.'

It took a blinking and blurred moment of recollection before the Engineer remembered where he was and what he was doing there. For a moment he had thought he was back accompanying the *first* Khanaphir expedition, making war on the city on behalf of the Many of Nem, rather than the other way around.

'The Scorpions are back?' he demanded, shrugging his way into a leather cuirass and locating his sword.

'Sir, we're . . . we're not sure what it is. The sentries don't think so, sir.'

'We're under attack?'

'Not yet, sir.'

Angved sighed, putting him down as the sort of overexcitable type who should never be left in charge of a night watch, for the good of everyone else's sleep. Still, now that he was awake, it seemed prudent to go and investigate what had spooked the watchmen. He dragged a woollen cloak over his shoulders to keep out the night chill, and shouldered his way out of his tent.

There was barely any moon, and only the torches and lanterns of the camp repelled the night. Angved tugged his cloak closer about him and let the lieutenant lead him to the walls, where a flick of his wings got him up on to the parapet.

'I don't see anything,' he grumbled, scowling into the darkness.

'Report, soldier,' the lieutenant instructed, stepping back and patently hoping thus to disappear from the angry major's notice.

'There's something big out there, sir,' one of the sentries said promptly. 'It's been back and forth three times now.'

'An animal,' suggested Angved dismissively.

'The only glimpse I had of it, it seemed like a man, sir. Or at least a little like a man. Most of the other sentries have seen it, too.' Even as he spoke, there came a shout from further along the wall, and Angved bustled over there to peer out beyond the range of the camp lights.

He saw it then, not very clearly but enough to confirm all that the sentry had said. The movement, as it slunk back into the night, was unpleasant – human but not quite, its limbs out of proportion, not quite on two legs, but not quite on all fours.

The Imperials exchanged unhappy glances.

'What was it up to, that time?' the watch lieutenant asked. 'It was . . . digging, was it?'

'Can you see something still out there?' one of the other sentries wondered, squinting. 'Looks like it left something behind.'

'Get me a strong flier with a lantern!' Angved snapped. Once this order was obeyed, he continued, 'You, fly out there and drop the lantern down where we saw it.'

The soldier looked none too happy at this, but the Imperial Light Airborne did not admit to being scared of the dark, so he kicked off from the wall and swooped in, making the pass as swiftly as he could and letting the lantern drop from ten feet up, ending tipped on its side on the sand, still burning.

At the sight revealed, one of the sentries swore. The rest were silent.

They could see a neat pyramid of human heads out there: Wasp-kinden heads, without a doubt. Angved felt quite equally sure that, asking around, he would find someone able to recognize the twisted features of Sergeant Stasric. Each of the expressions that the lantern picked out suggested that their deaths had not come quickly or easily.

At the far edge of the lantern's reach, something shifted, a hulking, long-armed thing with its knuckles resting on the ground, its massive fists clublike and thorned. It seemed as big as a Mole Cricket-kinden, but thinner and longer of limb. The head jutted from between broad shoulders heavily knotted with muscle, and although the eyes glinted, even the lantern light seemed reluctant to illuminate its face.

Angved felt its attention focus on him, as though it had somehow managed to identify him as the man in charge. His soldiers were thoroughly spooked, he knew, but they would still launch an attack on his word. And besides, this thing must surely be mortal, susceptible to sword and sting and snapbow bolt.

But still . . . 'Message understood!' he called out. 'You'll see no more of us in your city. That's not what we're here for. And we'll see no more of you, either. Agreed?'

His voice seemed to roll out for ever across the desert, as if the only sound in the world. He was aware that most of the camp was awake by now, with eyes on him alone.

The thing crouched even lower, leaning forward a little, and Angved caught a brief, stomach-twisting glimpse that made him wish its face had stayed hidden. The skull-like contours, that brutal tusked jaw . . . and yet those eyes were so human that they seemed to be agonized and appalled by the monstrosity that they were set in. Then it was gone, and it was Angved who cursed, this time, as it moved off, vanishing like wind and shadow in an instant.

'I dearly hope it understood you, sir,' said the lieutenant, standing at his elbow. Angved had feared that his actions might have made him seem weak before his men, but he realized then that he had gained their unexpected approval. Not one of them had wanted to go out and fight that thing, whatever it was, and no amount of tactical or technological superiority would change that.

There was nobody else at the camp either disobedient enough or venturesome enough to go treasure hunting, and their nocturnal visitor remained conspicuous by its absence, although Angved himself set up a searchlight for the night watch, just in case.

Subsequently it took them a single day to get the drill working, and a day after that to start the pumps. The machinery was designed to work in primitive conditions, sandstorms included, it being solid Beetle-kinden workmanship from Sonn that could survive being dragged all over the world by rough and ready Imperial soldiers. They were soon packing barrels with the mineral oil that generations of Scorpions had used for lighting lamps. Angved remembered them explaining its properties to him: wood was hard to come by, but the oil welled up in numerous places around the desert. If ignited, it would burn for days.

He had never come across mineral oil that would burn so steadily, in the quantities the Scorpions decanted into the bowls of their lamps. He had performed his tests and that simple artificer's inquisitiveness had led inexorably to this current pumping operation – and the similar stations that would soon be set up across the Nem.

He sent a messenger back to Khanaphes, and a few days later the first airship appeared, sailing serenely across the disc of the glaring sun, then scudding sideways in the crosswind as it tacked lower. Angved had the filled barrels ready for collection, and the airship crew and his own off-duty soldiers made quick work of hoisting them on board the vessel, which sagged a fraction lower in the sky with each additional load. The pilot brought news, too, together with supplies for the men and even three Dragonfly-kinden slave girls. The visit made a pleasant change from the brisk orders and hard looks that Angved had grown used to.

With evening coming on, he and Varsec stood outside his tent and watched the airship leave with its first consignment. The pumps were still going and everyone would have to learn to live with their noise, but the two engineers themselves were used to that sort of privation.

'There goes the future,' Angved observed, holding up a bottle to the fading light. It was good Imperial brandy, and the label denoted a vintage that he had only heard of, never been able to afford. 'If I were a more suspicious man, I'd think Colonel Lien was trying to poison us both with this.' The bottle had been marked for the two majors' personal attention.

Varsec smiled and shook his head. '*General* Lien hates the pair of us, as upstarts and troublemakers,' he mused, 'but he also knows full well that he needs us. Besides, the Empress knows our names, Angved. We can't just be made to vanish so someone else takes credit for our work. And Lien knows that I could have written how the Aviation Corps shouldn't be subject to the Engineers, but I was loyal enough not to. This is him saying that so long as we keep to our side of the deal, he'll keep his, *Major* Angved.'

'Why, thank you, *Major* Varsec.' Angved plucked from his toolstrip something that had not been particularly intended for extracting corks from bottles, but which artificers had been using for that purpose for two generations. The brandy was darker than blood, rich and smoky on the tongue, burning at the back of the throat.

'They're training the new pilots,' Varsec observed softly, once he had taken a first sip.

Angved remembered that other proposition to be found in Varsec's little book, regarding the sort of man they would need at the controls of one of his revolutionary new fliers. 'I didn't think they'd go for it,' he said, his tone hushed. 'You've put yourself out of a job, you know. Didn't you use to be an aviator yourself?'

'For me, it was never the flying, just the fact of us having the machines. I'll not miss it,' Varsec replied, although there was a touch of regret in his voice. 'Still, there will be plenty of jobs for the old batch of pilots – civilian roles, support roles. It's just that for our new type of air combat, we need the new type of men.'

His proposals had shocked Angved, visionary to the point of lunacy. 'It's going to be a very different place by the time we get home.'

'It was always going to be,' Varsec said philosophically. 'The only difference is that *we* will have made it so. The future, Angved – we're making the future right here, you and I. Even if nobody remembers our names, and the historians jabber on about how General Lien and Empress Seda revolutionized the world, it will be us, only us, behind it all.' He raised his bowl, and clinked it against Angved's own. 'The future,' he repeated.

'Our future,' Angved agreed.

He sipped his brandy. Life was good.

Nineteen

She heard the footsteps. She was still awake past midnight, on this night of all nights. How had she known? There was no explaining it, but a premonition had needled her and jabbed her, and filled her stomach with sinking dread – a premonition that the end of her little world was coming.

She was Seda, youngest daughter of the Wasp Emperor, a child of eight years old.

The footsteps were in no hurry. There was shouting elsewhere in the palace, but the man, that death-handed man, idled down the corridor towards their door. She sat up in her bed. Distantly, someone was cursing. Distantly, there was weeping, fighting. Slave sounds usually, but somehow she knew that it was free men and women who now wept and fought, on this particular night.

She slipped out of her bed, shivering, her bare feet cold on the stone. It was always cold here, the sun's fleeting warmth stolen away as quickly as it came, but there was a deeper cold now, and it came with those footsteps.

She knew who was approaching and what he intended. She knew what had happened: the terrible event that had hung in the balance for three days, and now was done.

Father? But he was dead, of course. His death had brought the footsteps.

Eight years old and intelligent enough to know what had

occurred, and what must follow. For a moment she considered the window, but she had no Art to climb or fly with.

Stripped of any options, she hunched down at her own bedside, hearing the footsteps stop at the door of her room.

In the bed across from hers, her brother Tarvec stirred, but slept on.

She retreated and retreated, but the only place to go was beneath the bed. When she had been very young, she had believed, after a vivid nightmare, that a creature dwelt there – red-eyed and its mouthparts honed into a long, hollow stiletto – waiting for her to sleep so that it could drink her blood. Now the space beneath the bed became her refuge, for the monsters were already abroad.

The door opened. There had been guards posted outside. Perhaps they still stood there, but they made no attempt to hinder the footsteps coming into the room.

Tap, tap, tap. Army-issue boots approached the side of her bed, and she pictured him staring at the thrown-back blanket. She tried not to breathe, tried to summon up some of the hiding Art that some of the lesser kinden practised. *Go away. There is nothing for you here.*

Then he was crouching, and she could not but open her eyes and look into his face. It was not a bad face, in itself: a Waspkinden man with receding, greying hair. A soldier, like so many others. An officer. Her father's friend.

But not today. She pressed herself back against the wall, as far from him as she could get, and jabbed an empty palm out towards him, as though she possessed the stinging Art that had made her people the greatest kinden in the world. She was only eight, though, and not so very precocious as all that. The intruder's face merely twisted in dry humour.

She heard Tarvec stirring, sitting up, her brother asking, 'Maxin, what—?'

Maxin's face vanished from her view as he stood up, and she heard the sharp crackle of his sting, a truncated exclamation as Tarvec died.

Then Maxin was kneeling to peer at her again. Was he making a decision on his own, or recalling instructions given to him by that other brother, her eldest brother – the one about to assume the throne.

The Rekef officer stood up again and she heard his footsteps cross the room. She breathed a little easier, because now she remembered how the rest of the dream went. He would go and murder her other siblings, a second brother and two other sisters, so that, out of the Emperor Alvdan the First's progeny, only the eldest boy and youngest girl would survive the night. Over the next tenday, eleven other Wasp-kinden – children or young men and women – would also die for the crime of having a mother whom the Emperor had found beguiling. Twenty-nine halfbreeds of various part-Wasp ancestries would follow them. Maxin was as thorough as the late Emperor had been lustful.

Then the third Emperor of the Wasps would take the throne, ushering in a new era.

She was so lost in this recollection that she almost failed to notice how the footsteps had not left the room. Maxin was standing at the doorway, and she knew he was looking back towards her.

A few hammering heartbeats before he moved again. He was coming *back*. But it hadn't been like this. He had gone off about his bloody-handed business, she recalled. But now he had changed his mind? Not for General Maxin the restricting bonds of history. This time he would guarantee his new Emperor's eternal reign by killing the only remaining threat to his power.

She was already screaming when he reached the bed, screaming as he dragged her out from under it, pushing her back towards the window with a hand about her throat. He was older now, with lines of cruelty and ambition written across his face which were the wages of eight years of service to the man he had made Emperor. He was just how she remembered him.

In the centre of the storm of terror wheeling about inside her head there remained one constant point, and she struggled for it like a swimmer in deep water. *Just how I remember you? But if you will be* that *man, then let us renew our old acquaintance, Maxin.*

With a great effort, she cast off her eight-year-old self enough to find the fabric of the dream around her and wrench at it, using strength without finesse. *Give me visions, will you? Then I shall have some of my own.*

The face of Maxin twisted and leered before her, and his grip was tight about her throat. With a fierce lunge of her will, she conjured hands on his shoulders, dragging him off her. In a moment she had squirmed from his grasp, watching the hated Rekef general hauled away by the two protectors that she had conjured from her own mind and pressed into service. Only one of them had been present for the real Maxin's death, but it pleased her to have the two of them side by side: Thalric, her regent, and Brugan, her new Lord General of the Rekef.

For a moment she found herself fighting back and forth for control, sensing the dream world all around her try to suborn her new agents, to make the two newcomers a part of the same nightmare. But they were *new*, and reacting to the new was most definitely not the strong point of Khanaphes.

Thalric had arched General Maxin over with a knee in the small of the man's back, thrusting his arms outwards so that Maxin could not sting. She saw Brugan's knife glint just as it had when the real Maxin had met his end.

'Hold,' she commanded, because if this was to be her dream, she would rip all the joy she could from it. She approached the straining Maxin, with her palm held out, watching him physically diminish, from ogre to a wretched old man weeping for mercy.

She took a deep breath and summoned her Art, and then her hand was blazing, again and again, the bolts of golden fire striking Maxin over and over, searing and crisping the flesh of his face, smashing its way into his skull.

She recognized another trap here: she could become just as lost in hollow triumphs as she could in terrors. So, instead, she turned away, banished it all from her mind and faced her unseen audience.

Are you satisfied? she asked the invisible watchers, and stepped out from the dream.

Che had a moment of clarity then, because she had been there herself: not with Maxin and the knife, but experiencing a horror that was personal to her. She had broken away from it, just as the Wasp Empress had done, which must mean . . .

And now she saw that well-remembered hall, high-ceilinged, with its pillars sculpted into surreal abominations blending the human and the insect. Braziers of blue-green fire leapt and guttered and, where Che herself had stood not so long ago, there was a single figure: Seda, supreme ruler of the Wasps.

An old man was curled up at her feet, and she knelt beside him, laying a hand on his shoulder and speaking softly until he twitched and cried out, as he escaped from whatever personal torment he also had been suffering. As with Che before her, Seda rescued her companion from the nightmares of the Masters of Khanaphes.

And Che heard the words in Seda's mind, her private thoughts: *It is just as I remember it, from the dream.*

A sense of dislocation paralysed her. *Who is dreaming, then? Was she with me all the way, when I came here before. Is she even now watching me watch her? When is this happening?*

Only when Gjegevey was able to regain his feet did Seda even spare a glance for the grand figures that towered over her. Three of them had come there to put her to the test: two women and a man, their voluptuous figures naked and clad only in a thin curtain of glistening slime. Che knew them well, their kinden and as individuals. These were the ancient Slug-kinden whose hands had guided the other peoples of the world out of the darkness of barbarism, or so they claimed. They had raised their great city of Khanaphes to be a wonder of the world. They had lived through the long days of their power, before the records of any save perhaps the Moths, who remembered a great deal else they never spoke of. When the great Inapt powers – the Spiders and Mosquitos and Moth-kinden – were struggling for dominance in that long-ago world, the Masters of Khanaphes were already in decline, their city subsiding into history as they retreated from a drying earth and the harsh sun, into the refuge of these subterranean crypts. Whether or not they were once the great lords and patrons of the world as they claimed, was lost to time, but one thing Che was sure of: within their own domain they preserved much of the ancient magic of the Days of Lore, which elsewhere had fled before the coming of the modern world.

And Seda stared them in the eye. 'Enough games,' said the Empress of the Wasps.

Thalric gazed out over the irregular hills that had been cut into steps for agriculture long ago, and repaired every year by a chain of farmers, father to son, following traditions that had been ancient before the Wasp-kinden ever dreamt of Empire.

'That's it, then?'

'Well, maps bicker, but just about,' Varmen confirmed. They were in the Commonweal now: the sovereign realm of the Monarch of the Dragonflies, and no longer just the pirated Principalities that had become such a twisted hybrid of two hostile cultures.

Skelling had turned back now, his business done. He had simply moved the draught insect from one end of his boat to the other, and the barge was already out of sight, leaving Thalric here where he had wanted to go.

But that, of course, was not really true. It was Che who had wanted to get here. It had been her plan, entirely. Thalric had no fond memories of the Commonweal, and he rather suspected that it had none of him either.

At first Che had been so full of talk about rescuing her sister, and then later about magic, and even about the Empress – though that was a subject Thalric had no wish to dwell on. She had carried him along with her because she had possessed a purpose, whereas he had none of his own. And because he had grown fond of her, and because they had more in common than he had with either his kin or kinden. From the interrogation chambers of Myna to the tombs of Khanaphes, they had grown close.

He knelt beside her, trying to see some clue that would help him unravel her, but she remained a mystery. She had not woken again since after the attack on the barge. She barely seemed to breathe. He had no way to help her, or even to understand what was wrong.

Varmen had not departed, not yet. He and his uncomplaining little pack-beetle were forever on the point of heading off, but somehow each new dawn saw him still hanging around.

Che refused to eat. Thalric had managed to force a little water down her, but surely not enough to keep her alive. Instead, whatever was holding her in this unconscious state seemed to be sustaining her as well. That was yet another thing he could not understand.

'Suon Ren,' he murmured. 'That's where she was heading.'

'Principality of Roh. East of here. Canals go to it,' Varmen explained.

Thalric looked at him almost with annoyance. 'How do you *know?* Why would *you* know a thing like that?'

'Been three times in the Commonweal now, since the war. You pick stuff up.' Varmen shrugged. 'Besides, I remember when we were marching on Shon Fhor, just before all that trouble back home kicked off and we ended up with that treaty. I was a sergeant, so I got to see the maps sometimes. We were going to surround Shon Fhor and scoop the Monarch out like eating an oyster, and the Fourth were going to press on south of the lake, to Suon Ren, and finish off taking the principality.

'Stead of which, everything fell apart round Maynes way. We lost our supply line, and wiser heads reckoned we'd bitten off enough for now on. Always wondered why we didn't come back here, instead of all that Lowlands business.'

'Rise of the Engineers and the merchants,' Thalric told him.

Varmen raised an eyebrow, baffled.

'Commonweal pickings were all very well, lots of art, some decent treasure, more slaves than anyone knew what to do with, but the Lowlands is *rich.* They had artifice and knowledge that exceeded our own, industry, real money. Once the Consortium and the Engineering Corps got their way, the Lowlander invasion was inevitable.'

'Goes to show you shouldn't be too clever, eh?' Varmen grunted, seeming much amused, then he pointed suddenly. 'She moved!'

Thalric was instantly over beside Che again, seeing her eyelids flutter. He spoke her name three times, but only when he tried the full 'Cheerwell' did she frown and twitch, and then stare up at him.

'Thalric?'

'Che, tell me what's happening.' He didn't like the hint of fear in his own voice, but there was no helping that.

'Thalric . . . I was in Khanaphes, with *her*—'

'Che, that doesn't help me.'

Abruptly she was clinging to him, as though about to be swept away at any moment. 'Thalric, it's not over. I can still feel her there. I'm falling back. Thalric, this is magic – you have to believe me. This is old magic, and I've got myself into it, and I don't know what to *do*.'

'I believe you.' His words came out without thinking, and it was almost a relief to cast off his responsibility for the situation by admitting such.

'Suon Ren,' Che told him urgently. 'Salma's father – foster-father – will have a magician at his court. He *must*! You can trust him.'

'Che, not without you there to make the introductions,' Thalric replied sharply. 'What can I say to him? That I'm the man who enslaved his son, and whose people killed him? I won't be welcome—'

'He will have to understand,' she gasped. He could feel her trembling violently, trying to brace herself against him as though a great tide was building up, ready to tear her away. 'There is no one else. Please . . . I need help, Thalric. Please help me.'

'Che, this is insane—'

But she cried out, wrapping her arms about him and, despite himself, he *felt* the moment when the invisible wave caught hold of her and ripped her away from him. So that, even though her body remained limp in his grasp, Che was gone again, fallen back into whatever abyss she had briefly clawed her way out of.

He laid her back down, scowling furiously, aware that Varmen was watching him, but not wanting to see the other Wasp's expression.

'You'll be wanting to hop one of the locals' barges, then,' was all the man said.

'They'd take me?'

Varmen shrugged. 'Can't hurt to ask. Maybe they'll try to kill us, or maybe they'll make us their new kings, who knows?'

'Us?' Thalric looked at him then.

The former Sentinel was sitting with one hand draped companionably across the pack-beetle's back. When he saw Thalric's scrutiny he shrugged, almost embarrassed. 'Can't see you manhandling the poor girl all that way on your own, even if you did hop a barge.'

'And I thought you wanted me dead, because I was Rekef?'

'Oh, *you*? Just don't press your luck, is all I'll say. She seems decent enough, though.' Varmen smiled. 'Wouldn't have thought I'd find a Rekef man so caught up with one of the *lesser* kinden.' His grin broadened as Thalric rounded on him, rising to the bait. 'Don't take offence at that, Rekef. We all need something to keep us human, right?'

The Masters of Khanaphes regarded Seda stonily.

'Little Empress,' said one of the women, 'we know why you have come. You have been expected.'

'Really?' Seda replied. 'And yet I feel anything but welcome.'

'Do you think that what you seek here should be *easy*?' the man asked acidly. 'We have hoarded our power for a thousand years, so would you resent us taking steps to discourage the unworthy?'

Seda gave a hard smile, gazing up at them amid the leaping, bluish light. 'Tell me why I am here, then?'

'You are here to learn,' the other woman told her.

'It is creditable.' The first nodded slowly. 'You have discovered in yourself the last drop of magic known to your people, but you do not know what to do with it. You have been diligent in seeking enlightenment, until it has led you to us, the first lords and ladies of mankind. You wish to learn from us.' They spoke softly, the Masters of Khanaphes, but their words created vast echoes that resounded – felt but unheard – about the cavernous spaces of this, their resting place. She was at the heart of it here, now, where all the remnants of ancient power had been hoarded and husbanded. Her body thrilled to it, telling her that she *belonged* here at their feet, as their humblest slave and servant, if only they would consent to let her *know* . . .

Seda nodded along with those thoughts. She saw Gjegevey staring at her worriedly, and wondered what it was she had woken him from. What constituted a Woodlouse nightmare?

When he saw that he had caught her eye, the old man shook his head. He must feel the leaden weight of their power and of all the ages they had stored up here. If they extended their hand to him, she mused, then perhaps he would already be kneeling before them in obeisance.

They were leaning on her, perhaps without even intending

to, pressuring her into following the path that they had already set out. No doubt they could not even imagine her saying no. Their confidence in her eventual decision was complete.

Was *almost* complete. For, of course, *she* – the other one who had stood here and also been given this choice – *she* had refused.

And I do not kneel. Not even before the Masters of Khanaphes.

'I think you underestimate the extent of my studies,' she declared. Seeing their disdainful expressions, she added quickly, 'Oh, Masters, I cannot pretend to match your many centuries. I can only guess at your long histories that the turning of the ages has overwritten. No doubt, when the world was young, you held the reins of power and the other kinden clustered around your feet like children. Perhaps, after that, you idled on your thrones while young races, those that we now think of as ancient and occult, squabbled for the scraps from your tables. Certainly I cannot guess how many centuries have passed since you last truly stirred yourselves or exercised your power. Until the Scorpions came to lay waste your city, that is, and you were forced to it. And which hand set those barbarians at your gates, if not my Empire's? Who could have then guessed what Brugan's foolishness would unearth?'

Her own words did not raise the same great, soundless echoes that theirs did. They raised only sharp, real echoes, that whiplashed across the faces of the Masters, for nobody had ever addressed to them in such a manner since the dawn of time.

'I am not here to *learn*,' she explained, speaking into the ringing silence. 'I am not here to sit at your feet and be satisfied with whatever pittance you grant me. I am the Empress of the Wasps, and I am no mere *subject*, not even for the first lords and ladies of mankind. You know what I am here for.'

There were more of them appearing now, their huge figures striding towards her between the pillars. They eyed her impassively, arrogantly, but she stared them down. *And do I detect the faintest quiver of doubt*?

Then one of the men sighed heavily and said, 'We are sorry that you have come such a way only for this. To stand before the Masters of Khanaphes and dare to make *demands* is only foolishness.' He did not sound angry, though, just disappointed. Even so, she felt a surge of their power building up, inexorable as an earthquake, readying itself to blot her out so utterly that the world would not even remember her name.

'Such promise,' one of the women murmured. 'She could have learned so much of our histories, such as no savage has ever known, and now this . . . Such a waste . . .'

'Majesty.' Gjegevey's voice quavered, and Seda realized that he was terrified almost out of his mind. Had he been here alone, he would have thrown himself before the Masters and begged for mercy, but she gave him strength and for her sake, for loyalty's sake, he clung to his staff and held his ground.

Several of the Masters were already turning away, not even interested enough to witness her being destroyed. The looming tidal wave of their power – a slightest handful of all they had saved up here, and yet still so much, such a vast fist to crush such small flies – was cresting all around them.

'You have your grand histories,' Seda conceded, betraying nothing but cool arrogance in her voice and stance. 'But I have an Empire.'

She could sense their amusement at such a proclamation, and it bought her a little more time – time to educate those who had thought she had come to serve them.

'At the lightest gesture of my army, half your city was razed. It would take a fraction of the soldiers now under my command to obliterate it from the face of the world. If I do not return safely to them, then that is exactly what I will do. More, they will bring in machines and Mole Cricket-kinden and they will dig. They shall tear apart the earth itself, until they uncover these halls, and then the sun shall become your only ceiling, and for all your power, and however many of my subjects you slay or drive mad, they shall take you eventually, and lead you through the streets of Capitas in chains. And so your histories, all of your histories, shall come to an end. I shall tear up every stone that bears your name or your likeness, and then I shall salt the earth itself so that your power may never revive.'

She sensed the massive hammer of their will poised in delicate balance above her.

'You cannot think—' one of them began, but Seda did not let him finish.

'If you harm me, then this shall come to pass. It shall come to pass even if you simply deny me. I am the Empress of the Wasps, and I am the inheritor of the ancient powers, by blood and by shadow, and there is only one thing I require from you. Grant that one thing, and I shall leave you to your darkness and your stone.'

This was the fulcrum moment on which the future hinged, with their power poised right above her, an invisible, irresistible weight that could crush her mind, send her stark mad, and none of her tricks of magic or statesmanship could withstand it. *But we are Wasps, and we do not beg. I shall have this on my terms or not at all, for there is no other path fit for an Empress.*

Gjegevey stood very close, almost clinging to her arm, his face sheened with sweat in this unwholesome blue light. She radiated strength, though. Even if, at her greatest, she seemed a mere gnat in the face of their might, she stood straight and defied them, and held firm to her demands.

Had it not been for that other woman, had it not been for those stolen dreams that had visited Seda so long ago, so far away – those dreams of the same echoing halls, the lamps, the solemn faces of the Masters – then she would have sucumbed. True, had it not been for those dreams she would never have come at all, but in that moment of crisis, facing the vast depths of the Masters' strength, she still held to that one scrap of knowledge. *They were defeated before, out-thought, tricked from their prey. The Beetle girl escaped them. Well, I shall go one better.*

'See my Empire,' she told them, and then filled her own

mind with it, all of its artifice and energy, its rapacious hunger, its unending hordes of soldiers, its fierce youthful fire. She summoned up all her own confidence, her belief in her people and in herself, and her unbridled and all-consuming *need* to control: to control herself, control her people, control the ancient powers, control the world. She did not know it, but she was grinning at them like a monster. She smiled like a tyrant and, just as their ancient power had weighed on her with its demands of *Worship us!* so she turned her mind on them with all the force of her Imperial will: *Submit to me!*

The air was full of soundless fury, of invisible fire, so that Gjegevey flinched from every moment of it. But in the physical world a great silence had fallen, and Seda's grin simply widened, and the Masters were suddenly uncertain. The world of the *new* and the *vital* was brought here before them, incomprehensible and threatening.

And, at the very last, an answer: 'What is it that you want, then?' said one of the women. 'Name it.'

'Validation,' Seda told them. 'Confirmation. You, with your great legacy, must accept me as your heir in the modern world. Just a nod, Masters – just the smallest nod. All of us here know how power is defined by such symbols.' She caught a glimpse of Gjegevey's face, and he was wide-eyed in horror, but she had come too far now to turn aside. 'Pass on to me the mantle,' she insisted.

The Masters of Khanaphes, and there were many more of them now, exchanged slow glances, and Seda knew that thoughts must be passing between them, not by Art or even magic, but by virtue of their having spent so many centuries in each other's company.

'You claim to be the heir to the Age of Lore,' one said at last, and when Seda nodded impatiently, added, 'You wish us to crown you, to acknowledge you.'

'You are the first-ever great magicians,' Seda declared. 'I will have you name me as your successor.'

'And are you prepared to share your throne?' asked another woman there.

Seda's eyes narrowed. 'With you?'

There was a murmur of laughter amongst them, more evident in the eyes than from anything she actually heard. 'You shall never be our peer, little Empress, but perhaps you are fit to be named queen of what scant magic this withered age still owns. With our blessing you might do great things – might even turn back the sands a little and bring back some shadow of the old days. We cannot bless you, though, unless we also bless your sister.'

The Wasp Empress stared at her, and it was a few moments before she could form the words: 'I have no sister. Maxin killed them all, years ago. I am the last of my blood.'

At her bafflement, the amusement among the Masters spread. 'She was not born your kin, but she is your sister now. You and she were bloodied by the same thorn. In the instant that you attained your power, she came to hers. And, though her understanding is behind yours, you are yet walking in her footsteps.'

Seda glared at them all. 'Explain yourselves!' she demanded.

'You have dreamt of these halls of ours,' another of the Masters interposed. 'But your sister was here before you. She broke our spells and made demands of us, though she was not so ambitious as you. You are joined, you and she, and though we bless you and grant you our acknowledgement, yet we must grant her nothing less. Your lives are intertwined, but only one of you can triumph in the end. You have a rival, Little Empress, and she is watching you even now.'

Che jerked back, trying to escape from the dream, trying to be anywhere but that subterranean tomb as the Wasp Empress glanced furiously about. *I am not here,* she had to remind herself. *This is just a vision. This is nothing—*

Seda's eyes found hers, and there was a physical jolt of recognition and enmity between them, whereupon Che stopped lying to herself.

'I see her,' the Wasp growled, and she thrust out a hand towards Che, as though to sting her across the hundreds of miles that separated them. There came no searing light and heat, though, and Che was just beginning to relax when Seda bared her teeth in a savage snarl, and a wave of darkness pulsed out from her, faster than any eye could follow. Che had only a moment to register its approach before she was struck. Then a hammerblow of the mind detached her from her disembodied viewpoint and cast her far away, down into endless night.

Part Three

The Huntress

Twenty

Tynisa had been left to her own devices amid the strange bustle of Lowre Cean's compound.

The old man himself seemed to drift between a dozen baffling pastimes, as though to actually commit wholly to any one occupation would be the death of him. Sometimes he was closeted with his little singers, the sight of which still made Tynisa's flesh crawl. At other times he would go off travelling through the snows with one band of reprobates or another, abandoning his servants and guards and vanishing for days. Tynisa was given to understand that all those armed bands that visited his estate were not, after all, bandits, or not *only* bandits, but also war veterans whom Lowre Cean had either commanded or fought alongside. Why the old tactician took the whole thing so personally, and what the precise relationship of duty and obligation was, Tynisa was not sure. Nobody spoke about it.

At other times, Cean would retreat into his workroom, where he would whittle away at tiny figures of soldiers and peasants and nobles, all carved out of a wood that could be found nowhere within a hundred miles, and that he had shipped in by infrequent barge. He would cook sometimes, inventing new concoctions and feeding all comers. He would tend his kadith ponds, adding his own blends of herbs and grasses for the insect larvae to knit into their cocoons, or he would retreat to his library and read some dusty scroll of centuries-old poetry.

He did not practise with weapons, or take a bow down to the butts to shoot at targets, as many of his people did. He did not talk about the war. He did not even seem to directly give orders to his guards or servants. They just went about their business, using their own best judgement.

Amidst all of this, Tynisa was left to amuse herself and she found that, rather than this leading to frustration and despair, she was oddly liberated by it all. Certainly she was waiting for Salme Alain to call upon her, as she was sure he would. Certainly she still had her great purpose, of bringing word of Salma's end to his mother, who did not seem to want to know. Still, until that part of her life interfered again, she was a free agent. The winter world seemed to have forgotten about her, and so had her own driving demons. Even the shadows grew infrequent, and sometimes whole days could go by without her glimpsing that hunched, accusing figure in grey robes, or her father's flayed corpse.

One morning she awoke in a sudden panic, hearing voices outside. For long moments she could not understand why the very sound of them had abruptly recalled to her all the guilt and fear that she had been hiding from. Then at last she placed it: a Collegiate accent, clear as day.

Outside in the courtyard she saw a covered wagon drawn by a brown-shelled beetle, and sitting on the driver's board was a Beetle-kinden, who was currently bawling at the top of her voice at some of Lowre's retainers. She was a stranger, and yet Tynisa felt she knew the woman instantly. She had seen plenty of that type in Collegium: stocky, bluff, forceful women striding about the city streets or College halls. They were independent, resourceful and practical, constantly making and selling and disputing, and always being *loud.*

The sight of such a woman here, wrapped in two layers of woollen robes and a long cloak, was bewildering, and Tynisa approached her cautiously.

'Excuse me,' she said, but the woman was giving strident

directions to someone about what to feed her beetle on, and so Tynisa had to repeat herself, even louder.

'What is it?' the woman snapped, obviously impatient with anything not immediately concerned with her current purpose.

'I was wondering . . . what can you be doing here.'

The woman stared at her, and suddenly let out a bark of outsize laughter. 'A voice from home, as I live and breathe!' she declared. 'A strange-looking Collegiate you make, too. I'd take you for a native, else. Sammi, come and look at this!'

From the round back of the wagon came an elderly Grasshopper-kinden with thinning grey hair and a frame that was all angles.

'Sammi?' queried Tynisa weakly.

'Well, it's – what is it? – Tse Mae, or something very like it,' the woman admitted, fighting with the man's name. 'But Sammi works for me, and so I get to call him that. Fordwright, by the way. Hardy Fordwright, Master of the College.'

Tynisa shook the proffered hand uncertainly. 'Tynisa, student of the same. But, Mistress Fordwright, how long have you been here in the Commonweal?'

'What is it . . . seven years now?' Fordwright asked her companion.

'Nine since we met, Harde,' Tse Mae replied, mangling her name equally as much as she had mangled his.

'On my life, is it really?' Fordwright looked genuinely surprised.

'But what are you doing here?' Tynisa pressed.

'Oh, old man Lowre's our patron, don't you know,' the Beetle woman explained. By now their animal was being unhitched and watered, and Tse Mae was arranging for the wagon to be put under cover. Fordwright beamed at him, then explained, 'You see, Sammi and me are here about a piece of research – You've heard of the Alchemical Theorem?' – and she went on as if Tynisa had, regardless. 'I was a chemical artificer back home, and Sammi here has spent his days cooking up elixirs and potions for the credulous. So I can put a bunch of ingredients together for a particular effect, and Sammi can do the same. The thing is that I can tell you why mine works, and he can tell you why his works, and neither of us agree *why* it works, but we both agree that it does.'

When Tynisa failed to react with immediate enthusiasm Fordwright pressed on impatiently. 'But don't you see? It's a process and result that makes sense both to Apt and Inapt minds, even if my sense doesn't work for him, and his doesn't work for me. Give me another few years and I'll stand before the College and tell them that I have found the exact field of study that Aptitude may have arisen from, and it's still being practised here in the Commonweal.'

This last was thrown over her shoulder, as she was striding off towards Lowre Cean's main hall, letting Tynisa and Tse Mae trail in her wake.

'And Lowre Cean is an alchemist too, is he?'

Fordwright beamed back at Tynisa. 'A little. He dabbles. Dabbles in just about everything, in fact. He's a patron of just about every art you can name. Painters and poets, itinerant Roach-kinden balladeers, stargazers and hocus-pocus merchants, and people who'll tell your future from your shadow. Lucky for Sammi and me that he's up for supporting some serious inquiry, as well as all those quacksalvers. My guess?' Even her colossal voice managed a crude sort of whisper. 'The old boy is up for anything that'll take his mind off the war.'

'But he was a hero,' Tynisa protested weakly.

Fordwright made a disrespectful sound that demonstrated precisely what she thought of war heroes. What she said made sense, Tynisa considered. Collegium's great figures were noted for their intellect, their diplomacy, their discoveries and inventions, and they left the glorifying of war to other kinden. In Tynisa, though, the fighting urge was strong: that need to test herself and her blade. She found in herself an unchallengeable insistence that all true heroes were warriors living and dying by the sword.

Like Salma. Like my father. Thus conjured, they both hovered just out of sight.

The young man who had fetched her from Gaved's home came to find her once again shortly afterwards. She had never even learned his name, about which he seemed to be unusually discreet. Her eventual conclusion was that the youth was some bastard by-blow of the old prince's, and that the Commonwealers had quaint ideas about fidelity and paternity.

'His Highness has ordered there to be a formal dinner tonight,' the youth informed her. 'Your presence would be welcomed.'

This would be the third such formal occasion since she had become Lowre Cean's guest. The old man usually ate by himself, at odd times and wherever he happened to be pursuing his own interests, but sometimes the prince-major would surface in him, and suddenly all his servants and followers would be galvanized into a culinary orgy of preparation, whilst those wayfarers lucky enough to be passing through would find themselves made guests of honour. Tynisa assumed that this time it was Hardy Fordwright and Tse Mae who had prompted the festivities.

During warmer months, the nameless young man explained, such feasts were held outside, under the stars, with places set so that everyone, from the prince's household down to the lowliest fieldhand, would take some part in the meal. During the winter, however, Lowre would ensure that some gift of food or drink reached each family that owed its livelihood to his presence, but he himself would feast within the doubled walls of his hall.

After sunset she made her way to the long hall, knowing that the meal would not commence for some time. She found Fordwright and her companion there already, plainly looking forward to the hospitality, among a handful of others who were guesting there too: a Dragonfly noblewoman, a Mercer out on business for the throne, and a Grasshopper woman in piecemeal armour who looked to Tynisa like a mercenary captain.

However, when Lowre Cean himself made his appearance, just as the servants were bringing through bowls of hot kadith, there was someone walking beside him that had Tynisa leaping up from her place.

'Alain!' she cried out, heedless of propriety. She had nearly cried 'Salma!' instead, just like before, which would have made her seem a complete fool.

Salme Alain grinned broadly at her. 'And here she is,' he declared. 'You have taken some finding, Maker Tynise, though I place the blame for that at my mother's door. Forgive me my absence, but I have been ensuring that our southern border is safe. The Turncoat tells me that he showed you exactly what we have to deal with there.'

It took her a moment before she remembered that 'the Turncoat' was Gaved, but then she nodded, recalling the wretched ruin that had been Siriell's Town.

Lowre Cean lowered himself into his appointed seat. A formal Dragonfly meal was set out much like a Fly-kinden feast: long, low tables, and everyone sitting on cushions on the floor, with the prince's place in the middle of one of the long sides. A moment later, servants began showing other people to their seats. Tynisa found herself at Lowre's left-hand side, balancing the nameless messenger seated on his right. Alain, who had presumably displaced some previously planned guest, was at one end of the table, seemingly as far from Tynisa as he could get. That seemed odd to her, and she turned to Lowre to ask about it. She caught the old man gazing at Salme Alain with a strange expression. If the two of them had not been Dragonfly nobles, and if Lowre was not so beholden to the Salmae, Tynisa might have read hostility there.

Alain was already talking animatedly with the people on either side of him, clearly making some new friends. He glanced at Tynisa once or twice, but without raising his voice more than would have been polite, there was no way he could speak to her. For her part, Tynisa picked at her meal in silence. She was aware that she must be missing something important, some unspoken axiom of Dragonfly society. She was used to reading people at a glance, sketching an instant picture of their motives and intentions, and it was not that the Commonwealers were too subtle for her, who had dealt with Imperial bureaucrats and Spider-kinden Aristoi in her time. It was simply that their language of face and gesture was different, following a code that she was still learning. While she tried to accustom herself to their ways, there were realms of suggestion and implication that were nevertheless passing her by.

She could catch not a word of Alain's conversation, either, for Hardy Fordwright was stridently holding forth about some matter of her own. In a bid to derail the woman's braying monopoly of the conversation, Tynisa leant over to her and, just as the Beetle paused for a draught, asked her, 'When did you last see our ambassador, Mistress Fordwright?'

'Our what?' the Beetle demanded, baffled.

'Gramo Galltree, at Suon Ren,' Tynisa explained. 'I was staying with him not so long ago. He did not mention any other Collegiates in the Commonweal.'

'I've never heard of the fellow,' Fordwright stated flatly. 'An *ambassador?*'

'Well, yes,' Tynisa said, now somewhat thrown. 'He said he was, anyway. He's a College man.'

Hardy frowned, quietened beyond Tynisa's wildest hopes. At last she said, 'Well, then, I suppose I should take a trip to Suon Ren. That's . . . Prince Vas Nares?'

'Felipe Shah.'

'Oh, the Prince-*Major*'s stamping ground. Well, perhaps Sammi and I will go south from here. Be good to hear another Collegiate voice.' Her tone so clearly equated 'Collegiate' with 'civilized'.

For a moment Tynisa felt guilty about dumping this brash, loud woman on poor old Gramo, but then she recalled the ambassador's lament on how he missed the familiar talk of his former home. Well, then, Hardy Fordwright would sate that need of his – or cure him of it for ever.

The meal was lengthy, the flavours of the food subtle and elusive, the wine tart and dry where a Collegium vintage would have been sweet. Tynisa, who had been happy, for months now, to drift along at Lowre Cean's aimless pace, was suddenly impatient with it all. Alain's arrival was like a stone cast into the clear waters of a pond.

Something is about to change. The world has been sleeping until now.

And, once the meal was done, he approached her with that smile which he shared with his dead brother.

'We are to celebrate, at Leose,' he announced. 'We have scored a great victory over the bandits and the dissenters.' He spoke loudly, deliberately including Lowre Cean, who was nearby. 'My mother wished you to know that she has not been idle, Your Highness.'

Again, Cean's look was coolly distant. 'I thank your mother for her kindness. I am too old, alas, to enjoy such festivities. I trust you will bear my apologies.'

'I will bear more than that, if I may.' Alain grinned at him. 'I would bear one of your guests away.' His glance at Tynisa was clear.

'But . . . when is this celebration?' she asked him.

'Oh, over several nights, but the greatest share of it will be as soon as I return,' Alain said carelessly. 'And it would be impolite to keep them waiting.'

'But Leose is . . .'

'Oh, I am here with Lycene, who will carry us both.' His smile flashed again, like a blade. 'You'll come, won't you?'

'Your mother didn't seem too fond of me, when we last met,' Tynisa said weakly.

'I am her heir, and she may not therefore turn away my guests,' Alain declared, with a rebellious spark.

She found herself glancing at Lowre Cean, which was

ridiculous. He was not her guardian, and she needed no one's permission. Still, she had hoped to see some manner of approval on the old man's lean face. He was quite unreadable, though, save that he had evidently no warmth to spare for Salme Alain, nor apparently for the young man's mother.

Strange, she considered, for Cean seemed to be guesting within Elas Mar province at the Salmae's invitation, and yet the fallen prince-major was obviously anything but grateful. *Is it merely that, then? Does he resent being beholden to them?* But that conclusion would go against all she had gathered of the old man's character. *Or is it his losses in the war?* She could understand that he might not wish to be reminded, by seeing those still in possession of what he himself had been stripped of. *Not lands, not castle, but . . .* She racked her memory, then decided, *Yes, there was a son of the house of Lowre. Someone has mentioned that to me. Perhaps that alone is enough to make him a bitter neighbour. He certainly goes to some lengths to put aside the trappings of a prince, and loses himself in trivial matters instead.*

The thought still did not quite sit right, but she had no better option, nor could she readily enquire of either Lowre or Alain. Gaved, she felt sure, would know, and would tell her, but the Wasp was not here to ask.

'I shall go,' she told Alain. 'I would be honoured.'

Twenty-One

'They are celebrating our demise even now, I'll wager,' said the broad-shouldered Grasshopper. His lean, scarred face had struck fear into enough hearts in its time, but it looked worried now. During three years of relative peace he had been happy running protection rackets and ordering thugs here in Siriell's Town, but it was increasingly clear to all that those days were gone. His real name was Ang We, but during the war he had fallen in with foreigners who had dubbed him 'Angry'. For good reason, the name had stuck.

'Half the town has left already. The smallholders are scattered all across Rhael province, hoping to forage. Most of the merchants and the artisans have slunk off to look for better markets.' This complaint came from a young Dragonfly woman who called herself Pirett, and who had claimed to be like a daughter to Siriell, the bandit queen's natural heir. Now that Siriell was dead, the hollowness of that boast had become clear. Siriell had left no heir and, deprived of the fallen woman's authority and her indefinable ability to yoke warring factions together in a common cause, the town was fast falling apart.

'Let them go. What's to stay for? She's dead, and we're done here,' said another Dragonfly, this time a man of stockier build than most, with a touch of grey to his hair and a square face that had seen a great deal of good times and bad.

'Cold words coming from the man who shared her bed, Dal,' Angry noted.

The Dragonfly-kinden, Dal Arche, shrugged. 'And you and your lads are staying, are you?' The Grasshopper did not reply.

The three of them, alone and without even their most immediate followers, had commandeered a room high up in the ruined face of the castle. Below them Siriell's Town was going about its business of falling apart, fighting with itself, lashing about in its death throes.

'I'm for the east,' Pirett declared. 'They say there's all manner of opportunity to be had at the border.'

'Then you'll be the first to know when the Empire comes knocking,' Dal told her. 'Or even when the Principality folks decide to take a bite. I've seen enough war for a lifetime. If you must go, go west.'

She shook her head stubbornly. The words went unsaid, but anywhere further west the land was unfamiliar, and it was said the Monarch's writ ran stronger there. Whether the spectre of the Commonweal's ruler truly had any claws left, none of them could say, but Pirett was clearly not ready to put it to the test.

'Rhael has life in it yet. All those weaklings who run from here, they'll set up elsewhere, in villages and farms. My lads want to follow them, keep them honest.' Angry gave them a patchwork smile of missing teeth.

'Meagre pickings,' Dal observed.

'That's what the lads want.' It was a curious trait in the Grasshopper brigand that he always hid his own desires behind the supposed will of his followers. 'The pickings'll be that much more meagre if someone else is trying to split the difference with me.'

'Have no fear. I've better to do than starve so hard that I take everyone nearby with me,' Dal Arche said sharply. For a moment the two men stared at each other, but it was Angry, the bigger and the louder, who looked away first.

'What, then?' Pirett asked him. 'You're going to throw yourself on Prince Felipe's mercy?'

He gave her a level stare. 'I would not go east, to the Empire and the creatures it has left behind. I have been a prisoner of the Black and Gold once, and never again.' He turned his regard on Angry. 'I have men and women to feed, who will demand full bellies, drink, action and prospects, or they will abandon me or else cut my throat. I'll not take them deeper into Rhael to plague those few poor beggars who've tried to turn the soil into a living.'

The Grasshopper sneered. 'Soft,' was all he said.

Dal Arche's smile had murder in it. 'You know I'm not one to stint in taking what I want from any that has it, but even I can't take what they don't have. No, since Siriell's Town is become a rotting corpse as of now, there's only one direction that I *know* has provision enough for my band. We march north.'

'You're not serious?' Pirett breathed.

'No? If they had just come here and killed Siriell, then perhaps it could be mended. I'm not a sentimental man. She knew the life she led. But come here and burn our stores . . .' He gestured at the window, where the shutters kept out all but the smell of the smoke. The Mercers had been thorough, and while their leader himself had slain the town's self-made ruler, the others had fired every warehouse and stockpile they could find. The accumulated harvests of the farmers and brigands and vagabonds of Siriell's Town had burned.

'Well then,' Dal Arche declared, in the silence that followed, 'they could have left well alone, and in ten years, perhaps, this place would become so tame I'd need to go rob some prince or other just to keep me from going mad with boredom. I thank the Salmae that they spared me the wait. They have food, north of the province border, and I see no better option than to take it, and spill what blood needs shedding.'

The other two brigand chiefs eyed him suspiciously, as though he was spinning them some particularly self-serving lie, but at last Pirett said wonderingly, 'Well, I wish you luck. Give my regards to Mother Salme when she has you hanged.'

Angry said nothing, but he nodded grudgingly.

Outside, with the other chieftains heading off to mobilize their followers, Dal Arche sought out his own three lieutenants. There was more in his mind than he had let on to the others, for his profession was never one to breed trust. He needed to steal a march on his rivals.

They were waiting for him, his most valued followers, his brothers of the wilds: a Wasp, a Scorpion and a gaunt and spindly Grasshopper passing a jug of beer between them as they waited for his return.

'We're moving out,' he told them, after dropping down beside them. They were the only occupants of what had once been a popular drinking den. Even the proprietor had gathered up what he could and fled. All the villains and renegades who had been concentrated in Siriell's Town were dispersing across Rhael Province and beyond.

'What's the plan, Dala?' the Wasp-kinden asked.

'I'm taking most of our lot north, like we discussed. I'll be raiding the borders in a tenday, strike and flight, like the old days. Always one step ahead of the Mercers. You three, though . . .' He looked them over: Mordrec, Barad Ygor and Soul Je. The four of them had been through a lot together since the Wasp had sprung Dal Arche from a Mynan prison. 'I want you to make a circle south and east. Go play the recruiting sergeant. Pick up every malcontent you can get who has a will to carve a piece of something better. You'll need to dodge Pirett and Angry's mobs, though. She's just heading to the border, but Angry will be after the same pickings, maybe, so you're best to keep ahead of him. Round up a whole new mob, get them fired up, bring them to me. We're going to teach the honest folk of Elas Mar Province how to piss themselves in fright.'

They stared at him, and he knew that these three, of all his followers, would not simply do what he said without question. They would be wondering how much of this plan was reason, how much rage. And how close had he been to Siriell, indeed, before she was killed?

'We've been a lot of things in our time,' he told them softly, 'but right now we're thieves, and there's only one direction we can go to find someone worth robbing.'

It seemed only minutes before she was seated astride Lycene, clinging to Alain's waist as the swift insect hurtled through the air. Tynisa could only huddle up against the prince's back and stare down, beyond the blurring wings, at the Commonweal countryside fleeting past. She thought she saw the lake, down there, that Gaved and Sef lived alongside, but then it was gone: her journey of several days to Lowre Cean's compound undone in hours only.

She had assumed that the dragonfly would bear them all the way to Leose before dark. Indeed, such was its speed that it seemed possible for the insect to take them anywhere, alighting in Collegium or in the Empire, or encircling the entire world. As night grew in the east, though, Lycene began to descend, either of her own volition or from some unseen signal given by Alain. There was a stand of reeds below them, that grew and grew larger as the insect drew closer, until Tynisa realized that she was looking at a dense stand of cane forest, with boles as thick as a man's body.

She had expected Lycene to make a demure landing on the open ground before the forest, but just as the dragonfly seemed about to alight, her wings gave a final flurry, casting her directly up towards the cane tops, so that she ended up clinging vertically, the tip of her tail just shy of the ground. Alain's own wings had caught him instantly, of course, feathering him down to the ground effortlessly, but perhaps he had forgotten how his passenger lacked that Art. Instead, Tynisa suffered a moment of utter fright, saved from a fall only by instinctively clenching her knees, left suspended head-down with her arms waving wildly. Then she recovered her balance, and clambered down the length of the hanging animal, thankful that her Art at least allowed her to climb.

Alain stood grinning at her, and she took the mockery as justified, thinking, *I'll be ready for that next time*. 'Perhaps I should have jumped into your arms?' she asked him acidly.

'That would have certainly put my wings to the test,' he agreed. 'We'd best make camp now. Lycene is tired and, though she can take to the air at night, she's not fond of it unless I insist.'

'I'm amazed your people bother with horses, when they have such creatures at their beck and call,' Tynisa suggested.

Alain shrugged. 'Horses are easier to rear, frankly, and cheaper to keep. Lycene will have to hunt half the morning, before we're ready to fly again. Besides, she is the mount for a prince. We couldn't have just anyone riding her, could we?'

The cold weather was returning, something else that Lycene was clearly not fond of, so Tynisa set up a fire close by the canes, where it might benefit the big insect as well as the humans. When she looked back, the work done as well as she could, she was startled to find Alain right by her shoulder.

'I've known a couple of Spider-kinden,' he said softly, 'but not with decent woodcraft like yours.' He knelt down beside her and made a few invisible adjustments to her efforts. 'A Mercer always knows how to make a good fire,' he explained. 'It's the first thing they teach you.'

She read his smile as self-mockery now. Abruptly she was completely taken aback by how *there* he seemed: how very close, elbow to elbow, hip to hip.

Salma . . . That familiar face, ready to cock a grin at her, but his eyes were measuring, appraising. 'My mother, now, she did not want me to become a Mercer. "You are a prince, Alain, and that should be enough."' His imitation of the Salmae matriarch recalled her tones perfectly. 'Mercers might one day find themselves in the wilderness without a full retinue of servants, you see. They have to learn skills more fitting to a lowlier class of man.' A wave of his hand signalled that her pyramid of wood had now reached his exacting standards, and she dispensed a final handful of wood shavings and scraps of paper for tinder, and then took out an ornate little metal firebox Lowre Cean had gifted to her, decanting some embers from it onto the tinder. Alain was leaning into her shoulder, with an expression suggesting that he was merely examining her efforts, but now almost cheek to cheek.

'My father was a real Mercer, the Monarch's own kind,' he murmured in her ear, 'although he wasn't much interested in teaching his sons. I think it was an excuse to absent himself whenever he wanted.'

'I'm surprised you were allowed to . . . Apprentice yourself?' There was a heat building now, as she fed tinder to the embers.

'Take the oath,' he corrected. 'I was all for running away to Shon Fhor, to swear myself to the Monarch. They had to bar the door and windows to hold me, some nights. So we compromised, as one does. Local Mercers are better than nothing, if you can't quite make it to the Monarch's court. And they still teach you how to make a decent fire.'

As the first flame glowed, uncertain and shy but gaining confidence, she risked a smile and found it answered.

'You, though, you are clearly a great lady of the Lowlands, where they have no Mercers. Where did you learn such a skill?'

'My father taught me what little I know,' she replied, and the words came out without the hesitation attending any earlier mention of Tisamon since his death. *And why not, since I'm sharing a fire with Salma – or his very image? Why should I be troubled about raising the dead?* With Salma at her side, she felt she could face anything, and her fire was now taking very nicely indeed. As she leant forward to blow gently on the flames, it seemed entirely natural for him to brush her hair back out of their way. 'My father, he was . . .' she started, then found herself on the brink of an abyss. How could she describe what Tisamon had been, before the end?

'Weaponsmaster?' Alain said abruptly, starting back from her. For a moment she froze, expecting the bloodstained Mantis shade to manifest itself, but the prince's eyes were now fixed on her neck, where she had strung the badge of her order. The sword-and-circle emblem swung free there, slipping from its hiding place beneath her tunic. There was a silent moment of re-evaluation between them in which certain possibilities demanded the correct distance, a blade's length.

'I never yet heard of a Spider Weaponsmaster,' Alain admitted at last.

Tynisa had almost replied, automatically, *He wasn't a Spider*, but from the way he had edged back from her after noticing the badge, how much further might he run if he discovered she was a halfbreed too?

'He was a remarkable man,' she stated, and he did not question further. The fire was going merrily by then, but it was just a fire, and they slept with it between them.

Tynisa remained awake for a long time after Alain's eyes had closed, watching his face in the dancing light. *Salma*, she could see only Salma there. Salma sleeping close enough to touch, as she had never seen him before. They had almost . . . hadn't they? She had not imagined that closeness? Why should he not be startled, be cautious, when something as weighty as a Weaponsmaster's brooch was abruptly dropped into the mix? But he would see past that, she knew, for the Commonweal had its share of them, after all, and it was no pariah's mark. She felt a great, confused knot of emotions surging within her.

Overhead, Lycene's great glittering eyes, which never closed, watched them both.

Castle Leose was in sight, poised on its buttress legs above the canal cutting through its valley. The snow had been descending in flurries for a while now, and Lycene's flight suffered from it, the creature fighting against the wind, dipping lower and lower. But now Alain dug his heels in, and the dragonfly fought its way higher into the air, shooting in at a sharp angle to clear the wall. A moment later, Lycene was clinging to the wooden lattice that enclosed the courtyard, the purpose of which now became clear.

It was an easier dismount than out in the cane forest. Alain simply dropped through the lattice with a flick of his wings, and Tynisa followed after him, hanging on by her arms for a moment before letting herself fall.

He had already commandeered a groom, who climbed up to lead Lycene off to wherever such animals were kept. Other servants had rushed inside the castle to announce the heir's arrival, for Leose's seneschal was with them in barely more than a minute. The tall, gaunt Grasshopper-kinden named Lisan Dea came hurrying out to greet them, but stopped with a disapproving stare when she saw Tynisa.

'I *see*,' she said primly. 'And what do you think your mother will say about this, my prince?'

'She may say what she likes,' Alain replied carelessly. 'We are to have a celebration of my victories over the brigands? Then I may invite who I wish to be my guest. If I wished to bring two Wasp generals and a convicted murderer, then you would find them rooms and show them all due hospitality. Or are you not a steward?'

Tynisa reacted to the word 'murderer' more visibly than Lisan Dea did to any of Alain's words, for not a single twitch or frown marred her long face.

'And she will stand amongst your family's other guests? She will eat and drink and dance with them, will she?' the Grasshopper demanded. Her harsh tone caught Tynisa by surprise. Despite her mistress's distant attitude, she had not guessed that this woman had taken such a dislike to her. Nothing of this had been evident at their last meeting.

'Why not?' was all Alain had to say, a study in boredom, practically rolling his eyes at this servant who dared to rise above herself.

'Does she at least have something fitting to wear?'

'This castle has stood since time began,' Alain replied. 'My family has lived here since the earliest days of the Commonweal. I am sure that there will be something hanging in some storeroom that will suit. Since *you* are the steward I leave that in your capable hands. Now, no doubt you will acquaint my mother with all that has passed between us two, then no doubt I'll be called to her presence to be railed at about filial duty. Might I kindly remind you of your station sufficiently for you to show my guest to suitable chambers, before you run off tattling to your betters?'

A moment's frozen silence was the only sign of Lisan Dea taking offence. 'Of course, my Prince,' she replied smoothly, and even bowed to Tynisa. 'If you would follow me, I shall have your room prepared.'

Tynisa glanced back at him once, but he was already giving instructions to another servant and, a moment later, the confines of Castle Leose closed about her.

The first hall they entered was high-ceilinged and airy, the windows on three sides casting a latticework of sunbeams. The next chamber was lower and darker, and so followed the progression, until Tynisa was forced to ask, 'Where are you leading me?'

Lisan Dea turned to face her and, to Tynisa's surprise, her expression was not simple disdain, but something closer to pity.

'What is your estate, child?' the seneschal asked. 'Are you a Spiderlands Arista? Are you some great lady of the Lowlands, whatever that might signify?'

'The Lowlands doesn't really have "great ladies" like that,' Tynisa muttered defensively, 'but I am the ward of an Assembler.' As she spoke the words, she realized that they meant nothing to the woman.

Lisan Dea shook her head. 'Yet he has brought you here, and asked me to house you and dress you, as if you were of noble blood. You do not understand, child.'

'I understand only that Alain has chosen to invite me here. I understand what it means to be treated like a guest.'

The flicker of a frown at this familiar use of the prince's name was almost lost in the curiously pained expression the Grasshopper woman assumed. 'You understand nothing,' she said grimly. 'You have no means of protecting yourself from them at all.'

Tynisa felt a sudden surge of anger, almost as if it had sprung from elsewhere, and within a moment her sword point was hovering close to Lisan Dea's breast. 'I have no difficulty in protecting myself,' she snapped.

But the seneschal simply looked back at her, without fear or even alarm. 'Why did you come here at all?'

'Because of Salma.' The answer came unwillingly. And then, because that would make no sense to the woman, 'I mean Salme Dien. I was his . . . his friend.' Abruptly she felt ridiculous, and slid her sword back in its scabbard, now ashamed at being goaded so effortlessly. *I have never been so shorn of grace before.* She found her killing instinct could not stand against the utter indifference of the Grasshopper.

'I remember Dien,' Lisan remarked, and a fond look transformed her face briefly, before it reverted to her professional blandness. 'But you should know that he has not dwelt in these halls for many years, not a trace of him.' And, with that cryptic observation, she walked on hurriedly, forcing Tynisa to follow her or become lost amidst the stones of Leose.

In the end, the room she was shown into was not so very poorly appointed, but was clearly not intended for a guest of honour either. It had bare stone walls draped with faded tapestries, and a single narrow window looking out over the gorge. They brought her gowns, then: objects of silk and layers, shimmering with colour. She found she could not wear them: they pinched in the wrong places, she could not walk properly without treading on the hems. Tynisa was used to Collegium robes, which were shorter and heavier, or else the breeches and arming jacket in which she had spent so long travelling. At the last she found a servant and prevailed upon her to fetch something more practical: a pale half-cloak over a long tunic of grey and gold that reached to her knees, with a belt that went three times round her waist.

The Lowlanders were never great arbiters of fashion, she knew, and Collegium's usual style was muted, borrowing any flair it possessed from seasons-old and mostly misunderstood Spider custom. The Beetle-kinden amongst whom she had grown up were a solid, pragmatic people to whom elegance did not come easily. Tall and slender and fair, she had walked amongst them wherever she wished, dressed how she wished, secure in the knowledge that they would deny her nothing. The other races that she had walked among were hardly different: blinkered Wasps, the rustic simplicity of the Mantis-kinden, the downtrodden grime of the Empire's slave races. She had never been obliged to *try* before. Certainly she had never strained to meet the standards of others.

Standing there in her borrowed garments, in this unfamiliar castle, she felt her self-confidence tarnishing by the moment. She did not know what to *do*, nor how to act, and a lifetime in Collegium had not prepared her for the web of intricate etiquette that bound these people together. Abruptly her simple room seemed close and crowded, and she heard Achaeos's spiteful reminder: *And you cannot even fly, which all these people take for granted. The Beetles have ruined you for polite company.* Tynisa shook her head, determined now to prove him wrong.

A dance, Alain had said. Well, it had indeed been a while since she had last trod a measure, but she knew that game. She knew the Beetle-kinden dances, which involved a great deal of romping back and forth in lines, changing places, turning round and, in the case of older, fatter or drunker dancers, falling over. She had skipped her way through enough of those, and even been admired for it. Then, again, there were the Spider dances, where the musicians set the measure and the dancers paired off and let their inspiration guide them, making grace and elegance their only standards. She felt she was ready for these Commonwealers.

The feast was disappointing. There were long, low tables seating a clear grading of guests, and she was placed at the end furthest from all the important people, meaning Alain and his mother and the more favoured of their noble invitees. She sensed Lisan Dea's hostile influence, but there was little she could do about it. Aside from herself, this gathering plainly represented Dragonfly aristocracy, resplendent in a rainbow of silks, cloth of gold, silvered leather and enamelled chitin. There was very little conversation between them, and none at all directed at Tynisa. If this gathering was to celebrate Alain's victories, nobody said anything about them, and his mother made no speeches. It was as though everyone had been thoroughly briefed beforehand, with only Tynisa left out. She ate in silence, finding the food too sharply and unexpectedly flavoured, and the portions small.

Then the gathering all adjourned into a further room, a circular space with a vastly high ceiling painted in patterns of blue and white and gold, where a little troupe of Grasshopper-kinden stood ready with instruments: long-necked lutes and rebecs and deep-throated drums. The guests spread out along the room's periphery, where Tynisa noticed several of them pairing off for the first dance. Her eyes sought out Alain, but he had already been secured by a coolly elegant Dragonfly lady, the two of them slotting together without preamble, as though the partnering had been arranged beforehand. Tynisa turned away, but there was someone unexpectedly at her elbow. For a moment she found her hand twitching for the sword she had left in her room, but it was a young man who had been seated near her at the table.

'Lady Lowlander, would you honour me with your hand for this dance?' he enquired.

She had no idea who he was, but his familiarity suggested

that they had already been introduced. In truth, she had not paid her neighbours much attention during the meal. Seeing him standing so solemnly before her, she began to feel curiously off-balance.

'Of course,' she said nonetheless, because she could not back down now. Even then the drummer was moving his fingers over taut hide, producing a patter of fluid sounds like no drum Tynisa had heard before. Dancers were moving into place as if drawn by some magical resonance, each to a precise spot.

'We shall join the lower tier, of course,' her partner told her bafflingly, and then abandoned her to take his position across the room. In the end, she only knew where to go when two concentric circles had formed, with a single glaring gap in the outermost.

Faster than she was expecting, the music struck as soon as she had found her feet there, and she tried to move with it, but in a moment she realized that a Commonweal dance was something far removed from her experience of either Spider-kinden or Lowlanders. The inner circle of dancers had taken to the air immediately, converging in the chamber's centre and circling one another, whilst the outer ring began following some complex pattern of its own that seemed to have no relationship to that of their fellow dancers aloft. Small groups of them would come together, turn about one another with solemn grace, now facing in, now out, and then their smaller circle would scatter in a single instant, each leaping to another point either on foot or by wing. It should have produced a chaos of tripping and collisions, but Tynisa realized very swiftly that each and every one of the participants knew their moves as if they had been rehearsed in them. This was no Beetle bumble with some half-drunk dance-master calling out the moves, nor a Spider-kinden improvisation where individual inspiration was all. These noblemen and women had been schooled in some intricate dancing art, move by move and step by step, so that they worked together to an invisible pattern that she had no access to.

Tynisa soon backed out hurriedly, because the alternative was to get in someone's way, and already she had hopelessly lost the rhythm of the music. Across the room she saw the young man who partnered her also retiring, his face kept carefully neutral.

She was embarrassed. It was a new feeling for her: she had discovered something that she *could not do*. Worse, Alain would have noticed her fail at it. Even though the dance went on, she felt all eyes on her. Achaeos's mocking laughter sounded in her head – and she knew that Salma's imaginary smile was merely polite now. She had failed his people, and he had witnessed it, for all he was a year buried in the earth.

Those angry thoughts kept her busy until the dance reached its preordained conclusion, and Tynisa hoped naively that they might pass on to some other entertainment. Instead, she saw a swapping of partners, hands changing hands, and a new pattern being laid out in feet and bodies, whilst the musicians conferred briefly. No signal had been given, but as soon as the drummer started tapping away, everyone there immediately recognized the measure and was ready for it, leaving Tynisa again clinging at the sidelines, frustrated and surplus to requirements.

This time, Alain was partnering another young noblewoman, an iridescent creature who reminded Tynisa far too much of the Butterfly-kinden that Salme Dien had fallen for. Grimly she watched the two of them pirouette and soar together, each beat of the music grating on her nerves, until she felt that she would have to quit the gathering, or else do something she might regret.

Instead, some stubborn part of her had rooted her feet to the floor, even as her temper wound tighter and tighter. The next dance proved even more intricate, dancers skipping from the floor all the way to the arched ceiling and back, hovering and darting and circling like so many mayflies. And, all the while, Tynisa just stared and stared.

She recalled now Lisan Dea's curious reaction to her, the

pity the seneschal seemed to show, even that question about how Tynisa would defend herself. Well, now she knew what the woman had meant. She, who had found her own way amongst so many different kinden and cultures, had now encountered heights that she could not ascend to. Whatever her gifts, or her Art, or her training, she was still a low-born Lowlander. In contrast, these people were aristocracy, and their world was different to hers.

An older world, a wiser world, Achaeos whispered in her ear, *but you were so bound up with your Beetle learning that you abandoned your own heritage, and what are you now? Apt? Inapt? You have lost them both.* He was a presence at her elbow, and she dared not look round to banish him in case she found him stubborn, standing there with that bloodstain spreading across his body and his hand held out to partner her. She felt herself begin to shake ever so slightly. Every eye seemed to slide off her, with contempt or pity or simple embarrassment in each look cast her way. She was scanning the host for Salme Alain, desperate to catch his eye. Just the once, she caught sight of his face amidst the crowds, and read only amusement there. At her? Who could know, but it cut her anyway.

She realized that she had stayed too long, and a waxing tide of bitter anger at being so *excluded*, beyond any ability of hers to remedy, was soon going to overtake her. The dancers had come back down to earth, moving out to the edges of the room, and she found herself stepping forward towards the centre, as if she ment to challenge them all, forcing them to face her on her own terms. Her sword had been left back in her room, but she felt its familiar contours against her fingers, only a shadow away from being in her grip.

She looked up to see a white-haired Mantis-kinden in a pale grey arming jacket stepping forward to meet her, and something in her said, *yes*, at the perfection of it. What better for her now than to fight and die against one of her own?

But Isendter, the White Hand, merely called out to the

musicians. 'Play a martiette.' After a moment's startled conference, the drummer began a new beat, stronger and more rhythmic than before, still slow but with the promise of growing pace within it.

Isendter now stood before her, one hand out as though he held a sword, and she matched his posture, dropping into her fighting stance and waiting for his move. She could almost feel their blades crossing – no, she *could* feel it, steel scraping against steel – even though there was nothing between them but air.

The drum spoke louder, a single beat, and Isendter began to move. Instantly she had matched him, giving ground as he sought her, keeping perfect distance. The pace was increasing and, just as she was about to step away, dismissing it all as a nonsense, he moved again. Her feet mirrored his, their hands almost touching, and the dance began. For a long time there was no sound in that great hall but the rattle and tap of the ever-speeding drum, as Tynisa and Isendter fought.

At first she just reacted to him, sliding left as he slid right, retreating and retreating to his lead, but soon she was throwing in moves of her own, lunges and advances, feints and darts, which he echoed perfectly with his ever-moving feet. She forgot all about the others. She forgot Alain. Even the music departed her conscious mind, speaking directly to her body, so that all that mattered was the grave old Mantis before her. She never noticed how the rhythm of their dance was led by the drum, each louder beat signalling a strike. She never witnessed how the expressions of disdain on the faces of the Dragonfly-kinden became watchful, and then wide-eyed, as she and Isendter spun and passed and came together again in the perfect collaboration of duellists.

She could have told, two minutes in, all there was to know about Isendter's martial history, just as he had laid her own similarly bare. She could sense which of his knees was slightly tender with age, where the past scars were that tugged at the fluidity of his movements – all those mementos of his long career. They knew each other like lovers, during the moves of that dance, and she realized that he was better than she was, made slower by years but made wiser by experience. And the fight and the dance were running to an inevitable conclusion, and . . .

The drum had stopped, and she tried to identify that final sound, that pulled her out of her trance. A familiar sound and a comforting one.

Steel on steel.

Her rapier was in her hand, as reassuring and impossible as dreams. Its blade crossed the metal claw jutting from the gauntlet that Isendter had not been wearing before, nor could have found the time to buckle on.

The dance was over, the room was silent, and the old Mantis nodded just once – but with a Weaponsmaster's approval. Somewhere in the room she felt her father was watching her, adding his own satisfaction to Isendter's curt approbation.

Then the applause came, not the rowdy cheering of a Collegium theatre crowd, but a pattering of fingers on palms as the nobility of Elas Mar Province allowed her into their world.

She looked across the room to meet Alain's eyes squarely, and he was smiling.

Twenty-Two

There was to be a grand hunt to celebrate the approach of spring, she discovered the next morning. The stags would soon be locking antlers in the woods, and apparently and there was no better time to match one's strength with them.

Nobody had specifically stated that she, Tynisa, would be accompanying the hunt, but after her performance the previous night, nobody forbade it either. She had often fought for her life, even been a prisoner of the Empire, and yet there at least she had understood the rules of the game. This bewildering society of the Dragonfly nobles was beyond her, until the Mantis-kinden had found a door into it and had shown her the way.

And Alain had *smiled* at her.

The thought had been growing in her that redemption came in many colours. She had failed to save Salma, and in losing him she had lost her rightful place in the world.

He was *mine*, she thought bitter daggers at the Butterfly woman who had stolen his affections.

She had lost Salma, yes, but here was his very image. If she won him, against his mother's apparent scorn, his steward's sneers and the airy sophistication of his peers . . . if she won him then surely it would be as though she had found her place in the world again? Surely *that* victory would go some way to repairing the damage she had done, to balance the scales?

She was just aware enough to know that she was clutching

at straws, and that if she stood back and looked at her position she would find it untenable. That way, though, led to a greater madness, because then she would have to face up to the guilt that, day and night, prowled around the outworks of her mind, looking for a way in. If she unlocked that door, then the ghosts fabricated by her mind would have her for good. Go forward, though, and look neither left nor right, and she could leave them behind for just a little while. Forward because ahead of her was Salme Alain.

As soon as she understood that there would be hunting, Tynisa had found drab garments of hard-wearing cloth: Mantis-kinden fabric that was more robust than the Dragonfly clothing she had seen here. She took a cloak too, green-grey and mottled, to help her stalk the prey, whatever it was. In truth she had never gone hunting beasts before, but she had heard Tisamon describe it, and observed Mantis hunters in the Felyal, east of Collegium, so she reckoned she knew how it was done.

The Dragonfly-kinden clearly had their own ideas about the art of hunting, however. The party that set off from Leose numbered perhaps a dozen riders, with twice as many servants, and none of them seemed to care if their quarry spotted them coming from miles away. The mounted nobles were all clad in bright silks: reds and blues and greens that shimmered like metal in the morning sun. They carried lances and most had a quiver of arrows and a shortbow holstered at their saddle. They were mostly of an age with Alain and herself, only two being older, and Alain's mother, the matriarch of the Salmae, was not present.

The hunting grounds were some days west of Leose, beyond Lowre Cean's compound. Tynisa had anticipated being able to ride alongside Alain, to talk to him and let him see more of her than the fragmentary glimpses that were all he had seen till now. What she had not taken into account was her horsemanship, a skill that the Lowlanders had precious little use for. The Commonwealer nobles all rode elegantly, as natural in the saddle as in the air, and whilst Tynisa could outdistance the mass of walking servants, the nobles themselves were lost to her as soon as the party set out. They rode ahead, frequently out of sight entirely, and she could not catch them up. When she could see them, they were engaging in mock manoeuvres and cavalry actions that she could not have joined in with. Alain was always at the centre of these, constantly in demand. Assisted by a small number of servants who had mounts of their own, the entourage of nobles even made their own camp, ahead on the trail, leaving Tynisa and the other menials far behind.

As they passed close to Lowre Cean's compound, and neared the hunting grounds themselves, she caught up. The pause had been occasioned by a pair of new riders joining the party, and she was surprised to see the prince himself and his young messenger, with no retainers of their own at all. The old man nodded gravely to her, as though they were the only two sane people in the whole ridiculous expedition.

They rode north and west for a few hours, following the contours of the land towards the dark line of a forest. The ground here was still patchy with snow, and the sky above slate-grey with clouds. Tynisa found herself shivering, because even the middle of a Collegium winter was considerably warmer than this, but none of her companions seemed to feel the cold, so she put the best face on it that she could.

There was another half-dozen of the Grasshoppers waiting for them at the forest's edge, and with them two more riders: not nobles but simply more elevated servants. One was the perennially disapproving Lisan Dea, clad in sober black in stark contrast to the nobles. The other was the Weaponsmaster Isendter, who gave Tynisa a small nod of acknowledgement.

'Well?' Alain demanded of them.

'We have tracked a suitable quarry, my lord,' the sour-faced seneschal confirmed. 'The family has several females and calves, and a few younger males. The prince stag is somewhat large, though. I was concerned—'

'You're always concerned,' Alain dismissed her. 'Come, let's see this prodigy. It is time to hunt!'

They pushed into the woods, and now it was not the pace, but the simple business of guiding her mount through the trees, that taxed Tynisa.

'The Lowlanders plainly hunt afoot,' one girl remarked, on seeing her lamentable progress. 'Well, there is honest work for the infantry, too, in this.' Her tone was disdainful, plainly equating 'honest' with *demeaning*. Tynisa could not help but notice that the Dragonfly-kinden rode and that most of their unmounted servants were Grasshoppers. For a moment she felt herself on the edge of an uncomfortable comparison, thinking of the Wasp Empire and its slave-Auxillians of many subject races. This was the Commonweal after all, though, so it was not the same thing, not at all.

'Perhaps the lady would honour me by riding behind me.' The speaker was a smiling young man dressed in scintillating turquoise, his finery enhanced by a breastplate of silvered leather. His manner was shorn of mockery. 'Lady, I am Telse Orian, and you are Maker Tynise, are you not?'

'Close enough,' she admitted. A study of Lowre Cean's expression revealed no reason why she should not avail herself of Orian's offer, so she took his arm and let him pull her from her saddle and up behind him. Most of the nobles had a saddle that was built up before and behind, but her new companion's was something lighter and more recognizable. She was realizing how very little she knew about the whole business of horsemanship.

'So tell me, Maker Tynise.' The arch-looking Dragonfly girl guided her horse closer as the riders set off at a comfortable pace, their servants loping with long strides all around them. 'Tell me of your Lowland accomplishments. We have already seen your dancing.' She put a peculiar stress on that last word, clearly wanting to make it an insult, nevertheless not quite able to do so. 'You are great archers, perhaps, in the Lowlands?'

'Not that you'd notice,' Tynisa replied, trying to match the woman's tone. In truth she would have been hard pressed to even find a bow in Collegium, where the crossbow was the weapon of choice – but a weapon denied to her because of her Inaptitude. Tisamon had been a fair archer, but it was a skill he had never tried to teach her.

'Skilled horsemen, then, surely?' the girl needled.

'Not that either,' Tynisa replied coldly, feeling the anger inside her respond to the taunting. In her youth, in Collegium, such petty barbs as this would have been beneath her notice, and she had been master of her own emotions. Her experiences at the end of the Wasp war, the loss of too many loved ones and the guilt, they had all conspired to throw her irretrievably off balance.

'Why then surely—?' the Dragonfly girl started again, but Orian snapped at her, 'Velienn, enough.'

'But you have raised her up and made her one of us,' Velienn protested slyly. 'Is she to be starved of conversation?'

'If you wish to see what I excel at then I shall meet you on foot and with blades,' Tynisa declared flatly, not even returning the woman's gaze. She sensed Velienn ready herself for a retort, but then no words came, and she imagined the Dragonfly's eyes flicking over her Weaponsmaster's badge. Alain rode past them just then, and he must have caught Tynisa's words, for he grinned at her briefly.

They ventured deeper into the wood following Isendter, the horses picking their way between the trees, now together, now wending their ways separately. There was barely a sign or a sound of life about them save for the trees themselves, which had retained a mantle of needles weighed down by the snow. Every so often, one of the horses or footmen would brush against a branch and dislodge its load of white in a swift recoil of branches, and once or twice the sound of distant breaking would echo through the quiet forest, as some flawed limb gave way beneath its burden.

Ahead of them, Alain raised his hand, and the company slowed and then halted. Tynisa peered through the trees, trying to see what they had been led to. For a surprisingly long time she missed seeing the animals despite their size, caught out by the vastness of the empty woods stretching in all directions. Then a movement caught her eye: a dozen beetles rooting in the snow, or attacking the tree bark with blunt mandibles. They seemed unexceptional creatures, dull black and brown, some full-grown adults and some smaller ones that had probably still been grubs in the ground last spring. Then a further movement caught her eye, and she spotted what must surely be their quarry.

The stag, as Alain had named it, was a grand patriarch of beetles, considerably larger than any of his family, and armed with magnificent branching antlers that were half as long *again* as his bulky body. At first they seemed too large to be useful, but then the beetle's feathery antennae twitched, and it lifted its horns threateningly, moving them with a casual speed and strength.

Alain glanced back at his followers and raised his lance, apparently the signal to ready themselves.

'We will announce our presence,' Telse Orian murmured back to Tynisa. 'The stag will stand firm, to let his wives and family flee. The beaters and huntsmen will form a ring about him, and try to ensure that he does not make his escape. It is thus we will take him. Know that there is an order of precedence, in the hunt. The prince must strike first, and then the others by rank of family, so that honour and protocol are satisfied.' He twisted in the saddle to face her. 'I myself am here only with my bow, so if you wish to strike at the stag, you may wish to find another mount.'

The various servants were now spreading out on either side, moving forward cautiously between the trees. One or two of the beetles stopped feeding, antennae fluttering. The horses stamped and snorted, surely plainly visible and audible by now to the grazing insects.

Then some of the servants began making noise, beating

sticks against tree trunks, whooping and calling out, and the herd was instantly galvanized, females and younger beetles turning to thunder off, shouldering clumsily between the trees and dislodging curtains of cascading snow. The stag reared up, his great horns brandished fiercely against the sky, and abruptly Alain spurred his horse forward, lance in hand.

Tynisa could hardly breathe, in those brief seconds of his charge, as he propelled himself forward into the gape of those enormous mandibles. The huge stag was further away than she had thought, though, and Alain's mount darted off to one side even as the beetle lowered its antlers. The horns ripped furrows in the earth, and Alain cast his spear just as his steed galloped past. The weapon glanced off the beetle's thorax, dancing in the air for a moment before falling away.

The next rider was already in motion, his steed also hurtling forward as though he was deliberately trying to throw himself into the insect's jaws, then veering to the other side, as another spear was cast. This shaft found some purchase at the base of the stag's wing cases, thrumming there for a moment before rattling off, as the enraged beetle swerved and gave chase. The disdainful girl Velienn was next, seizing the opportunity of the insect's distraction to pitch her lance into the creature's abdomen, where it stuck and held firm.

The stag turned and lumbered away, with a surprising turn of speed, but by now the servants had completed their loose circle, and continued to shout and beat sticks directly in the creature's path. To Tynisa's astonishment it flinched away from them, rounding back towards the riders even as another of the nobles began to make his pass. The man was slightly slow in turning aside and, without warning, the great antlers were scything at him, so that Tynisa was convinced he would be crushed. Instead he just kicked up off his saddle, his wings pulling him up into the branches and well out of the beetle's reach. His mount fled the enraged insect instantly, which gave chase.

The clamouring of the servants made no impression on the

horse, and a moment later they were throwing themselves aside, as it charged through their ranks with the stag right behind it. Tynisa winced when one of the Grasshopper-kinden caught a blow from one clawed foot and was hurled aside with a shriek.

The next moment all the nobles were kicking their steeds into motion, chasing after the ponderous insect. Tynisa saw Alain draw alongside it and drive a second lance into the creature's side, leaning halfway out of the saddle with his wings flaring for balance. Then Telse Orian was drawing level on the opposite side, with Tynisa still clinging breathlessly to his waist. With casual grace, the Dragonfly nocked an arrow and let it fly, even as he steered his horse away, and Tynisa saw the shaft ram into place between two of the beetle's legs.

Abruptly the huge creature was no longer rampaging after the riderless horse, but making a break for the deeper forest. It went thundering off between the trees, in a blizzard of falling snow, the riders in hot pursuit and the footmen left to follow as best they could.

Alain took the lead, and Tynisa could not say whether this was more noble precedence, or whether he was simply the most skilled rider among them. When the stag scrabbled to a halt unexpectedly, his mount nearly ended up galloping up its wing-cases and on to its back. Tynisa could not see what had made the great insect stop, but it turned towards them now, at bay despite the open forest behind it. The riders pulled slightly away and passed back and forth before it warily, whilst their servants caught up.

Tynisa glanced from face to face, trying to understand if this was normal behaviour for the beast, but the young hunters were flushed with the chase, none of them seeming to find anything unusual. Looking beyond them, though, Tynisa noticed Lowre Cean frowning, while the Mantis Isendter glanced about him with narrowed eyes. She opened her mouth as if to warn against . . . what? She could put no words to it, but she had sensed something too.

Then Veliemm gave a shrill cry and charged at the stag, nimbly guiding her steed beyond the range of the arc of its jaws to plant another spear between the plates of its carapace. Then the hunt was back on, and another two nobles made their passes – one missing entirely, to the derision of his fellows. Alain headed forth next, but the beetle charged even as he was making his approach. After having apparently made its stand, this move was wholly unexpected, and the prince's steed was not yet moving fast enough to swerve out of the way. Tynisa heard the prince curse briefly, and she was already vaulting off Orian's mount, her sword leaping into her hand.

Alain kicked up out of his saddle, wings flowering from his shoulders. The unstoppable bulk of the stag struck his horse head-on, its great barbed mandibles, that each reached almost the whole length of the wretched steed, clashed together, and lifted the horse's jerking body clean off the ground, shaking it in fury. One flailing hoof clipped Alain even as he strove to spring clear, and sent him arcing over the stag's back to land awkwardly in the snow beyond.

The stag turned on him, the horse's ruined form dropping bonelessly from its jaws, but then one of the other riders gave a high, challenging cry to distract its attention. A mounted figure flashed past, his lance not held for throwing but couched in the crook of one arm, and only after he had gone did Tynisa recognize him as Lowre Cean. She saw the colossal beetle rear up before this new challenger, and saw Lowre begin to veer away. In that same moment, she thought he had left it too late, because he was cutting his escape much finer than the others had done. Lowre rammed his spear home with all the momentum his charging steed could provide, and only the high back to his saddle saved him from being thrown backwards by the shock of impact. He passed virtually under the stag's raised foreleg, crouching low along his horse's back, and in his wake, the beetle was already collapsing, his spear driven so deep between its jaws that more than half the shaft was hidden from view.

Alain was already starting to rise, shaking his head groggily, but Tynisa began running towards him.

'Still!' she cried out. 'Alain, stay still!'

She had a brief sense of other hunters reacting to this – with puzzlement or with annoyance at such familiarity – but then Isendter was also moving.

'My prince,' he snapped, 'heed her and be still.'

Alain froze, his eyes flicking from Tynisa to the Mantis, then to the stag's great rounded body, and back again. Behind Tynisa, the nobles had gone suddenly quiet, aware that something was amiss but not at all sure what.

She was close enough now that she could not keep running, so she made herself as still as she was willing Alain to be. She was poised at the very edge of a boundary that was invisible, and yet glaringly apparent to her and to the other Weaponsmaster. It was a boundary that Alain had unwittingly crossed.

The thing that loomed over Alain, so motionless as to be utterly unnoticed amongst the trees, now shifted slightly, swaying a fraction, and a murmur of shock ran through the noble hunters. Tynisa heard the slight creak of a bow being drawn.

'Make no moves,' she instructed, without looking back at them. 'Not while he is *there*.'

'This is absurd—' she heard a familiar disdainful voice start, and then another woman hissed, 'Velienn, *shut up*.'

Isendter was standing at that notional boundary, and dropped to one knee as if to survey the ground. He shot a glance at Tynisa, and understanding passed between them without the need for words.

He nodded, just once.

Tynisa began to advance, not in a headlong rush as previously, but at a slow shuffle, pushing the boundary back and back, her sword extended before her as though she were facing a fellow duellist at the Prowess Forum. Her eyes were fixed on her opponent, which meant tilting her head back considerably.

Isendter reached out a hand to his master. 'To me, my

Prince – but slowly. Move as the girl moves, stop when she stops. *Do not look back.*'

Alain gritted his teeth, keeping his eyes only on Tynisa. She shifted forward three steps, and he crawled the same distance towards Isendter. Two cautious steps in, matched by two careful steps out. Behind and above Alain, the great forest mantis shifted again, its all-seeing eyes watching each of them simultaneously. Alain was still well within the range of its spined forelimbs.

Tynisa could sense something else now, the same presence that had caused the stag to turn at bay. It was not the predator – though that was surely up to making a meal of the huge beetle – but something beyond it.

'Do your own people live here, Whitehand?' she hissed at Isendter from the corner of her mouth.

'Once they did,' he replied, which was the worst answer for her to hear. She had known places before where the Mantis-kinden had once lived, but dwelt no more. Sometimes they remained there, even though their living bodies had departed. She had not expected to find such a place in the Commonweal.

Another few steps in and she had passed Alain, usurping his place within reach of the insect's killing arms. As she held up her tiny needle of a sword, a subtle succession of sounds behind told her that Alain had made good his retreat, and was being drawn away by Isendter.

Which just leaves me, she thought. She heard the creak of the bow again, and knew it was Orian, and that the young nobleman was intending to do something noble and foolish. She thrust her left hand back towards him, palm out: *Wait!*

No arrow sped past, although the insect's head was cocked to one side now, the mandibles twitching like knife-tipped fingers. Slowly she reached for her brooch, tugged it from her jacket and held it up at arm's length. *You recognize this, don't you?* her gesture said.

Its triangular head tilted further forward, and she somehow

knew that it was regarding the Dragonfly-kinden arrayed behind her. 'They are under our protection,' she murmured, knowing that Isendter was still there and ready to back her up. The overarching mantis swayed again, as though trying to study the situation from all points of view.

Then it was picking its way backwards, with its killing arms still raised, until it reached a precise distance from her where their circles of influence no longer intersected. Whereupon it dropped down and moved off unhurriedly between the trees, a long, dark insect that was soon lost amid the confusion of trunks.

In its place, Tynisa now saw what she had known must be there. Twenty yards behind where the mantis had reared up was a circular clearing. It was not large, and the vegetation had made ample inroads into recolonizing it, but the weathered stump at its centre had been a totem once, such as she had seen far south of here on the same night she had earned the badge that was still clutched in her left hand.

A Mantis-kinden ritual site. Any questions she might have had about whether the Commonwealer Mantids were substantially different from their Lowlander kin were now answered. Blood had been spilled here, year after year, and though the Mantis-kinden had moved on, their legacy remained.

And then she saw him, hovering grey in the air above the ruined idol. Filmy and translucent he might be, but unmistakable. She risked a glance at Isendter, then at Alain, and it was clear that neither of them could see. Only she could preceive how, coalescing into view within the Mantids' sacred place here, was her father. Not that bloodied walking corpse that had lurked at the edge of her vision since his death, its outlines rendered barely human by the hacking treatment the Wasps had inflicted. This was the man unwounded and whole, for all that the trees showed through him, and though she stared and stared, he did not vanish, but grew stronger, heartbeat to heartbeat.

There was a moment when her three imagined haunters encroached on her, looming at her shoulders – Achaeos with his load of guilt, Salma's bright smile, slaughtered Tisamon. In contrast to it, though, they were faint echoes. She had known hardship and horror, loss and remorse. She had seen her father hacked to death, had lost her beloved, had dealt a friend a mortal blow, and small wonder that she had peopled her world with reminders. Only now did she realize that they had been merely her crutch, forever distracting her, forever swatting her mind away.

She appreciated how far she had been from being mad until now, for the momentary glimpses of those three dead men were nothing in comparison to this. *My father. Tisamon.*

He was gazing at her with that smile he sometimes wore as he fought. How hard he must have fought, indeed, to claw his way back thus from death. She wanted to drop to her knees, but instead she found that she was holding her stance, keeping her blade up ready to fight.

I do not believe in magic. But those words became a distant, waning refrain, banished utterly as soon as she heard his familiar lost voice inside her head.

My daughter, spoke Tisamon. *I am proud of you. I have so much left to teach you.*

He had his hand held out towards her, and she had a dreadful sense of vertigo, as though she stood at a cliff edge, with a fathomless void below her, and she was leaning out . . . and leaning out, and . . .

Surely this is a terrible mistake. The dead must stay dead. But he was her father, and she was far from home and lost, and more in need of help than she had ever been.

She reached and took his hand.

Twenty-Three

The fires would be seen for miles, making a statement that Dal had not quite wanted yet, but the fire-starters had intended just that, and he had not felt it politic to stop them.

Dal Arche had not known this village's name before he arrived here, or at least he had not been sufficiently interested to find out. Sara Tela was the name they had later supplied to him, though a piece of knowledge growing fast obsolete. All the houses were alight by now, those nearest the storehouse just starting to catch fire, whilst the first couple to be torched were blazing skeletons, with their outer shutters peeled away, and the inner walls merely ragged strips of charred wood. The wholesale destruction was a little ahead of schedule, for sparks were already drifting on to the storehouse's sloping roof even as his people were still loading up inside. There was food here, and wine, jars of kadith, bales of silk and cotton, all of it intended for onward barge to Leose. Unexpectedly there was also a small trove of old gold: inscribed lozenges dulled by time that had surely been pilfered by the local headman from some nearby ruin or mound. This discovery had put new heart into Dal's men, who had been less and less enthusiastic about this particular plan.

'Speed it up!' he shouted, letting his wings whisk him on to the storehouse roof, stamping on a few embers as he landed. His watchman was already there, the lean Grasshopper-kinden named Soul Je, one of the three companions who had accompanied Dal Arche since before he came to resume this bandit life.

'Any sign?' Dal asked him.

The Grasshopper shook his head. He had kept an arrow nocked to his longbow, but his chief purpose was keeping watch. When Dal arrived here, he had anticipated the possibility of someone taking notice. With the smoke forming a pillar all the way to the sun, such attention was guaranteed.

For the last tenday, Dal had been just testing the waters of brigandage. First there had been a few isolated individuals: a crofter, a herdsman, Dal's band making free with what little they possessed, slaughtering animals for meat, taking their food and drink. Dal had gathered around twenty men by that point and the pickings had been slim, even if their victims had been quick to surrender them.

Then there had been the attack on a convoy of pack-crickets led by a Dragonfly functionary bringing in some taxes. He had a quartet of Grasshopper guards escorting him, but Dal's people had caught them utterly by surprise, leaping or flying from all around with bows drawn back. The tax-gatherer had sat glumly by and watched the bandits whoop and cheer as they salvaged this unexpected haul. When they were done, Dal had considered letting his people shoot the witnesses, as many had wished to, but had ruled against it. Word was going to spread in any event, and if he got a reputation that suggested surrender was useless, then a great many such fights might get a good deal harder to win.

He had taken his men to ground after that, let them enjoy the meagre spoils in the heart of a small wood while he planned his next move.

It reminded him of the way it had been after the war. The Wasps had changed his life, but he could not say whether that was for the better or not. Before the war he had been a woodsman, hunting and tracking game to keep his village fed, spending his days out of doors and his nights in a variety of beds – a loner, but not an outsider, and with more than a few admirers. It was a better living than many enjoyed, surely. The village headman had not bothered him, and the nearest noble had barely troubled the headman. It was a way of life that had been turning its slow circles for ever, and could have done so for ever more – or so it seemed to all concerned.

Then the Wasp Empire had mounted its grand invasion – a people and a nation that nobody in Dal Arche's village had ever heard of, and originating so many miles away it might have been something out of a folk tale – until, that is, the prince's recruiters came. There was to be a levy, and the headman had been given a quota: young men and women to be sent off to the war.

Some had volunteered, most had been put forward by others or decided by the headman's fiat. The old man had even sent his own son, acting from faith or guilt. They had been supplied with spears and padded cuirasses, and Dal had brought along his little woodsman's bow. And so they had gone to war.

Of those young men and women conscripted into the Commonweal's grand army from Dal's village, only Dal himself survived. The others had died, almost all together, charging the Wasp lines: scorched by stings, lanced by crossbow bolts, butchered by the sword. Only Dal, the archer, had lived, to be taken up by the princes and put into another force. He had been one of several such archers, but he had been a swifter flier and a better shot, and more than that, he had come to understand that few of the nobles directing the battles had the slightest idea of what they were doing. The Wasps had come against them with their flying machines and their automotives, their ordered formations, their ballistae and their stings. In return, the Commonweal had brought its massed ranks of spears, its vast, untrained and frightened peasant levy, within which, studded like gems, were the glittering retinues of individual nobles and princes.

Dal never went home again. He did not want to look into

the faces of villagers he had grown up with, and see their eyes accuse him of the crime of being the only man to return. Nor could he go back to being a simple woodsman.

He had sworn that he would never be the subject of princes again.

After the war the Commonweal was a different place. The Monarch's lands had already possessed their share of vacant provinces, gone to seed without a noble's ruling hand and becoming a haunt for the lawless and the wild. The war had killed off many of the old families, and at the same time released onto the land far too many men who had known war, and would not take up the plough again.

Dal had thus become a bandit, and a leader of bandits. Then he had been caught, not by some aggrieved prince but by the Empire, near whose borders he had strayed. Escaping eventually from Imperial custody, he and three comrades had tried to make a living by hunting down fugitives, but business had been bad, and princes were poor paymasters. In the end it had been the free outlaw's life again for Dal.

He remembered Siriell, and how she had been building her own principality in miniature: yoking together violent men like Dal and making them work in partnership, laying the foundations of a community.

So much for that.

A few days ago he had acquired another thirty men, the first batch that Mordrec and the others had recruited, so he had decided it was time to go hunting once more. They had found a barge heading for Leose and captured it – there had been no guards, for word of Dal's activities was slow in spreading, and there had been little brigandage in these parts for years, thanks to Siriell's moderating influence. Dal had thought the barge attack had passed without bloodshed, but then the barge's master, for inexplicable reasons, had attacked one of the brigands as they were exploring the hold. In the fracas that followed, five of the barge's crew of six had been killed, but Dal shed no tears for them. If it was useful to have a reputation that said those who surrendered would live, it was similarly useful to make it known that those who resisted would die. That was the code of wise robbers by land and sea all over the world. As a compromise, he had let the final bargeman go unharmed, just to spread the tale.

The barge had originally been heading here to Sara Tela, and Dal and a few companions had then seen it to its destination. On arrival the headman had come down to the quay with his servants and household, eager to get the goods unloaded and ready for the tax collectors. Sara Tela was a wretchedly poor place, Dal had noted, the houses small and shabby, the land around it half barren, the fields mean. He had grown up in just such a place, living on land that could barely support the people farming it, let along a hierarchy of increasingly distant nobles.

Even as the man approached, Dal had put an arrow into the headman, before the eyes of his family and followers. Some of the rest had fled, others had tried to fight, but the bandits outnumbered them, and had arrows already nocked. It had been a short and miserable piece of business, and most of the locals had not run, but simply watched, not remotely minded to step in to save their headman or his henchmen, and maybe curious as to what Dal would do next. They had gathered their children close to them and watched. *We are poor*, their silence seemed to say. *Will you take that from us, too?*

A ripple had gone through them when Dal had sent his Scorpion lieutenant, Ygor, over to the storehouse to force open the door. Barad Ygor was a showman at heart and, after severing the rope ties with his claws, he had thrown the door wide and stepped back dramatically.

Now Dal Arche's followers were finishing up their looting, taking everything of value and loading it on the barge, before burning whatever was left behind. Those villagers who had fled would find all the days and months of their lives undone, and perhaps they would starve. Where would they go? Perhaps they would seek solace from their betters, begging at the steps of the nobility whose solemn duty was to provide for them and protect them. Dal did not rate their chances highly, for he had seen the face of the nobility, and by actions such as this he was going to hold a mirror up to it.

See what your rulers truly are, he thought. *I have seen, and so shall you.*

He would wager that the Salmae would be slow to offer succour to those he was now making homeless, but they would be quick to avenge this slight on their honour and this infringement of their feudal rights, just as they had not been able to leave Siriell's Town alone and in peace.

Soul Je jogged him with an elbow abruptly. Company was approaching: a party of riders galloping alongside the canal towards the blazing buildings.

Dal squinted, and counted half a dozen. A quick glance at the sky showed no sign of dragonfly-riders up there, nor had there been time for cavalry to come all the way from Leose itself. This must be some band of Mercers who happened to be in the area, perhaps investigating Dal's earlier misdeeds.

He kicked off from the roof and landed in the village's heart, surrounded by the collapsing skeletons of houses and a flurry of glowing embers. 'Get it stowed right away. They're coming!' he shouted, and his people, new and old, doubled their pace, practically throwing everything on to the barge. The draught-nymph was already in place ready to drag the bulky craft back the way it had come, though of course the riders could outstrip it easily.

There were Mercers and Mercers, Dal knew. If this little band turned out to be the Monarch's own – those wandering hero-magistrates who kept the peace, helped the needy, defended the weak, and put people like Dal Arche in his place – then his plan was sunk even before it could get under way. The Monarch had such good intentions, Dal knew, and would be horrified to learn that a peasant woodsman was gnawing at the fabric of Commonweal society in such a way. The Monarch was far, far away, though. The Monarch also, in Dal's firmly held belief, reserved righteous indignation for the unruly peasants of this world, and turned a blind eye to the evils of the great and the good unless they ventured into outright treason.

The Monarch dispatched Mercers across the Commonweal to do her will, but the Commonweal was vast, and they were few. So it was that each noble house maintained its own elite, and called them Mercers for all that the title had never been earned. Dal was betting a great deal that these riders were locally grown. They would still be well trained and equipped, with glittering armour of steel and chitin, with bows and swords and majestic steeds. They would also be equipped with a thousand years of tradition telling them how much *better* they were than the wretches who dared offend against the natural order of the world.

Dal shrugged his recurved bow off his shoulder, one hand selecting an arrow from his quiver.

The Commonweal had always had brigands, like a beast had ticks. They had included disaffected peasants, criminals, the estranged and the misfits. They had preyed on good and honest folk, and the princes had hunted them down and brought justice back to the land. Everyone knew that, of course.

There were fewer stories about those times when a noble had gone bad: second sons and daughters not content to be left without an inheritance, the cruel, the mad, the feuding – those who rallied evildoers about them and set themselves up as petty tyrants. It was considered bad luck to tell stories about such fallen princes, in case their virtuous kin should take offence.

Dal watched as the band of horsemen galloped closer to the burning village, while sparks drifted either side of him or landed, stinging, on his skin. The now-empty storehouse would catch fire soon enough, completing his day's work.

It was always the case: a few of Dal's people had not withdrawn soon enough, still chasing some last piece of loot, or just believing they knew better. One of them caught an arrow in the chest, the lead Mercer standing up in the saddle to loose it without his mount's speed slackening at all. The rest scattered as the six riders thundered between the burning ruins of the houses, aiming directly for the barge.

In the past, brigands had been nothing but angry, maladjusted farmers, with perhaps the odd woodsman amongst them who could string a bow. Mercers, even the local kind, were a constant terror to them. Even now the stragglers among Dal's people were fleeing in all directions, while the Mercers rode past them, turning in the saddle to aim and loose arrows at every target, and hitting them more often than not.

Dal took careful aim and loosed, too, but the rearmost rider shouted a warning even as he did so. The shaft struck the approaching woman's shimmering breastplate and glanced off, knocking her sideways and half out of the saddle. A moment later, she had taken to the air, as did half the others.

Soul Je took careful aim and put a three-foot shaft through the Mercer woman, striking an inch over her breastplate's collar and plucking her out of the sky. Dal's shaft was supposed to have provided the signal, but it was her blood that prompted the brigands to counterattack.

Of those fleeing to the barge, perhaps a dozen had courage enough to turn around and face the horses, bending bows and setting spears. Amongst them was the Wasp, Mordrec, his hands flashing fire as the Mercers came on. On all sides, though, Dal's people were suddenly springing from behind bushes, from the perilous shadows of burning buildings, from the waters of the canal itself. Arrows danced and sang through the air, mostly to no avail, but three separate shafts managed to strike the same man and throw him from his saddle. He was still alive as he hit the ground, his mail preserving him from the onslaught of the flimsy hunting bows most of the bandits carried. Then there were spearmen converging on him, three or four of them together, and within six or seven stabs they had found some part of him the armour did not cover.

The other Mercers were circling, two on horseback still and two in the air. Had they chosen to flee then, they would have got away with it. Dal could see their faces, though, and realized that they could not believe what was happening to them – that peasants were taking such liberties with their lives.

Dal Arche selected another arrow, then waited for a target to present itself. He saw one of the horses rear and fall as Mordrec's sting lashed into it. The rider tried heading for the sky but one of Dal's men struck him across the back with a cudgel, and another, a Grasshopper, leapt high in the air and grabbed hold of him, bringing the stunned man down to earth again. Another Mercer had gone down with a crossbow bolt in the leg, courtesy of Barad Ygor, and now Ygor's pet scorpion was busy savaging the victim, claws prying apart mail and plates to get at the meat beneath.

Dal Arche sighted carefully, as calm as a man on a practice range, and sent a shaft through one of the fliers' throat even as the Mercer was drawing back his own bowstring.

Their final opponent was ascending, up and up, still staring downwards in incredulous horror. Dal called up his own wings, but Soul was aiming, string pulled back beside his ear as he sighted almost into the sun. The arrow leapt from his bow, so fast as to seem invisible, and all Dal saw was the shuddering impact, and then the Mercer was tumbling from the heavens.

In the old days, bandits had been those unable or unwilling to live under the rule of princes, and perhaps that had not changed. What had changed, though, was the number of disgruntled peasants who had been ripped from their land and forced to fight in a war, who had seen their friends and comrades and families cast away in one doomed battle after another, as the Empire ground its way across the Commonweal map. They had died in their droves, those levies of the Commonweal, given spears but no training and scattered like chaff against the greatest armies of the world. Those who had survived, though . . .

Those that survived had learned soldiering the hard way. Men like Dal Arche himself, baked hard in the fires of war, tough men with sharp edges. They had lasted out the war itself and then found they could not go home, either because it was now beneath the Imperial flag, or because they had changed so much in character that nowhere in the Commonweal seemed like home to them.

They were the men who had learned what comes of following princes.

When the fighting was over, Dal flew down to confer with his lieutenants, as the rest of his men prepared the barge for its departure.

'We won't get it that easy again,' Mordrec remarked.

'When have we ever had it easy?' Dal asked him. 'I want you three to go back south and keep recruiting. We'll need more men.'

'The Salmae are going to be riled,' noted the Wasp. 'We're sure we know what we're doing?'

Dal looked from face to face. 'The Salmae have already shown us that they won't accept us as neighbours. They wrote that message clear enough. Now we've sent them our reply, in proper noble language.'

'We've declared war,' Mordrec translated.

'That's what I said,' agreed Dal, seeing Soul Je, who seldom spoke, nodding in agreement.

Dal turned to view his followers, casting his gaze over all of them. The new faces, those who had formerly been the peasants of Sara Tela, were staring at the dead Mercers with a world of possibilities in their eyes.

Twenty-Four

Salme Elass, Princess of Leose, felt herself poised on the brink of a great height, and the time had come to cast herself from it.

She sat in the chamber she governed from: not for her a garden, like Felipe Shah, but a high-ceilinged room where lofty windows let in coloured shafts of light that crossed each other like sword blades. There was a warrior statue on either side of her, the kind that the ancient magicians of her people had supposedly been able to imbue with life in order to defend their royal charges. *All lost,* she thought. *Yet another thing lost, and nobody will do anything to stop these sands running through our fingers.*

There were some, she knew, who had already grown sick with that loss, so that they turned away from the destiny that princes lived for. Felipe Shah had grown weak after the war, cut so deep by his losses that he feared to take any action, lest some further calamity befall him. Lowre Cean was another, although Elass still had a use for him.

And the Monarch is a third. A strong Monarch would make a strong Commonweal, but there was only silence from Shon Fhor. The land might as well now be leaderless.

It is time for someone of will and ambition to take a stand and recover what we have lost. The Commonweal can rise again, but those of us who are not grown palsied by doubt must act.

On either side of the two statues stood her chief servants:

Isendter Whitehand, her champion, and Lisan Dea, her seneschal, both of them bound to her by the iron chains of loyalty. Both also thinking they knew best, but they were not prince or princess. They were not even Dragonfly-kinden, merely servants.

The brigands to the south were growing bold, no doubt expecting the usual Mercer patrols in response, just enough manpower diverted in their direction to make their raids difficult and costly and persuade them to look elsewhere for their loot. Thus the Commonweal had been dealing with its internal problems for years, either letting the villains run riot in abandoned provinces, or passing them on to a neighbour, who passed the problem on in turn, all motivated by some hope that time itself would smooth over the growing cracks.

No more. Elass had already sent out summonses to those minor nobles who she knew would heed her, and would therefore act. They were few enough, a half-dozen tiny families with a handful of house guards and a minuscule levy available to them. There were others, though, who had the resources but lacked the will. She needed a standard to inspire them, for the name of the Salmae was not yet great enough in its own right.

Ungrateful wretches, she thought bitterly. Her husband had died in the war, and her eldest son, too, and then her middle son had been taken by Felipe and sent to die in the Lowlands. *And still they will not rise up at my bidding.*

It would be different, she knew, if it were Lowre Cean sounding the horn and leading the charge. The old man's name still carried weight, one of the few Commonweal leaders who had won any significant victories against the Empire. The effort of it had worn Lowre out, though, since he had lost his lands, his wife, his adored son. Even though he lived on Salmae soil, and by her graces, he would not draw his sword for her.

Until now, I hope, for something had changed. The girl had come, the one who had been trailing Alain's footsteps so much. Elass was unsure of the Lowlander's significance, but apparently Felipe Shah had been much impressed with her, and now she was part of old Lowre's household, and obviously held in some esteem. Then there had been that business with the dance, and some piece of drama at Alain's idiot hunt. She had made a name for herself, and it was not hard to see the direction her affections were pointed in.

It would not be the first time that Alain had come back with some beggar girl following at his heels, believing . . . what? Believing that the sanctity of princes would make her an exception, Elass supposed. And of course, they had no princes in the Lowlands, no royal blood, nothing but a grubby overclass of merchants, so she understood. The Spider girl would never be a suitable match for Alain, but likewise she would never understand the barriers between them. But she might be useful: a tool to take in hand and turn against the world, for old Lowre Cean was sentimental, and had clearly taken the girl to heart. Where a princess's pleas might fall on deaf ears, the same words from Maker Tynise could sway him. So long as Elass could control her. So long as Alain had not already overplayed his part.

The nobility of the Commonweal observed complex strata of love-play, tiers and hierarchies, subtle distinctions, all the soft arts and their related games – the degrees of distance and attachment. There were the casual attractions, involving a single meeting and a parting, and no more. There were the soul-mates married and matched and bound together. There were the comrades enjoying a closeness of delicate balance not to be marred by fierce passions but no less a bond of love. The Spider girl hardly merited either of the last two, but Elass could only hope that her son had not already made of Tynisa the former – already had her and had done with her – leaving nothing that Elass could use.

For of course there was another relationship, to be held close and yet not touched: that of the useful servant, the special tool that will only be persuaded by promises. *And let Alain remember his station, what he is and what she is, and not raise her too high nor cast her too far away . . .*

'You are sure she will come here?' she asked, speaking into the silence that had held sway for more than an hour now, while she reflected.

'My divination tells me so – and soon. Today most likely,' Lisan Dea replied.

'Then you must be ready to greet her,' Elass instructed, with a gesture of dismissal. Lisan was unhappy about the business, she knew, but it was not her seneschal's place to comment on the designs of her betters.

'The girl has changed since she was last here,' Isendter observed, as the echoes of Lisan's footsteps faded.

'In what way?'

The Mantis was silent for a long moment before he spoke. 'It is hard to tell. She may seem a Spider, but there was always something of my people about her, perhaps granted to her by the badge she bears. Now that part has become greater. I look on her now and my mind says *Mantis,* whatever my eyes tell me.'

'She has thoughts still for Alain, however she's changed, I am sure,' Elass decided. 'Will she join the fight?'

'Yes,' came the immediate and firm response. 'You may have no fear of that.'

Tynisa had expected a change of weather heralding the spring, but instead the skies had opened up with fresh snow, which lay in foot-thick drifts as far as the horizon. Lowre Cean had told her this was perfectly normal.

'I understand it is different in your Lowlands,' he had mused, 'but here the winter does not let go without a fight.'

And something had twitched with approval inside of her, and she had smiled without meaning to.

'I must practise now,' she had told him, and departed for the courtyard where, before an audience of Roach-kinden travellers and a gang of Bee-kinden Auxillian deserters, she had thrown herself through all the paces that her father had ever taught her, every trick of footwork and bladework, as the snow filtered down around her.

She did not recall coming back here after the hunt. Her mind had been so seared by that impossible image of her father standing there before the Mantis icon, gleaming and translucent, holding one spined hand out to her. She remembered nothing else. They told her that she had collapsed.

When she had awoken, the nobles were long gone, but one of their party had remained by her bedside. She had opened her eyes to see the severe features of Isendter Whitehand.

'It has been two days, almost,' he had informed her, before she could ask him.

She had stared into his face. *I saw . . .* but what would it mean to him? Instead, what had emerged from her lips was, 'Alain . . .'

'Is in Leose by now.'

'But he asked you to stay with me,' she had pressed, hoping.

'I would have stayed of my own will, unless ordered away,' he had told her but, after a pause in which she felt sour disappointment creeping in, added, 'You are correct though. Prince Alain wishes to know when you are well again.'

She had swung her legs out of bed, staring at the floor just to hide her smile from him. 'And now?'

'I shall return to his side and report.' Yet he had made no move, and she glanced up at him. His expression had been measuring, almost wary. 'You have been . . . touched by something. I am no magician, but I sensed it there, at the shrine.'

'Yes,' she had confirmed, giving him no other details.

'Be wary of such contact, Maker Tynise. The world of the living does not easily walk hand in hand with the world of either spirits or the dead.'

'I have no fear of it. What else can I trust, if not this?' she had replied blithely. His troubled expression had remained as he bowed and left her.

While dressing, she had looked about for some sign of her

father, but he was not to be seen. Instead she heard an echo within her head, words remembered from long ago. *You must practise. How else will you honour your gifts?*

It was true that, since Tisamon's death, she had not kept to the rigorous training he had prescribed for her. In the depth of her loss that had not seemed important, but now she suddenly felt that she had betrayed his memory by her laxness. She had a duty to the badge she wore, to a thousand years of heritage.

With the thought, she felt a distant surge of approval.

She did not believe in ghosts, but suddenly there was something new for her, a hand on her tiller to steer her course true. She could *not* have seen her father, of course, but even so, she felt him near her.

You must face the world without fear. Life is struggle.

Of course it is, she told herself. That was the Mantis way, after all: meet the world with a drawn blade, to either conquer or die.

What do you want? had come the question, the one she asked inside her own head, couched in that cold, far-off voice.

'Salme Alain,' she murmured in response, savouring his name.

Then you must stalk him and win him, she told herself, in that same voice. *And I shall show you how.*

Some days later she had left Lowre's compound, in thick snow, and headed for Leose. The Commonweal weather, which had previously seemed something almost supernatural, was put in its place as just one more way for a Weaponsmaster to test herself.

She did not stop at Gaved and Sef's hut. A Wasp and a Spider, what were they to her?

On waking up after the hunt, the world had seemed more simple, its colours brighter, the divisions between light and dark that much more clear. The endless round that her mind had kept treading – all those paths of guilt and worry – had fallen away from her. That her father and Salma were dead did not sting: they had died as warriors after all. That Achaeos was dead . . . She explored the thought like touching a rotten tooth. *Regret is for the weak*, came her inner voice. *Do not hide from what your blade has done. If you slew him, then surely he was your enemy.*

She had not yet let go of regret, but her grip was loosening. How attractive it would be to rewrite her personal history so that her stabbing of Achaeos became not a crime but a justified exercise of her superiority.

Her trek to Leose was almost completely solitary, with the vast expanse of the frozen Commonweal like a canvas about her: a world picked out in white and grey and dark shadow. She might have been the last living thing in the world.

Each day she would travel until noon, then pause to eat and to train, finding once again her perfect balance with the blade, all the old moves and passes that she had allowed to rust while she indulged her sense of guilt. Each session of bladework cleansed her of another layer of useless distractions, honing her to a point.

She had a purpose now, or rather, the purpose that she had been standing on the brink of for some time had now coalesced. *I want Salme Alain.* And the answer came, *And you shall have him, but you must perfect yourself until he cannot deny you.*

So it was that she found herself at the gates of Castle Leose, under the wary eyes of the guards in shimmering armour.

They sent for Lisan Dea, of course, and the Grasshopper seneschal came out, eventually, to regard Tynisa wearily.

'You have some message from Lowre Cean?' she asked grimly.

'You know why I am here,' Tynisa told her evenly. *Do not make me prove myself to you.* A part of her weighed up the woman and found her wanting. She was nothing but a grand clerk, after all.

The Grasshopper stared at her, stepping close enough for Tynisa to impale her just by drawing her rapier from its scabbard, one fluid motion so swift that the guards would barely see it before it was done. The thought played itself out in her mind, and she had to fight against simply letting her body follow suit.

'Go home,' said Lisan Dea softly, giving her another of those hidden looks. 'Lowlander, go home.'

Tynisa smiled keenly. 'I have no home in the Lowlands. That is why I've come here.'

The seneschal opened her mouth to utter some further dismissal, but then a shifting amongst the guards heralded a new arrival. Without fanfare, the princess herself was with them.

'I thought I recognized the Lowlander girl from my window,' she remarked. 'Tell me, why have you taken it upon yourself to turn away our guests?'

Lisan Dea stood very straight, looking ahead and not daring to glance at her mistress. She made no reply.

'You are a capable enough servant for peacetime, Lisan, but perhaps not fit to act as my seneschal in war. Return inside and contemplate that,' the princess ordered. Tynisa expected a glare from the Grasshopper as she obeyed, but instead caught an unguarded expression: she read sadness on the face of Lisan Dea, and not as a response to her mistress's anger.

'You seek my son, no doubt,' the lady of the Salmae observed. 'I have heard about your actions during the hunt, and the Salmae recognize our debts. Come with me.' She turned and strode inside.

Elass led the girl to her throne room, never once glancing back but confident that mere curiosity would draw the Lowlander after her. *She should appreciate that I am doing her a great honour.* But these foreigners seemed to have little grasp of propriety, and who could blame them, being bereft of proper rulers, no great familes, no royal blood. They should be congratulated for not declining into utter savagery.

Taking her accustomed seat between the two statues, she saw Tynisa hovering uncertainly in the doorway.

'Sit,' she said, the word sounding somewhere between an invitation and an order. Tynisa entered cautiously and Elass saw her eyes flick towards the friezes adorning the walls, all the life-size figures carved in high relief. Noblemen and women of the Commonweal led horses or drew back bowstrings, waged war in elegant mail or played musical instruments. The girl obviously possessed some latent courtesy, Elass decided, for although distracted, she proceeded to the correct position where a petitioner should kneel, and sank to the floor.

For a moment, Elass adopted a stern face, studying this Spider-kinden waif before her. *Whitehand is right: something has changed within her.* There was now an edge to her that had not been evident before, a purpose. Even sitting, the girl exuded a sense of being kept still only under restraint, and that if her leash were slipped she would explode into violence. *And how may I channel that?* Elass let her expression lighten, like stormclouds dissipating from the sky.

'I learn that you performed admirably on the hunt,' she stated. 'Most importantly, my champion speaks well of you, and his faintest praise is worth the applause of many.'

She saw no flush of pleasure at the words. The girl accepted the praise as Isendter himself would have, impassively.

'Alain is not here, or doubtless he would have met you at our gates himself,' Elass began. Just then, and as she saw Alain's name spark life from the girl's expression, a servant entered with a pair of scrolls for his mistress. She laid one down and scanned the contents of the other, apparently forgetting Tynisa's presence. Another servant was suddenly at her elbow, placing bowls for kadith.

'I understand that you are Maker Tynise of Collegium,' the princess continued absently.

Tynisa merely nodded.

'Alain will not have given you my personal name. The boy never was one for proper introductions. I am Salme Elass – although, of course, you should address me as "my Princess" or "my lady."' As she mummed reading the scroll she was watching the girl obliquely.

Of course, revealing one's name was a privileged concession, but Elass was not sure whether the Lowlander knew that. She saw an understanding somewhere in Tynisa's eyes, though, that names represented power to the Inapt, and so she would think she was being given some great gift.

Elass followed this indulgence with a smile, transforming her face from stone to flesh. 'My son will need you, in the near future,' she said.

Again Elass read that curious reaction: the eagerness of the young woman that became the eagerness of the Weaponsmaster to prove her skill. For a moment, Elass found herself disconcerted by the latter, sensing almost a personal danger here. *She is so young, and of such an unusual kinden, that I had forgotten that she must have earned that badge.* For a moment she wondered whether using this tool would be wise, but then she dismissed the doubts. *So, she is a sharper blade than I had thought. No matter, though, as long as I hold the hilt.*

'We are at war,' Salme Elass declared flatly.

'War?' Tynisa was startled into speech, and that same eagerness for combat waxed like a flame behind her eyes.

'Ah, you have a tongue, then?' Salme Elass permitted herself another smile. 'You will not have heard of this, while in Prince Lowre's care, for he always seeks to isolate himself, but this province is under attack, and even now Alain has flown off to scout the enemy. This coming spring we will be obliged to fight.'

'Is it the Empire?' Tynisa enquired, even though she must surely know how far they were from the Wasps. Unconsciously, her hand curled towards her rapier hilt, and Elass found herself delighted. *How I shall use her against Lowre Cean!*

'Not the Wasps, but a considerable danger nonetheless. There is a brigand army assembling at our southern border, challenging our rightful authority. The winter has seen them coming to seek easy prey amongst my people, and for that they must be destroyed. Alain shall be in the vanguard of the assault, and I hope, Tynise, that you shall be alongside him.'

'Of course.' The words came without the need for further thought.

Salme Elass nodded, looking down at the scroll again. 'There is one matter in particular that you can aid us with.' She paused to ensure Tynisa was listening. 'I have few swords that I can call upon here at Leose. My people are diminished since the war, and these brigands are many. Therefore I need to call upon my allies, but I fear they may not answer me. There is one, in particular, whose skills would hasten our victory and so save many lives. His mere presence would hearten those loyal to the Monarch, and strike fear into our enemies. He is old, however, and he suffers from a curious condition whereby he seeks to hide from what he was, by losing himself in mundane pursuits unworthy of him.' She looked up again, and saw that the girl understood.

'Lowre Cean,' Tynisa offered, thoughtfully.

'I will ride to visit him shortly,' Elass explained, 'but I am unsure of the welcome I will receive there. However, if there was one of his own household who spoke on my behalf, and had already softened his resolve, then my task would be that much the easier. We need him.'

There was a brief moment's pause in which Tynisa surely weighed up all that she had experienced of Lowre Cean: an old man bumbling aimlessly from one pointless pastime to the next. But Elass knew that Lowre had acquitted himself admirably on the hunt, at the last moment, when no other would step in, and Tynisa had surely seen that, too.

'I shall do it,' the girl confirmed, and Elass carefully restrained her smile from growing any wider.

A tenday later, Salme Elass herself arrived at Lowre's enclave, a nearly unprecedented occurrence. The old man met her in his main hall that was, for once, cleared of most of his other transient guests. He sat at one end of it and, though wearing only a darned robe, his posture and bearing had transformed him again into Prince-Major Lowre Cean rather than the semi-recluse normally to be seen pottering about the compound.

A little late to try and recapture all that authority, she reflected. Elass sat across the room from him arrayed in her full and formal robes of silk ornamented with gold trim and silver threads. Isendter knelt at her right hand, his head bowed in deference.

'My lord,' she said, instilling available humility into her tone, for all that this whole enclave of his was but guesting on her land, 'you have heard now how the people of Elas Mar are oppressed, how villains are come north from the unclaimed provinces to burn and rob, and prey on the honest folk who live under my protection. I cannot stand idly by at such a time and, my lord prince, I am sure that you cannot either. You fought with my husband against the Empire, and your victories are famed throughout the Commonweal, so I am sure you will take up arms to defend what was his. Having dwelt here in Elas Mar all the years since your own estates were lost, I am sure that you would defend your newfound home. You have been a Mercer in your time, and surely you cannot stand by and see evil done. Therefore I ask you now to attend my war muster at Leose and give us the benefit of your wise counsel, strengthening my few followers with your own. What do you say, my lord prince?'

Lowre Cean looked away from her and pinched at the bridge of his nose. Elass let her eyes flick across to Tynisa, sitting on the sidelines, and found the girl's attention was fixed firmly on the old man. *She has already done her part,* the noblewoman decided. Tynisa had obviously hurried back to Lowre's compound full of righteous purpose, and how could the old man say no to all that? How could he have lessened and lowered himself in the eyes of his new ward, by refusing to go to battle?

Elass particularly enjoyed the slightly baffled expression she saw on the girl's face. There was a war on, and Tynisa plainly could not understand why Lowre Cean would not gladly cast aside the mundane in order to don his armour once again.

The Prince-Major sighed. 'I am an old man and I have long put aside warlike pursuits. Your husband was a comrade to me, before the war took him away. He was a comrade to my son, before the Wasp-kinden killed him also.' He was speaking so softly that Elass had to lean in to catch the words. 'I am no necromancer to know the wishes of the dead, however.'

He paused then, as one of his servants produced kadith, Isendter pouring for his mistress and Lowre's young messenger performing the same duty for his master.

'Nor can I allow the happenstance of residence to move me, for all I was invited here in your husband's fond memory,' Lowre continued, at last. 'The Commonweal is wide, even that part of it left to us by the Wasps, and there are no longer so many of us to people it as before. There are other places for a man such as me, if need be.'

Another pause, age-old conversational paths meandering between them.

'As for evil, that is a dangerous word that can turn like a centipede and bite its holder. I will make no judgements regarding evil,' Lowre added. 'These arguments cannot move me.'

Elass nodded, nothing daunted. 'And if I extend the invitation to all your folk here, so that they may join me in this venture, be we however few, be the enemy so many? I am sure that there are some here who will do what must be done, even without your leadership to guide them. Or perhaps there is some other reason whereby you might agree to lend us your skills.' She pointedly did not look to Tynisa, but Lowre knew exactly what she meant. *Join me or not, the girl is mine now. She would stand in a fire if I told her my son would applaud it. So, Cean, what does she mean to you? Is she a mere distraction that you will let go easily? If she does mean something, will you let her go off to war while you remain behind? Another name to add to your list of the fallen, Cean?*

The Prince-Major gave a long sigh, looking older than he had ever done before: just a frail old man, now. The messenger beside him put a concerned hand on his arm. 'Oh, I'll come,' the old man agreed at last. 'My counsel you shall have, even though you may not like it. I shall bring my few followers to join your new grand army. I shall not plan your battles for you, though, Princess Salme Elass. I have enough blood on my account already.'

It was the smallest of defeats, now that he had agreed to lend his name to her offensive, but for a moment Elass found even this thwarting response hard to bear. So the great tactician, the hero of Masaka, would just watch idly, would he? Did he fear that his skills might have rusted from disuse? Or was he looking forward to laughing at the mistakes of others? Anger rose inside her, but she fought it down and was all calm once more. 'We will be honoured by your presence, my Prince,' she told him. 'I shall hold a muster of all those who will lend their strength to mine – within a tenday I shall hold it. I shall look out for you there.'

Twenty-Five

The barge brought them to within sight of Suon Ren and offloaded them – two Wasps and an unconscious Beetle girl – without comment. The vessel's crew had spoken barely a word to them throughout the long journey, but had just as obviously been glad to have them aboard. They had treated the two renegade Imperials as though they were guard animals of proven ferocity. The horror of the Twelve-year War would resound in Commonweal minds for decades yet to come.

Che had not been comatose the whole way. She woke sporadically, clawing at the air, talking feverishly, staring about her. Thalric then made it his business to get some water into her, and sometimes even food. She would wander about the barge, bumping into things, flinching from objects invisible. She spoke to him, too, but it was seldom him she actually saw. Often she would explain something at great speed, something mystical that the two Wasps could not follow. Sometimes she was trying to flee from something, and had to be restrained from simply flying off the barge. Once . . .

Once she was being tortured, or under threat of it, and Thalric knew with a sick feeling that, this time of all of them, she saw him for who he was.

He wondered at what point he had changed, that he no longer considered just abandoning her.

Some nights, as Varmen slept, Thalric would sit and gaze

down at her, as she trembled and twitched in the grip of whatever affliction had befallen her. His feelings of despair, during those lonely hours past midnight, were nothing he would ever admit to in the light of day.

The journey from the Commonweal's borders to Suon Ren had proved steady and untroubled, and in Thalric's mind was a simple thought, *What now?* They had come here at Che's behest, for reasons to do with her foster-sister, yet it seemed unlikely to him that Tynisa was now within a thousand miles of them. Che seemed to have picked Suon Ren randomly from a map of all the places she had ever heard about and, now they were here, she was in no state to capitalize on it. Thalric himself did not know the plan. *I don't mind making my own way, I don't mind receiving orders, but this in-between business is no use at all.*

'They have a prince at Suon Ren, don't they?' he asked, casting his mind back to the war. *Isn't this where Stenwold Maker was heading in search of Commonwealer allies?*

'A big one, I think,' Varmen agreed. 'Going to seek an audience, are you?'

'I need help.' Thalric glanced down at Che. 'I need a doctor, or at least what passes for one in this place. Problem is, I can't see how two war veterans like us will carry much weight when it comes to exacting favours from princes . . .' A flicker of movement caught his eye, and now he saw a handful of Dragonflies approaching. Two of them were armoured in a way that was depressingly familiar, provoking a momentary recollection of men and women like that seen on the battlefield, glittering and graceful, and doomed.

They landed in front of the two Wasps: two warriors in shimmering mail, and another man who was lean and grey, wearing what Thalric took to be fine clothes of the local cut. Whereas the warriors held swords and were watching the Wasps warily, their leader had eyes only for Che.

Something twitched in the Dragonfly's face, as he studied her, and he said, 'She must be taken before Prince Felipe.'

Thalric exchanged a glance with Varmen. 'Then we must go with her.'

The Dragonfly regarded him narrowly, but nodded agreement at last, and Thalric wondered whether the man simply felt it was too dangerous to leave two Wasp-kinden running loose. 'Send for a stretcher and bearers,' he ordered one of his fellows. 'She must be shown respect.'

At that moment Che awoke, wide-eyed, flinging an arm out as though to protect herself, crying out wordlessly. There were tears in her eyes.

Thalric looked at the Dragonflies to see if this display had diminished their 'respect', but to his surprise he saw that, if anything, they were eyeing Che with a measure of superstitious awe.

Entering Suon Ren, Thalric caught Varmen's eye, and thought he saw a kindred look of recognition on the man's face. For both of them equally, this pure Commonweal architecture must provoke memories of once putting it to the torch.

Their escort took them to the exact centre of the town, a broad area of open space that must serve as a meeting place or muster or market for the people of Suon Ren. All the locals were staring, perhaps wondering if this was some precursor to further Imperial aggression. The adults' faces were hostile, yet fearful, as though even just two Wasps posed a danger to their entire town. The children, however, pointed and whispered, and soon the oldest of them were exercising their Art wings, seeing who could swoop closest to the dreaded enemy. Some even mimed being seared by stingshot, spiralling from the air to collapse with great theatrics. To Thalric it all seemed in horribly bad taste, from these children who had surely lost relatives in the war.

'We will now take her to the prince,' explained the leader of the escort. 'You will stay here.'

'Now wait – where she goes, I go,' Thalric insisted, but the man merely raised an eyebrow. He jerked his head slightly in the direction of the wooden-frame castle on the hill, and Thalric saw that another half-dozen soldiers had appeared from it, with bows in hand.

'You will wait here,' the Dragonfly repeated, as though instructing a slow student. The stretcher-bearers took up their burden once again, and they set off for the castle.

There was just a moment when Thalric thought of going after them, bows or not, but then his common sense reasserted itself. He had no feeling to suggest that the Commonwealers actually meant Che any harm, and perhaps it was sensible for a prince to avoid private audiences with the Wasp-kinden.

Varmen himself sat down, and his pack-beetle drew close and nuzzled at him until he unwrapped a parcel of nuts for it to grind away at. After a while, Thalric joined him, as there seemed little else to do. The adult Commonwealers around them were studiously not paying the strangers too much attention, but at the same time were not dispersing either, each finding some reason to stay within sight of the two Wasps.

'Executions all round, you reckon?' Varmen asked eventually. 'Reckon this prince is one of the fierce ones who're still smarting from the war?'

Thalric shrugged. 'It would make sense. This is the man the Lowlanders approached, when they wanted Commonweal aid against us.'

Varmen grunted. 'Nice to have been told *that* before.'

'I didn't ask you to come.'

'That'll teach me to do the decent thing,' grumbled Varmen. Deftly, he drew open the beetle's pack and took out his breastplate. 'You up to doing a few buckles? It's a lot quicker with someone helping.'

They're going to shoot us any moment, Thalric suspected, but then reckoned that might be true whatever they did. With that in mind, he turned his back on the Dragonfly archers and helped Varmen on with his armour, finding a certain calming quality in the ritual of latching and tightening wherever the ex-Sentinel directed. Soon enough, Varmen had breast and back armour, pauldrons on his shoulders, tassets hanging from his belt, the gauntlets on and helm at the ready.

'That'll do,' he decided. 'Besides, they're coming this way.'

Thalric glanced up to see that the soldiers' leader had returned, and now the whole pack were approaching cautiously. He took his stand alongside Varmen, hoping that his copperweave shirt would turn away a few arrows, if need be. For the first time in a long while, he found himself wishing for some black and gold livery to match the other Wasp's armour.

The Commonwealers stopped short of the Wasps, and Thalric could practically see the ghosts of the Twelve-year War in their eyes. At last, though, their leader said, 'My prince wishes to speak with you,' uttered as though the words were bitter gall.

So it was that two Wasps, armoured and armed, came to visit the court of Felipe Shah.

Thalric had seen enough during the war for Felipe's garden serving as an audience chamber not to surprise him. There were a half-dozen Dragonflies scattered irregularly about it, kneeling in attendance, but it was clear who was the prince and who merely the hangers-on. Felipe Shah had dressed himself formally in robes that were stiff and elaborately embroidered, and edged with plates of gold. Their colours shimmered and changed with his slightest movement and at every shadow or change of the light.

The soldiers and their belligerent leader were obviously intending to stay as close as possible to the Wasps, to forestall any treachery, but the prince shook his head.

'Coren, no,' he said simply, and the archers backed away until they were loitering at the very furthest limit of the castle, a grey area where the open-sided design of the walls muddied who was inside and who was without. The man called Coren retreated to some nook behind his master's back.

For a long time, Prince Felipe Shah just stared at the two Wasps – long enough for Thalric to become uncomfortable. He had plenty of history among the Commonwealers, but none of it on a social footing. He had no idea what to expect, or whether this scrutiny was simply considered good form for a Dragonfly-kinden.

At last the man spoke. 'What do you seek here?' His quiet voice sounded weary.

Every kind of grand response marched through Thalric's mind, but all he finally said was, 'Help.'

'The Empire seeks help?' It was said without rancour, indeed almost matter-of-factly.

'I seek help. We are neither of us good sons of the Empire – not any more – and we seek help for *her*, not for ourselves.'

'Why here?'

'Because here is where she was going, when . . . when it happened.' It appeared that candour must be the order of the day, but Felipe's reaction proved encouraging, a little of his reserve dropping away.

'Do you know what she is?'

'Cheerwell Maker, the niece of a previous guest of yours – or so I'm told,' Thalric replied promptly. 'Your Highness, I don't know what's wrong with her, but . . .' The words would not come, perhaps because of Varmen's solid Apt presence beside him. Felipe Shah did not assist him either, merely waited. Thalric gritted his teeth, feeling acutely embarrassed to even contemplate coming out with the words.

Khanaphes, he reminded himself. *The tunnels, the Masters, all that inexplicable misadventure that we shared there. The Empress, for the world's sake! The Empress, who drinks the blood of slaves and is . . .* He shuddered. *The Empress, whom Che spoke of, just before* it *happened. I do not believe, I cannot believe, but even so . . .* 'Something unnatural has happened to her,' he got out, the word 'magic' faltering on his tongue. 'She has been . . . attacked in some way.' His expression, if he could have seen it, was mutely appealing, begging the Dragonfly to fill in the gaps without him having to be too explicit.

The prince's eyebrows lifted in surprise. 'Yes, she has,'

he admitted. 'My seers have examined her, and they are . . . disturbed.'

'Can you help? Or your . . . seers? Doctors . . . you must have doctors here, of any kind.' There was an edge of desperation in Thalric's voice that he could not prevent.

'They say she has departed her body, and that she is now a ghost,' Felipe Shah informed them.

Thalric felt Varmen shift beside him, his credulity strained to its limits. 'A ghost . . .' he managed. 'But ghosts . . . I've never heard a ghost story where the person wasn't . . . dead.'

'Her body lives – for now. But her *self* has been cut from it, and cannot find its way back. Soon enough the body will die, and she will then be as you suggest.'

'Help her,' Thalric snapped. It sounded almost an order.

Instead of taking offence, Felipe lowered his gaze, considering. He gave a great sigh, as his shoulders sagged slightly. From behind him, the man Coren stepped forward.

'My Prince, no. You know what the seers said, how this girl could pave the way for terrible things. Perhaps it would be best to let matters take their course.'

'And if she is so terrible, will her ghost not be more terrible still?' Felipe murmured. 'There are enough ghosts clinging to me already, Coren, without adding one more. And she is Maker Stenwold's niece, and there is a debt there.' Abruptly he looked up again, meeting Thalric's gaze. 'My seers can do nothing, because they fear her, and their skills are of a different nature. To call her *self* back, you must find someone skilled in speaking to the ghosts of the fallen, for that is what she has become, whether her body still breathes or not.'

'You are saying that you cannot help her, then,' Thalric stated flatly.

'I keep none about my court gifted at speaking with the dead,' Felipe said softly. 'I have no wish to hear such a clamour of voices, for there are too many I would recognize.' His penetrating gaze fixed on the two Wasps, and Varmen shuffled uncomfortably. 'Those who come to my door offering such services are turned away. Perhaps they do not go far. Coren,' and his seneschal was at his elbow, ready for orders.

'You know the woman I mean,' Felipe instructed him. 'Some tendays ago she came, and was refused entry. Unless you have grown slack, you will have a good idea of where she has gone.'

'Peddling her trade about your villages, I think,' Coren replied. 'I was not sure . . . but you had never forbidden it.'

'I would not deny to others whatever comfort the words of ghosts can bring,' the prince told him philosophically. 'Find the woman and bring her here.'

They had placed Che in another garden chamber, open to the sky, and also to the horizon on two sides. Seeing her laid out there, surrounded by spring flowers, Thalric felt a lurch of emotion inside of him. *And they have sent for some kind of mystic undertaker. Is she . . .?* He could see her breast rise and fall with shallow breathing, but death seemed to hang about her, as though only waiting for the right moment.

The idea of placing her fate – *and my fate!* – into the hands of some raddled old hag, some morbid chanting charlatan, disgusted him. *Have they no doctors?* Part of him railed at it, but experiencing the inexplicable had made inroads enough into his mind that he did not truly believe mere medicine would carry the day: not the herbs and poultices of Commonwealer healers, nor good Imperial surgery.

Varmen joined him later. The big Wasp looked sober and thoughtful as he stripped his armour off again.

'Not under threat any more? Or are the odds so bad that the armour wouldn't help?' Thalric needled him, needing something to take his mind off other things.

Varmen just shrugged. 'I reckon your woman's on her way – the ghost-talking one, I mean.'

Thalric nodded morosely. 'If this doesn't work . . .'

'What, waving her arms around and talking to spirits and

magic, not work? What are the odds on that?' Varmen's smile was weak. 'Curse me, but I remember the last year of the war, you know? 'Wealer armies bunching up to defend Shon Fhor, and leaving all their civilians behind them, villages and towns full of them ripe for the Slave Corps . . . We were first in, a couple of times. You'd find them on their knees around some sage or seer or magic-maker, begging their spirits to do something, to protect them from us. You'd find tens of them, hundreds even, singing and dancing and chanting, and then we'd walk in, us heavy-armour lads, and they'd go quiet one by one, then all of 'em. If we could see who their wizard-type was, orders were to shoot 'em dead. The rest would cave in soon enough after that. You could see it in their faces, like you'd just come and tilted their world on its side. And now nothing worked like they thought it should, poor bastards.'

'And now we seem to need to tilt it back again,' Thalric said wryly, just as Coren came marching in with a couple of his glittering soldiers, and also a woman.

In that moment, it was clear to Thalric that nobody had explained to the necromancer what she was being brought to Suon Ren for, and that the seneschal had not only copied but actually intensified his prince's dislike of the breed. The expression on the woman's face was that of a prisoner on her way to an execution, and seeing a pair of Wasp-kinden there did not change it.

She was not what Thalric had expected: not a crone, nor even a Dragonfly-kinden. She was considerably younger than he was, and her skin was a curious shade: pale underlain with lead-grey highlights, so that she herself looked half a corpse already. Her face was narrow, and her eyes held no irises at all, just pinpoint pupils amidst a pale field. She was a slender creature, dressed in a robe that had seen much darning, her dark hair streaked messily with white and hanging raggedly about her shoulders. There was an empty scabbard attached to her belt, for a short-bladed sword, and she clutched a travelling pack.

Thalric guessed that some conjoining of Moth, Roach and

Mantis inheritance had led to this particular miscegenation. *How many flavours of mystic nonsense am I getting, combined in this one woman?* He awaited the inevitable outpouring of curses, benedictions and portentous threats that all these quacksalvers seemed to come out with.

Instead, the seneschal gave the woman a shove towards where Che was laid out, and she rounded on him as soon as she was out of arm's reach.

'What do you want, you bastard lackey? Selling me to the Empire, is it?'

'Make her well,' the Dragonfly ordered her. 'The prince demands it.'

The necromancer looked rebellious. 'The prince didn't want my skills a few days ago. How about I tell him he can go —'

Coren's hand went for his sword, but Thalric stepped forward pointedly, making them both flinch. 'I'll take it from here,' he announced. The Dragonfly seneschal stared at him, blankly hostile, then turned on his heel and left, his men following him.

The halfbreed woman hugged her satchel and eyed the Wasps doubtfully. 'So, what?' she asked, sneaking a glance at Che. 'She's not dead. What am I supposed to do with someone who's not dead?'

Thalric forbore to ask what she might have done with a corpse, had one been offered. 'Examine her,' he instructed. 'They said you could help.'

'They say a lot of things.' The woman was already retreating. 'This isn't anything to do with me. I'm not the woman for it.'

Bitterness rose inside Thalric and he advanced on her angrily. 'Is that what the mystics of the Commonweal have come to? You're not even going to make a few passes in the air and then vomit out some ambiguous prediction? Come on, you might at least go through the motions, woman – or what's a charlatan for?' After just a few steps, he had backed her into a corner, trampling over Felipe's flowers. 'Because they claimed you could help, and now I'm cursed if I have anyone else to turn to. They said her *self* had been cut loose, whatever that's supposed to mean, and all I know is that *something* struck her down, and I can't tell what's wrong, and it might as well be . . .' He realized that he had her by the shoulders, in a grip that must surely have hurt, and was staring her right in the face, and about to do who could know what.

Her expression had gone from alarm to calm acceptance, and now to curiosity. 'Magic?' she whispered.

Feeling suddenly defeated, Thalric let her go and stomped back over to Che. 'Why not?' he asked. 'What's left except lies like that? Why not magic?'

'My name is Maure, sir,' she told him. 'Will you pay me for my work?'

He turned back to her, frowning. 'What sort of magician are you?'

'One that has to eat,' she stated. 'And there's no payment promised by Prince Felipe, and living off the gratitude of princes is like to leave me hungry, in any event.'

'Recover Che and I'll pay you,' he told her gruffly. 'And no "sirs". We're neither of us in the army any more. I'm Thalric, that's Varmen, she's Cheerwell Maker.'

Maure approached Che's body almost casually at first, but then she flinched back, eyebrows vanishing under her uneven fringe. 'Oh, now,' she murmured, 'what am I looking at? What did they *do* to her?'

'The consensus of the prince's seers was that she represents some kind of menace best destroyed, or so the steward said,' Thalric said acidly.

'Is that the truth?' Maure wondered. 'Well, then, I should do my best to bring her back to herself as quickly as possible, if only because it will annoy that man so. Now, you two, sirs, give me room and time to work, and don't expect too much too soon, sirs – and, yes, I know you said not to call you that, sirs but, as a halfbreed and a woman and a Commonwealer to boot, I've not enjoyed the best experiences with any of your people, so you'll appreciate if I keep myself on the windy side of civil.'

Twenty-Six

The hall of Leose was busy now, far more so even than when the young nobles had danced here. Salme Elass was holding her council of war.

She held pride of place, with Alain sitting to her left, and Isendter Whitehand to her right, whilst the seneschal, Lisan Dea, hovered in attendance behind. Around the room she had assembled many of those same aristocrats that had been hunting the stag, together with their own champions, their war leaders and headmen of their retinues.

Elass watched the Lowlander take her place. Telse Orian gave the new arrival a companionable nod, and young Chevre Velienn was scowling at her as an upstart, but Tynisa ignored them both. Partly that was because the girl's attention was directed instead at Elass's son, who was, after all, the hook that the princess had caught her on. There was more, though, for there was a casual arrogance about the girl suggesting that opinions of the assembled nobility were now beneath her notice.

In truth, it is a shame that she is a Lowlander. Were she of our kinden, and of halfway decent blood, then perhaps she might make a good match for Alain after all. He could profit from being taught that kind of self-assurance.

Almost directly across from Elass sat Lowre Cean, with some of his own people about him. Tynisa's chosen seat placed her on the periphery of his influence, which was fitting enough, for she was the thread by which Elass had hauled the old man in, after all.

She surveyed the mustered war leaders and let her wings shimmer a moment about her shoulders, her signal that she was about to speak. 'You all know why I have gathered you here,' she addressed them. 'Elas Mar has suffered grievous incursions from the lordless lands to our south. For a long time that wilderness has been a breeding ground for bandits and killers, and yet nothing has been done. For reasons I cannot guess at, our Prince-Major has not deigned to purge those lands of their lawless inhabitants. So now my villages are burned, my people killed, and I cannot sit idle. We have a force here that is superior to the brigands in discipline, and whose cause is just. We will drive them from Elas Mar, and then we will scour their own territory of them, so they shall find no rest and no home. I shall take back these lawless lands on behalf of the Monarch.'

'And the Monarch will recognize your efforts, Princess?' Lowre Cean asked sardonically. 'And what has Felipe Shah to say about this?'

'I have sent to him for aid,' Elass returned, quite calmly. 'Our prince has written to me: he declines to come. He will not support us, for all our cause is plainly a righteous one.'

'And does he give any reason?'

Elass considered the terse missive she had received back from her liege, the Prince-Major. 'None,' she said, which was both true and false. Suffice to say that half of Felipe Shah's reasons had been incomprehensible, the other half anathema.

There was a pause, into which Lowre was clearly being invited to add something more, but he held his peace.

Elass nodded. 'Our southern border is heavily wooded, and the brigands take advantage of this to more easily cross into and out of our lands. Already four villages have suffered their depredations. That is where we must meet them: we must scout them even as they venture forth to raid. We must follow them back to their dens. We must drive them from the trees and ever southwards. We must capture their leaders, kill any that follow them. We will deliver the Monarch's justice that these wretches believe is sleeping.' Again she glanced at Lowre Cean. 'Does our strategist have any wise counsel? Your victories against the Wasps are well remembered.'

'I am not your strategist,' Lowre said tiredly. 'Make your own plans.'

Elass's mouth tightened into a thin line. 'My son will fly for the border, taking with him a band of our best, to deliver a message to these criminals that they will clearly understand. He will make a severe example of whoever he can catch. By the time our main force has joined him, the bandits shall no doubt have lost their stomach for the fight. And I believe, Prince Cean, there is one amongst your household who wishes to accompany Alain.'

Lowre Cean's face was stony, but he said nothing.

'Maker Tynise,' Elass named the girl, 'you see here beside me my champion.' A nod towards Isendter, who had knelt motionless throughout. 'My son will lead the attack on these villains. Will you be his huntress, *his* champion, when he does so?'

She could see the Lowlander wanting to glance at Lowre for his reaction, but she had said 'Yes,' already, her response following eagerly and inevitably after Elass's question. Lamplight glittered, caught on the badge that she wore.

Elass smiled pleasantly at her, saving the razored edge of her expression for the old man opposite her. *Oh, I know, my Prince.* Felipe Shah had apparently sent a personal request to his old friend Cean, to look after this girl. Elass had no idea why the Lowlander was so important, whether she might be some great dignitary whose death would tarnish Shah's honour, or whether this represented just one more inexplicable fragment of sentiment from the prince. *But it is enough that I have taken her from them. Let them fret, and now let her live or die by her skills.*

Staring across the room at Lowre Cean, Elass knew the old man could read all of these thoughts in her face. She revealed them there clearly, just for him. *I will turn you to my purpose, my Prince,* she reflected. *When I asked you on to my lands I sought a hero, not this senile wreck of a man I see before me. You shall either recover your earlier glories or I shall strip you of all you have. And as for Felipe Shah . . .*

The girl, Tynisa, had first arrived at her door with news of her son, Salme Dien. As always, the foreigners did not understand how life was amongst a civilized people. She had no such son, nor had she for many years, since long before the Lowlanders' own wars had claimed Dien's life. Felipe Shah had taken her son from her, and reworked Dien into his own creature. She still remembered the day that he had quite publicly made the request of her. Oh, it was an honour, no doubt, and because it was an honour she could not refuse it, and so she had been deprived of yet another child, and only Alain left at her side, the least promising of the lot.

But I have found a way to strike back, at last, through this Lowlander girl. Perhaps, in the end, I will kill her myself – have Isendter challenge her and then cut her down. Or perhaps the brigands will spare me the trouble.

And, of course, after that rabble of thieves is dealt with, I have other plans. Then perhaps you shall find, Felipe Shah, just what happens to a prince who forgets what it means to have noble blood.

'When were you going to tell us that this was the plan?' Mordrec demanded, chasing after Dal Arche, as the bandit leader tried to walk away. Receiving no immediate response, the Wasp-kinden simply dogged Dal's steps all the way out of the encampment, still demanding, 'When, Dala? Or did you think we wouldn't notice?'

Dal's other two lieutenants, tall and close-mouthed Soul Je and the stocky Scorpion Barad Ygor, followed a few paces behind, content to let Mordrec draw their leader's ire.

At last Dal rounded on them. 'What do you want me to say?' he asked.

'I want you to tell me the truth about what this cursed *plan* is!' Mordrec insisted. 'Let's go raid the Salmae, you said. They've got plenty of what we need, you said.'

'And have I led you astray, in that?'

'Dala, what you failed to mention is that you thought we needed *people*. You had us running about picking up thieves and malcontents to bring to you, when all the while you had this business ready to spring on us.'

'Mord, this was never the plan,' Dal protested.

The Wasp blinked. 'Then what in the pits *is* it?'

Dal looked back at the encampment, seeing a messy aggregation of tents, lean-tos, fire pits and sleeping rolls. *Spring's turning out mild, which is just as well. Most of these people never thought about where they'd be sleeping, fools that they are.*

'Four villages,' Ygor the Scorpion reminded him. He spoke in an absurdly cultured drawl that originated somewhere half the world away, in a place ruled by Spiders.

'Victims of our own success,' Dal murmured.

'Success?' Mord hissed, back on the offensive again. 'I know what success looks like, to a bandit. It looks like a little loot, and nobody about to catch you yet. It doesn't look like piss-near all the people of four villagers deciding to sign up with you. What are you planning to be at the end of this, Dal? A general?'

Dal tried to recall where generals featured in the Imperial scheme of things. *Ah yes, at the top*. 'You want me to turn them away?'

'Yes, I want you to turn them away! Maybe one in five is some use, good to hold a spear or pull a bow. We've got *children* out there, and old people, too. What's the point of them? Why are they even here?'

'Victims of our own success,' Dal repeated.

'Stop *saying* that,' Mord snapped.

Soul Je held up a long-fingered hand. 'He's right,' the Grasshopper intoned.

'How is he right?'

'Mord,' Dal addressed him, 'you know that pile of loot we're sitting on, all the food, the drink, the cloth bales, the honey, the kadith, the gold? You do understand that was taxes intended for the Salmae, yes?'

Mordrec nodded , with an expression stubborn enough that Dal knew he already understood. Still, he pressed on.

'And you can see the actual villagers from here, yes? Do they look as though they got much of that stuff? You'd describe them as prosperous? Well-fed?'

'And who's going to feed them now? Do they reckon they're better off with us?'

Dal shrugged. 'Because at least we're fighting, is how they see it.'

'We're not fighting, we're robbing,' the Wasp pointed out mulishly.

'I don't mean fighting the Salmae specifically, although we will. I mean fighting what *is*,' Dal told him.

'Since when were we idealists?' asked Barad Ygor slowly.

'We're not. We never were.' Dal threw his hands up suddenly. 'I'd go back south, right now, if there was anything there for us, but the reasons that brought us here still hold.'

'Dala, we came to raid. That lot behind us isn't a raiding party,' Ygor stressed. 'We can't move fast. We can't get ourselves out of the way, if a hundred Mercers suddenly turn up. Or at least *they* can't.'

Dal looked past his lieutenants, at the camp beyond. 'You're right. We need to do something about that.'

They exchanged uncertain glances.

'You're going to turn them away?' Mordrec asked. Although it was what he had been arguing for, he sounded uncertain now.

'Separate out those who can fight,' Dal instructed. 'The three of you, take half of them, and all the non-combatants. Lead them to Siriell's Town, with your pick of the supplies.'

This was greeted with silence.

'There's nothing at Siriell's Town any more,' Ygor started slowly.

'There will be once you've repopulated it with this lot,' Dal told him. 'And before you ask me what's to stop the Mercers attacking the town again, we've shifted the battle lines. While we're here gnawing at their vitals, they won't be sending any punitive expedition further south.'

'I was wrong. You're not a general. Inside your head you're a prince,' Mordrec accused him.

'I'm a brigand, Mord, like all of us, but think of this. Four villages raided, now, and most of the locals just came right over to join us. We've got half again as many fighting men, even after you take the non-combatants away. If we keep rolling in that kind of support, we can raid as far as the gates of Leose itself. And where will they be able to raise a levy from, if all their peasants are under *our* flag, hmm?'

'We're not exactly equipped for a siege,' the Wasp pointed out, although he sounded less adversarial now, the spirit of the idea working on him.

'Let them keep their walls. I doubt that they can eat them, once they get hungry,' Dal Arche declared. 'I want the three of you gone by tomorrow for Siriell's Town, or whatever's left of it. Get your charges lodged there as soon as possible, and bring me back anyone you find who's able to fight. Bring me weapons too, as many as you can: spears, arrows, axes even – whatever you can get. We've got plenty of hands all of a sudden, and nothing to put in them.'

He looked from face to face, seeing Ygor and Mordrec still unhappy, Soul Je merely impassive. 'Or what?' he asked them. 'No, we didn't ask for this. We came here to raid some villages, put a little thorn in the side of the nobility, get a little plunder. We knew that the Salmae taxed hard and all we thought was that the locals wouldn't risk their necks to defend the tax collector's haul. Well, fate's dealt us more cards than we know what to do with. What would *you* do with what we've been given?'

‘Where does it end?’ Ygor asked quietly. ‘We break the Salmae, and then what? Felipe Shah? The Monarch?’

Dal shrugged. ‘Where does a bandit’s life normally end? What were you expecting?’

‘Dying rich in a Spiderlands whorehouse, for preference,’ the Scorpion considered. ‘But, seeing as I’m a few hundred miles out of my way for that, why not raise an army? Next-best thing, isn’t it?’

‘Damned right it is,’ Dal confirmed. ‘And you, Soul?’

The Grasshopper had remained silent a long time, but now he nodded, just the once. ‘Let’s do it.’

With that said, Mordrec gave in with poor grace. ‘We’re dead men from now on. They’ll stamp down hard when they think it’s bandits. If they find out we’re stealing their peasants, they’ll keep on stamping till we’re just a stain on the grass.’

Dal’s smile was resolute. ‘There comes a time in a man’s life when he gets the chance to be free, even if it’s just for a day or so. That chance doesn’t often come twice.’ In his mind he saw the marching armies of the Twelve-year War, as viewed from the midst of a block of terrified peasant levy being thrown headlong at the black and gold, without a choice, without understanding, just bodies for the grinding Wasp war machine to chew up and spit out. Who should a man blame for that kind of memory? Blame the Wasps? Oh, too easy. The Dal Arche of back then had no grievance with the Wasps, had barely heard of their Empire. When they come to throw you into the fire, he considered, don’t blame the fire for burning you, blame the hands that threw you.

‘I want to be free,’ he told them fiercely. ‘I want to be free of the nobles and their wars, just this once, and if they won’t let us retire free in Siriell’s Town, then the only way any of us can be free is to take the fight to them and give them a hard enough slap that they won’t come back. Now, round up your charges and be ready to head out with the dawn. The Salmae and their cronies will be on us soon enough, and I’ve got to make plans.’

*

She could now ride a horse, without help. The facility had come to her along with so much else, in that moment at the end of the hunt. Some level of calm and concentration in the saddle had been gifted to her, unearned and unasked for. Still, she was not the equal of the Commonwealer nobles and their retinues, so she brought up the rear as they hurried through sparse woodland towards the latest pillar of smoke. Some way behind them followed a grumbling levy of Grasshopper-kinden peasantry, given only spears and orders, and making the best time they could. Telse Orian had decided not to wait for them, though, once the smudgy pillar of black had been sighted.

He had mentioned the name of the village, but Tynisa had forgotten it already. The Commonwealer names all seemed interchangeable, and were a matter of supreme indifference to her. All that mattered was that the avenging Mercers arrived there in time to catch the brigands still at their pillaging.

Alain himself was scouting aloft with a few other nobles, perched on their glittering insects with the countryside speeding past below them. Perhaps he would be at the village ahead, she hoped, feeling a familiar eagerness steal over her. She had wanted to ride with him, but inside her a voice had said, *You must prove yourself first, then he will not deny you.*

Let there be blood, she proclaimed to the world, for she had accepted the truth now. *In nothing do you so excel*, the voice said, *as in the spilling of blood. It is your calling.*

So she had joined up with Telse Orian and his followers, judging him a man who would not be slow in joining battle, and even now the smoke of a murdered village blotted the sky above them as they surged through the trees.

Abruptly, Telse Orian had put the spur to his mount, and all around Tynisa the rest followed suit, breaking into a charge as they passed the treeline, and leaving her behind. Her horsemanship, however acquired, was insufficient to keep up with them at a gallop, so all she could do was tag along behind, losing ground with every hoofbeat.

Ahead she saw the village itself, much of it ablaze and a crowd of men and women clearly setting the next house alight. Telse lowered a lance now, and Tynisa saw the brigands scatter left and right, or straight up into the air. Arrows were already skimming towards them, several of the Mercers drawing and loosing smoothly from the saddle, which was another skill Tynisa did not possess.

But the voice within told her, *You will have your chance*, and she trusted it implicitly, kicking at her mount to get all the speed from it that she could.

A half-dozen of the arsonists were down already. They seemed poorly prepared for the assault, getting in one another's way even as they tried to flee. Telse left off the attack, circling his horse in the centre of the village even as another roof began to smoulder with burning embers. He was peering down at the corpses.

'Hold!' he cried, but most of his followers were too busy chasing down the enemy, and only Tynisa heard him say, 'What kind of bandits are these?'

To her eyes, they were dead bandits, and the only shame was that she had not slain them herself. Telse Orian stepped from the saddle, though, and knelt down beside one.

'No armour – not even armed . . .' He stood, frowning. 'Hold!' he called again. 'These aren't bandits. I'll wager these are the locals themselves.'

'Then what are they doing?' Tynisa demanded.

'Perhaps they seek to deny the real brigands the use of their homes, and—' Telse started, as an arrow slanted from the gleaming chitin of his breastplate, knocking him off his feet.

There was now a second band of men breaking from the trees, and they were a far more fearsome prospect than the fire starters had been. Most of them had bows, and Tynisa saw swords and spears, leather and chitin mail, and even a few battered pieces of armour that had surely graced some Mercer or noble scion once.

Telse sat up again, still winded, but his people were already reacting without any guiding plan. She saw two of them cut down from their saddles by bandit arrows, as the rest flurried and circled, some passing one way and some the other. The advancing bandits were loosing arrows at every target that presented itself. One shaft nipped past Tynisa herself, to bury itself in the ground.

Now, came the voice in her head, and she felt her father's hands guide her as she whipped the reins and dug her heels in, her mount breaking into a gallop. She heard Telse Orian call her name, but he was irrelevant now.

There was some ground to cover before she reached the first of the brigands, but they could hardly fail to spot her. An arrow danced to her left, another to her right. She had her sword thrust out, and the next shaft, impossibly, struck the blade, its impact jolting all the way to her shoulder. She was close, then, levelling her rapier as though it was a lance.

They were a vicious-looking crew, she noted distantly. Dragonflies and Grasshopper-kinden, with a couple of other breeds too. One in particular stood out like a leader amongst them, a burly Dragonfly-kinden with greying hair. He had an arrow nocked at the moment she marked him, and it was loosed as soon as she saw it. She felt the impact shudder all the way through her horse, as the shaft plunged into the animal's breast right up to the fletchings.

Another two strikes followed rapidly from other archers, but the luckless beast was already toppling forward, its forelegs giving way. For a moment Tynisa stood in the saddle, then hurled herself forward, landing on her feet and rushing the last few yards to the bandit leader.

He bounded backwards with a ten-foot leap, his wings briefly glimmering, then his next shaft, drawn and loosed with remarkable speed, struck the rapier's curved guard even as she lunged forward, the sword seeming to guide itself as it defended her. She saw his eyes widen, then she was laying about left and right, catching two of the brigands neatly between the ribs, both as good as dead in the same instant. A Grasshopper spearman tried to get in her way but the tip of her blade made a ruin of his face with an almost leisurely flick.

Then the enemy were fleeing, and she could hear the drumming of hoofs behind her as Orian's people finally rallied. Tynisa thought the brigands had broken at first, assuming that the horsemen would follow the enemy into the woods. There was a core of discipline to the bandits, though, enough of them turning at the treeline to shoot that Telse Orian called his people back. Tynisa stood firm, arrows skipping at her feet, but she was not touched.

I will remember you, she warned the bandit leader in her mind. *Whether you are a captain or a mere lieutenant, I will remember you.*

Twenty-Seven

Che . . .

Behind her, the river Jamail flowed steady on its course, heedless of time or the deeds of mayfly humanity. The current chaos disturbing its slow waters, namely Amnon's fish hunt, was a mere nothing, gone before the river could notice. It was just as irrelevant to Che.

Somewhere ahead of her, amid the moss-hung tangle of the trees, was the grey smudge that she told herself was Achaeos's ghost, which had dragged her from her fellows to set off like a madwoman into the swamp. She had never been able to refuse him anything.

Some part of her knew she would discover, in time, that the apparition was not Achaeos at all. Instead, the parasite clinging to her mind was some fragment of Tynisa's father, Tisamon, who had died destroying the Shadow Box. Somehow, the Mantis's ghost had crawled from the very clutches of oblivion and into her head, then had lacked the strength to get out again.

So that was why she was here, as it led her a merry chase through the channels and mudflats and twisted greenery of the Jamail delta, impatient and demanding, and she followed gladly, because she thought it was Achaeos. Even though she knew that she was wrong, living through this a second time, she could not force herself to do anything different. There was a comfort in keeping her hand off the tiller and knowing the outcome, however painful it would be.

At last she had burst into the open, and found the little Mantis village: the reed-and-thatch circle of huts surrounding their sacred place of sacrifice. Even as she broke in upon them, the stunted Mantis-kinden of the delta were herding their latest two victims towards the wicker idol in the centre, its outstretched arms forever reaching for more blood.

Che had stepped forward, as she remembered, but realized there was now someone keeping pace with her. She glanced sideways, annoyed that the sanctity of her memories was being invaded, and saw a complete stranger, some halfbreed woman who looked as though she had Mantis blood herself. The intruder did not return her glance, but continued staring ahead at the two Wasp prisoners the swamp-dwellers had captured.

'It is him, isn't it?' the other woman remarked, apropos of nothing. 'I don't know the sickly one, but your other man, that's definitely . . . oh, what's his name?' And finally she glanced at Che, as if looking for help.

And Che had always been helpful. 'Thalric,' she supplied automatically, and found that mentioning the name opened up a whole world of other memories, unwelcome because she should now have been safe from them. *But none of that has happened yet,* and, as she thought that, she felt the world around her unravelling, unable to retain its integrity in the face of her returning knowledge.

No – it's Achaeos! But instantly she felt embarrassed, caught pretending ignorance, when all the time she knew it was not her dead lover. She could not live this over again. It was false—

A solid catapulted stone thundered down nearby, indicating that the Wasp artillerists positioned on the roof of the governor's palace had finished moving the piece into place. Their angle of attack was awkward, but it still showered the nearest Mynans with sharp chips of masonry. Che shrank back, throwing an arm up, even though none of the fragments came anywhere near her.

Kymene stalked past just then, a retinue of self-appointed junior officers trailing after her. The night was dragging on, and the Wasps occupying the palace remained stubborn in their resistance. Everyone knew that Imperial reinforcements were on their way, and if there were still Wasp soldiers within the city when they arrived then the revolution that everyone had fought so hard for would be caught between the two, and most likely crushed.

Another detachment of Mynans was forming up, getting ready to rush the gates. The great doors to the palace were already gone, but the Wasps had put up a makeshift barricade, and were holding there with crossbow, spear and sting. The Mynans massively outnumbered them, but the Imperial defensive position was formidable. A dozen similar assaults had already been thrown back. Che stared at the citizens readying themselves for the push: men and women of all ages from mere youths to white-haired veterans, and most of them wearing either captured Wasp armour or the old black-and-red Mynan breastplates and peaked helms. The front half held triangular shields, the rear had a motley collection of crossbows. They were not trained soldiers, but then Myna had been occupied and enslaved for almost twenty years. These men and women were tough, bitter street fighters who had cut their teeth during the resistance, but this now was a soldier's job, and they were not trained for it. And even professional soldiers might have balked at the task that awaited them.

One of them stepped out of the line: not a Mynan, this one, but some kind of muddied halfbreed woman not much older than Che herself.

'At first I thought this was before the war, but you're too young for that,' she observed, approaching Che with her hands behind her back, as if the scene about her was intended merely for her personal amusement. 'I suppose the Empire has been fighting all manner of people elsewhere, but in the Commonweal it's almost impossible to get any news of it.'

'Commonweal?' Che eyed her blankly, but even as she said it there were new thoughts trickling into her mind. *Yes, I will travel to the Commonweal, but that's later, much later*, and with that thought she was forced to accept that all of this, all the frenzy and bravery of the Mynan resistance, was history.

'I charged the gates,' Che murmured, recalling the moment in awe. She looked at the strange woman, who was holding a hand out to her.

There was pain, concealed in the palm of that hand, and Che wanted none of it. She turned away.

In Solarno, the angry crowd surged back and forth, the supporters of the Crystal Standard and Satin Trail parties shouting slogans, clashing messily with their slender, curved swords. Che had backed away as far as she could from them, waiting for the moment when this angry demonstration of Solarnese government-by-mob would flow over the low wall of the taverna and wash her away. But the fight flowed back and forth, prowling about the wall's edge like a hungry animal, repeating the same round of violence over and over, and she knew she could wait for ever, the world trapped in amber, and be safe.

'You Lowlanders live lives of such violence,' the strange half-breed woman remarked. 'Cheerwell Maker, come to me.'

The sight of her filled Che with a nameless fear and she turned away, searching for somewhere . . .

It was quiet here in the farmhouse cellar, and she could almost believe there was no army camped above. A few tens of thousands of Wasp-kinden and their Auxillians, but she would hardly have guessed at their presence had she not been their prisoner.

On the morrow no doubt they would question her, torture her most likely, but she had all night to think about that, and 'all night' could last as long as she wished, this little moment of shadowed calm stretching out indefinitely.

It was a strange place to find sanctuary, but she could not fault it.

This will do, she decided, and then the door above opened, and a solitary figure was stepping down into the dark. She thought it was Totho, at first, as it should have been, but instead it was—

The jolt of recognition was physical this time. That same halfbreed, the woman Che had never met, and yet who seemed to be acquiring a grim inevitability.

'Cheerwell Maker, listen to me,' the woman started, but Che did not want to listen to her. *There must be somewhere . . .*

The Prowess Forum was well attended today – some favourites were listed to fight and the connoisseurs of the amateur game were looking forward to some interesting matches. *None of which will involve me*, Che reflected, and the thought was reassuring. *I am nothing special here. Nobody will trouble me.* Eventually they would call upon her to fight, of course, and she would match swords with the clumsy nephew of some Collegium magnate, and she would lose, of course, and be mortified at letting her friends down. The thought now brought nothing more than a wry smile to her face: back when the trivial had mattered.

I will hold time still here. In the Prowess Forum, with her friends about her, and the stern Ant-kinden Master Kymon just stepping out into the circle, many months before he would end his life transfixed by a Vekken crossbow bolt.

She smiled, and took a seat on the lowest step of the tiered stone benches. How little she knew, how young she was! Whatever joy the future held, the hours took more than they gave, in the end.

'I have no idea where this is, now,' said a woman sitting beside her. For a moment Che felt a surge of outrage and horror: *her, here?* But the sensation was gone almost as soon as it had arrived, for she was home, here, ignorant and safe.

The halfbreed woman had stood up, and was gazing over at Che's fellow duellists. Her accent had been oddly familiar, Che decided.

'Excuse me, but are you a Commonwealer?' she asked timidly.

'I have that honour,' the woman replied. 'My name is Maure and you are Cheerwell Maker.'

Che blinked, fighting down a queasy feeling of discontinuity. 'Are you a friend of Salma's?' she asked. 'Salme Dien, that is.'

Maure's eyes flicked towards the elegant Dragonfly youth preparing to meet his opponent. 'Ah, no – but I know of him.' She seemed sad about that, and Che had to forcibly prevent herself from remembering why that might be.

She realized she was desperate to make the woman *go away*, but at the same time she was meek Cheerwell Maker, who was always polite and had never really been hurt. She clung to that. It was all that was left between her and the storm.

'I am sent to be your guide, Cheerwell Maker,' Maure stated.

Che flinched from her. 'I don't know what you're talking about.'

'Oh, you do, you do. Ah, look, your friends are coming over to see you.'

Che cast desperate eyes over towards those familiar faces, and recoiled when she saw them. Somehow, while she had not been concentrating, something had slipped badly within the Prowess Forum. The audience had gone, and her friends . . . her friends . . .

Salma was dead, she saw, a sword wound splashing his front with red. Hard-faced Totho wore intricate armour of interlocking plates, overlaid by a grey surcoat showing an open gauntlet. Tynisa . . . Tynisa was gone.

Tynisa was gone, and was that not why Che was doing . . . whatever it was she had been doing when . . .

‘No,’ Che whispered. ‘I’m home. I’m safe here. Go away.’

The halfbreed woman sighed, looking out over the fighting ring where the Master Armsman, long-dead Kymon, still stood. ‘I understand this is a place of learning,’ she remarked.

Che blinked at her. ‘Yes, yes it is.’

‘I would like to visit here, some day. Most necromancers are ignorant fools making a living from the hopes and dreams of others. They paw at the dead, enticing fallen friends and dead relatives out to perform like trained crickets, and they have no *understanding*. They just know what works and what does not, and never mind the *why*.’

‘Magic?’ Che said slowly. ‘You’re talking about magic.’ The false Prowess Forum was falling away now, but the world seemed to be uncertain as to what to replace it with. ‘But I don’t . . .’

Believe in it . . . But before Maure’s sharp gaze, she could no longer deceive herself. ‘But you do not talk like a magician.’

‘Thank you,’ the halfbreed said drily. ‘I was trained in Tsolshevy, amongst the Woodlouse-kinden. Some *experiment* of theirs, I was. They treat their magicians like scientists and their artificers like mystics, there, and perhaps they know more about either than most do because of that. They taught me necromancy, and I understand it like nothing else.’ She patted the stone beside her companionably, the bank of seats that somehow had survived the dissolution going on around them. Lacking alternatives, Che sat.

Maure leant back, propping herself on her elbows. ‘Any quack will tell you about ghosts haunting battlefields,’ she continued, ‘old buildings, ruins, deathbeds; about ghosts that linger where their living selves were murdered; ghosts within the weapons that slew them, or that their hands had once wielded; ghosts in treasured objects, or attached to grieving relatives, or simply hanging in the ether like a goggling fish waiting for someone of my profession to cast down a hook. That is not all, however. Few enough know it, but a ghost may also end up haunting the insides of her own head, retreating into memories – driven away from the world and fearing to return. There are many kinds of haunting.'

'But that's not haunting,' Che objected. 'That's madness.'

'Perhaps that is why the Inapt kinden have, in my experience, a better understanding of what madness truly is,' Maure murmured. 'The time has come to move on, Che.' She rose abruptly, catching hold of Che's hand and pulling her up. Behind her there was a bright light eating away at the misty world.

'No,' Che said again.

'What are you afraid of?'

I'm not afraid, I'm really not, I just want to go home – home where there's nothing to fear . . .

'*Her*,' She finally confessed. The word was wrenched out unwillingly.

Maure stared at her for a long moment. 'A magician has practised on you, to make you fear her so,' she understood at last. 'She has stamped herself into your mind as a thing of terror. Cheerwell, if you hide for ever, then you will die. Your body will die and you will haunt your own corpse until it is food for worms and beyond. Come with me.'

'No, don't make me, please.'

'Cheerwell—'

'I don't want to face her. I can't.' Che was shaking now as the memories began to slide back into place, like great weights of fragmented rock, and at the heart of them was *her*. 'You don't understand who she is.'

'That I don't,' Maure admitted. 'So let us face her together.'

She still clasped Che's hand, but in that moment it did not seem to matter. The blazing radiance was half the world already. Maure had held her still long enough for time to catch up with her.

Go, said a voice in her ear, and she thought it might have been Salma, but with just the one word to work on, she would never know.

She held tight to Maure's hand and walked into the light.

All at once, something stooped down on them, keening its rage. Che looked up to see Seda, wings afire, Wasp Art making her hands glow like coals.

'I told you!' the apparition screeched. 'Back where you belong, Beetle! Back beneath your stone!'

A wave of flame washed over them, and Che heard Maure scream, her hand ripped abruptly from the woman's grip. For a moment the fear of this *thing* – not even the Empress herself, but a mere phantasm she had left behind – was paralysing.

Then, from somewhere came the words that had been spoken by the Masters of Khanaphes. A final piece of memory shaken loose, which Seda had been at pains to conceal from her.

Whatever it was that you demanded from them, they gave it to me as well. We are sisters, in this, if in nothing else. And Che reached out, and swatted the screaming thing into dust, nothing but the echo of another woman's voice fading inside her head.

Che awoke.

It was not a gentle waking, either. She jackknifed up, jerking sideways off the pallet she was lying on, her stomach cramping viciously. She was aware of a certain amount of shouting from nearby, but in those first few moments it was all she could do to suck breath into her lungs.

The sequence of dream images remained with her, that thread of beads she had made of her life. *A ghost, she told me?* In that convulsive moment, Che wondered whether she really had come back from the dead.

Then there were arms about her, and at first she tried to fight them, but she heard a voice speaking her name over and over, and relaxed. She remembered everything just then, the real and the imagined and the far-seen, all in order and neatly labelled, memories like specimens stored in a College master's cupboard.

'Che, do you know where you are?' It was Thalric, of course. 'Do you know who *I* am?'

She forced out a little laugh, at that, her racked body already becoming easier. 'Oh, yes, to be sure. I'm not likely to forget you, Thalric, for any number of reasons. And, of course, I know . . .' She frowned, staring about her. 'Come to think of it, where am I?'

She sensed a tension going out of him, one that had been held in check through iron discipline, but was no less great for all that. 'You're back.'

'It looks that way.'

He still had not let her go, but she decided she could live with that for now, saying only, 'Back where, precisely?'

'Suon Ren, this,' said another voice, and she only placed it as she looked upon its owner's face. It was Varmen, their guide, and still with them as far as Suon Ren, apparently.

'Then . . .' For a moment she was going to ask about Tynisa, but then someone groaned – another woman – and Che stared round. 'You . . .'

It was the halfbreed, her guide from the inner recesses of her own past, where Seda's might had banished her. The woman was lying on her side on the floor, and perhaps had lost consciousness for a moment, but now she was shaking her head, clambering up on to hands and knees. 'Ah,' she began, to nobody in particular, and then, 'You have a great line in enemies, Cheerwell Maker. The Empress of the Wasps, no less.'

Che felt Thalric instantly go still and tense, and Varmen's eyes almost popped from his head at the unwelcome revelation. She decided that she herself would have to be the one to put a brave face on it. 'Well, the Spider-kinden say always judge people by their enemies, so I must be doing well in life, don't you think?'

The woman – *Maure* – gave a choked laugh, and looked up at her. The laugh died, and she flinched back from Che, as though she saw her own death revealed in the Beetle woman's face . . . *No, as though she sees something about my brow, or above my head.*

This reaction was gone in an instant, covered up so well that Che would never have known, had she not seen. 'What is it?' she asked, knowing already that the other woman would simply shake her head and disown the whole thing.

'Nothing, there's nothing.' Maure sat up straight, looking haggard and drawn. 'It's no easy road, that's all, and I wasn't expecting . . . *her* to be waiting at the end of it. Since when is the Empress of all the Wasps a *magician?* What's the world coming to.'

Varmen looked faintly embarrassed at this suggestion, but Che glanced back and noticed Thalric's expression was unhappy and thoughtful. *He knows. Despite all the Aptitude in the world, he knows it, too.*

'You have my thanks,' she said simply to the halfbreed woman. For a moment it seemed that Maure would not accept the gratitude, but then she acknowledged Che's words with a twitch of one hand. Che remembered the wretched Grasshopper mystic in Myna. *These pleasantries have power, amongst the Inapt.*

'Ah,' Maure murmured again, stretching a hand out to Varmen and waiting until he shuffled over to pull her to her feet. She brushed herself down meticulously, flicking her uneven fringe back in place, tugging at her clothes in what was obviously a little ritual for her own mental wellbeing. 'They'll tell you, the Commonwealers, how talking to ghosts, speaking to the dead, is a natural thing: that it's all part of a well-rounded life to honour your ancestors face to face, to bid a posthumous farewell to your peers and your relatives.' The smile she directed at them was tight-lipped. 'Mantis-kinden, they're even worse, you know? They worship death, practically. Spend all their living days hoping to die, so long as they die well. The best necromancers are always the Mantis-kinden.' She took a deep breath. 'You know what, though? Prince Felipe has the right idea, even if it took losing a dozen battles and a hundred friends just to educate him. Death's a miserable bloody business, and only a fool would go poking at it. Why else d'you think all the necromancers in those stories are after eternal life: they've seen just what death's like.'

The silence following this remark was only broken when Varmen commented, 'Why do it, then?'

'I'm *good* at it, Wasp-kinden,' she told him.

'So I was good with wood, when I was young. Doesn't mean I had to become a carpenter,' the big Wasp grumbled.

Maure smiled at him, but Che saw how the expression only just covered over the cracks in this woman's life. 'That's because, if you give up being a carpenter, the wood doesn't come hunting you down, demanding that you hammer some nails in.'

Twenty-Eight

Che did not hang up the dreamcatcher that same night. It was not that she wished thus to avoid her dreams, more she had accepted that there was no getting away from them, not any more. She had fought her newly Inapt nature at first, then she had tried to master it, as though in Khanaphes she might find some secret that would let her put the ancient world and all its magic back in the box . . .

The Shadow Box, of course, she interrupted her own musings. *All this stems from the Shadow Box. Tisamon and the Empress and I, all linked.*

. . . And Achaeos, too, but where is he? Why hasn't his ghost really come to call? He was more closely linked to that box and its contents than I was.

Standing there by her hammock in the Lowlander embassy, her thoughts turned inexorably to Maure. *She could . . . surely she could . . .* She owed the halfbreed woman a great deal, and it was plain that Maure had suffered, in order to bring her from the depths of her own mind and back to the waking world. *Can I ask this of her? No, I cannot.*

But the thought did not go away.

In Khanaphes, the ancient world had almost destroyed her that first time. She had nearly drowned in a sea of half-understood hieroglyphs. Then the real world had intruded, sending her down into the catacombs beneath the city, where waited the Masters. There, for the first time, she had been forced to confront her new self. She had almost enslaved herself to the Masters, as an easy way to avoid taking responsibility for what she had become. In the end she had defied them, though, shamed them into doing what she wanted, been rid of the ghost that had been haunting her – Tisamon's, not Achaeos's – and then escaped with her life, and with her companions. With Thalric.

Since then, she had been trying to control what she was, but the dreams had got the better of her, till at last she had come to the notice of the Empress – *my sister, they said* – and been swatted by her like a fly.

But it had not been merely her intrusion that had so enraged the queen of all the Wasps; it had been that intangible kinship that meant that . . .

Whatever she forced out of the Masters, it came to me as well as to her. I have shared in her blessing, so what was it that Maure saw, when I awoke . . .?

Lying in the hammock later, probably she dreamt, but she had now gone so far into that other world that it was impossible to tell dream apart from just *seeing.* As if revelations had been backing up all the while she had been a prisoner of her own mind, now she was deluged. It was a wild flood at first, too fierce for comprehension, that buffeted and tumbled against her, filling all the land around her until she was at the centre of a vast ocean of foretelling, which stretched on all sides, beyond the horizon. Then the world became still, and she had silence for once, and for a moment she saw it all.

Too much, too much to hold on to, each insight displacing the next within her memory, those countless drops of understanding plunging through her mind and impossible to hold . . . but for that single moment it was all apparent, all clear to her, and she was something more than human with it, godlike in a godless land.

She was floating over Khanaphes seeing its dark, hidden

heart beat sluggishly beneath her. Imperial soldiers were enforcing a curfew, the Empress's airship gone already, as Ethmet and his ministers sat in the resounding unheard echo of the double coronation that the Masters had enacted. Praeda and Amnon were already sailed for Collegium.

In the desert of the Nem, the Wasp artificers furthered their plans, feeding into the great darkness all the terror and pain and fire of the future, all the pieces of their scheme laid out before her. Yet she could not understand it at all; an Apter mind was needed, and the Apt would never see as she saw now. It struck her that this must be how the Moth-kinden had felt on the eve of the revolution. Those ceaseless parsers of the future must have realized their world was about to end, and been unable to stop it, unable to even comprehend the disaster that was rapidly befalling them.

In the Empire's capital, Seda had gathered her power about her, her servants and her generals. Che could see the manifest destiny of the Empire limning her like a golden halo, but Seda's footsteps seeped blood, the blood of countless kinden. There was a hunger in her, a lust to consume and control. Had she been no more than a temporal empress then she would have been considered a terror to the world. She was crowned, though, as Che was crowned, and her ambitions could no longer restrict themselves to mere land and slaves, for there was a new hunger in her that would never be sated. But why now those dark Mantis forests, and a gateway of rotting wood? From whence came those twisting, devouring forms that writhed, shackled in the earth beneath? In that dislocated instant it seemed as if the whole world became merely the skin covering some darker place, locked away out of sight and yet never quite gone . . .

For a moment, Che saw it all, the entire map of it, a prescient dream such as any Moth-kinden skryre would have wept at, and experiencing the full horror of what might happen stole her breath away.

But when she woke, after midnight, it was only with fragments like shards of ice melting, the sheer enormity of the vision defeating her, and all it left her with was a sense of dread – and an aftertaste of the Empress's hunger.

I am running out of time, she told herself, *I am here for a reason*. When she slept again, her mind was focused not on the grand tapestry but on the threads, and there she saw Tynisa.

She let the rapier carry her forward, its needle point penetrating the chest of the Grasshopper-kinden before her, then whipping out again at her command, before flashing behind her without her even having to turn and look. She felt the slightest resistance as it carved into another enemy, and she exulted briefly in the sheer purity of the sensation. A spear was heading her way, its wielder scarcely seeming relevant. Her blade caught the shaft, bound around it in a circular motion that put her within the spearman's reach, her point darting inside his guard until it had lanced him under the armpit.

For a moment she seemed clear of it all, unthreatened and alone in the midst of the skirmish, although Telse Orian's people were still hard-pressed on every side.

Aerial scouts had reported a band of brigands lurking in the woods here, perhaps a score of them. Orian had set out with half as many again, a handful of nobles and Mercers backed by an unruly levy of Grasshopper peasants. The bandits had anticipated them, though, and then had come the ambush. The Salmae forces were outnumbered two to one, and many of the brigands carried bows, whilst of Orian's party only the nobles were archers. The latter were better shots than the brigands, for sure, but numbers still counted. About half the panicking peasant levy had been scythed down, and several of the horses killed, before the ambushers had finally broken cover and attacked.

Those who met Tynisa regretted it, albeit briefly.

She had seen the ambush for what it was straight away. She had heard her father's voice in her ear, felt him guide her eyes: they would be concealed *here* and *here*, and the main body of them *there*. She had said nothing to the others, feeling a need for blood building up in her. *Let them come.*

She picked her next target, a raggedly armoured Dragonfly cocking back his spear, about to drive it into a Mercer's back. Levelling her rapier, she let it carry her to its inevitable destination, running the man through the ribs and out again, with barely more resistance from the flesh than from the air. She caught another before he even saw her, virtually by accident as he walked through the deadly path of her blade, and then she was passing on again, passing through the conflict like a plague, instantly striking down all who came within her orbit.

The rage was upon her, but it was harnessed now, tamed to her will. Her sword, her body, her father's memory, all of them were working in seamless harmony, so that she could ghost through a scrum of half a dozen enemy, their spearheads and blades passing on every side, and barely have to sway or parry, their blows falling wide as if by prior arrangement. Once or twice an arrow flashed towards her, but she caught it with her sword, each shaft slanting away, spent or broken.

There was something in the faces of those she killed, and it was adulation. It was her due. In that succession of fatal moments, she became real and fulfilled, and so did her victims. She rescued them from a lifetime of greed and murder and made something great of them by using their bodies as her canvas.

She realized that they were gone, all the brigands. They had fled into the woods rather than face her. The ground was littered with them, and with the dead of her own side as well. She was not even bloodied, though. She was not touched. Instead she was smiling, and perhaps it was that smile alone that had finally driven them away.

As she looked round, something miscarried within her. For a moment the fierce killing flames guttered.

Telse Orian lay cradled in the arms of one of his fellows, an arrow sunk so deeply in his neck that the point must surely be jutting out behind. He was not dead, not quite yet, but beyond the skill of any healer they had brought with them, and it was plain that moving him would be certain to bring his end that much the sooner.

He was looking at Tynisa, or at least his staring eyes were turned towards her. His mouth worked, bloody at the corners, but no sounds came out.

Tynisa gazed about with fresh eyes. Of the score who had set out, only she and six others remained, four of the armoured nobles and a couple of the most fortunate peasants. The two of them, lean spearmen clad in leather cuirasses and helms, stood close together and regarded Tynisa with fear and awe. They did not look so very different to the bandits, and it seemed to her, in that moment, entirely possible that some of the flesh that had fallen before her blade might not even have been the enemy's.

What am I doing? She asked herself, looking again at Telse Orian. His eyes were still fixed . . . no, not at her exactly, but as though he saw something – or someone – at her shoulder.

She saw the light go out, the last spark of what had been Orian, who, out of all Alain's peers, had shown her kindness. For a moment she felt that she should run, should flee this place while she was still free of . . .

Tynisa shook her head to clear it of such foolishness. 'We must report back to Alain,' she told the survivors, assuming command effortlessly. 'We must report how the bandits are driven back.'

For a moment they stared at her blankly, trying to equate her triumphant tone with the scene around them.

Che woke up into perfect awareness in the pre-dawn greyness, staring up at the ceiling. The previous night's images stirred in her mind, but most of all she remembered Tynisa, fighting with breath-taking elegance and grace, and not alone. Her every move had been shadowed by a twisted figure always at her back, one hand on her shoulder, corded with vines and racked with thorns.

Tisamon had found his daughter, and Che had witnessed how he was moulding her. What part of the Mantis Weaponsmaster that was still left to haunt the land of the living had obviously decided to cling to the ancient values of his kinden: blood and death, fierce and uncompromising, with not a hair's-breadth gap into which mercy or regret could pry. Che remembered Tisamon, and what she had heard of the man's last days. From what she gathered, regrets had eaten him alive, unable to reconcile his humanity with the impossible and terrible ideals his people aspired to.

It was plain that his ghost did not intend to let his daughter go the same way, even if he had to cut out her humanity to do so. *What will Tynisa become?*

Her sister was suffering, and there was nobody else who could go to her aid, but Cheerwell Maker.

By the time dawn had claimed the east, she was ready. She had dressed, recovered those of her possessions that Thalric and Varmen had brought with them, and now sat waiting impatiently for the light to waken her companions.

First up was Gramo Galltree, whom she had met briefly the previous evening, before she abandoned the world for much-needed sleep.

He eyed her cautiously. 'You seem recovered.'

With what she now knew, such small talk seemed an unconscionable waste of her time. 'Will the prince see me?' she asked flatly. 'Alternatively, will he mind if I take my leave . . .? Why are you smiling?'

Gramo coughed into his hand, a perfectly Collegiate way of hiding amusement. 'Prince Felipe Shah departed, with his retinue, even as you were being . . . recovered,' he told her. 'He had an audience with one of your Wasp friends, and then he set off for Esselve. Today is the first day of spring. A prince-major is expected to visit his vassals, although for the last few years Prince Felipe has not been too prompt in that.'

After an audience with one of my Wasp friends . . . Che considered, hoping that Thalric had not managed to offend one of the most powerful men in the Commonweal.

The two Wasps rose soon after. Varmen was first to appear,

bustling out of the embassy with only a brusque nod to her, off to check on his pack-beetle. Thalric stepped out a moment later, finding Che sitting near the door, looking towards the centre of Suon Ren, at the Dragonfly-kinden going about their business there.

She glanced at him, expecting that familiar closed look, the cynical Thalric armoured against the world, but instead she caught a strangely vulnerable expression there. Relief at her recovery, yes, but more than that. He stared at her without words, and at last she found her feet, with a flick of her wings, and walked over to him, holding his gaze.

'You put me to a great deal of trouble, Beetle girl,' he told her, but his voice trembled slightly, and she put her arms around him and hugged him tight, feeling his own embrace respond a moment later.

'We must set off north, as soon as you're ready to go,' she murmured into his chest. 'Tynisa needs me.'

He grunted. 'Does *she* know that?'

'No. Quite the opposite, probably. But I can't abandon her to . . .' She remembered that he would almost certainly not understand, and just let the sentence tail off.

'Well, then, I can't think of any urgent social engagements here that I can't put aside,' he told her. 'Let's beg some supplies and we'll set off.'

Thalric had looked out a map, soon after they had arrived, in preparation for this moment. He produced it with something like embarrassment, because it made no sense to him, lacking the careful proportion and measurement of the charts used by the Imperial army. Che studied it with interest, though, seeing how the Inapt cartographers had set out their world, places and trails, landmarks and directions. She understood it perfectly.

When they were ready to set off, they found Varmen waiting for them, his laden beetle at his heels.

'You're heading back east?' Che asked him.

He shuffled his feet. 'Thought I'd come with you.'

She glanced at Thalric, who was frowning, clearly as surprised as she was. 'You've been paid off?' she pressed.

Varmen shrugged. 'Paid, certainly. Listen, where you're heading, it's Rhael Province – bandit country. You're saying you can't use an extra sword?'

Che scrutinized his face, trying to detect treachery. She sensed a crack in his bluff and simple exterior, but she did not read guilt there, exactly. 'What is it?' she murmured, feeling obscurely that she should be able to tell precisely, to extract the knowledge from his face or his mind.

'You were with Felipe Shah,' Thalric noted, and Che readied herself for a display of suspicion, but instead the former Rekef man was nodding. 'He's hired you, hasn't he, to look after Che?'

Varmen shrugged awkwardly. 'He wasn't exactly going to pay me anything to look after *you*,' he said, still evasive. Thalric seemed satisfied with his own deductions, but Che could sense the gap, the discontinuity. Not that Thalric was wrong, but she knew there was more that was going unsaid by Varmen.

They set off shortly after, following a path that was little more than an animal track. They were barely a quarter mile from Suon Ren's outskirts, though, when someone was calling them back. Glancing behind them, Che saw a figure swathed in a dark cloak hurrying to catch up.

'It's the world's least subtle assassin,' Varmen murmured, mirroring Che's thoughts so closely that she could not suppress a bark of laughter.

'It's Maure,' Thalric observed, 'the . . . healer.' It would be a desperate day indeed before the word 'necromancer' passed the Wasp's lips willingly.

With that, there was no choice but to wait for the halfbreed to catch up. She stopped a little short of them, glancing from Wasp to Wasp, but looking mostly at Che.

'What do you want?' Thalric asked, a little harshly.

‘You just happen to be going the way I was heading,’ she told them, still hovering at that awkward distance, neither with them nor apart from them.

‘And what way’s that?’

‘Away from Suon Ren’s a good start,’ she told them. ‘Or you may not have noticed how I wasn’t exactly loved there, hmm? Got thrown out by that boot-faced seneschal on his master’s orders, first time round, and next thing I know is the prince’s soldiers are dragging me back, so I can look at you, lady.’ The nod she gave Che seemed overly respectful, endowing Che with the sort of gravitas that a great prince like Felipe Shah should own. ‘Now you’re well again, there’s no welcome for me here.’

‘So there’s a wide world,’ Thalric told her. ‘What do you want from us?’

‘Well, much as I love the thrill of travelling these roads on my own, what with the threat of robbery and rape to keep life interesting, I thought I might try walking in your shadows for at least a while.’

Thalric was opening his mouth to issue some fresh objection, but Varmen quickly said, ‘Let her come. Why not?’ And, in the moment before Varmen was reminded by Thalric that he had no vote in this issue, Che was saying, ‘Enough.’

They all listened to her. That was the frightening thing.

‘Maure,’ she said simply, ‘I owe you a great deal, and if Suon Ren has no gratitude, then don’t think we’ll repeat that failing. Travel with us if you wish. You’re welcome.’

Again she felt that these words carried more weight to them than the simple meanings she was used to. It was as though she was now some great queen whose merest nod or favour carried unthinkable importance. Maure seemed relieved, but at the same time in no great hurry to come closer. ‘That is all, is it?’ Che pressed her. ‘Safety in numbers?’

‘Oh, of course,’ Maure said, and the lie was obvious, but Che let it pass.

Twenty-Nine

In the end, Che let Maure choose their path through Rhael Province, by roads that the woman had obviously travelled before. They made a point of keeping under tree cover whenever they could, and it was clear that the halfbreed was deliberately avoiding settlements along the way.

'You don't like doing business with brigands, then?' Che had asked her.

'I do business with anyone, if I have to. Brigands pay better than princes, and they pay in advance. I thought you wanted to get to Elas Mar as quickly as possible, though, so best to avoid the locals. They're a curious lot, and might ask pointed questions.'

Che found herself still convalescing, lacking something of her customary Beetle stamina, which left her trailing behind whilst Varmen strode on ahead, his beetle ambling at his heels. Thalric, however, kept pace with her, which she found by turns comforting and annoying. She was not used to being indulged as an invalid.

After a while, she stopped paying much attention even to Thalric, because the long trek was wearing her down. She cut a walking stick to lean on, and still she laboured her way at the rear, so that Maure and Varmen were perpetually having to stop and wait for her. *A shame no northbound barges are expected any time soon.*

Towards the end of the first day she glanced up from her plodding feet, for the first time in a while, and saw the halfbreed necromancer leaning in towards Varmen, talking closely, and then the big Wasp's head cocked back as he laughed at something she had said. Maure had never seemed much of a humorist to Che, but then the woman's reaction towards her had been curious from the start. Plainly, with others she felt able to let go a little more.

'Look.' She managed a gesture towards them, for Thalric's sake.

'I see it.' His tone of voice was not approving.

'Surely you're not . . .' Che caught her breath, 'still toeing that line of Imperial dogma? Superior races and all?'

'Che, I don't know why *either* of them is still with us. Allow me my suspicions, and I'll let you remain trusting as a newborn, and we'll agree to differ.'

She glanced at him, and could not suppress a tired smile. 'Looking after me, is it?'

'Someone has to. I'm only surprised I've not had to rescue you from something over the last few days.' His tone, delivering acerbic banter calculated to hide whatever deeper feelings were hidden there, reminded her irresistibly of their time in Khanaphes together, first as ambassadors and then as fugitives.

'I don't know what I'd do without you,' she said, trying to put a smile into it, but the words came out as far too solemn, and he gave no reply.

That night, after an argument over how hidden they should remain, Varmen stubbornly set a fire, albeit low down in a dip between trees. The pantries of Suon Ren had come up with some peculiar travelling provisions: a spiced hotchpotch of seeds, nuts, shreds of meat and dried fruit that could be eaten dry or cooked up into a kind of stew. It was filling, but promised to become dull eating after a while.

'Honey would set this off well,' Che opined, between heavily chewed mouthfuls. 'They don't seem to like it much around here, though.'

'It was one of the commodities the army shipped in by the ton, during the war,' Thalric agreed. 'That and good wine, since Commonweal drink is an acquired taste.'

'I'm sure you managed to acquire it.' The simple act of eating was wearing her out, and she glanced up to offer her half-finished bowl around, but found Varmen and Maure were both missing.

'Where are . . .?' she started, but, on registering Thalric's look, she abruptly understood. 'That was quick work.' She felt a sudden and irrational stab of envy that such casual liaisons had never been something open to her: raised as she was in Collegium, city of propriety, under the guidance of a respectable public figure and, besides, when had she ever even had the opportunity?

Of course, Tynisa had never let Stenwold's high station stop her enjoying herself . . .

You are not here for that, anyway, she told herself. *You have a higher purpose.* If she closed her eyes, she could feel the faint thorn-point that was the spectre of Tisamon, penetrating Tynisa's mind like a wound that could only suppurate with time. It seemed very far off, and she seemed altogether too weak a vessel to provide any great aid to her wayward sister.

The night was cold, and Che felt very alone just then, so when Thalric put his arms about her, she gave herself up to his embrace, leaning into his chest, feeling his chin butt gently against the back of her head. His hands rested across her stomach, and she felt a little shiver at the thought of their killing power, the Art that slept within them. Reclining against him, his arms seemed to form a barrier keeping the world at bay. His very Apt ignorance was a shield, and she felt that she would not dream whilst he held her. Some part of him would stand sentry, and burn down any dreadful revelations that tried to ambush her.

His breath was at her ear, and so it was simple enough to tilt her head back and find his mouth with her own, expecting him to start with surprise, but the pointed absence of Varmen and Maure must have led his thoughts along the same path, for he kissed her hungrily in return. A moment later, and his hands were moving up to cup her breasts, brashly at first but hesitant just before they came to rest, a fulcrum moment when he was plainly unsure whether she had meant to allow him so much.

Then she was slipping to one side, but only so she could draw him down over her, one hand working at his belt, and their lips never quite parting, no matter what contortions they went through. His killing hands remained firm on her, like another Imperial conquest.

There was a moment, the inevitable moment, *Achaeos!* as she contrasted the gentle touch of the Moth with Thalric's fierce strength. And after that came the thought of what Stenwold would say if she took this last step, this final fall from grace. *I can't lie with Thalric. I can't, not after all he's done, no no no . . .*

And he sensed the sudden tension, and she saw complete understanding appear in his face as she twisted her head away from him. *It's wrong, it's wrong . . .* The well-bred Collegium girl, Maker's niece, the enemy of the Empire, all shouting that reproach at her.

To the pits with the lot of you. She'd had enough of being haunted by herself, and it had been a long time, and she *wanted* this. She almost lunged at Thalric, arms dragging him down towards her again, feeling all those walls of propriety and repression shatter like glass. The two of them now fighting out of their clothes as though they were being reborn, a new stage of life – clutching at each other in something as much relief and catharsis as it was desire.

Che awoke in the chill hours before dawn, her back pressed against his warm chest, aware of hearing quiet movement nearby. With a start she sat up, fumbling for her sword hilt, but it was only Maure poking at the embers, trying to leach a little more warmth from the corpse of their fire. Thalric woke up with a growl, glared at the world balefully, then turned over, wrapping himself in the cloak, that had previously covered them both. On the far side of the fire, Varmen was snoring with a beehive drone.

Maure added some kindling to the fire, with obvious pessimism, but soon there were a few brave flames venturing forth, and she had quickly nurtured a steady little blaze. Seeing Che's eyes still fixed on her, she retreated over to Varmen's side of the fire, raising an eyebrow. On that invitation, Che carefully got to her feet and followed her, leaving Thalric to sleep alone.

'My mystical intuition tells me you have questions,' Maure said, with a slight smile, which only broadened when Che could not help glancing down at Varmen.

'Thank the world for Apt men, hmm?' said the halfbreed.

Che frowned at her, caught unawares. 'I don't understand.'

'No? But surely you do,' Maure corrected her. 'I mean men to whom everything *we* are and do, the very world we live in, is a fiction. You don't see the advantage in that? No questions, no requests, none of the reverence that's equal parts fear and distrust. I thought that's why you were with him.' One finger indicated Thalric's supine form.

'No, that's . . . complicated,' Che replied, but even as she spoke she was thinking, *And yet perhaps she's closer to it than I give her credit for. Oh, it's frustrating, sometimes, that he cannot understand, but still . . . would he stay with me, if he did?*

'Complicated, you can keep,' Maure declared. 'I like men to be simple. I've rolled the lucky dice with this one.'

Che nodded companionably, and felt almost guilty when she threw down, 'And your reasons for travelling with us, they're just as simple, are they?'

Maure paused, and her expression was both hurt and guilty. 'That was uncalled for.'

'You're making Thalric nervous, the pair of you, and I can see why. He's had plenty of people try to put a knife in his back, and he's right that Varmen should be heading back east by now, and you should be going . . . wherever it is that you go. So tell me.'

'Varmen's reasons I don't know, but I can guess.' Maure's eyes were downcast now. 'He has a ghost on his shoulder. No surprise, you'd think, but most Wasps I ever met see the world in a way that paints everything they do with the Empire's colours. No guilt, you see, and guilt lets the ghosts in like nothing else does. But then you knew that.'

She now caught Che's eye, and for a moment the Beetle girl could not answer.

'And you?' she challenged at last. 'Don't ask me to believe you came running after us to save you from the brigands you're obviously familiar with, or to get inside Varmen's mail. Help me to trust you, Maure.'

The halfbreed mystic looked away again, her good humour ebbing and leaving her vulnerable again. 'Ghosts, Cheerwell Maker . . . do you know what ghosts are?'

'They're . . .' *They're what happens to us after we die? But that can't be right.*

Maure had apparently read her mind. 'Nobody knows what happens to us when we pass on – the vital spark that animates our crude flesh. Perhaps we are merely gone, after all. Or perhaps we fly back to rejoin our ideal, thus Beetles to the essence of beetle-ness and so on, although that begs the question of what happens to someone like me. Perhaps there is another world, yet, a metamorphosis into something splendid, out of this coarse life. Some Woodlouse-kinden even believe we may simply be born once again. But we don't *know*, and that's not what ghosts are. Ghosts are . . . it's as if we were a nymph or larva all our lives, and in our dying moments, we hardened our skins, made of ourselves a chrysalis, and then . . . the spark of us, the thing that made us live, flies free somewhere else, but something's left behind that still has our shape, our nature. It fractured, when the life burst forth and flew away, and most of the time that's all there is left, just shards of the husk blown by the wind, but some deaths – horrible deaths, terrible deaths, deaths cutting short unfulfilled lives, deaths of magicians especially – those can leave a husk behind that is still *them*, or part of them, some fragment or aspect of their being that still possesses urges and needs. They can be spoken with, and bound to service even, and they can haunt others, or objects, places. Broken things, they are, most often, but still recognizable as who they once were. Even the smaller fragments may contain some ounce of self, some emotion – a hate, a love.'

Che shivered at that suggestion. 'But that still doesn't explain—'

'It's not the actual requests I mind,' Maure spoke over her. 'Trawling for someone's dead husband, or someone's lost child, there's a science to that – and I almost enjoy it. But all the rest of the time . . . all the rest of the time it's just hearing the whispers, the fragmentary voices, the odds and ends of memory, the wasted splinters of other people's lives. The world is full of the husks of the dead, and they all talk to me, and I can't blot them out.'

Che just watched her now, waiting to hear more.

'They went quiet when you woke up, though,' Maure whispered, trying to find her smile again. 'I can't hear a single one of the wretched, abandoned bastards. A whole ghost, well, that's different. I reckon it wouldn't be so in awe of you. But the chaff, all that disintegrating chaff, you brush it away because of what they gave you – what they gave to you and *her*.'

Che felt her hand rise to touch her forehead, without knowing why until she realized that Maure's gaze had led her there.

'What do you see?' she demanded, but the woman merely shook her head and would not say.

For a long while they sat in silence, during which Thalric turned over twice, threatening to wake again. Maure mustered a shamefaced grin, but it convinced neither of them. At last she said, 'Ask your question.'

'I was haunted,' Che told her. 'The ghost . . . I thought it was the ghost of my lover, but it wasn't. It was a Mantis-kinden I had once known, and the Masters of Khanaphes cut him from me and set him loose in the world. And now he's poisoning my sister, and I have to stop him, and . . .'

Maure nodded. 'Ask it,' she urged.

'My lover, he died . . .' Che said, realizing how she was stating the obvious, yet surprised to find the pain so raw and immediate, after so much time and distance. 'He . . . I was with him, in a way, but I never had the chance to speak to him, to say goodbye, to say . . .' She clenched her fists. 'Would you . . . could you . . .?'

Maure's grin failed, and she was now nodding grimly. 'I could hardly refuse a request from someone like you, now, could I? But let that wait until we reach Elas Mar, at least. Let me find some place there that I can fortify and protect. Let me . . . let me have this journey without ghosts, Cheerwell Maker.'

'Call me Che.' The Beetle reached out and put a hand on the necromancer's arm. Then Varmen's snoring ceased, and the Wasp was stretching, yawning. And Che backed off as Maure sat down again beside him.

Four nights later, they ran into the bandits.

It was so much a meeting of chance that it was almost embarrassing. Varmen laid a small fire, as on each night previously, but by the time he had it going they had all spotted another fire through the trees, a hundred yards away or so, and the makers of that fire had by now surely spotted theirs. There followed a hasty discussion about the virtues of fleeing further into the woods at night, of awaiting whatever might befall them, or of confronting the other fire and its owners. In the end, Che was the only one amongst them advocating anything other than confrontation, so she gave in with bad grace.

After a little preparation, they set off in that direction, knowing that their opposite numbers had been given ample time to prepare.

Che, Maure and Thalric proceeded first, approaching the

campfire as obviously as they could, finding just two men there, neither of them locals, and with three horses tied nearby. One was a squat Scorpion-kinden, and a loaded crossbow lay beside him as he ostentatiously burned a hunk of bread in the flames. The other was a solid-looking Wasp-kinden man with dark hair, who was watching their approach bright-eyed.

'I swear I'm meeting more Wasps here in the Commonweal than I ever did in the Empire,' Che murmured.

Thalric stopped within range of their firelight, having counted the horses, and Maure leant in to say to him, 'The third is in the trees to your right. He has a bow.'

He nodded, then announced, 'We seem to be neighbours for this night, so perhaps it would make sense if we shared the same fire.' They had already discussed this, and it seemed marginally safer to have their opposite numbers where they could see them, rather than out in the dark planning who-knew-what.

'There's logic to that,' the dark Wasp conceded. 'You have food?'

'Some,' Thalric returned. 'We're no danger to you, so perhaps your friend could come and join us.'

The two men exchanged glances, and the Scorpion shrugged his broad shoulders. 'Come on out, Soul,' he said. A moment later a tall, angular man glided out of the darkness, his face expressionless. He was Grasshopper-kinden and, tall as he was, his bow was taller, an arrow fitted to the string, but pointing towards the ground.

'They've a friend also, a big man still out there in the dark,' said the Grasshopper.

The Wasp raised an eyebrow. 'Is that so?' He reached down beside him, retrieving something from under a blanket. It took Che a moment to recognize that the object now resting across his knees was a nailbow, a weapon she would not have expected to find in the Commonweal.

Thalric nodded, recognizing this game of escalation when he saw it. He opened his mouth to call out, but Varmen was already responding to his cue and strode out of the darkness to back up his fellows. They had decked him out in all his armour, and for a moment the three strangers just stared at him. Probably the nailbow bolts could have pierced his mail, some of them at least, but it was clear that the dark-haired Wasp knew a Sentinel when he saw one, and he reacted in almost superstitious awe.

'Well,' the man said at last. 'I reckon you won that round.' He set the nailbow back down, though still within easy reach. 'I've not seen one of your kind since the Twelve-year War.'

'Not since you deserted, you mean?' asked Thalric, sitting down by their fire as though he had just taken possession of it.

The Wasp's face showed that he was about to make a retort, but the Scorpion's sudden snicker took the wind out of him. 'I reckon we're none of us here with the Emperor's orders in our packs,' he stated.

Che had been watching the three carefully, and something tugged at her notice: nothing she could put a name to, but she was abruptly sure that there was a fourth one somewhere. It was hinted in the way that they sat, something implicit in their placement.

'Your other friend might as well come out,' she said pleasantly, 'now that we're all getting on so well.' She saw the Scorpion-kinden's eyes shift and she drew her sword smoothly, pointing it behind her in the direction he had glanced. 'Or is that not the case?'

For a moment everyone was very still, but then the Scorpion grunted, holding out a hand. A moment later, something surged from the undergrowth to let him run clawed fingers over its segmented carapace. It was a fine specimen, Che considered, perhaps two-thirds the bulk of its master, its claws looking well able to scissor a man's leg off at the knee, and the needle point of its sting was swaying suspiciously as if regarding the newcomers.

'Scutts,' the Scorpion gestured with one talon. 'Barad Ygor,' he added, pointing to himself. The Wasp was Mordrec, the Grasshopper Soul Je.

Introductions made, the two groups of travellers settled down about the single campfire, watching each other very carefully. Varmen remained in his armour, a hulking presence weighing down the corners of everyone's attention.

Che busied herself with sorting out some food, readying a pot for boiling, reckoning that such signs of unconcerned activity would go some way to allaying suspicions. Soon enough, she saw Thalric and Varmen fall into cautious talk with the dark-haired Wasp-kinden, but before long they had broken off and retreated back to silence around the fire, to the other man's obvious chagrin. She shifted over to ask, out of the corner of her mouth, 'What is it? Something wrong?'

Thalric gave a derisive snort. 'Slave Corps,' he muttered, as if that explained everything.

'What, *still*?'

'He used to be.'

Che gave Thalric a level look. 'And you're in a position to care?' she demanded, still trying to keep her voice to a whisper, but failing somewhat.

'You wouldn't understand,' he told her, and he grimaced even as he said it, realizing how unwise the words were. Immediately, Che was storming over to the three travellers, aggressively enough for them to scrabble for their weapons.

'You,' she pointed at Mordrec. 'You enslave people much these days?'

'Not me.' He looked at her levelly. 'In fact my current troubles are more to do with too much pursuit of freedom.'

Che glanced back at Thalric and Varmen. 'Then stop being so stupid, the pair of you.' To make her point she sat down beside Mordrec, hooking her pot over the fire. 'Why did you leave the army, then?'

He blinked at the question, then shrugged. 'Killed a Rekef man. An officer.'

Thalric had the grace to smile slightly at that. 'There's a coincidence.'

'And the debts,' Ygor muttered. 'What he's not telling you is how he owed the man money. Don't go taking him for some kind of hero.'

'Well maybe we should get on to what you and Soul did,' Mordrec retaliated, whereupon Ygor held his hands up hurriedly.

'All right, you're a hero. The less said about us mere mortals the better, especially as *that* business could still come back and bite us.'

Other people's histories, thought Che, noticing significant looks pass between the men, and knowing that she would never find out. She lifted her eyes to the third member of their band, and found him staring at her.

'What?' she asked.

'I don't know,' the Grasshopper replied softly. 'Something, though.'

Ygor and Mordrec would be Apt, of course. She wondered if Soul Je just had particularly good sight, or whether all the Inapt would end up staring at her like that, trying to work out what had marked her out in their eyes.

Later, she sought out Maure's company again, after Thalric and all three of the travellers had bedded down, leaving just Varmen and the scorpion Scutts staring at each other over the fire. The halfbreed woman was plainly about to seek sleep herself, but she sat up again as Che approached.

'These three,' the Beetle girl murmured. 'Any ghosts there?'

'Hah, it's strange,' Maure replied. 'They share one, but it's not a dead man's. You can be haunted by the living in a strange sort of way, as you yourself have cause to know. They'd rather be elsewhere, maybe even not in each other's company, but I can see the same hand rests on each of them. Loyalty to a living friend can haunt you as much as the ghost of a dead one.'

The next morning the two travelling parties parted company, and Che would not see any of the three again until much later, and in much-changed circumstances.

Thirty

There was precious little cover out here, and Dal and his followers were lying low in a copse of twisted trees, an old orchard gone wild decades ago. Had the Mercers been scouring the sky above them, then this mob of brigands would have been discovered almost at once even under cover of night, for there were more than fifty of them, filling the space between the trees to bursting. The Salmae's hunters were not here, however. They were further south, which could mean one of two things, depending on who was in control.

Either they've cut us off from our retreat into Rhael, Dal considered, *or we've stolen a march on them.* So far, the skirmishing between Dal's people and the Salmae had lasted over three tendays, with a dozen vicious hit-and-run engagements, ambushes and surprise attacks from the bandits punctuating a history in which the Salmae's Mercers chased all over the Rhael–Elas Mar border, trying to pin them down. Their conflict to date had been so mobile that Dal reckoned neither side could be sure who had the advantage in numbers. Dal's people were split into smaller groups, because it would have been impossible to feed them otherwise, and so, of necessity, the hunters had split up as well, to try and contain them. The only numbers that mattered at any given time were those who were in evidence here and now.

The Mercers were better equipped, Dal knew, even if their luckless levy of peasants was not. If Dal had met them toe to toe, fighting them with honour and dignity, then those iridescent suits of armour, their masterworked swords and man-length recurved bows would carry the day swiftly. Not only were his own followers just a rabble under arms, but they had no stomach for a hard fight either. They had not signed on to die for him, just to get rich and fill their bellies. The Mercers, on the other hand, were relentless, and their peasant troops were just as scared of Salmae retribution as they were of Dal's arrows.

And yet we're not losing. It was hard to claim whether they were actually *winning*, in this chaotic shifting battlefield, but the simple fact that the Salmae had been unable to tie them down or force them into a serious battle seemed a victory in itself. Dal had lived the last few years in and around Siriell's Town, jostling for power with the other bandit chiefs and sporadically wooing Siriell herself, playing his part in the chaotic running of that renegade province, which had depended wholly on the relative strengths of the major players there. Throughout this time, he had known that the people north of Rhael considered him their enemy.

A fair proportion of the population of seven villages had now turned out to swell the ranks of his followers. Several had burned their own homes. The mere appearance of Dal's people seemed to spark off a madness of new horizons, people who had known nothing but gruelling work and taxation suddenly seeing for the first time *another way*. For Dal, the experience was like being carried away by a river current, but carried towards a destination that had never been within reach before. He knew, from personal experience, that a peasant's life was hard, and that the privations of the war had only made it harder, but the people of Elas Mar had been living on the wrong side of poverty for years now as the Salmae settled their war debts through tithe and appropriation, without deigning to suffer privation themselves.

It would not be true to say that the people here wanted

revenge, but they did want freedom. It took a desperate kind of squinting to mistake rule by brigands for *that*, but these were desperate times.

The thought kept occurring to Dal Arche now: *What if we win?* Would he set himself up as a local prince, put on the tyrant's shoes and simply continue the way of the world, armed with everything noble but a bloodline? And what would the Prince-Major do about that? Reports suggested he had refused to come to the Salmae's aid, and certainly none of his people had been seen yet, but that might change quickly if Dal started getting too many airs.

Well, I'm about to push my luck. There was another village right ahead of them, and on the far horizon the moon picked out the crooked silhouette of Castle Leose. After avoiding the most recent attempt by the Salmae to entrap him, Dal had decided against leading his people back south. Instead, while his enemies hunted for him at the border of Rhael, he had gathered this band of desperadoes and taken them north, to within sight of the Salmae's stronghold, albeit still the most distant sight possible.

'He's coming back,' someone muttered, and Dal saw a figure hurrying – no, running – from the village outskirts towards the copse. It was his unofficial ambassador, a renegade Spider-kinden who called himself Avaris, and who had practised a variety of confidence tricks and crooked games up and down the Imperial border until he had alienated so many powerful people that he had been forced to flee into the Commonweal. He was a fast talker, though, and very protective of his own skin, which was why Dal had picked him.

'Speak,' he instructed as Avaris reached the cover of the trees.

'They're up in arms – but not for us,' the Spider replied shortly. 'They'll have sent someone with news for the castle. I told you this was a bad idea.'

Dal did not reply, but took a moment to consider how he

felt about this development. There was a plan for this sort of reception, of course, but recently the peasantry of Elas Mar had offered him a run of easy victories. His banditry had virtually been sleeping in its scabbard, but now he was put to draw it forth once again.

'What do they think?' he asked.

'That the Salmae will protect them,' Avaris reported. 'I told you that, this close to the castle . . .'

'I know,' Dal cut him off, because he had seen all this before. Closer to a castle, the peasants were less discontented, the headmen hailing from families that had served thus for generations. They had grown to love the boot on their neck. The headman of Dal's own village had been the same way, no doubt.

'Pull back?' Avaris prompted.

'They're well armed? Well defended?'

'Spears and staves.'

Dal turned to address the rest of his followers, who had been following this exchange intently. 'You may have had some illusions about what we're here for,' he told them, his voice just loud enough to be heard by them all. 'Some of you have been telling stories, from the old times, about peasant heroes, about good deeds and just causes.' He knew it was so. The conflict so far had sufficed to give their venture the illusion of righteousness. 'You all remember the war. Many of you fought in it. There's not a one of you that hasn't known friend or family that's ended up a corpse on some battlefield or other. Well, know this: the Wasp Empire killed off the old times. The Wasp Empire put paid to all that talk of heroes. Where were those heroes when the Wasps scythed us down in our hundreds?' He heard his voice shake slightly, and brought his emotions to heel. 'Our glorious nobility will tell each other that *they* were heroes, dying to defend their people, but for each one of them that fell, there was a carpet of our dead to cushion them. We're no heroes but, for all that, they've shown us they've no right to lord it over us, and those that uphold their damned right to do so can burn.'

He watched their faces. He did not consider himself any great leader of men, but he was leader enough to keep hold of a group like this.

Without another word he turned away and strung his bow in one smooth motion. A moment later he was out of the trees, his wings flaring into being to coast him towards the village – and soon his bloody-handed retinue was following.

They coursed uphill towards the village outskirts, and Dal knew that if the headman had made swift preparations, then they would meet a fence of spear points at the summit. But there were no defenders, no attempt to stop them. *Maybe they're with us, after all?*

Looking ahead towards the village's heart he saw a confused gaggle of men, women and children. They were Grasshopper- and Dragonfly-kinden, most of them unarmed and many only partly dressed, blinking in the moonlight as their headman addressed them in moderate tones, not shouting or ordering. And Dal Arche saw the headman look across as the front-runners in the bandit charge pelted in amongst the houses, with torches and blades. The man's face fell apart, that was the only way Dal could think about it. He was an old Dragonfly whose whole life must have been spent in this same village. When the war came, Dal would put money on it, the Salmae had instructed him on who to send off to fight, and told him to stay here safe with his family. Here was a man who trusted implicitly the traditional order that set him over his fellows, and under his betters. He knew that Leose would protect him, and did not have it in him to credit Avaris. He had dismissed the garrulous Spider-kinden as a mere trickster.

Run, thought Dal, even as he plucked back his bowstring, and some of the villagers were running. The mothers, the fathers, those who had the most immediate things to protect, they began breaking free of the headman's spell, even as the old man continued to urge them to stay where they were. But not all of them were running; some were turning to fight. Others just stood staring, mesmerized by the certainty in the old man's voice, as he kept croaking on at them despite the shock fragmenting his lined features.

Dal put his first arrow between the headman's wide eyes and counted it as a mercy to the village as a whole, as more people started fleeing.

Lycene banked over the smoke, and then cut a wide arc around the ruined village's perimeter. Astride the insect's back, Alain looked down, with Tynisa clinging to his waist.

She had risen in the ranks of the Salmae's soldiers since the fighting had started. The peasant levy now regarded her with almost superstitious awe, for she never flinched from bloodshed, never feared, never retreated. The brigands had learned to recognize her, too, and her arrival would sometimes send them fleeing even before she drew steel. Those that were bold enough to go up against her, she slew, or her flickering rapier cut their arrows from the air as she sped closer and closer.

But she could be in only one place at a time, whilst the brigands always seemed to be everywhere, or elsewhere. When Salme Elass led her forces down en masse, the bandits would be gone, or some small pocket of them all that could be found. Meanwhile they would strike somewhere else, not defending any of their gains but making daring inroads into Elas Mar Province like this – pillaging, burning and murdering even within sight of Leose Castle.

The Salmae kept a dozen dragonflies trained to carry a rider, and they were all of them deployed now, scouring the ground below for signs of the bandits. There had been some successes, and only a few days ago a mob of thirty ruffians were cut down to a man, after Alain had spotted them from above. Most of the time, however, the brigands were in and out of the trees, following shadowed and hidden roads to seek out their prey.

'There,' Tynisa snapped, squeezing Alain tighter with one arm as she pointed. He took a moment to read her direction, then nudged Lycene with his knees, propelling the insect across the speeding ground. In the first pass he missed them, but at Tynisa's insistence he swung back, before spotting a score of figures hurrying across between stands of trees. No doubt these were the very villains who had set the fires.

Alain gestured in the direction they had come from: *We must fetch help.*

She leant close and spoke in his ear. 'Set me down.'

He glanced back at her, so that for a moment they were almost kissing. Tynisa felt her blood race. *Almost. I almost have him. Perhaps I shall win him with this deed.* She had been bold in the fray, since finding her new purpose, and none bolder. She knew that Alain and his mother had both been impressed by her fury and her skill, the many lives she had taken in their names. Surely her success was working on Alain's mind, in this bloody wooing. He could not but acknowledge her as the perfect partner, predatory and loyal as any Mantis-kinden should be.

'You're sure?' he said.

Does he have to ask? 'Set me down,' she repeated. 'I shall trail them, track them. Bring on your nobles and your levy as fast as you may, you shall find me there.'

His grin sent fire flashing through her, and then he was guiding Lycene down, far enough to avoid watching eyes but close enough for Tynisa to soon regain the enemy.

'Good hunting,' he said.

For a moment she wanted to tell him, *For you, I do this for you,* but he must know her by her actions, not by hollow words. Then she had slipped off the dragonfly's back, while the insect hovered just clear of the ground, and a second later Alain was darting back for the skies and she was alone.

She entered the woods, slipping from shadow to shadow with her sword eager in her hand, like some trained beast that she had often hunted alongside. Her feet did not falter: some additional sense told her just where her quarry was, as though a guiding hand led her this way and that to pick up their trail. Before long she could hear them: a score of men and women doing their best to be quiet, and she skulked silently closer, the woods they relied on now betraying them by hiding her from them.

They were laden with sacks, and she saw a few handcarts, the spoils from the latest ruined village being hauled southwards as fast as could be. If they were intercepted by the Salmae's forces, she knew they would abandon the loot without a second thought. They were still being called bandits by the angry nobility, but such pillaging seemed to have become secondary to them, as if pride of place in their plans went to resisting their lawful masters.

She was just a dozen feet now from the stragglers, and saw they had sentries out on either side of the main group, and doubtless scouts ahead, but nobody bothered looking back the way they had come.

How best to . . .? the thought began, but these days she seldom had to finish such a question before that inner voice – in the authoritative, confident tones of her father – provided the answer.

Kill their watchers, was the solution. *Kill their scouts. Make them fear.*

She picked up her pace, virtually tasting their blood in her mouth already, skirting the edge of the moving band but keeping them always in sight. Her first victim made himself obvious by standing still as the rest moved on. He stared into the greenery, narrow-eyed, but he was not peering at her. He was Dragonfly-kinden, dark hair stippled with grey and his face gaunt, holding a spear in two hands at waist height, and wearing a leather and chitin hauberk that was slightly too large for him. Dragonflies had good eyes, she knew, but she was Tynisa, daughter of Tisamon, and the shadows loved her.

He was moving on again, a few trees out from the main herd, spear levelled ahead of him, but he heard nothing, saw nothing, as she sidled closer. For a moment the sheer power of it all almost overwhelmed her, deadly as a knife, quiet as a ghost.

Her rapier's needle point speared through his ear, grating a little as it sheared bone. As he dropped, she was gone and her blade with her, licking its lips and hungry for more.

Her first mark had not been discovered by the time she killed the second, this one a bony Grasshopper woman with a noble's long-hafted sword resting on her shoulder. She was inconveniently tall for a slit throat, so Tynisa struck her from a crouch, inserting her blade under the ribs and into the heart. The woman died without a cry, her mouth gaping emptily, eyes already sightless as she hit the ground.

This time the victim was noticed in seconds, but Tynisa was already moving on. There were cries and exclamations. Names were called out. Then they spotted the absence of the Dragonfly man she had slain first, and the group milled, bunching closer. They seemed to have no clear leader.

She killed her third and fourth around the other side of the group, then moved on.

The fifth almost surprised her: a young Dragonfly who had been standing so still between trees that Tynisa virtually walked into her. For a second she thought she had gone unnoticed, since the other woman was looking inwards at her fellows, not outwards as a good sentry should. Tynisa drew her blade back, but the movement must have reflected in the corner of the Dragonfly girl's eye, for she leapt up with a shout, her wings flashing about her shoulders. She was still not quite fast enough, the rapier's blade following her up, arrow-swift, to lance up beneath her sternum and bring her to earth. Then there were arrows cutting through the trees, and Tynisa faded back into the shadows, feeling her father's guiding hand on her shoulder again, letting her Art turn all eyes away from her, becoming *still*.

They were coming after her now, a vengeful rabble. She let the first dozen rush uselessly by, becoming more scattered as they went. The thirteenth she killed, dancing from her hiding place to slash his throat and sever his bowstring in the same movement, and then away. A couple of them had seen her, then. The closest was too near to hide from, so she put out his eye with a swift lunge, seeing how his arms lifted his spear-haft to parry even after she had killed him. The other witnessed that, and she saw her casual poise reflected in his eyes, his bravado souring to terror in an instant. He backed away, struck a tree, turned and ran. She savoured the moment. Fear was a form of worship, after all. It was her proper due for her skills, just like coins thrown into a minstrel's hat.

By then the bandits had realized their mistake, and they were calling out to each other, drawing close again. Uncaring, she slew another three as they did so, and knew they would be counting heads as they reassembled, realizing by just how much their force had been diminished.

No order was given, but they were running now, abandoning their spoils, fleeing through the woods. She kept pace with them effortlessly, feeling strength flow into her with each successive stride as though the very earth was urging her on. Those that stumbled or fell behind were her rightful prey.

Are you proud of me, father?

And she was sure she heard his voice reply, from far away, *There is more yet to do.*

Something had caught her eye ahead, and it was a while before she realized what. Her fleeing victims were not alone now, but seeking sanctuary with their fellows. Ahead of them, hidden neatly in the deeper woods, was a larger band – twice as many at least as the runners had started out with.

She slowed, watching carefully, seeking out the weak points. These were a better breed of brigand, she decided, with more sentries, and more alert ones, too. There were soon two score arrows pointed into the trees as the word spread.

So, a challenge.

Then she realized: *Alain.*

He would be bringing what men he could spare to put down an insurrection of fifty, not one hundred and fifty. He would not be ready.

I have to warn him. He can go back and find more soldiers. But in the meantime these bandits would be long gone, one step ahead of them as always.

But if they fight, we might lose . . .

She sensed a disappointment in the air around her. *What are you thinking like? You are thinking like a cowardly Beetle, like a* Spider. *What is win? What is lose? Merely to fight is all. If you go back and warn your man, there will be no fight. How will you impress him then?*

And there was no answer to that.

The fight had been glorious. Alain had brought perhaps ninety with him, a dozen nobles and the balance in peasant spearmen. The bandits had more archers, though Alain and his kin were better shots. The forest had not been grown with archery in mind, though, and although arrows picked off a handful on both sides, the spears met in short order, and then the real bloodletting commenced.

Tynisa had led the charge, exulting in it. The brigands she had picked as her targets had faltered, clearly recognizing her as the killer in the woods from just an hour before. They tried to keep her at the end of their spears, but they could as easily have penned in the tide. Like the tide, she flowed past them, leaving bloody wounds in her wake, her blade a cage of razors all about her, lopping spearheads clean from shafts, hands from wrists, inexorable as death.

Behind her she had felt the shock as Alain's spearmen met the line of the enemy, pushing and shoving with their clumsy weapons, but surely they had to be exulting too, knowing that they were in the right. Surely the very vileness of the brigands' cause had hindered the defenders. There was justice left in the Commonweal, and the bandits had discovered it at last.

Arrows constantly sought her, even in the midst of the fray, the best of the enemy bowmen trying desperately to find a way to kill her that did not involve coming within reach of her fatal sword. Her father stayed with her, guiding her left and right, letting the lethal shafts fall short or find other targets; or she would snip them from the air, her blade slicing swifter than they flew. Then she would go in search of the archers themselves, hunt them down, cut a red path towards them.

There had been one, she particularly recalled. She remembered him from before, and clearly he knew her also. She had tried again and again to reach him, but his wings had carried him clear, and he had shifted the defence with him, his followers keeping pace. Only then, for a moment, had she hungered for the greatbow that her father sometimes used, finding all her speed and skill not quite enough to bring her close to him.

But I will take you, she had silently promised him. *I will bring you in chains before Alain, and he will love me for it.*

Now, the conflict over and the bulk of the bandits fled, the survivors of Alain's followers had rejoined the larger force, alongside the soldiers of Lowre Cean and Salme Elass and of the other leading nobles, camping between the trees in a great, sprawling network of fires and tents and hammocks. Tynisa strode through it all with her head held high, feeling their envious eyes upon her.

While in the midst of a conference with Lowre and some others, Alain saw her, and smiled. She could read fondness there, and admiration, and it lit her like a brand, and warmed her as she settled down to sleep.

She did not dream these days. She had not dreamt since the hunt, as though that energy within her that fed her dreams was being somehow siphoned away to feed something else. When she awoke in the forest with everyone gone from around her, then she was unsure for a moment whether it was all real or imaginary.

Her sword was in her hand, of course; whether in reality or dream it was her constant companion.

'Who's there?' she demanded. She could tell that she was being watched, though she could not see another living soul.

The woman who appeared there suddenly, a dozen feet away, between the trees, was a stranger to her. She was a mongrel halfbreed with enough Moth in her for her eyes to lack irises, and dark hair with pale streaks running through it. She looked wary and harrowed, and abruptly something rose up inside Tynisa, something sharp-edged and unfamiliar that she took too long to recognize: *fear!* In the dismal surroundings of this empty forest, the sudden arrival of this robed figure could only signify a magician about to practise some evil on her. Tynisa remembered . . .

I remember . . .

In Jerez, when we had the Shadow Box, and Achaeos opened it . . . there was a terrible forest of thorns, and a dark figure in robes, and I . . . and I . . .

And she had stabbed Achaeos, although not realizing it at the time, and he had died of that wound afterwards, so she was a *murderer*, the slayer of her sister's lover, and she had not been able to live with that, and had fled . . .

Here . . .

Tynisa screamed and lunged at the robed woman, again and again, but each time she seemed to miscalculate the distance, for no matter how far she reached, the stranger was still a foot beyond the rapier's dancing point. At the same time the blade felt heavy and sluggish, and fear was building and building inside her at this blatant magic . . . and fighting against the memory that her sword *had been heavy that night too*, as though it had been trying to dissuade her from the murder.

What am I doing? But, even as she asked herself the question, another voice was commanding, *Kill her!* And she tried, she really tried, but the forest seemed to trip and baffle her, even though it let the magician slip through untouched, and thorns plucked at Tynisa's clothing as the trees around her twisted into that other place.

What am I doing now? What is my body doing now? What of Alain? Am I killing Alain?

Her blade still directed with a straight arm at the magician, she froze. 'No,' she whispered to herself. 'No, no, not this. Please, not again . . .'

'This is shameful,' the woman chided. 'Come now, there's no need to hide. I'm right here. You want me dead, I can see that, and you're not the first. Come try me, then. Perhaps you'll succeed, for I understand you had a reputation in that field. But not through this girl. What courage does that show, Mantis-kinden?'

Tynisa stared at her wildly, not understanding what she meant. The woman suddenly seemed to really focus on her, although she had been looking her in the face all this time.

'Tynisa Maker, I am sent by your sister. She is coming for you. She wants you to be strong, do you understand? Be strong, and do nothing unwise.'

'My sister . . .?' *Cheerwell?*

But then the magician was looking not-quite-at Tynisa again, giving out a mocking little laugh. 'Oh, is this really all you're cut down to? I thought they called you a hero over Collegium way? The man who killed the Emperor, and here he is hiding behind his daughter's skirts?'

And she felt someone move behind her, rushing forward, and in that instant something had *left* her, surging out from her in raging fury. The magician was already dancing away between the trees, though, and she saw the indistinct form of Tisamon chasing after her, his metal claw drawn back to strike, but forever just too far away, receding and receding and . . .

She woke up, crying out, and leapt to her feet still clutching her blanket. There was a faint lightening through the trees to the east, and all around her the earliest risers were already about their business.

She stared at them blankly, the foot soldiers of the Salmae's army, those glorious, exultant bringers of justice. They sat in their huddles, spears leaning haphazardly nearby: Grasshopper-kinden and Dragonflies in padded cuirasses that were dirty and torn. Many were wounded, and she saw at least two who must have died overnight.

They looked frightened, she realized. They were tired and abused, men and women who had no taste for this conflict, but had been brought to it anyway, sore and bloodied and unwilling. It struck her that some of them probably had family and friends in the village that had been burned, or in places like it, and they had not been able to defend them or get them away to safety. *They none of them want to be here.* The revelation, in the face of the frenzy she had felt before, was shocking.

And how many had she consigned to death by not warning Alain of the trap? Was that costly victory really worth it?

'This has gone on long enough,' she said, and went off to seek out Lowre Cean.

When she arrived at his tent she found him sitting up in his hammock, dressed in a crumpled white silk robe. There was a bowl in his hand, two jugs at his feet, one lying on its side, already empty.

'Morning, Maker Tynise,' he addressed her, with a slight and melancholy smile. There had been no guards nearby. If she had been an assassin, she could have slain him right there, and walked out leaving his followers none the wiser. She briefly wondered if that was his intent.

She sat down, cross-legged like a schoolchild, and gazed up at him. 'Prince Lowre, there is a question I have to ask you – and then a request, after that.'

'I thought as much. I'd expected you sooner, but you seemed to be so . . . so caught up in this . . .' His hand made a vague gesture encompassing a world of skirmish and conflict beyond the cloth walls of his tent.

'You are a war hero,' she said flatly.

His smile turned sour and he shrugged, before hooking another bowl from beneath the hammock with one bare foot. He stooped to reclaim it and the full jug, then divided the remaining wine between the bowls, with some juggling, before eventually handing her one of them. Had she not been watching carefully she would have taken him for a drunken clown, save that he did not spill a drop.

The wine she drank was the colour of blood, dry and sharp. After a mouthful, she repeated, 'You are a war hero,' almost accusingly. 'They all say so. When the Wasps came, you commanded an army, and of all the Commonweal tacticians, you alone slowed the Empire down. You commanded at Masaka, when the Sixth was destroyed. In the Lowlands a man like you would be found at the heart of things, a statesman and a leader. When times of trouble come, such a man would be the man persuading others, rather than having himself to be persuaded.'

'Ah, the war,' he sighed, as though he was just catching up with her first words. 'You've had war in the Lowlands, of course. For two years, was it? But then the Wasps had learned a lot of lessons after they finished with us. They had no idea, poor fools. I think, if they'd truly understood the *size* of the Commonweal, just how *many* of us there were, they'd never have started. It was a mad venture, and we outnumbered them massively on many of the battlefields, especially at the start. What could they have thought when they saw the size of a true Commonwealer army?' He raised one white eyebrow at her, and she looked back at him uncertainly.

'Contempt,' he pronounced precisely. 'Because if they had ten thousand, and we had a hundred thousand, still they had real soldiers, and we had . . . farmers, tradesmen, labourers. We depended on men and women whose lives were spent tilling the land, who had the next harvest to worry about, whose hands reached for the hoe and the rake, not the spear.'

She made to retort, but he silenced her with just a small motion of one hand. 'I was at the Monarch's court when news first came of the Wasp invasion. We had known that they were seizing the cities at our south-eastern border, of course, but we had the castle at Shol Amen, that had never been taken, and we . . . we had not believed it was possible, that those hill tribes would even *dare* to step on to the royal earth of the Commonweal. I remember . . .' He drank, eyes looking into a lost past. 'I remember how the Monarch called for his greatest seer, and demanded to know what response the crown should make to such impudence. She said . . . she said there were one million reasons to surrender and only one reason to fight. One of us, it might even have been Felipe Shah, asked her what that one reason was. "Freedom," she replied. The Monarch ordered that we should resist the Empire to our last breath. He was a bold man. His daughter, who is Monarch now, might not have done the same.'

'I don't understand,' Tynisa admitted. 'Surely there is nothing greater to fight for than freedom?'

'One million reasons,' Lowre intoned solemnly, before draining his bowl. 'I had a son, you know. My son, my Darien. He was a hero. I planned the battles, but *he* fought them. He even continued fighting after the Treaty of Pearl. He would never accept that we had lost. They killed him, of course, as they always do. My bold and dashing son. And all the men I led, in my *victories*,' he spoke the last word with an unexpected bitterness and force, 'where are they now? How long do you think I kept them alive, after all, after victory turned to ashes? All those farmhands and smiths and woodsmen and artisans, with spears in their hands. All my clansmen, my Mantis warriors, my nomads. All the many many who followed my banner.'

He turned his aching red eyes on her, for a moment appearing such a fierce figure that she felt a shock of fear run through her.

'I have known so many people during my long life, Maker Tynise, and most of them I led into a just war, for a good cause. What, as you say, is sweeter to fight for than freedom? Surely freedom is worth any price? But one million? One *million*? Can you even conceive of that number? Nobody asked the seer what the one million reasons to surrender were: men and women and children, families, communities, friendships, all that would have been saved had we simply bowed the knee to the Empire. If I could do it over again, I know what I would counsel.'

'But the Empire may come again,' she insisted. 'It may come against the Lowlands again. Are you saying that you . . . that we should simply surrender?'

He just stared at her, the empty bowl dangling loose in his hand. 'Ask Felipe Shah how he feels. Ask the Monarch for her thoughts. We were there, and we saw it all, from beginning to end, and all the fine nobles' sons and daughters who buckled on their armour to the tune of a just cause and then never came back; all the village men and women whose lives would hardly have changed, tilling the earth for their prince or for some Wasp governor, but who instead we mustered up and gave spears to; all the idealists, the reformed thieves, the fierce warriors, who followed us, and believed us. I remember them all, every one. Of all the people I ever knew, the dead far outweigh the living. And they are dead before their time, before their children could grow, before they could even *have* children. We murdered a generation on the battlefields of the Twelve-year War. We extinguished a score of noble lines and a million lives. And we *lost.* And you ask me if freedom was worth it?' His bitter smile, out of context, could have been taken for humour. 'I led all the people I ever knew onto one battlefield or another, Maker Tynise. And in the end, here I am, and where are *they*?'

'But this . . .' She was off balance now, and the only thing she had to cling to was her purpose in coming here. 'These brigands, surely this is a . . .?' But she found that she could not now utter the words 'just cause'.

For a long time they just stared at one another, and then she finished her wine.

'But they are dying anyway,' she said at last. 'Because this bandit leader out-thinks us, even though we have more soldiers. And whether you took up the tactician's blade again or not, they would still die. Fewer would die, surely, if you took control here and guided Salme Alain and his mother to victory.' As he started to speak, she interrupted almost viciously, 'Yes I *know*. They would die under your command. They would be yet more corpses to lay on your back. But it's beyond that now, and we need you. Is that load so great that a few more corpses will break you, Prince Lowre?'

'You are cruel.'

'I know the weight of blood, and I will not claim this is a just war. I say only that it must end.'

His lips tightened, and she thought of the way he had lived before she had talked him into coming: hiding away in his secluded compound, pottering from one idle hobby to another, always at home to his old friends – to those he still had left – keeping his little court and offering no harm to anyone, for fear . . .

'I know,' she whispered. 'I'm sorry, but there's no other way. We have to bring this to an end.'

And at last he nodded, or perhaps his head sagged. 'I know,' he echoed her dispiritedly. 'I know.' He took a deep breath. 'I suppose I will have to dress as befits a war leader, then.' Some small ghost of his customary humour touched him, as he indicated his current state. 'Let Salme Elass know that I wish to have counsel with her, but I may be some little while.'

She stepped out of his tent and her father was waiting for her, laying his hands on her shoulders, guiding her, reassuring her, reminding her of her true purpose. And she then forgot a great deal of what she had just felt and heard and said, and knew only that, once more, *There will be blood.*

Thirty-One

As the three of them galloped up, Mordrec kicked off from his saddle, his wings coasting him over to Dal Arche, while letting his horse find its own way. Dal looked up as he landed. 'You've taken your time.'

'Getting them set up for a fight back in Rhael wasn't as easy as you might think.'

Dal grimaced. 'They didn't take it seriously?'

'They took it *too* cursed seriously,' Mordrec told him. 'We dumped a load of bows and spears and swords on them, and they had the wit to ask us how they were supposed to put them to use. We ended up staying there half a tenday more than we'd hoped, just drilling them in the basics. You should see Siriell's Town now: everyone and their grandmother's going about armed. You got the weapons we sent ahead?'

'I did.'

The two of them turned, as Soul Je and Barad Ygor rode up, too, and dismounted.

'Have you told him?' the Scorpion demanded. His companion clung to his back, her claws crossed beneath his collarbones, and her stinging tail curled about his waist.

'I was getting to it,' Mordrec snapped back. 'Dala, we've seen the Salmae on the move between here and the Rhael border.'

'I know,' Dal agreed. 'The game's changed, and we're pulling back. What have you got available in Rhael now?'

'There's close on five hundred just over the border, waiting for the word. If we don't use them soon, they'll go sour on us and either head back south or start fighting with each other,' Mordrec declared.

'We had them just where we wanted them until a few days ago, but then they got wise to us,' Dal explained. 'We were running them all over the place, keeping them guessing, and they were going for us every chance they got. We could lead them any way we chose. Then they went on the defensive all of a sudden, and wherever we decided to raid we'd find at least a handful of them on watch for us, with fliers ready to spread the word. We still scored a few hits, but our luck's turned. Time to regroup and take stock, I think.'

'If they're on the defensive, shouldn't we take advantage of it?' Ygor suggested slowly. 'I mean, if they're backing off, and we're also backing off, where will the fight be?'

Dal Arche shook his head. 'The way I read it, they *want* us to chase them, so instead we're going to creep quietly back to Rhael Province and join up with your force there, and wait for reinforcements from Siriell's Town. After that, we'll have enough numbers to come back and up the stakes a little.'

'How many are you here?' came the dry voice of Soul Je.

'Right now? About three hundred and fifty. I've a raiding party out at the moment of somewhere near seventy-five. We're moving as soon as they get back. What size parties did you see on the way here?'

Mordrec opened his mouth, but it was Soul who spoke. 'Move now.'

'What do you mean?' Dal demanded.

'Head south now,' the Grasshopper insisted. 'This is wrong, I don't like it.' It was a lot for him to say.

The four brigands exchanged glances, because Soul seldom wasted words, and his intuition had been right before, when they had ignored him to their lasting regret.

'You may be right,' Dal said slowly. 'I'll get a messenger off to the raiding party, and we'll pull back. Can't be too careful.'

Almost as he said it, a young Grasshopper-kinden dropped down beside them. 'Enemies coming,' he panted. 'Couple nobles, maybe forty levy.'

'Fight?' Mordrec asked.

'Too few of them,' Dal stated, eyes narrow. 'Been a while since they were parading about in groups that small. Any word of the raiding party?'

The young Grasshopper shook his head.

'Move out,' Soul Je urged.

After a moment's grimacing pause, Dal nodded. 'We've outstayed our welcome,' he decided. 'Let's get back across the border and regroup. I don't like the feel of this.'

Within moments, he and his lieutenants were kicking their way through the camp, getting everyone moving. Brigands and their hangers-on took what loot they could carry and readied their weapons. Dal had conditioned them to a rudimentary order: those with bows spread left and right, whilst spears, swords and miscellaneous blunt implements formed the central block. At the vanguard rode their cavalry, consisting of Dal and his fellows and half a dozen others who possessed stolen mounts and the ability to ride them.

'You're thinking that raiding party won't be coming back?' Ygor pressed as they got under way.

Dal shrugged. 'I reckon all that quiet we've been hearing was the Salmae finally getting their act together and moving into position.'

They broke from the trees not in military order, but not a mob either, heading south at a good pace. There was another stretch of woodland ahead, and once there they could travel under cover of the canopy almost all the way to Rhael.

'Double pace,' shouted Dal abruptly, kicking at his own mount. There was a baffled grumbling from the men and women around him. 'Run, you bastards!' he berated them. 'Head into the trees.'

Most of them obeyed, in the end. He had done just enough to turn them from a gang of thieves into an army, whether he had originally wanted to or not. As his horse lurched into a canter, he swung it to the right, bringing it around and along the flank of his suddenly piecemeal force, and watching the complaining, stumbling brigands as they picked up speed.

'Archers, fall towards the rear,' he shouted. 'Be ready to let them have it when they come.' He guided his steed all the way around the back, galloping along the left flank and repeating his orders to the bowmen there. About half of them would have the wit or the courage to obey, he reckoned. The others, once running, would just rush full-tilt until they had the trees around them.

'They can't be on us already?' Mordrec complained, as Dal rejoined the other riders at the front. Even as he said it, though, Soul was pointing. Along the treeline ahead of them could be seen the glitter of sun on armour, and then they saw the enemy cavalry. So far, in the skirmishing, they had faced individual nobles on their mounts, and each noble had brought his own levy of peasants travelling on foot and slowing him down. There had not seemed enough of the aristocracy to mount the cavalry charges that traditional Commonweal war had centred on. Now here they were, surely the majority of the nobles under Salmae command, and they were racing to catch the brigands in the open. There were perhaps forty of them in all, noblemen and noblewomen with their favoured mounted retainers, but Dal knew the bandits could not stand up before a cavalry charge. They would break and then be ridden down, however many of them there were.

If the brigands had been moving at their usual slower pace before then they would have been caught right under the hammer. Even running as they were, it would be touch and go, but they had bought themselves a chance to get under cover now, and safe from the worst of the charge.

Dal Arche's wings took over, parting him from his saddle as he coasted over his fleeing people. He had his bow in hand, an arrow fitted to the string.

'Archers!' he bellowed at them. 'Hold till my mark!'

As he had expected, at least half of his bowmen were running headlong for the safety of the trees now, but a number had stopped to form a ragged line, and now Soul Je leapt down to join them, drawing back the string on his man-high bow.

The approaching cavalry exerted a fearful fascination, and Dal nearly missed his chance. 'Loose!' he shouted suddenly. 'Loose, cut and run!'

He watched as the arrows rose high, before curving in mid-air and falling upon the riders like rain. Soul's shaft caught one man near the point of the enemy formation, cutting between his helm and breastplate and sending the luckless target lurching back across his saddle. None of the other shots found a human target, but they struck home amongst the horses, causing them to jerk sideways, rearing and plunging. The gleaming perfection of the charge faltered just enough, and then the archers were following their fellows into the trees, on foot or wing, and Dal followed after. He realized that he had not actually loosed his own arrow at all.

Did I ever really want to become a leader of men? he asked himself. Surely the answer was no.

This long arm of the forest – this brigand's road – would take them to within striking distance of the Rhael border, but he doubted that a few trees would keep the Salmae off his back from now on. They were obviously pushing for the endgame, and Dal found that he had overextended his people, driven them too far from home, too close to Rhael. *But we were doing so well!* Then he remembered the war, and the way that every victory against the Wasps, however striking, had seemed to be the prelude to an ever-greater defeat. *Just my luck that I find a Commonweal noble who actually learned something from all those cursed battles.*

He drove his followers hard, keeping them moving and keeping them organized. He had scouts on either flank, and Soul Je leading a band of the fleetest in the vanguard, whilst Mordrec and Ygor marshalled the main force, chivvying stragglers and keeping some semblance of order.

The pursuing riders had plainly lacked the nerve to simply charge straight into the forest, where their advantage would be swiftly lost, after which so would they. However, Dal knew there was more. Cavalry on their own won few battles, so there would be somewhere ahead where the Salmae would have picked out an ambush point – or at least that would be how Dal himself would arrange it. After all, it was hardly a great secret as to which direction the bandits would take . . .

So perhaps we jump the wrong way? Dal sent a runner ahead to fetch Soul back. 'You know how the land lies ahead?' he asked the Grasshopper. At Soul's terse nod he continued, 'What do you say to us breaking left, out into the open? Where can we find woods again, after that?'

'A half-mile east and there's a fair stand of cane forest, but it's commune land.'

Dal stared at him hard, even as Soul loped along beside him, keeping pace. 'Stick-kinden?' he said, expressionless.

'You don't believe in them?'

'I'm sharper than that, but even so . . . Three hundred brigands heading through Stick-kinden land, someone's going to get it wrong, and we don't need more enemies.'

'We can always skirt the edges. Salmae might not follow,' Soul suggested. 'Break for the open again, quarter-mile, there's denser woods. We can hide up there, set watch and stay overnight.'

They got clear of the woods without delay, despite a fair proportion of Dal's people demanding to know where they were going. They lacked the discipline and the stamina of true soldiers, and the march was already beginning to tell on them.

But out in the open they found new motivation: the thought

of the Salmae cavalry looming in every mind. Dal rode back and forth along the length of their ragtag formation, keeping them together and on the move. Soon enough, one of his people had spotted the enemy: a small shape dark against the sky. That was one of their nobles, high above on a dragonfly, hovering as its rider located the brigands and worked out where they were going. The sight sparked a certain satisfaction in Dal Arche. *So, you didn't guess we'd do this, eh?*

Still, the Salmae were making the most of their new discipline, and their first troops were in sight just before the brigands made it to the edge of the cane forest. Footmen and riders both were approaching, but far enough away still for Dal's people to get themselves under the suspect cover of the bamboo without trouble.

Once they had all assembled amongst the boles, Dal halted them. Around them the countless tall stalks remained ominously still, the field of close-packed verticals playing tricks on the eye. The sky above was darkening now, cloudless enough to promise a chill night. As the brigands stamped and shuffled, Dal waited on Mordrec and Ygor, who had gone to the perimeter to see what the Salmae would do next.

They were holding off, came Mordrec's report at last. Nightfall had seen the sparks of Salmae campfires out beyond the canes, where they seemed to be settling down and waiting for dawn.

'Which leaves us with a few possibilities,' Dal remarked. 'They might be tricking us and come for us at night, which'd mean a mess for all concerned. We could try and make our own move at night, and hope they won't notice. Or perhaps they reckon they can match us as we move around the cane-forest edge, and pen us in here.'

'We don't want to be in here any longer than we need to,' Ygor stated. 'Mord and me, we saw something, we think. Like a man, a very tall man, watching us.'

'Well, we're still alive for now,' Mordrec added, pragmatic as always. 'What'll it be? Make camp or make our move?'

‘Soul?’ Dal asked, and the Grasshopper seemed to materialize at his shoulder. ‘You know these places, yes?’

‘A little, from the war.’ Soul Je had been an Imperial Auxillian in the Twelve-year War, and not enjoyed it much.

‘The . . . locals, they might come for us at night?’

‘It’s possible.’

‘They can be reasoned with?’

‘They like their privacy, Dala.’

Ygor muscled in, then. ‘Looks like they’re around a third of our number.’ The skin over his eyes creased, where a man with eyebrows would have raised them. ‘Fight? Attack them overnight?’

‘Sounds like they’re inviting it,’ Dal agreed. ‘Which is why we won’t. There’ll be more of them, for sure. They wouldn’t have kept us hopping all day just to fail so badly now. We need to get clear of them. If we fight, we fight when and where I choose. Soul, I get the impression you can talk to our . . . hosts in here? You’ve done it before?’

The Grasshopper looked sour. ‘Wouldn’t say it worked well, but I’ve seen it done. I know a little of their speech.’

‘Then I have something for you to tell them.’

The brigands made camp, with plenty of eyes keeping watch towards the dimly glimpsed fires of their pursuers. By his own orders, it was only Dal Arche who allowed his gaze to turn the other way, watching Soul as he sat some way deeper into the cane forest. Dal had always had good eyes, even for one of his kind, and at last, an hour later, he saw Soul standing up. For a long while there was nothing more save that he could hear the distant murmur of the Grasshopper’s voice. But then there was a movement, and Dal realized that the Stick-kinden were here, or one of them at least. The newcomer was freakishly tall, standing a good two feet higher than Soul, who was as lofty as most of his kind. Beneath the shrouding cloak, Dal could make out broad shoulders, but there seemed to be little more substance to this creature, just a great gaunt scarecrow, two long-fingered hands moved, making patterns in the air, but Dal heard no voice other than Soul's. The conversation, such as it was, went on for a long time, the Grasshopper giving soft replies to the signs that the Stick-kinden used. When Soul talked at length, Dal lost sight of the tall creature entirely: standing utterly still as it did, its Art cloaked it in shadows and led the eye astray. Only when it spoke with its hands did it attract the attention,

There could be dozens of the things all around us. Dal forced himself to keep calm. If that was so, there was little he could do about it.

At last, Soul Je came back, looking worn down by his negotiations.

'Get everyone up,' he said, and Dal quickly kicked the nearest half-dozen awake, and sent them grumbling and complaining to wake up others.

'They're going to kill us?'

'They're going to guide us through their lands,' Soul replied. 'Don't ask why, because I don't know. We've nothing they want. Perhaps they just like lost causes.'

'Not lost yet,' Dal decided.

'One condition, though: blindfolds. Everyone must be blindfolded. They'll kill anyone who so much as peeks. We'll be passing through their heartland, Dala. *Nobody*'s ever seen it. They want to keep it that way.'

Dal nodded grimly, and began to pass the word along. *It's not going to work*, he already knew. The temptation would be too great. Worse, it could be a trap. They might none of them come out of this alive. 'You trust them, though.'

'They're not like us,' Soul replied. 'They don't care about politics, they don't pay taxes, they don't want more land. They're apart from it all.' His voice sounded almost wistful. 'If they didn't like us, then we'd be getting shot at right now, or we'd just never see them at all. They have no need of betrayal.'

Studying him now, Dal thought he saw why the Stick-kinden

had been so compliant. Perhaps they had seen in Soul some little fragment of their own nature.

By that time the bandits were all awake, though not happy about it, and even less happy once they were told to blindfold themselves. Mordrec tied together every rope and cord he could lay his hands on, supplemented with torn cloaks and tunics after they ran out. Soon everyone was holding on to a section of of his makeshift lead, the brigands making a long, untidy string of baffled and angry people. Beyond the forest edge, the Salmae camp was waking up too, hearing the disturbance and no doubt expecting the brigands to make a break into the open under cover of darkness.

Of course, that break never came, so the followers of the Salmae milled about and watched intently for hours, as the bandits melted away into the heart of the cane forest.

Dal Arche had been expecting an eerie, almost mystical experience, but a couple of hundred brigands, all blindfolded and tied together and being led through a forest, made enough noise for the entire business to sound more like a particularly raucous troupe of travelling clowns. Not a moment passed without someone falling over, stumbling into the hard, ridged bole of a bamboo cane, or stepping on someone else's foot. It should have been hilarious. Instead, Dal was on edge the whole time, thinking of what else those noises might be covering.

There would be those amongst his followers who could not bear not knowing, so they would find a moment to lift the blindfold, despite his strict instructions. They would regret it, too; Dal was sure of that. He had a sense that all around them loomed the Stick-kinden: towering, angular and silent, staring with mute antipathy at these clumsy intruders, their hands stayed only by their anonymity. There were occasional screams amidst that chaos of stumbling and complaining. They were brief, cut off even as they started, but they were unmistakable.

How long it took them to cross that forest of cane, he could not say. The enforced darkness seemed to blind him to the passage of time as much as it did to the stars and moon. Eventually, though, he became aware that he was no longer being tugged along, and all around him people were standing still.

'Eyes open,' he snapped, hoping he was right, and that this was not some cruel trick of their hosts. When he pulled the cloth from his eyes, though, he saw that the canes gave out only yards ahead, and open ground lay beyond.

He located Mordrec and tugged at his arm. 'Make a count,' he suggested, and the Wasp nodded. As he passed through the band, counting heads, Dal spotted Soul and Ygor, and felt a sudden rush of relief when he saw them still alive.

The Scorpion was already moving out into the open, crouching low and with his companion beast ranging ahead of him, its claws and tail raised threateningly. Dal moved towards him but, as he approached, Ygor raised a hand abruptly and dropped to one knee.

Dal crept up beside him, but he had spotted the problem before he could ask about it. There were campfires visible out there, quite a large band of people, perhaps the same size as the group they had left behind.

'This is impossible. Nobody could be that far ahead of us.' A sudden thought struck him. 'They must have a seer, a really good one, to be able to see in such detail.'

Ygor snorted, for he was Apt and didn't believe in any of that. 'They've got us to rights here, anyway,' he replied. 'I don't reckon we'll get back through the woods again, either.'

Mordrec and Soul Je joined them quietly. 'We're down thirty-seven,' was the Wasp's grim report.

Dal nodded. *We would have lost more, had we turned and fought, though.* He could not guarantee that, but it seemed overwhelmingly likely. Thirty-seven? Thirty-seven men and women who could not bear to stay blind in an unfamiliar place – and had that one last glimpse been worth it?

'Soul, Ygor, scout them out,' he ordered. 'See how alert

they are, their sentries, their preparations. We outnumber them and, even though they're here, they might not be expecting an attack. We might get out of this yet.'

The Scorpion and the Grasshopper padded off into the darkness, with Ygor's pet slinking along between them. Dal sat back on his haunches, staring out at the campfires.

'We've been in worse,' Mordrec reminded him philosophically. 'Remember the steppes, hmm?'

'Oh, certainly,' Dal agreed, feeling suddenly very tired. *I'm just slightly on the wrong side of youth to be indulging in these all-night capers.* 'That double-cross at Mie Salve wasn't much fun either.'

'Only because of your bloody taste in women,' Mordrec reminded him. 'Matter of fact, the steppe business was women too.'

'Well there's no woman here now, Mord.'

'There was Siriell,' Mordrec suggested, impoliticly. At Dal's responding glare he shrugged, setting the nailbow swaying on his shoulder. 'I'm just saying.'

Dal was formulating a scathing reply, when he saw movement, and identified it a moment later as Soul and Ygor on their rapid return. *The fools, they've been spotted,* was his instant thought.

Without being told, Mordrec was heading back into the canes to rouse the others.

'Report,' Dal snapped angrily, but Ygor was grinning broadly.

'You'll love it,' the Scorpion promised. 'You'll kiss me for it.'

'*What*, Ygor?'

'It's the raiding party. *Our* raiding party.'

Dal stared at him dumbly, then looked to Soul for confirmation.

'It's true,' the Grasshopper confirmed. 'We spoke with that Spider, Avaris. They got lost. Been wandering around for a day or so trying to find us.'

'Just shy of a hundred fighting men and women now, they've got,' Ygor added with great satisfaction.

Dal weighed up the numbers in his head.

'Come morning, we head south,' he decided. 'We move fast, and in one group. When we meet the Salmae, we fight. There's nothing else for it. We'll break through them, or break against them. We've reached the end of it.'

Thirty-Two

'They're now moving in force towards the border. This leader of theirs is a resourceful fellow, it seems,' Lowre Cean remarked mildly.

Salme Elass was not in the mood for mildness. 'I want him brought alive to Leose. I want him executed before his followers, for denying the order of the Commonweal.'

Lowre raised an eyebrow at her, for that. They were in full war council, with two dozen other nobles crammed into her grand campaigning tent this evening, so he said nothing, but she took him up on it nonetheless.

'By taking these liberties, it is not *me* that these wretches defy,' she snapped, 'it is our entire society. In turning on their betters, they are traitors to the very Monarch.'

'No doubt it is as you say,' Lowre replied softly, but with a slight edge to his voice that made the others stir uncertainly.

Tynisa glanced at Alain, sitting beside her. He had his arms folded, head cocked to one side. Catching her gaze, he raised his eyebrows. *We'd both rather be out getting things done,* his look seemed to say, and when she grinned a little, he repaid her twice over. She felt something stir and leap within her. *I'm winning.*

'They have greater numbers than us,' Lowre continued after a pause. 'Certainly more numbers than any force we could intercept them with before they reach Rhael. However, I suppose we must make the attempt, or they will doubtless return in even greater strength, and we will never be done. I want this business finished.'

'As do we all,' Elass confirmed.

Again, Lowre eyed her, but said nothing. Like an Imperial general, he had a map to hand, on which stones of various colours marked the last known positions of the brigands, and of their own forces. 'Our chief aim is to place a force in their path that will suffice to delay them. We have limited numbers, however, who can move swiftly enough to cut them off. Also, if we put too strong a force in their way, they are likely to change their course once again. We must tempt them into a fight they believe they can win quickly. Once they are engaged, our remaining forces can catch them up and close the trap. This will necessitate everyone moving throughout the night. Our forces will thus not be best fit for a fight in the morning, but I see no alternative. For those who stand in the brigands' path, things will go hard. If our main force is delayed for any reason, it might be the end of them.'

'I will stand there,' Tynisa declared flatly. She was no noblewoman, no member of the Commonweal hierarchy that Salme Elass was so devoted to, but nobody denied her a place here, and those nobles who had once looked askance at her when she danced or hunted now stayed out of her way. She had gained a reputation written in blood.

Lowre Cean winced but nodded, accepting the inevitable.

'With your permission, my Princess?'

Tynisa looked around for the speaker, recognizing the voice of Isendter Whitehand, the Salmae's champion. She caught Elass looking at the white-haired Mantis with concern, as though she wanted to refuse to let him go, but feared looking weak.

At last she nodded. 'With my blessing,' she said.

One by one the nobles spoke up, those who had been in the thick of the fighting already, those who had suffered burned villages or lessened revenues. Others pledged their servants, those who could ride swiftly enough to hold the pace. The pledges trickled in until Lowre Cean raised a thin hand.

'Enough,' he said. 'That will be enough.' He looked to Whitehand. 'Isendter, I give you command over this business.'

Several of the nobles hovered on the brink of outrage that a mere servant should be given that honour. The calm, pale gaze of the Mantis-kinden soon silenced them. In that moment, Tynisa realized that Alain would not be coming, that she would make her stand without him there to admire her prowess. She glanced at him, and saw him frown at his mother. *She will not let him fight, but how else will he grow strong?* The thought crossed her mind that perhaps she would need to do something about Salme Elass, at some point – for Alain's own good. How else could he become the man that Tynisa wished him to be?

As Lowre had decreed, they rode all through the night, and Whitehand set a punishing pace. Tynisa's newfound skills were just sufficient to keep her on her mount, and at the back of the pack. The others, the nobles and their picked retinues, were better horsemen and women by far, but their skill had been learned over the years rather than dropped unearned on their shoulders.

Towards the dawn, she knew, Lowre would send a dragonfly rider, perhaps Alain himself, to scout out the whereabouts of the brigands. Their timing was tight. Too slow overnight and they might miss the bandit army entirely, or perhaps even run straight into them.

I would not mind if we did, Tynisa decided. *It will save time. We will kill them all the sooner*. That Whitehand's little contingent would be outnumbered at least five to one was important only in giving her a greater opportunity to demonstrate her skill, and thus allow her to woo Alain on that much grander scale.

She had no idea of their progress, hanging on grimly at the rear, and the night passed in a series of swift rides across the countryside, interspersed with short breaks for the horses to be watered and fed. The Commonweal steeds had been bred for both speed and stamina, she could see: the Lowlands had nothing like them. *Perhaps if Salma had used such beasts . . .* but nothing was served by thinking of such things now.

When Whitehand called a halt, Tynisa did not realize that this was *it*, that they had already reached their goal, and were presumably ahead of the enemy. The sky was greying with pre-dawn towards the east, towards the Empire, and all around her the Commonwealers were dismounting, and tending their horses. They were a mixed band, and she had barely paid them any attention throughout the night's journey. To her they were just 'the nobles', and she had dismissed them as such. Perhaps half of them were aristocracy in fact: graceful Dragonfly-kinden in glimmering armour of many colours, chitin and enamelled steel over mail and quilted cloth. They carried tall bows, long-hafted swords and short punch-blades, and Whitehand passed amongst them, singling out those whose steeds had lasted the journey best, setting them aside to fight on horseback in the morning. The balance of the force was made up of the retainers that had been promised, men and women of Whitehand's own station or below. Dragonflies mostly, but with some Grasshopper-kinden amongst them, and a lone Wasp.

Tynisa stared at him for a long while until, as though he was one of those clever pictures the Collegium mathematicians drew, that flipped from one image to another as the eye adjusted its perspective, finally he turned into someone she knew.

'How long have you been with us?' she demanded.

'All the way,' he replied. It was Gaved, whom she had not seen since she was his guest on the lakeshore.

'You weren't at the council.'

He shrugged. 'I asked Prince Lowre if I could join you.'

'I'm surprised he didn't have you thrown out. I'm surprised he ever wants to see another of your people, after the war.'

'Then perhaps you don't understand him,' he replied, maddeningly calm. 'Sef asked me to see that you were all right.'

Tynisa narrowed her eyes, smelling the lie, and he made a curious gesture, of proffering his fists as though wanting her to guess which one held the stone in it. She realized it was the Wasp equivalent of holding up open hands to stave off a hostile reaction.

'It was a request,' he admitted, 'but from Felipe Shah. *He* wanted to know that you were well, and that you stayed that way.'

She was suspicious at that. 'Why would *Felipe Shah* even know you exist, Gaved?'

For a moment he just stared at her, but then he shrugged. 'Man in my position, it's good to let people know I'm useful.'

'And you're being paid, of course.'

'Gratitude of princes.' He shrugged. 'Still, as princes go, Felipe's word is better than most.'

Whitehand passed nearby. 'I've set watches. Get what sleep you can.'

Sleep? Tynisa felt too fierce and full of fight to sleep, but a moment later some part of her had made its own calculation, and she knew that she would sleep undisturbed, and wake in an instant, fresh and spoiling for blood. Another gift she had not enjoyed a month ago.

'I don't need looking after,' she warned Gaved.

'Should make earning my wage that much easier, then,' he replied, frowning a little as though he was trying to work out what was different about her. Abruptly, she turned her back on him, stretching out on the ground to sleep, as though she spent every night in the wilds. It was not so much that she wanted to dismiss him from her thoughts as that she felt her hand being drawn towards her sword hilt by the Wasp's mere presence.

It was barely dawn when she awoke, sitting up abruptly with her blade in her hand. The sentries Whitehand had posted were just at that moment rushing into camp. It seemed the brigands were approaching.

'They're later than we'd thought,' the Mantis was saying. 'They must have rested up at least part of the night, and they'll be fresher, but we only need to hold them until the rest arrive. Fetch me all of our archers.'

By the dawn light Tynisa could see their surroundings better: to their right the land rose in rocky steps, to the left, whence they had come, the ground was scrubby and uneven, fit pasture only for goats. The ten who Isendter had picked to fight mounted were already assembling there, a little way from the main force, leaving room for a charge. Northwards was a ragged forest edge, but Whitehand had chosen this clear ground for their stand, ground that the retreating brigands would be forced to cross.

'They're on their way.' Gaved appeared at her elbow, and she had to fight fiercely to keep her sword still.

'How do you know?'

He pointed upwards, and she saw a shape pass across the lightening sky: a dragonfly rider circling. *Alain, is it?* She was abruptly convinced that it must be, for even if his mother had kept him back from the fight, he would still want to play his part. *And he will see me.*

Whitehand had set the archers up on their right flank, up amongst the rocks, leaving perhaps thirty spearmen and swordsmen to hold the centre. Tynisa saw what would happen if a large force struck them: *we will be folded back against the high ground.* It would guard their backs, but they would have nowhere to go. The meagre cavalry could charge in then, but if the enemy were ready, then the horsemen could meet a rain of arrows.

'What if they just stand off and shoot?' she asked.

Whitehand glanced back at her. 'They have few good bows amongst them. Our reach is greater and our aim better, or else the flower of the Commonweal has fallen far since last it was tested.'

The last time it was tested was the Twelve-year War, she

reflected. Even though she *knew*, as a matter of absolute faith, that the odds did not matter, that the greater the foe the greater the glory, and the more chance she had to show her skill, some small sane part of her was noting that this action would stand or fall on the organization of the brigands, and the speed with which the relief force arrived.

She met Gaved's gaze, and saw the same knowledge reflected in his eyes. *And you will fly for your life, if it comes to that.* The thought occurred to her, almost hungrily, that it would be easy enough to be rid of him in the fight, and nobody need know. The idea of shedding a Wasp's blood seemed vastly attractive: this Wasp, any Wasp . . .

For a moment she felt almost dizzy with the number of conflicting thoughts inside her head. She remembered Sef, and the former slave's simple happiness. She remembered how she had been a guest in Gaved's house, that she had fought alongside him.

'Stay away from me, when it starts,' she forced out, fighting with herself to get the words spoken.

He regarded her doubtfully and she spat, 'I don't care what Felipe told you to do, just stay clear of me. I might . . . I can't . . .' She bit down on the words, either reasserting control or losing it. Something of the strangeness about her had got through to him, though, and he backed off. She could only hope it was enough warning. She also hoped it would not be enough. She had saved him, she would kill him: she felt a desperate need to simplify her world by going elbow deep in the blood of her enemies. Any enemies.

At that point she spotted the first outrunners of the brigands, a few scattered bands at first, but it was as though the woods were oozing with them, forming ever-deepening pools of shabby, patchily armoured men and women that gathered at the treeline, staring outwards. Whitehand walked to the fore, waiting for them with his clawed gauntlet on his hand, distinctive in his pale grey leathers. Tynisa guessed that his name would be passing among their enemies: the champion of the Salmae had come in person to meet them.

She moved to the Mantis's side. 'And if they won't come against us?'

'Then they're more craven than I thought,' he replied smoothly.

'Our archers may outreach them, but they have more. Once they've found their range, why should they not stay out there and just drop arrows on us?'

He glanced at her, expressionless. 'Then we shall have to go to them.'

She nodded, satisfied, and went to find a horse. There were plenty spare, of course, but few of them in any proper condition to go out and fight, worn down as they were by the night's ride. *But then I won't need one for long*, Tynisa reflected, and saddled the most promising mount, as best she could.

The brigands were advancing from the woods now, creeping forward cautiously and no doubt trying to discern where the rest of Whitehand's force was hidden. They gathered out of bowshot, a great unruly mass of villains, and milled and tried to order themselves, clearly unwilling to commit to the fight. They could see the glittering armour of the nobles and even now, at the height of their rebellion, the sight of their former lords and masters in such numbers was unsettling them. No doubt they were expecting hundreds of peasant levy to spring up from the earth. Still, the idea must be trickling through their ranks: *What if this is all there is?*

'Archers ready,' Whitehand called, not loud, but his voice carried to the last of his followers. The brigands were building up their courage, realizing that, yes, they really did outnumber the enemy five to one. A quick strike now could stand as revenge for any number of punishments and slights received from the aristocracy.

Isendter Whitehand's eyes narrowed, watching their hesitant approach, one hand half raised. Every bowman kept that pale glove in the corner of his eye as they chose their target. At Isendter's smallest gesture, they all loosed together.

With so many close-packed enemies, it would have been near-impossible to miss, and Tynisa saw several brigands crumple in their front line. Then returning arrows peppered the air, mostly shot from the small hunting bows the bandits carried and falling far short. A few of the enemy must be better equipped, though, for the odd shaft flew far enough to land between the well-spaced defenders, and the man beside Whitehand took a shaft in the shoulder, between the plates of his mail.

Whitehand's own bowmen let fly again, determined to make the most of their advantage, but Tynisa had seen just how many arrows had flown in reprisal. If the bandits gathered the courage to close half of the distance, they would have enough bows to devastate Whitehand's people in short order.

She pulled herself up into the saddle and guided her newfound steed around the edge of their lines, until she came alongside the front rank. At first the brigands had fallen back, out of longbow range, but she saw that they were re-forming, organizing. If she looked carefully, she could see a few of their number hustling the rest into order, exhorting them to press forward. One of those, she knew, must be their elusive leader. She had seen him, she was sure, a Dragonfly-kinden man with greying hair and a fiercely determined manner. He had nearly put an arrow through her on more than one occasion, and she had nearly put her sword through him. *But today I shall catch you,* she thought. *You shall be my gift to Alain.*

For a moment the brigands refused to be drawn, stepping into the light rain of long arrows and then flinching back, but at last their leaders motivated them enough to surge forward, with the Salmae arrows picking at them but unable to slow them, and then they were within their own bowshot, and arrows from the more optimistic brigand archers began to feather across the gap. The rest of them were urged forward another dozen yards, to a range where their weapons might do the most good.

Tynisa noticed Whitehand's little detachment of cavalry ready itself, but a charge of only ten riders into that great mass of men would surely vanish without a trace.

So what about a charge of one? she wondered, as the arrows started to come down, first a few, then thicker and thicker. She saw Whitehand gather himself to give the order, but could not know whether it was to retreat or to charge. She would take the responsibility of that decision away from him.

She dug her heels into her horse's flanks and the beast rushed forward blindly, She caught a brief glimpse of Isendter's expression, as she coursed into the space between the two massed forces, her horse drawing an oblique course towards the right-hand extreme of the enemy's front line.

The bandits saw her, of course, and she saw them react. There was a flurry of motion within their ranks, and then the arrows were speeding for her, cutting past her on both sides like the flight of dragonflies. She had her rapier directed straight at the enemy, alongside her horse's head.

Behind her she heard shouting, and then Whitehand's order to charge. *You will thank me*, she thought, her mind as calm as a pond, *for showing you the right decision*. Retreat was cowardice. The only way was onwards. Whitehand himself must be Mantis enough to recognize such a fundamental truth.

She felt the shuddering impact as the first arrow found her mount, then a second a moment later. A shaft tore across her shoulder, another nicked her thigh. By then she was on them.

Her mount failed at the moment before she would have smashed into them, collapsing to its knees with a sound of agony, but she was prepared for that. Giving the dying animal no thought, she leapt to the ground over its bowed neck, now within reach of the brigands, and began killing those closest. They had made their front lines out of archers whose weapons were suddenly useless to them, and for the first few seconds her fight consisted entirely of killing defenceless people in the act of dropping their bows and reaching for knives. She spun and glittered amongst them, her rapier etching red lines in the air on all sides, creating a steel web that caught anyone within her reach until she had cut a space amongst them. They might have been able to use their bows against her in that moment, but she was already leaping on, driving a one-woman wedge into the very heart of their formation.

She felt the reverberation as the cavalry struck home almost unopposed, and the balance of Whitehand's force was not far behind, though enough of the brigand archers had kept their heads to make the Mantis's charge a difficult one. That was his problem, though, as Tynisa's thoughts were all now focused on the perfection of her dance.

The Spiders used the word 'dancing' to refer to their endless round of politics, but for the Mantis-kinden, Tynisa's true inheritance, it meant something far cleaner and deadlier.

The enemy were all around her but, because of that, they were crippled: unable to run, unable to bring their spears to bear on her or to swing their staves and axes without striking their fellows. Her rapier seemed able to pass through them as though they were air. She gave the weapon its head and it leapt joyously about her, weaving its killing patterns. Soon they started trying to scatter, shoving their own allies aside in their haste to remain amongst the living.

Isendter had now arrived. She felt the movements of the enemy mob change as he struck against them, sending their foremost scattering. She kept forcing her way inwards, lashing her rapier behind at those who thought her back would be an easy target. She was looking for the telltale signs of someone giving orders.

A brief glance told her that her own fellows were having a hard time of it. Whitehand was giving a bloody account of himself, but the sheer numbers of the enemy had brought his charge to a standstill, and his followers were dying left and right of him. The archers up on the bluff continued to drop arrows into the close-packed brigands, but were taking twice as many in reply. The cavalry had broken off and were wheeling for another charge, after leaving two of their number behind.

Tynisa's ears were suddenly ringing with thunder, causing a moment of utter confusion in which an opportunistic spearman almost killed her outright. *I know that sound.* A nailbow, she realized with shock, dragged out of her bloody reverie. Who in the Commonweal would possess such a thing?

The weapon spoke again, and this time she spotted its wielder. A determined-looking Wasp-kinden had begun unleashing it on Whitehand's people, its impact punching men and women off their feet. Tynisa went for him without a further thought, clearing others from her path like chaff.

He noticed her at the last moment, or someone had warned him, and she saw the Wasp drag the nailbow around towards her, but too late. He hauled on the trigger and the weapon boomed, a single bolt zipping past her ear even as she thrust her blade into the device's workings. That was not a feat a rapier would normally have been capable of, for the nailbow was made of heavy steel, solid and durable enough to withstand the percussive recoil of its use, but her blade nevertheless sheared through some vital part of it and silenced the thing for ever.

Withdrawing the blade, she noted with approval the Wasp's expression of disbelief, then an arrow rammed her shoulder and knocked her down.

For a second the pain of it utterly destroyed her, so large in her mind that there was no room to think of anything else.

Then it was gone again, caged away in the furthest recesses of her skull, and she had already leapt to her feet, the sword that had flown from her right hand now secure in her left.

She saw him again: the same Dragonfly with greying hair, the man she had picked as their leader from the moment she saw him. He was right there in front of her, hauling the Wasp out of the way. His eyes met hers and the shock of recognition was mutual.

He suddenly shoved the Wasp away, his off hand reaching

for his quiver. She thought she had him then, for she was closing the ground between them so swiftly that he could never have drawn the bowstring, but his wings flowered at his shoulders, casting him backwards over the heads of the scrum, and an arrow lanced from his bow even as he reached the apex of his leap. She felt the arrowhead already in her shoulder grating shallowly against her flesh as she ducked, felt his shot kiss the blade of her sword, enough to divert the shaft from her, and then she was going after him, felling anyone luckless enough to get in her way. The Dragonfly already had another arrow nocked, but he was clearly loath to risk killing one of his own, so she used that against him, not allowing him a clear shot until she was almost on him. A spearman tried lunging for her, and she whipped her rapier across his throat almost casually, her eyes still fixed on the brigand chief. She saw the moment when he understood that he would have no choice but to shoot, and she shared it with him. As he let the arrow fly she was already moving, tipping the collapsing spearman into the way so that the shaft ploughed into his dying flesh and not into hers.

The Dragonfly's wings flashed once more, as she lunged for him open-handed, catching his ankle and feeling the pull of his wings, almost fierce enough to wrench her arm from its socket. For a moment she was off the ground, and then the two of them tumbled back into the fray.

Her left hand, which had been weaponless for a moment in order to seize him, found the comforting grip of her sword in it again, the weapon coming and going obedient to her will in accordance with the secret lore of the Weaponsmaster. *Alive, he must be alive.* She lanced for his leg, seeking to cripple him, but he rolled aside, coming up into a crouch with his bow raised and ready. In the frozen moment she could only admire his mastery, delighted to find a worthy opponent amidst all this dross.

Just as he had the string drawn back to his ear, she drew the tip of her blade across the taut arch of the bow, cutting the weapon in two.

The arrow struck her ribs, his aim a moment from driving it through her body. As it was the shaft spun at her sideways, staggering her but drawing no blood.

The loose and jagged end of the bow whiplashed back into his face, and he hit the ground hard with his shoulder, one hand pressed to the wound.

She had a fight on her hands then, for all around were his followers, and enough of them had registered their leader's jeopardy and were trying to save him. She disposed of three with swift, economic passes of her blade, but then Whitehand's men were on all sides of her, the Mantis himself leading their rescue attempt.

She dismissed them, let Whitehand fight the minions while she went after their leader. The man had got back to his feet now, although there was a bloody weal across his face. In one hand he had a Commonwealer punch-sword: a short, vicious blade projecting straight from a shielded knuckleguard. He must have known that she was by far the better duellist, and she expected him to take flight again and force her to chase him, but he went for her instead, trying to get in under her longer reach.

She drilled him in the thigh, where she had intended to catch him all along, and he fell back on to one knee, but his eyes remained watchful and waiting.

There. She turned, sensing a threat from her right, but it almost caught her anyway. Not a man but a beast: a low-slung hunting scorpion bolting towards her from the melee, one pincer opened wide and reaching to crush her ankle. She hopped aside, awkward with surprise, and its sting missed her leg by only inches.

The Dragonfly took advantage of the distraction, but she tilted aside from his lunge, letting the punch-sword pass within an inch of her back, while smacking her elbow into his chin. She stepped this way and that, dancing an angled course around the scorpion's claws as it tried to pin her down, and then her blade severed the last three inches of its stinger and stabbed down to pierce the beast amidst its clustered eyes.

She felt the swirl of fighting humanity about her eddy and shudder, and knew without seeing that the relief force must have arrived at last. That meant they had held up the brigands long enough for Lowre's trap to be sprung, so it only remained for her to ensure that the bandit chief himself did not escape.

He was not trying to, however, or perhaps the wounds he had taken had deprived him of his flying Art. He glanced briefly at the dead scorpion and then went for her again, grimacing as he put his weight on to his injured leg. She stayed outside his reach, because his eyes promised further surprises, and when the spear came at her from behind, she was ready for it – turning to slash at the wielder, who got himself out of the way faster than she had expected. She saw a long-faced Grasshopper-kinden now staring at his truncated spear-shaft.

All around them the brigands were fleeing, some taking to the air to run the gauntlet of the Salmae's own fliers, while others tried to reach the treeline again. The counterattack was mopping up most of them, throwing a ring around those that remained and driving them in towards Tynisa. The bandits continued fighting, but she guessed that those with any sense would start surrendering soon.

The Grasshopper was neither fighting nor fleeing. Instead he was still trying to find a way of coming against her to rescue his leader. That told her all she needed to know.

Thinking that she was distracted, the Dragonfly thrust at her again. She took his sword with her raper's quillons and twisted it in a way that would have disarmed anyone with a Wasp-issue shortsword, but just sprained his wrist, and then she stepped back. As she finished moving, the razor edge of her sword was right under his chin, drawing a little blood, then she remained absolutely still, and so did he.

Without looking at the Grasshopper, she could sense him frustrated and angry and fearful for the life of his leader – and his friend, she decided. Had he been a Mantis, he would surely not have let such sentiment cripple him, she told herself.

'Drop your weapons, both of you,' she called out, loud enough to be heard over the fighting. 'All of you,' she added, because she saw she now had a wider audience. The brigands immediately around her were already surrendering, not out of love of their leader but because Whitehand and his followers had started killing any who did not throw down their arms. Tynisa glanced at the nearest. She saw the Wasp, now with an Imperial shortsword to replace his ruined nailbow. She saw the Grasshopper, and she saw a squat Scorpion-kinden man holding a short-hafted halberd and looking at her like blood and murder.

'All of you,' she repeated, with a tiny shift of the rapier. The Dragonfly hissed and dropped his sword.

'You can't kill us all,' the Wasp tried.

'Of course I can,' she replied earnestly, and it was the utter conviction of her tone that finally disarmed him, and the Grasshopper. She turned her gaze to the Scorpion-kinden, who seemed disinclined to join them.

'Ygor,' the Dragonfly hissed, 'it's over.'

'She killed my wife,' the Scorpion growled. 'She killed Scutts.'

He was going to swing his halberd at her, she knew. He was mired enough in grief to throw away his life, and those of his fellows too. She almost saluted him for it. It was the proper thing to do.

But then he sagged, and let the heavy weapon fall, the head burying itself in the earth, and the next moment the followers of the Salmae were binding the wrists of those bandits who, by surrendering, had bought themselves another tenday of life.

They insisted on extracting the arrow before she rode for the camp. A solemn Grasshopper healer removed the protruding head, and then carefully eased the shaft back out. As she sat gritting her teeth, she felt all the pain that had not dared trouble her during the battle, now returning with a vengeance. She did not cry out.

When the healer had bandaged her, she rode on to the place where Salme Elass had decided to pitch her tents. There was a lamp burning in the princess's pavilion, but she had not come to make her report to the matron of the Salmae.

She found Alain in his own tent, and he turned as she entered, still bloodied from the battlefield and with her sword at her hip. The tales that had already reached him would not have been silent about her own particular exploits: she had led the assault, she had taken the bandit leader. *My gift to you.*

She almost threw herself at him. In her mind she was duelling, and had beaten down his last parry, exposing him to her blade. It was now that balancing moment when one protagonist was utterly at the mercy of the other.

He caught her, as she reached him, and their lips met. The shock of it made her heart stutter, as that long-familiar face, that maddening smile, all of a sudden they were *hers*.

He drew her down on to his sleeping mat. 'Salma,' she whispered, when she finally could.

And, of course, he replied, 'Yes.'

Part Four

Broken Threads

Thirty-Three

Surveying the field from the forest's edge made for a grim sight. The battle had not been large, compared with some that Che or the others had seen, but this aftermath had a particularly abandoned air. The bodies of, they assumed, the losers were strewn haphazardly all about, as a score or so individuals picked their way through them, hauling corpses aside into an untidy line. Others were digging a great pit, the final resting place that the dead here would all lie in together.

The winners had already departed, leaving these menials to assign the losers to the worms and the burying beetles. These undertakers moved without speed, hunched up against a chill wind that coursed unchecked across the open ground.

After pausing long enough in the trees, the four travellers set out again, plotting a path that would skirt the field of combat. Che saw Maure steel herself before moving on, and wondered what additional horrors a necromancer might witness in such a place.

'We need news,' Thalric decided. 'I'd not expected to find this sort of slaughter in the Commonweal. A good few hundred fighters a side, surely.'

Some of the gravediggers glanced up at them, but looked away just as quickly, obviously wanting these wayfarers to be none of their problems. They spotted one man standing apart, though, leaning on his narrow-headed spade. He was a greying

Grasshopper, the same kinden as most of the workers, but he regarded the travellers steadily as they approached him. As they drew near they saw that there was a dead man lying by his feet, another Grasshopper, with the arrow that had done for him standing up like a tiny standard.

If the old man had any fear that the newcomers might attack him, he did not show it. Perhaps he felt that even the Wasp-kinden could not make his current surroundings much worse.

'Good day to you,' Che called out, and then she grimaced, deciding that her words were poorly chosen. 'Well . . . anyway,' she continued vaguely. Closer to, she had ample opportunity to study the strewn corpses. They seemed a poor sort of soldier, badly armoured and clothed like the peasants seen on their travels, not like men and women for whom fate had chosen this violent end. 'What happened here?'

The old man cast his eyes over the carnage, and then back at her, as if to say, *Is it not obvious?*

She nodded, waving his unspoken words away. 'Who fought here? Who won?'

'Was the Salmae fighting bandits, so they say. Salmae won.' He shrugged. 'Or we won, perhaps. They said it was for us, when they made us fight. Protect us against the raiders, they said.'

It took Che a moment to deconstruct 'the Salmae', and to understand that the man must mean Salma's family. 'Where did the winners go from here?' she asked quickly.

'North. Leose. They'll have some great celebration there, no doubt.' The gravedigger, looked underwhelmed by the thought.

'Tell me, if you were fighting here, was there a Spider-kinden woman . . .?' Che's words tailed off as she noted a telltale tightening of the lips, a tensing of the way he stood. 'She was here.'

'Oh, she was here,' the Grasshopper agreed, but said no more.

'Come on,' Thalric decided. 'We can't be far behind them, and we'll move faster than their army.'

'Why are you just standing here, old man?' Maure asked softly. 'Why linger by this body?'

He looked at her, and perhaps something about her told him what she was. 'I knew him,' he told her. 'From my village, he was. Knew him all his life. He was never happy, him. He always said someone should take up a blade against the taxes and the nobles, and I was always telling him, "Life's not that way." There's nothing a man like you or me can do, I'd say to him. Still, when men came from Rhael and offered him a blade, he took it, even so. Here's a man that died of dreams. The arrow did him not half so much harm. But I won't see him buried with the rest. I'll keep with him here, and the least he deserves is his own hole in the ground, when all of this is done.' They were philosophers, the Grasshopper-kinden, so Che had once heard. They might till the earth for their Dragonfly princes, but they were philosophers nonetheless.

Maure nodded thoughtfully, staring at the corpse. 'Do you want to . . .? I could see if he . . .' Words failed her, as so often on the subject of her profession, but the old man was already shaking his head.

'Don't know what I'd say to him now. Don't think I could tell him why I wasn't fighting on his side.'

As they moved on, following the path the army had clearly taken, Varmen commented, 'He didn't seem too impressed with your Spider lass.'

Che nodded unhappily.

'With what rides her, I'm not surprised,' Maure put in. 'I've come across nothing like it. Mantis ghosts, yes, and all of them hungry for blood – but this one has *power*.'

'It has the power of the Darakyon, or what's left of it,' Che murmured, too quietly for any of them to pick up. That was the conclusion she had come to, after all her visions and insights. All Maure's talk of ghosts only highlighted how Tisamon's shade had gone beyond the normal petty limits that such spirits were bound by. *He and I and the Wasp Empress are all of us bound together by the Darakyon, somehow.* She could not quite see the link, nor did she have all the pieces, but she was becoming more and more sure of it.

And now I have another reason to find Tynisa, for she actually saw Tisamon die – she saw Tisamon kill the Emperor, and surely the Emperor's sister was nearby . . .

'Maure,' she asked, 'would you visit my sister and try to drive away her ghost again?'

The necromancer shook her head vigorously, for her previous attempt had left her sweating and trembling. She had professed success in prying Tisamon's hold off Tynisa's mind, but only for a little while. 'Not again,' she insisted. 'He would be ready for me now, and he'd kill me. Put me before the woman, and I will try my usual rituals and incantations, but only from within my own body, where I'm safer. In dreams I'd not give much for my chances, now he's ready for me.'

The two Wasps exchanged glances, but by now they had given up attempting to understand the strange world that these women inhabited. For Thalric, it was enough that the Beetle girl was walking and talking. Anything else he could learn to live with.

I'd love to think that this halfbreed was just conning Che, he mused, *and that at the end of it there would be demands for money or such, but . . .* He remembered the Twelve-year War and all the mysticism that the Commonwealers had laid claim to, and which the invading Empire had laughed at. *Well, I'm loath to admit it, but perhaps this old lore of theirs has a few teeth left to it – not enough to turn back an army but sufficient to drive a mad Spider-kinden even madder than she was.*

And following on that thought: *Better that the Empire had taken the Commonweal entirely and wiped out all this mind-rotting mysticism. Reason enough for the conquest had it been fake, but all the more reason if there is some truth behind it.* He knew Che would not understand, but she had never been a good arbiter of her own best interests. *If I could take you away from this, then I would, but there remains a shard of it lodged inside you, wherever you go . . .*

By evening they could see the Salmae's army by its campfires, and it was plain that they would overtake it the following morning. They had a brief, divided discussion about whether to make contact meanwhile, with Thalric and Varmen both arguing that the victorious troops might mistake them for stragglers from the defeated brigands, so contact would be better made once their army had reached its destination and disbanded. Che would hear none of it, though. Tynisa was accompanying that force, and that was all that mattered.

Varmen insisted on taking the first watch, and even spent the time getting into the bulk of his armour to do it. The big Wasp had been growing more distant as they travelled, and it was clear to Che that whatever burden he had carried within him from Suon Ren was only growing, whether through time or distance. Still, he looked such a forbidding figure in all that weight of steel that she found that she did not quite have the courage to broach the matter. After Thalric and Maure had gone to sleep, she found herself still awake, staring at his plated form looming in the darkness which her eyes could pierce so easily, the black and gold of his mail dimmed to black and grey in her Art-sight.

At last his helm turned towards her, and he spoke. 'If you're not going to sleep, you might as well come over and keep me company.' His voice sounded hushed and hollow.

Into the surprised silence that followed he explained, 'Your breathing. I could tell from your breathing. People don't realize how, if you spend a lifetime wearing this stuff, just how much you can see and hear and sense.'

Blankets wrapped around her, Che shuffled over to him. 'Did you want to talk?'

'You're Beetle-kinden, and yet you understand all this magic business the Commonwealers talk about, right?'

'Some of it, some of the time,' she admitted.

'Fate and destiny, that sort of thing.' he added vaguely. 'It's just . . . I remember the war, and how we came through here, won our battles, took over their places, set up governors. We killed a lot of their people. I did myself. Pride of the Sixth, you know. Even then, there were moments . . . there was a girl, a Dragonfly girl, one of their nobles. We fought . . .'

'You killed her?'

'I never did. I liked her. Nice voice, she had. I like a nice-sounding voice in a girl. So I let her go. But then the Second bastard Army rolled through. I tried to find her, later . . . Stupid thing to have regrets about, eh?'

Che waited, watching him. He was no longer looking at her, just staring off into the night. At last he said, 'I never before and never after had any second thoughts about what we were doing, except then, after that fight . . . She was brave, you see, and I liked her. And then they re-formed the Sixth, under General Praeter, and we marched off into the Lowlands, and there's Malkan's Stand . . .' One gauntleted hand touched the rough-edged hole in his breastplate. 'After that I don't have an army, and even if I went back, and they took me back, I wouldn't be what I was. No more Sentinels, eh? They've no use for Sentinels any more, not with snapbows ready to drill a hole in the strongest plate. A lifetime of training and being special, then it's all down the drain. And what was I left with? When I sobered up, when I stopped trying to die . . . I was left with *her.* Crazy Dragonfly girl with the nice voice. I came back, you see. Hovering about the Commonweal border, plying some sort of useless bastard escort business. After all that, after getting shot through my mail, after the defeat, after losing it all . . . just her. Some dead Dragonfly girl that I'll never find. The only thing left in my head, after all that, was remembering her.'

'You're still looking for her?' Che asked.

'She's dead.'

'You don't know—'

Varmen's helm had twitched towards Maure's sleeping form, so Che understood when he repeated, 'She's dead.'

Che could have asked him, then. She could have asked, *Did you speak with her?* Or enquired what a long-dead Dragonfly noblewoman might have had to say to a representative of her murderers. She might even have asked if Varmen's continued presence at her side was the result of some request or atonement demanded by this notional ghost. Or perhaps this duty was one that the Wasp had assumed himself, like another piece of ultimately ineffective armour.

But in the end she did not ask. Better that the man kept his secrets.

The Commonwealer force was still mustering by the time they reached it the next day, and even Che could see that this was chiefly because the bulk of it was anything but military. She was willing to wager that these peasants-turned-soldiers had been up at first dawn, but forming themselves into a marching column was clearly not part of their usual morning routine.

The arrival of the four of them caused a nervous stir amongst the common soldiery, their carefully constructed formations eddying and swirling aside as though to even be close to a Wasp-kinden was to invite extinction. Che expected this disturbance to swiftly attract the attention of the officers or the nobles in charge, but it quickly became apparent that there were few of their kind available. The small band of Dragonfly-kinden who eventually showed up spent more time staring at Thalric and Varmen than reordering their troops, and for a moment Che feared that the four of them, by their very presence, would somehow reverse the recent military victory and rout the entire army.

Then order was finally restored by the appearance of one man, and Che could see why. Her first thought was, *Tisamon*, but of course it was not. The dead Weaponsmaster had been in her thoughts so much that any Mantis of a similar bearing, and wearing the same badge above all, would have instantly brought him to mind. This man was older, with silver hair, and was wearing an arming jacket of pale grey leather, where Tisamon had favoured forest green. He seemed calmer, too, in a strange way. Che would never have described Tynisa's father as agitated, but there had constantly been a high-strung tension to Tisamon, which this man had conquered. Here was Tisamon as he might have been, had he never loved Tynisa's Spider-kinden mother, had he never become friends with Stenwold Maker.

'What is your business here?' he asked, not loudly but in a voice that could not be ignored.

'Please, sieur,' Che said, falling back on the Solarnese title for no reason she could think of, 'we're looking for my foster-sister, Tynisa.'

'Tynisa?' For a moment his face was blank, then something fell into place. 'Ah, Maker Tynise. And you are her sister?'

'Foster-sister,' Che explained. 'I've travelled a very long way, we all have.'

'She's left the column,' the Mantis told her. 'She's flown off to Leose, along with most of the nobles.'

So close. Che sagged a little. *A day gained somewhere and I'd have caught her.* 'You're taking your soldiers to . . . Leose then?' she asked, stumbling a little over the name.

'I return there myself, so accompany me if you will.' He was still studying Che's face, without expression. She wondered how much he could read there of her recent history.

'We'll make better time on our own,' Thalric suggested. The Mantis's eyes flicked towards him sharply, a man with no love for Wasp-kinden, nor fear of them either.

'You'll do better to approach Leose with a friend to gain you admittance,' Maure murmured. 'The Salmae's doors don't open even as wide as Felipe Shah's, I've heard.' She wore a wry smile, no doubt thinking of her reception back at Suon Ren.

Che glanced between them, keenly aware of the Mantis's gaze turning back to her. 'Then, yes, we'll travel with you, and gladly,' she told him at last. 'Cheerwell Maker of Collegium,' she introduced herself, then named her companions in turn.

The Mantis's name was Isendter, pronounced with a typical Commonweal flourish that Che found almost impossible to replicate. He was called Whitehand also, apparently, so she settled for that. As the day wore on, it became clear why he had set himself aside as the only one who would reach Leose. Little detachments of the makeshift soldiers were constantly abandoning the column, their ranks thinning and thinning as time wore on: the peasants were returning to their farms and villages, their herds and crops, Che realized, and clearly glad to be putting the military life behind them. It was spring, after all, and a farmer had better things to do than go chasing about with a spear. She thought of those soldiers of Collegium, who were repurposed tradesmen, artisans and shopkeepers, yet had still accounted for themselves well enough during the war. Then she thought about the Empire, whose every male son was given a uniform and a weapon, and allowed no other trade but fighting.

How did we ever beat them? she asked herself, but then had to admit, *We did not. They were not beaten: they just stepped back to deal with a little infighting. And they have since whipped their rebel governors into line, and they now have their new Empress, and surely I can hear the sound of a thousand thousand swords being drawn even now. What is to stop them?*

'Che?' Thalric touched her arm and for a moment she wanted to run away from him and from his brutal birthright. Instead, she hugged him tight because he was surely proof that redemption was possible, even for the Wasp-kinden.

Thirty-Four

Che had the impression that Whitehand was a man who spoke little, yet he broke his rule to ask her about Tynisa, and through his few terse questions he managed to prompt from her a great deal of the curious story of Stenwold Maker, of Cheerwell, and of Tynisa's mother. Che approached the subject of Tisamon carefully, never quite naming him as Tynisa's father in case Isendter held any great grudge against halfbreeds, but making the strength of their relationship clear. Whitehand's face remained impassive throughout, but Che had the impression that he had been waiting for a figure such as Tisamon to turn up in this account.

As she recounted what she knew of Tisamon's death, Isendter nodded fractionally, but that small movement spoke volumes, the only acknowledgement he had made. 'And they were close?' he put in.

'Very,' Che agreed. 'And I believe . . .' For a moment the old Collegium Che rebelled against the words, or perhaps felt embarrassed at speaking them before Thalric, but she pressed on. 'I believe that he is haunting her now. I think that his ghost takes its duties as a . . .' she almost said 'father', '. . . as a mentor very seriously indeed.'

'It may be as you say,' was all Isendter Whitehand replied, but Che knew that he had sensed something or seen something in Tynisa. 'There was a shrine of my people, in the woods, out west. We came upon it while hunting. After that . . .'

Che nodded, seeing the perfect gateway through which the ghost could have stepped, directly into Tynisa's mind.

By the time they came to Leose, most of the impromptu army had disbanded, hurrying back to lives that had no need of conflict or bloodshed in them. Che found herself and her companions quickly abandoned in a great courtyard, lined to one side with ranks of stables, and roofed by a wooden lattice that Maure explained was for dragonfly steeds to land on. They had just enough time to wonder if they had been forgotten, when a lean Grasshopper-kinden woman wearing dark colours came out to them, looking them up and down with that crisp and slightly disapproving expression of senior servants the world over.

'The champion tells me you are here to see the Spider-kinden girl,' she remarked. 'Which of you is her sister?'

'Her foster-sister.' Che raised a hand. 'Cheerwell Maker of Collegium. This is Thalric, this Varmen, and this—'

'Maure,' said the mystic quickly, cutting her off, and Che wondered if magicians were supposed to introduce themselves, or whether being named by another might diminish their power, or some such. *And is that real, or just superstition? There's so much I don't know.*

The Grasshopper stared at the halfbreed necromancer for a long moment. 'Lisan Dea, seneschal of Leose,' she named herself.

'There are those who might use my services here? The lady of the house, perhaps?' Maure enquired, as though simply having turned up there as a solitary vagabond.

'Not the lady, I think,' Lisan Dea replied, 'but there are others, nonetheless.' She had clearly somehow recognized the services that Maure could provide, and there was a hint of some small tragedy written in her features, some impenetrable loss that Che would never dare ask about, and that Maure would never report. The Grasshopper nodded suddenly, gathering her composure about her like a cloak. 'You are welcome here, Maure, for the gifts you bring. You are welcome, Cheerwell

Maker, as the sister of our guest. Your companions are not so welcome, however.'

Che opened her mouth to protest, but the Grasshopper held up one lean finger. 'They will be lodged with other servants of the Salmae.'

'Go,' Thalric suggested. 'Do what you've come to do and then we'll be well rid of this place.'

Stepping into the shadow of the Commonwealer castle caused an almost physical shock, so that Che was forced to clutch at Maure's arm, feeling disoriented by the shift between what she saw and what she felt. That it was daylight outside, channelled in by the high windows, seemed to be denied by every part of her but her eyes. That the high-vaulted ceilings made the halls beneath airy and spacious, her senses insisted was false, a mere gloss. She felt as though she was entombed underground. She felt as though those lofty arches were not for the convenience of a flying kinden, but simply to accommodate ponderous forms of much greater stature than herself, and that these Commonwealers were merely living in their discarded shells.

In short, although the design was as different as several hundred miles of distance, and perhaps several centuries of time, could account for, she felt that she already knew the builders of this place. Their presence, even the last decaying scraps of it, oppressed her. Of all the kinden of the world, and of all the secrets of history, she'd had enough of *them*.

She glanced at Maure, but it was impossible to tell whether the necromancer recognized her disquiet. In front of Lisan Dea, the mystic was all business.

'Your sister came to us at the start of winter, from Suon Ren,' the Grasshopper was saying. She had deliberately slowed her long-legged pace to let Che keep up, but because of that she seemed to be watching always from the corner of her eye, reading every least twitch of Che's features. The Beetle girl made a dutiful show of listening.

'It seemed she was not in favour, and had little to offer us, nor did she know our ways or how to behave. It seemed that would be the end of it, and that the spring would see her dispatched back to the Lowlands.' Lisan Dea recited the words neutrally, taking no side.

'This has changed, then?' Che put in, because she felt it was expected of her.

'After winter she demonstrated talents that fit the times,' the seneschal replied. 'So she is in favour, so long as those times last.'

Talents that fit the times. Under Tisamon's tutelage Tynisa had devoted herself to one particular talent and, now that the man's ghost was guiding her through this time of conflict, the seneschal's words were not difficult to understand. 'She was always skilled,' she managed. The presence of Tynisa, through walls of stone, seemed palpably closer, and Che was wondering what manner of reception she might receive. What would the ghost drive her sister to do?

Then the Grasshopper made an abrupt turn, leading her guests through an arched door flanked by tapestries of red and gold – and there was Tynisa.

The room she stood in was lit by oblique shafts of light descending from windows cut high into one wall, a light so crisp and clear that Che wondered whether guests were only received in this chamber at this one particular time. The rush matting on the floor, left mostly in shadow, spoke of martial practice. At the far end of the room stood Tynisa herself, where the floor stepped up to a raised platform from which instructors had no doubt guided their charges through their paces.

She was not alone, though. A Dragonfly-kinden man was speaking softly in her ear, and Che had the impression that Tynisa must have just completed some fencing passes on the floor. He seemed young to be a mentor, though, and stood too close, so for a moment Che hovered awkwardly in the doorway, realizing that she was intruding, hesitant to press on and yet even less willing to lose this opportunity.

Then Lisan Dea was stalking across the room, and the Dragonfly looked up and took a step away. The Grasshopper seneschal practically radiated an icy disapproval directed, in so far as Che could tell, solely at the man.

There was something curiously familiar about him, now that Che saw his face: some passing likeness that she felt she should recognize. Then the Grasshopper had drawn him aside and hissed something in his ear, and his crooked grin transformed into incredulity as he stared down the length of the room towards Che.

That was it, she suddenly realized: he looked a little like Salma, or at least more than most young Dragonfly men did. Given where they all were, he must be some manner of relative.

Then, without ceremony, Lisan Dea was shepherding him out of the room. Che could not see his expression as he gazed back briefly at Tynisa, but his parting look at the Beetle herself was nothing short of contemptuous, making plain his surprise that *this* woman could claim a sisterhood with *that* one.

Maure had hung back – no, Maure had ducked out of sight entirely and was now gone from her side. Unexpectedly, after the varied escorts Che had enjoyed since leaving Khanaphes, she was left alone with Tynisa.

She approached, skirting the edge of the fighting mat as if it was the ground of the Prowess Forum in Collegium. From her elevated position, Tynisa watched her closely, and there was nothing in her face or stance that recognized Che at all. Her expression was bleak as winter, and her hand hovered near her sword. Che was no great warrior, scarcely a warrior at all, but as she drew near she became acutely aware of an invisible circle about Tynisa dictated by the broad reach of her blade, and that to cross into it uninvited would be fatal.

In that stance, in that arch expression, it was Tisamon who stood before her, or part of him at least. That segment of the Mantis-kinden which had been so devoted to Che's uncle Stenwold was repressed or excised, along with those few times he had smiled or laughed, or shown himself something like human. Instead this was a sharp-edged and brittle creature of skill and bloodlust that was poised to strike at her, the same despairing figure of tragedy that had dashed itself to death against its love for the Dragonfly Felise Mienn, as Mantis heroes were traditionally wont to do.

Then something flickered in the girl's eyes that owed nothing to that thousand years of dark and bloody heritage, and she said, 'Che?'

'No other,' the Beetle replied, edging closer and feeling that circle around Tynisa flex as she touched it, like a tripwire, and then vanish, the danger gone as if it had never been. Feeling as though she had been given permission, Che stepped forward and embraced her near-sister.

'What are you doing here?' Tynisa asked of her, not annoyed as Che had anticipated, only wondering.

'Looking for you,' she explained. 'You disappeared, remember?'

'Yes, yes, I did,' Tynisa agreed. 'And if you'd found me just a few months ago, I'd not have been grateful for it, I think. Still, things have changed since then. Life's better than it was.'

Che regarded her cautiously. 'Is that so?'

The smile that met her gaze was unfamiliar. The Spider-kinden girl Che had grown up with had possessed a grand stock of smiles, knowing, subtle, gleeful, suggestive, a veritable arsenal that had brought about the ruin of many a young man. Tisamon, in contrast, had smiled rarely: his killing grin when shedding blood, and a more human expression reserved for his conversations with Stenwold. This smile belonged neither to the dead father nor to the daughter, as she had faced the world back then, but Che had a feeling that, had Tynisa ever let anyone into her heart, without masks and mirrors, this is what they might have seen.

'You saw him, saw Alain?' Tynisa asked her eagerly.

Che frowned for a second before connecting the name to the man. 'I did,' she conceded.

'Well?'

There was obviously some immediate comment she should be ready to make, but Che could not find it.

Tynisa shook her head impatiently. 'How like his brother he is. The very image, yes?'

Che looked her in the eyes, reading a lot there. Oh, Salme Dien had mocked Che, in his time, but fondly, always fondly. He would never have assumed that expression of condescension that Che had seen on the face of Salme Alain as he departed. But she said, 'Yes, very,' nevertheless, because this was not the time, nor the challenge she had come here to deliver. 'Tynisa, you must know . . . You say things have changed for you?'

'I have a purpose now,' Tynisa agreed. 'I have Alain.'

'And was there a moment, when that change occurred?' Che pressed.

Tynisa looked at her oddly. 'I don't know what you mean.'

'Your father, Tynisa?' Because to barrel on, at this point, seemed the only way – whilst keeping a weather eye open for some murderous reprisal from the man's ghost. Yet Tynisa's expression seemed honestly baffled. 'Tynisa, I know. I saw him for myself. I know that the ghost of your father has sought you out, and I'm here to help you.'

For a long moment Tynisa just stared at her, and Che tensed, waiting for that glint of steel in her eyes that would herald Tisamon clawing to the forefront of her mind. Then she laughed: a snort of amusement that emerged despite all of Tynisa's attempts to control it. 'Ghosts, Che? There's no such thing as ghosts. Don't tell me fifteen years of College education didn't teach you that.'

Che stared back at her, caught utterly off guard. 'But . . . you can't tell me you haven't felt him, seen him even . . .?'

Tynisa's expression sobered. 'Oh, I won't deny I've enjoyed some strange company when I've been on my own – on my way here and during the winter. I won't say I didn't see him.' She held a hand up to forestall Che. 'Achaeos, too, and Salma.

You can't imagine the fright it gave me to see Alain for the first time. I thought that I really was going out of my mind. But that was just me, Che, because I was all alone and I'd lost . . . everything, or so it seemed. I don't think anyone could blame me for indulging in a few fantasies. But that's done now, since I found Alain. I'm a new woman now.'

Gazing at her, Che could all but see the malignant form of Tisamon lurking at her shoulder. She could feel the dead Weaponsmaster's presence like a chill in the air, but Tynisa kept smiling slightly condescendingly.

'Ghosts, Che? Seriously? You'll find plenty of people here who believe in them. But we know better, surely?' Her smile was so brittle that Che could almost detect the cracks, but in Tynisa's eyes there was absolutely no recognition of that looming presence which Che felt like a physical pressure.

'We have to talk, Tynisa,' Che said at last, recognizing defeat in the first skirmish, and retreating to a prepared position. 'But I've come a long way, and I need to catch my breath. Tomorrow perhaps?'

'And where were you?' Che asked Maure, when she had tracked her down, after considerable searching.

'Looking after your best interests by absenting myself,' the mystic told her. 'The ghost *knows* me – and knows me for its enemy. It wouldn't have helped, me being there. When I meet it again, I want it to be somewhere that I've warded. Besides, I've been asking questions on your behalf.'

'Oh?'

'That steward wanted my services, so I said I'd help her. We talked. She was close-mouthed, but I worked out what put the sour look on her face.'

'Tynisa?' Che suggested glumly. 'They don't think she should be associating with their prince, I suppose.'

Maure gave her a curious look. 'Well, you've got it completely backwards but, other than that, you're right. Prince

Alain has a reputation with women, and I get the impression that Lisan Dea was doing her best, as warden of the castle's hospitality, to keep the two of them apart. But that's all gone to the pits now, as you saw.'

Che closed her eyes briefly. 'That's a complication I don't think I can deal with just at the moment. Let me stay with my brief and free her from the ghost, if I can. She's never had any difficulties with relationships before.' Even as Che said that, she saw Tynisa's face again in her mind, all those layers of social accomplishment stripped away, leaving something as raw and vulnerable as her father ever was. Had not Tisamon himself made such unhappy personal relationships the very meat and drink of his downfall? 'If that's how this Lisan Dea feels, why hasn't she warned Tynisa?'

'And betray her mistress and the family? Unthinkable.'

'And yet she told you.'

Maure shrugged. 'There's a saying: no secrets from the dead. It generalizes to those of my profession. We do more than clutch at the memory of the departed. Sometimes those grieving simply need a sympathetic ear amongst the living rather than an audience with the dead. Our seneschal didn't want any spectres raised. She wanted . . . confession. Your sister is in danger from Alain, and she's being used as a weapon by the Salmae princess, as well. Only, the way I hear it, that weapon turned out to be sharper than anyone guessed. I think we both know why that is.'

'We need to act on the ghost fast, then. Advise me, Maure.'

'Bring your sister to a place of my choosing – one that I have properly prepared. I will then throw open the doors, and see if he will emerge. If he does, I will fight him for her.'

Che regarded her doubtfully. 'And that will work, will it?'

'No guarantees.' Maure's mouth twisted. 'He may just sit there in her mind, like a grub in a tree and not be drawn. He may prove too strong for me, in which case I'll need your help.'

'Me?'

Maure shrugged. 'Your strength, the power you've been gifted with, the authority you've assumed, whatever you prefer to call it. With you beside me, I'm willing to venture it.'

Che thought about that. 'When you say "open the doors", does that mean other ghosts might . . .?'

'Well, if I set my wards correctly, we should have an exclusive audience,' the mystic declared. She noticed Che's expression. 'But I can leave them open, just a little while, and if there is some other ghost, some echo of someone linked to you . . .?'

Che was silent for a while, reaching out for an empty space within her. *I have thought about it since I first met this woman. Would it do any harm? We had so many things we never said.*

'They have the Wasps lodged in some retainer's hut outside the walls,' Maure informed her briskly, breaking the mood. 'I have the directions. I don't know about you, but I don't feel welcome enough to spend the night in Castle Leose, and besides, I find I miss Varmen more than I expected. Have your sister come to that hut, which is far enough from this castle for me not to have to deal with generations of Salmae ancestors battering at the door. Then I'll see what I can do.'

Thirty-Five

Tynisa had wondered how a Commonwealer noble would be able to confine her enemies, in a castle of the Inapt, where there were no locks, and where those prisoners could most likely possess the Art to fly. It was an eventuality that the ancient builders of Leose had apparently anticipated, however, for there were so many cellars underlying the castle that it seemed remarkable the structure was not undermined to the point of collapse. The largest and most central of these was reached by a narrow and easily defensible stair leading down from the guards' quarters on the floor above, and alternatively through a trapdoor set into the courtyard, wide enough for a horse to be lowered through it should the need arise. The lords of Leose clearly did not want to see their enemies dragged through the castle halls on their way to imprisonment. So, when the surviving chiefs of the brigands had been brought in, it was a simple matter to decant them straight into the bowels of the castle.

There was only one cell down there: a pit excavated into the floor, some fifteen foot deep, and walled in smooth, slick stone. Of course, that would prove no obstacle to most Commonwealers, but the grille that covered it was held down at each corner by a heavy block of stone. Tynisa had watched the captives installed there, seeing those same weights swung into position on ropes that were balanced by counterweights. It was as intricate a system as the Inapt had ever designed, and plainly dated from whatever ancient era the castle was first constructed in. Only the cane grille and the ropes themselves would have needed periodic replacement, and the masters of Leose had held their enemies here in such a manner since time immemorial.

She had now come back to view the prisoners – *her* prisoners as she felt justified in considering them. For had *she* not led the charge? Had *she* not been the vanguard of the assault that had scattered their army and captured them? She looked upon them, almost fondly, with a proprietorial air. *My gift to Alain.*

As she approached, stepping lightly down the narrow, winding stair from above, she heard a hurried movement, the flurry of wings, and knew that one of the prisoners must have been crawling about the underside of the grille, testing it for weak points. The canes themselves were as thick in diameter as Tynisa's arm, and they were bound together with wire, as well as cord that had been soaked first and then dried tight. Even those prisoners whose Art had furnished them with blades would not be able to pry this prison apart.

As she stepped to the edge, they were all waiting with upturned faces, pale or sallow or the gold of Dragonfly-kinden. The only one bound was the Wasp-kinden, who had his arms twisted behind him and lashed together, that being a lesson the Commonwealers had learned well enough. She gave them time to recognize her, as she stood gazing down on them like an empress.

A mixed bag they were, too, about a score of them, looking more like tired, wretched vagabonds than dangerous brigands. They included a ragbag of Grasshoppers and Dragonflies, the one brooding Scorpion, the Wasp, and a Spider-kinden who must have been very far from home. The Scorpion's glare was baleful but defeated, and only one seemed to retain a spark of defiance. She almost smiled at the sight of their leader: the Dragonfly known, she had since learned, as Dal Arche.

'Come to gloat?' he asked, and the walls of the pit took the soft words and conveyed them up to her easily.

'To see justice done,' she retorted, and he nodded philosophically.

'That time is it, then? Are you the executioner?'

'You have a few days more to brood on your defeat,' she declared, noting the shadows of anger and despair that passed across their faces. In truth, Salme Elass was saving them for something suitably public. She had sent messengers to cordially invite Felipe Shah to witness the death of these enemies of the Monarch's peace, and Tynisa knew that the woman would then press for the retaking of Rhael, so as to finish off the extermination of all the scum that had gathered there in defiance of the rightful authority of the princes. Still, the brigand's suggestion had some merit in it. 'I shall ask to be appointed as your executioner, and why not? For who else has that right, more than I?'

The Dragonfly looked up at her, almost smiling, with eyes narrowed like a man looking into the sun. 'Since you're in a talkative mood, what's all of this to you, girl? They paying you well, are they?'

'I'm no mercenary,' she told him. 'I just know what's right. You're lawbreakers and rebels against the Monarch.'

'Well, that makes us sound grand,' Dal Arche replied wryly. 'I hadn't realized you'd met the Monarch. I never saw her myself.'

'You know what I mean.'

He shrugged. 'I won't deny that the laws of princes don't sit happily on my shoulders. I travelled a long way to get out from under them but, wherever you go, it seems there's always someone trying to tell you what to do, whether they call themselves prince or emperor. I thought I might as well come home, in that case.'

Tynisa shook her head, crouching by the edge of the grille to see him better. 'Oh, that won't carry weight, brigand. I've seen the Empire, and you can't equate Imperial rule with the Commonweal.'

'Lived there, have you? And lived a life here, to compare?' Dal challenged her.

'*His* people killed my father,' she hissed, jabbing a finger at the Wasp, who flinched back, startled.

'Don't drag me into this. I quit,' he muttered, but Dal was already shaking his head.

'If you want to play that game, then one prince or another has killed pretty much everyone I ever knew,' he said. 'Oh, certainly it was the Wasps who held the sword, but it was my own kinden, my glorious *betters*, who threw the victims onto it. It's been some prince or other who's taxed my kin so that we could only live hand to mouth, and never build anything more on what we had. It's been your darling prince and his mother here who knocked us down when we tried to set ourselves up like decent folk in Siriell's Town.'

'I saw Siriell's Town,' Tynisa snapped. 'There was nothing "decent" there.'

'Well, I'm sorry we didn't all live in the castle,' Dal Arche retorted, a little more fire in his voice now. 'Perhaps then we'd have fitted your idea of how decent folk live? Tell me, who are you to judge us, living here without care as a guest of the Salmae?'

Tynisa leant closer, feeling obscurely gratified that she had made him angry at last. 'I've seen more of the world than you, old man. I've seen the Empire and I know what they value there: tyranny and slavery. I've seen Helleron and I know half the Lowlands is just greed running riot, or places like Collegium where good intentions are never quite enough. But I know . . . I *know* the Commonweal. The Commonweal makes good people, who fight for the right things: heroes. I know what the Monarch believes in. I recognize truth and honour and honesty when I see it. A friend taught me about the Commonweal, by the example of everything he ever did. He was the best man I ever knew, and he knew what was right and what was wrong. That's how I can judge you, thief and murderer that you are.

You have rebelled against your rightful rulers, and for that you'll die.'

She waited for an explosion of wrath, of counter-accusation, even of pleading, but it did not come.

Instead Dal Arche leant back against the wall of the pit. 'Oh, that does sound grand. If you ever find this mythical place you're talking about, let me know, I'd like to see it. Until then, I suppose I'll have to live with the merely *human* nobility who got so many of us killed in the war. At least I won't have to live with them very long.'

Something nagged at her briefly, some echo of Lowre Cean's words before the battle, but she shrugged it away. 'I can judge,' she repeated. 'And I can be the one to wield the blade, when your time comes. Better that than suffer the crossed pikes of the Empire, no?'

'And in your Lowlands?' he asked her.

'They were always too soft in Collegium,' she replied, getting up and turning to go. A thought struck her, and she gave voice to it: 'You can hardly deny that you've earned this, having robbed and pillaged your way across half of the province?'

'Oh, no, not at all,' was his reply. 'We took what we wanted and went wherever we would. But more joined us than fled from us, and for a while at least, we were free of princes. And I will maintain, to death and beyond, that those who condemn us are themselves murderers and thieves greater than we are, and no amount of law and heritage will change that.'

She opened her mouth for a scathing rebuke, but the words did not come to her. *They are criminals going to their just punishment,* she assured herself, but abruptly she had no stomach left for taunting them.

'When the time comes, I'll look for a sharp blade and a quick end,' Dal Arche stated. 'We're owed that much, I think.'

She nodded, thrown off balance but not sure why. Inside her head, her mantra whirled: *I love Alain. Alain is a prince. Alain is virtuous, as a prince should be.* And always at the back of that was the knowledge that Alain *must* be virtuous, because Salma had been virtuous. But Salma had been removed from her grasp by his Butterfly lover, and then by death, and so Alain was what she had, and he *must* be as much the man as Salma was. She would not countenance any other option.

The brigands were all staring at her, and she was aware of having stood in silence at the pit's edge for too long. She turned quickly and stalked away, hoping that such an exit would seem part of her disdain for them, yet all the while wondering what part of her thoughts had been readable in her face.

Castle Leose was busier now than she had ever seen it, for Princess Salme Elass was about to hold some grand piece of festivity, calling all and sundry of noble blood to congratulate her on putting down Dal Arche's little insurrection. There seemed to be twice as many servants as was usual, a general summons for itinerant entertainers to amuse the anticipated guests. In the castle's courtyard, Tynisa watched Grasshopper musicians tuning up, whilst their long-legged acrobats leapt and balanced. A troupe of Roach-kinden had appeared, presenting themselves as jugglers and magicians, although it seemed more likely that they were opportunistic wayfarers looking for a free meal. Most disturbing to Tynisa was the trio of dancers apparently brought here at the princess's express command. They did not practise out in public view, nor did they mingle with their peers, instead clustering together out of the way in a corner that would be shadowed if they had not brought their own light to it. Tynisa had only ever seen one Butterfly in her life, but the woman had been a dancer too, and stirred no fond memories. The mere sight of these shimmering, glowing girls, with their ethereal grace and beauty radiating from every pose and motion, stirred ugly thoughts within her.

When she found Alain again, he was amid a gaggle of other Dragonfly nobles, the same crowd of the young and elegant that had attended the dance – less a few faces like Orian's, that had been claimed by the fighting. Tynisa paused in an archway, looking out across the sun-splashed open garden, where, in the shadow of carefully intertwined trees, these brightly clad aristocrats were laughing at something the prince himself had just said. She could see how their entire society revolved about him; without him they were nothing, and their status and standing could be read in each individual stance, and in the distance they stood from their prince. She saw how the women amongst them desired him, but she knew that it was only for the chance of becoming the lady of Leose after Salme Elass died. The men admired him and envied his power and bloodline.

Tynisa's mind seemed to cast shadows over the gathering, painting their faces in darker colours, poisonous and dangerous: bad influences. *Alain would be better away from this place, not entombed in stone and etiquette, not leeched at by these sycophants.* After all, *she* did not care whether he was prince or pauper, so long as he bore Salma's face. It would make a better man of him if he was removed from all this pointless distraction: just the two of them travelling the world, seeking out any just cause. Perhaps they would end up as Mercers in the service of the Monarch, or fighting the Empire when it inevitably turned its attention westward.

She felt a pressure in her mind that told her she would have to take action soon, just to save him from this wasteful life. Her hand itched for her sword hilt, but she restrained herself. Whilst it seemed likely that such a course as she intended would bring her into fatal conflict with others here, Whitehand and Princess Elass most of all, she must at least try to achieve her ends peaceably. After all, it was possible that Alain was not yet so corrupted by his hangers-on, and that he would come with her willingly. Otherwise she might have to take action, for his own good.

One of the noblewomen had spotted her, and Tynisa noticed the look of disdain on the Dragonfly's face on seeing the Spider-kinden duellist in her tired old arming jacket, in stark contrast to the shimmering hues of the court. Tynisa smiled at her keenly, enjoying the automatic flinch of the other woman's response, then she stepped further out into the courtyard. Her approach caused a small flurry, minute changes of pose and position effecting an arrangement that attempted to exclude her, but failed because none of them would interpose themselves between her and Alain. They could sneer at her all they liked, but their derision remained hollow so long as she could see that they were afraid of her.

Only dare challenge me, she thought, finding that none would even meet her gaze, *and we shall then see who looks down on whom, at the end.*

'Alain,' she said. He had no fear of her, at least, and he put an easy arm about her shoulders, drawing her close to him. It seemed to her that he was equally amused by the way that she unnerved his compatriots. Secure at his side, she gave them all a sharp-edged smile. *See who he chooses, out of all of you. See who he considers his own?*

'Later,' the prince told his followers. 'We'll discuss later.' So dismissed, they drifted away in ones and twos, until he and Tynisa were alone, with only the walls and the cloudless spring sky.

'Discuss?' she enquired, as the two of them found their way past the twined trees to a half-hidden garden beyond, fragrant with herbs and early flowers and the drone of bees.

'Discuss the celebrations of our victory – your victory, my huntress. Everyone wants to demonstrate their loyalty and fealty to my mother, for fear of being overlooked when any rewards are handed out. Everyone wants an estate in Rhael when we retake it.' He grinned at her, that maddening and familiar grin. 'Another opportunity for you to bloody your blade?'

'There is more to life than fighting,' she remarked with raised eyebrows.

His grin intensified. 'As my wicked huntress has already shown me. Still, I'd assumed that blade-work was your first love.'

She did not say, *You are my first love*, but the words were written on her features clearly enough as she faced him. It was true, as well – if one took him for his brother.

The pause between them was a long one, but his smile did not slip. 'Do not fear, for I have claimed you as my own, huntress, and you have served me well. You shall be rewarded as well as any.'

'So tell me,' she pressed, because that pause concerned her and she sensed adverse influence, perhaps his peers or his family trying to take him from her. 'What do you promise me, Alain?'

'Time for that later,' he assured her. 'At our celebration we shall bestow all manner of honours on those who have served us well.'

'I don't want such a promise from the grand family of the Salmae,' she pointed out. 'I want only one from you.'

Still his smile remained constant. 'And you shall have it, in time.' Abruptly he broke away from her. 'But I was summoned some time ago to meet with my mother.' His grimace was wholly unfeigned. 'Forgive me, as your company is sweeter by far, but duty is duty.'

She watched him as he left: a flash of wings and a flutter of silk robes, and he was gone in a way she could never follow.

There was a small cold stone suddenly in her heart. *They are taking him from me.* She did not want to act against the Salmae. It seemed absurd, in the face of her recent words to the captive brigands, that she should be contemplating her own insurrection. Still, she could see what was right and what was wrong, and since the hunt she had never been so sure of her judgement. The world was writ in black and white for her now. *I will have to save him from himself* seemed like an inescapable conclusion.

Exiting by way of the twisted trees, she found herself come face to face with Lisan Dea's severe features, as though the woman had been lying in wait for her.

‘What do you want?’ Tynisa demanded. The surprise had put her sword in her hand instantly.

‘Please recollect that this is my lady’s castle, of which I am seneschal and chief among her servants.’ Despite the woman’s calm tone, the reprimand stung, and Tynisa took a step back, her blade in its scabbard once again. The steward nodded at this concession, and continued. ‘Your part-sister Maker Cheerwell sends word. She has gone to the Turncoat’s home, to be with her travelling companions, and she asks that you join her there. I understand there is some manner of ceremony or ritual that she wishes to carry out – something from your homeland, perhaps?’

‘A ceremony?’ Tynisa blinked at that, wondering if Che intended to stage a one-woman re-enactment of the opening of the Amphiophos or something. The sheer banality of this, and the thought of foolish, amiable Che, brought her out of her reverie, pushing away those thoughts of blood and honour that seemed to cling to her ever closer these days.

‘Perhaps I did not understand her.’ Lisan Dea shrugged bony shoulders. ‘Still, she was very insistent about wishing to speak with you there.’

And leave Alain? was the first thought that came to her, but some rebellious part of her wanted to seize this opportunity to absent herself, even for a brief while, because otherwise she would have to take action here, and she could feel the repercussions of that looming in her near future like a thunderhead. Today’s Tynisa, steeled with newfound purpose, did not shy from that necessity, but some part of the woman she had been until recently was trying to pull away.

But, no, Alain always came first.

A moment later came a recollection of who ‘the Turncoat’ was, and her stomach lurched. *Che is with Gaved*? Che was with the Wasp who had witnessed Achaeos’s deadly wounding at her hands. He would surely poison her against Tynisa, tell the impressionable Beetle . . . tell her . . .

Tell her the truth.

It was surprising just how great was the feeling of horror that now gripped her, welling up from a time past when she had still felt guilt and grief. Che, poor Che, her sister . . . her awkward, endearingly clumsy playmate. It took her wholly by surprise that having Che finally turned against her, that last door into her old life closed . . . it suddenly mattered more than Alain. She could not bear Che to think badly of her.

The spined, rigid part of her twisted in her grip for a moment and then settled into a new groove. There was an easy way out of this. Kill Gaved. Kill Gaved and Sef, and the problem would die with them.

Thirty-Six

Gaved had not been happy with the news.

'You've called her here – to my house?' he demanded. Che and Maure had come upon the three Wasp-kinden expatriates sharing a jar of wine and reminiscing about who could say what. From the voices heard as she approached, Varmen had been doing most of the talking.

'I needed to get her away from the castle. There was not a chance that we could accomplish anything with the Salmae and their people listening at every door,' Che protested.

'What do you possibly expect to accomplish? That woman's mad, dangerous and mad,' Gaved said flatly. 'She was shaky enough when I ran into her at Siriell's Town but, believe me, something changed her over winter. You've no idea how difficult it was watching out for her during that last scrap with the bandits, because I had to make cursed sure I was well out of her reach at every moment. I know I'm on her list, Beetle. I could see that clear enough.'

'Yes, something did happen over winter,' Che confirmed, solemnly enough to quieten him. 'I won't try and explain what, because you'll neither believe nor understand it . . .' She broke off as someone entered the house, sliding aside the door panel. It was just Sef, and the Spider-kinden woman gazed at them curiously.

'They're bringing that killer here,' Gaved informed her darkly.

Sef cocked her head at Che. They had never met before, but the Beetle girl had heard the stories of her remarkable origins. Out here in the Commonweal, she seemed no more than just a young Spider-kinden with unusually pale skin.

'Ask her why,' Gaved prompted. 'She won't tell me. Apparently I won't understand.' The burn scar on his chin had flushed dark.

'She is possessed. A ghost is haunting her, and it prompts her to act in the way she does,' Che explained. The words produced a perfect silence, and she could almost imagine receding ripples, as though she had thrown a stone into a pool.

Gaved's face had screwed up in disbelief, but the other two Wasps silenced his protest. It was not that Thalric and Varmen were nodding along with what had been said, exactly, but they were not exactly jumping in with objections, either.

'Nonsense,' snapped Gaved at last. 'Come on, there's nothing like that in the world.'

'Don't look at me. Nothing to do with me,' said Varmen, shrugging easily. 'The girl thinks it means something. None of my business.' He gave a smile at Maure, who returned it.

'Thalric,' Gaved prompted, 'you're piss-damned Rekef, or you were. You must know this is nonsense.'

Che met Thalric's gaze, wondering if he was revisiting their shared adventure beneath Khanaphes, or perhaps thinking about the Wasp Empress's secret practices. He did not believe, she knew, but even so . . .

'I cannot say for sure that these things are fictions,' he pronounced at last. 'I cannot explain so many of the things I myself have seen. I don't say there's no natural explanation, only that I cannot explain them. I think I'm better off not knowing the truth. I leave that for those better qualified.' He nodded at Che. 'But to suggest that Tynisa Maker is a dangerous lunatic, well, no great change there. I have few fond memories of her, even from before this supposed change overtook her. To bring her here is to invite disaster.'

'Maure and I will ensure that she does no harm.'

'Absolutely not. Not under my roof. You're not risking me and mine,' Gaved snapped. 'You can go back to the cursed Lowlands and get on with your bloody business there . . .' He tailed off, because Sef had put a hand on his arm.

'There *are* ghosts,' she said. 'I have seen them in the deep water, and I have seen them here.'

Gaved bared his teeth at her, but that simple laying of a hand on his arm had drained the anger out of him.

'Tell me this,' Che put in, 'when you saw her last, did she not remind you of Tisamon?'

The Wasp looked at her blankly for a moment, as if reluctant to admit it, but then he nodded. 'Perhaps, a little. But there are reasons . . .'

'Of course, there always are,' Che confirmed.

'We will go to Prince Lowre Cean,' Sef declared confidently. 'He cares about the Maker girl enough, so he will understand. He will believe.'

'Abandon our own house?' Gaved demanded.

'It is a house. It will still be here after they are all gone,' Sef explained reasonably. 'And you must all come, all of you.' Her gesture took in the three Wasps.

'Now hold on—' started Thalric, but Che cut him off.

'She's right, best that you're not here. As you said, you and Tynisa have a good deal of history, and besides, Wasp-kinden are not what we need to confront her with. It would be too good an excuse for her to give in to temptation and draw her sword.'

'Not that she ever needed much of an excuse,' Thalric recalled sourly.

'Quite,' Che agreed. 'Thalric, please.'

Thalric nodded tiredly. 'When she saw the two of us off in Collegium, setting off for Tharn during the war, she was ready to swear all manner of oaths that she would come and kill me if anything happened to you, Che.'

She eyed him wordlessly, but with a single nod.

'Then I swear this: if she harms you – whether in her madness or her sanity – then I will hunt her down, you understand? If she so much as draws a bead of your blood, then I will see her die in flames.' He was abruptly once more the merciless spymaster, the killer of children, the fatal hand of the Empire, and it was for *her,* for Che alone, that he would become such a thing again. The feeling of power, having him on her side, shocked her.

'She won't hurt me,' Che did her best to assure him.

His expression held no confidence in that, and his threat, his promise, still hung in the air as Varmen said, 'Well, then, who's this fellow we're to impose ourselves on? Prince Lousy, was it, you said?'

'Lowre Cean,' Gaved said quietly. 'Prince-Major Lowre Cean.' He gave the name some weight, and waited for the other Wasps to catch up.

Thalric was ahead of Varmen, but it was plain that the two of them registered the name.

'You can't mean their general?'

'Yes, Thalric,' Gaved confirmed, 'none other.'

'The man who crushed the . . .?' Thalric's words tailed off, his eyes drawn inexorably to Varmen. 'The man who crushed the Sixth at Masaki.'

'Pride of the Sixth,' the big Wasp echoed. For a moment the strange pensive expression taking up unfamiliar residence on his face was enough to silence the rest of them. 'Oh, yes, let's go visiting. Why not?'

Gaved shot him a dangerous look. 'He's well liked, loved even. Don't get any ideas.'

'I'm not noted for them,' Varmen replied. 'What, you think I'm going to go take vengeance on him for a whole army? If I was going to do that, I'd dig up our old General Haken and spit on his corpse, I would. But I want to see this fellow. I want to see the face of the man behind Masaki. I knew there was a reason for me to come so far, and maybe that's it.'

*

When Maure announced, without warning, that the ghost was nearing, presumably with Tynisa in thrall and in tow, Che opened the external panels of the house, so that her sister would see it as an invitation. Oh, she would be suspicious, of course, and it would not take Tisamon's shade to prompt that, but she would enter nonetheless.

Inside, Maure had already made her preparations. A circle was drawn on the floor in bone ash and charcoal, and she had hung lanterns in each corner of the inner room, each housing a constellation of fireflies within. She had marked out the circle with symbols that were not letters but pictograms, which looked frighteningly familiar to Che. Testing the water, she asked the necromancer, 'What do they say?'

'Say?' Maure shrugged. 'They don't say anything. They're just the warding marks that we use, passed down from teacher to pupil, generation to generation.'

Che nodded dully, while interpreting, *By Ephisemnas Queen of the Veiled Night I adjure you. By Telephian the Wise, Lord of the Seven Guards, I stay your hand. By . . .* On and on, a rote of power rooted solely in the terror of ancient names and titles, but she could sense that power there. *First the castle at Leose, and now this. How far did the reach of the Masters of Khanaphes stretch, in their heyday?*

There was incense too, little smoking stacks of it on leaves floating in brass bowls of snowmelt water, and also sprigs of herbs tied to the eaves. Maure caught Che's look and nodded grimly. 'I know, you're wondering which of it works and which doesn't, hm? Well, who can say, but with this visitor I'm not minding to leave any of it out.' Around the edge of the circle, she sprinkled a trail of white powder, and Che wondered if it was ordinary salt.

'And what will this accomplish?' she asked.

'Assuming any of it has any staying power at all, it will prevent the ghost from simply striking me dead.'

Che blinked. 'He can do that? Himself?'

'No, but your girl there has a sword, so he only has to put the idea in her head. From Gaved's evidence, she's not exactly inhibited in that way.'

I cannot deny it. Che nodded unhappily. And then Tynisa came stalking into the room, with drawn sword.

She stopped, as though having struck a wall, and stared about her. 'Oh, my word, what's this?' she got out, with a choking sound, and a moment later Che realized that she was laughing.

'Tynisa,' she greeted her sister, feeling a slight tension as she did so. *For names have power.* 'This is Maure, a friend. She and I are conducting . . . an experiment. I want you to join us for it.'

Tynisa eyed the paraphernalia with contempt, and moved to kick out at one of the bowls, but something stopped her, clearly to her own surprise. 'You called me out here just for this?' Her eyes narrowed. 'Where are Gaved and his woman?'

'Away,' Che said firmly, seeing in that instant how wise it had been to ensure that the Wasps were absent. 'Sit down, please.'

'More ghosts?' Tynisa asked her mockingly.

'Possibly. Will you sit?'

The Spider girl shook her head, her expression pitying, and she seemed about to turn and leave when Maure said, 'Do you not know me, Tynisa? Have you not seen me before?'

'No.' But Tynisa frowned. 'Have I?' Her sword, which had been hanging loose by her side, was abruptly levelled across the circle, directed at Maure's heart. For a moment Tynisa went very still, save that Che could see a slight tremble in her, as though she was fighting with her own body. 'What . . .?' she got out, 'I should . . .'

'You want to kill me,' Maure observed.

'No, why would I want to . . .?' Tynisa was staring at her own arm, which seemed to be warring both with the rest of her and with the rapier itself. At last, with a great effort of will, she rammed the weapon home in its scabbard. 'What's going on?' she demanded, with a tremor to her voice.

'Sit down, please,' Che repeated, and Tynisa did so, looking all of a sudden uncertain.

'Tell me what's going on,' she asked, with a hint of pleading in her voice.

'Maure is going to perform a ritual,' Che explained. 'A ritual to try and call up certain ghosts that are near to us. You and I have both lost loved ones. We . . . the Inapt believe that there may be traces, shadows of the dead left in the world. Wouldn't you want to speak to them?'

'No,' said Tynisa hollowly, but she did not get up. 'Che, I have seen . . . On my journey to this place, I've had them at my elbow every day. Just in my own mind, but that's enough ghost for me. I've only recently got rid of them, so . . . even if it was possible, I wouldn't want to see them again.'

'Even if they could then let you go? Give you their blessing?' Che pressed. She was not sure whether she was now speaking for Tynisa's benefit or her own.

For a long while Tynisa stared into the circle sketched in ash and charcoal. 'You're mad,' she said at last, but her voice had a plaintive tone. 'This woman's led you on. How much money did you give her?'

'Tynisa—'

'But perform your nonsense. Go on, get it over with. I'll sit here and listen. Why not?'

Che nodded, somewhat mollified. 'Maure, would you . . .?'

'You must think of him, both of you. Draw into your minds all your recollections, the precise shape of him, the shadow he cast on the world.' She closed her eyes and began visibly steeling herself. Che had expected incantations, mystic words, a high-blown patter to go with all the props and clutter that the woman had assembled here, but there was none of that, simply a name.

'Tisamon.' It was dropped like a stone into a well, and

although the walls around them were not capable of it, Che was sure that there was an echo.

'Tisamon,' Maure repeated. 'Tisamon, I name you—' names signifying power to the old Inapt kinden. The air within that central room twanged with tension, the incense smoke coiling but refusing to rise properly. In the lanterns, the fireflies seemed to spell out strange sigils with their lights.

The beating of rain on the sloped roof above them was sudden enough to make Che start, an abruptly descending hiss as the skies broke open, soon joined by the sound of a miniature waterfall as the water began sheeting off the roof's lower edge. Not the thunderstorm that traditionally belonged to this kind of venture, but a moderate shower remarkable only for the timing of its onset.

'Tisamon,' Maure repeated, over the sound of it. 'Come forth and speak your piece. You have grievances, let us hear them. Speak to us, Tisamon.'

But there was nothing. No shadowy figure stepped into the circle. No voice croaked from beyond the grave. There was no sign that the influence that had laid its hand on Tynisa would unmask itself.

'What's wrong?' Che demanded. 'Make it come out.'

'Che . . .?' Tynisa herself looked almost embarrassed.

Maure grimaced. 'It's not so simple. I have never before needed to force a ghost to do anything. Normally they're only too glad to get the chance to speak, to make their demands, to set right old wrongs. Normally they have messages to impart. Believe me, Che, normally I'd have to beat one off with a stick, given this kind of opportunity.'

'But it's here, it's right here.' Che knew it in her heart. She could almost taste the metallic, sour savour of Tisamon in the air. 'Call it out.'

'I've called. It won't answer. It's staying where it wants to be,' Maure explained. 'It doesn't *need* to talk to anyone else.'

'Che, this is ridiculous,' Tynisa said. 'What money has this woman had from you?'

'Listen to me!' Che stood up, ignoring Maure's attempt to hush her. 'I know you're here, Tisamon. I know you're with Tynisa right now. I can practically see you riding her shoulders. Is this what you wanted? Is this what you're reduced to? Come out and face me, will you?'

Only the rain answered her words. No spectre made itself known.

'Che, this isn't funny,' Tynisa remarked after a suitable pause. 'I don't appreciate my father's name being abused like this. If I thought this halfbreed put you up to it, I'd kill her right now, but it seems that you're driving all this nonsense yourself. I know you got hurt in the war, Che, but to resort to *this* . . .?'

Che stared at her, seeing the embodiment of calm reason in Tynisa's face, whilst the invisible shade of Tisamon lurked secure behind her eyes. She had assumed that Maure would haul the ghost out by main magical force. She had thought this must be what the necromancer's work entailed. But now it seemed that the shade could continue simply to squat within Tynisa's mind, like a creeping poison, and they could not touch it.

She looked helplessly about the room until she met Maure's cautious gaze. 'Well then,' she said sickly. 'If not that, then I must find some way myself. Whatever mantle I've been given must be good for something. I'm not done with this.'

'Che—' Tynisa started again, but the Beetle girl made a slashing motion in her direction, prompting an astonished silence.

'Another,' Che instructed Maure. 'Call up another.'

'I need some link, at least. I can't just—'

'His name was Achaeos, a Moth-kinden of Tharn. He was my lover, and he was dealt a wound by Tynisa, before his death,' Che spat it out harshly, ignoring the way her sister flinched from the words. 'Tell me that's not enough.'

'It will do.' Maure grimaced again. 'Achaeos of Tharn, then . . . Achaeos, beloved of Cheerwell Maker.' She closed her eyes again. 'Wherever your spirit resides, whatever still remains of it, come forth. Here stands your lover, Achaeos. Surely you must desire some words with her?'

Che sought within her mind, trying to piece together a complete picture of the man she had known. But it was like stepping out over a yawning chasm, because she now found that she was barely able to. For so long after his death she had borne her grief, had been tormented by dreams, had even thought that his angry ghost was haunting her. The actual man himself, the sum of the feelings she had invested in him, had receded under the weight of those mostly self-imposed torments. So now that she came to find him again, the surviving impressions were distant and cold.

But it must be enough. It will be enough. Achaeos!

Maure kept shaking her head, though. 'There is nothing.'

'Call him again.'

'You don't understand, Che. There is nothing.' When it was plain to her that Che genuinely did not understand, she elaborated, 'When I called on the Mantis, I felt the tug, a connection, even though he would not come forth. With this Achaeos, there is nothing. No touch, no contact . . . no ghost.'

Che stared at her. 'What do you mean?' she asked tightly.

'I'm sorry, Che. No ghost. Whatever happened to him, he's left nothing behind. Either some greater force has claimed him, or he has passed beyond, without so much as a scrap of him remaining. That's rare, in fact, very rare, but it can happen.'

Che felt her hands begin to shake. 'Some greater force . . .' she managed to get out. As he had died, Achaeos had been in communion with the cursed Mantis spirits of the Darakyon, channelling their power into a grand ritual taking place in Tharn. Che had been helping him, lending what strength she could. She had felt the cold death sent by the Darakyon surge down the link, and she had known at once when Achaeos had died, the connection between them severed as if by a knife.

And they got him, and then the Shadow Box was sundered, and they ceased to be – and whatever was left of Achaeos went with them, scattered to the four winds.

No last reconciliation. No apologies. No parting words. No closing of the wound. No final blessing that would let her live her life again without all the grief.

Only then did Che realize how she had staked far more on that, emotionally, than on trying to draw the poisoned dart of Tisamon out of Tynisa's mind. Her intentions had become hopelessly tangled and self-involved.

She glanced from Maure to Tynisa, as though looking for an escape.

'Che, listen to me,' her sister said patiently. 'None of this is real. I understand why you've resorted to it, but you've got to face the real world.' Confronting that bland scepticism, Che now almost believed her. After all, how much easier life would be if everything, from Khanaphes onwards, had been only a bad dream?

But she knew it was real, and she knew that if Maure could not so much as detect a loose thread of Achaeos, then the Darakyon had got him, and that was that.

And, with that revelation, she could not stay in the incense-heavy air of the claustrophobic room, so she fumbled a panel aside and dashed out into the rain, unable to face either of the other women any more.

Maure was on her feet instantly, chasing after Che. It was not clear whether it was to comfort the Beetle girl or because, for all her words and wards, the mystic did not feel safe close to Tynisa's rapier without Che there to protect her.

Tynisa shook her head, listening to the rain. Che was out there getting wet, but experience had told her that running around after her sister, once the girl got upset, achieved nothing. Che was best left to herself to calm down, then come back embarrassed at whatever outburst she had been provoked into. And the best medicine after that would be to act as though nothing had happened, and thus spare the girl's blushes. Still, Maure obviously had not known Che long enough to learn that lesson. Now that it seemed the mummery was over for the evening, Tynisa decided to wait out the worst of the rain under Gaved's roof, and then set off on the long road back for Leose. She had unfinished business there, for certain.

And such foolishness, she considered. *Still, Che is my sister, in fact if not in kinden. She called and I came, despite this waste of my time. Nobody can ask more of me than that.*

She stood up and leant over the circle, trying to fathom how people could imagine that such marks on the ground could have any power in the real world.

Tynisa . . .

The world seemed to lurch around her. Her name whispered, at the very edge of hearing. For a moment she felt a tide of fear rising up in her, primal and unreasoning, and tainted by memories that she had cast off or locked away. *But no, I do not believe . . .*

Tynisa . . . have I found you? It is so hard to tell.

Although the voice came from everywhere and nowhere, and within her, she conceived the feeling that someone stood behind her . . . someone familiar.

There is a door here half open, the voice whispered, still coming from just beside her, and yet far, far away. *I see you only as in twilight, but it is you, is it not?*

The room seemed darker than before, the fireflies no longer lighting anything but themselves, the incense smouldering into ash. The rain outside had blotted out the sun and covered the entire house in shadow.

She swallowed. *If I speak, I will admit to hearing it. I must not answer it.* But she knew that voice now, beyond all doubt, and she could not stop herself from saying, 'Salma.'

It is you, then, truly? But who else would venture so far to call on me?

'I'd have thought your cursed Butterfly woman, if she cared.'

The vindictive words were out of Tynisa's mouth before she could stop them, and she did not know now whether she was more afraid that he would speak to her again, or that she might have driven him away. In her mind resonated the comforting mantra: *All is not lost, I may simply be mad. I saw him at my elbow before, so why not hear his voice now?* But that faint voice, barely audible over the rain, was still something vastly more real than any of her hallucinations had been.

Her kinden's magic is of light, not these shadows, came his response to her outburst. The voice sounded fondly amused, and that, more than anything else, broke her reserve.

'Salma . . .' And she turned, but he was not there. 'Salma, speak to me, tell me . . . Tell me how to help you.'

Help? Ah, I need no help now. Now that you have called me.

'But you weren't called. She called for Tisamon, then for Achaeos, and neither of them came.'

But you called me, Tynisa. Not the mystic. You.

His hand settled on her shoulder, a comforting and familiar pressure that scared her half to death. Again he was behind her, and she could feel his breath on the nape of her neck.

'You're dead,' she got out, her voice barely more substantial than his. 'You know you're dead.'

It seemed likely, he agreed wistfully. *But you live, so we can't have done so badly.*

'They . . .' She was helplessly reminded of her audience with Felipe Shah, when recounting Salma's history for her friend's mentor. 'They named a town after you. Your followers built it, after . . . Please let me see you, Salma.'

I cannot. Tynisa, I have to go. I've stayed so long, this shadow of me, just for this purpose only.

'For what? Why do this at all, if you just have to go again?' she hissed.

Because of you. Because we parted badly. Because I never did get to speak to you again, before . . . She came between us, I know, and I loved her, but do not think I did not love you also. In all the world, against the tide of death, this scrap of me stays on to ask your forgiveness, and to say goodbye.

'That's cruel.' The words barely emerged. She could not stop herself reaching out for his hand, and when she touched it, invisible as it was, she felt a living warmth there. All she needed to do was turn around. She could practically see him now at the edge of her vision. 'Please, Salma.'

You've met my brother. The words sounded less fond now, and she could only nod, thinking, *What now? Am I betraying you with Alain, is that what you mean?*

She heard him sigh, the breath rippling her hair. *Do not return to Leose, Tynisa, please. Leave there and never look back.*

'Salma, I . . .' She could not have said this before any other listener. 'I've nothing left now. Too much blood on my hands, too little reason left to live. I've nothing else. If you have to go, show me how to come with you, please.'

Not yet, not soon either – or so I hope. I do not know the country I shall be travelling to, but if it were pleasant, why would the wisest of us take such pains to stave it off. Do not wish that, Tynisa. Bid me a good journey, and let me go.

A thousand protests came to her then, but she felt a clarity of mind that she had not known in a long time. *And in a way it does not matter if I am mad or not.*

'I love you, Salma,' she told him – or perhaps her memory of him. 'But you know that. You cannot ask me to forgive you for having loved another woman, or for dying as you did. But, even so, because I love you, I forgive you it all. Go in peace.' Her voice was shaking almost too much for her to form the words now. 'Go with my love. And when you get where you're going, wait for me. I'll be following along. There's no place so dark we can't face it together, just like old times.'

She felt him lean closer, and then his lips brushed her cheek. The hand beneath her own was cooling rapidly, and she now realized that she held only a fold of cloth from her cloak there, and the only sound was the rain, and she stood alone in Gaved's inner room, and the incense had stopped smouldering. Inside, she felt like a tower of glass that one knock could shatter into a thousand pieces.

The rain seemed to be passing. Indeed, as she listened, it pattered to a halt almost as suddenly as it had begun, leaving only a sporadic dripping from the eaves.

Avoid Leose? she wondered. *But what, then?* The answer came clearly for once: *Go with Che, wherever she went*, for her sister surely needed her help. Return to Stenwold in Collegium, for a reconciliation. Visit Princep Salmae even, for she had never gone there and felt strong enough to try, now.

She stepped out of the house, away from the incense and the painted signs, and abruptly something seemed to seize her in a grip of iron that made her gasp.

She could not walk away from Leose, it told her. She had unfinished business there. She had made a vow to win Alain, and such vows were inviolable, no matter how much blood was shed over them. That was the Mantis way. That was her way, too. There was no avoiding it.

She fought furiously for a moment, clutching for her free will, for any mastery of her own fate, but that rigid hand was still guiding her, steering an inexorable course. She had a role yet to play in the Tragic History of Tynisa Maker. The closing act was about to begin and her story would be as glorious and terrible as all Mantis-kinden stories were. Salme Alain was waiting for her.

She saw Che and Maure a short distance away, only now noticing her, and for a moment she reached out towards them despairingly, as though drowning.

Then she was marching away towards her tethered horse, heading for Leose and for her destiny.

Thirty-Seven

'Pride of the Sixth,' pronounced Lowre Cean carefully. 'Oh, yes, I remember that.'

'You were at Masaki, sir?' Varmen asked him, sipping at the kadith the old man had poured. They were sitting, not in some formal audience hall, but in a little wood-carving workshop, with curls of sawdust underfoot and, on shelves to either side, ranks of miniature figures that the prince himself had whittled: peasants, craftsmen, dancers, all compact and stylized and yet bursting with frozen energy.

'Some way from the front lines,' Cean admitted. 'My son led the charge.' He was watching the Wasp-kinden carefully. 'And you were not there?'

Varmen only nodded.

'Of course you were not. The Imperial Sentinels never run. They fight to the last. *Can't* run, in all that armour, I'd imagine. But Darien, my son, told me how the centre held, even when all the rest, all the Light Airborne and artificers and support and the like, had been blown aside. They stood and fought to the last man.'

The Wasp grunted. 'They'd sent some of us off after some scouts that got holed up. We fought, as well. Pair of your nobles tried to flush us out, over and over. We heard from them that the Sixth had gone.'

'I recall hearing about that,' Cean acknowledged. 'You must have been relieved by the Seventh, I think?'

'The Second, sir – the Gears, General Tynan's command. And wasn't that just a joy for us, to be beholden to them? Almost as bad as fighting with the Seventh at Malkan's Stand. That time, I didn't miss the action. Most everyone else of the heavies died. I sometimes think . . .' Abruptly he decided that he had said too much. The old man's mild voice had led him into letting his guard down, and now he stood up rebelliously, feeling tricked and trapped. 'Why have you even let me in here? What if I killed you? We're enemies, after all.'

'Once,' Cean admitted. He had not moved or reacted, save to look up. 'But now, years later, we have more in common than you might think. We were both there, after all, and although your army won, perhaps you have more right to hate me, as a commander, than I do to hate you, being just a soldier. Would casting you out of my house bring back a single dead man or woman from the war? Would killing me with your sting redeem the fallen Sixth? We are united, Sergeant, by the memories of our dead. That is something we share. You ask me why I let you in, and I ask you why did you come here?'

'Avoiding the crazy Spider-kinden girl,' Varmen explained, but Cean was shaking his head.

'I meant here to the Commonweal. Here to revisit your past and your losses?'

Varmen stared at him stubbornly, but sat back down. 'Seemed like a good idea at the time.'

Cean poured more kadith, watching him with slightly raised eyebrows, but saying nothing.

'Should have died at Masaki, I reckon, sometimes,' Varmen added unwillingly. 'You know how that feels, that one blind bit of chance takes you out of the way of the axe?' Seeing Cean nodding, he went on, 'And at Malkan's Stand, I nearly did. Got a snapbow bolt through me, armour and all. Should have died there, too. After that, the army had no use for me – the

Sentinels were being recalled. No point in all that armour if it couldn't stop the shot. They just cut me off, like I was an embarrassment for surviving. A freak. I kicked about in Helleron some, but I used to dream of the Commonweal, of the Sixth as it used to be, before that useless tinkerer Praeter got put in charge. I used to dream of being holed up with them scouts, and . . . there was a girl, can't even remember her name now. One of your lot, nice voice. I ended up going one on one with her, because I had to buy time for my men. I dream of that a lot. Seemed like my life went downhill from there, really. Now doesn't that sound stupid, eh?'

Cean regarded him solemnly. 'To a Wasp, perhaps, but my own kinden would understand. Mantis-kinden, too. There is a time for all things, especially for people. You and I, our time was then – that year, that month, at the height of our powers. We have neither of us ever been quite who we were then, do you not think?'

Varmen regarded him bleakly, but at last he nodded tiredly. 'Reckon you've got the right of it, sir.'

'We lost our purpose, after that. No matter that the war still had a few years left to run, our great work was done, and all we had left was to preside over our decline in the face of progress. It is a terrible thing to outlive one's destiny.'

'I don't believe in destiny,' Varmen said automatically, and then, 'but, yes.'

'You won't believe in guiding spirits, either,' Lowre Cean decided, 'but in the Commonweal it can happen that a man whose destiny has passed him by may yet find a way to make something of himself. He may find himself taking strange paths, in order to seek out that elusive sense of purpose. Such as a Wasp coming to the Commonweal, perhaps? Who knows?'

'Is that so?' Varmen shrugged.

'You're heading back to Leose, of course?'

'No chance. Won't let us through the doors of that place.'

Lowre Cean sighed. 'Prince Felipe Shah, my old comrade

and friend, has asked me to look after the girl, Tynisa Maker. He believes he owes her a great debt. He also believes that she is travelling into darkness: that she is being led into it. I'm no fortune-teller myself, but he seems to think that she will need friends, and even a poor old man such as myself can sense that there is a storm brewing at Leose. So I think you should gather up your fellows and return there as swiftly as possible.'

'I owe the girl nothing,' Varmen challenged. 'Why should I?'

'Her name was Felipe Daless,' declared Lowre Cean, looking the Wasp right in the eye. 'She was Felipe Shah's daughter.'

Varmen could only stare at him. 'What did you . . .? How could you even . . .?'

'I could baffle you with talk of mind-reading and magic now, could I not, Sergeant? But it was as simple as this: I knew her, and she told me of a duel with a Wasp Sentinel – of how you held her and her people off until more soldiers came to your rescue. It must have been you, for I doubt such events happened twice during all the war. And here you are – and no doubt you'll say you were drawn here by blind coincidence.'

Varmen's expression had become very fixed.

'She bore you no ill will. I even think she respected you,' Cean continued. 'The duel of champions is a proud Commonwealer tradition, after all, and she had not expected it in an Imperial.'

Still Varmen said nothing, but Lowre Cean waited for him to conquer his internal demons to finally ask, 'What happened to her?'

The old man's smile was sad. 'She died, of course. Just one more casualty of the war.' He did not say, *your people's war*, nor did his gaze accuse. His expression suggested, instead, that they all of them were victims of the same vast and unthinking tormentor. 'I envy you your unbelief, Sergeant, for I *do* believe in fate, and I have seen enough of its workings to know that it does not have our best interests at heart. Will you help the girl, Tynisa Maker?'

'Did he know?' Varmen asked hoarsely. 'I spoke with the man . . . with your Prince Felipe. Did he *know*?'

'I would not be at all surprised,' Lowre Cean stated.

'Bastard,' said Varmen vaguely, and then, 'And yes. Yes, I will.'

But when Tynisa returned to Leose, Alain was gone, and instead she found herself summoned to meet Salme Elass. The princess received her in the same formal room as when she had first recruited Tynisa to her cause, where servants set out kadith and sweet cakes for them, everything in elaborate order. Elass finished writing something on a scroll laid out before her, her calligraphy elegant and unhurried, whilst Tynisa fidgeted and shuffled.

'I have need of you, you must be aware.' The scroll was finished with, apparently, for Elass handed it to a new servant whilst yet another bore away the pen and ink.

Tynisa said nothing, which the princess apparently took for acceptance.

'When I host my fealtor nobles, when they come to partake of our celebrations, they must see you here – especially those who were lukewarm in sending aid. They must see the fabled Spider Weaponsmaster. Perhaps you could challenge some of their champions? Or give some display of your skill, certainly. It shall be part of the entertainment.'

An ugly scene was called glaringly into Tynisa's mind's eye: an arena, tiered seats packed with baying Wasps. Her father.

'Where is Alain?' she asked quietly.

Elass made a dismissive snort. 'He was getting fractious penned up here, so I gave him an entourage and sent him off to chivvy my guests along.' She eyed Tynisa, calculating. 'He will be back before long.'

'Before long' is unacceptable. With a start Tynisa realized that she had reached the end of her patience with the games of Salme Elass. Whilst they helped her towards her prize, giving

her an opportunity to display her skill and to woo Alain, then she had played along at being the obedient tool of the Salmae. She had accomplished her purpose now. She had Alain. He had lain with her. He was *hers*. She did not need to waste her time with this woman any more. Her duty was to secure Alain and take him somewhere he could become the man she wanted him to be. Suon Ren, perhaps? After all, there was precedent.

A distant part of her, the part that had talked to Lowre Cean and listened to Salma's ghost, was aware that she was utterly out of control now, and that Salme Elass had no idea of this. The face that Tynisa showed the world was still unblemished. All the cracks – so many cracks – were still on the inside.

'While you wait, I want you to report to my armourer,' Elass told her. 'It is fit that you dress like a warrior of the Commonweal. There is no time to fashion something to your measurements, but no doubt the castle has some spare pieces that may serve. You should be seen wearing my colours: the red and blue and gold.'

And Tynisa smiled quite naturally, knowing that she would never put on that yoke, and she sought out Lisan Dea as soon as the princess had finished making her doomed plans.

The steward was busily overseeing the castle's servants in frenzied preparations for the festivities to come. Once she saw Tynisa, however, she perhaps read the girl better than her mistress did, for she sent the remaining attendants away and retreated into a storeroom where they might not be overheard.

Tynisa wasted no time. 'Where is Alain?' she demanded. 'You know all the comings and goings of this place. Where has he gone?'

The Grasshopper-kinden stared down at her with a curious fascination. 'And am I now obliged to answer to you?'

Tynisa's hand was at her sword-hilt. 'Or else I will kill you. I will cut you until you tell me, and then I will kill you. If you tell me now then you will live, but only then.'

'Have we come this far?' the steward wondered, showing no

fear. 'Is your metamorphosis complete, now? Just a killer and nothing else?'

'I want Alain. Tell me.' Suddenly Tynisa scowled. 'Oh, I know, you look down on me because I'm not part of your precious nobility. You've always tried to stand between us two. You think you're protecting him.'

'Oh, not him,' Lisan Dea corrected her. 'But perhaps that which I thought I was protecting has already been corrupted. Perhaps there is no reason for me to stand between the pair of you any more.' Abruptly the seneschal's reserve disintegrated, and something welled up from behind her broken mask that made Tynisa flinch, savage as she was. Behind the meticulous steward there was something raw and vicious, something that must have been festering impotently a long time. 'Now you've shown what you really are, why should I try to prevent such a blessed union? Alain's gone west, just a day ago, with half a dozen attendants and a couple of entertainers. They'll not have made much time, so you could catch them by tonight, if you ride hard.'

For a moment Tynisa stared with horrified fascination at the vitriol writ large across the woman's face. Then her iron purpose reasserted itself: no matter what the woman's motives, Tynisa knew what she needed to know.

She was going to find Alain. She was going to take what was hers.

'Gone west,' had been so vague that it should have taken her longer than a day to find Alain's party, but whatever had given her skill enough to ride a horse had enabled her to find a trail, too. The Commonweal had few roads, and her eyes soon picked out a track that looked recently used, and by a medium-sized party making no efforts to hide their progress. Indeed, casting her gaze across the ground was just like reading a book, a library of information set out for her. She was astonished that she had never noticed such evidence before.

She pushed her horse to the limit, knowing she had a bad reputation amongst the grooms of Leose, after killing a half-dozen of the beasts during the war with the brigands, but then the dumb animals were there to serve. She could not understand how anyone could get too attached to them. A handful of dead mounts was a small price to pay for the destruction of Salme Elass's enemies.

Alain would not be expecting her, of course, and she tried to imagine the look on his face. He would be glad to see her, and discover that she had come to take him away from the confines and restrictions of Leose. His retinue might not be so pleased, of course. They would have their instructions from the princess, so they would resist.

She considered simply killing them all, but suspected Alain might not take kindly to that and, besides, it seemed inelegant, like a prostitution of her skills. Better that she stalked them, then took Alain from them without their noticing. That would satisfy her more. And if they gave chase, well . . .

At the back of her mind were pangs of doubt that she had to quell from time to time. *What would Che think? What about the things Salma said? Surely this is not what I meant?* But she was now in the grip of a fierce and borrowed certainty: qualms could not touch her.

Evening had drawn on, and her quarry obliged her by revealing its location with a campfire, which made everything so much easier. Of course, the Dragonfly-kinden could see well in the dark but, huddled close about their fire, they would be spoiling their own night-vision. There would be sentries, of course, in case some scraps of the brigand army remained, but they would not notice Tynisa.

Their camp was situated in a hollow excavated into a wooded hillside, deep enough to retain the heat and stave off the cold. No doubt this was a place maintained by the local farmers and herders for just such a purpose. She approached sideways on, slipping from tree to tree, eyes picking out the individual members of Alain's escort against the blaze.

She crept close, closer than was wise, but she might as well have already cut out all their eyes. The armoured Mercers sat with the warmth of the fire at their backs and stared bleakly out into the darkness, unhappily waiting out the chill of the night with their breath pluming. A half-dozen others were huddled up close to the flames, and she picked out faces, builds, trying to identify her man. At the last she was forced to steal all around the site and approach it from further up the hillside, where the trees were denser, away from the main gaze of the watchmen. Their lax vigilance eventually allowed her to come all the way into camp, to stand in silence amongst them and mark each face. *I could kill them all right now*, and for a moment it was all she could manage to simply stand there without doing so. *They deserve it for such poor service. Alain merits better followers*. But her sword kept to its scabbard, and she had another matter to occupy her mind. Alain himself was not there.

The firelight let her read the ground, and she saw a recent scuffed track heading up the hillside. No doubt Alain, too, was sick of his idle retinue and had taken himself away from them. Perhaps he was even waiting for her somewhere. She pictured him in the moonlight, standing tall between the trees, smiling a greeting. And they would leave this place and make their own life, and to the pits with the Salmae and the Makers both. His princely virtue, her mastery and skill: together they would hunt down bandits and kill the enemies of the Monarch, he shorn of the ambitions of his mother, herself rid of the concerns of her sister. It would be perfect.

She left the camp, following his trail, each step a study in quietness, until she heard him up ahead.

He seemed to be murmuring to himself, which surprised her. She could just make him out, a crouching form in the darkness, hardly touched by the moon. And, yet, was there not a dim radiance there, from beneath him, that picked out his form in silhouette?

She waited until she was almost on his heels before she spoke.

'Alain?'

He turned with a start. And she saw.

In that first moment she did not take in how the girl's clothes were torn, nor the look of despair on her face. She saw only that Alain had been crouched over one of the Butterfly-kinden dancers, his robes open down the front, his abruptly shrinking genitals exposed to the cold night air.

Thirty-Eight

'Beheading, isn't it, in the Commonweal?' the Spider-kinden Avaris asked.

'Beheading is just for their own, nice and quick and dignified. They'll weight our heels and string us up,' said one of the Dragonfly-kinden, a hard-faced woman named Feass, dropping down from her ninth inspection of the grille. No flaw in its workmanship had turned up yet. The weights still pinned it down at each corner, and the brigands were still securely imprisoned in the dungeon pit of Leose.

'Just count yourself lucky you're on this side of the border,' Mordrec the Wasp growled. 'They'd use crossed pikes in the Empire, and in the Principalities, too.'

'I always wondered about that,' Feass said, frowning. 'I mean, do they just leave you to starve, after tying you to the pikes? What's to stop someone coming to cut you free?'

Mordrec gave her an odd look. 'They don't *tie* you to the pikes. They shove the pissing things in under your ribs, so the point of the pike goes right through your body into your arm on the other side, like so.' He made a violent gesture for emphasis. 'If they know what they're doing – and it's a valued skill, where I come from – then you hang there dying slowly for hours.'

'Lovely relatives you have,' Avaris remarked drily.

'And things are better in the Spiderlands?' Mordrec challenged.

'Oh at least we have the benefit of variety. Hanging's customary, but the local magistrate has free rein, you see. Anything goes: flayed alive, dismembered by machines, tied between four beetles and pulled apart, fed to the ant-lion, eaten alive by maggots, you name it. I once heard of a woman who had a wasp sting her – not your kind, just a little hand-sized one. Then, when they let her go, she thought she was the luckiest criminal in the Spiderlands. Of course a week later the grub starts eating her from the inside, and she's history. So don't you come your crossed pikes with me. We invented being cruel bastards. Your lot are just amateurs.'

'You are so full of lies, you probably piss them,' Mordrec retorted, but without much fire.

'Have you not got some other topic of conversation?' Dal complained, after that.

'Of course, surely. So, what were you thinking of doing tomorrow, anyone? Because if the weather lasts I thought I'd go to the *theatre*,' Avaris said, slumping down tiredly. 'Or maybe a brothel, if it rains. I know this lovely place in Helleron, the Veil. You should come along. They cater for all tastes.'

'Shut up,' Dal told him sharply.

'Well you're the one who wanted to talk—'

'No, shut up. We're not alone.'

That silenced them all, and they peered upward into the gloom. There was just a single torch up there, shedding precious little light.

'Is it time?' Mordrec asked softly.

'It's night,' stammered Avaris. 'They'll make it public. Won't kill us at night.'

'*Quiet*,' hissed Dal Arche, and then, 'So, come back to gloat some more, have you? Or is it remorse? An odd thing for someone like you to be losing sleep over.'

As he spoke, Tynisa's pale face appeared above them, staring down. She said nothing, but would not quite meet the Dragonfly's gaze.

'Come on, out with it,' Dal prompted. 'What's the bad news?'

She twitched unexpectedly. Perhaps only Dal's eyes were good enough to spot it.

Tynisa backed away from the grille, out of direct view. A few grumbles of protest arose, but the bandit leader's hiss silenced them. She put down her bundle and turned her attention to the nearest corner weight.

For a long while she just stared, even the simple mechanics of it evading her. The mechanism had been designed by the Inapt for the Inapt, though, and she had watched it in operation. Eventually something fell reluctantly into place in her mind, and she saw that if she moved this piece of wood *here,* it would free the counterweight to swing aside. She could not quite see how that would make this corner weight light enough to be heaved aside into the appropriate channel cut into the stone, freeing that quarter of the grille, but nevertheless that was what seemed to happen. Instead of trying to wrestle with cause and effect, she followed by rote what she had witnessed, as perhaps the jailers of Leose had done for generations, each in empty mimicry of his predecessor.

That done, she paused, and realized that she would have to repeat this performance for each of the corners in order to render the grille movable at all, after which she would then have to find some way of actually shifting it. She moved on, and now the bandits were watching her, wide-eyed and bewildered, but with a dawning sense that all was not as it should be, and that some opportunity might come their way. She glanced down at them, as she moved the second weight. The burly Scorpion-kinden was glowering at her still, murder burning in his deep-set eyes, but the rest had hope writ large on their faces, all save their leader, Dal Arche, who remained profoundly suspicious.

'What are you doing, girl?'

'You're mine. I caught you, more than anyone did, and I had

a purpose for you, at the time,' she said tiredly, putting her back against the third weight, which grated heavily across wood and stone before it fell clear. 'But now I've changed my mind. You're mine, all of you, so that makes you mine to set free, if I want.'

She released the counterbalance for the final corner and, when she turned back, Dal was already crouching up against the grille, and others of his people were taking up position, too, using their wings or clinging to the walls, ready to jointly shoulder the confining bars out of the way.

'That's not it,' Dal said patiently, as though he was not a prisoner, and she was not dangling his freedom in front of him. 'What happened to all that truth and justice and the golden law of the Monarch? What happened to right and wrong? Or do you reckon we're heroes, now?'

Tynisa paused and stared at him. 'Oh, you're murderers and robbers and bastards, the lot of you. But you know what? I realize now that I can't judge you. The right and the wrong of it seem to have slipped away when I wasn't looking, and I see clearly enough, now, to understand that I *can't* see clearly enough to sit in judgement. And why should you suffer because of my blindness, and why should the Salmae benefit?' She paused, staring down at their hungry faces. 'I'm undoing it. I'm undoing it all – all my interfering. It'll be as though I was never even here.' Her voice trembled over the last few words, and she clenched her teeth.

'Except for all the bodies,' their Spider-kinden pointed out.

For a moment she went very still, fighting down a wave of nausea that rose up inside her, and she closed her eyes in case some spectre of her imagination should resurface, and plunge her back into that well of guilt she had only recently crawled out of. 'Yes,' she whispered, 'except for the bodies.' When she looked up she wore a hard, bleak smile. 'You and the Salmae can go tear each other apart straight away, for all I care.'

'Not likely. It's south for Rhael Province, for us,' Dal decided.

'Not staying to kill Princess Elass in her sleep?' Tynisa enquired, shifting the last weight.

'You're a bloody-handed sort, aren't you?' At Dal's signal, his people braced themselves to shunt the grille two feet aside. That gave enough room, and moments later they came crawling out into the dubious freedom of the prison chamber. Tynisa calmly picked up her bundle again.

Dal was staring up the ramp that led to the courtyard. 'Trust the Salmae to want to keep their prisoners nicely out of the way of their spotless private chambers. If we can make the courtyard, we're free.'

Tynisa knelt down and unfurled her burden, revealing a random collection of knives and swords, whatever she could take easily from the little armoury she had found. Dal knelt down and took up the shortbow she had found.

'Just the one?'

'Don't complain,' she snapped.

He shrugged, and she assumed he would keep the weapon for himself, but he passed it, along with the slender quiver, to one of his Grasshopper-kinden. 'Soul, you're the best shot. You take it.'

'You didn't happen to find a replacement nailbow on your travels, did you?' asked the Wasp-kinden.

Tynisa gave him a narrow look. 'You'll just have to make do with shooting fire from your damned *hands*.'

The Scorpion-kinden reached down and took up a short-hafted spear. When he straightened up, his pose had subtly altered, and she took a swift step back, whisking her sword from its sheath.

'You killed my wife,' the man rumbled through his tusks.

The words threw Tynisa completely. 'Your *wife*? I remember killing your nasty little pet.'

'Where he comes from, you're not considered a grown man unless you've a companion like that,' murmured the Grasshopper, Soul. 'They call them wives, because it's a partnership for life.'

'You killed my wife,' repeated the Scorpion, his hands clenching the spear shaft.

'Ygor, not now—' Dal started, interposing himself between the pair.

'Out of my way, Dala.' The Scorpion hunched his shoulders, as if readying himself to rush at Tynisa.

'No, not now,' Dal insisted. 'Look, she's not running from us, and she'll be happy to hack it out with you any other time. Right now we need to get *out*. Later, Ygor, later. She's up for it, that I guarantee, but not now.'

For a moment it looked as though no amount of calming words would do, but then something went out of the belligerent Scorpion-kinden, with a long hiss of breath. 'Then let's move,' he snarled.

'There's some way of getting out front?' Dal asked.

Tynisa glanced at the doors to the courtyard, barred on the outside of course. She herself had come here via the narrow stairwell leading from the guards' quarters. In truth her planning ended here: free the prisoners, undo the results of her meddling, then leave. She had not thought it through. Indeed thought barely came into it.

Something in her said *fight*. Rouse the guards, slay the Salmae, *avenge the insult*. But surely she had done enough avenging already, enough for a lifetime and a half.

'I will go out and open the doors. Just stay here, and be quiet.'

'Oh, no,' Dal told her straight away. 'You think this makes us your followers, to stay or go at your say-so? And what if this is just some game of yours, or of the nobles? You slip out of here and suddenly they come down on us, catch us trying to escape, have a little sport?'

The Scorpion, Ygor, rumbled deep in his chest, and she sensed the brigands weighing up the odds, a pack of them against her, their stolen blades crossing with a single rapier. She felt her smile grow, and was helpless to stop it. *Why not? Free them, kill them – what's the difference? Be but true to your own nature, wherever it takes you, and then you need bear no guilt nor blame.* She suppressed the insidious feeling, but something of it had communicated itself to the brigands, and none of them made a first move.

'Soul, you go with her,' Dal directed. 'Besides, the bar on these doors is huge, a two-man job at least.'

Tynisa looked the Grasshopper up and down. He was a tall, lean specimen with his kind's usual lanky frame, but there was a stillness to him that marked him out as dangerous. He nodded to her and, when she ascended the stairs, he fell into step so naturally that it was as if they had worked together for years. He was silent too, padding past the sleeping guards with barely a scuff of his bare feet. The one sentry still awake saw Tynisa coming, recognizing her and not challenging her, just as he had let her pass through on the way down, no doubt imagining her to be on some errand of the princess's. This time Tynisa made herself nod, forcing a smile, while Soul Je crept past unobserved, as though the pair of them had spent an hour planning the move.

The castle beyond was quiet, at a time when only a few of the most menial servants would be abroad and about their tasks. Tynisa led the way, passage to passage, heading for the open air: not using the main gates, which were closed, with guards close at hand within, but a window on the first floor, the shutters drawn back and just large enough for her to squeeze through. In truth she was not sure if he would be able to follow her, but with a twist of his shoulders he was out, too. While she let herself down the wall hand over hand with her Art, he simply dropped straight down, crouching for a moment all knees and elbows, before straightening up and making his swift way across the courtyard to the hatch leading to the prison.

They heard the fighting from the other side of the trapdoor even as they approached. Clearly, at least one of the Salmae's guards had decided to see what Tynisa had been up to, or had simply wandered down to check on the prisoners. Sharing a glance, Tynisa and Soul Je took hold of the bar and hefted it out of its rests, letting the heavy wood thud to the ground. The doors burst open almost at once.

Tynisa saw the Spider-kinden, Avaris, fall back with a mailed Dragonfly poised above him, his punch-sword drawn back to strike. She did not stop to think, and any distant guilt she might have entertained about causing the deaths of innocent servants simply doing their jobs vanished on the instant. Her blade took the man between shoulder and neck, where his armour was weak, and she killed him in that one surgical strike. Avaris scrambled out from under the corpse, and wasted no time running for the main gates to the courtyard.

The brigands came piling out into the open air without plan or rearguard, spilling the Salmae's guardsmen in their wake. Tynisa counted a mere half a dozen of the latter here, with a couple lying dead around the empty pit, and at least one of Dal Arche's people fallen too. There would be more, though, for the alarm would have been raised, and Elass's forces here were bolstered by the retinues of her early-arriving guests.

Her sword lashed out again, and they fell back before her, even as the brigands rushed for the main gates. She was left alone to face the guards, but they stayed back and would not engage her, and their faces showed only fear. In that moment she finally saw what Salme Elass had made of her: not a champion, not a huntress, most certainly not a fit match for her son. Instead, a tame monster was what Tynisa had been cast as, to terrify the Salmae's enemies and keep their allies in line; just a pet killer to be let off the leash for special occasions.

Well, I am off the leash now, and she retreated back towards the gates, even as another flight of Dragonfly-kinden dropped down, armed retainers of the Salmae and her visitors.

'Get the gate open!' she shouted, and risked a brief glance over her shoulder to see that the brigands had the bar off, but were being attacked even now. Airborne guards began swooping on them, and she saw Soul Je's little bow sing, spitting shafts through the night air with a calm, sure aim, backed by the fierce flash of Mordrec's Wasp-kinden sting.

She went after them then, turning her back on her opponents and trusting to her reputation and her reflexes to keep them at bay for just long enough. Half the brigands were already through the gates now, and running, and she saw Dal Arche trying to muster the rest to get them moving. She arrived in a flurry of steel, picking one of the attackers from the air even as he swooped down. 'Go!' she heard herself yelling. Dal's expression made it plain that was exactly what he was attempting, but then his eyes fell on something behind her, and she read his face and turned.

There was a pale figure emerging from the hatch leading to the prison: a white-haired Mantis-kinden that she knew well.

The guards dropped towards them again in renewed numbers, and for a moment it was all they could do to defend themselves. Most of the brigands kept going, getting clear of the castle, putting more and more of a burden on those few that remained. The first few guards flying over the courtyard wall, in pursuit of the escapees, met with Soul Je's bow as he kept watch and picked them off.

'Go!' Tynisa shouted, and then realized that they had, that even Dal Arche was now backing away as Isendter Whitehand approached, and that there was only one left there beside her to hold off the guards. It was Ygor the Scorpion-kinden, the short spear bloody in his clawed hands. Behind them there was a flurry of wings, an arrow singing through the air, as Soul Je waited on to keep the fliers at bay.

A reverent hush fell over the guards of Leose, and they started backing off, giving room for Isendter himself. Imperial soldiers would have brought Tynisa and Ygor down by now, with these superior numbers, and sent Light Airborne out to kill the fleeing brigands, but they did things differently here in the Commonweal, and as the Salmae's champion took the field, he was given time and space to act.

Whitehand stepped to within a few yards of them, his face

expressionless, and Tynisa had a moment of wondering what he was waiting for. Then she realized: *Single combat, a duel of Weaponsmasters – that's what he wants.* The Mantis intended to accord her the honour due to her badge, before he killed her.

Tynisa did indeed feel honoured. It was the right and proper way, such a fight, and such a death. For a moment she straightened up, directing her sword towards him, but then the crippling thought came, *That's what* Tisamon *wants as well*, the spectre of her father pulling her strings just like before, tugging her down the road of Mantis tragedy. She faltered, and was not ready as Isendter's stance shifted, impatient for the strike.

They had both forgotten Ygor. The Scorpion moved in a sudden, ugly lunge that would sully the name of any Weaponsmaster. For a moment it seemed that he intended to spit Tynisa herself with his spear, and she had a split second's glimpse of those eyes, mad with fury and vengeance for his dead pet, his lost wife. Then he was past her, throwing himself at Isendter.

He hurled the spear, and that nearly won him the fight. Isendter was not expecting the enemy to disarm himself, and if he had simply swayed aside, then one of the Dragonflies behind would have taken the shaft in the chest. Instead he struck the spear to the ground with a swift motion of his claw, as Ygor charged him with taloned hands spread wide.

Dal Arche was unexpectedly back, dropping down beside Tynisa. 'Time to move,' he said hoarsely. The Dragonfly was staring after his friend, his face creased with emotion, but he was already backing away, drawing her after him, putting distance between them and the fight.

When they turned again, they saw Ygor strike twice, three times, savage and furious, but not one blow landed, and then Isendter killed him with a single clean strike to the throat, using the same deadly blow that Tisamon had always been so fond of. In that moment Dal made a single choked sound, the only grief to escape his control, then he was gone, his wings lifting him away, and Tynisa was running after him.

Thirty-Nine

The irony was that they had forgone the chance to make camp at nightfall. At Che's behest they had pressed on after dark because Leose was so close, and now that she had regained the two Wasp-kinden she was anxious to catch up with Tynisa again and try once more to persuade her to return home. Had they simply been content to finish the rest of the journey in the morning, then they would probably have gone overlooked that night. As it was, however, the patrol swooped on them within sight of the castle itself, nine Dragonfly-kinden dropping out of the night with spears and swords and bows, forming a loose ring at a wary distance from the four travellers.

Varmen's pack-beetle started at their sudden appearance, so he lost valuable time hauling on its leash and trying to keep it to heel. Thalric already had his hands ready, an open palm extended to either side, whilst Che found her sword springing to hand, assuming these were yet more of the brigands Tynisa had been dealing with recently.

Her Art sight leached any sense of colour and, whilst aware that they were well armoured, she could not distinguish their livery. It was left to Maure to state, 'These are the Salmae's people.'

By now Varmen had his beast under control, and had also thrust a palm out threateningly. The Dragonflies, having descended on them so swiftly, now seemed to be unsure of themselves, or perhaps unhappy with the odds.

'What is this?' Che asked of them. 'We're no enemies of the Salmae. We're travelling towards Leose even now. What's happened?'

'You're the Spider's sister?' one of them challenged.

'Foster-sister,' Che clarified, for what seemed like the hundredth time. 'Please, tell me what has happened.'

'You're under arrest,' the man snapped. 'The princess has ordered you brought to Leose.'

'I was already *going* to Leose—!' Che started, but Thalric interrupted.

'What's the charge? Or does Commonweal justice need no reasons?'

Che was about to warn him that he was not helping, but the ring of Dragonflies had widened, slightly but perceptibly, as he challenged them, and she thought she understood why.

'She has freed the prisoners, the brigands. She has killed our people,' the leader of the patrol snarled. He gripped his sword in both hands, plainly readying himself to strike. Two of his followers were archers, both women with arrows already to the string and aimed, one at Varmen, one at Thalric, and each of them recipients of the Wasps' attention in return. Che knew that there was only so long a bowstring could be restrained.

'Tynisa did that?' she asked hurriedly and, when the man gave a brief nod, added, 'And you saw her?'

'I did,' one of the archers declared flatly.

'We have to act now, to get the drop on them,' Thalric hissed between his teeth.

'Wait,' Che said, for everyone's benefit. 'Hold, there's no need for bloodshed.'

'You have to come with us,' the patrol leader insisted, but there was now a tremor to his voice, his eyes flicking between Thalric and Varmen. It was a familiar reaction from all through Commonweal lands, the scars the Twelve-year War had left on the minds of the losers. Three-to-one odds were not enough to overcome such a legacy.

Still, something was likely to snap any moment, either one of the archers or one of the Wasps, and things had obviously gone badly wrong at Leose. *I have to know what's happened,* Che decided.

'You just want me, then,' she informed them. 'Your orders were to bring back Tynisa's sister?'

'Che—' Thalric started angrily, but she silenced him with a look.

'They meant . . .' The patrol leader grimaced unhappily. 'I'm sure . . .'

'Take me to Leose. I have committed no crime, nor harmed anybody. I will come of my own free will to see what my sister has done, and to answer for her if I can. But my companions have no part in this, and if you attempt to take them, then . . .' she almost said, *they will fight,* but decided a little more drama was necessary, 'they will kill you.'

She could see that they believed it, the same fear stamped on each face.

'Che, not again,' Thalric hissed.

'I am not being taken prisoner,' she insisted. 'I am going of my own free will.' This was more to save her pride than to reassure him, for he had mocked her about the number of different cells she had seen the inside of, his own included.

I do not want a fight here, though, for the odds are not good, and besides, I do not want to make enemies of Salma's own family. Surely there must be a sensible solution to this.

'Trust me,' she told Thalric, although she felt far from certain herself. She stepped forward, away from the others, a slow and careful movement, aware of the bowstrings loosening and hoping that the Wasps would not see this as an opportunity.

'Take me to Leose,' she instructed the patrol. 'I have my wings, so I can fly at least part of the distance.'

She had half expected to be brought before Salme Elass in her throne room, surrounded by the woman's court and servants, to give whatever account of her sister's actions she could. Diplomacy, she told herself, had always been one of her stronger suits – at least she had not been killed for it yet. A more pessimistic prediction anticipated stone walls and bars, and perhaps worse. Neither prediction bore fruit.

When she was brought into the courtyard of Leose, the place was alive with hasty preparations. There were armed men on horseback, inside the gates and outside, and a ragged company of spearmen was being assembled even as she entered. Whatever had happened here at Leose, a great many people now seemed set to leave it. Aside from a handful of servants, everyone she saw was armed and ready for battle, and their faces spoke of bloody murder.

'My Princess!' the patrol leader called, and the nearest rider cocked back her helm and glowered down at the new arrivals. In that face, Che could read the same lineage that had produced her friend Salme Dien, and the briefly glimpsed Salme Alain.

'You have her,' the woman remarked, neither praising nor condemnatory. Her eyes, resting on Che, were loveless and bleak. 'Bind her, put her on a horse, bring her along. I'll speak to her once we have an idea of where the vermin have gone.' Her eyes narrowed. 'And her companions, too.'

'She was the only one who surrendered to us.' The faces of the patrol were united in a conspiracy of omission.

Minutes later, Che was sitting astride a solid, patient beast moving alongside the one being ridden by the patrol leader, who had clearly hoped to be rid of her by now. Whether Che would have ever taken to riding if left to her own devices, she would never know, but having her wrists roped together to the saddle bow only meant constantly wrenching her arms every time she slid sideways. If the column had not been limited to moving at the speed of the foot soldiers, then she would probably have soon broken her neck somewhere along the way. As it was the progress was merely painful and difficult rather than fatal.

At last, with the dawn light appearing in the east, they stopped, but nobody dismounted. Che sagged against her restraints, feeling more exhausted than if she had been forced to walk the whole distance. She could see woodland ahead, and wondered if there was fear of an ambush, but shortly she spotted a scattering of figures winging their way over. One of them was clearly not Dragonfly-kinden, and she recognized him long before he landed.

'Gaved,' she greeted him, and he started in surprise just as he was about to go and deliver his report. The Dragonfly scouts had landed directly in front of their mistress, but Che guessed it was safer for the Wasp to approach humbly on foot.

'They came looking for me on dragonfly-back,' he murmured as he neared the Beetle girl. 'Every tracker the Salmae can call in is here. I've not slept since then – they sent me right out after the runaways. Your sister, she finally did it then? She finally snapped.'

Che said nothing, but he read her expression well enough to add, 'I'm sorry. It happens to the greatest. What can I say?' And then he was hurrying off to add to the other scouts' briefing.

Shortly after dawn, Che was sent for. The warband, hunting party, retinue, whatever it was, had not set off again, but scouts had been back and forth, flitting into and around the woods, and Che assumed that either the brigands and Tynisa were lying low or waiting in ambush, or they had disguised their trail so well that the princess did not know which way to follow.

Che's bonds were cut before she was presented to Salme Elass, but she did not get the impression that she should feel encouraged by that. It was more of a ceremonial matter, as if some tradition prevented bound prisoners from being allowed in the royal presence. *What manner of meeting will this be then?* she wondered; *a group inquisition or a private word?* Even as she considered it, she saw that matters were going to be a good deal more public. Salme Elass was holding court.

The princess herself, clad in her mail of red, blue and gold, knelt on a woven mat, while all around her were other nobles, a dozen of them in their own uniquely patterned mails. Beside and behind the princess knelt lowlier specimens, presumably her followers and staff, and each of her tributary nobles had their own orbiting system of retainers, so that what appeared just a random assembly of kneeling men and women resolved itself into a precise map of station and status, comprehensible even to Che's eyes. The hollow in the ground Elass had chosen had thus become her courtroom, as thoroughly as if her people had put up walls.

Che found herself standing at the far end of that notional space, on an invisible threshold that she could somehow sense and not argue with. Her escort let go of her arms, and she felt the gravity of that system of interlocking circles draw her forward almost against her will, each noble and his followers forming a wheel that moved her on towards the princess who was the centre of it all, and yet who at the same time seemed quite alone in the midst of it.

Che put on her bravest face, straightened her shoulders, and made the approach as proudly as she could, though feeling all around her the disparaging looks of the mustered aristocracy and their creatures. She knew what it was to be looked down on as lesser kinden, she had experienced quite enough of that when amongst Wasps, Moth-kinden and the Masters of Khanaphes. Halfway towards the princess, it seemed suddenly too much, too unfair, and she felt something slip within her, opening up a crack in the dam of her reserve. There had been a slight rustle of movement, a mutter of inaudible but barbed words. Che stopped and closed her eyes for a moment, and heard the background murmur die away abruptly. When she looked again, the expressions visible to her had changed. Mouths were shut, eyes were wide or wary. *What had they seen?* But she might as well ask what Maure had seen in her, for it was that same mark: the anointing of the Khanaphir Masters, the inexplicable coronation that the Wasp Empress Seda had inadvertently procured for both of them. It rested inside her like a stone, something she had not asked for and could not yet make any use of, but just for a moment then it had been visible. She suspected that none of them could quite know what had flickered momentarily about her, but all of them were silent, and none sneered at her or mocked her any more.

Only Elass's face had not changed. The cold mask of her displeasure was unaltered.

'So, you claim to be her sister,' she pronounced, when Che was still ten feet away from her.

'By upbringing if not by blood, Your Highness,' Che confirmed. 'Your officer told me that she has freed your prisoners.'

She sensed at once that she had got it wrong, yet that was a feeling she was familiar with, and it no longer stung her like it used to. Instead she concentrated her gaze on Salme Elass, noting the seething fire behind her eyes, the raw emotions the woman held on a fraying leash behind that icy expression.

What has Tynisa done? But she did not ask. Any words from Che, without full knowledge, would only harm her position, and she could see truth rising up behind Elass's expression like a fish out of deep water, towards an inevitable breaching of the surface.

And Elass was on her feet, in a single, almost brutal motion, with fists clenched. Despite this, her voice was stony calm when she declared, 'She has killed my son.'

Che held that furious, knife-edged gaze, and registered no surprise in herself at all. The fact, now it was spoken, seemed as though inevitable from the first moment Che had seen the two of them together. Tynisa had killed Salme Alain, and any misdeed regarding the prisoners was a poor second.

'I see,' was all she said. Che was waiting for a rush of feeling, the guilt, the sense of grief, the apologies, all the usual baggage that seemed so inseparable from her normal dealings with the world: taking responsibility for all sorts of of aspects of it she could do nothing about. The reaction remained conspicuous in its absence and, for once in her life Che remained wholly calm. *Thalric would be proud of me.*

'We will hunt her down and execute her like the base criminal she is,' Elass hissed, stepping closer. 'And you will help us, Beetle-kinden.'

Che sighed deeply, mostly in regret for what she was going to say, because she was now about to make Uncle Sten proud of her, too, in a curious way. She felt his presence close to her, remembering his bold speeches delivered in the Collegium Assembly, his lack of compromise, his locking horns with his adversaries and casting them down, through rhetoric and logic and simple truth.

'Princess, you have lost two sons,' she stated.

The very words brought Elass up short, and there was a world of things to be read on her face for a moment, and none of them pleasant.

'I knew Salme Dien. He was a good friend of mine, and a hero of the Lowlander war with the Wasp-kinden. They named a city after him, back home. He was a good man, and he knew a great deal about justice and responsibility. I think Tynisa and I, coming here, therefore expected a land of law and justice.'

The gathering remained utterly silent, waiting for Elass's next words: likely a death sentence hanging in the air, and awaiting only her order to see it carried out. The princess just stared, though, as if struck dumb by the temerity of this short and ungainly foreigner.

'You have taken me prisoner. Am I a criminal? If so, what is my crime? I have done nothing against you, or against your people. I came here of my own free will to see what could be done to resolve matters concerning my sister. That is all. Imprison me, harm me, and you have no justice.'

'And how do you plan to resolve matters, as you put it?' Elass demanded.

Che met her venomous gaze without flinching, remembering another Dragonfly-kinden she had known: Felise Mienn, who had died alongside Tisamon. Stenwold had brought that woman back to the Commonweal, shortly beforehand, and Che recalled very well how Commonwealer justice had then treated Mienn, the kinslayer.

'My sister has killed your son,' she stated. 'She has freed your prisoners, all of them criminals. Why do you think she has done these things?'

'It hardly matters,' Elass snapped.

'She has done it because she is not in her right mind. Because madness has touched her.' And she felt a sudden freedom that she could say what she was about to say, and not one of them there would dismiss her as mad herself. 'The ghost of her father, who died in violence and fury, has come to haunt her, and leads her astray. She is not responsible for what she does, and I know that, in the Commonweal, that makes her something other than a criminal.'

And she had got it exactly right, not overstated, but her point clearly made and understood, and everyone there looked to Salme Elass, knowing that Che was correct, but they said nothing.

'It matters not,' said the princess, at long last. Her tone was very quiet, but the silence was its match, and everyone there heard her. 'It matters not whether she was mad or sane or haunted. She killed my *son*. I do not want justice. I do not want a trial. If *she* may go mad and murder who she will, so shall I. I will ransack the whole world in order to have my vengeance on that bastard Lowlands girl. You say I had *two* sons? Do you think I care what happened to that traitor boy who ran off to Felipe Shah's court and abandoned me? Alain was all that was left to me, and I will have your sister executed in front of me. If the justice of the Monarch or the Lowlands or the bloody-handed Empress herself stands in my way, I shall batter it *down*.' Her fierce glare cowed them all, her subjects and her followers, making them accomplices in all that she said. 'I shall have vengeance for my son's death, written in the blood of Tynisa Maker. And as for you . . .' Abruptly there were guards holding Che's arms once more. 'We shall see how mad she is that she will not give herself to me to save her sister.'

Forty

The silence that had fallen around the fire was total: with the startled brigands-turned-fugitives staring at her in its guttering light. They had dug in to make camp, excavating a hollow between the roots of a great tree with practised skill and turfing out years' worth of dead leaf mulch until the arching ribs of its roots had become the vaults of their low ceiling, and thus their fire would be hidden from any nocturnal hunters the Salmae might have sent out.

Or no longer the Salmae, for Salme Elass was the last of them now.

'You killed the prince,' Dal Arche said slowly. 'I knew you'd make a play for my role sooner or later, but I think you might have overdone proving your qualifications, girl.'

'I have no wish to be an outlaw,' Tynisa snapped back.

'Whoever does?' remarked Avaris the Spider. 'It's more an honour that someone else pins to your chest, Bella Tynisa.'

'The road leading to where we sit now is the same for us all,' Dal stated, 'although some of us apparently choose to ride it at a gallop. We've all been where you've been, girl; it's just you've decided to achieve in grand style, and all at once, what most of us have made the work of a lifetime.'

'Next you'll be telling me that it's a noble calling, to be a brigand. Or are you claiming to be a revolutionary, set on casting down the nobility?' She tried to sound disdainful, but there was a curious note of need in her voice, despite herself. *Can that be it? Can these ragged wretches have been right all along? Because that would mean I could justify what I've done . . .*

'A bandit, a man-hunter, a lawbreaker, a bow for hire,' Dal replied. 'I never wanted any grand cause. If it looks like I'm fighting tyrants, it's only because the world's so damned full of them that you can't draw a sword without crossing some of their laws.' He sighed, staring at the embers of the fire. 'Easy as easy, it is, to become an outlaw. Come the war, they drafted me for their levy – emptied my village, and got pretty much everyone I knew from there killed. When the war was done, well, there was nothing to go back for, and nothing to eat. Twelve years of fighting and the farms had been turned into battlefields, or just left fallow because the labour was all off trailing the pike. And what food there was, half of it went to the Empire, can you believe? Terms of the Treaty of Pearl said that the food out of our mouths went to feed their soldiers. The other half went to the nobles, and you can bet *they* didn't starve. Or maybe I'm too harsh. Maybe some of them stinted themselves and fed their people, but I never saw sign of it. They were our lords and masters after all, our *betters*, so there was hardly an incentive for them to help shoulder the burden.'

'And so you lowered yourself to their level, is that it?' she asked him.

His look was sharp. 'I learned how easy it is to abuse power, girl. When you're a soldier without a war, with a bow in your hand and nothing in your stomach, and you meet a man who has food and no bow, with no soldiering in him, it's easy. He might be a merchant or a tax gatherer or a barge master or some noble's prize messenger, but he has food, and you're hungry and you can kill him for it. That's all it takes. And next time maybe you don't have to be quite so hungry, and eventually it's become a way of life to take from others and, though you try to make a living at hunting fugitives or some such nonsense, the time will always come when someone has food and you don't, and you'll do it again. We've all been there, and now you've come to visit.'

There was a pause, and the Grasshopper, Soul Je, carefully added some more wood to the fire. Beyond their scooped-out hollow, Tynisa knew the fickle light would be all but invisible amongst the trees.

'I don't want to be your leader, and I don't want to be a brigand,' she said, and had to fight down a part of her that *did*. The ugly, violent thing that had driven her this far would relish it: somehow it seemed that one could have the same honour in killing thieves for a prince as killing princes for the benefit of thieves – so long as there was blood. She shuddered.

'Then you've no need to share our fate, win or lose,' Dal pointed out.

'I . . .' The world was out there, dark and harsh and unforgiving, and she had once again excised herself from it. If she left the company of these ragged creatures, then she would have nothing at all.

Perhaps Dal saw something of the truth from her face, for he did not press the issue.

There was a rustling above, and immediately all hands went to swords and knife hilts. It was Mordrec, though, squeezing in to take up all the available space, and with a bundle in his arms.

'Just where we left it,' the Wasp confirmed, slightly out of breath. 'Glad we listened to you, now. Never thought we'd be coming back this way, myself.'

He unfurled the oilcloth, spilling out a meagre collection of knives, shortbows and an untidy stack of arrows. None of it looked like good workmanship, but the brigands helped themselves gladly, so that all of them save Mordrec now had a bow and at least a few shafts.

'Any sign of their scouts?' Soul asked.

'How the pits should I know?' Mordrec hissed back. 'They can see better than I can. I just concentrated on keeping my head down, all the way.'

Tynisa sighed. 'I'll go look.'

They regarded her doubtfully, and at last Dal Arche said, 'One of us, then?'

'And not your leader,' she insisted firmly. 'I need to get away. You need to get away. I'm willing to bet that they want me more than you.'

That had to be explained for Mordrec's benefit, and the Wasp goggled at her. 'Shame you didn't go report to the old woman before you sprang us,' he said. 'Could have wiped out the whole family. Make the Rekef proud.'

She glared at him, but the words hit close to home.

'What's the plan, then?' asked Mordrec, settling down. 'I reckon we're a few points off the compass, but that's just runner's instinct. You got a plan now, Dala?'

The Dragonfly nodded slowly. 'I reckon the reason they've not caught us already is because most of their people headed south, thinking we'd just repeat our dash for Rhael. As you've noticed, we've made best time by going due east, instead. Now they've got airborne scouts and cavalry, so they'll catch our trail soon enough, and it's only a matter of time before they overhaul us. Not many options for us, then. Too few of us to make much of an impression if we stand and fight. We could scatter, each to his own, and some of us would likely remain free, and others would be hunted down like beasts. That has an appeal to it, if only because it puts our enemies to the most trouble. However, I've a third way, if you want to hear it.'

'Speak,' Soul Je prompted.

'We just hope to keep out of their reach, as we run east, and then we cross the border. It's not as far as you might think. Don't forget how half this Principality ended up on the wrong side of the Imperial lines, at the end.'

Mordrec spat. 'You know what it's like in the Wasp Principalities? You think they're any easier on brigands there?'

'I reckon they're not *already* hunting us as brigands over there, nor as prince-killers either. So I think, right now, we're better off risking our freedom with the slave-takers than our lives with the Salmae.' As Mordrec was about to speak again, he added, 'You sprang me from a Slave Corps cell in Myna, Mord, so it's not something I'd suggest lightly. Still, by my reckoning we've just about outstayed our welcome here. Split off from us tomorrow, anyone that wants, but I'm for the border, and see how bold Salme Elass gets then.'

He met Tynisa's gaze, and she asked him, 'You've fought all this while against the Commonweal aristocracy? Don't you think the Empire will be worse?'

'Oh you're right,' Dal replied lazily. 'We might be enslaved and forced to work their farms and do their will. They might conscript us for their armies. They might execute us for turning our back on their laws. How different is that from the old Commonweal, eh?' He nodded to Tynisa. 'You go spotting for their scouts, girl. Put your eyes to good use.'

They kept Che constantly bound, travelling awkwardly on horseback before one of the Salmae's retainers, or dumped at night alongside the stores and provisions. She managed to pick up little detail, but their search was plainly not progressing well. The initial hopes the pursuers had of overhauling the fugitive band had been dashed and their second-guessing had been found wanting. After that the trackers, Gaved amongst them, had been sent out on winged errands to try and find some other sign of their quarry. A day later they were back, and it was plain that Salme Elass had been leading her avenging force in entirely the wrong direction. The cavalry set off as soon as the news was in, and Che bundled along with them. The miserable conscripted levy were left to follow on foot at their own best pace.

She wondered idly if this was how the Commonwealers had conducted the war, and whether that explained everything. From that reflection, her mind turned to Thalric and her other companions. They were close, she knew: she could feel Thalric's arrowhead of a mind out there, seeking ways to cut at the knot of her captors and set her free. She dared not let her mind wander too far, or exercise her little-understood powers too much. The Empress was still out there, and who could know how far her feelers might stretch from her nest in the heart of Capitas? Surely she had not forgotten Che, her unwished-for peer and sister. And if the Beetle girl's consciousness should brush against her, then who knew what new magical attack Seda might unleash? Che had no wish to be banished into the back of her own head once more.

This night, as the advance force camped, the scouts seemed to have more positive information. They had already made up a lot of the lost ground, Che came to understand from the snippets of talk she overheard. Another day, or even less, and they would catch up with the brigands, and Tynisa. And then Salme Elass would have her revenge.

There were perhaps forty or fifty in the cavalry party, and they were the cream of the Commonweal, nobles and their retainers armoured in glittering shell and steel, skilled with bow and sword and lance. Che had glumly concluded that it didn't matter how much help Tisamon's ghost could lend to his daughter, Tynisa would not be able to triumph over her enemies this time, not even with a motley collection of brigands at her back. And she would not run for long, Che knew, for Tisamon would not have run. Perhaps Tynisa did not even think of her actions so far as *escaping*, rather than just escorting and guarding the villains she had freed. The moment she thought that she was running *from* something, then she would turn and fight. It was what Tisamon himself would have done, and the instinct had surely killed enough Mantis-kinden over the years. Che had a fairly strong conviction that Tisamon's ghost had only one aim in its damaged mind: that Tynisa would die as a Mantis should die: bloody-handed and in company.

So, the ghost's play had reached its endgame, and Che's own had clearly failed. She was in no position to save Tynisa from anything, nor even herself.

She started as someone crouched down next to her, sitting back on his haunches. She recognized him as Isandter, the silver-haired Mantis-kinden. His eyes were wintry and cold, and Che knew well enough the sword-and-circle brooch he wore.

'What do you want?' she asked him.

He was studying her with a slight frown. 'You are a noble of the Lowlands, a woman of importance?'

She almost laughed at that. 'We don't have an aristocracy. Bloodline won't get you far on its own, where I come from. But my uncle Stenwold is a man of note, back in Collegium. I imagine he'll take it personally if he hears that something bad has happened to me. Not that it'll do me much good by then, of course.'

Isendter nodded soberly. 'Maker Stenwold,' he enunciated carefully. 'That is the name of the Lowlander who spoke to the Monarch at Prince Felipe's court.'

Che raised her eyebrows. 'The very same, Master Whitehand. You've a good memory.'

'It was much talked about, at the time. And you are important, then, so it's a mistake to treat you thus.'

She waited, but the words were not a prelude to any attempt on his part to secure her freedom. Instead he surprised her by sitting down beside her, as though the two of them were simply exchanging pleasantries.

'You know our ways a little. You learned that from your uncle, no doubt. You were right, in what you said: the girl is not in her right mind, not her own master. My lady has erred by setting herself on this course. No good will come of it.' He spoke low, so that his voice would not carry further than Che's ears. She had a sudden insight that he had come to speak to her because these words, prying their way out of him, were too dangerous to voice to any other.

'If you're looking for sympathy from your prisoner, you'll find none here. She's *your* mistress.'

'Not by choice. I am the tithe paid by my people: the service of a Weaponsmaster in exchange for my kin to live untroubled in the deep places. I have served the Salmae most of my life.'

'No doubt the prince was a better master, when he lived,' Che suggested. For all her caveats about sympathy, she could not retain a stern face. The old man seemed oddly frail and vulnerable in thus confessing to her, for all that he was a Mantis-kinden killer and a master of the blade.

'He was not.' Isendter stared up at the stars. 'He was thoroughly vainglorious, and he would not listen. He died in the war's early years, leading a pointless charge against a superior foe, because he could not conceive of ever being wrong. He did not die alone.' The Mantid's expression was sour, hollow. 'Others of the Salmae fell in similar ways, serving their Monarch, and yet giving precious little of value, until there was the princess and her son. Her *sons*. But, then you said you knew the boy, Dien.'

'Very much so,' Che agreed. 'He was a good friend.'

Isendter let out a long breath. 'Felipe Shah took him into his household, as kin obligate. It was a great honour, of course, but the Salmae would have refused it, if they dared. Prince Felipe thought he saw something in the boy worth saving, and took him to Suon Ren to raise as his own son. And he was right, it would seem.'

'I take it Alain wasn't of the same stamp?'

There was a long silence then, and Che assumed that the man's unburdening had come to an end, but at last his voice emerged again, in barely more than a whisper. 'Without honour, he was, and with no sense of a nobleman's responsibility. Not one of the old nobility, like Felipe Shah or Lowre Cean, men who take their duty seriously. Instead, a boy who was denied nothing, who acknowledged no boundaries, around whom no woman was safe. Who bred vice instead of virtue, resentment instead of loyalty – and I am bound to avenge him, or die trying.'

'Why are you telling me this?' Che asked him.

'Because you alone here might understand, and who else would? I would have warned your sister, save that she was under Alain's spell before I ever met her. I know Lisan Dea did her best to turn the girl away. This time, though, the boy took on more than he could manage. A Weaponsmaster, wounded in mind, unpredictable, fierce, a killer – that is your sister. He thought he could keep her spinning about him like a moth about a candle but, this once, he mistook who was the flame.'

'She killed him,' Che said flatly, 'She killed your prince.'

'She is a fugitive, a murderess, she has robbed the family of its cherished son.' His brooding expression deepened. 'Still, I can feel no grief in me that the boy is dead.'

Forty-One

First he donned his cap and arming jacket, their padded cloth now the worse for wear, still bearing all their old stains of blood and sweat like badges of honour. The hauberk came next, a long-sleeved coat of mail that fell to his knees. Not the heavy chain of an Ant-kinden line soldier but fine links that flowed like water, yet would bunch like solid metal under the impact of sword or arrow. The weight of it pressed on his shoulders, resting against the additional thickness of the arming jacket there, but it did not burden him. Instead, he felt lighter and freer with that comforting pressure about him. He donned his coif, a hood of the same delicate mail, shaking his head a little to centre it, tugging the collar straight.

Then came the breast- and backplates, fitted together and hinged shut to form the centre of his steel carapace. Both pieces bore a punched hole, the edges long since filed blunt, where a snapbow bolt had winged its way right through him, armour and all, and thereby ended the era of the battlefield sentinel.

The end of my world, thought Varmen, but then they did not have snapbows in the Commonweal.

All this he could do alone, from long practice, but it was easier with a companion to arm him. Back in the days when he had belonged to an army, he and his comrades had garbed each other, like a ceremony and a ritual before going into battle.

A belt strapped around the lower edges of the breast- and backplates to keep them closed, and then Thalric buckled on his leg armour, piece by piece: cuisses for the thighs, poleyns for the knee, armoured boots for the feet, and then greaves over them for the calves. The ex-Rekef man made a slow job of the work, having to be ordered and directed, segment by segment, but he grew more confident as he progressed. Had Varmen been on his own he would have had to start with the feet and work up; with the breastplate already on, he could not reach down that far.

A skirt of segmented tassets overlaid the cuisses to just above the knee, hooked to both breast- and backplates, and then Thalric had turned to the arms, fitting the same sequence of articulated, overlapping plates, defending from all angles and allowing only the bare minimum of gaps – and those backed by the light mail – and yet none of it encumbering, none of it slowing Varmen at all, not after a lifetime spent encased in armour such as this.

About his neck was fastened a crescent-shaped gorget, denying his enemies the gap between the breastplate rip and his helm. He drew on his own gauntlets, as a point of pride, while Thalric laced and buckled on his pauldrons, three curved plates on each shoulder, with a vertical crest rimming the innermost to protect the side of his neck. He buckled on his swordbelt then, fingers still finding their way surely despite the steel about them. The heavy blade was a comforting presence at his side.

'I'm ready,' he proclaimed, and Maure brought his helm forward, her expression solemn. Varmen nodded to Thalric, who made a wry face and stepped back, giving the two of them their privacy.

'You've seen the ghost about me, haven't you?' Varmen muttered.

Maure just nodded and the Wasp scowled.

'I don't believe in ghosts. No such thing.' He took the helm from her and stared into its faceless visage. 'A Dragonfly girl.'

'Even so,' Maure agreed.

'So tell me, is she real? Or just in my head? I fought the girl once, one on one. I was trying to save my men.' His face was blankly uncomprehending. 'It's stayed with me, all this time. She had a good voice, a beautiful voice: even when she was demanding our surrender and telling us we couldn't win out. It's odd what you remember.'

'It doesn't make a difference whether it's a ghost from her death, or a ghost from your mind. It's no less real,' Maure told him. 'Or no *more* real, seeing as you don't believe in them.'

'Not in the slightest,' Varmen agreed. 'You're going to stay back, you hear? No getting in the way.'

'I'm no warrior, me,' she agreed. 'I'd tell you all the ways in which I'll be helping you, but you wouldn't believe me in that, either.'

'Probably not.' He tried a smile, but it was a bleak and stillborn thing. 'Back in the bloody Commonweal. I feel like this place has been waiting for me ever since the war ended. He took a deep breath that set the plates of his armour rising and grating against one another. 'I should have died on the field with the Seventh, when their snapbows cut us down like wheat.' Balancing the helm in one hand he touched the entry hole with an armoured finger. 'But I'd rather have died fighting that girl here in the Commonweal. Then I'd not have had to see the end of us, the end of all of our ways.' He glanced off into the darkness. 'Just like all the old Commonweal magic, eh? They used to put such faith in us, and then one day . . . nobody believed in us any more.'

He reached up and placed the helm on his head, his world reducing to a slit, and yet he felt that he somehow saw more, sensed more, now that his armour was complete. He had regained a connection to the world, feeling all of its tricks and changes. He was something elemental.

'Pride of the Sixth,' he murmured, tugging the chinstrap

tight. He swung the helm to find Maure, saw her expression. 'Such a long road just to come back here,' he said, his voice loud in his own ears.

Thalric stood waiting for him a short distance off. Varmen had dug out an old tunic for him, creased and stained but recognizable still in its colours. Varmen's mail had once been immaculately painted in black and gold and, although it was chipped and scarred, the hues were still plain to see. It would take more battering than that to rub away the hand of the Empire.

Maure watched them go, and then set about her own work. It was nothing she had discussed with the two Wasps, for she thought they would not understand or appreciate it, and their scepticism would merely damage her efforts. Having exchanged those few words to Varmen, though, she wondered whether she had done the right thing in staying silent.

Their plan to rescue Che had been both simple and desperate. Just the two of them against a camp filled with Dragonfly warriors. They had almost ended up making their assault in broad daylight, for Thalric reasoned that the Dragonflies saw better at night, and so why bother relying on the stealth of it? In the end, neither of the Wasps quite had the nerve for that, but even at night their business seemed just a shaving away from suicide. They had only one advantage over the Commonwealers: they were Wasp-kinden, they were the Empire – they were the fear at the heart of a conquered people. That was little enough to even the terrible odds, but Thalric claimed that it would buy them enough time for a sudden strike: just grab Che and go.

Maure had heard him discuss it, and knew that he did not believe his own words, but he was now in a corner with nowhere else to go. She had not realized – perhaps he himself had not realized – his depth of feeling for Che, until she was taken from him this last time. He had reached the end of his wire, now, and action was his only release. Win or lose, the outcome was going to be bloody. Since Che had been lost to them, something else had surfaced in Thalric – or perhaps resurfaced. Maure sensed a kind of murderous capability in him, a man who would do anything to achieve his goals.

She took a deep breath. All her life she had used her skills sparingly, as she had been taught. A Moth Skryre or some such grand magician would think of the practice as accumulating power, but she had been taught that she was accruing credit with the world, especially with the world of the dead. Every spirit she helped to its destination, every ancestor who could share a few posthumous words with a descendant, every legacy passed on, it all added up; and though the coins were small, yet she had a lot of them by now. She was not powerful, as magicians measured themselves, but she had a deep well to draw on, now that she needed it.

Setting a ghost to haunt someone was an old necromancer's trick, both risky and difficult and seldom worth the effort. Each person had their own weaknesses, each vengeful spirit its own small remit. Such skills would be little use in confronting the numbers that Thalric and Varmen now went to confront.

But they had provided her with the answer, of course. Thalric's plan was better than he knew.

She took a deep breath. None of the mummery of before, involving candles and circles. She did not want to pacify these ghosts, and indeed she was not sure that calm was even in their nature. She wanted them fighting mad.

They would be drawn from the minds of the Salmae's followers, from each and every one, either from personal experience or from second-hand fear brought on by the stories they would have heard.

She closed her eyes and concentrated upon the black and gold.

Thalric and Varmen: representatives of the Rekef and the invincible Imperial army, those spectres that had poisoned the Commonweal over twelve years of bloody warfare, that had left fearful ghosts in every mind: that had even replaced blood-drinking Mosquitos as the terrors invoked to caution children with. Terrors that any moment could march back across the border to continue their slaughter. Terrors of the machine-handed, the disciplined, the cruel, slavers and butchers, rapists and child-killers.

The ghost she raised and sent to follow Thalric and Varmen was the nightmare that troubled the sleep of the entire Commonweal. The two Wasps themselves would never know, never see, but they were trailed by a wake of black and gold shades with flaming hands and red swords.

The Salmae's warband had entered dense forest now, following the recaptured trail of the fugitives. Under such cover, Thalric's party had been able to move far closer than they could while pursuing the Salmae through hilly open countryside. Now he hoped to use the same cover to get within sting range before he was spotted. There must be sentries, he knew, for nobody was fool enough to hunt brigands through woodland without setting plenty of watchmen. Still, he was already within sight of the camp's edge, a chaotic gathering of tents spread out in a maze of canvas between the trees, and he was just beginning to think that he should have left Varmen behind. It seemed entirely possible he could sneak into this place, find Che, and get her out again, all on his own.

Then a scout dropped from the branches above, her bow already bent back. Thalric could not see the woman's expression, but he was sure she was next to laughing at him: just one man come to storm half a hundred of the Commonweal's finest. He tensed himself to dive aside behind a tree, his hands warming to sting. Then Varmen caught up with him.

The archer swung the arrow towards the newcomer and then recoiled away, her back rebounding from a tree trunk and her arrow skipping off one of Varmen's pauldrons. She tried to shout something, but for a moment nothing emerged but jabber, the terrified stutter of a warning as she fumbled frantically for another arrow. The flash from Thalric's outstretched palm struck her down, and then the two were moving again.

Just the two of them, because Thalric *knew* that there was only himself and Varmen in this raiding party. But as he rushed past the first tent, it seemed that the forest all around was alive with running feet, the rattle of armour, even the distant sounds of heliopter engines. For a moment, this chill Commonweal night intermeshed with one from his memories, and this was no longer a doomed rescue but the inexorable weight of the Empire's military might descending to crush yet another disorganized Commonweal force.

He saw armoured men and women ahead, spears and swords glittering in the firelight. An arrow lashed past, far to his left. He let his hands speak for him, taking any target that presented itself. He knew that the scintillating Commonweal mail could scatter stingshot from itself at the right angle, but it did not seem to matter. He and Varmen had become an unstoppable force, and the Dragonflies did not even try to resist. They scattered right and left or straight up, a few falling to Thalric's sting, but none staying to chance Varmen's sword. Then the two Wasps were charging through the heart of the camp, trees looming on all sides, Dragonfly-kinden came rushing half-dressed from their tents, to stare or flee at the sight of Varmen's armoured form,

This won't last, Thalric thought and, even as he did so, a Dragonfly noble dropped down to engage Varmen, his face a fixed mask of self-control. His long-hafted sword swung three times at the Wasp in rapid succession, bounding back from breastplate, shoulder and helm, and leaving barely a dent. He made to dodge around his bulky enemy, to use that restricting helm and the weight of mail against him. Varmen turned the other way, faster than Thalric could quite believe, and flattened the attacker against his shield, wheeling again to stab the

Dragonfly in the leg as the wretched man staggered. The glittering mail, the work of master armourers with a thousand years' experience, did not stretch to protecting the inner thigh, and the nobleman went down without ceremony.

Arrows clipped from between the trees, but Thalric was running in Varmen's shadow. The shafts sprang back from his shield or slanted from the planes of his mail, as the armoured man stomped his way forward.

Where is Che?

Three of the enemy mustered sufficient understanding and courage to attack Varmen from behind. Thalric, unseen beside the black and gold ironclad, killed one as they rushed in, the assailant arching backwards with a blackened hole in his face, for the Commonwealers had never designed full helms. Another man rammed his spear full strength into Varmen's back without any understanding of the weak points of heavy mail. The point struck in the middle of the backplate, rather than seeking out the joints, and Varmen lurched forward a step under the impact, as the spear shaft bent and then snapped. The Sentinel swung round, his cleaving stroke knocking the third man's blade from his hands. For a second the blank visor stared at them, and then Varmen had turned and was striding further into the camp.

And Thalric heard her call his name. Those Commonwealers had no idea about how to secure prisoners either. She was merely tied to a tree beside a rank of restless horses, not penned up, not even gagged.

'Varmen!' Thalric began running for her. A Grasshopper groom or functionary came dashing along the row of horses, quite possibly for purposes unconnected with the rescue, but Thalric took no chances and stung him down anyway. He heard the clatter of steel behind him and knew that the Commonwealers were regaining their dented courage, and coming in greater numbers. He dared not look back to see how Varmen fared.

There were no chains, no locks. He had his sword out,

hacking at the ropes and cutting jagged gashes in the tree itself, and in a moment Che was free.

An arrow dug into the trunk just above her head, even as she slumped forward. Thalric hauled her to her feet, but she sank back on to her knees, and for a moment he thought that she had been shot.

'Been on a horse for days,' Che gasped. 'No idea how *sore* I am . . . barely walk.'

'You're going to have to,' Thalric cautioned her. 'Running would be even better.'

She cursed as he dragged her upright again, but at least she managed to stay standing. Thalric calculated quickly, deciding the swiftest way out of the camp. True to his bad luck, the Salmae had tethered their animals safely towards the centre, and of course their prisoner too. For a moment he considered stealing a horse, but his riding skills would barely manage a sedate trot in daylight, let alone a mad gallop at night.

'Varmen!' he yelled again. Glancing back, he saw the armoured figure striding in the opposite direction. From here, all ways led out, and it seemed that the Sentinel's shadow allowed room enough for a bruised Beetle girl as well as a former Rekef man.

Even as they caught up, Thalric forcing Che to keep the pace, another flurry of Commonwealers attacked. A brace of arrows bounded from Varmen's raised shield, and then there were airborne forms about him, wheeling and darting, striking at his head and shoulders. They were trying to keep him off balance, first one attacking and then another, but it seemed as though Varmen was in another world, within his helm, and no matter how hard they made it ring, none of their feints could fool him. The Sentinel's skill was not simply in bearing the huge burden of his mail, but in fighting with complete focus and awareness, so that the mail was no burden, the visor no restriction. As each attacker lunged downwards, Varmen was ready, taking their blows on his shield, striking back only when it was economical to do so. He brought down two of five, leaving them, crawling away bloodied on the forest floor, and he did not stop for them.

There was a voice calling out, ahead, and Che's head snapped up at the sound.

'That's *her*,' she whispered, and Thalric had no idea who she meant until he saw. They had somehow taken the one path that led them further in, to the absolute centre of the camp, or perhaps Varmen had been well aware of where he was going all along. There was a chaos of activity here, half-armoured Dragonflies flying back and forth, some rushing out to locate a threat that had already arrived at their doorstep, others trying to form up into some semblance of military order. In the midst of it all stood a woman in glorious armour of red and blue that reflected the firelight fiercely. She was practically shrieking orders, striking out at any of her people that came within fist range.

Princess Salme Elass, last of her line.

'We need to get out, not in. What are you doing?' Thalric demanded. Varmen's entrance had been noted, and the tail end of the Imperial awe that had got them this far lashed into the assembled Commonwealers. They did not see Thalric or Che, just that one indomitable armoured form – and, behind him, all the horrors of the Twelve-year War.

'Varmen, we have to go!' Che called. 'They have a Weapons-master.'

The armoured man turned briefly, helm tilting to stare over his shoulder. His sword levelled past them, indicating the direction *away*.

Varmen took the next sword on his shield, long-honed instincts telling him where his new foe would be even without seeing him, calculating back from the angle of strike. He brought his sword back from signalling Thalric and Che, and chopped it into the path that he knew his assailant would take, feeling a solid impact and knowing that he had caught the man somewhere unarmoured. There seemed to be a host all about him, pressing behind and on both sides, not seen, not even heard, but felt through the weight of his mail. When he now advanced, the foe fell away as though he had a regiment at his back.

Another wave of Dragonfly-kinden dared him, and broke against his shield, passing him by as though they were so many autumn leaves. He felt the impacts of their blades and spearpoints, and had they simply stood against him, probed for the weak points in his mail, then they would have brought him down in short order. They would not stand, though, and these fleeting strikes were all they were good for.

His narrow frame of reference scanned about him: noting the campfires, the running and flying enemy, the tents.

He thought he saw the black and gold banner beside him, shadowed forms in striped mail, his comrades the Sentinels, but they were not really there. They had perished at Masaki, they had died at Malkan's Stand, they had been disbanded by an Empire that no longer had need of them.

'Pride of the Sixth,' he croaked to himself, and took another step.

For a moment he thought he saw the Dragonfly girl, not this chaff that was sleeting past him but the girl he had duelled so long ago, in that moment his life seemed to hinge on. *When I was alive. For I was never so alive as in that moment.* He thought that she smiled at him, and nodded, and then turned to go. *Where I cannot follow, alas. I'd have followed her then, or had her follow me. She was a beauty and no mistake, even when she was trying to kill me. Especially then. After all, I've thought about doing the deed myself once or twice, after Malkan's Stand. I can hardly hold it against her, then, can I?*

Another staccato rattle of weapons striking home, arrows, most of them, One shaft stuck in his elbow-joint, clipping in under the shield, but it failed to touch him. None of it touched him.

He saw her. Not the ghost-girl now, for she had gone, or never been. He saw the leader of the enemy shouting her orders. Thalric and his Beetle woman were fleeing fast, he hoped, but he would detain his audience a little longer, to let them make their exit.

For my next trick . . .

He broke into a run then, and was willing to put money down that none of the enemy had realized he could do it. The weight of his mail made him unstoppable.

He saw the woman straight ahead of him, gorgeous in armour that would have taken ten times as long to make as Varmen's own, and cost just as much more, even without the gold chasing, and would protect her far less from his blade. She spotted his approach in mid-shout, and he had her face framed perfectly within the slot of his visor, saw her anger stretch and split, shouldered aside by the horror now hatching behind it.

Salme Elass screamed, and her wings sprang into life, hauling her back into an ungainly leap to put more distance between her and the Imperial behemoth now closing with her.

Abruptly there was someone in between them: a pale figure with a twisting blade hooking out from one hand. He struck four times in swift succession, curving past Varmen's shield each time, his metal claw feeling out for the strength of the Imperial mail.

Varmen's steel held, and he forged forward. Whatever the antagonist had expected, it was not that. Presumably, when a Mantis-kinden stopped to fight you, you were supposed to stay fought, but Varmen shouldered on towards the Salme woman, and carried the Mantis with him. The man was too quick to get caught by the sweep of the Wasp's blade, but Varmen gave him no time to seek out the joints and cracks in his armour, and all the while the Mantis was desperately trying to turn him aside from the princess.

The claw-blade came for his eyeslit, but Varmen just ducked a little, feeling it scrape off his helm. The next blow chopped between neck and shoulder, but that was why his pauldrons had those high ridges protecting his throat. A strike to his groin found only layers of mail and the articulated lames of his tassets. As the Mantis gave yet more ground, Varmen caught a glimpse of his face: blank frustration growing behind the warrior's mask.

Others were also attacking. He felt the punch of arrows and spears against his back. It seemed impossible that one of them had not brought him down yet. *But I feel as if I have the whole army with me, the glorious Sixth. I feel like they could never take me, not all the Commonwealers in the world.*

The Mantis was suddenly right before him, one hand hooking a thumb into his eyeslit, trying to force his head back, claw-blade ready to strike at his throat. It was a mistake, for now he had sacrificed all his speed and skill in order to brawl like a common soldier, and Varmen was the stronger man. He swept his shield around, feeling the rim catch his enemy somewhere in the side, forcing him away, and then Varmen simply swatted his enemy with the flat of it, knocking him aside.

There was nothing between him and the leader of his enemies, and he was immortal.

'Pride of the Sixth!' he roared, and charged. The princess had her blade out, but she was backing away still, stumbling as she ran into a tree. Her people had been all about her, but they were running too, not one of them willing to face the Wasp-kinden.

Then the old Mantis was back, and he had a spear levelled, coming in from Varmen's sword side, the tip of the weapon already past his guard. Varmen lifted his blade to cut the man down, but something struck him a solid, jarring impact that left him completely still, all his surging momentum stolen away. The glory of the Sixth ebbed from him. He was immortal no longer. The dream had passed.

He stared at the Mantis, who met his visored gaze evenly, even respectfully. The white-haired old man still held his spear, but the head of it was gone, the shaft splintered. This moment between them seemed to last for ever.

Then Varmen nodded, understanding, and turned to go. He heard the princess's voice shouting after him, demanding his death, but not one of her people would approach him, not even now. Feeling numb, more distant with every step, he trudged out of the camp, and they did not follow him, not yet, not then. It was almost as if a rearguard had taken up station behind him, the shadows of the Sixth guarding his slow retreat.

Maure found him just as his strength gave out and he was forced to sit, backplate resting against a tree, as he slumped down on to the forest floor. He felt her tugging at his helm, but managed to lift a hand to stop her.

'Like this,' he wanted to say. 'Go as I lived . . . when I lived.' But the words were so soft that they did not leave the quiet of his helm.

Her hands found the spearhead where it had lodged in that same hole the snapbow bolt had made at Malkan's Stand, when progress had killed off his way of life. She did not try to remove it, just knelt there beside him, with her arms wrapped about his dented and bloody mail, and waited for the end.

The spectacle of Varmen had not been enough to distract all of Salme's defenders, and when Che and Thalric broke from the camp there were enough who decided that chasing a fleeing Wasp and Beetle through the forest at night was safer than facing up to a defiant Wasp by firelight. The arrows kept skipping through the air even as Thalric tugged at Che's arm, forcing her to run at his longer-legged pace and brutally hauling her to her feet again whenever she stumbled. The pain was vicious, legs sore from so many days enforced riding now shooting fire into her with every step, but the enemy were ahead and above, and outpacing them no matter how fast Thalric dragged at her.

'Can you fly?' he called back to her.

'Easier than run,' she agreed. Not necessarily faster, she

knew, for her kinden did not have it in them to be graceful in the air, but on the other hand . . .

She gripped Thalric's hand tight and took off at a tangent, wings unfurling from nothing and shimmering about her back. She was heading for the densest part of the forest, wheeling around tree trunks and between branches. There was an initial tug as Thalric resisted her, asserting his own judgement over hers, but then he let her guide him into the deeper, darker woods, with the Dragonfly-kinden at their heels.

They had good eyes, the Dragonflies. In daylight they could hover high in the sky and still watch the details of the land far beneath. In the night, their sight was as good as a Mantid's or Fly-kinden's in piercing the dusk. Not as good as Che's, though. To her gifted eyes, the night itself was banished, the world picked out clearly in shades of grey, enjoying that rare Art of her people that let them see the world as their former Masters, the Moth-kinden, did. She was not graceful but she was sure, choosing her path through the upper reaches of the forest as though it were plain daylight. Now the Dragonflies' swiftness betrayed them. They could not navigate as she could, so they must either slow down to her speed or risk losing her amongst the interlocking branches.

Still, the arrows went on coming, in ones and twos. Thalric kept them busy in return, flashing back at them with his free hand, the fire of his sting going wide, scorching wood, warning them off.

It was still not enough. Che had led them a dance, but she could see enemy ahead now, looping round while following their fellows' voices. She dropped lower, hoping to cut underneath them before they realized she was quite so close.

An arrow lanced through her calf and, in the sudden shock of pain, her wings were gone. Abruptly she became just a weight on Thalric's arm, and he could not support them both. He would not let go, and the two of them spiralled helplessly down to the ground. Che's leg gave way the moment she tried to put weight on it, and immediately Thalric was standing over her, both hands out and his sting lancing towards their attackers. Che saw one of the Dragonflies reeling back, the armour over his shoulder burned away. There were too many, though. Arrows hissed past Thalric in the poor light, but closer each time. Che saw an archer drop down to Thalric's left, unnoticed, drawing a bowstring back with patient care, and using the flare of the Wasp's own stingshot to guide his aim.

When the arrow struck, it was swift enough that Che had no sense of its passage, only the missile suddenly sprouting from the same archer's jaw, the force of it knocking him back. She saw Thalric start aside at the last moment from a sword stroke, then step in to grapple the attacker, the two of them wrestling in near-pitch darkness but every movement clear to her. Another Dragonfly, a woman in partial armour, landed with a spear levelled, trying to get a clear strike at Thalric, but an arrow struck her breastplate, staggering her. Che craned back and saw newcomers, a little pack of vicious-looking men darting between the trees. Most had bows, though one was a Wasp, and, as she watched, his hands flashed with a fire that looked pure white through her Art-vision.

A boot came down on her chest with shocking suddenness, and she saw another of the Salmae's people standing over her, eyes narrowed as he drew back a spear, plainly intending to run her through and then escape while he could. She reached for the spear shaft, missed it and cut her fingers on the blade. Then a thin lance of steel had struck its way into her attacker's armour, punching through as though it were made of eggshell, and he fell back, the spear clattering aside. Che looked up at her rescuer, and a jolt of mixed emotions ran through her.

Tynisa.

Forty-Two

With Che an increasingly stumbling weight in his arms, Thalric took in very little of their new companions. It was all he could do to keep up, pelting ahead into the dark, through the trees. Che's wings flickered in and out as she tried to keep weight off her injured leg. He could feel her tense each time, gathering her waning strength, and after the second blur of wings he timed his bursts of speed to coincide with them, staying just on the heels of the fleeing Spider-kinden man ahead of him.

Abruptly he was alone, his escorts vanished like spectres. He skidded to a halt, Che crying out in pain, and someone tugged at his boot. He had a moment of fumbling Che's weight, trying for a free hand, before he realized that there was a hollow here, excavated amongst the tree roots, where his guides had taken shelter.

He dropped obediently down, then was suddenly tumbling forwards as the hole turned out deeper than he had thought. His wings slowed him partially, then Che's weight wrenched onwards, so he ended up on his knees, with the girl clinging to him.

For a moment all was dark, Che's whimpering breath his whole world. Then he noticed a flicker of light, a familiar crackle that had him extending his palm into the dark, a single candle guttered into a wan glow. The Wasp who held it had just touched it to life with the slightest ember of his sting.

That Thalric recognized him instantly came as no surprise now. It seemed that the Commonweal formed a web of strange chances, of elaborately intertwined destinies. *No wonder the superstitious bastards believe so many stupid things*. But he could not hold to such a dismissive thought with a clear conscience any longer. He had witnessed too much of the wrong side of the world. *Give me a month in a sane man's town, with automotives on the streets and gaslight at night, and I'll recognize all this as a bad dream.*

'Mordrec, isn't it?' he recalled wearily.

The other Wasp eyed him blankly for a moment, then cursed. 'You . . . and the Beetle girl. Why not? Where are the others that were with you?'

'Expected any moment,' Thalric replied, although he felt a cold certainty that he would not see Varmen again.

'We were just creeping out to take a look at the Salmae, see what the bitch had brought with her.' Mordrec's free hand was by his side, but Thalric sensed the threat implicit there. 'And how come we found you setting fires and causing chaos?'

'Because of her.' Thalric nodded past the man's shoulder. There was a whole cave nestling here, a rent in the earth left where the roots of some vast forest giant had withered and died. Towards the rear he could make out a huddle of figures lit by a further candle, a good ten feet away. Between the two lights, though barely touched by either, he could make out the figure of Tynisa.

When Mordrec noticed her there, and saw her expression, he stayed well clear of them, ducking off to one side, holding his candle out like a talisman.

Her blade was drawn, Thalric saw. He would almost have been disappointed otherwise.

'What have you done to her?' Tynisa hissed, the words he could have put in her mouth, given two guesses. He glanced pointedly at Che's leg and saw, with a wince, that the arrow's fletchings had snapped off at some point during their escape.

'Yes, that's right. Obviously I shot her myself. I'm that well known for my archery.'

Her narrow blade was lined up with his throat, the tip of it within his arm's reach, but something about this woman had always brought out in him a need for bitter words, and he felt too tired to restrain himself.

'I rescued her from the Salmae, who seized her for reasons I can't guess at unless, as they're hunting you, they wanted to use her as bait.' He felt his Wasp temper slip its leash. 'She says your father's ghost sits on your shoulders like a cloak but, frankly, I don't know. After my getting you out of Capitas after the war, bringing your sister halfway across the known world, and then snatching her from the Commonweal nobility, of fond memory, I don't think even that bloody menace Tisamon would display quite such a level of ingratitude.'

He tensed as he said it, his wings and sting both at the ready, but the light of Mordrec's candle caught an unexpected look on her face: stricken and lost.

'He wants to kill you,' she whispered, and it seemed that she lowered her sword only by great effort of will. 'He doesn't remember gratitude. He doesn't remember his friends even, or barely, but he remembers his honour, and the Mantis way – and his enemies. Keep clear of me, Thalric. I don't know if I can stop him. I couldn't before . . .'

'Before what?' he asked, suspiciously.

'You killed their prince.'

Both of them looked down at Che, now almost forgotten.

'We killed him, both of us,' Tynisa confirmed. 'I don't know where I end and Tisamon starts. You were right, Che, and your magician was right, too, and now . . . I missed my chance, and it's too late.'

'Not yet. Not quite.'

They started, all of them, and Mordrec swore fiercely as Maure dropped down into the cave with a flurry of wings.

★

I remember his face, Tynisa considered. In stories she had heard of berserking warriors from the Bad Old Days – after the fit left them they would recall nothing of what they had done. The climax of a dozen Mantis tragedies was when the hero discovers too late whose blood is on her blade. *That would be a mercy,* Tynisa decided. *Let their fabled heroes weep and gnash their teeth. Remembering is worse than finding out second-hand.* She recalled Alain's expression as he had looked back and seen her there, the faintest shadow of guilt quickly brushed away, to be replaced by an all-too-ready smile. It was an invitation for her to forgive his dalliance, born from his confidence that he would talk her round, and that the world would continue dancing to his tune. He had mistaken her, though. He had thought that she was lovestruck, enamoured of him. He had never realized that she had loved him only for the image of his dead brother. Later, after the hunt, after Tisamon had lodged inside her like a poisoned arrow, she had not loved him at all. She had claimed him, made his approval the justification for her every bloody act, and he had used her, his mother had used her, and both of them had thought of her as a tame beast.

The Butterfly-kinden girl had read Tynisa better than Alain ever did. As soon as he was no longer pinning her down, she had fled in a flurry of golden wings, holding her ripped garments to her. By then Alain was dead.

'Do it. Make it go away,' she instructed.

'It's not so easy, but if you really wish the ghost gone, that is half the battle,' Maure replied.

The brigands had spent an entire day without discovery, Dal Arche keeping them inside the hollow beneath the trees, while the scouts of the Salmae ranged far beyond them. That night they had crept out and made best time heading north, all the better to baffle the trackers. Out of the woods, across a stretch of open ground, and then into the decaying remains of a small village, barely a half-dozen houses, most with only three walls still standing at best. The flimsy-looking Commonweal architecture was surprisingly durable, however, and where the outer walls had fallen away, panels decaying and overgrown, the inner rooms often still stood, and the slanted roofs remained more intact than not.

The Salmae search had already progressed further east, and Dal reckoned they had at least a day to catch their breath before the hunters realized they had been tricked. He was already hidden away with Soul Je and Mordrec, plotting their next move, working out the next cover between here and the border.

Che, Tynisa and Maure had chosen one ramshackle hut as their own. After dressing her wound as best she could, Che had sent Thalric to keep watch on their doubtful allies. Maure's exorcism would not be helped by a Wasp-kinden sceptic tutting over her shoulder.

'We must draw him out first,' Maure explained. 'When we attempted this before, he simply sat there in your mind like a beetle beneath a stone. With your help, though, we can startle him out, to where you can confront him and cut the bonds that hold him to you.'

Tynisa glanced around them. 'Che, you believe . . .?'

The Beetle girl nodded soberly.

'But the College, Collegium, your people . . . everything they taught us when we were growing up . . .' Tynisa's whisper was almost pleading. 'The world can't be like *this*? Can't I just be simply mad?'

Che took her sister's hands, which were shaking. 'Do you trust me?' Despite her wound, despite everything, she seemed now more solid and grounded than even Stenwold had been, an anchor of stability.

'I have no one else to trust,' Tynisa said, in a small, scared voice. 'Do it. Do it now before I change my mind.'

'Right.' Maure clapped her hands, businesslike, then hurried out of their wretched little hut to harangue the bandits. 'I need candles – all the candles you have. Incense, herbs. Just lay it all out. Serious ghost business! Don't make me put a curse on you. No stinting!' She would not take no for an answer, would not give up, and, although the Wasps stared at her as if she was mad, the bulk of the brigands were Inapt and obviously took her extremely seriously. Within a few minutes she returned with a surprising haul, and began sorting through it, trying to duplicate all the artefacts of ritual that she had left behind at Leose.

She first set out all the candles she had been able to scavenge, almost twenty stubs of varying sizes, and then had the Wasp Mordrec light them through his Art, which he seemed able to focus and control more than most of his kinden. In place of her firefly lamps, the little flames attracted dozens of insects that wheeled and circled about the tiny flames, before giving themselves to the pyre in brief, crackling sacrifice. Maure drew her circle in flour commandeered from some brigand's provisions, and marked out symbols in splashes of liquor, those same Khanaphes pictograms that she herself could not read. She had sorted through what meagre herbs, medicines and spices Dal Arche's people had donated, burning some, mixing others, in a ferocious magical improvisation, and doing everything she could with the makeshift tools at hand. Che watched it all but, more than that, she *felt* – understanding how Maure experimented to bring the circle to the right pitch of preparedness; until she could name the very moment when the necromancer had succeeded, that moment when the correct taste and strength of power had arisen, harsh, at the back of her throat.

Tynisa had watched it all blankly, but now at last Maure turned to her. 'Kneel,' she said. 'Kneel, for we are ready.'

Grimacing, Tynisa did as she was asked, acutely conscious of her sword as she tilted it to keep the scabbard-tip from scraping the floor. Che had knelt as well, then winced and thought better of it, so ended up sitting awkwardly with her injured leg straight out in front of her.

'We will now go into your mind, we three,' Maure announced. 'We will take you somewhere that your ghost cannot bear to be.' Her long face, with all its diverse heritage, looked drawn and lean. 'You will not relish that place either, but you must seize on to it, as if it were a thorn.'

'You mean a nettle,' Che said automatically. 'Nettles don't hurt if you grasp them, but thorns still do.' For a moment she was again the pedantic student that Tynisa remembered from the Great College.

Maure stared at her. 'If I may continue?' she asked, and Che nodded apologetically. 'Close your eyes, please,' the magician requested, 'both of you. We are going to travel back a little way. I know enough about you, Tynisa, to find my path. Che has told me of the hooks your life is hung from, so we will go to see something of worth, I think. Che, you have wished to see this too, and there are answers here for you. Simply concentrate on my voice, nothing more. Eyes closed, and listen . . .'

Sitting in that oddly peaceful ruin, with the bandits sufficiently involved in their own business not to intrude, Che felt oddly at rest, almost on the point of dozing. A moment later she jerked her head, sure she had missed some of Maure's intonation. The woman kept repeating the same few phrases, changing the order but never altering her tone. The day was clear and still, though, and sunlight shafted through the cracks in the roof. This was surely no suitable time for magic, let alone necromancy.

And yet closing her eyes allowed her a darkness that even her Art could not penetrate, and the droning cycle of Maure's words seemed to throw layers and layers of distance between her and the rest of the world, as though she was receding in a direction she had no precise word for.

And, unable to stop herself, she opened her eyes – or they were opened for her.

By opening them, she let in a wall of sound. For a moment she could make no sense of the images, but the heaving, roaring bellow all around her seemed to take and shake her until her teeth rattled. There were surely a thousand Wasp-kinden all around, in tiered seats arranged in a huge ellipse about a pit of sand. She knew enough to recognize it as a blood-fighting arena, but she'd had no idea that they could be so large.

Her attention was already being shepherded though, to a knot of fighting at the lip of the pit. For a moment the movement there was so swift and brutal that she could not make it out, but then she felt Tynisa invisibly with her, felt her sister's horror as she attempted to squirm away from the sight, and she knew.

Tisamon and his lover, the Dragonfly Felise Mienn, were fighting. Dozens of Wasp soldiers descended on them, throwing themselves in the way of the avenging pair, dying on their blades. For a moment Che could not see why the Wasps did not simply stand off and use their stings, but then she absorbed the greater picture and she understood. Tisamon and Felise were not simply shedding random blood: they had a goal in mind.

Way above them, and yet so close, was the Imperial box, a cloth-walled chamber where cowered a crowned young Wasp who could only be the Emperor, Alvdan the Second. Beside him Che saw the unforgettable face of Seda, who would become Empress in his stead. She was not yet the imperious sorceress that Che had locked horns with, though. The aura of power that Che expected was absent, had yet to touch her. The girl was staring at the approaching pair with an expression of fascination and fear, but her fear was not for her own life, or at least not at the hands of Tisamon. There was a thread extending from her, invisible yet apparent to Che, that touched on a dark-robed man seated on the far side of the Emperor, a pinch-faced, emaciated old creature who held in his hands an ornate knot of wood that Che knew at once, though she had never seen it.

For this was the heart of it all. This was the Shadow Box, born from the failure of a twisted and terrible ritual, the soul of the blighted Forest Darakyon and the prison of a thousand Mantis-kinden warriors and magicians over five long centuries. Achaeos had nearly died in failing to secure this box, and here was the man into whose hands it had come. Gazing upon it, Che was struck by the sheer dark power of the object, and it was a power she recognized, as she might know a poison the second time she tasted it.

Felise was dead now, Tisamon still trying to battle his way onwards, but the Wasps threw themselves upon him in a storm of blood and vengeance. The Emperor gripped the arms of his throne, staring at the Mantis Weaponsmaster in terror. The withered old man, the Mosquito-kinden, invoked the Shadow Box, and Che saw a hideous creature flower in the Emperor's shadow: a twisted hybrid of insect and woman and briar thorn. The Emperor died without ever knowing it, and his stolen power flowed into the box, and into the hands of the robed magician.

There was another thread, which led away from the arena, and even by thinking of it her viewpoint pulled away so that she now saw the events around Tisamon as though lit by one candle, whilst another candle sprang up in the great night to show her a gathering of Moth-kinden atop a mountain. *Tharn*, she knew, and Achaeos was there, injured and weak, but charging a ritual to drive out the Wasp-kinden invaders from the Moths' halls. She knew it, knew it well, because here, as she watched, he reached out for strength, and here was her younger self to lend it. Another thread.

The Darakyon answered Achaeos's call and she remembered, all too well, that bleak and icy grip in her mind as it seized on them both. Her younger self was screaming now, in Myna all those miles away, as the Moth ritual rose to a bitter, wrenching climax.

And in Capitas, at the same arena, Tisamon broke away from the pack and struck down not the Emperor, who was already dead, but the magician who clutched the soul of the Darakyon. That bloody metal claw drove down and shattered the Shadow Box, and killed its bearer, and the great knot that was the Darakyon was abruptly undone, ebbing from the world. Achaeos was dead by now, the strain of enacting the ritual more than his body could bear, and Che's younger image had gone mad, charging towards the Wasp lines, and never knowing that the spectres of the Darakyon were at her back, ready to engage in their last battle before the world was rid of them for ever.

Or not quite all, and not quite for ever. Che reached out and held the world still, examining the net that linked them all, seeing each thread glitter as though dipped in diamond. Here the line from the dying magician to Seda, a conduit for the last of his power; here from Achaeos to Che and through him to the collapsing Darakyon. Here . . .

I see it now.

Here to Tisamon. Here the Wasps killed him, but his blade had cut into the heart of the Darakyon, and his spirit was now held within the knot. As the forest's ghosts were drawn away from the world, he went with them – but there was yet one thread that he could use to drag his way back into the world.

Che finally noticed Tynisa in the dead magician's shadow, chained and bound like a plaything, nothing but a spectator to her father's death. No thread touched her, though, and Tisamon's ghost re-entered the world by a more tortuous route by far. But, of course, Che had already known that, for she herself had been linked to the Darakyon, and she saw now, in crystal detail, how Tisamon's ghost had crept into her own mind: the spectre that had haunted her in Collegium and Khanaphes, and that she had wrongly believed to be Achaeos's tortured, bitter spirit.

And in Khanaphes the Masters had rid her of her parasitic companion, and thus set Tisamon free to roam the world. And, naturally, he had sought out his daughter, fulfilling his unfinished task: to mould her in his own image, with all the doomed tragedy that must imply.

She could sense Tynisa alongside her, forced to witness again the death of her father and her own inability to save him.

Maure was close too, and Che felt the necromancer's frustration that this tableau had not drawn the ghost out into the open. Che understood it, though, as only a sister could. Despite her determination to be rid of Tisamon's shade, Tynisa held tight to him still.

A further shock is needed, she firmly resolved, and knew what it should be. She smothered a brief stab of guilt as she reached for Tynisa's memories once again. With her sister's mind at her disposal, she knew that she must see *one* image, *one* moment, whether it would aid in their efforts against Tisamon or not. *I have to know.*

The interior of the shack was wretched, walls and ceiling leaning and bulging at odd angles as its slipshod construction surrendered, by degrees, to the constant damp. The room was crowded, some of its occupants on their feet, others strewn across the floor, struck senseless the moment the Shadow Box had been opened. The artefact's dark, twisting influence was everywhere, like the smell of rotting meat. Che took a deep breath before identifying the players: on the floor lay Tisamon, Tynisa and the Spider girl Sef, while Achaeos, her lover, sat hunched over with the Shadow Box clutched in his hands. She saw now how he had tried to pry into its secrets, but instead it had drawn him into itself, along with all those around him.

Staring down at the bodies were two Wasp-kinden – Thalric and Gaved, both utterly bewildered by what had happened. Their Inapt minds had been ignored by the Shadow Box, leaving them unaffected, and at the same time they could not see the cloaked figure that walked between them. It was another Mosquito-kinden, a pale, cadaverous woman dressed in trailing robes, now stepping invisibly past the Wasps and taking the Shadow Box neatly from Achaeos's unfeeling hands. Then the shadowy figure had touched Tynisa, and the Spider girl was waking up even as the thief retreated.

Awake but not herself: her face was blank, her eyes staring

blindly. The two Wasps started and stared at her, as she stood over Achaeos with her sword in her hand.

Che sensed her sister's mind kicking away from that moment, and understood that these were memories that Tynisa had never known she had. That moment had always been a blank for her, the Mosquito-kinden's magic raising a barrier she had not been able to penetrate. Now she saw herself clear as day, in that filthy hut in Jerez, and she waited for the terrible stroke to descend, for the blade to lance Achaeos through.

Abruptly Che realized that she did not want to see this, after all. She knew what the outcome would be: Achaeos would receive a wound that would nearly kill him, and the strain of it would prove the death of him during the Moth-kinden ritual later on. Seeing him fragile and helpless, she tried to pull herself away, but the moment she felt doubt, her control of the vision escaped her, and she was held – as unwilling a witness as Tynisa – watching as the same moment played itself out.

And still Tynisa stood there with sword out, and Gaved and Thalric were questioning her, demanding answers. Her hand was shaking.

She fights the geas imposed on her, Maure's thought came. *She could have killed them all by now.*

Then, with a hopeless, graceless motion, Tynisa lashed out with her blade, lancing Achaeos through. But even Che could see that her stroke had gone awry, her blade and her arm conspiring to spoil her aim.

There was more then, Tynisa fighting with the two Wasps, but Che felt a great shudder, and the image was abruptly fragmenting. She became aware of her own body through the pain in her leg, which had been mounting up in her absence.

'You told me,' she heard Tynisa gasp, and then opened her eyes. The Spider girl was already on her feet, her blade drawn again, and for a horrible moment Che thought history might repeat itself. It was not Maure or Che that Tynisa was confronting, though.

In the air before her hung a shape pale and indistinct, a spiderweb of lines that resembled something like a man – but a man transfigured, his body writhing with briars, his skin rippling with chitin. Only the face remained untouched by the taint of the Darakyon.

Tisamon.

Tynisa was staring at this tattered spectre, and Che had no word for the expression on the girl's face.

'In Jerez, after Achaeos . . . I tried to throw my sword away . . .' the Spider girl got out. Whatever emotion had hold of her was shaking her with all its force. 'But you told me then that I had been the victim of magic, and that the sword did its best to stay my hand. You told me that, then, but I had forgotten.'

The ghost made some almost dismissive gesture, but Tynisa's face was abruptly twisted into a snarl.

'You told me that, then, and I didn't believe you, and I thought I must have had some reason to do it, because in Collegium there is no magic and people do not stab their friends without purpose,' she spat out. 'But here in the Commonweal, after you came to me, you had me believe that I stabbed him because he was an enemy – that he had earned his death, and that I should rejoice in his blood. All these things you whispered to me, telling me to feel no guilt but to be satisfied at the downfall of a foe. Where is the man who comforted me, and told me I was bewitched, and that even my blade had fought against the deed? Why not tell me that, and lead me away from . . .' and her voice broke momentarily, 'from doing it all *again*!'

Mantis-kinden know no guilt. Che heard the voice as if it was a whisper of leaves.

'You did!' Tynisa snapped. 'It made you *human,* that regret, but where is it now? Where is the man who was Stenwold's friend, and who loved my mother?' Her jaw clenched, and Che thought she had finished, but then she shrieked out, loud enough for everyone among the ruins to hear, '*Where is my father?*'

The movements of the ghost tried to claim that title, but its voice was too faint to hear. Instead, it was Maure who answered her anguished cry.

'This is but some part of him that has clung on,' the magician explained sadly. 'Some handful of shards of him, mere fragments of the man that once was. Ghosts are just broken pieces of us. The hard slivers of him stand before you, with nothing to sheathe their sharp edges. This is the Mantis, not the man.'

A fragile calm touched Tynisa and she let her hands fall to her sides, pointedly no longer resting one on her sword grip. 'You made me kill Alain, and without you . . . perhaps I would not have been so hasty. I will not say he was a good man, and he was certainly not his brother, but I became a murderer in truth when I shed his blood.'

Tisamon's shade made an angry gesture, and Che faintly heard, *You are above their laws and morality.*

'Stenwold would disagree,' Tynisa replied, and the mention of that name seemed to strike the ghost like a blow, making it ripple and shudder. And then she said, 'I cast you out.'

There was an utter silence after those words, and the twisted and changing face of the ghost remained still for a moment, then it rushed forward, to within inches of Tynisa's face. Che heard it cry out, *You need me!*

'My true father would tell me I need nobody but myself.'

With my aid, you will never lose a battle, triumph in every fight!

'You lie, spirit,' Tynisa snapped. 'I would triumph in every fight except the last, because you would drive me to some impossible conflict eventually, just to have me die as Mantis-kinden should. I cast you out. I cast you *out.* I deny you. You are not my father.'

Che held her breath, waiting and still waiting as the spectre shimmered and hung in the air. A disturbance was building up within it, and it writhed and twisted as though strung up on hooks. Her gaze sought out Maure, and found the magician pale and tense, as if awaiting an explosion.

Then, like an exhalation, it was gone, vanishing into infinite distance, yet without seeming to leave the walls of the decrepit hut they sat in, even as the very sunlight seemed to creep into the shade's absence.

Maure let out a long, ragged breath. As the only one of them to know the risks intimately, she looked more relieved than Che cared to think about.

'It's done,' she confirmed. 'The shade is gone.'

'Gone where?' Tynisa asked, sounding shaky, but all Maure would say was, 'Away.'

The Spider girl glanced at Che, tentatively probing her expression. 'You saw it all? Tisamon? *Achaeos*?'

Che nodded tiredly. 'I've never held Achaeos against you, Tynisa, nor has Stenwold, nor did Tisamon when he truly lived. The only one who ever did was you yourself. Do you at least accept that you're not to blame for his death?'

Tynisa nodded. 'I tried so hard not to believe in magic. I thought it was just a convenient excuse. You came a long way to tell me that, Che.'

'Well of course I did,' Che replied, almost offended. 'We're sisters, after all, despite everything. And you'll be needed.'

Tynisa blinked. 'I'll . . . what?'

'As we all will be needed.'

Tynisa and Maure were both staring at her now, but the words just fell from Che's lips, her face slack and expressionless.

'Falling leaves, red and brown and black and gold. A rain of burning machines over a city of the Apt. The darkness between trees. The Seal of the Worm is breaking.'

A beat of complete silence followed, as though the world outside their ruined hut had been utterly stilled. Then Che blinked at them and demanded, 'What? Why are you looking at me like that?'

'Che, you said . . .' Tynisa frowned. 'I don't understand what you just said.'

'No?' Maure asked. 'The Moths call their magicians seers, and set them to sift the future for visions of what may come. Sometimes the visions arrive unasked. The Seal of the Worm, that's what you said.'

'Meaning what?' Che asked, entirely thrown, but a man's voice broke in, startling them all, Tynisa snatching for her sword.

'The Seal of the Worm. That's a bad old story.' It was Soul Je, the Grasshopper-kinden brigand, crouching just outside the shattered doorway of their hut. Che guessed he had come to investigate the shouting of just a moment before.

'Tell us,' Che instructed him immediately, but the man shook his head.

'Best not repeated. Old wars, old enemies banished to the depths, and let them long remain there. Besides, who knows the truth these days?' He shrugged.

Che was frowning, her face screwed up in concentration. *Something of the Moth lore* . . . In trying to understand Achaeos she had read all that a Beetle might readily acquire, including mouldering histories that no other College hand had touched in centuries. 'Worms . . . some old war?' *And what had happened at the end of that war?* But, of course, Moth histories were opaque, dense with allegory. The Moths had fought off so many challengers in the Inapt world of the Days of Lore: all of them defeated, hunted down, destroyed wherever they could be found, or else . . . *banished?*

Sealed away . . . came the uncomfortable recollection.

She opened her mouth to question Soul Je again, but he shook his head, discouraging it. A moment later the Wasp Mordrec bundled past him.

'We've spotted their scouts! Time to move!'

Forty-Three

Salme Elass's tactical problem now was that her entire force, including all the peasant levy and footmen, could not reliably keep up with the fleeing brigands. A large force was always slower, trailing its supplies and its unwilling conscripts. If she mustered her strength in one place, she might never catch her enemies.

She had taken the only step she could, by sending her followers out in detachments at varying speeds, trusting to the fastest to bring her quarry to bay so that the rest of her strength could regroup and finish the business once and for all.

At first the bandits faced only airborne opposition, the fleetest of the Dragonfly-kinden – nobles and their retinues in light armour. They were few in number, for their strength had been spread wide to locate the fugitives, and the wiser of them simply waited high over the chase, signalling by their very presence the whereabouts of the enemy.

The rasher of the scouts, those keen to make a name for themselves, tried to harry the brigands on the ground, stooping on them with spears or loosing arrows as they dived past overhead. They soon found, however, that Dal Arche and Soul Je were both easily capable of hitting a mark whilst still running, twisting back and up to follow the flight of a passing warrior and then letting fly without ever stumbling or slowing. The scouts had minimal armour, the better to fly far and fast, and after the brigands' shafts had brought several down the rest kept their distance.

The column of scouts, circling like some bizarre localized weather, would serve its purpose, though. Soon enough, Avaris the Spider called out, '*Riders*!' as the first elements of the Salmae cavalry came in sight, still distant but gaining.

A handful still, but they would be harder to turn away than the scouts. Dal wordlessly changed his direction, striking out against the rise of the land. It was not clear to anyone if he had an actual destination in mind, and so Tynisa exerted herself to fetch up alongside him.

'We can get under cover before they reach us?' she got out.

He shook his head, saving his breath. Aware of her exasperated look, he grimaced and rasped, 'These we kill. The next? Depends how soon, how fast.'

Tynisa nodded, dropping back. 'Thalric, Mordrec,' she snapped. 'Rearguard.'

They both glared at her, neither of them happy to be taking orders from her. Thalric was supporting Che, who was still slowing them all with her injured leg. Wordlessly he passed her to Maure, who did her best to lend some strength to the toiling Beetle girl.

'I count six,' Tynisa stated. 'Your stings, my blade.'

'They could just go round us,' Mordrec pointed out, half-breathless.

'Then the archers must take them,' Tynisa declared.

'Let me take the lead,' Thalric put in. 'We need a horse kept alive for Che.'

The riders were closing swiftly, thrashing their horses to make up the distance, each one of them wanting to win the favour of Salme Elass. When they saw who awaited them, however, they faltered a little, two reining in and the rest swerving away. *They fear us*, Tynisa thought with satisfaction, and then she was rushing towards the nearest rider, even as he tried to haul his mount aside. He had ventured too close, though, and

Thalric's sting struck him against his breastplate. The scintillating mail turned most of the heat away, but the blow still sent the rider reeling back in his saddle, and before he could regain control of the reins Tynisa had lunged up, her blade piercing the chitin shell of his armour and running itself to the hilt into his side. She saw the man's golden skin turn suddenly pale, and he toppled from his mount.

'Maure!' Thalric shouted. 'Take the beast!'

The magician rushed forward but the panicking horse shied away from her, and as she stumbled after it, another rider charged her with lance levelled. Her wings lifted her from under the hoofs, but not fast enough to evade the weapon's point. An arrow flowered in the rider's neck, though, between pauldron and helm, throwing him sideways, jerking the lance aside. Maure dropped down onto the horse's neck, kicking and elbowing until the rider fell from the saddle, and then snagging the reins with one hand and dragging the beast back towards Che. She looked around wildly to see Dal Arche fitting another arrow to his bow whilst, beside him, Soul Je aimed upwards, warning off the boldest of the scouts.

Two more of the riders had chosen the same moment to attack, and the Wasps had made them rue it. Whilst the armour of a Dragonfly noble might scatter some of their stingshot, the horses were not so protected. Thalric and Mordrec brought them both down in short order, lashing the wretched animals with both hands until they reared and plunged and fell. One of the cavalrymen kicked himself free and flew, darting in the air to avoid Dal's next shot, and putting as much distance between himself and the brigands as possible. The other fallen rider had just got to her feet, swaying but reaching for her sword, when Tynisa reached her and finished her with a single straight thrust.

The remaining two horsemen kept their distance, keeping out of arrowshot but no further. There was movement beyond them, which could only be the rest of the Salmae's forces, or at least a fair proportion of them.

'Keep moving!' Dal shouted. 'There'll be more cavalry soon.'

Maure had Che perched before the saddle now, although the horse protested at its double load. She kept a steady pace, keeping the animal on a tight rein, well aware that if she outdistanced the bandits, the circling scouts were likely to drop on her.

A glance back confirmed that there were more riders splitting off from the main body of the Salmae force, some making straight for the fugitives, others peeling off to circle round and ahead of them, intending to cut them off.

'There!' Dal cried out, putting on an additional burst of speed. They were still slogging up the rise of the land, but now they could see woods ahead, and within the trees some suggestion of stone.

'A castle?' Thalric asked him.

'Not quite. A tower, though. Should be enough of it left to defend.'

'Defend? For how long?' Thalric demanded.

Dal's backwards look told him all he needed to know. The leader of brigands was running out of plans.

A half-mile on and the whole bloody business was played out again, even as they were running for the treeline along the hill's crest. The faster outriders had caught up with them, perhaps only a dozen, but to stop and fight them would give more of Salme Elass's people time to catch up. Again Tynisa dropped back, the two Wasps shadowing her automatically now.

'Ride!' she shouted, and Maure kicked at her stolen horse's flanks, making a break for the trees. A couple of the scouts swooped on her, but Soul Je shot one from the air in a single fluid motion, and the other darted away.

On either side of Tynisa, the Wasps' stings crackled sporadically, a sound that made some inner part of her twitch away, from long experience. *How can they now be on my side?* The first flashes were at extreme range, though Thalric still made his target rear up and shy away, almost unseating the rider.

Then arrows came hissing past them, most of the riders choosing to stay out of sting reach. Their small horse-bows were still enough to outdistance Mordrec, and of course many of them would have had first-hand experience of the Wasp Art during the war. Tynisa backed up, remembering how, when the spirit of Tisamon had been with her, she had batted arrows from the air as though they were juggler's balls.

Thalric sighted down his arm and sent off a sizzling bolt of fire that struck one of the archers clean from the saddle, his bow springing apart, the string charred through. That bought them a little more time as the other riders swung their mounts aside, circling for more distance. It seemed ridiculous that the three of them could stand off a dozen cavalry, but the reputation of the Wasp-kinden was ground deep into their foes. The man that Thalric had knocked down was clearly not getting up again.

Tynisa only distantly heard the cry of warning, but her sword came up and back without the need for thought, catching a blade as it rammed for her back, and turning the strike aside. The scouts had now sensed their chance, or else they feared the wrath of the Salmae if they did nothing, and they were dropping down all around, some with bows and some with swords.

An arrow spiked Mordrec's shoulder and he went down on one knee with a curse, the other arm flung out to sear its way across the bowman's chest. Another archer loosed a shaft at Thalric, but hurriedly, the shot flying wide despite its close range, and then Dal Arche shot the man in the back, shouting, 'Run for the woods! We have to move!' In truth, by now only Tynisa, the two Wasps, Dal and Soul Je were still left.

Tynisa let her rapier twist about the sword of the scout attacking her, flicked it aside with a circular motion of her wrist and then jabbed into the opening she had created, pricking him through the throat. The cavalry had meanwhile regained their courage, and a couple were plucking lances from the holsters beside their saddles. She risked a glance behind her, gauging the distance to the treeline.

A bowman was there, the string drawn back to his ear and the arrowhead directed at her face. Even as she spotted him, he loosed.

She felt the impact like a hammer blow, but it had fallen on the guard of her blade, the weapon and her arm both finding their way by the age-old Weaponsmasters' partnership. The impact drove her sword hand back to her chest, and the archer's jaw dropped as the arrow sliced to one side of her, deflected from the curved quillons.

So it was me, and not him. She killed the bowman even while registering the thought, leaping into a lunge that drove her blade through the chitin of his armour, barely slowing. Then she was running, Dal Arche helping Mordrec along beside her; as Soul Je and Thalric sent arrows and stingshot at the oncoming riders.

Abruptly the trees were above and around them, the riders behind them slowing and turning aside, and then they were running uphill towards tumbled stone walls.

Within the trees, the bows were of less use, which was just as well, as the enemy were bringing up considerably more of them than the brigands could muster. The cavalry would be next to useless, too, unable to charge or manoeuvre between the trunks. There would be a moment when the front-runners of the attacking force hesitated, waited for their fellows, fearing some trap, perhaps brigand reinforcements. It was enough to give Dal Arche's people a headstart on reaching the ruins.

The airborne scouts were ahead of them, though, and a half-dozen had the wit to try and claim the ruin before the brigands could get there. The tower itself had been a circular structure, its height undeterminable now, but the lowest storey remained almost intact, surrounded by a broken area of fallen stone coated with moss and entwined by creepers. The fleetest brigands arrived just in time for one of them, a lean Grasshopper, to take an arrow in the throat from a Dragonfly archer crouched in the doorway. The others then scattered, taking cover amongst the trees. More arrows sped from the pair of narrow slit windows flanking the door.

Tynisa took in the situation the moment she arrived. Dal and Soul Je were shooting from within the trees, but the doorway lent cover enough that they were getting nowhere. She grimaced – but somehow it turned to a grin.

A moment later she was running forward, her sword levelled before her. She saw the man in the doorway draw back his string, focusing on some other movement within the trees, before one of his fellows shouted a warning and he saw her. His expression was all she could ask for, fright and shock making him twitch away, the arrow flying harmlessly high. Another shaft from one of his comrades hissed past her like a breath of air, and then she was amongst them. Her sword lanced the closest man under the ribs, but she just carried on running, plunging into the gloom of the interior while dragging her victim round until her blade slid free. The men within were dropping their bows, reaching for swords or daggers instead, but the walls close about them gave nowhere to run to. Her mind plotted a pattern on the dusty, leaf-blown floor and she let her feet trace it, treading in a jagged star with each point punctuated by blood. The rapier was never still, flicking and dancing through the air like a silver insect, fending off their strikes at her, leaping over their guards to pierce their armour of leather and chitin as though it was nothing but cloth. The last man got by her and ran through the doorway out into the open, only to meet Thalric's sting that hurled him off his feet.

The brigands raced inside. Che limped in next, leaning on Maure, and finally Mordrec aided by Soul Je. It was now crowded company there, but even so it was plain that several of them had not made it. Aside from Dal and Soul, even now trying to extract the arrow from Mordrec's shoulder, there were only half a dozen brigands left: two apiece of Grasshoppers and Dragonflies, a halfbreed and the Spider, Avaris.

'They're hiding in the trees now,' someone called out, and

bandits moved to the slit windows, arrows nocked. Tynisa herself went to the door, waiting for her next challenger. Overhead the sky darkened, the evening coming on fast. They had been constantly on the move for most of the day.

And I don't feel tired, not at all. She suspected that she would, though, as soon as the rush of it all had drained away, but for now Tynisa felt as though she could run for ever.

The first wave to come against them included a fair number of noble retainers amongst the levy, their armour glittering in the last rays of the sun. They met arrows and stingshot from the defenders – and then they met Tynisa in the doorway.

For a moment she felt fear: not fear of them but that the spectre of her father, or that murderous piece of her father that had been left behind, would descend on her again and make her his creature. Instead, she felt her training, her skill, her heritage and her blade all converge within her, a council of war that was resolved in moments, and she swayed away from an arrow and then met the first blade, flicked it aside with a small motion of her wrist and then laid open the wielder's forehead, beneath the rim of his open helm, sending him staggering backwards with blood in his eyes. She cut aside spearheads as they quested for her, darting to gash hands and arms, to sever fingers, making a mockery of their reach. Then another noble was rushing at her, a Dragonfly woman with a fixed look of hatred, and Tynisa let her try to strike, let the sword cleave empty air, and then put an elbow in the woman's eye and ran her through as she stumbled, dropping her neatly. The longer she held the door, the more damage the others could do through the arrowslits, and now Mordrec had hauled himself over to a window, so that stingshot was crackling from both sides.

The enemy fell back, the levy giving way first, and their betters following suit rather than be left exposed.

The next wave, after a pause of almost half an hour, was a throng of armed peasants: a mob of desperate, frightened Dragonflies and Grasshoppers lacking armour save for quilted jackets or the odd cuirass of chitin scales, and armed only with spears. Tynisa steeled herself, and took a lot less joy in staving them off, but the confrontation was a brief one. With no inbound arrows, other bandits had the courage to back her up with bows, and the wretched peasantry broke and fled a minute after they had reached the door. By then the dark had fallen, and she knew that, whilst Dragonfly eyes were as good or better than hers, their Grasshopper levy could not see well at night.

And besides, she suddenly considered, *how many of them are left?*

It was an unexpected thought, but a salient one. After all, how many had Salme Elass been able to muster for her grand campaign against the brigands? And how many remained with her now, of her guests and their retainers, and whatever peasants she had pressed into service along the way? Oh certainly, she would still have a force that greatly outnumbered the defenders, but even so, not vast by the standards that Tynisa was used to thinking of: not the resources of an Ant city-state or a Wasp army, or even a Collegium merchant company. Not enough to waste.

Enough to kill us, she had to concede, but the odds she faced were simply extremely bad, not actually overwhelming.

That thought made her laugh, startling her fellows, but then her reputation amongst them was for bloody-handed madness, so this did not seem out of character.

Tynisa stood watch, peering into the gathering darkness and waiting for Salme Elass's next assault. Occasionally she thought she heard wings overhead, but no onslaught came from the trees.

How many of them have we killed, in all? she wondered. With her blade to aid them, and with the great doomed assault Varmen had made on the enemy camp, the brigands had certainly given far better than they had received. This was helped by Salme Elass's lust for vengeance, which had made her throw her people pell-mell at them, in whatever numbers could be mustered, rather than conserving her strength. Still, that vengeance would mean the end of the bandits, however long it took. She would keep spending the lives of her own people until nobody was left, and most of all until Tynisa herself was dead.

If I walked out there now and gave myself up . . . She glanced back at her companions: Che she would die for certainly, Thalric, probably not, and she barely knew Maure. Of the others, they were desperate, violent men, and scarcely worth a grand sacrifice.

She found, though, that she liked and respected them, their leader most of all. She had seen him shepherding his people all the way from Leose to this forsaken place, and decided he was a man to admire. If the Commonweal could have recognized such qualities in a man of common blood he would no doubt have become a war hero, an officer, a tactician. But all that life had granted him was to be a leader of criminals.

Che appeared at her elbow. 'I'll take over now.'

'You get your sleep,' Tynisa urged her.

Unlike the meek girl she remembered, Che managed a smile with about a hundred years of pain and wisdom in it. 'And you're so fresh, after a day running and fighting? We'll need you tomorrow, so go get something to eat with the others, then sleep. And be thankful the nights are still long.' When Tynisa opened her mouth to protest, Che added, 'And I can see in the dark, like a Moth.'

Her tone was almost commanding, imperious, and Tynisa found that her natural reaction was to nod and obey. *But you and I will talk, about what has happened to you.*

The bandits had stoked up the embers of a fire, and the walls around them helped a little to confine the heat. They all looked ragged and drained, but they were passing around jerky and grain cakes, and someone had a little pot reluctantly coming to the boil. To her amusement they were making kadith, Soul Je producing a roll of sad little dry bundles to steep in the water.

'How the other half lives, is it?' she asked, elbowing herself some room and sitting down.

'Kadith is an ancient and inviolable ritual,' Soul Je replied softly, almost reproachfully.

'And besides, what are we saving it for?' added Dal Arche. The brigands produced a motley collection of drinking vessels, from clay bowls to tin cups that still bore the stamp of the Imperial army.

Thalric was carefully bandaging Mordrec's shoulder with torn cloth. The Wasp's armour, metal plates sewn into cloth, had taken some of the force, but the arrow had still driven in some way.

'Well,' he said, after the kadith had been shared out, just a half-cup for each, 'this will be it then?'

There was sober nodding about the fire.

'We've given them a run, though,' one of the Dragonflies remarked.

'We were close, too,' added the other. 'They won't forget us.'

'Small comfort,' Thalric muttered.

'Oh?' Maure challenged him. 'And when the next leader comes along to rouse up the underclass, is it no consolation at all that the work of those gathered here will inspire them?'

Thalric gave her a bleak look. 'Rouse up the underclass? And how did that ever solve anything?'

'Ask Collegium that question,' Che called back from the doorway where she sat watching, wrapped up in cloaks and her breath steaming. Tynisa saw Thalric about to argue, but then he stopped and, to her surprise, he tacitly conceded the point. A moment later Che squeaked – there was no other word for it – and then got out, 'Alarm! I mean someone's coming! Attack!'

They were up and to the windows instantly, peering into the darkness.

'I don't see . . . yes, yes I do,' Dal started, nocking an arrow. 'Is there . . . just one?'

'Wasp-kinden,' Che replied. 'Approaching, walking with hands closed – Gaved? It's Gaved.'

'And who's Gaved?' the bandit leader demanded.

'He works for the Salmae,' Tynisa said, and added hurriedly, 'so they may have sent him with a message. Especially if he's on his own. He's no hero.'

'We see you,' Dal Arche yelled. 'What's your business?'

'Just to talk,' came the Wasp's voice, from the night.

'Let him talk from out there,' suggested one of the brigands, but Tynisa shook her head.

'Let him come in,' she decided. 'I know him.'

They looked to Dal questioningly, but the Dragonfly nodded. 'Any tricks and he's a dead man, even if he's your lover or your brother,' he warned.

'Approach, Gaved,' she said, pitching her voice sufficiently to carry out of the window. He did so cautiously, until the faint light of the fire touched him. For a moment he stood just beyond the doorway, plainly debating the wisdom of entering, but then he ducked under the lintel and stepped inside.

'Salme Elass sent you?' Tynisa observed. She, Che and Thalric had stayed to talk with him, while the rest of the brigands returned to their fire, save for Dal Arche, who remained by one of the windows, plainly not convinced that this might not be some kind of distraction.

'She did and she didn't,' said Gaved. He looked tired, having no doubt been kept busy trying to track them down across half of Leose Province. 'She sent out all her scouts, and there are a dozen of us around this place, making sure nobody slips away.' He shrugged. 'But I came to say goodbye.' He looked from face to face, seeing matching frowns. 'The game's changed. I'm lighting out, while I can.'

'But Salme Elass . . .' Che started uncertainly.

'Will take it badly, I suspect. She took it poorly enough when I didn't pitch in against Varmen, as though I could somehow conjure up some kind of Imperial magic to counter him. They want me to *fight* for them. Because I'm a Wasp, they want me to be a soldier.' His eyes flicked about the ruined tower's interior.

'I guessed Varmen didn't make it, after there was no sign of him yesterday. They don't know for sure, though. They can't be certain he's not going to rise up again. They never found his body.'

'But what about Sef?' Che interrupted

'I sent her to Prince Lowre, he'll keep her safe enough until I can find her again. I knew, before the start. I knew the deal was going sour.'

'I'm sorry,' Tynisa said.

He blinked at her, taken aback. 'Not your fault, girl. Maybe you stirred the pot, but Salme Elass has had this planned from way back – stir up the brigands, get them marching in strength, put them down, and then swallow up Rhael under cover of keeping her own lands safe. You helped, of course, and certainly the bandits put up a better fight than she'd guessed, but her plan's still on track right now. Except of course she's down a son, which might complicate her plans for keeping up the dynasty.' He sighed wearily. 'They're going to come for you soon after dawn,' Gaved stated flatly. 'You must know that already. You've cut a dent into her numbers, with all your fun and games, but she's not giving up, not now, not ever.' He looked over at Dal Arche. 'You've given her a better run than I'd ever have guessed, but it ends here – you must know that.'

'You say it as though we planned this,' Dal said dourly.

Again Gaved shrugged. 'I wish I could do something to help, but right now I've got my hands full just helping *me*. I have to go and dodge my fellow scouts now, and most of them can see in the dark.'

'Luck go with you, Gaved.' Tynisa put out a hand and he took it cautiously, clasping wrist to wrist. It was, she reflected, a Lowlander gesture, therefore unlikely to see much use amongst Wasps.

After he had gone, and Che had taken up watch again, Dal turned back to his fellows. 'When they come tomorrow . . . if we can beat them off just once, then we'll sally out,' he suggested.

'Those that can get away, go. Split up and lose them in the trees.'

'They'll be overhead and waiting for that,' said his halfbreed follower.

He shrugged. 'We're at the end of the wire now. Maybe someone will get clear. But wait till tomorrow for that talk. Let's have something more cheerful now. A song, anyone?'

One of the Grasshopper-kinden had a little instrument, a holed gourd small enough to be cupped in one hand, but she played something soulful on it, pleasant in its way but hardly qualifying as cheerful. After that the Spider, Avaris, told them some unlikely story about ghosts and buried treasure, and told it well enough to take their thoughts away from their cramped and grim surroundings. Then the other Grasshopper tried for a song, with a voice that was strong and pleasant at first, but the refrain seemed inexorably to speak of things past, things lost, time's hand closing the book of days, until a quaver came into the singer's tone, and he let his words fumble to a halt.

'Ah, well,' said Mordrec, into the ensuing quiet. 'This is it, then. I'm glad we gave them the run in the end, but all we've done is move our prison cell eastwards a ways. No last-minute schemes, Dala? You always did have a head for them.'

Dal Arche's expression suggested not. 'I'd rather Ygor was with us now. He was always a good man in a scrape.'

Maure took a deep breath. 'And Varmen, too,' she said, and there was an odd tremble in her voice as she said it, suggesting something more than mourning.

'And him,' Mordrec agreed. 'Why not? In fact, I'd rather we had about two hundred old friends and relations.'

'But Varmen . . .' Maure cast a guilty glance back at Che. 'Varmen had a way out. Because Varmen was in this place before.'

'Varmen's dead,' Thalric declared, probably more harshly than he meant, but Maure barely flinched.

Dal's face remained expressionless. 'What are you talking about?' he demanded. 'Explain.'

'He told me about a time during the war when he and some of his people were penned in by us Commonwealers, no hope of getting out – only of holding on a little longer before the end.'

'Maure—' Che started, suddenly understanding, but the magician hurried on with her story.

'He challenged them to duel of champions. That's the old way, here in the Commonweal. Before the Empire, that was the way that lords and ladies did it, to spare their people. Of course, the Wasps never saw the need, but Varmen used it to buy time.'

Tynisa saw that every pair of eyes had turned to her, inexorable as the dawn.

'No, absolutely not,' she heard Che saying distantly. 'They have a Weaponsmaster with them. A real killer.'

'I thought we had one here, too,' Dal Arche said quietly.

'But how will it help?' the Beetle girl demanded.

'Che, when two Weaponsmasters fight, people watch,' Maure pointed out. 'Even in the Commonweal it is a rare thing to see. There will be a chance to escape, win or lose. More of a chance than by staying trapped in here until . . .' She faced up to Che's accusing stare and shrugged unhappily. 'Che, I want to live. I agreed to help you, but not to end like this. I want to *live*.'

'As do we all,' Dal Arche agreed.

'You can't ask her!' Che snapped at him.

Dal stood up abruptly, with enough threat in his posture that Thalric intervened, hand extended, getting between him and Che. With that, everyone was on their feet, hands reaching for weapon hilts – everyone save Tynisa and Maure.

'Hold! All hold!' Dal snapped. 'Listen, Beetle,' he addressed Che, 'we are due to die on the morrow. I have no illusions about the justice of our cause. We are robbers and killers, and so are those that oppose us, and all the justice in the world won't tilt those scales an inch. But if there is a chance that any of us could live, then I *can* ask anyone anything. Death is a long road, Beetle girl, and trodden one way only, and those who put honour and principle before life belong in stories, not here in this ruin along with us. A challenge of champions might win us time to scatter and get away. If it means only another half-day of life for one of us, then I *can* ask.' He shook his head. 'She's right regarding the old ways from before the war. They don't apply to bastards like us, peasants and villains, but if the girl puts herself forward, I'll wager the Salmae will agree. That way the princess'll get to see the blood she most wants to.'

'How can you even—' Che started, but Tynisa just said, 'Che.' Not spoken loudly, but the word brought silence in its wake.

'It's a good idea,' she continued. 'I'll do it.' And when Che started protesting again, 'I've seen the man fight, so who knows how matters might fall out? And, besides, I'd rather die at the hands of another Weaponsmaster I can respect, than fall to some chance spear or arrow.'

And in her head she heard the echo of the words, *With me, you can win any battle*, and they were followed by hollow, bitter laughter.

I could ask him back, even now, and he would come, but she knew bleakly that she would not. *I will live or die according to my own merits, in the final analysis. The real man that my father was would appreciate that.*

Forty-Four

After that it had simply remained for them to choose who should deliver the challenge.

In the grey light of a mist-laden dawn, Thalric emerged from the tumbled tower, passing Dal Arche, who had watched out the last hours of the night.

'Good luck,' the Dragonfly wished him.

Thalric gave the man a sour look. This was, he was fully aware, a stupid idea, and he had no faith in it, whatever the late Varmen might have said. Still, it was marginally less stupid than sitting in the tower until the Salmae finally cracked their defences.

All I need to do is get Che out, he decided. Win or lose, he would manufacture the opportunity somehow.

And they take this seriously? This clash of champions? Now that it had been mentioned, he did find an old memory surfacing from the earliest years of the war. Imperial generals being called out, gorgeously armoured Dragonfly-kinden Weaponsmasters standing before the automotives and the massed infantry, and then pointing a levelled sword, trying to face down the future.

He frowned. There was a great deal of idealism in the Commonweal back in those days – amongst the nobility, at least, who didn't need to worry about where their next meal was coming from. Storybook lives, princes and castles, dances and hunts and mock tourneys. Then the Empire had come and burned away centuries of accumulated romance inside the engines of its war machine. So where did that leave Salme Elass? Was she still the honour-bound idealist?

Emperor's balls she is, Thalric decided. He would rely on two things: that there would be empty-headed idle nobles among her retinue by whom this nonsense would be taken seriously and that Salme Elass knew what she herself wanted.

He spotted their picket line even as he entered the trees, mostly because it recoiled from him at a distance of twenty feet, the scouts flitting back towards the safety of the camp. He guessed that they had spread themselves thin, a cordon about the tower with plenty of airborne keeping watch for attempts at an escape to the sky. *But, then, they know Tynisa, therefore they know she cannot fly.*

'I am an emissary with a message for your princess,' he called out. 'You will take me to her.'

After a pause, a handful of them approached him, clustered together for shared courage, as though they were stepping between the jaws of a beast. Thalric regarded them coldly, facing down the spearheads trained on him. They were a handful of peasant levy, he realized, and terrified of him. *Varmen did some good work, then.*

'I come under truce,' he informed them, raising one hand. A red flag was apparently the truce sign in the Commonweal – another gap in the Empire's knowledge, as far as he was aware, though he guessed that wouldn't have made much difference to the course of the war. Oddly, none of the brigands had been carrying one, back there in the tower, but eventually it had been discovered that Avaris was wearing three shirts, one of which was something close to russet. It had then been pressed into service, tied about Thalric's wrist so as to leave both hands free.

One of the soldiers, a Grasshopper-kinden with short greying hair, stepped forward and took a deep breath. When

Thalric failed to strike him dead, he bowed slightly. 'Come with me,' he beckoned.

Word had clearly outstripped his arrival because some semblance of a court had already assembled, with Salme Elass, partly armoured, at its heart. Thalric regarded the Dragonfly matriarch speculatively: whatever rage she harboured for the death of her son was kept deep within her. Her glance towards him was merely imperious. Even so, there were a great many spears directed his way, some arrows too, and he saw plenty of sidelong glances and people shuffling a few inches back as he passed by. It was as though death by Empire was something that could be caught merely by proximity.

If I cried 'Boo!' now, I'd make half of them crap themselves. And I'd get shot, too, about nineteen times, so over all not worth it.

'Emissary!' He held up the rag tied to his wrist. 'Sent from Dal Arche of Rhael to Salme Elass of Leose.' He only hoped he had the province names the right way round. And no wonder his people had renamed most of the places they conquered. The place was easy enough to get lost in, as it was, without all their baffling and oddly pronounced towns and villages.

'"Dal Arche of Rhael"?' echoed Salme Elass archly. 'The villain styles himself thus, does he?'

'I'd assumed this was the heart of your disagreement,' Thalric replied easily, as though he was not the focus of such utter fear and hatred. 'You'll forgive me, but these Commonweal customs are unfamiliar to me. I merely bring you the message.'

She gave him a calculating look. 'So this is not the Empire's fight, then?' and it was plain that the subtraction of one Wasp-kinden from the equation was greatly to be desired, most especially if that Wasp might then just walk away. 'What is your name, emissary?'

'Thalric,' he stated simply, for the momentary luxury of having an audience to whom it would mean nothing. Then, because he had a reputation to keep up as a figure of terror and nightmare, '*Major* Thalric.'

Salme Elass affected to look bored. 'Every Wasp lordling from across the border is a colonel at least.'

'Whereas I come from the Empire itself, and not your lost principalities, and so am only a major,' he replied equably. 'But you're right: this isn't the Empire's fight, nor mine.' He had to bite his tongue to keep it at that, because the idea of the Empire even *noticing* this petty little brawl was ludicrous. This was not war. It was barely civil disobedience.

And yet people have died, and will die. It remains to ensure that Che and I are not amongst them.

'What is your message, emissary?' Elass snapped.

'I am sent to invoke an old Commonweal practice, as I understand it. We challenge you.'

An expanding ripple of silence followed his words. When Salme Elass's only response was to stare at him, he added, 'Dal Arche challenges Salme Elass or, as tradition will have it, his champion shall meet yours.'

'And what victory does your bandit-prince offer me, should I lower myself to accept this challenge?' she hissed.

'Himself and his followers, with no further loss of life amongst your servants,' Thalric elaborated. 'If he wins, he and his are pardoned, absolved, let loose to leave your lands unmolested. I think that's what they have in mind.'

'He and his half-dozen are now trapped inside a pile of stones, just waiting for my spears to pry him out, like a snail from its shell,' she pointed out with a slight smile. 'Is this the only way he could think of improving his odds? He is no prince, therefore I need accept no challenge. Why should I?'

Even as she said it, Thalric sensed a shifting and a frowning from some quarters, most especially those he had identified as nobles. Dal Arche was indeed beneath a princess's notice, unfit to clean her boots, let alone challenge her, but, even so, the refusal did not sit well. *Perhaps there are simply those who value their followers' lives more than she does.*

'Why should you?' Thalric echoed. 'I'd thought you wanted

to see Tynisa's blood, Princess. How better than if your own Weaponsmaster whittles her down for you? I understand he knows his trade.' He looked around, spotting the pale-haired old Mantis not far off, and instantly recognizable. 'Having her spear-riddled corpse dragged before you over a carpet of your own dead soldiers would be less satisfying to you? It would be to me, certainly.'

'A strange way to speak of your champion,' she remarked drily.

'Mine?' He raised his eyebrows. 'As I said, this is not my fight.' He felt the tide of honesty rising, and let it take him where it would. 'I care only for myself and for the Beetle girl I arrived with, Princess. For the others, the brigands, I care nothing. I have no doubt that you feel you've just cause to put them on the pikes, or string them up, or however else you like your executions around here. But as for Tynisa, well . . .' His grin was harsh. 'You have no idea how much *simpler* my life would be without her. If she got carved up by your man, why, I'd be dancing with joy inside. We've tried to kill each other enough times in the past, and whenever she had me at her mercy she made me regret it, every punch and kick she did, and even when I did her a good turn, she cast it back in my face with a curse. To have Tynisa dead would be the world's own gift to me, Princess. Let her come and let her die, and then I shall depart with Cheerwell Maker, and the rest are for your justice. Why would you say no? Why would you wish victory any other way?'

Finishing his speech, he examined his feelings on the matter. *And how much of that did I mean, and how much was just for show?* He found that he had absolutely no idea. The vein of bitterness he had tapped surprised even himself.

'Let her come then,' Elass said, just loud enough for him to hear. 'I grant this Dal Arche the honour of my agreement to his challenge. Let the murdering bitch come, and my champion will be waiting for her.'

Thalric nodded, then raked his black and gold gaze across the assembled court, seeing plenty of them flinch or drop their eyes rather than meet his.

'In one hour?' he suggested.

'An hour,' agreed Salme Elass, whereupon Thalric sketched a brief, almost disdainful bow to her, and went to spread the good news.

Gaved the Turncoat darted across the sky, the patchy forest rushing beneath him. For a Wasp he was a fair flier, which made him at best adequate and workmanlike by local standards, and normally he would not have tried to travel these distances trusting to nothing but his Art. He needed his high vantage point from which to search the land ahead, though. A great deal was resting on him just then.

That he was selling out one ally for another was a depressing weight in his stomach. He had tried, sincerely tried, to be an honest man, but nobody in the Commonweal wanted an honest Wasp. He seemed to have spied on everyone for everybody else, told each that they were the only one, like a faithless lover. He had lost track some time ago of precisely where his loyalties were supposed to lie.

The thought that he and Thalric had all this in common was a miserable one.

The weather was taking a turn, he felt – the air become crisp, snow on the way most likely. Just another way for the world to make his life harder just then. *Let it snow when Sef and I are out of here. Let it snow all it likes.*

And where the pits are they?

He pulled higher in the air, feeling the wind buffet him, taking his bearings, even checking his compass against the landmarks on offer. The Commonweal was so cursed *big*, and so much of it looked just like this, especially in Elas Mar Province. That was assuming he was still in Elas Mar Province, of course. The bandits' flight had taken them some way east, and if Gaved had got his compass points wrong he could even be over the border by now.

But there: he saw them now – the riders. They had been a further distraction to the Salmae scouts, or so the word had come to him: a party of riders plainly not under Salmae command, an armed force with unknown intent. When the scouts had gone seriously hunting them, though, no trace had been found. Gaved could only envy the woodcraft.

He dropped down, hoping fervently that nobody was going to shoot him. Bad first impressions were likely to be fatal in this sort of situation. He had his arms out, fists closed, but who knew whether these people remembered civilized conventions like that, any more.

There were a dozen riders there, and the contrast to the Salmae's people was plain: these were military, or at least the next best thing. There was a quiet discipline to them that put all the posturing of the local nobles to shame. Their armour was more functional than fancy, and they had a feel to them of men who had killed, and would kill again, and were utterly dedicated to their cause.

Gaved did not meet their gaze, because he was most certainly someone they would not hesitate to slay, given the order. Instead he hurried towards their leaders, two men he was at least on speaking terms with, even if those words were just orders that they gave him.

In the face of their stern looks, he had to fight the urge to salute.

'I must report,' he told them. 'Please, hear me. There is a great deal I have to tell you.'

Tynisa stood there in the morning sunlight, feeling the easy weight of her rapier, like clutching the hand of an old friend. The Salmae's people had started gathering at the trees' edge, some venturing up the slope a little. There was no sign of Elass or of Isendter yet.

She sheathed the blade, its point finding the scabbard's narrow mouth automatically, and took out her badge. The sword-and-circle glinted in the sun, looking polished as new. With care, she pinned it over her right breast.

The brigands had ventured out behind her, with plenty of nervous glances up at the sky. They held their weapons ready, and Tynisa realized that nobody cared about their supposed pledge to surrender themselves if she lost. When the tide of Salme Elass's followers descended on them with spear, sword and bow, they would soon be scattered and killed. Some might make it back to the tower, or halfway back up the hill, but that would avail them little.

She glanced back, her eyes seeking Che. Her sister sat resting her leg, with Thalric standing guard over her, and the halfbreed Maure nearby. The magician was looking guilty, and Che had pointedly turned away from her, but Tynisa could feel philosophical. *She was right, after all, this is the best way. I have done many bad things, and made many bad decisions, and I cannot blame them all on Tisamon's ghost.*

Even as she had this thought, the echo of his presence returned to her, almost like a plea to be allowed back in. *I shall make you win. You will carve your way through them, spill the blood of your enemies. What else is there?*

But she shook her head. *If I die, it will not be undeserved.* That was the bare truth of it. The Commonweal of Salme Dien, with its moral certainties, enlightened nobles and happy serfs, was already a lost world, and she had believed in it for too long, to her detriment. Perhaps men such as Felipe Shah and Lowre Cean did their best, but human nature was the same the world over. There was nothing magically pure about the nobles of the Commonweal. She had simply been lucky enough to know Salma, and he had been something special.

There was a murmur in the ranks, and she saw Salme Elass had arrived. *Alain's mother.* Dien's *mother.* The woman stared at her, the hard sun glinting and shimmering on her armour, then a servant brought forth a chair for her and she sat down, for all the world like the guest of honour at some theatrical presentation. Into the silence that followed stepped Isendter Whitehand.

The pale-haired Mantis paused a moment at Salme Elass's side, gazing down at his mistress. His gauntlet was buckled on, its blade jutting out between his middle fingers, and he flexed it in and out as he watched her: now forwards like a punch-dagger, now folding back along his arm. For a moment Tynisa sensed uncertainty in him, and she wondered whether he might have some reason to fear her, after all. Then he came striding to meet her, and the silence seemed to grow and grow around them both. The light touched brightly on his brooch too, the match for her own.

'You have lost a companion, I think,' he told her, when close enough to be heard without raising his voice. For a moment she thought he meant Varmen, but then she realized that he must have sensed the change, the absence of the ghost.

'I sent him away, in the end,' she declared. 'The price was too high.'

He regarded her levelly. 'Some might say that it was now that you would most need such aid.'

She forced a smile. 'I'll beat you on my own. I need no crutch, Master Whitehand.'

His nod was brief but approving. 'You are worthy to wear the badge, then,' he said simply, but the words seemed to strike her deeper than she could account for, drawing out parts of her that had withered in Tisamon's shadow.

I am a Weaponsmaster, after all. Live or die.

'And the justice of your cause?' he asked, nodding towards the little pack of brigands.

'And the justice of yours?' Because his words had practically invited the comparison. 'The fight is all.'

'We understand one another.' In a single step, he had put a very precise distance between them, a fighting distance, and her sword was in her hand without her needing to reach for it.

Even as he cut for her, she heard in her mind the beat of the Martiette, back in the ballroom of Leose. She already knew him, knew his skill and his style, the pattern of how he fought, taught to her in that dance. He perhaps thought he knew her just as well, but she had been playing host to Tisamon since then, and been twisted in his grip. She was no longer the same dance partner as before.

The first series of cuts came as though she and he had arranged them by prior agreement, as he made to step within her reach and bring his shorter, more agile blade to bear, twisting his wrist to lash at her from all angles, and she stepped back and round, circling, letting him drive her, and adjusting her stance for the sloping ground but catching each blow as it darted towards her, turning it aside with her blade and, once, with her quillons. Then, without warning, she had taken two steps to his one, widening the gap between them and putting him at her sword's point, and she lunged without giving him a chance to react. It was unfair, perhaps, that it was a move he would not see coming, not part of their previous course of dealings, but her sword led her into it, and she took the opening as soon as she had made it.

He did not even step back. Instead, his metal claw cut across his body, her sword's tip almost trapped between it and the spines of his arm. Then he moved further in, for a moment almost body to body, then past her, turning as neatly as any dancer – even as she spun on the ball of her foot, drawing her blade free, backing up to allow space again.

Two sharp lines of pain were clamouring in her mind, torn through her arming jacket below her right shoulder, dug there by the spikes of his off-hand arm.

His face bore a slight smile, and his eyes were encouraging, almost genial. He was enjoying himself, but not at her expense. She was impressing him, even though it was her blood glistening on his spines.

Then he drove straight at her, destroying all the distance she had tried to create. His swift blade flicked past her face, only her last-moment sway saving an eye from it, and then it was back to cut across her body, too close to be parried. She let her left leg fold, shoulder almost touching her knee, letting the strike pass her by. A heavier weapon would have left him open but, when she tried to jab at him with her sword, twisting her wrist and arm inwards to bring the needle tip to him, his weapon was in place to scrape down the length of her own blade, nicking her elbow to draw a single bead of blood.

She slapped him with her off-hand. She had no needles or spines of Art there, but it was a move both unbecoming and unheralded, and she felt the inside of her fingers connect with his chin, hooking his head aside. She used this tenuous purchase to swing her back foot round and retreat, then kick off and move forward again, even as he started to close once more.

She should have had him then. Her technique had been faultless: not a spare twitch or quiver to warn him that he would be driving himself on to her blade. His body was abruptly sideways, though, feet skipping him aside so that the slender lance of her rapier scoured a gouge in the grey leather of his jacket but drew no blood, and then he drove his clawed gauntlet down at her like a scythe-blade.

The first jolt passed through her, though in that moment she could not have recognized what it was. She pressed forward, ducking almost under his armpit, feeling the descending blade rake through her flurrying hair as she put on a rush of speed, clearing ten, twelve paces before she turned with sword outstretched and ready for him. She found him standing, as before, without having deigned to follow her. His expression was patiently encouraging, maddening because there was a meaning there that she could not quite grasp.

Her heart and innards felt taut and out of balance. He had bloodied her twice, and he was improvising. She had the measure of him, yet had barely touched him.

Some small, clear voice in the back of her mind explained it to her patiently: *This is fear.*

He approached again, his steps confident but without arrogance, a man who has seen the history of his duel written out like a play, and intends to perform his role without melodrama.

She seized the initiative, a three-step lunge from a standing start before he had even neared her, her sword lashing down on him, demanding an answering parry as he tried to catch her blade in the crook of his. Instead she drew her weapon back, whipped it at his face so he swayed aside, then was already drawing it back across her to pierce between his right-side ribs. His blade shadowed hers, his parry waiting for the strike to land as if it were a fly. Instead she wrenched her lunge up and stabbed straight at his face again, a strike meant to take him through the eye, but dropping for his throat even as he brought his blade up, hoping to slip under his guard.

Something rang across her skull, scattering her vision with sparks and lights, and she felt a solid impact on her sword-guard, a complaint of steel, and a pain in her side that seemed to spring from nowhere. For a second she could not see, but instinct brought her blade about to fend his off even as she stumbled back, and he let her go again, a second break, providing punctuation in the meticulous rhythm of the duel in his head, that he was carefully teaching to her.

That was what his expression meant, she realized miserably. It was the look of a hard teacher whose student is proving capable, if not exemplary.

He had punched her with his gauntlet even as he had the blade hinged down to catch her blow. Somehow she had warded off his first riposte, but the next had gashed her just above the waist. There was a trickle of blood down the side of her face where he had broken the skin.

The cold, ill feeling within her had crystallized. *I am not as good as he is*. The gap between them was certainly smaller than should be expected, given the difference in their years, but Isendter had been a master since before she was born.

He was stepping forward again, ready with his next lesson,

and she felt a tremble inside. *Save me – he's going to kill me.* She had never acknowledged such before. When she had fought Tisamon, so long ago, she had been too young and foolish to quite understand what losing a duel meant. Since then, she had fought many times, but no single opponent had really challenged her, not like this.

She tried another attack, putting her sword through a half-dozen feints and lunges, keeping him at its far end, and herself out of his reach. In her arm, her side, her face, the pain seemed to grow and grow. His metal claw had become a thing of horror, a torture implement. *I don't want to be hurt. I don't want to die.*

He let her stave him off for a little while, demonstrating a parrying style that moved his arm faster than she could flick the tip of her blade.

I am going to lose. The small voice was growing louder within her.

Dal Arche watched, and he knew enough to see how the fight was going. Everyone else was watching, too – all save one. Someone tugged at his elbow urgently.

'Dal, we have to go.'

He dragged his eyes away from the contest to see the Spider, Avaris, hopping anxiously from one foot to another.

'Dal, it's the plan, remember. We leg it now, maybe some of us get clear, come *on!*'

He glanced back at the duel, saw the pair separate again, another flash of red on the girl's body. *I owe her nothing, not even enough to watch her die. She's not one of mine.*

But he realized, with sour reluctance, that somehow she was, even though it was she who had got them into this mess. She was his champion, after all. He was a peasant woodsman gone to the bad, but in this moment he owed her something of that feudal loyalty that princes never quite seemed to grant to their underlings.

'We're going nowhere,' he growled.

'What? *Dal!*' Avaris hissed, and then, when the brigand chief rounded on him, he bared his teeth in a rictus of desperation. 'I want to live, Dal. Don't do this.'

However that loyalty to his followers cut both ways, and Dal sagged and nodded, feeling off balance, and unfamiliar to himself. 'Those that want to, go now, creep off, but no sudden moves. The Beetle girl and her Wasp are staying, no doubt, and so am I. Maybe they won't notice those that leave, if some of us stick around.'

He turned his eyes back to the fight, hands clenching and unclenching on his bow, hearing the careful, wretched sounds of his people taking their chances. Someone stepped up to his elbow, though, and he glanced sideways to find Soul Je nodding to him.

'Go and take your chances,' Dal advised, but the Grass-hopper shook his head.

'Mordrec, then?' Dal asked.

'Right behind you, Dala. Don't feel up to running, anyway.'

At that he did glance around. As he had known, the Beetle girl and her escort had remained, and their magician too, though she seemed perilously close to flight.

'A man can die in worse company, it's true,' he decided, clapping Soul Je on the shoulder, and settled down to watch the conclusion of the duel.

He saw the Beetle girl shift, coming half to her feet before the Wasp dragged her back down.

'Look at them,' Thalric snapped, his eyes not on the fight but on the Salmae's followers. 'See how many of them? And if you break the rules and interfere, why not them?' And then, perhaps in answer to some stubborn expression on the girl's face, 'And if you interfere by . . . *other means*, do you think they'd not know? They must have some two-stripe conjuror amongst them, if I'm to credit any of it.'

And Che sagged in his grip, but her eyes had never left the antagonists.

Tynisa backed and backed again, keeping Isendter away from her, but he simply walked into her reach, unhurried, careful and inexorable. When she tried to use this against him, to pin him at the far extent of her sword's length, he slipped by her guard like water, and his claw was already ready for more blood. Her little wounds were beginning to work at her as a pack, snagging at her every time she moved, trying to drag her down. Inside she was fighting a similarly losing battle with her fear. She had never realized just how bitterly she wanted to keep on living, for a tenday, a single day, an hour more. How terrible it was to have already seen her last dawn.

She worked up some alchemy to transmute that fear to anger, and her next strike almost caught him off balance, breaking the rhythm that she had let herself succumb to. For a precious few steps she was driving him before her, the air suddenly filled with the dull clatter of steel. He parried and parried, his gauntlet making circles in the air as he took her sword's point aside, over and over, but her blade was as insistent as a fly over food, and she nearly blooded his arm, nearly gashed his ribs, then flicked a drop of blood from his ear. *Now you fear!*

But he was calm, weathering the storm until she overreached, and was then ready to take the initiative from her as easily as if she had held it out for him to grasp. That last strike went too far, he had taken only a half step, and her sword's point went past his head. The claw was ready, its metal darkness driving for her throat as he snapped his arm out. She kicked back, trying to regain her distance, too slowly, but from somewhere she got her off-hand up, slapping for the side of the blade.

She felt the keen, cold razor of it slide across her fingers, stumbled back on to one knee and then forced her legs to lift her up again. Her left hand was awash with blood, the wound so sharp and clean that she barely felt the actual pain, though it was waiting for her just a little way distant.

He let her back off, yet again, and she now felt that she knew him better than she had known any opponent save her own father. This fight was an intimacy she had shared with nobody else. She had learned respect for Isendter Whitehand the hard way. She could not hate him, or even dislike him. Her Mantis nature, however much she might wish to deny it, recognized the *rightness* of this moment. There was no shame in a duellist's death at the hands of a master.

He was coming again. From his expression, he judged her an encouraging student, whose education he would rather complete than cut short, but such was life. *Learn*, his look seemed to say to her. *Improve.* She backed off, intently watching his face, his eyes.

The justice of your cause? he had asked her. Simply by being here she had vouched for the thieves and thugs behind her, and his regard for her had not suffered. When she had turned the question back on him, however, as he must have known she would, she had seen the pain in his eyes. He was a man worth more than his service here, and she could only think how even the seneschal Lisan Dea had seemed to turn on her mistress, there at the end. How much more, then, would a creature of honour like Isendter wish to walk away? Understanding that, she deciphered his expression at last.

So help me, he wants me to win, she realized with a shock. He had no faith in the noblewoman he was championing. He would far rather lose the duel and see justice done. But he could never fight to lose. To do so would slur his honour far more than would fighting for a bad cause. He was *willing* Tynisa to improve, to match him blow for blow and let him lose with dignity.

She was not equal to it, however. She risked repeated assaults on his perfect defence, and came back wounded and bleeding each time, like someone trying to reach into a thorn bush, suffering a thousand cuts. She had not let him land a fatal stroke on her, not yet, but even her best defence could not keep him from whittling her away.

She put some additional distance between them, because that thought had led to another, darker one. She remembered old Kymon drilling her and the other College students in the Prowess Forum. *What is the most important aim of the duellist?* And always some fool would pipe up, *To hit the enemy, Master Kymon.* And the old Ant would snap back, *By no means! It is to avoid being hit!*

But she had failed at that. Her best skill had already gone into minimizing the damage that Isendter had caused her. She had no more resources to bolster her defences with. His siege of her swordcraft breached the walls further with every foray.

She wondered if she had read it in his eyes, but it was a terrible bleak thought, more fearful almost than his claw as it hunted her, twisting the hundred paths in the air between them, closer and closer with every motion.

A quick exchange of steel, a gash to the back of her hand, and she was clear again. The thought sat like a leaden weight within her, *no, not that,* even as she planned out how it might be achieved.

For a moment she thought he stumbled, the sloping ground treacherous beneath his feet, and she leapt for this opening instantly, faster than thought. Thought, catching up, cried, *It's a feint!* but she had taken the bait already, lunging in even as he struck out at her whilst twisting aside from her blade.

There was barely an impact felt, but she heard a scream and thought it must be her own. Her sight was filled with red, and the slope of the ground seemed to roll under her feet, pitching her half a dozen reeling steps downhill, sword raised to ward him off, blindly covering one of a hundred approaches his blade might make.

It was Che who had screamed, she now realized. She herself kept silent as the tomb. There was blood in her eyes, and she drew a sleeve across them. *That* hurt, a burning pain shooting across her face where his blade had lashed her. *My face—*

One eye was still running with blood, but she had the other one clear, enough to see him approach again, steady and measured in his pace. The searing pain had not stopped, but she forced it away, locking it in the depths of her mind, perhaps in one of those chambers where Tisamon had so recently resided. Her mouth was full of blood, refilling each time she spat it out. He had cut her across her face . . . her *face*.

She had lived in two worlds, once. The Mantis child in her had fought, the Spider had smiled and plotted, painted herself in the mirror, charmed her enemies and made them fools. She had even smiled a path all the way to the Imperial palace at Capitas, because swords could not be relied on to win every fight.

She felt the Mantis path before her feet now, all others cut away. One-eyed, she met his gaze, and thought that he would understand. It was not true that every Mantis tragedy ended with a body on the floor. Some had two.

When he came for her next, she turned her body in a vain attempt to let his blade slide off her, while her own blade was already in motion. Her expected parry did not come, that he angled his blade to anticipate. Instead she dragged her hand back and up, the point of her rapier remaining almost motionless as she pivoted the rest of the sword around it in the air. The solid shock of contact came as his claw drove into her hip, driving a choking gasp out of her as she spat blood. His own left hand was lifting to catch her blade, but she drove it down anyway, calling on every ounce of strength to speed it on its way.

He had his hand almost in place, but the edge of her blade flayed his palm and cut the web of skin between thumb and forefinger down to the bone, and he could not put enough force into his gesture to deflect her.

Angled downwards and inwards, the point then dug into his pale leathers, just below his left collarbone, and it did not stop until the quillons were an inch from his ribs.

Through a film of new blood, she saw Isendter's head cock back abruptly, his eyes closed. His expression was that of a man listening to musicians in some private, peaceful place. She felt his blade grind against bone and, for a moment, they were propping one another up.

She drew in a breath raggedly, and let go of her sword hilt, gifting him with the blade. When his own drew clear of her, from the bloody landscape it had left of her hip and thigh, she let out a brief, horrified bark of pain.

For a moment they just stared at one another. Blood had begun painting the grey of his arming jacket, welling slowly around the inch of steel she had left showing.

Something tugged at the corner of his mouth. It might even have been a smile. Then he let himself go, slumping down to one knee with a grating whoosh of breath. The whole world was silent.

She looked beyond Isendter and saw Salme Elass standing there, her face a picture of rage and denial. There came no instant command, though, no immediate breaking with the Commonweal's ancient traditions. The princess was too shocked even for that.

Tynisa felt her legs tremble, and knew that if she also fell now, she would lose. She was the winner only so long as she stood. Salme Elass's paralysis would not survive any show of weakness.

Tynisa turned, very carefully indeed, to see Che's agonized face, Thalric's grim one, and fewer bandits than she had remembered. They were standing uphill from her, of course, curse them.

The pain had become a constantly expanding fire in her,

battering at her mind, demanding that she give in to it, tearing at her self-control. She remained upright only by application of pure will.

With the utmost precision she placed one foot in front of the other and began to walk.

Forty-Five

They could do nothing but watch Tynisa's tortuous progress back towards them, even as some of the Salmae's people began to approach their own kneeling champion. Tynisa swayed, and each time she put weight on her right leg a shudder went through her, like a dying thing, but somehow she was still on her feet when Che reached out to clasp her arm, and take her weight. The duellist's face was a mess of blood, the wounds impossible to trace beneath it. One eye was clear and open, but focusing on nothing. Her teeth were clenched together hard enough for Che to hear them grinding.

'Into the trees,' Dal Arche snapped. 'Get beyond the treeline. Keep her on her feet until then.'

When Che rounded on him furiously, he made a wild gesture at all the Salmae's people. 'They're staying where they are because she won, and even when the princess gets her voice back and starts telling them that the fight meant nothing, a lot of them will hold back. Tradition, just useless, rotten tradition, but this once it works for us. Our champion won, so going after us now counts as *bad form.*' He spat the words disgustedly. 'Oh, they'll come, sure enough, but we have some time so long as it's us that won.'

'But . . .' Che started, already moving for the trees with Tynisa leaning on her, barely more than a dead weight.

'That fellow she took down is still alive back there, for all her sword's sticking in him,' Dal shot back. 'If she just keels over in full view, well, she might be dead, then. In that case *their* man won, and *we're* all dead a moment after that.' He glanced back anxiously. 'Tell the truth, I'm not sure who *did* win there. Bloody mess, all of it. Soul—'

'Stay by the treeline and watch what they do,' the Grasshopper pre-empted him. He had an arrow to his bow, his eyes flicking left and right across the breadth of the enemy host, and then up to the sky.

The trees loomed sooner than Che had expected. 'A doctor, there must be,' she said. 'We have to . . .' She looked down in horror at the sheer quantity of blood. 'Bandages, medicines, something . . .' She tried to catch Maure's eye but the magician would not look at her.

'Carry the girl into the woods,' Dal stated flatly. He glanced at Thalric, who bristled for a moment, but then got an arm round Tynisa's back and simply gathered up her knees with the other, hoisting the girl in his arms. She gave out a wretched, rasping cry, and Che almost hoped she would pass out, escape for a moment from the agony she must be in. But instead, Tynisa rested her head on Thalric's shoulder, sheer willpower twisting her face.

'Go,' Dal urged, and he and Mordrec set the pace, letting the other two keep up as best they could. Released from Tynisa's weight, Che's injured leg took the chance to register its own complaints, for all her durable Beetle nature. She let herself lean on Maure's arm, while Thalric strode and stumbled ahead, trying to balance Tynisa's weight. If Mordrec had been unwounded then the two bandits might have got clear of them and simply vanished into the trees, but his shoulder was troubling him still, sapping his strength, and Dal hung back to match his friend's pace.

'She's dying!' Che called out, not caring who heard her now. 'I need to tend her wounds, please!'

Dal looked back, and she saw the internal conflict on his face, the man who wanted to run for it fighting desperately with the man so many had chosen to follow. He cast his eyes about furiously, trying to judge how far they had come. *Not far enough*, was written plainly in his expression, but then one finger jabbed out, indicating a dip where the land fell away, offering some pitiful shelter from enemy eyes.

Thalric manoeuvred his trembling burden down, skidding a little on the slope before coming to a halt with a jar that made Tynisa clutch at him tightly. His face could not be read as he looked at the injured girl, but Che supposed miserably that he would rather she died as soon as they were out of sight of the Salmae, just to rid him of the burden.

As soon as they had stopped, Che was fumbling in her packs for some bandages, and a few little jars of medicine to clean wounds and to ease pain. *And thank the world they didn't take them off me, when I was caught.* 'Start a fire,' she gasped. 'Boil up some water.'

'No time,' Dal told her flatly.

She glared at him. 'She'll die—'

'She may well die,' he replied, 'but we all will, if they catch us. You have minutes here only. Do what you can.'

The mistake Che made was in going for Tynisa's face first, wetting a bandage with water from her canteen and then wiping away the mask of blood she had been left with. What she saw beneath made her recoil, for the blade's single stroke had carved her sister from forehead to lips, in a long, crooked line. The mercy was that both eyes were still intact, one gummed shut with blood, but the wound had opened up Tynisa's cheek and slit the corner of her mouth. The old Mantis-kinden had given her a new face to frighten children.

Che reached for her needle and thread, but Maure was already dragging at her sleeve. 'No, Che,' and she was indicating the wound at the Spider girl's hip.

When she looked, there was so much blood that it seemed impossible that Tynisa could lay claim to it all, yet more kept coming. When Che peeled back the soaking rags of the wounded girl's clothing it started to gush with a frantic rhythm while Tynisa arched back, ravaged face screwed up against the pain.

'Stop the blood, stop the blood,' Che said to herself, thrusting her hands against the wound, but she could not stem it. There was just too much. The life of her sister was emptying itself out between her fingers. A shadow fell over her, a presence looming at her shoulder. 'Go away!' she snapped, pressing harder until a brief, choking sound came from Tynisa's lips.

'Get out of the way, you stupid woman.' A hand was on her shoulder and then she was abruptly slung aside. She heard the man grunt with pain as he did it, and recognized Mordrec kneeling at Tynisa's side.

He's going to kill her, so she doesn't slow us down, she thought. Thalric had a palm extended, but was hesitating, as Mordrec put his own hands flat on to Tynisa's hip, wrist-deep in blood instantly. Maure was holding her back, pleading, 'No, Che, no,' as she tried to lunge at the man, to drag him off her sister.

Tynisa keened, with a high sound like a saw biting into iron, one arm flailing madly at the Wasp, then Che saw a stuttering glow between Mordrec's fingers, and smelt burning. Burning blood, burning skin.

She wanted to cry out, *What is he doing?* but realization came to her even as she opened her mouth.

After Mordrec stood up, whatever blood Tynisa had left inside her would be staying there, and the imprint of his big hand was seared into her skin in a glossy burn-scar that would surely stay with her for as long as she lived – however short that looked likely to be.

'I didn't know Wasp Art could do that,' she admitted weakly, glancing at Thalric.

'Don't look at me. Mine tends to the opposite direction. I'd have blown her leg off.'

She saw Mordrec's pallid face, sheened with sweat from the effort. 'We have to go,' he rasped.

Dropping back down beside Tynisa, Che took her wound-cleanser and soaked bandages in it, using every last drop. Her sister writhed and fought as she applied it, and from personal experience she knew how it stung, but Collegium doctors had long known how the difference between a fatal and a trivial wound would be whether it turned to corruption or not. She swabbed swiftly and aggressively at Tynisa's face, cleaning away the blood and trying not to look at the twisted line of the scar, and then did her best with what Mordrec had left of the major wound on her hip. Tynisa looked paler than Che had ever seen another human being, or at least one who was still alive. The loss of blood might still kill her, or the shock, or any number of other things. Impulsively, Che took her hand, and was startled by the faint squeeze back. Tynisa was still conscious, and not through any of it had she let go, perhaps fearing that a temporary darkness could become permanent all too easily.

In Che's mind was a great deal of dread, a terror of a future that did not have this woman in it. *We came so far, and it cannot just have been to lose you now.*

And: in the midst of her whirl of panicked thoughts, *I will not have it.*

She blinked. For a moment she had seemed to feel the world shudder, just a little, around her – the air and the earth trembling minutely, out of step with each other. She found herself meeting Tynisa's gaze.

'We have to move,' Che whispered urgently. 'I'm sorry . . .'

Tynisa squeezed her hand again, stronger this time, and then Thalric stepped in without being asked and picked her up. Straightening with a grunt, he glanced towards the sky, where a flurry of white was blowing between the branches. The last echo of the Commonweal winter had picked this time to enter its death throes.

Soul Je suddenly arrived, a shape leaping and bounding between trees. In one hand he held his bow, an arrow clasped across it.

'All kinds of shouting,' he reported. 'Princess is telling them to get moving. They don't like it.'

'It won't last,' Dal decided. 'Some of them will be keen enough to retain her favour. It won't be all of them, but frankly it won't need many.'

Thalric began walking away, almost at random, and a moment later they were all on the move.

Dal squinted up at the white-grey sky. 'The snow's a curse when it's light. We can't hide our tracks. If it's heavy, though, there'll be no tracks. We might hide in it all the way to the border.'

'If it's heavy, the cold will kill her,' Che chided him.

'Then find a way to stop the snow,' he replied with a shrug. When Che just halted, he carried on.

She looked up at a lattice of branches with the flakes flurrying through.

'Maure.'

The magician glanced back. 'Che, no.'

'Then what good is it, any of it? Or is that the great secret of magic, that it's dwindled to uselessness, and that's why the armies of the Apt run roughshod over the world? Have I come so far just to join the losing side?'

'Che, you've power, but you've no direction, no training, and the power you have, it's . . . not native to you. It was never intended for a Beetle-kinden to use.'

Che shrugged. 'One thing about Beetles is that we adapt.' And with that, she thrust her arms out into the chill air, directed back the way they had come, towards the invisible Salmae. For a moment nothing happened, and she could conceive of no possible way that she could affect the world. Magic was a fiction, of course, and all her early years of study confirmed that. Then she sensed the faintest catch, as though her fingers had brushed some kind of trailing veil, invisible in the air.

'Masters of Khanaphes, you crowned me,' Che murmured, less to herself than to the world at large. 'You made me something new, me and the Empress – you gave us some mark or mantle of yours, made us your champions, however it works. After a thousand years of exile beneath the earth, you have *recognized* us. Does that mean nothing? Does that mean that when I speak to the wind, it just whisks my words away? What good is it all, then? What is the point of it all?'

She heard Thalric calling to her distantly, but the wind was picking up now, and she caught none of his meaning.

'I am caught between two worlds,' she considered, as Maure shifted from foot to foot beside her, keen to get away. 'Child of the new, but scion of the old. Nobody could have intended that, but it has happened, and I refuse to let it become nothing more than a handicap.' She was speaking quietly, calmly, but with that last word she summoned her will and pushed it through both hands, tearing at the sky with invisible fingers, clutching and dragging and *throwing* . . .

The wind changed direction with an audible *whump,* and was abruptly whistling past her, back towards the pursuers that were surely coming. She heard it keening through the trees, followed by the snow, thicker than it had been a moment ago, rushing to fly in the faces of their hunters, while obliterating all tracks.

She felt something go out of her, as if some great reservoir had been emptied all at once – expended in a flood of power sent to batter the very heavens into submission.

But had I been skilled, oh then . . . For in that moment she saw that given a little application, a little care, she might have achieved the same result from so much less effort, and thus have something still in hand to deal with her enemies when they did finally catch up. For now, though, she felt leaden, hollowed out, and could only stumble behind Maure as the magician led her after the others.

The fierce snowstorm that would now be making their followers' lives a misery was well behind her, and it stayed behind her as she hurried to catch up with Thalric. The air ahead and immediately around her remained crisp and still, the wind itself waiting for her to pass by before claiming another yard of ground.

Her progress was a mad lurch through the forest, the snow always building right behind her, gusting about her heels as though she was the harbinger of a second winter. Maure, helping to take Che's weight, was shivering, the tips of her ears and nose turning blue with cold, but Che herself felt none of it.

Consequences, she thought to herself. *I must be more careful whenever I try to move the world. My standpoint is more solid than I thought.* At the same time, though, the scholar in her was considering, *And though I believe I moved the weather, yet Thalric would simply claim that this snow was fortuitous. Magic must creep, now. It is not the fire and grandeur of the Bad Old Days.*

She heard Dal Arche cry out from ahead of her, his words lost in the wind, but they could mean nothing good. Maure put on an extra burst of speed, without being asked, and a moment later Che saw Thalric, his hands outstretched, looking wildly around. Tynisa crouched at his feet, plainly awake and aware. Her eyes locked on to Che's and she shouted hoarsely, 'Look out!'

The snow had not been enough. Even as Tynisa called her warning, a horse thundered between them, close enough to nearly shoulder Che aside. Something whistled by her head, like a large insect, and she only realized afterwards that it was a sword blade.

The horse reared as its rider tugged at the reins to turn it back. Soul Je's arrow nipped past him, clipping the armour on his shoulder. Then there were more of them. The snowstorm had stripped Salme Elass of most of her force, losing them in the labyrinth of trees and foul weather that Che had turned the forest into. They would have had other magicians, though, to cut a course for them through the wild wind, and now this handful of cavalry had found them, and there would soon be more to come.

Another rider bore down on Che and Maure, a spear

couched in his arm, but Dal Arche's arrow flowered suddenly from the horse's neck, and the luckless animal rolled forward and over, its rider's wings flourishing briefly to bring him down firmly on his feet. A moment later Thalric's sting knocked him down, cracking his intricate armour like an eggshell. A further crackle of stingshot sounded further off, as Mordrec defended himself from more of the Salmae's followers.

The swordsman had now turned to ride down Soul Je, who kicked himself backwards in a long arc, fifteen feet of leap at least, loosing another shot even as he sprang from the man's path. Then Che lost track of him, because an arrow drove deep into Maure's arm, and she cried out in pain and sat down hard.

The archer was mounted, holding his horse still to improve his aim. Che saw him select another arrow from his quiver and nock it to his bow. His face, those pleasant, golden-skinned Dragonfly features, was dispassionate, almost bored.

She knelt over Maure and reached out for whatever magic she could find.

'Go to her!' shouted Tynisa, or at least she tried to shout, pushing Thalric away. He gave her an exasperated look, then was flying towards Che, but surely too late to stop the arrow. Tynisa ground her teeth together and stood up, clutching for the sword that she had left behind. The mounted archer sighted carefully, and then his hand flew open in release, the string invisible as it whipped the arrow straight at Che.

The fist of wind that buffeted them all at that moment had to be a freak of the unseasonal weather, Tynisa knew. She saw Che stagger under its battering, and the archer's horse reared madly. Where the arrow went, she could not discern.

Then Thalric had reached him, grappling the man off his horse under the full speed of his wings, and Tynisa heard the hiss of his Art burning into the archer's body from point-blank range.

There was a tremor in the ground, a flicker of motion, and

Tynisa tried to cast herself aside, managing only an ungainly collapse, the pain roaring through her like a fire, just as the next horse passed by, hoofs inches from trampling her. Without looking up, she *knew*, and was already forcing herself upright, determined to meet her fate on her feet. The strength – borrowed from who-knew-where – ebbed and flowed within her, always on the point of running dry, and yet she found herself standing up again, swaying and shuddering.

Salme Elass stared down at her icily, a long-hafted sword resting on her shoulder. The moment seemed endless as she studied her prey, and it was all Tynisa could do to stay standing and return the woman's gaze.

'Child of the Lowlands,' the Dragonfly princess said, 'what brought you here to kill my son? Tell me it was the business of the Empire. Tell me I have an enemy in some Beetle city. Make me understand.' Her hand flexed on the sword's grip, and Tynisa could envisage the diagonal cleaving stroke as Elass leant forward in the saddle to hack into her collarbone and come near to decapitating her. The princess was a skilled horsewoman who had judged the distance precisely, her victim well within reach.

None of Tynisa's comrades seemed to be close enough to intervene, this time. Thalric was still protecting Che, and the bandits were looking after their own.

Well, then, let it be this.

'Alain made me his sword to use in war,' she said simply. 'But when it then came to peacetime, he was careless and so he cut himself. Do not blame the sword.'

Elass's face contorted in fury and her blade whipped forward even faster than Tynisa had anticipated. She closed her eyes.

The sound of steel on steel came in a single ringing impact, and then she heard Elass's horse whinny, and its mistress curse. When Tynisa's eyes opened, Elass was on foot, thrown from her horse, and the animal running off with its bridle swinging. Between her and Tynisa stood a pale figure. In fact Tynisa had never seen a paler. It was not just the grey leathers, which were torn and stained, but he carried the bloodless pallor of a dead man. Isendter, named Whitehand, stood before his mistress with his claw upraised. He was breathing like a dying sprinter, the red on his lips vivid against his blanched skin, and the web of bandages about his wound was running with fresh blood.

'Traitor!' Elass screamed.

'This is shameful,' came Isendter's reply, his voice as weak and ragged as Tynisa's own. 'I swore to defend your honour. She *won!*'

'Traitor.' This time the word was flat and ugly. Tynisa saw the blow before it landed, and cried out in warning, but Isendter must surely have foreseen it too. He made no move, did not dip his upraised blade by so much as an inch, accepting the rebuke of his mistress.

She ran him through, ramming the straight blade beneath his ribs, hard enough to lift him on to his toes. With a scream, Salme Elass wrenched her blade free from his body, and he dropped to his knees in the snow and keeled over. Tynisa needed only a glance to know that Isendter was dead.

Then Elass's blade was in motion again, scything in a flat arc towards Tynisa.

She turned it with her own and, though the impact seemed to shock half of the remaining life from her, her form was perfect and the smallest motion of her wrist deflected the heavy blow by just enough. In the back of her mind, where her father's ghost had once lurked, she felt a long chain receding into the past, master and student in an unbroken line of tradition: *Weaponsmasters*, just as Isendter had been, who had deserved a better end than that. The chain that bound her to that antique order was purchase enough to hold her on her feet – just as it had sufficed to bring Isandter to her aid – although the pain of her wounds had its teeth in her and would not let go.

Elass stared at her, then at the rapier in her hand. Where it had been until now, after they had so carefully removed it from

Isendter's body, Tynisa could not say, only that it had come to her when she called. Isendter's last breath had changed something in her. She had given up on a passive, easy death. She was a Weaponsmaster, of Spider and of Mantis blood, and neither of her parents would have stood and waited for the headsman's axe.

Then Elass struck at her again, putting all her strength into the blow, to batter through Tynisa's guard. The cut would have been impossible to stop, but Tynisa felt her arm and sword move along paths made easy by her training, not blocking but simply deflecting, so that in the aftermath of the ringing clash, Salme Elass had struck her rapier from her hand, but the noblewoman's own blade had been thrown wide by the narrowest of margins.

There was renewed shouting, now, from the other Salmae riders, the movement around them intensifying, the thunder of more hoofs, but Tynisa and Salme Elass were in a vicious little world made for two.

Elass's eyes flicked to the rapier, lying in the snow and out of reach, but in the heartbeat it took her to draw her blade back, the slender weapon was in Tynisa's hand again. A Weaponsmaster was never to be parted from her sword. Just as she had awoken with the ancient Mantis weapon in hand, so long ago in Collegium, now it stayed with her no matter what.

The sight seemed to enrage Elass even more than the death of her son, as if the rapier and not the injured girl was her enemy. She struck again – at the sword itself, as if she were a rank novice, knocking it from Tynisa's slack grip, and yet there it was again, directed at her, even before it had time to hit the ground. Had Tynisa possessed an ounce of strength, she could have ended the fight then, a riposte past the other woman's blade and a clean and instant kill, but she could do nothing but hold her trembling stance.

And then there were more horses flashing past on every side, their riders' armour gleaming even through the snow, cloaks rippling behind them, and Tynisa realized that it was now too late.

She still waited for the next strike because, even if she was doomed now, even if a spear or sword was about to plant itself in her back, it was not in her nature to surrender. *Let the bitch work for her blood!*

There was a confusion of horses all around, a score of riders perhaps, circling, breaking fights apart, archers training arrows on everyone they found, and one cried out, standing up in the saddle with his wings flaring, 'Mercre Monachis!'

Salme Elass was no longer attacking. Her sword hung like a dead weight in one hand as she stared about at the newcomers. These were not her own followers. Allowed a moment to herself, Tynisa took a better look at them. Their armour looked both plainer and more functional than Salme Elass's people's, and their horses were a hand taller at least. These were lean, fierce, men and women, guiding their mounts with the casual synchronization of a shoal of fish. She saw both Elass's people and the brigands, all of them separated now, staring about at the strangers who had cut between them and now surrounded them. To Tynisa's left, Thalric was helping Che to her feet, and the halfbreed magician was sitting up, grimacing at the shaft in her arm. On the far side, Soul Je stood over Mordrec, the Wasp propped up on one elbow, with his metal-lined armour cut open and a bloody wound in his scalp.

One of the newcomers was sharing his steed, Tynisa noticed. Sitting ahead of an armoured woman, his wrists tied behind his back to the saddle pommel, was the Spider-kinden Avaris, with his face bruised, looking wretched and miserable. It was plain the newcomers had been busy.

Ten yards away from Tynisa, Dal Arche still had an arrow nocked and half drawn back as though waiting for a target to present itself. Perhaps it now did, although Dal wisely chose not to loose the shot. Two new mounts were picking their way between the trees, the riders cloaked against the gusting snow that only now seemed to be letting up. Tynisa knew them both, even before they were close, and so did Salme Elass.

The man lagging behind slightly was Lowre Cean, looking older than ever, as if physically pained to be drawn from his recluse's life for this belated adventure. The man he followed was his fellow Prince-Major, Felipe Shah.

Prince Felipe approached Princess Salme slowly, his face expressionless. 'I see you have caught your bandits,' he noted.

The look that briefly flashed in the princess's eyes was pure venom, but her voice remained controlled as she said, 'A shame the Monarch's response is too late.'

'Or just in time,' Felipe remarked mildly. 'How many years have you been cautioning us against the great uprising from Rhael, I wonder?'

'And I was right!' she snapped. 'The traitors have defied the law of the Monarch and raised an army, burned villages, murdered . . .'

Felipe guided his horse on a little further until it was beside her. 'And here you have bearded their great chief, I believe,' he said mildly. 'Am I right?'

Another figure stepped from the trees, though keeping a careful distance from Salme Elass. 'You are, my lord. Dal Arche, they called him at Siriell's Town,' explained Gaved, looking as though he would take to the air at the first hint of trouble.

Elass's hand clenched on her sword hilt, but she simply looked aside, as if disdaining to notice the Wasp.

Tynisa had no such compulsion. 'You live more lives than most, Gaved,' she called out to him. 'Changing your stripes already, is it?'

The look the Wasp gave her was a study in equivocation. 'You'd be surprised, when a man sets out to have no master, how often he collects two, or even more,' he replied philosophically.

'Dal Arche,' Felipe Shah called.

The brigand chief tensed, arrow still in place, but the newly arrived riders had several shafts already trained on him, and he simply held his shot, the string slightly tensioned, as though he had forgotten it was there. 'These are the real thing, then, are they? Mercers?' he enquired. 'Servants of the Monarch's throne, not just lackeys to some provincial princess-minor?'

Again Elass quivered with suppressed rage, but she held her tongue.

'Indeed, and I'm lucky I was able to gather them so quickly. They – we – are spread wide these days, fewer of us each year, and the Commonweal as vast as ever,' Felipe's tone was conversational. 'I've heard much of your exploits, Dal Arche.'

The bandit chief glanced first at Soul Je and Mordrec, then at Avaris, and Tynisa read the man's thoughts in his eyes. *He's wondering if he can spare them somehow, wondering if his confession or his surrender might do it.* But the Dragonfly brigand's face then hardened. *He knows there is no way out.*

'This is the man who has rebelled against my rightful authority,' Elass declared, her voice pure winter. 'This is the Monarch's enemy. If you are her Mercers, then do your duty, and I only wish that you had heeded me sooner, and that we had purged Rhael of this filth before they grew so bold.'

To Tynisa's ears she was overacting, playing the outraged voice of law and justice to cover the terrible, personal hatreds seething under the surface.

'And *this* one is a murderess! She turned her blade on my own son! On my *son*, Prince Felipe!'

Felipe looked at Tynisa with a sad smile. 'I have already mourned one of your sons, Princess Salme. You yourself must mourn the other.'

'Is that all you have to say? What will you *do?*'

'I will ask why Siriell died, and why the stores at her town were burned.'

Elass stared at him blankly, utterly thrown.

'Did you think your concerns were ignored, Princess? And did you forget that I served the Monarch as spymaster during the war? As my agents spied out the Wasps then, so they were in Siriell's Town, evaluating your concerns. They told me that the wild and savage people of Rhael Province were at last working their way to something approaching civilization. And then your son and followers came, and killed the woman who had wrought such progress, and destroyed their foodstocks, and ensured that some, at least, would strike back at you, and thus give you your excuse to take Rhael for your own – as I had forbidden you time and time again.'

'But they were *outlaws*!' Elass snapped, not even attempting to deny a word of it. 'They had turned away from the Monarch's grace. They had defied our rule! That land had been left fallow for too long. I had a duty—!'

'Your duty was to obey your Prince-Major, and no more. You do not owe fealty to the Monarch, but to me, and it is I who judge how best you should serve. For example, this girl . . .' He nodded at Tynisa. 'She is under my protection. She has rendered a rare service to me, and I am in her debt. Thus I absolve her of all acts committed in this, my principality.'

Elass gaped at him, aghast. 'But my *son*—'

'Has benefited from just such leniency on many an occasion, under your own justice. He chose to live by that sword. If you will maintain an arbitrary rule, learn to be ruled arbitrarily in turn.' He held her incandescent gaze for some time, with no further sound but the echo of his voice in every ear. At last he turned those keen eyes on the brigand chief. 'Dal Arche, you fought in the war, I'd guess.'

The brigand chief nodded curtly, his expression not inviting further questioning, and Felipe went on, 'Your home is under the black and gold now, perhaps? Or maybe you're no longer the same man that called such a place home. I hear much of you from my agents, and some from your own men.' He nodded at Avaris. 'But Salme Elass is correct in one thing: Rhael cannot be allowed to slide back into anarchy. I had hoped Siriell would tame it, but alas . . . Now I shall be cruel to you, Dal Arche, more so than you might expect. You would have your followers live beyond today?'

Again that terse nod.

'Then you must do something for me, O leader of outlaws. You must swear fealty to me, body and mind, abject and without condition. For I will have you made Prince of Rhael.'

Somewhere nearby Salme Elass let out a screech of protest, but in that moment Tynisa was wholly taken up with the greying brigand's face, and the battle there between hate for the aristocracy and fear for his fellows. She saw his hand twitch twice on the bowstring, making as if to pull it taut, but somehow he held himself back.

'It's that, is it? Is that the choice I get?' he grated.

Felipe smiled bleakly. 'Do you like my Mercers? I wonder what they represent to you. Do they populate your nightmares, these the Monarch's most skilled servants, thief-takers and bringers of justice? And would it surprise you to know that the greatest duty of the Mercers is to keep watch on the nobility and punish those lords and ladies who use for selfish ends the power the Monarch grants? As I say, they are few, and the times are wicked, but they are enemies of more than just brigands. Your answer, Dal Arche?'

'You're a madman,' Dal told him.

'I'd not be the first prince-major to be so,' Felipe replied implacably, and then demanded again, 'Your answer.'

Tynisa genuinely believed the brigand was going to refuse, his loathing of the nobility stronger even than his love of his friends, but then his shoulders sagged. 'Let it be so, though it's a mad world.' He looked more like a man condemned to death than a candidate for the nobility.

The movement, when it came, was so swift that Tynisa nearly missed it, and she was caught by a weird sense that she had been here before: only then she had been the victim, and another's blade had stood in the way. Salme Elass had taken more than she could bear, and Tynisa would never know whether it had been the loss of her son or of her ambitions that snapped her.

Her blade whistled up towards Felipe Shah, who had not even drawn his own. The world seemed to stand still.

Tynisa found that her own blade was already moving to intervene, but the angle was wrong to simply flick the woman's blow aside. To beat it away from herself would only be to speed it on its way. Instead she snaked her narrow sword between Felipe and the blow and put all the strength she could into her parry, so that Elass's sword swung round at her, narrowly missing her torn face as she fell backwards. Elass was screaming, blade raised to impale her, heedless of rank and station, and Tynisa lifted her own weapon with trembling arms, knowing she was not strong enough even to roll aside.

The arrow struck Salme Elass in the jaw and drove in halfway to the fletchings, snapping the princess's head sideways at an unnatural angle, a brief, bloody choking sound the only exclamation she could muster. The sword fell from her fingers, end over end, on to the snowy ground, then she collapsed.

Dal Arche lowered his bow, his hand automatically reaching for his quiver, but finding no more arrows there. If he was satisfied that he had, at least, been permitted one last act of rebellion, his face showed none of it. Indeed there was a tense silence that overcame everyone there, each face frozen as they waited for the prince's response. The only true mourner of Salme Elass, judging from his expression, was Felipe Shah himself.

'Another dynasty ended, then,' he murmured, so that only Tynisa could hear him. 'Another prince to find.'

His private thoughts seemed to exercise a magical power over the watchers for, although Felipe's head remained bowed, all other eyes were drawn to Lowre Cean.

'No, no.' The old man shook his head. 'Not that. Not again. Don't ask me, Shah.'

'There must be someone, or Elas Mar will become a new Rhael within a year. Find me an alternative. Give me their name, their pedigree. I must work with the tools that I have, Cean. You must rule from Leose, or what have we gained, out of all this?'

The slump of Lowre Cean's shoulders indicated a despondency every bit as profound as Dal Arche's.

'Gather up, all of you,' Felipe Shah called out, his voice again reaching all ears. 'Followers of the Salmae, know that at the end your mistress betrayed her Monarch and her prince. You serve the Lowrae now, and may that bring you more honour than your service to the Salmae.' The words were merely formal, for Tynisa knew well that Cean was the last of the Lowre bloodline, just as Elass had been the end of hers.

The motley collection of followers that Elass had kept with her formed an awkward group, sullen and uncertain, whilst their former enemies drifted together into a distinct band with Dal Arche – *Prince Dal* – at their head. Tynisa took the chance to sit up painfully, grateful when Che reached out to help her.

'This is the will of the Monarch,' Felipe Shah stated 'declared through me, her Prince-Major. I hereby invest Lowre Cean as Prince of Leose, and Dal Arche as Prince of Rhael, and I charge them both to keep a better order in their new domains than has been the case there before now. Let us have peace and prosperity, as much as this late age allows it.' He broke off, looking beyond the gathered groups, and Tynisa followed his gaze. Another rider was coming, and she recognized the same youth who had served Lowre Cean as messenger.

'Marcade, what news?' Lowre called out, for the young man's expression was pale and terrible, and he gripped a scroll in a hand that shook when he proffered it to the old man.

Lowre read the contents grimly, and passed it wordlessly to Felipe. Watching him, Tynisa saw something go out of the Prince-Major, some briefly kindled flame of hope. When at last he spoke, his gaze found hers.

'My agents report . . . The Empire has brought its armies to Myna. The war has started again. They are coming for us,' his sombre gaze passed from Tynisa to Che. 'Or for you.'

Epilogue

Capitas: some months before

Since the business with the Mosquito-kinden, the great and the good of Capitas had begun to look forward to the Empress Seda's welcoming of new ambassadors. Whether she charmed or whether she punished them, she was equally entertaining, as good as a visit to the fighting pits. This, she knew, was how the court felt. Returned from Khanaphes and on her own throne again, she gauged the mood around her, noting with amusement the swelled numbers of courtiers eager to see her latest reception.

But they were the Empire, or at least a certain face of it, the powerful and the ambitious whose desires she yoked to haul her Empire forward. She had divided and wooed them, played favourites, cast down, raised up, and always she had walked with the knives of the Rekef in her shadow. There was no union or alliance of them strong enough to bring her down, not for the moment.

She was aware of how most of them looked at her. She had won them, for now. She was a woman more Wasp-kinden than her brother had ever been. She met the world head-on. She was fierce when ferocity was needed, cunning as required, and when she punished, her abrupt sentences were often carried out before the whole court, less a lesson than a spectacle. She thought that they loved her most of all for that. There was an arbitrariness to her – the one thing she shared with her late brother – that well became a master of the Empire.

For these qualities, they forgave her a few foibles, such as the mystics and Inapt scholars she kept about the court. After all, even the Wasp-kinden had to admit that the Moths and their ilk had ruled the world centuries before, had been great powers in an age when Wasp history was not even being written down. What other great power of the modern world had seen their ambassadors come so meekly and humbly? Was there a Lowlander merchant prince or Assembler who could boast the same?

And now she had some new visitors, and she reclined on the throne to watch as they were escorted through the great doors at the far end of the chamber.

They were three men, all in full armour, and although they must have been aware of the unfriendly attention of the whole room, they made a brave show by marching in step, the last of them bearing a banner sloping across one shoulder: a simple checked field in familiar colours. The style of their mail was familiar to most of her court, or certainly those in active service a decade before: curved plates of chitin overlaying silk and leather and fine chainmail, in shapes elegant and graceful, and slightly too extravagant for an Imperial armourer's more practical tastes. Where the spectators might have expected scintillating greens and blues and reds, though, all three wore identical colours, segments painted over or enamelled, and the leader's breastplate newly wrought, so that the chitin's sparkling finish was resplendent in their colours: black and gold.

They had bunches of moth-antennae plumes, cloaks lined with butterfly scales, torcs of gold and mother of pearl. These Dragonfly-kinden had clearly gone to great pains to impress, unaware that in the Empire such excess would seem quaint and barbaric. As they progressed towards the throne, presenting a study in pride and defiance, they were followed by an undercurrent of derision and mockery. What did they think they were, these savages decked in the livery of Empire? Was this some kind of joke?

'Speak.' Seda's voice rang out, halting them. 'What do you bring before me?'

There was a small exchange of sidelong glances between the two at the rear, but their leader knelt without hesitation. His brow gleamed a little with sweat, and Seda saw him swallow away a dry throat before he announced, 'Your Imperial Majesty, accept me as your servant General Torste Sain, here to bring you word of the Principalities.'

At his proclaimed rank, a tide of laughter welled up, and an eddy of angry calls for the crossed pikes, amid jeers and threats. Seda held the gaze of Torste Sain the Dragonfly general, noticing his jaw clench and his shoulders hunch, as though readying himself for the rod.

She stood up abruptly and the room went silent, waiting for the Imperial verdict and for the downfall of these strange visitors. Instead, she turned her gaze upon her own court, and few enough of them dared meet her eyes the way the Dragonfly had.

'How dare you mock?' she demanded, not loudly, but sharply enough to reach the back of the room. 'What do you find here that is worthy of your humour? Is there a general of our Empire who would dare to stand thus in the heart of a foreign state, facing every expectation of a swift execution? Would any of you risk your lives in the halls of the Spider-kinden Aristoi, or the royal court of some hostile Ant city-state?' Torste Sain was regarding her impassively, so she invited him, 'General, speak to us of the Principalities.'

At her words the kneeling Dragonfly stood up in a single smooth motion. 'Great Majesty,' he announced, 'I am sent from the Principalities as a humble messenger. Since the borders of Empire shifted, you must know how we have been beset on all sides by the Commonweal to the west, by Myna and its allies to the east. We have had to forge ourselves a new state from the pieces that were left to us, guided by those of your people who remained and being taught the ways of Empire by your former servants. It is with joy that my people have learned the power of the new, Highness. I am proud to bear the rank of general, for I am the first of my kinden ever to do so.' And he was indeed proud, it was plain to see. Seda wondered if any Wasp-kinden within living memory had felt that honour quite so keenly.

'And do you seek to rejoin the Empire, General?' she asked softly.

Taking a deep breath, he braced himself. 'Your Highness, no.'

There might have been a uproar then, but her outstretched hands rendered it stillborn.

The general's two companions were standing markedly closer together now, but he himself had not moved. 'We honour the Empire,' he stated. 'There is no need to take what can be freely given. We shall have tribute for your treasury, Highness. We shall have soldiers to fight alongside your armies. We ask only for recognition as your friends and protection against our mutual enemies.'

This time she let the protests run a little longer, because there were many traditionalists still in her court, and the Empire had always recognized only two classes of geography: those parts of the map already in black and gold, and those parts yet to be painted. That mentality had served well enough to let a single hill tribe swallow up its kindred neighbours, and then put a score of other cities in chains. *But the times have changed.*

'The word you seek is "protectorate",' she declared, and her court quietened quickly, because speaking over the Empress was seldom forgiven. She looked around at them all, seeing plenty there of shock and outrage, with the old guard ready to decry the insurrection of the Principalities' Wasp-kinden, and to call for the subjugation of pretenders such as this Torste

Sain. There were other expressions to be read too, though. There were thoughtful Consortium merchants, calculating tacticians, scholars of recent history and politics, Beetle-kinden diplomats and agents of the Rekef Outlander. They were thinking as she was thinking, using a logic that had nothing to do with Apt or Inapt.

'Consider Collegium in the Lowlands,' she urged her court. 'How is it that Collegium is not beneath our flag already? Because Collegium never stands alone. When we fought Collegium, we were also fighting Tharn, the Spiderlands, the Sarnesh, Solarno and the Commonweal, not to mention the rebellions in Myna and Szar which Collegiate agents incited. That is how Collegium staved us off.' She gifted them with a smile fierce as the sun. 'You have all seen the statue that stands within the palace doors. Who are the defenders who stand at my back there? Soldier, artificer, merchant and *diplomat*. Wars are won by more weapons than swords and snapbows and artillery. General Torste, the Empire is glad to recognize its errant children, and to extend to them a hand of friendship and protection, and in return, and with our aid, you shall guard our border with the Commonweal, whose stratagems your people are best placed to understand. And when we march on the Lowlands once more, when we stand before the gates of Collegium, you shall be with us to see it, and this time we shall not turn away.'

Capitas: Now

There had been many changes in Capitas over the last few years. It was the Empire in miniature, and the Empire had been forced to deal with a great deal of turmoil since the strength of its armies had broken at Collegium and Sarn, Myna and

Solarno and elsewhere. The ill-educated, within the Empire and without, claimed that the death of the Emperor had been the blow that rocked the Empire, but just as the death of a general would not halt an Imperial army, so the death of Alvdan II would have been nothing but a footnote in history, if only his armies and his battle plans had been sounder.

After the end of the external war had come the internal: renegade governors refusing to acknowledge Seda, setting themselves up as their own masters. The Empire had teetered on the brink of a disintegration that would have taken it back to its feuding tribal origins of three generations before.

That the Empire had survived to regain its territory and its strength was due to two saviours. One was embodied in Seda, her sharp mind and her adroit handling of both her allies and her enemies ensuring that she was never forced into a position from which only force could extricate her. The second saving factor was the other kinden, the Wasps' second-class citizens.

There had always been a fair number of Beetle- and Fly-kinden in the Empire, and they were counted Imperials of a sort, not as good as Wasps but better than the rest. While the Wasp-kinden ran their armies, the Beetles and Flies tended to find work as clerks and merchants and administrators, and when the Empire had cracked apart, they had stepped into the breach. The efficiency of the Consortium of the Honest, of the Quartermaster Corps, the Engineers, the Capitas bureaucracy, had proved the glue that held the Empire together, and that was able to re-join each piece seamlessly. No demands were made, no threats, but by the end of the insurrection there was a notable number of influential Beetles and Flies who had found promotion and power, as well as the covert gratitude of the Empress.

But there was more than that. The doomsayers had predicted a hundred revolts, every enslaved city striving for its freedom. In truth, except for the cities of the West-Empire – Szar, Maynes and Myna in their new Alliance – the majority of the cities to rise up were those whose governors had forced the issue. The enemies of the Empress had turned out to be other ambitious Wasps rather than her subject peoples. There had been a few attempted rebellions, but most of the subject cities had otherwise simply gone about their business. In the aftermath, Seda made sure to reward both governors and slave-subjects for their loyalty, just as she had punished treachery without mercy or hesitation.

One result of this new mood within the Empire was that Capitas's citizens were taking a keener interest in the subjects of their Empire, which in turn had led to the founding of the Imperial Museum. It was a Collegiate concept of course, though the Lowlander Beetles preferred exhibits representing the domains of the historian, naturalist or artificer. The Imperial Museum was just that: a museum of the Empire. The building itself was still being constructed, half of its halls and wings still just foundations surmounted by the skeletons of scaffolding, but the completed sections had already seen a brisk trade of fascinated Wasp-kinden come to learn more about their slaves and servants.

There was a Bee-kinden wing, where artefacts from the city of Vesserett were on display: their graceful yet functional carving, their elegant illustrated scrolls, all the trappings of their emergent power from the days in which they had been the nascent Empire's first challenge. There was a hall of Grasshopper-kinden art from Sa, where slave musicians would play on certain days. There was a cellar tricked out to look like a Mole Cricket-kinden dwelling from Delve. There were three halls devoted to the Commonweal, one lined with the swords and armour of two score Dragonfly nobles, all of it recovered during the war, and many displaying the damage that had done for their original owners. The Wasp-kinden strolled through these rooms and learned a little about those far-flung cultures, those disparate peoples, but most of all they learned how they were superior because these things were all the spoils of conquest. It was the same lesson as taught by the deaths of foreign combatants in the arena, but more lasting.

The Empress herself had made her fondness for this establishment widely known, and the Beetle-kinden Consortium family who were behind it had been richly rewarded. It was well known, indeed, that after dark, when the museum was locked up, she would use its empty halls to speak to those who had particularly attracted her notice. It was, everyone knew, a sign of great favour.

Her companion tonight was one Major Karrec, a man of good family and good standing in the Consortium. As she paced the length of the Commonweal hall, the vacant helms of fallen nobles regarding her gravely from either side, he regaled her with stories of his war exploits and his cleverness in the face of the enemy. He was a man of middle height, running slightly to fat from a life far from rigorous, but there was a spark about him, she thought. *As there should be.*

Behind the two of them, a pair of her Mantis-kinden bodyguards paced silently, the metal claws of their gauntlets folded back.

He smiled at her, did Karrec, and walked closer than was appropriate, and she realized that he was crossing that old familiar line, as she thought he might. As the Empress, on high, she was only female in the abstract, but if she allowed her underlings any familiarity, then some of them would begin to treat her as women had always been treated in the Empire: as something to be possessed and controlled.

As they reached the end of the hall, Karrec stopped and stared. He had been discoursing on some of the suits of mail, obviously familiar with the exhibits, but now he frowned. 'Your Imperial Majesty, forgive me. I don't recall a hall beyond this one.'

'It is not for public viewing yet, Major,' she said sweetly. 'However, I have asked our curators to open it tonight, just for us.'

He was encouraged by that, she saw, and she wondered just how deluded he might be about his prospects. Still, it was all to her advantage, so she let him dream while he could.

The chamber beyond was small compared with the museum's other halls, a simple box of a room that seemed as though it had been left to moulder for decades, until the walls had grown a patina of mould and lichen, the plaster decaying and falling away to turn the smooth surfaces into a maze of canyons and eroded topography, all of it made to shiver and move under the light of two ensconced torches. Karrec was not quite so oblivious as to take *that* sight in his stride, and he hesitated in the doorway, until she turned back and smiled at him.

'A remarkable effect, yes? I understand the craftsmen laboured at it for days.'

'But what is it for?' he asked, entering cautiously.

'This is the Mantis-kinden hall,' she explained. 'It is small, as there are few such in the Empire, but they possess a fascinating culture nonetheless.'

He glanced back at the two guards, who had stopped at the doorway. 'And they're friends to the throne now, I see.'

'Oh, they were gifts from the clever Moth-kinden of Tharn,' she explained. 'Half a dozen Mantis-kinden warriors to guard me from enemies both within and without the Empire. As if I would take such a gift unquestioned. Spies, of course, for their masters in the mountains, their loyalty already pledged before they were sent to kneel to me. However, I have shown them where their true path lies, so they are mine now.' As Karrec would surely question that, she took up a torch and brought it over to her prize exhibit, hearing his astonished gasp. As a Consortium man, and a man of independent wealth, Karrec was a collector. She took it on faith that he would already be placing an exorbitant price on what she was showing him.

It was a suit of armour, full mail from the closed helm down to the boots. The closest equivalent still in use would be the heavy Sentinel plate that was even now being retired from the Imperial armies, but this had been fashioned for Sentinels of another age. Every piece had been made with loving care, backed by centuries of skill. The elegant curves and lines recalled the Dragonfly mail in the previous room, but their message was far less one of idle beauty. There was deadliness written in every line and edge of it, so that the helm glowered down at them and – even hanging at rest – the metal held itself in such a way as to suggest it was a moment from leaping forward and striking them both down. The ruddy torch flame flickered over it, picking out the ancient greens and russets as various shades of black.

The colours alone betrayed the compromise she had been forced to make. There was no sizeable Mantis-kinden hold in the Empire, and the kinden themselves did not ever sell their antique heirlooms. This suit had been pieced together from a half-dozen incomplete sets that were loot from the Twelve-year War or from the fall of the Felyal, then commandeered by the throne from the collections of the wealthy. It had been the best that she could do, even with all the resources of the Empire behind her, but here it was: the closest to a complete suit of Mantis-kinden Sentinel plate that any non-Mantis had ever owned, and in truth she guessed that precious few of them remained even in the hands of their original creators.

She saw Karrec's forehead wrinkle suddenly and he observed, with the absorption of the true collector, 'It's incomplete.' His hand approached the empty steel cuff where the right gauntlet was missing, but he did not touch.

'For now,' she admitted, 'though not for long.' She moved about the room until her torchlight flared up at the object positioned to face the armour. She heard Karrec give a startled hiss, and saw him recoil with a palm directed at the effigy.

'Remarkable, is it not?' she asked.

They had taken it from the Felyal in its entirety, although by the time it had reached Capitas the rot had turned parts of it to wood dust, and her bodyguards had become restorers, splicing in fresh wood to maintain the icon's form, without ever quite removing the rot that was part of its essence. Eight feet tall and brushing the ceiling, it was a pillar carved unevenly with insect sigils: centipede and woodlouse and beetle grub, all the creatures of rot and renewal. It was built with two arms, arching out and then down, but even then the resemblance to a mantis was rudimentary. It should have been a thing of clumsy ugliness that the people of Capitas would come and laugh at, deriding the superstitions of the primitives. Instead, in torchlight and darkness, it had the brooding, malign presence of a living thing.

Karrec had backed a few paces towards the door, forgetting that two of her guard were still stationed there. Then she moved her torch a little, and another armoured form was revealed beside the wooden effigy. She saw him relax for a moment, and then freeze motionless, as the figure moved smoothly forward: another of her bodyguard, and a fourth from the icon's far side, padding into the gloom towards Karrec.

He was not, in the end, quite the fool he had been playing. 'Majesty, if I have offended you in any way . . .' he began desperately, but she silenced him with a gesture.

'Your crimes are well known to me,' she said flatly. 'That the gold of the Empire sticks to your fingers before it reaches our treasury, this is no rare thing in a Consortium man. That you have underlings who rob and kill for you, to swell your private collection, this is but ambition and no great transgression. That you have correspondents in Helleron to whom you over-boldly speak of Imperial affairs, well, you know little enough. What could you betray, even if you tried? None of these mere errors warrant a death sentence, Major.'

He stared at her, his throat working but no sound coming out, and the two Mantis-kinden seized his arms.

'But nevertheless you will die,' she told him softly, once his hands were secure and he was unable to sting. 'Not for any fault of yours, but because my grandfather, Alvric the Great, first Emperor of the Wasps, was a man of broad-spread appetites, and because of that he was your grandfather, too. The blood of Empire runs in your veins, and a cruel old man taught me well that it is a currency which commands respect.'

He was protesting now, but the Mantis-kinden hauled him over to the effigy and, while one held him still, the other took long nails and hammered them home, pinning his arms within the carved grip. His screams echoed the length of the empty museum, until they finally cut his throat and collected the first of his blood in a chalice, which she took from them.

'The glove,' she instructed them, and noticed their moment of hesitation. In shedding blood they were quick as water, but this . . . they did not know whether she was right or wrong in this, whether it was high honour or high treason she was about. Like most of their kind, they feared magic, even as their whole culture had been trained to revere the old days when magic had walked freely over the world – before the Apt revolution.

Still, after she had returned from Khanaphes with the invisible brand on her brow, the mark of the Masters, they had given themselves over to her, heart and soul.

One of them knelt before her, presenting the object she had called for: a battered leather gauntlet with a short, vicious blade jutting from between the second and third finger, connected to a metal bar the wearer would grip, able to flex its killing point in and out: now standing straight, now folded back. The archetypal Mantis weapon, lethal beyond swords in the hands of a master, laughable when wielded by the untrained. But she had seen what it could do. She had been given a detailed and graphic lesson on just what carnage a man could wreak with such a thing.

She nodded, and the Mantis-kinden secured the glove to the armour's empty cuff. She put a hand on the elegantly spined pauldrons, feeling the emptiness, a vacancy that went beyond a simple, unoccupied suit of mail, as though the breastplate enclosed a vast lonely abyss, and in its depths . . .

She sipped from the chalice, tasting Karrec's blood. His life of small cruelties and petty selfishness had given it a bitter flavour, but there was a rich aftertaste there, his unknown heritage that she had parsed out. It was not that the Imperial bloodline was special in some objective way that an artificer could discern through analysis in glassware and measurement, but so long as an emperor or empress held sway, commanded the terror and the adoration of a hundred thousand and more, as long as the citizens of the Empire *believed* that blood and destiny rode side by side, then the blood of emperors was a power and currency in the magical realm of symbols and significances. It was a trick the Commonwealers, too, had mastered an age before, and then forgotten.

Almost gently she touched the lower rim of the Mantis-crafted helm and tipped it back, the empty visor staring at the ceiling. With a smooth motion, she emptied the chalice of Karrec's blood into the helm, hearing it gush down into the further reaches of the armour.

No words, at first. She reached out, still reinventing the discipline she practised moment to moment. Had anything such as this been attempted for five hundred years? She felt not. Something urged her on, though, some spirit of the magical traditions she had been unwillingly initiated into: the twisted darkness of the Mantis-kinden leaching from the shattered Shadow Box of the Darakyon, and the blood and hatred of the Mosquito-kinden from her late mentor Uctebri, combining in her now, funnelled into her until she became something quite new: a walker between two worlds, a thing from another age.

And far away, in a direction that had nothing to do with the compass, she felt him answer.

'Come to me,' she whispered into the blood-spattered helm. 'Come now to me, great killer. I, Seda, call to you. I have your blade, your Weaponsmaster's blade that is more a part of you than it is the smith's art. I have your heritage embodied in this shell of steel and chitin. I have the blood of royalty for you to drink. Come to me, speak to me. Serve me.'

The armour moved and, despite herself, she took a quick

step back. At first it was a subtle shifting of the plates that could have simply been the old metal settling on the stand, but then, and without any definite, identifiable motion, something about it had changed irrevocably, and it was no longer a lifeless object but a man standing, faceless behind the helm.

She was very aware of the blade, the same blade that had shed the blood of so many of her father's soldiers, that had broken the Shadow Box and killed Uctebri, and condemned her to be what she was now.

'Look upon me,' she instructed it. 'See what I am. I am the heir to the old ways. I am the successor to the Masters of Khanaphes. I am old magic's envoy in the world.'

Its reply chilled her when it came, in a voice like the rustling of old leaves, the creaking of branches.

One of them. You are the second I have met, to bear that mark.

Something hard crystallized in Seda, a seed of anger and jealousy. 'Do not fear that. It will not be for long. So, the Beetle girl has sought you also? Well, no matter. She is not so free with the blood of others as I am. She lacks the qualities to command one such as you. Serve me, Mantis-kinden. Tisamon of Felyal, I name you, Weaponsmaster, gladiator, slave and killer. Serve me, be mine.'

And why? came that cold voice once again.

'Because where else would you find a fit mistress for one such as you, save in me?' she replied. 'Because I shall let you fight, and I shall give you blood. Because you shall be the champion of an Empress, her executioner and her blade. But, more than this, you shall serve me for the same reason your living kin here also serve me.'

And what is that?

'Because I shall bring them all back, those days that you yearn for, the elder days of magic. I am the immortal magician-queen of the Empire, and I shall remake the world in my image, the Apt and the Inapt both. Where your kind's old masters, the Moth-kinden, have tried for five centuries to turn back the clock with spells and potions, I shall usher in a new age with armies and conquest. The Days of Lore will return, the days of darkness and fear, and I shall rule over them, and you shall be my right hand. Serve me.'

She watched and waited, and saw his blade quiver and flex. Eyes glittered suddenly in the empty night of the helm.

Tisamon nodded.

Glossary

Characters

Aarth – Wasp merchant in the Principalities
Achaeos – Moth-kinden, Che's lover, killed in a ritual
Alvdan II – former Emperor of the Wasps, Seda's brother, killed by Uctebri's magic
Alvric – first Emperor of the Wasps, Seda's grandfather
Amnon – Beetle-kinden, former First Soldier of Khanaphes
Angved – Wasp engineer
Ang We ('Angry') – Grasshopper bandit chief
Avaris – Spider fraudster and bandit
Barad Ygor – Scorpion bandit
Brugan – Wasp general of the Rekef
Cheerwell Maker ('Che') – Beetle-kinden, Stenwold's niece, now Inapt
Chevre Velienn – Dragonfly noblewoman
Dal Arche – Dragonfly bandit chief
Dariandrephos ('Drephos', 'the Colonel-Auxillian') – halfbreed Master Artificer, leader of the Iron Glove
Emon – Bee artificer with the Iron Glove
Ethmet – Beetle First Minister of Khanaphes
Feass – Grasshopper bandit
Felipe Shah – Dragonfly Prince-Major of the Principality of Roh

Felise Mienn – Dragonfly duellist, killed with Tisamon in Capitas
Gaved – Wasp mercenary, Sef's lover
Gjegevey – Woodlouse-kinden, Imperial adviser and slave
Gramo Galltree – Beetle-kinden, self-styled Collegiate ambassador to the Commonweal
Gryllis – Spider-kinden, business partner of Hokiak
Halter – Wasp slaver in the Principalities
Hardy Fordwright – Beetle scholar and alchemist
Hokiak – Scorpion black-marketeer in Myna
Isendter 'Whitehand' – Mantis Weaponsmaster
Jons Allanbridge – Beetle aviator
Karrec – Wasp Consortium officer
Kymene – Soldier Beetle-kinden, Mynan stateswoman and former resistance leader
Lien – Wasp colonel of Engineers
Lioste Coren – Dragonfly-kinden, seneschal to Felipe Shah
Lisan Dea – Grasshopper-kinden, seneschal to Salme Elass
Lowre Cean – Dragonfly-kinden, Prince-Major and strategist
Lowre Darien – Lowre Cean's son, died after the Twelve-year War
Ma Leyd – Mole Cricket, proprietor of the Hitch
Maure – halfbreed necromancer
Maxin – Wasp general of the Rekef, died alongside Alvdan II
Mordrec – Wasp bandit
Pirett – Dragonfly bandit chief
Praeda Rakespear – Beetle-kinden scholar
Salme Alain – Dragonfly Prince-Minor, son of Salme Elass
Salme Dien ('Salma') – Dragonfly Prince-Minor, died fighting the Wasps in the Lowlands
Salme Elass – Dragonfly-kinden, Princess-Minor of Elas Mar province
Scutts – Barad Ygor's pet scorpion
Seda – Empress of the Wasps
Sef – Water Spider-kinden exile

Siriell – Dragonfly bandit chief
Skelling – Skater bargeman
Soul Je – Grasshopper bandit
Stenwold Maker – Beetle spymaster and statesman
Telse Orian – Dragonfly noble
Thalric – Wasp-kinden, former Rekef spymaster, Che's lover
Tse Mae ('Sammi') – Grasshopper alchemist
Thanred – Wasp colonel and governor of Capitas
Tisamon – Mantis Weaponsmaster, died in Capitas
Torste Sain – Dragonfly general from the Principalities
Totho – halfbreed artificer, second in command of the Iron Glove
Tynisa – halfbreed Weaponsmaster, Tisamon's daughter
Uctebri – Mosquito magician, killed by Tisamon in Capitas
Uie Se – Grasshopper seer in Myna
Varmen – Wasp former Sentinel, now mercenary
Varsec – Wasp aviator and engineer

Places

Aleth – large forest south of the Exalsee
Barrier Ridge – cliff boundary between the Lowlands and the Commonweal
Capitas – capital of the Wasp Empire
Collegium – Beetle-kinden city in the Lowlands, home of the Great College
Commonweal – the Dragonfly state north of the Lowlands, partly conquered by the Empire
Darakyon – formerly haunted forest in the north-east Lowlands
Elas Mar – province governed by Salme Elass
Exalsee – inland sea south of the Empire
Felyal – Mantis forest on the Lowlands coast

Helleron – Beetle-kinden city in the Lowlands noted for its industry
The Hitch – fugitive community at the foot of the Barrier Ridge
Jerez – Skater-kinden lake town in the Empire
Khanaphes – ancient Beetle-kinden city
Landstower – city in the Principalities (formerly Lans Stowe)
Leose – centre of Elas Mar province and castle of the Salme family
Lowlands – the city states south of the Commonweal and west of the Empire
Maynes – Ant-kinden city of the Three-city Alliance
Myna – Soldier Beetle city of the Three-city Alliance
The Nem – desert west of Khanaphes
Porta Rabi – Solarnese port
Princep Salma – New Lowlands city named after Salme Dien
The Principalities – that part of the Commonweal conquered by the Empire
Ren – Province governed by Felipe Shah
Rhael – untenanted province in Roh
Roh – Principality covered by Felipe Shah
Sara Tele – village in Elas Mar province
Shon Fhor – capital of the Commonweal
Siriell's Town – bandit town in Rhael province
Solamen – fortress in the Principalities (formerly Shol Amen)
Solarno – a city of high artifice on the Exalsee
Suon Ren – town and castle of Felipe Shah
Szar – Bee city in the Three-city Alliance
Three-city Alliance – a state composed of Maynes, Myna and Szar, former Wasp subjects
Toek Station – Scorpion trading post north of Solarno
Tsolshevy – believed Woodlouse-kinden community, unknown location
Vesserett – Bee city within the Empire

Organizations and things

Consortium of the Honest – mercantile arm of the Imperial administration

Iron Glove – trading cartel of artificers led by Dariandrephos

Landsarmy – the army of refugees led by Salme Dien during the war

Loquae – a speaker for a Mantis-kinden community

The Many – Scorpion-kinden of the Nem desert

The Masters – the ancient, legendary rulers of Khanaphes

Mercers – Dragonfly-kinden knights errant

Monarch – the ruler of the Commonweal

Nailbow – a weapon that shoots bolts via a firepowder charge, powerful but inaccurate and of limited range.

Rekef – Imperial secret service and police, divided into Inlander and Outlander

Salmae – Dragonfly noble family led by Salme Elass

Scriptora – the Khanaphir seat of government

Shadow Box – artefact linked to the Darakyon, destroyed by Tisamon

Skryre – a magical leader of the Moth-kinden

Snapbow – a weapon devised by Totho that projects a bolt over a long range with great force and accuracy

Twelve-year War – the war between the Empire and the Commonweal

Way Brothers – a philosophical order providing hospitality to travellers

The *Windlass* – Jons Allanbridge's new airship, replacing the *Buoyant Maiden*